I0761993

Mafia Wars

Forget Me Not Bombshell

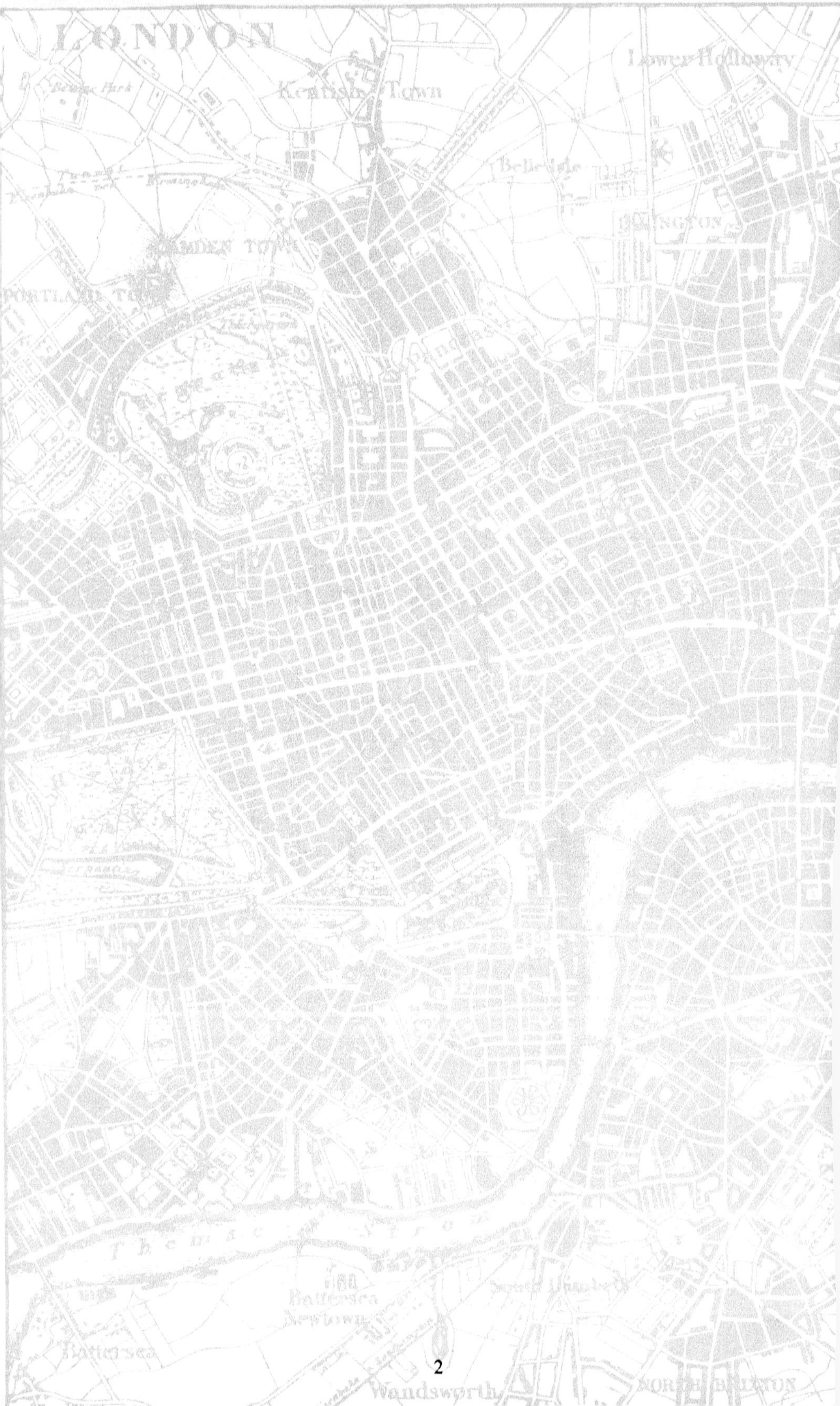
LONDON
Kentish Town
Lower Holloway
Belle Isle
Battersea Newtown
Battersea
Wandsworth

Mafia Wars

Forget Me Not Bombshell

Caroline Peckham & Susanne Valenti

Forget Me Not Bombshell
Mafia Wars #6

Interior Illustration & Formatting by Sloane Murphy

Forget Me Not Bombshell/Caroline Peckham & Susanne Valenti – 1st ed.
ISBN-13 - 978-1-914425-22-6

This book is dedicated to anyone who understands this...

I was headin' up the apple and pears, then thought 'Cor blimey' I really fancy a cup of Rosie Lee. So I took a ball and chalk to the pub and ordered myself a nice brew, and while I was there this nasty little Berkshire Hunt took a swing at me. So I knocked him on his bottle and glass, then kicked him in the cobblers just before the bobbies arrived. I got away with it though, because no one in these parts would dare breathe a dickie bird about what happened. But when I went back to finish my Rosie Lee, someone had half inched it, would you Adam and Eve it?

PROLOGUE

TEN YEARS AGO

My fist thumped on the door hard enough for the noise to pound out above the torrent of the tropical storm which crashed down over my head, plastering my dark hair to my scalp and turning my white dress shirt transparent.

Bermuda. Who the hell thought of coming to this fucking place in the middle of hurricane season? Probably the Russians – they were always coming up with dumb as fuck ideas. Like that time I heard one of them had tried to hijack a plane with no fuel in it. Come to think of it, maybe that was the Mexicans…

Well whoever it was, they were probably the ones who were responsible for us enduring this ridiculous fiasco of a weather pattern. Give me good old fashioned British rain any day of the week. A thunderstorm where I came from would soak you good and leave you shivering, but she wouldn't try to fuck you up the arse the way this bugger was attempting.

My jaw ticked as I was left waiting in the rain, fingers flexing with an ache for violence which would be well quenched before I'd be heading to any damn meeting. If it had been down to me, I'd have bailed on account of our dear old pa passing outa this world at the start of the week anyway. But of course, the old motherfucker had managed to rasp out a dying wish in earshot of our ma while his heart pounded its final beats and he slumped to the floor of the shitter. Yeah. That's right, our pa, Trevor Butcher, most feared man on all the streets of London town and all-round fucking tyrant had been taken out by bad cholesterol and tachycardia while taking a shit.

Fucking tragic that.

And yeah, I meant that on some level. What boy didn't love his pa? Even if their old man happened to be of the brutal, hard-faced kind. The kind who showed love by offering up a swift back hand coupled with wildly infrequent praise. So on the one hand, I was all kinds of cut up over the loss of the head of our family, the kingpin, leader, don, whatever the fuck you wanted to call him. But on the other, I was a prince who had just become a king.

Joint king anyway.

My gaze cut across the alley to where my twin brother Danny lurked in the shadows, waiting like a fucking ghost about to shout boo whenever this arsehole opened the goddamn door. He had that look in his eye tonight. The feral one. The one that said I wasn't gonna be happy by the end of this and our ma would be clutching her pearls back home as a shiver tracked down her spine.

Not that she'd ever admit it. Poor old ma still believed we were good lads, sweet boys, just a little misunderstood. When I was nine years old, she'd told my teacher that when he called up to complain about me setting alight to his desk. He'd made the mistake of disrespecting me by suggesting I should work on my focusing skills. Of course, she'd also told the neighbours that whenever one of their pets turned up dismembered thanks to Danny's fucked up hobbies.

See, that was the difference between me and the man I'd shared a womb with. I was the kind of cracked in the head that made people keep the fuck away from me, stay outa my damn way and mark a cross over their hearts when I passed them by. But that was all it took to avoid my wrath. Outa sight outa mind. I didn't waste time hunting prey who weren't dumb enough to cross me. Danny on the other hand was the kind of cracked in the head which meant his brains had spilled into a puddle on the floor and he'd lost a lot of the important stuff. Like impulse control, empathy and the appreciation for the cuteness of puppies over the desire to see their insides.

Yeah. That was us. The Butcher boys. Fucked in the head and just plain terrifying. And now we were kings in our own right. God save the people who came against us now. Like tonight's little job for example.

The door swung open, a confused looking old gal blinking up at me in my funeral suit and wondering what the fuck I was doing pounding on her door in the middle of a hurricane.

"Alright, love?" I asked, flashing her my winning smile. The one that made my ma pinch my cheek and call me her sweet boy. The one that also got virgins bending over for me in back alleys while I fucked the innocent clean out of them and made sure they never forgot their first time.

"What do you-" she began, but of course fucking Danny couldn't stick to the fucking plan.

"We got business with your neighbour," he said, grinning widely as he moved to my side and butted his shoulder against mine. "So how about you let us in, or I kill your family and make puppets out of their skulls. I can put on a damn good show with enough severed heads."

The woman screamed and I shoved Danny aside as I knocked the door wide against her attempt to slam it and slapped a hand down over her mouth. She kicked and punched but she was frail, and it did nothing to slow me as I backed her up and moved her into her own bathroom.

The look she gave me before I threw the door closed in her face said she thought I was a demon, but little did she know I'd just done her a favour by putting her outa Danny's way.

"We shouldn't leave witnesses," Danny pointed out as I wedged a chair beneath the handle of the bathroom door to lock the old woman inside it.

"You got any plans to return to Bermuda any time soon?" I asked him, shoving a hand through my black hair and sweeping it out of my face, causing droplets to speckle the walls. "Because I don't see this place becoming a new holiday spot for me, so I see no reason to kill some old woman. But if the great Danny Butcher thinks killing old ladies proves how big his balls are then by all means, go right ahead and prove it."

Danny snorted, his gaze swinging from the bathroom where the old woman was still yelling to the glass door at the rear of the house which led out to the courtyard we'd come here for.

"Nah," Danny said, moving away from the old woman like I'd known he would. "I got bigger fish to fry."

I fought off the urge to smirk to myself as I followed him towards the patio door through the little orange kitchen. Everyone thought Danny was a feral dog without a leash, but that was bollocks. *I* was his leash. He just didn't fucking realise it. I knew how to play him, how to make him do things my way without him even cottoning on. He didn't like it when I laughed at his attempts to prove his macho bullshit with things like killing weak old women. But if I'd flat out told him no, he'd have done it just to prove he didn't take orders from me. So there you had it, he thought he'd made his own choice and I'd just saved that old lady's life. I was practically a fucking saint. But would she thank me for it? Not likely.

That was why I wasn't worried about sharing the top dog spot with my identical twin though. Because I knew I'd be the one who was really in charge. Danny mighta been the one who handed out the worst nightmares, but I was the one smart enough to rule.

I plucked a kitchen knife from the block as I passed it – airplanes didn't much like the idea of me bringing my own murder weapons after all – and I followed Danny back out into the rain.

We stepped into the courtyard which served the four brightly decorated houses surrounding us and turned our gaze on the turquoise one ahead of us as the rain sheeted down on our flesh once more.

"Top floor?" Danny confirmed, craning his head to look up at the third floor of the house and I nodded.

"So we were told." I didn't much like relying on tip offs like this without having the chance to check it out myself, but we hadn't had a choice in this one. We were here for a meeting with the families that ruled the underbelly of this fair world, and if my watch was anything to go by, we were already going to be pushing it to get there on time. Not that I was overly concerned about that. A wise man had once told me that it was better to show up late than not at all and that all souls waited for important men anyway.

So what better way to make sure the other families knew not to fuck with us than to make them sweat, wondering if The Firm were going to be showing our faces or not? After all, whatever this deal they wanted to make involved, they'd be needing the most powerful crime family in Europe to ensure it came together. Without us, nothing could be decided, and they'd do well to remember that.

"So who gets to creep in the window?" Danny asked, that manic glint in his eyes saying he wanted the honours, but fuck that. I had the bloodlust in me tonight and I wanted it sated too.

This fucker had stolen from us and run off to this beautiful little slice of paradise, making the foolish mistake of believing we wouldn't follow him here. And sure, it had taken a couple of years to track him down, but that was the problem with stealing from men like us - we never forgot. And once we got our little tip off to his location, it was only ever a matter of time before this day came. Our meeting with the other crime families only bumped it up on the agenda.

I held my fist out to Danny and he tsked as he reluctantly held his out too, the pair of us mirror images of the same dark souls in that moment. My twin brother and me. A pair of demons born into power on the streets of fair lady London. Boy did the underworld tremble when we made it out into this world. We were both tall, broad and all the right kinds of intimidating. We had our pa's imposing auras and our ma's dark hair and eyes, our souls had been spat right out of hell into our black hearts to complete the package and there was no way of not noticing that when you looked on us.

We bounced our hands in rhythm and he kept his in a fist as I flattened mine. A sneer pulled at my brother's lips as he lost the game, violence flashing in his dark eyes. Sometimes, when he looked at me like that, I had to wonder if he might really try to kill me one of these days. There had been a time when I would have sworn to hell and back that that would never happen, but I could see it on occasion now. The jealousy, the hatred simmering in there with the love neither of us had asked for but had been forced upon us. Each of us could have ruled alone if it wasn't for the other and that hadn't mattered so much while pa was still kicking, but now all bets were off. I was confident in my own abilities though, so I wasn't losing sleep over my psychotic brother's possible intentions towards me. For now, his love for me outweighed any hatred or resentment, so the two of us would keep on just as we were.

"Looks like you're taking the back door," I mocked, jamming the kitchen knife into my waistband as I looked up at the building and picked out my first foothold.

Danny stalked away with a curse and I smirked to myself as I used the closest window ledge to heave myself upward. Smart shoes and howling rain weren't the best choice of outfit for scaling buildings, but I was long since used to making do with what I had to hand. Butchers make the best of it - as my pa used to say.

I climbed up, finding cracks in the plaster and using the windows to heave myself higher while the sound of breaking glass announced Danny entering the building from below.

There was a scream followed by a gunshot and I would have feared for my brother's life if I hadn't heard the unmistakable sound of him laughing a moment later.

I climbed faster, cursing him for not waiting for me to make it in as I heaved myself up to the window on the third floor and shoved it open. I tumbled inside, shaking the rain from my hair and leaping to my feet as I found myself in a badly tiled green bathroom.

The sounds of more screams and shouts continued downstairs but I ignored them, pulling the knife from my belt and striding to the door. I threw it open, hearing a thump from beyond the closed door to my left as I made it onto the landing and headed that way.

I kicked the door open and a yell of fright met me before three gunshots were fired in my direction and I was forced to take cover by the wall. The gun rang empty with a dull click and I took off running, diving into the bedroom and colliding with the motherfucker we'd come here for as he tried to make a run for it.

Rodney screamed as my weight crashed into him, his fist slamming into my side over and over before I landed a solid punch to his temple to knock him back beneath me.

"You seriously thought you could steal from us and get away with it?" I taunted, glaring down at him as I placed my knee on his chest to hold him there.

He'd been little more than a grunt in our establishment, and I wouldn't have cared to track him down at all if he'd just cut and run. But he had to go a step further than that. Had to dip his hands in our coiffeurs and take a payday he wasn't owed. More fool him.

"I'm sorry," Rodney gasped. "Sorry. So sorry. I just wanted out. I just wanted-"

I punched him again and he seemed to realise I wasn't here for an apology as his nose broke and his screams of agony filled the air.

He started bucking and kicking beneath me, his fist slamming into my side and sending the air crashing from my lungs. I let him get a few good strikes in if for no other reason than me wanting to feel alive. Because there was nothing like a taste of agony to remind me of that, nothing like the kiss of pain to wake me up and get the monster in me growling. And it was growling alright. Baying for damn blood.

I slammed the blade down into his chest before he could land another blow against me, and I was lost to the beast in me as I ripped it free and stabbed him again. Again and again and a-fucking-gain, his blood splattering me and staining the white shirt I'd worn to Pa's funeral, giving him the kind of send-off he woulda wanted.

I shoved myself to my feet once I was certain he was dead beneath me, kicking his corpse several times before spitting on him too.

No one crossed the Butchers.

No one.

Certainly not some greedy little piece of shit like this cockroach.

When the adrenaline finally began to calm in my veins, I released a slow breath and let the bloodlust fade from my limbs. I left the knife where it was, embedded in Rodney's chest, taking a moment to wipe my prints from it, though I wasn't too concerned about leaving evidence. We had a fall guy ready and waiting to take the hit for this one if it came to it, though I didn't expect that to be necessary. No one gave a fuck about scum like this being taken from the world.

I moved over to the closet which stood ajar, kicking it wide to see what Rodney had been trying to get to before I'd shown up to ruin his day, and my lips lifted a little as I spotted the bag of cash which had fallen to the floor.

I dropped to one knee as I gave it the once over, taking a mental count and smirking at the figure.

It wasn't even close to the amount he'd stolen from us, but it was something. I pocketed the cash. Leaving the bag behind and keeping what I couldn't fit in my pockets in my fist as I kicked the closet door closed and was gifted a bloody reflection of myself in the mirror that hung there.

I looked every inch the animal I was, my shirt and skin painted with flecks of red, dark hair falling forward to shadow my eyes. I was all Butcher today and I was loving every second of it. This was who I was at my core; brutal, savage, merciless. And it suited me better than any flashy funeral suit and listening to false condolences at the wake of a man everyone had feared and hated.

I headed for the stairs with my fist full of cash, calling out to Danny in the now empty house.

He didn't grace me with a reply, but I found him downstairs, grinning manically as he stood amongst a trio of corpses and a heavy breath escaped me.

"What happened to us only hitting Rodney?" I growled, making my brother smile wider.

"I decided to go for a different approach," he said with an innocent shrug that did nothing to take away from the butchered remains of Rodney's wife and kids surrounding him.

The teenage boys looked older than I'd been when I'd first started in this line of work, but I still doubted their deaths had been called for. I pushed my tongue into my cheek as I attempted to stamp down my irritation with my brother for going against our plan. He wanted a rise from me. I could see it in the depths of his dark eyes where he still hungered for more blood.

A clock chimed on the wall and I glanced at it.

"We're late," I grunted, biting my tongue on my irritation and shoving the handful of cash at my brother as I turned for the door.

He took it and followed me, moving up close behind me and making a prickle run down my spine at his nearness. I had the feeling I was offering my back to a predator, but that didn't make me pause. My twin might have been an animal, but I was confident that he wasn't a match for the monster in me if it came down to that.

Danny strutted along like a peacock, whistling happily as he followed me and I led the way back out into the storm.

The wind was howling more insistently now, no fuckers in sight anywhere as they all took cover and waited for it to pass. The only ones mad enough to be out in a hurricane were the two of us.

I stepped into the sheeting rain and strode away down the street. A hurricane wasn't going to be the end of Benny Butcher. Karma just wasn't that kind to the world.

I made it to the car we'd rented and dropped in behind the wheel, sparking up a cigarette as I waited for Danny to climb in beside me.

"The others will be pissed at us for showing up late," he joked, taking a smoke for himself and lighting up too.

"Fuck 'em," I said dismissively, smoke pouring between my lips as I spoke. "No one tells us what to do or when to do it and they'd do well to remember that."

"So why are we showing up to this thing at all?" Danny questioned and I knew he'd just as happily turn towards the airport and forget this whole peace deal. But I wasn't gonna let that happen.

"Because I'm not having the five of them make some bargain we ain't a part of," I said firmly. "Then they might start getting ideas. And we don't want none of those ideas encroaching on our turf. So if there's gonna be peace, then we'll be taking part in it. And if it turns to war instead then I'll happily fire the first shot."

Danny grinned as he looked out past the racing wiper blades into the storm and the near invisible streets, and I let the satnav guide us to our destination while I drove through it with my heart pounding in anticipation of this meeting.

This would be the first time me and Danny had stood tall at the head of our family and I guessed we'd be making an impression turning up covered in the blood of someone who had betrayed us. Not that I was fool enough to think any of them would fear a little blood and gore, but it was always nice to remind the old arseholes in attendance that we still got our hands bloody on the regular and weren't afraid to do our own dirty work.

We pulled up at the luxurious hotel where our meeting was to be held and I parked before its double doors, ignoring the sign which discouraged parking in that particular spot.

I was out before Danny, flicking my cigarette butt aside and striding towards doors that were pulled open for us by a guy who was working not to show any reaction to our appearance.

Danny barked at him like a dog and he only flinched a little before encouraging us to follow him to our meeting. Clearly he knew who we were and I couldn't say I hated it when our reputation proceeded us like that.

The atrium was empty, most likely down to people hiding out from the storm so we dripped water across the white tiles and followed him down a corridor to a conference room which held the world's most dangerous men.

"We've got it from here," I told the guy who'd shown us the way before he could make a move to open the door for us. He bobbed his head before turning and scurrying away again.

"I say we just toss a grenade in there and do the world and ourselves a favour," Danny said in a low tone, his shoulder knocking mine and bringing tension to my limbs.

"You heard pa's final wish," I said in a flat tone, refusing to bite. "He wanted us to take part in this peace and I mighta hated him, but I'm not gonna spit on his grave by refusing his dying request."

"Yeah, yeah," Danny muttered, moving to push past me and enter the room first, but that would be a fuck no.

My shoulder butted against his and I yanked the door open hard enough to make it smack against the wall and draw all eyes in the room to us as we strode over the threshold.

They were all there, all of the major crime lords who ran this world beneath the noses of its upstanding citizens and provided the vices so many people ached for.

My gaze swung over them all, calculating, assessing, just as they looked at us in return. There were two from each family. Old men and their first-born sons for the most part. But we were the young blood at the table, the ones they knew least about now that we'd taken our pa's place.

We'd killed people from most of their organisations and they'd killed people from ours, not that I could think of a single fucker I grieved over because of any of them. It was a hard won thing to find a place close to my heart after all, so I wasn't surprised they hadn't yet managed to strike at it. Not that that meant they wouldn't have been glad of the chance to once. But not anymore apparently. No, now we were here to make peace. Or at least we would be if the price was one I could stomach.

Danny tried to beat me to the single seat left at the table, but I quickened my pace and dropped into it first, fighting a smirk as he snarled beneath his breath. Yeah we ruled together, but if there was a seat at the table, I'd be the one filling it and he needed to get used to that. Luckily, his temper held and he just took his place standing behind me the way the sons of all the other kingpins in this room were.

I glanced to my left where the Mexican Cartel sat, followed by the

Sicilians who ruled the Cosa Nostra in New York, the Irish Mob who ran Boston, the Russian Bratva from Las Vegas and finally the Italian Outfit who owned Chicago to my right. None of them held a candle to London in my humble opinion and as mine was the only opinion I cared for in this room of thugs and heathens, I was damn tempted to think of myself and Danny as the true power in this place.

They all looked to be carrying weapons which made me and Danny the only unarmed men here. Some mighta called that foolish, but I liked to think it only proved how little we feared these men. They couldn't kill us. They wouldn't fucking dare. And I was confident enough in that to let them know we didn't even fear them trying.

"You're late," Giovanni Moretti snapped, his cigar pointed at me as he seemed to think he could tell me off like I was some young boy. He mighta been the head of the Italians, but he certainly wasn't the boss of me.

"We're here, aren't we?" I tossed back, shrugging insolently as I leaned back in my chair and spread my legs wide, letting him know I gave no fucks about wasting his precious time. If he wanted a rise from me, he'd have to try better than that. "Count your blessings, Giovanni, that we came at all."

Danny snorted in amusement at my back and I let the corner of my mouth lift into a grin. This here was when the Butcher boys shone brightest. When it was us against an enemy. Then we were thicker than thieves, an unbreakable bonded pair that nothing could divide or stand against. All rivalry parked at the door.

Niall Kelly muttered something to his son which I was guessing was meant as an insult to us, but as the Irish arsehole didn't have the balls to raise his voice and speak in plain English, the only response I gave him was a wider smile and the offer of his death in my eyes.

"We all know why we have come together today," Carlo Rossi said loudly, pulling our attention to the Sicilian. The head of the Cosa Nostra didn't look our way, his hatred for our organisation more than clear in the way he was trying to avoid so much as looking at us. But it wasn't our fault that The Firm dominated the whole of Europe while they, the Russians and the Irish all snapped at our heels like a pack of hungry mutts. We let them have the scraps we didn't want, but everyone here knew The Firm was top dog. "Every head of family sitting here has come to the realization that to preserve our way of life, sacrifices need to be made by all. We must put past grudges aside in order to guarantee our future."

The Russians and Irish started baiting each other across the table and I yawned as I tuned them out. It was always the same with them, 'you almost killed me,' 'I swear vengeance on your bloodline,' yada, yada, yada. I say they should either shoot each other or shut the fuck up about it. But apparently the Russian heir, Alexi, was still salty about the scar the Irish heir, Tiernan, had put around his pretty neck.

My phone buzzed in my pocket and I pulled it out, smirking at the video Danny had sent me of a man who looked a whole lot like angry Alexi getting spit roasted by a guy who held a certain similarity to the head of the Cosa Nostra and a dude who looked big enough to split him in two.

The argument continued at the table and I glanced to the Mexicans who were on my left, tilting my phone to show the son, Alejandro. He tried real hard not to look amused but as his gaze flicked up to look at Alexi in recognition of the joke, I swear a smirk touched his lips. Yeah. That shit was funny.

"We came here to ensure peace and that we can continue our livelihood. That will not happen if sacrifice and pride cannot be set to the side." Don Rossi continued with less vehemence in his tone.

"That's a tall order to make, old man," I piped up because that motherfucker wasn't going to keep pretending we weren't in the room if he liked the arrangement of his face the way it was.

"It's an order that will ensure you get to be as old as me. Or is life so dispensable where you come from?" he asked in a flat tone which said he wasn't in the mood to play with me.

"Depends on the life." I shrugged dismissively, wanting this done.

The bickering continued and I turned my attention back to my phone as Danny messaged me again.

Danny:
We could take 'em.

Benny:
No doubt. Probably best not to for now though

Danny:
Spoilsport

I glanced around again, hoping Danny didn't really have any intentions of starting shit here. But I was pretty confident he didn't. He'd loved pa more than I did and I knew he wanted to see his final request fulfilled, even if he was going to bitch his way through the execution of it.

"It has been a year since we started our deliberations, and the time has come to put them into action. I admit it will take some time to get used to this new reality, but resistance is futile," the head of the Cosa Nostra went on.

I rolled my eyes at the theatrics, texting Danny with a Darth Vader gif and a short message.

Benny:
"Resistance is futile."

Danny barked a laugh which was ignored by almost everyone, but

Alejandro got it, I could tell by the cold, flat 'I could kill you with my pinky finger' look in his eyes. I was sure. Or maybe not. I wasn't the best at making friends in all honesty - I had a tendency to get suspicious of their reasons for wanting my friendship and then I just got stabby. It didn't make for all that many lasting friendships, that was for sure.

Really though, these old bastards took everything so fucking seriously. I'd taken a look over the agreements that had been drawn up while our pa was taking part in all of these little peace talks, and I was happy enough to agree to the terms. As far as we were concerned, it didn't make all that much difference to our operations anyway. Everyone just had to keep to their own turf. We didn't have the issues the others had with their drug distribution problems across the states. We'd always held England in an iron fist and our hold over the rest of Europe was practically unrivalled too. We just had to agree to making a few allowances for the Irish, Sicilians and Russians to continue their operations and I guessed it was worth those concessions for the benefits of a lasting peace.

"Agreed," everyone around the table rattled out, not noticing that I stayed silent. But this was the one sticking point for me because I'd read into the agreement here and I was fairly certain I knew the way they wanted to bind us to it.

"To ensure blood will stop flowing, we need to mix the families together," he went on like he thought it was his place to speak for all of us, but still I held my tongue, listening, waiting. "We must make sure we are all connected in some way, so no one thinks twice before waging war on us."

"Agreed," the heads of each family replied in sync, and again I held my tongue. I'd never been a sheep and I wasn't about to become one now. I'd make my own decision here even if it cost us this peace.

"We all have daughters and a woman's reason for being has always been to use for alliances purposes, so it fits that they be the ones to be sacrificed here."

Sacrificed.

I didn't like the use of that word one bit and my posture tightened even while I remained leaning back in my seat like I didn't give a single shit about any of this. But I did. Because me and Danny weren't it so far as our family went. There was one more child of sin born to the Butcher family, though our little sister, Dahlia, had escaped the worst of our bloodline thanks to the fears of our father. I barely knew her really. He'd sent her away when she was only five and she'd been educated in private boarding schools ever since, kept away from us and the dirt we coated ourselves in to pay for her pretty privilege. I used to envy her of that, then later I'd been glad of it, glad that innocent little creature had been gifted a way out of our mess if she'd wanted it.

But not anymore. If we agreed to this peace deal then she'd be in it just like the rest of us and I wasn't sure how I felt about that.

"Once the girls are of age, they must marry the leaders of their family, or soon to be Dons. This exchange must be done all within the same time frame. We don't want to have anyone back out because they got cold feet and are no longer interested in the union. Can we agree on those terms?"

I'd been caught up thinking about my sister's fate and had almost forgotten this concerned my fate too. Well, mine or Danny's. One of us was going to have to marry the daughter of one of the families in this room if we were to uphold our end of the deal.

I didn't much want a stranger for a bride, but I also doubted I'd ever meet a woman I did want to walk down the aisle anyway. I didn't get time for that shit. Besides, no woman had ever held my attention long enough for me to consider it, though I guessed as I was only twenty-four there was time for that.

No one disagreed and I held my tongue too. I didn't love the idea of shipping my little sister off to one of these fuckers for a bride, but we could cross that bridge when we came to it.

"Good. Now seeing as my daughter is only eight and the youngest of the girls, I propose marriage should only occur in ten years' time when she's of age."

"That's preposterous!" Miguel exclaimed, his face going all red and angry. "My daughter is of age now. How can you expect Rosa to wait to be married until she's almost thirty? People will think there is something wrong with her!"

"When has public opinion ever been a concern for us?" I asked with an arched brow, goading him and wondering if he might try and act on those hungry demons in his eyes which clearly wanted my death. Hell, if I was gifted his daughter for a bride, I'd take great joy in fucking her and knowing how much he hated it.

My phone buzzed again and I tuned out the arguments over the details as I looked at the message from my brother.

Danny:
If she looks anything like him then I'd say there is something wrong with her.

Benny:
Shit, I didn't think of that.
If our girl turns out to look like a goat then you can be the one to marry her.

Danny:
Deal. It don't matter what they look like so long as you bend 'em over anyway. Besides, the ugly ones are always grateful, so they go at it harder.

Benny:
I wouldn't know, my standards aren't as low as yours.

Danny:

Which is why I get my dick wet so much more often than you do, brother.

The arguing in the room grew in intensity until the Irish leader shoved to his feet. All around us scary arseholes reached for the guns at their belts and I watched them with a little more interest as I wondered if coming here unarmed was the wrong move. Not that I'd let a detail like that be the end of me. I'd kill them all with my bare hands if it came to it.

I watched Niall Kelly as he strolled away from the table to the breakfast spread which I hadn't noticed before but suddenly wanted to take full advantage of before he grabbed the bowl of fruit from the centre of it.

He walked back towards us, tossing the fruit over his shoulder and making me grin as I watched the apples and oranges roll away. Hell, I might have even liked this fucker in another lifetime. He had an *I don't give a fuck* attitude that called to my soul. Damn, I kinda wished he wasn't an Irish mobster who hated me and all that shit, just so that we could go out fruit throwing together getting wasted on cheap booze.

Niall dropped the bowl onto the table and grabbed a pad of yellow paper before jotting his family name of Kelly onto it and dropping it inside the bowl.

Danny:

Are we having a fucking raffle to pick a bride??

Benny:

Looks like it. Do you think there's a chance I get to win a bottle of wine instead of a woman?

"We all pick a name. Should the name pulled out be of our own daughter, we pick again until we have a new name," the Irish kingpin said as he finished.

"A little childish, but I guess it serves the purpose," Danny said, not bothering to hide his amusement.

"Aye, but I find simplicity always gets the job done. Why make a mountain out of a molehill, I always say."

Benny:

Like we always said, brother - the Irish mobsters are simpletons.

Danny laughed loudly behind me as the rest of the family leaders began writing their names on a piece of paper and tossing them into the bowl too. When it came to my turn, I wrote BUTCHER in block caps and drew a little carved up corpse beside it just for fun before adding it to the tombola.

All around us men looked sombre, but I wasn't going to be feeling any kind of way about this right now. Ten years? That was a lifetime plus some in the violent world we lived in. If I was still here in ten years' time, I'd worry about this shit. But until then I was happy to go on living my life just the way I was while adjusting to this new layout of our family dynamics with our pa dead and buried.

The leader of the Italians, Giovanni, stood abruptly, ashing his cigar and picking up a pen from the table, using it to slice into his palm.

"On my blood, I swear to protect and care for the woman who will ensure the life of the Outfit. Let her sacrifice bring union to the *famiglias,*" he said firmly and I had to admit, I respected him for that. I might not have known our little sister well, but I wanted her to live a life of safety and his promise ensured that if she ended up with them. At least so far as the word of a man of his character could be trusted anyway.

He went on to pull a name from the bowl and I lost myself to my thoughts, only paying enough attention to be certain it wasn't our sister's name that he called out.

My gaze slid between the remaining families as the rumours and reports of the atrocities they'd all been responsible for ran through my mind and I tried to decide if there was a single one of them who I might have been happiest for our little sister to end up with. I wasn't sure I could claim to trust any of them like that though.

Giovanni pushed the bowl to me next and I blinked down into the bloody pieces of paper that might just have held my fate on them.

I wet my lips then raised my hand to my mouth, using my own teeth to draw my blood from the heel of my hand and letting it drip down over the folded paper too.

"I swear to look after the woman who comes to us," I said, deciding in that moment that I could offer them that promise. I'd marry her myself. I wouldn't inflict Danny upon her to be used as his plaything. Because I knew his cruelty wouldn't be contained if I allowed her to go to him. But I could offer that much. Even if I wouldn't make any promises of anything more than her safety and my name. I wasn't a man who could give her love or adoration, but she'd be safe, a princess kept in a tower at the very least.

I pushed my hand into the bowl, feeling the way the pieces of paper slipped across my fingers, wondering if I'd get some sense of fate from one of them to help me pick. But there was nothing. Just smooth paper brushing my fingertips and the warm dampness of the blood that decorated the pieces.

I tugged one out and opened it, lifting my eyes to look across the table to the Russians as I read the name of their daughter out, my voice hanging in the air between us.

Between the two of them I could read nothing of how they felt about this, nothing at all in the darkness of their gazes or the hard lines of their faces. But it didn't really matter anyway. Because it was already done.

"Anya Volkov. Looks like I just got myself a Russian bride."

PART ONE

TAKE ME TO CHURCH

ANYA

CHAPTER ONE

TEN YEARS LATER

I slid another straw between Adrik's lips as he slept beside me, my big ass bodyguard like a tank filling out his entire seat despite the huge size of it. He had fourteen wedged between his lips now and every time he let out a snore, the sound rippled through them and a few fluttered down onto his lap. I put them straight back in, obviously.

I knelt up on my seat as one flew down to land on his left knee and I had to reach over carefully to try and grab it. The moment he'd fallen asleep, I'd stripped out of my leggings and changed into my black Van Halen band tee which was too big for me, but it still didn't cover my ass at all while I was bent over like this. Someone was definitely getting an eyeful of my panties behind me, but I didn't give much of a fuck.

"Um, excuse me, miss, the seatbelt light is on, you need to sit down," a soft female voice carried from behind me just as my fingers grazed the straw and I accidentally sent it sailing down between Adrik's thighs. My endlessly long blonde hair tumbled down around me so I got lost in a sea of platinum and the scent of passionfruit shampoo floating around me.

No, you whore of a straw. Come back here.

I waved a hand in the flight attendant's vague direction to try and hush her, leaning down and bracing myself on the arm of Adrik's chair as I reached to the floor and my face lined up way too precisely with his crotch. There was a bulge in there the size of Texas and I really didn't want to face smoosh it.

Adrik was like a big, silent uncle who stood vaguely nearby on Christmases and birthdays. He was a constant in my life. And I was a constant in his. Mostly a constant irritation. But still. My life's mission was to make him crack a grin and in all my years of trying, I'd never managed it. Not once. And I was funny when I could be bothered to be. Like, not comedian funny. But I had my moments.

"*Miss*," the attendant hissed more urgently. "You really must sit down."

The airplane suddenly bounced with the turbulence and my head flew up then whacked down into Adrik's cock in one furious movement that gave me whiplash. Which was better than the dicklash Adrik got as he roared in pain and straws exploded from his mouth, flying in every direction, one of them jabbing an unsuspecting two year old in the eye. The kid started screaming and his mother shot Adrik a death glare.

My cheek had felt too much of Adrik's cock for my liking and I had the icky feeling it was imprinted there as he caught me by the back of the neck and practically shoved me back into my seat. He rounded on me with a fury in his dark eyes that could have killed a man at ten paces.

"You little hellion." He lunged at me, grabbing my seatbelt and yanking it into place, grabbing the cord and jerking it hard to tighten it to the point of pain. My long hair got caught under the belt and I winced, working to pull it out.

The attendant gawped at us and I looked up at her, painting on a smile. "Can I have another juice box?" I asked, pushing my toes against the stash I had under the chair in front of me to try and hide the source of all my straws. Not to brag, but I was kind of the queen of pranks. My brothers had fallen prey to my games a thousand times. It was one of the very few joys in my life.

"Another one?" she asked in surprise.

"Ignore her," Adrik barked, pointing to direct the woman away and my scary ass bodyguard's voice did the job as she bounded back down the aisle.

My gaze fixed on an old guy across the way who was staring at me with his glasses on the end of his nose and a shocked expression that said he'd been a front row voyeur to my ass. I shot him a wink and he looked like he was going into cardiac arrest as he continued to stare.

Adrik leaned across me, yanking the divider into place to block his view. Perks of flying business class and all.

"What would your father say if he was here to see you dressed this way?" he growled.

"Um, he'd likely be more interested in getting his hands on the free drinks seeing as he's been burning in hell for years. He's probably parched," I deadpanned.

"Your insolent tongue is going to get you in trouble at the end of this journey. You do understand where you're going, don't you Miss Volkov?"

Of course I understood. How could I not understand that my life had been sold to a British asshole who was one of the most feared men in Europe? My tongue burned with acid at the thought of him and liquid fire ignited along the inside of my flesh. Danny Butcher. My fucking fiancé.

"No I don't understand, Adrik," I said sarcastically in my sweetest voice. It was a game I liked to play. How sarcastic could I be before someone realised I was mocking them. "Please explain it to me."

"You're going to be a wife, Miss Volkov," he said, taking my words very seriously.

"A wife?" I breathed innocently. As if I'd forget that I was being sent to marry a man who was eight years older than me and painted in more sin than I could tally up. At twenty six, my life was officially not my own anymore and I was destined to be nothing more than a gangster's property. "Am I really to be a wife?"

"Yes and – wait, you're doing that thing again, aren't you?" he muttered.

"What thing?" I asked, giving him my biggest eyes. I looked like a doe, all sweetness and virtue and Adrik's gaze narrowed on me in suspicion.

"Don't mock me, Miss Volkov. I may be your bodyguard, but I am also your guardian. Your brothers asked me to look after you. So I am in command here."

"Yes and you are such a big, scary commander man," I said, nodding as I fluttered my lashes.

"Stop it," he grunted. "Now listen to me. I may be an old man who never married, but I've learned a thing or two about men like Danny Butcher in my time." He reached into his pocket, taking out a folded piece of paper which I recognised from Mother's writing desk. It had pink roses on it and smelled like vanilla. I used to take a piece of that paper to bed with me every night after she died, trying to hold onto her, refusing to let go. How did she die? Well that was just a violent little headfuck I didn't fancy indulging in right now. But even as my mind turned that way, I could hear The Killing Moon by Echo & the Bunnymen playing in my ears, louder and louder until the fear that bound me to that memory dug deeper.

"I believe the best way to keep you safe is for you to obey your new husband," Adrik said.

Obey? I didn't obey. Obedience was for dogs and boring people. Not wives. Certainly not twenty first century wives, even if they were sold into marriage like we were living in the eighteen hundreds.

I took my chunky, over-the-ear headphones from my bag as Adrik started reading out what was bound to be a vom-fest of misogyny as I casually hooked my headphones up to my iPod with Bluetooth. Sure, an iPod Touch was seriously outdated, but my brother Zakhar had given it to me when I needed it a long time ago, and I was never going to give it up.

"If you are asked to do something, don't question it," Adrik continued and I fought the urge to roll my eyes back so hard they never returned from the inside of my skull. "You are best to keep your head down and answer his questions promptly and honestly until I have time to deal with him."

I was an urn. An empty one. But it was soon going to start filling with the blackened, charred remains of me if I didn't deal with my new owner swiftly.

I knew Adrik was saying these things to try and protect me, but the idea of walking into some monster's home and becoming his house-trained pet was abhorrent to me. I'd rather slit my throat now and be done with it. No, actually I'd rather slit his. But sadly, it probably wouldn't be me driving the knife into him. That was Adrik's task. He was coming all this way with me to be my assassin. And if I was Danny Butcher, I'd be cowering in my little British knickers right now, because Adrik was a monster with a violent streak that rivalled that of my brothers.

"Wear what he asks you to wear. If he buys you a dress for an occasion, don't nit-pick the colour or style."

I gave him a blank look. That simply wasn't gonna happen. I wasn't interested in shoving my body into flappy, flouncy things that pushed my tits up. No, I was the disappointing tomboy my father had never wanted. He'd tried to force me to be his little princess. Turned out, you could threaten a girl into a dress, but you couldn't change the colour of her soul. Mine was grey, like the colour of steel or concrete or the eternal nothingness of my waking life.

My brothers liked me as I was, at least. They'd let me be *me*. They'd liked that I was rough around the edges, they didn't expect anything of me for simply being female. Father had been…difficult. Although that was probably the understatement of the whole damn universe. All credit to him on the feminism though, he hadn't been prejudiced in who he used his fists against. My body had been as fair game as my brothers', and I wouldn't have had it any other way. Except the way where none of us had been beaten – duh.

He was a fool really, hitting his boys even as they grew into savage men. It wasn't that surprising that they'd killed him in the end. You can't raise monsters and expect them not to be monstrous - I should get that on a t-shirt. Bit wordy though.

I glanced at Adrik as he kept reading from the page, casually placing my headphones over my ears and tuning him out as I slipped into my escape. Music was freedom to me. A magical place which I could carry anywhere and disappear into the moment I grew tired of the world's bullshit. I was obsessed with old school rock and blues, and the only saving grace of me being carted off to London to marry a psychotic Butcher boy was that I'd be living in the land which had birthed The Beatles, The Rolling Stones, Pink Floyd, The Who and so, so many more legends.

Butcher.

The wedding.

London.

The panic bloomed slowly at first then it built and built, raking at the inside of my chest. Adrik and my brothers may have concocted a little plan together, but it wasn't going to be quick. I'd belong to Danny for a while before Adrik would be able to get close enough to kill him. I was pretty sure he was going to make it look like an accident, but I hadn't been invited to the plan party. I'd simply been told to stay out of it. My brothers always protected me, and I loved them for that, but sometimes I felt like a wasp kept in a jar. I had a sting of my own, but I was rarely able to use it. It was difficult to fight your own battles when every time you remotely pissed someone off, three massive Russian tanks showed up to defend my honour. Four if you counted Adrik.

I turned the music right up and slipped the eye mask down which was perched on my head, falling away into the bliss of House of the Rising Sun by The Animals. The numbness found me at last and the panic washed away just like that. Nothing could touch me here. I was gone, a million miles beyond the sun and still travelling at the speed of light.

Adrik either didn't notice I was absent, or didn't bother trying to grab my attention again. He never did when I put my music on, probably because I bit him that one time when he interrupted me during a session with The Eagles. I mean, okay, I'd been singing along in the back row of some family friend's funeral, but said family friend had pinched my ass and called me his little slut two weeks prior to the deathly peanut allergy reaction which had landed him in that coffin. Apparently his epi-pen had gone missing and he hadn't made it to the hospital in time. Funny how I'd acquired an epi-pen not long before that. Not that I was a psycho or anything. It was the pedo porn on his laptop that had pushed me over the edge. I was a bit of a rare gem when it came to cracking people's logins.

I bobbed my head, falling into the music, feeling like I was sinking deep underwater and drifting into a wide, open ocean where anything was possible. My heart found the rhythm of the music and I was gone, somewhere far away where no one owned me, not here on an airplane, heading towards an inescapable fate.

I may have seemed semi-calm about this marriage thing, and maybe I was. But I had good reason for that. See, the thing was, Danny Butcher was a dead man whether Adrik pulled the trigger or not. I may not have had that many opportunities to kill in life, but while my parents had been busy ignoring me, my brothers had raised me to be a wild animal of a girl. I'd been wrestling with them since I could walk, and continued to do so up until this very morning before all three of them had brought me to the airport. They were double my size, but they'd shown me ways to beat them that didn't depend on physical strength. My brain was my greatest weapon, my brother Alexi always told me that. I had the smarts of a vicious little house cat and I knew where to stab to bleed out a man and kill him quicker than I could shout *die motherfucker!*

I knew how to make poison from everyday household items too, and how to disguise the scent of it in food, leave no trace of my involvement. I also knew how to make an array of bombs given the materials, but my greatest gift? Oh baby, my greatest gift was the void in me.

My emotions had a kill switch and I could put on whichever mask suited the occasion. At political functions and snooty parties for the rich while I painted on fake smiles and laughed so believably, you'd really think I was happy. My ability to show up and pretend I was a warm-blooded creature with a soul had become my greatest asset, because the moment you believed that, I was at my deadliest. Even my brothers didn't know the extent to which I numbed out in my adult life. I was barely here these days, a living ghost.

Oh and not to boast, but my face was kinda nice. I'd inherited my mother's beauty and knew how to enhance my features when I had to. But whenever I wasn't performing, I always stripped down to my panties, put on a band tee, tied my long, Rapunzel hair up in a messy bun and curled up with my music. It was my happy place. And I didn't get to spend nearly as much time in my happy place as I would have liked.

My brother Zakhar had encouraged it, he'd told me if I didn't have something that was mine, then people would come along and take away every piece of me for themselves. They'd chew me up and spit me back out when they were done. But so long as I had something truly untouchable just for me, I'd never be broken. And in this world of blood and mobsters and cruelty, there had been far too many chances to be broken. I hadn't survived all of it, I'd seen things no one should see as a child, I'd had blood splashed on my face more times than I could count and the taste of it never really went away.

But sometimes I was still sort of here, sort of awake. Like when I laughed with my brothers or when I bought myself a new band tee and put it on for the first time. But the place I was the least broken was in my head when the music was playing. Then everything just felt…bearable. Even when all hell was descending around me. The world could probably burn and so long as I was listening to Bob Dylan, I'd smile my way through it.

Zakhar had been the one to make me my first playlist. He used to come to my room, slide my headphones over my ears and block out the sound of Father beating one of our other brothers. I loved him for that, but there was sadness in it too. My brother trying to shelter me from this violent life we were all born in to for as long as he could. Then Alexi had been the one to suggest training me in the ways that could truly protect me from the cruel men I was likely to encounter in life. And both Nikolay and Zakhar had agreed, wanting to protect me too as always. But they couldn't in the end. Because today, I'd had to say goodbye to the three men who I was sure were the only ones in this world who would ever truly love me.

Outside of them, I was just a sold woman, sent to the bed of a man I despised even before I'd met him. I'd heard of the sick things Danny Butcher did to people. When he went against his enemies, he didn't just target them, he bled their whole family dry, children and all. And the truth was, deep down, I feared the hands of a man like that touching me, possessing me, hurting me. Which was why I wasn't going to rely on a long-game plan that Adrik would be enacting. I wasn't going to play the submissive wife while the boys decided when was best to kill my husband. I'd be doing it myself before I had to offer up a piece of my soul on a platter.

My brothers had their own wedding to deal with, an Irish girl was landing in their lives right about now. And I didn't really know how to feel about that. I hoped she was a badass with a backbone of steel though, because my brothers were men forged in the pits of hell. They'd all decided to tie themselves to her in some twisted marriage, and I hoped she was prepared for that. I didn't even want to think about the poor girl in all honesty, but then again the Irish were known for their hearts clad in iron and maybe she would be strong enough to handle them. Men so easily dismissed our gender in this cutthroat world of gangs and bloodshed, believing the meat swinging between their thighs made them somehow more powerful than us. But strength didn't equal power. Power could be quiet, unassuming, power could creep into your bed and slit your belly open without you ever seeing it coming. That was the downfall of arrogant men. Assuming women weren't a threat to their grand empires.

Anyway, I had bigger problems to focus on right now than men and my brothers' wedding. My own wedding night was coming up on me fast. Tomorrow, I'd walk down the aisle and bind myself to a monster, but when we were left alone in the dark, I'd strike like a cobra. My stowed luggage contained a set of new knives, the smallest of which would easily slide up my sleeve, ready to slice its way across his throat.

I am your death and I am flying towards you on metal wings, Butcher.

I put on the playlist Zakhar had made for me and the first song tugged on my heartstrings, begging me to cry. Because for now, this was goodbye to my brothers, and though I prayed my plan would all go smoothly, I didn't know for sure that I could pull it off. And I might not get out alive even if I did manage to kill Danny Butcher. But giving myself to that monster was not on the cards for me, and so long as my music was playing when I went, I was sure I could handle death. What sweeter way to die than to be carried there on the back of your favourite song?

The tears didn't come. They never did anymore. I slipped into the numb place inside me once again and switched off all the bad emotions that were battling to claim me.

All Along the Watchtower by Jimi Hendrix filled my head and I let it steal my pain away and feed it back to me in the form of rock and roll. And suddenly I was fine, just fine.

I stood on the sidewalk outside London Heathrow Airport in the darkening evening light, my fingers twitchy as music blasted in my head and Adrik stood beside me like a solid wall. The English assholes were late to pick me up and rain was washing down from the sky, the landscape more vividly green than anything I'd ever seen in my life. I was used to the red rocks of Vegas and the blaring sunshine which dried the air within an inch of its life. Here, the air was wet, cool and tasted like trees and living things. I didn't hate that, but I did hate the way the rain somehow swept across the ground and drenched my leggings despite the fact that we were standing beneath an overhang.

I toyed with the idea of running away, diving into one of the black cabs which kept pulling up in front of us, but then I remembered Adrik was holding all of my credit cards hostage and I doubted I'd be getting my hands on them again until my escort arrived. Besides, he had a plan. I did too. Between the two of us, we'd figure this shit out.

I was glad Adrik was with me. He'd stop anyone from manhandling me before I even had to consider a dick kick. He might have been a dull fuck, but he was damn good at his job and if my ass needed protecting, he'd throw himself over it like a human ass shield.

Someone started honking and I turned, a frown pinching my brow as I spotted a classic red Mini Cooper tearing down the road toward us, swerving past black cabs and undercutting them at highspeed, the headlights flashing and the wipers swinging back and forth. The roof held a Union Jack flag in red, white and blue and I grimaced at the gaudy thing as it pulled up right in front of us.

Rock music still blared in my head, and I swear the guy got out of the car in time with Fortunate Son by Creedence Clearwater Revival like he was the star in some cheesy romcom movie.

Despite the rain, he only wore a bright blue tank top over dark jeans, his inked arms on display, showing a myriad of tattoos that all seemed to be some form of English symbol, from a gleaming crown on his shoulder, a red phone box on his bulging bicep and a roaring lion on his right forearm. I spotted a British bulldog on his other arm too, alongside a red first-class postage stamp with the head of the Queen on it and what I was pretty sure was a five pound note curling around his wrist. His hair was a mess of blonde curls on the top of his head which fell into his silvery eyes.

My heart jolted out of rhythm with the song in my head and I blinked for the first time in a while. Looking at him made me sort of...wake up for a second. It was like my music, only louder.

His jaw was in need of a shave and as he rounded the Mini, I noticed he was wearing muddy green rubber boots nearly up to his knees. His skin was vampire pale but his muscles were werewolf worthy and I let myself stare as I took in the self-assuredness in the way he gave absolutely no fucks about the attention he was drawing. It looked like the Queen had invited him to high tea then thrown up every English cliché in the book all over him. Damn, why was that hot though?

I'd gone through a few wild years of fucking men in the hopes of finding one worth keeping around. Like, not for a relationship or anything crazy like that. But to get me off. Turned out, most guys weren't any good at that. And after a while, I'd upgraded from men when I found my soulmate in the form of a vibrator. So this guy might have been as hot as the inner rings of hell, but as he wasn't pink, rubber and built in with twenty five different pulsation settings, he wasn't my type.

He strode straight over to me and I glanced elsewhere, figuring he was lost, but he kept coming until he was right in my breathing space. I looked up at him as he chewed on gum in the very corner of his mouth, a grin aimed at me. The scent of spearmint and rain carried from his flesh and coiled through my senses, drawing me in despite my rock solid decision to ignore him.

I curled my hand into a fist in case I needed to dick punch the guy. Weirdly, Adrik wasn't making any move to push him back and one glance at him told me all I needed to know. *Great. This tatted dickwad is my escort, isn't he?*

The guy started talking but my music was still blasting and I decided I didn't care what he had to say as I shut my eyes and remained in the numb place I preferred over most interactions. But then he touched my headphones *–touched my fucking headphones!!* – plucking them right off my head and placing them on his own.

"Well she's got fuckable lips, but does she have good music taste?" he said as if to himself in a very British accent which was nothing like the Queen's. It was rough and full of grit and sent a ripple of desire straight down to my pussy. "Oh shit, she does. Fuck me, Fleetwood Mac? Sound choice."

"Wow, it's almost like I asked your opinion," I said lightly, reaching for my headphones, but he batted my hand away, tapping on his ear and pointing out a Bluetooth earpiece as he dropped my headphones around his neck.

"Not talking to you, darlin'." He winked then looked me up and down while my eyes narrowed on this rude asshole. "Yeah, her face is a ten out of ten, but her tits could be a four. I can't tell, they're hiding in a Van Halen t-shirt like two whack-a-moles. Want me to check?" He reached toward my top and I snatched his thumb in my grip, twisting it sharply in a move my brother Alexi had taught me, making his eyes widen as a curse left his lips.

"Hang on, she's doing something interesting now," he said. "I'll see if I can get a rating on her arse." He jerked his chin at me as I shoved his hand back into his chest and he sucked on his sore thumb. "Turn around, darlin', and be a dear and bend over while I take a pic for the boss."

Without my music, the numbness was wearing off and this guy was grating on my nerves.

He had his phone out ready for the photo he was so confident he was gonna get and I snatched it from his grasp, flipping it around and snapping a photo of Adrik's backside which was the most muscular ass I knew, his cheeks permanently clenched as his pants hugged the rigid planes of it. I threw the phone back at the blonde asshole and he caught it out of the air, looking down at the photo with raised eyebrows.

Adrik glanced at me with a faint frown, but remained resolutely silent, watching our interaction without comment.

The blonde guy released a wild, untamed laugh that sent a rush of heat to my clit which had absolutely no business heading on a trip there.

"That's enough," Adrik tried, side stepping into the new guy's way as he tried to snap a photo of me.

I stepped around my bodyguard as I locked my gaze on the headphones now sitting around the asshole's neck.

"She's an eight for humour," the guy spoke to who I guessed must have been my future husband. "Tits and ass to be confirmed. I'd place a bet her pussy flaps are neat but she's probably as hairy as a husky's tail down there, want me to check or are you cool for the surprise reveal tomorrow night?"

My upper lip curled back and I nudged Adrik. "Take some notes for me."

He frowned, but took out a pen and paper from his pants' pocket as I ran my gaze up and down the British piece of shit.

"Eight out of ten for the arms, the muscles are nice but the tattoos are trash, the face is pretty, but the words spewing from it bring it down to a solid six, and the outfit is a two," I said lightly, whipping my headphones off the guy's neck before he could stop me and placing them around my own.

He ran his tongue across his teeth. "I'll call you back." He killed the call, taking out his earpiece and stuffing it in his pocket, then looked to Adrik. "You can fuck off back to the City of Sin now, my boy." He clapped him twice around the cheek and Adrik growled low in his throat.

"He's good standing right there beside me actually," I said, glancing at the tiny car behind my escort. "And he won't fit in there, so we'll just take a cab back to your little Hobbit hole or whatever it is you live in."

He laughed, but there was no humour in it this time, just cold, dark savagery. "Oh poor little darlin'," he taunted. "Your brothers didn't tell you, did they? Your boy here ain't staying. He's fucking off home, ain't that right big fella?"

I scoffed, looking to Adrik, but his throat worked and for the first time, he frowned at me with a blazing emotion in his eyes that resembled an apology. *Wait...what?*

"Adrik?" I hissed, needing way more assurance in his eyes than I was getting. He had a plan. Him and my brothers had made a plan. So there was no chance he was leaving.

"Sorry, Miss Volkov, what he says is true. My flight back to Vegas is in an hour."

You've got to be fucking kidding me. I was being handed to the wolves alone? Danny Butcher could lock me in a goddamn basement for the rest of my life if he wanted. This was bullshit. My brothers wouldn't do that to me. They wouldn't.

"But you said-" I cut myself off as he dropped his eyes, shame washing over his features.

A lie. They'd fucking lied. My brothers. Him. They'd gotten me here compliant thinking there was some grand rescue plan in place, but it had been fucking bullshit!

Cold betrayal dripped through my gut and left me shellshocked. Adrik was really going to leave me here, it was already done. And I may have been trained for violence, witnessed it my whole life, but I'd still never known the reality of standing in a room full of my enemies with only myself to rely on to survive the fight.

"You can't leave," I croaked out, my walls splintering. I hadn't realised how much I'd been relying on him being here through this, on him running off with me the moment I killed Danny Butcher. He was my steed – my fucking steed!

"Adrik?" I pressed when he didn't answer, but he just bowed his head like he was out of the game, out of my life.

I was being abandoned. Ignored. Little Anya swept under the rug and dismissed. I'd never been allowed to be involved in the family business, always kept at a distance from it even when I told my brothers I was capable of killing as well as they were. But they'd never allowed it. And I'd assumed that was to protect me, but this was the opposite of protecting me. They'd sold me out. They'd finally found a use for me, and this was it.

I loved my brothers, but they'd actually agreed to this. How could they do this to me? Was I really just a sacrificial lamb to them after all this time?

"Weeeeell," the blonde asshole interjected, sticking his head between us and looking from Adrik to me. "This is fucking awkward, isn't it? Tell you what, I'll make it easier."

He lunged at me, sweeping me off my feet and making me gasp in alarm as he yanked the door of his Mini open, pulled the front seat forward and tossed me into the back. I scrambled around with a curse as he slammed the door in my face and the locks clicked. He casually wheeled my suitcase along and gave it a hard shove that sent it rolling off into the middle of the road before offering Adrik a middle finger salute and dropping into the driver's seat.

"Miss Volkov, remember what I told you!" Adrik called, looking frantic for the first time in his life. To be compliant? Fuck that. Fuck him. Fuck my brothers.

"Let me out," I snarled at the guy as he started the engine and accelerated towards my suitcase. "Wait!" I cried before he drove over it, the wheels crushing the case and sending my clothes scattering everywhere across the street. My favourite band tees, lost to the wind and the rain and I screamed at the loss of them, punching the asshole in the back of the head. "No!"

He swerved violently then turned fully around in his seat, driving faster and faster and making my stomach lurch into my throat.

"You got something to say, darlin'?" he asked through a manic smile.

"Watch the road!" I yelled, my heart thrashing.

"What road?" he asked through a smirk, driving even faster as we came up towards a sharp corner. "Ohhh *that* road."

"You're fucking crazy!"

"Crazy…or cute?" he taunted. "Now sit in your seat nicely and I'll consider looking where I'm going."

I dropped onto my ass, clicking my belt into place and half hoping we'd crash so he'd go flying through the windscreen.

He looked around just before we reached the corner and turned the wheel so hard, I slammed into the window and had to brace myself against it for several seconds as he straightened out the tiny car.

His biceps flexed and he whooped, speeding along the darkening road and I winced as he headed onto a roundabout so fast that a truck blared its horn at us. He entered a highway just as fast, and I felt every bump and rivet in the road as the small car sped along it and the engine roared inside my brain.

For the first time in a long time, I was wide awake, my senses screaming, adrenaline thumping. And I found I didn't want to fucking die.

"Name's Church by the way," he said casually like we were on friendly terms. "And you're Anya, right darlin'?"

"No, it's Brian," I spat and he snorted.

"I can tell I'm gonna like babysitting you," he said with a grin in his voice. "How's those pre-wedding jitters going for you? I hear they can be a bitch."

"Church?" I asked sweetly, trying to calm my wild heart and sink back down into a more familiar place of detachment.

"Yes, darlin'?" he asked, cocking an eyebrow at me in the rear-view mirror.

"Can you do me a favour?" I asked.

"Anythin' for a pretty face," he said, tossing me another smile which set my flesh on fire.

"See that monstrous plastic bulldog bobbing its head on your dashboard?"

"That's Barkley," he said seriously, petting the creepy thing.

"Can you shove it in your mouth as far as it'll go?" I asked in a sugary voice. "Just all the way down your throat until you stop breathing, kay? Thanks." I put my headphones on, blocking out his reply to that and closed my eyes as I put on Voodoo Child by Jimi Hendrix, letting the music flood over me and drown my emotions. It was the only way I could work through them. The fear, the loss of Adrik, my brothers' betrayal, the fact that my suitcase and every one of my valued possessions were gone, and my chance of stabbing my new husband with them.

There'll be other knives. Other weapons. It's not over.

Fuck, my credit cards were in Adrik's pocket.

Panic wasn't my style. But I was cracking a little. I just needed to think, figure out how best to proceed from here. But as we sailed further and further towards the depths of London, I started to feel the echoes of my father's fists on my flesh and my brothers running into the room to try and stop him. But it was always too late. And I never wanted them to come anyway, because if they did, they faced his wrath ten times worse.

The difference between then and now, was that I'd never wanted them to save me before, but they always had. I knew they'd show up and have my back and do anything within their power to keep me from harm. But this time they'd put me directly in the lion's den by dangling a shiny lie in front of my eyes. They'd left me in the hands of a heathen and at the very least I thought they'd sent Adrik to protect me.

I hadn't told them what I was planning myself, but maybe they knew. Maybe they expected me to fight back. But what if they didn't? What if they really did want me to marry a Butcher and be his dutiful wife for the sake of their fucking peace treaty?

I ground my teeth, feeding the piercing pain of that possibility into the rhythm in my ears and letting the music steal it away.

Everything I'd ever learned was about to be put to the test. I'd killed fools and perverts before, but I'd never been challenged with a true enemy. Someone with so much blood on their hands they could have filled two swimming pools with it and still had some to spare.

I was taking on the Devil with a teaspoon. And it looked like I was on my own.

CHAPTER TWO

I was forced out of my safe space by strong hands tugging me from the back of the car and I kept my eyes clamped shut as I tried to remain there a moment longer. But the same hands pushed my headphones down to hang around my neck and my eyes snapped open as I found myself in a concrete parking lot, penned in against the Mini Cooper by the blonde-haired maniac.

Up close, his eyes were like two silver quarters, gleaming and hard. He smelled like the rain, and the minty smell of his gum drew me in, begging me to lean into it and steal some of the life I could see thriving within his gaze. My life always felt so grey, monotonous, but I'd bet if I was able to gaze at the world through his eyes, it would be full of so much colour I'd be blinded by it.

"Wanna trade secrets?" he asked, his cocky overfamiliarity back intact.

"Is your secret that you're a terrible driver, because the cat's out of the bag, Church," I said lightly, innocently, using my words to cut, but keeping myself too sweet to appear like a true threat. It was a fine line to tread, but one which was as natural to me as breathing. So long as men couldn't quite figure me out, they were on my hook, constantly questioning my motives while being unsure whether I was insulting them or flirting with them.

"You're mistaking driving fast for driving shit. Did I crash us, darlin', or did we get here in record time?" Dimples dug into his cheeks as he smiled a broad smile and my gaze hooked on them for a second, wetting my lips. Who was this guy? My fiancé's right hand man? His friend? *Best* friend? He was important enough to be sent to collect me, so he had to be valued by the boss. And I needed to figure out how to twist that to my advantage, because now I was down my weapons, I needed to figure out how to get one before tomorrow night. And how to flee the clutches of The Firm without Adrik's fists and killer instincts to assist me. *Argh, fuck him.*

"What's your secret then? Tiny dick?" I guessed, pushing his boundaries, seeing what made him tick.

He lowered a hand to squeeze his cock through his jeans. "Wanna check?"

"And what would your boss think of that?" I feigned a gasp and he chuckled.

"You're his tomorrow, not his right now. And seeing as I'm the only one here, I guess that makes me your hen."

"My what?" I frowned.

"Your hen. For your hen do."

My frown grew. What the hell was he talking about?

"For your bachelorette, darlin'," he sniggered. "I'll double as your hen, your stripper and your last free fuck, if you like?"

"Oh wow," I breathed like I was considering it, looking him up and down. "That's so damn tempting, Church. But there's just one problem."

"Oh yeah? What's that?" he murmured, resting one hand on the roof of his car while leaning in close, crowding my space and making my breath hitch. Fuck me, that face was Adonis hot. Maybe it wouldn't be the worst idea to fuck it. Of course, then I remembered him driving over my suitcase and a snarl built in my throat, hatred swiftly following.

I pressed two fingers to his chest, giving him a hungry smile which made his pupils dilate as I started walking my fingers up towards his neck. I kept my voice low and sultry as I spoke every word, planning on maximum damage as I lured him into my trap. "You make me want to push you onto the ground and crawl all the way up your body..."

"And then?" he pressed, practically dripping sex as he shifted even closer, devouring the space between us.

"*Then* I'd tear your shirt off and kneel either side of your head…" I purred and he nodded in encouragement, his cock growing hard against my hip and showing me the reason for that huge ego of his. "Then I'd drive a blade into your pretty face again and again until there's nothing left of it." I booped him on the nose, ducked under his arm and walked away towards the elevator.

His laughter followed me and he caught up a beat later, slinging his arm over my shoulders, locking it tightly there so I had no chance of getting it off.

"I just love strangers touching me inappropriately," I said dryly.

"So, our secret trade," he continued like he hadn't heard me and I wondered if this dude had an off switch. He was so…peppy. "I'll go first seeing as you just flew three thousand and a bit miles to see me."

I rolled my eyes. Was this it? The big, bad Firm? Were all the Brits like this? Because this guy might have been a little cuckoo, but he wasn't exactly scaring the panties off of me.

"I'm related to someone famous," he said. "My name's not actually Church, see? It's a nickname because of my heritage. Wanna guess who?" He grinned smugly and I tried to tune him out, wishing for my music as he kept going. "It's Winston Churchill," he said dramatically. "I'm like his great, great, great, grandson's cousin or something."

"Oh my god," I gasped and he nodded, that smug as pie smile continuing to grow.

"I know, right?"

"No, I mean, oh my god, I literally couldn't care any less. Like, imagine the amount you think I care and divide that by a billion, then you're getting close." I twisted out of his grip on my shoulders as he punched the button for the elevator.

"You'd care if you knew anything about him," he said, not giving up on trying to impress me with this. Though why he gave a fuck what I thought, I had no idea.

"He was your old president or whatever and led your country through the second world war." I shrugged. "You don't get to claim any of his glory."

"Firstly, we don't have presidents, Miss America, we have prime ministers. And secondly, I get to claim *all* of his glory because his blood runs in my veins." He pounded his fist against his chest like a gorilla.

"Well how about you hand me a knife and I'll deal with that for you by spilling it all over the floor?" I batted my lashes and he growled, literally growled like a beast.

The elevator doors opened and he hounded me inside, making me back up until my spine hit the far wall. The doors slid closed and seemed to suck all the air out of the space as he rested his hands above me on the mirror, teeth bared, animal on show. I could see the evil in him at last, peeking through the illusion of safety painted on his skin. He wasn't some dudebro asshole, he was dangerous. And suddenly I felt exposed, vulnerable, and I craved my music more than ever, my fingers twitching for my iPod, the urge to pull my headphones on and numb out nearly consuming me.

"Don't listen, Anya," my brother Zakhar's voice whispered in my ear. "You can stay in your own world so long as the music is playing."

I so wanted it to play right now. Because I desperately didn't want to feel like that small girl who could hear her daddy's footsteps heading toward her room. I always despised the relief I felt when he kept walking, when he chose one of my brothers instead to sate his rage. And the guilt was only ever eased by the music. The crash of drums and the roar of a guitar in my head. So long as it was loud and booming and didn't stop, then the world outside me didn't exist.

"Scared, darlin'?" Church purred, knocking his knuckle under my chin as he took one hand off of the mirror. The elevator started rising beneath us and I tilted my head back to hold his gaze. No fear would cross my features, indifference was my friend. Because if he knew he was getting under my skin, then the game was up.

"Fear is for children," I said with a shrug.

"Then why are you shaking, Anya?" he asked, twisting his fingers into a lock of my platinum hair.

God, the way he said my name. It was like he owned it, every letter wrapped around his tongue never to let go.

"It's cold," I lied smoothly, the sound of The Killing Moon by Echo & the Bunnymen playing in my head again from the past. *Don't go there*. It was the one song I couldn't listen to anymore, despite how it had helped me at the time. But now it was an embodiment of that night, of the screams the lyrics had helped me blot out. "I was born in the desert."

"And now one day you'll die in the rain." He smirked as if he liked that idea, wrapping the lock of hair tight around his knuckle and pulling so my head was jerked forward, our mouths burningly close.

I tasted his next words more than I heard them, the brush of his lips against mine like the seven sins combined. It was as terrifying as it was thrilling, and I found myself surprisingly drawn to the darkness I saw lurking in his eyes. "You're ours now, Miss America. Branded, bought and sold. Butcher might put a ring on you tomorrow, but I'll always be your watcher, the one who keeps an eye on every move you make at every minute of the day. And if you think I don't see the plan to run away swirling in your pretty onyx eyes, you're so very fucking wrong, darlin'. There's a treaty to uphold and I take that as serious as a chip butty on a Sunday, you get me?"

What the fuck is a chip butty?

My upper lip curled in a sneer, my anger rising like a sea swell only for me to push it down deep within me again. Now wasn't the time to lose my head. I was only going to get one shot at killing Danny Butcher and this douchebag wasn't going to get in my way. Church thought I was planning to run, which was good, because that meant he didn't think I had the balls to try and kill his boss. But I did. Big invisible man balls which hung between my thighs like two grapefruits. And he'd realise that the moment he found his precious boss in a pool of his own blood. *Oh I won't run, baby, I'll fight.*

"Do you get me, Miss America?" he pushed.

"I got you," I said coolly.

He shoved off of the mirror as the doors opened once more then gestured for me to walk past him into the plain corridor that awaited us. "Now if you don't mind gettin' a trot on, darlin', I have an ass to judge while you're walking."

I kicked off of the mirror, striding away from him and flipping him off over my shoulder. "You owe me a new collection of band t-shirts."

"Alright, suck my cock and we'll talk."

I bared my teeth, glaring back at him over my shoulder, finding his eyes firmly on my ass. "I'd literally rather swallow a cold, dead fish whole."

"That would make for some interesting evening entertainment," he said thoughtfully. "I'll see what I can do. Would you rather deepthroat a trout or a carp?"

"Surprise me." I hooked my headphones onto my ears as Church walked past me, taking hold of my elbow and leading me to a door across the hall. It was some old apartment block and I drowned out the sound of some guy screaming at his wife as I hit play on She's Not There by The Zombies.

Church led me into the simple studio with a kitchenette on one side, a double bed on the other and a door that led off into the bathroom. There were posters of bands which I was irritated to admit I loved plastered on the far wall alongside a grungy looking British flag and an assortment of ticket stubs which were jammed into the side of a mirror, documenting the amount of time he'd spent in the company of live music. I envied him that.

The windows were large and gave a view out onto the street below which was brightly lit now that night had fallen, and I caught a glimpse of London as rain washed against them. I could see The Gherkin and part of The Shard too, the iconic buildings making my pulse spike a little as I drank in the sight of them. Red buses weaved along the narrow road in queues of heavy traffic while cyclists risked their lives whizzing between all the vehicles. It was a furious buzz of frantic energy and close-packed bodies, and yet something about it called to me on a primal level, the history of this place seeming to sing from the ancient streets and work its way through the cracks in the walls I held tight around my heart. It was beautiful. Even in the drowning rain, painted in tones of endless grey, there was something so full of vitality and life to the city that I couldn't help but feel drawn to it.

A bleep sounded within my headphones that made the bottom drop out of my stomach and I wrenched them off in a panic, backing up to the door.

"I need to go to the store to get a new charging cable for these." My back hit the wood and my fingers locked around the doorhandle, jiggling it frantically but it was locked.

Church ignored me, pulling his shirt off and tossing it on the bed, turning to face the window and revealing a Spitfire airplane inked across his back with bombs dropping from beneath it down his spine. Damn, that ink was fucking nice, but fuck if I'd ever serve him a compliment over it.

"Church," I barked and he looked around lazily.

"I'm gonna get an early night," he said, kicking his shoes off and yawning as he walked to the bed.

No you're fucking not.

I ran forward, leaping onto it before he could make it there, my pulse wild as I slapped a hand to his shoulder to stop him advancing. "I need a fucking charger and if you don't get me one, I will scream and scream and scream until the cops come."

His flesh was searingly hot against mine and I swear I could feel his dark soul dancing at the edges of his skin, daring me to come closer.

"What do I get out of it, darlin'?" he asked in a low voice, hooking an arm around my back and yanking me closer as he gazed up at me with the Devil in his eyes.

I sneered at him, my fingers itching for a blade to drive into this asshole's chest.

"What do you want?" I hissed, despising him, but I would have sold my soul to keep those headphones alive. I couldn't live without my music. I'd get no sleep, and eventually the demons would break in again and I'd fall prey to their claws and teeth. They were always waiting to come in, but the music kept them at bay, it closed the doors and bolted them tight. Without it, I didn't know what would happen. And I didn't want to.

He frowned as he took in my expression and I worked to mask the desperation in my eyes, but when it came to this one thing, I was weak. And it looked like he was working that out fast.

"A kiss," he said, not blinking, his eyes sliding down to my mouth as his muscular arm tightened around me, becoming a rigid, immovable cage.

A kiss? A fucking kiss? Was he for real? I was his boss's fiancé. I'd be walking down the aisle tomorrow, bound to a man he served.

"What about Danny?" I whispered, knowing I'd already made my decision on this. A kiss was a low price to pay for my music. And a twisted part of me knew I'd have given more, given anything to keep the music playing.

"Don't let it stop playing, Anya," Zakhar begged, his face twisted in pain. "Look at me. Just me. Let the music fill you up until there's nothing else."

"Like I said, darlin', he's your tomorrow. You don't even have an engagement ring on that pretty finger of yours. So what harm's a little kiss between friends?" His lips twisted into a psycho's smirk and his dimples looked more like bullet holes in his cheeks as he stared at me. And he really did stare, like he was hungry for what he saw, a beast with an empty belly and an appetite for American girls in baggy t-shirts.

"Then you'll get me my charger?" I confirmed, my teeth grinding at giving in to this. But he was just some trash guy, what did it matter? I'd kissed dudes like him before. The only difference was I hated this one.

"I swear on my ma's grave," he said sincerely.

I swallowed the rising lump in my throat, letting my fingers sail over his shoulder and slide around the back of his neck. He watched me like a predator luring in its prey, but I was no rabbit in the claws of a leopard. I'd take this kiss, not give it.

I leaned down, digging my nails hard into his flesh as my pussy clenched and the intoxicating aura of him enveloped me. My breaths quickened, mingling with his as his arm unlocked from me and both his hands cupped my ass instead, yanking me flush to his body. He tipped his chin up as I leaned down and I swear I heard the sweet serenity of music thrumming between us, but the tune wasn't one I knew. I'd heard endless songs, knew countless lyrics, but this was new to me. Something that resembled the rampant, primitive rhythm of life itself. A life I so desperately wanted to live.

"Did you really think I'd kiss Butcher's girl?" his cruel voice crawled over me like an infestation of termites and I froze, still so close to him, he was all I could see.

His eyes weren't full of colour anymore, they were shadowed and villainous and they were shutting me out like two iron walls. He started laughing, squeezing a handful of my ass then shoving me back so I fell onto the bed like a sack of shit. I stared up at him with my cheeks scalding and I slipped readily into the monster that lived in me. I was music-less and merciless. And he was going to fucking pay.

"Ten out of ten for the ass, by the way," he said, still laughing as he walked away with his back to me.

I shoved off of the bed, stalking up behind him on silent feet and kicking the back of his knee hard. He buckled, his knee hitting the floor as he let out a yell of surprise and I slipped my fingers into his back pocket, tugging out the keys to the apartment. I was already running by the time he was coming after me, hooking up my headphones on the way and unlocking the door before he caught me. I slipped outside, slamming it behind me and the weight of a beast collided with it.

I sprinted for the elevator just as it opened and an elderly couple stepped out. Their shocked faces said I had a pursuer hot on my heels but I made it inside, twisting around with a sharp inhale of breath as I saw him coming for me like a charging rhino. I jammed my finger on the shut door button over and over again, but as the doors started to close, he leapt through them with a victorious laugh and collided with me like a battering ram, whirling me around in his arms with the momentum of his run before setting me straight on my feet again.

But instead of the beating I expected to come, he wrapped his hand around mine and started fucking whistling as he pushed the ground floor button.

"That was fun," he said, shooting me a grin. "Let's do it naked next time."

The doors opened and he dragged me out of them onto the street, still shirtless and without shoes like he gave no fucking shits about anything. I growled as he towed me towards an electrical shop, weaving through the endless sea of people with ease, somehow guiding me between the crush of bodies without a single one of them so much as brushing against me despite how closely packed they were. Rain peppered my cheeks before he led me inside the store, earning himself a lot of odd looks as he guided me up to the storekeeper, snatched my headphones from my grip and placed them down on the counter.

The woman's lips parted and her eyes dipped to take in Church's abs for a second before she blinked several times and looked up at his face. "Can I help you?"

"I bought these headphones for my girlfriend last week, but they're broken so I want a new pair, darlin'. Can you sort me out?" he asked smoothly and I frowned up at him, still trying to jerk my fingers out of his vice like grip.

"Oh, sure…do you have a receipt?" she asked.

"Not unless you count the one in my memory," he said with a smirk.

"Do you have the box they came in at least?" she asked, her lashes still acting like demented butterflies.

"No, my girl sat on it, didn't you darlin'?" He nudged me then looked back at the girl. "Look, beautiful, I need a little helping hand here, see? My girl's halfway through an audiobook about a chick who gets abducted by an alien with a tentacle dick and she'll listen to it without the headphones all night long if I don't get her new ones. I mean, sure, I'm happy for her to come climbing onto my cock at three am sobbing because the tentacle bloke almost died, and I'll even let her paint me blue before she rides me like a horny space cadet that needs breeding, but I got work to do before then. Can't you just slip these little broken ones into the trash, hand me a new pair and I'll get outa your lovely hair?" He winked at her and I scoffed, but then the girl looked at me like I was a tentacle porn addict and my scoff died in my throat as she apparently believed his whole story. And far be it from me to let the embarrassment rest solely on my head.

"Well, you do owe me after you watched that milking porno and asked to suckle my teets like a newborn calf," I said in a purr and Church looked at me with his grin growing even wider. Shit, were we having…fun? Ergh. Not a chance.

"Well, you didn't have to go the extra mile and wear the cow costume, did you darlin'? But fuck me, I wasn't complainin'."

"No you were mooing loudly as I remember, honey, and then you told me take your bull horn like a good little bovine." I tickled his chin and glanced at the attendant whose flirtatious expression had now twisted into something much closer to horror.

"You're always horny for my horn," Church murmured, making me almost snort a laugh.

"Here," the girl said quickly, placing down a brand new pair of headphones which looked like an upgrade from mine.

"Cheers, sweetheart." Church's smile fell away just like that and he handed them to me before guiding me out of the store.

He glanced at me as we headed up the street and I had the feeling he was looking for a thank you. Well he was looking in the wrong place because it was shoved right up his ass.

"Got you a new iPod charger too." He produced it from his pocket. "And a mini torch." He waved a tiny pink flashlight at me, clicking it on and off to blind me before pushing it into my free hand with the headphones.

"Is this supposed to make up for you running over my suitcase and destroying everything I own?"

"Not really." He shrugged. "Could a tiny torch really make up for your suitcase going boom and all of your prized possessions exploding across the road in a shower of memories?"

My spine prickled with anger.

"So is it me you hate or my family in general?" I asked icily.

"Both."

"Wow, imagine how hateful you'd be if you got sold into a lifetime of misery without your consent," I said airily.

"Hey, I didn't sign no treaty, Anya. If it was up to me, I'd still be in a bloody war against your family along with the rest of the cunts."

"So you're against what your boss did?" I snagged hold of that bit of information and he glanced at me, his jaw pulsing.

"I didn't say that."

"You kinda did," I pointed out and he glanced around the street like he was worried he was being watched before towing me back to the building and into the elevator once more.

He didn't speak again until we made it to the apartment and he locked the door tight behind us, finally releasing my hand. My fingers felt bruised from how tight he'd held on and as he moved away across the room to grab a bottle of brandy out of the kitchen cupboard, I started ripping into my headphones box.

"Listen, I ain't on your side," he said, taking a box of cigars from a drawer and tucking one into the corner of his mouth. This dude really was taking the Winston Churchill thing too far. "I'm just sayin', I woulda done things different."

"Yeah, I heard you. You'd rather be at war." I dropped to my knees by a socket, pushing the three-pronged plug into it and connecting the cable to the headphones. I sat on the floor with them in my lap, my anxiety putting on a parade through my chest as I pressed my back to the wall. *Come on, little headphones. Let's get your charge on.*

"Uhuh," he agreed then pointed at me with the cigar. "Anyway, you owe me a secret and I know which one I want. And seeing as I got you those headphones and I can take 'em away again anytime I fancy, you're gonna answer me straight."

My grip tightened on the headphones, but the look in his eyes said I'd lose the fight for them if he went through with that threat. "Fine. What do you want to know? My bra size?"

"Nah, I'll be able to tell that the second you wear somethin' fitted, darlin'."

"Note to self, never wear anything fitted."

"You ain't seen your wedding dress yet, have you?" he taunted.

Fuck.

"And you have?" I demanded.

"Nah, but Danny's fucking predictable. He likes his women with their tits pushed together and their asses on show. You'll be his prized possession, at least until he gets bored. But from the look of you, I'd say it'll be a while."

Silence echoed for a moment as my skin crawled with biting ants and I almost could have sworn there was an ounce of pity in Church's eyes.

His throat bobbed as he puffed on his cigar and the sweet smoke carried to me on the air. "So here's what I wanna know, Miss America." He jerked his chin at the headphones. "What's with the music? I ain't never seen someone panic over headphones like they're the goddamn Queen's corgis gone missing."

I clutched the headphones tighter and let a lie spill against my lips as I formed the right words. Because the truth wasn't ever to be told. It was mine to keep, to bear. And I didn't want this arrogant dipshit having anything to do with it.

"It reminds me of home," I said and he nodded slowly, placing his cigar in an ashtray that was shaped like a red British mail box.

"See…that's a dirty, filthy lie, Anya," he said in a tone that set my veins buzzing with violent energy. "So when you're ready to tell me the truth, I'll be all ears."

He finished his cigar then unbuckled his pants, pushing them off along with his socks before heading into the bathroom to brush his teeth. When he returned, my gaze travelled up his athletic body, tracing the ink over his chest, reading the quote there which I recognised as the words of Winston Churchill - '*If you're going through hell, keep going.*' There was a ring of truth to those words which gave me pause and made me wonder what hell this beast of a man had lived through. I had to guess he was five or six years older than me, probably into his thirties, plenty of time to have lived through several hells in this kind of life. My gaze continued to soak in the sight of his bare chest, moving on from that quote and trailing lower to the V that dipped deep down beneath his black boxers.

"Are you coming to bed or are you gonna sit on the floor all night? It gets fucking cold in here, so be warned. The floor's an unforgiving mistress," he said as he got into bed.

I glanced around the place, realising there wasn't even so much as a chair in here to sleep on. It was the bed or the floor. But frankly, I wasn't moving anywhere until my headphones were charged anyway, and what was a little cold? Sure, I was used to a much warmer climate, but how bad could it really get?

Silence fell between us and Church turned the light off with a switch above the bed, plunging us into near total darkness, though the headlights from the traffic rippled across the ceiling.

I remained there for an endless amount of time, trying to slip into my numb place by repeating songs in my head, but it wasn't the same. I needed the din in my ears, the constant beat, the deep tremor of a rocker's voice.

The longer I sat there, the more the darkness crept in on me.

Tomorrow, I'll be married.

Tomorrow, my fate will be sealed.

Tomorrow, I'll kill my husband or I'll die trying.

Tick, tick, tick. The obnoxious clock shaped like Big Ben was so fucking loud. But not loud enough to steal away my thoughts.

The memories started pouring in and I heard screams rattling in the back of my skull as claws seemed to tear down my spine.

"Play the music, Anya."

"I can't," I whispered, pressing the button on the headphones for the hundredth attempt. But this time, they flashed on and relief swept through me as I placed them over my ears and quickly hooked them up to my iPod.

As Panic by The Smiths wrapped around me like a hug, I released a steadier breath and realised it came out in a fog before me. *Holy fucking hell, it's freezing.*

I shivered my way through eight songs before I gave in to the inevitable and got up, heading into the small bathroom. There was only one toothbrush and I eyed it for an intense moment before snatching it up and coating it in toothpaste, stuffing it in my mouth. I glanced at myself in the mirror, my head bobbing to the tune as I scrubbed my teeth clean, the scent of peppermint washing over my senses. When I was done, I kicked off my shoes, pulled off my leggings and slipped back into the bedroom, creeping up to the edge of Church's bed.

He was passed out, his arm slung over the pillow above him and a crease between his eyes that said his sleep wasn't restful. I vaguely wondered what haunted a man like Church and wished I could hear his thoughts now so I could wield them against him in the morning.

I pulled the covers back and climbed under them, the heat of Church's body radiating to me and making a heady sigh fall from my lips. *Damn radiator man. At least you're good for something.*

I shamelessly put my ice cold feet on his legs and he grunted in his sleep, the discomfort on his face growing and causing a satisfied smile to pull at my lips. I curled up like a cat, wedging my feet more firmly between his muscular thighs and drifted down into the blissful numb. Where no one on this earth could follow.

ANYA

CHAPTER THREE

One Day Like This by Elbow drifted into my consciousness and my chest filled with the sunlight which seemed to be contained within the song. I'd always thought the rise and fall of this rhythm might be how it would feel to fall in love, the music seeming to build towards some cathartic conclusion that would ensure everything was right in the world.

But the world didn't work like that. I'd been raised in the shadows and exposed to the cruelty that lay in the dark. I'd seen lovers turn on each other at the prospect of money, I'd seen sisters draw blood on each other's flesh over men, I'd seen fathers cut off their children in the name of pride. But I'd always thought the love I shared with my brothers was different, unbreakable. Until now. Because I was waking up in a stranger's bed alone, with no shield around me, no plan in place to protect me. They'd been a wall of safety between me and my enemies, whether they were there or not. An invisible shield I could always feel the touch of on my flesh despite never asking them to provide it. But now my flesh was barren, and I realised for the first time in my life that our love wasn't the unshakeable force I'd once believed it to be. If this was love, then all the love songs ever written were a lie.

Someone started shaking me and my headphones were jolted off my head as their hands tightened on my arms to the point of pain. I squinted up at my attacker with a snarl, finding Church rearing over me with his toothbrush jammed in the corner of his mouth and his eyes full of sleep.

"Get up, darlin'. We're fucking late." A few stray blonde curls fell forward into his gaze, making him look wilder than he had last night.

"Stop. Shaking. Me. Then," I gritted out as he continued to bounce my whole body on the mattress.

He laughed around his toothbrush, continuing to scrub his teeth as he sat back and let go of me. He was in his boxers, his abs tight as he watched me slink out of my cocoon and the cold in the room found me, making my nipples peak and my mood descend further.

"Don't you have a heater?" I asked through chattering teeth, wanting to stay within the warmth of the bed as more of the cold air found its way beneath the comforter. England sucked ass so far. Where were the tiny teacups and cute little hedgehogs wearing aprons? Oh right, they were tattooed on this asshole's body. A body I was paying far too much attention to.

"That would require me paying my landlord to fix it," he said around his toothbrush, so much frothy toothpaste building up in his mouth that it was on the verge of spilling out. "And I ain't payin' him until he replies to my email about him being an exorbitant cunt. I'm expecting a reply any day now."

I released a snort of amusement, caught off guard, then flattened my features into a scowl. Church was a jackass with an emphasis on the ass. I got out of bed, taking my iPod with me as I headed to the bathroom, feeling his eyes on me as I went.

"Jesus, your legs are a ten too. Three for the cold feet though, darlin'. I gave you a free heat sesh on my legs, but next time you wanna use them to heat up those icicles I'll expect somethin' in return."

I flipped him off and kicked the door shut, placing my iPod on the basin and playing Day Tripper by The Beatles, letting it fill up the space. I pulled my t-shirt off, wondering what the fuck I was even supposed to wear today, but too cold to worry about it as I dropped my panties and stepped into the tiny shower unit with red, white and blue tiles on the walls – *of course*. What was this guy's obsession with Britain anyway? He was freaking raised here, wasn't he? I might have lived in Vegas my whole life, but I didn't go around tattooing slot machines and Elvis impersonators on my tits, did I?

The shower products were all contained within bottles that looked like British bulldogs and I muttered under my breath about his terrible taste before twisting the shower on.

I screamed, like motherfucking screamed my lungs out as the ice-cold water hit me like a punch to the face.

Church walked straight into the room without knocking and rinsed out his mouth in the sink, tossing the toothbrush into the red bus holder. I cursed, turning my back on him and covering my tits with my hands.

"It's fucking freezing," I snapped, glaring back over my shoulder at him.

"Yeah, you have to jiggle it," he said, dropping his boxers and striding straight into the shower with me.

I was so taken aback that I didn't even move, just stood there as his huge body rutted up against mine and my gaze dropped automatically to his dick. Which was massive, at half mast, and had a piercing in the end of it. It was the kind of cock I imagined a porn star would get a lifetime contract for, and I tried not to stare too hard before snatching my gaze away from it.

"Of course you have a fucking Prince Albert," I muttered and he smirked, not seeming bothered by the cold water as it ran over his hair and soaked him.

"Jiggle it then," Church said, a dare in his voice and I scowled at him, fronting this out as I reached for the knob on the wall and jiggled it without breaking eye contact.

He licked his lips, tasting the icy droplets running over them and I had the crazy desire to do the same.

"Try the other knob," he suggested, mischief in his eyes and I glanced at the wall.

"There is no other – ergh, you are such a pig," I hissed as I realised he meant his cock and he roared a laugh. "There's no hot water is there?"

"Nope. I can give you a golden shower if you like though, seeing as you enjoy my body warming you up so much," he taunted and my upper lip peeled back.

I grabbed his shampoo and fixed my attention on the wall as I washed my hair, my teeth locked tight. But his cock kept grazing my ass and I swear every time it did, it was harder, bigger. *How can it be bigger? It's already giving the shampoo bottle a run for its money.*

"How's it feel taking a shower with a relative of Winston Churchill? I suppose you'll be posting all over social media about it to your little American friends. But don't mention my name, yeah darlin'? I'm kind of a big deal."

"Oh I won't. I'll be sure to keep it a secret in my journal." I put on a dreamy voice as I continued. "Dear diary, today a man named Church brought me to his skanky apartment full of trashy tourist crap. He talks like the teapot from Beauty and the Beast and acts like he lives in the Queen's palace instead of a tiny studio apartment with no heating-"

"Hey," he snarled angrily, spinning me around and pointing in my face. "Mrs Potts is an insult to Brits. She speaks like Oliver Twist's grandma and not a single cunt in this country likes her. And if they do, they ain't a true Brit to me, they're a cunt just like Mrs Potts is a cunt."

He looked so serious about that that a surprised smile quirked up my lips. The rage slid from his features and the hand pointing at me reached out to cup my chin. He started studying my face like he'd never seen it before, a crease forming between his eyes. I wanted to reach up and push his hand off me, but I was frozen, and not just by the arctic water. By him and his dominating aura which made something grow in the empty space within my chest.

"What about Chip?" I breathed, my voice suddenly not working all that well.

"Chip's a little cunt too," he said and my smile grew wider, making him shift even closer so the hard, silky shaft of his cock pressed to my hip.

"When you smile, it's hard to remember I despise you, Miss America," he said in a deep growl that made my clit throb and my knees threaten to buckle. I wasn't the swooning type. Fuck, I was the type who kneed guys like this in the balls and threw their Playstation out the window if they pissed me off. But when he was this near to me, looking at me like *that* with this few clothes on, maybe I didn't entirely despise him. Or at least I liked him enough to consider hate fucking him.

I flattened my lips, building up my defences against this stranger again, reminding myself of who he was connected to. My dreaded fiancé. "Thanks for the tip. I'll remember not to offer smiles out so easily in future."

I ducked past him, grabbing a towel and wrapping it around me while taking another for my hair as I picked up my band tee and walked out of the bathroom.

Now what the hell was I going to wear?

I dried myself off before heading to the set of drawers near the bed, tugging them open one at a time and finding an endless amount of brightly coloured clothes in there. Most of which were either red, white or blue. Was he for real?

I grabbed some blue boxers and pulled on a white Beatles t-shirt which I was officially claiming as mine seeing as he owed me a whole closet full of band tees. Shame that it smelled like him though. Not that his smell was bad, but as it belonged to him, I'd be sure to wash it out of this shirt as soon as I could.

I realised I'd left my iPod in the bathroom and the music had changed to Psycho Killer by Talking Heads.

Holy fuck, did I just go somewhere without taking my music with me? Yikes, it must be the jet lag.

I'd been doing pretty well so far in not thinking about where this morning was heading, but time was ticking by and the reality was starting to creep in now. The wedding was coming. This afternoon, I'd be announced as Mrs Butcher, and honestly that made me want to open the window to my right and hurl myself out of it onto the street below. One swift fall and a painful crack to the head would end all of my problems. I'd have to incriminate Church in a final act of defiance, so I'd punch myself in the face and go backwards when I went to give the illusion of being pushed. Little wins and all.

Church appeared from the shower, butt naked and towelling his hair dry as he strode across the room, his still giant but now deflated cock telling me he had just dealt with his morning glory.

His cheeks were slightly flushed and my throat thickened at the post orgasm face of this British demi-god, his smirk still intact as his gaze fell on me wearing his clothes.

"I'll be wanting those back at some point, darlin'," he warned.

"We all want things we can't have, Church," I said lightly. "Personally, I'd like to punch you in the balls and hop on a one way flight back to Vegas after I set your quirky little shithole of an apartment alight. Sadly, it's not to be."

He grunted before grabbing some clothes out of the drawers and pulling them on. He chose a fitted blue shirt with long sleeves and a badger silhouette on the front of it, pairing it with black jeans which hugged his ass and a belt that had the buckle of the Big Ben clocktower on it. *Oh, come on.*

A loud knock sounded at the door and Church moved quickly to the bed like a ninja, reaching under his mattress and taking a fucking cricket bat into his grip. He headed to the door, looking through the peephole as I searched the space for a weapon in case a fight was coming.

I slipped to the kitchenette, opening a drawer and taking out a sharp little fish knife, holding it in such a way that the blade was concealed against my palm, my pulse thumping erratically at the base of my throat.

I moved closer to the door as Church yanked it open, the bat going slack in his hand just as I prepared to fight.

A man stepped into the room who was the size of a tank; he was mixed race with dark skin and unusually blue eyes that seemed to hold a bigger void than the one which lived in me. His face was chiselled into perfect straight lines, his jaw a work of art, the symmetry in his features so exact he was like a model. His hair was shaved and made him look shit hot, like some sort of action movie star.

Who in the name of the motherfucking United Kingdom was this?

"Morning, Frank," Church said brightly, clapping him on the shoulder. Frank didn't seem to like that, his face twisting in a slight sneer as he looked at Church.

"You're late," he snapped in a deep baritone voice that sent a shockwave down to my pussy. *Woah, back it up*. "The bride was meant to be at the hotel an hour ago." He spoke like I wasn't there and it immediately rubbed me the wrong way. Which was a shame, because I was pretty sure if this guy rubbed me the right way, I'd be coming all over his fingers in no time.

"Keep your knickers on, she's heading there with you now, aren't you darlin'? I've got a job to run before I can join in with the fun," Church said, throwing me a grin.

I shrugged, not giving a shit as I headed to the bed to get my headphones while having some internal stern words with my tingling clit. *These guys are not your friends. They're your enemies.* My clit seemed to be even more excited about that, so I gave up on trying to reason with it and ignored the message it was trying to communicate to me in Morse code about fucking the two assholes in the room.

I took a moment to slide the fish knife into the waistband of the boxers I was wearing, keeping it flush against my hip. My music was still playing in the bathroom, Hurt by Johnny Cash carrying through the air, but it was starting to sound too far away now and I didn't like it. The arrival of this new guy was setting me on edge, reminding me that I had an aisle to walk down today, and I wasn't anywhere near prepared for that.

Frank looked furious and I was kinda surprised there wasn't steam billowing from his ears as I moved to grab my things.

Headphones – check. iPod – check. Van Halen band tee – check. Chargers – check. Well, I guessed that was it thanks to Church.

"Don't forget your mini torch," Church said, picking it up from where I'd abandoned it on the floor last night. He dangled it in front of me on the little chain attached to it and I gave him a dry look.

"Oh no…please don't let me forget that," I deadpanned and he grinned, stepping forward, tugging up my shirt a little and tucking it into the waistband of my boxers. My heart thrashed as he caught hold of the fish knife, tugging it out and giving me a wolf's grin as he promptly tucked it into his pocket, keeping the movement hidden from Frank. My breathing stuttered but I kept my expression neutral, bored, and he dropped the shirt again a beat later.

Fuck.

"You'll be a good girl today, won't you Miss America?" he purred, his eyes dancing with our secret. There was a warning in his words and I had to wonder why he was sparing me the wrath of his boss by covering for my ass. Or maybe he was going to call Danny the moment I left and tip him off about my obvious intentions.

He could fuck up everything if Danny took the threat seriously. But that wasn't going to deter me. I'd made my mind up and I was going to kill the man who thought he could own me. Tonight. My biggest problem was fucking up this whole treaty my brothers had sacrificed me for. But if they really expected me to spread my legs obediently and birth the spawn of my enemy, then they didn't know me at all. There *was* a chance they expected me to fight, however. And that was an idea I preferred to believe, because the alternative made me question everything they'd ever been to me. So I was going to hold onto the image of me turning up at home with Danny Butcher's blood dried on my skin and imagine their faces splitting into perfect smiles as they congratulated me for doing just as they'd hoped. Okay, maybe I'd wash the blood off first. Airport customs and all.

"What are you not understandin' about the word late? Move. Now," Frank barked at me, making my heart flinch and Church stepped aside to let me go.

I tightened my lips as I kicked on my sneakers and stepped into the hall, not looking at the knife-stealing dickwad again.

Frank followed me out of the apartment like the Grim Reaper at my back, his shadow consuming everything I was and if it was possible to get even colder, I did.

"Bye, darlin'," Church called. "See you at the wedding."

I didn't respond, my heart beginning to thump to an anxious beat in my chest that wasn't like any song I'd listened to before. This one was calm and deadly. Frank gripped the crook of my elbow and his large hand locked tight around my skin like a shackle.

He guided me into the elevator, his gaze fixed on the doors and I glanced at the large knife strapped to his hip. If I grabbed it, stabbed hard and furiously up into his throat, I could take him by surprise. One, sharp, swift stab and then

I could run. Run and run and run until my feet were bloody and no one could find me.

But then where would I go? What would I do? How would I get home?

No…it was too irrational an idea. And if I was caught, I'd lose my chance to kill the man I really wanted dead. The one who would be bound to me in marriage by the end of this day.

I took a slow breath and Frank turned his head, looking down at me with a menacing glare on his face. To say he hated me was well off base. This man looked like he wanted my skin to melt under the intensity of his gaze and expose the bones hidden beneath it before turning them to ash. And he wouldn't even wince while he watched.

There was something about that energy which was both terrifying and dangerously hot.

"Church may have shown you decency, Miss Volkov, but that decency ends here. I will not tolerate disobedience, do you understand me?"

My eyes narrowed at his bossiness and my demons rose to the challenge of it. "And what will you do if I'm bad? Spank me?" I arched a brow, causing a sneer to pull at his lips and I just couldn't help but goad him like I always had with Adrik. "Are you going to go all Christian Grey on me and tie me up at your mercy?"

He came at me in a move that could only have been professional and I ducked fast with skill of my own, narrowly missing his outstretched hands. But there was nowhere to go inside this steel box and as I darted around him, he caught my arm, twisting it up behind my back and shoving me against the wall hard enough to make me gasp in pain. His mouth fell to my ear as I panted, blonde tendrils of hair fluttering against my lips as he held me in place with a terrifying strength.

"My job is to deliver you to a location in town, and I'll happily tie your hands to your ankles and gag you while I do it."

"Kinky," I rasped, wincing as he gripped my arm even tighter.

"I'd fuck a Volkov the same day I'd slit my own throat," he spat.

"Whatever gets you off," I said, jerking against his hold once more, but it was pointless.

He grunted as the elevator doors slid open and dragged me through them while keeping me pulled tightly back against his body. We approached a white van parked near to Church's Mini and I dug my heels in, deciding I wasn't in the mood to be compliant.

"I want to ride in the front," I demanded.

"Tough shit," he muttered, releasing me with one arm as he slid the side door open and shoved me inside. I crashed onto the hard surface on my knees, twisting around to face him and finding purest hellfire awaiting me within that desperately hollow gaze of his.

"You'll probably want to hold onto something." He smirked then slid the door shut hard, plunging me into absolute darkness.

My heart rate shot up and screams ripped through my skull like they lived here, now, in the present.

"No, Mom," I gasped, my voice childlike, echoing the past.

I squeezed my eyes shut, fumbling with my headphones as I put them on and started playing Gimme Shelter by The Rolling Stones to drown it all out.

The van took off at speed and I was thrown backwards with a yelp, rolling across the hard floor and hitting the back wall with a thump that made my head spin. *Asshole.*

I managed to get myself upright, a growl leaving me as I dug my heels in and cranked the music right up to keep my demons at bay.

We drove on and on and I was glad that Frank didn't drive like Church despite the obvious speed we were moving at.

When the van finally stopped, I'd listened to several tracks and had returned to the beautiful, detached place inside me where no fear lived.

The side door rolled open and I squinted against the light pouring in as strong hands caught my right ankle and dragged me toward the exit.

I gasped as Frank lifted me up, throwing me over his shoulder like a sack of shit and I raised my head, having one second to take in the narrow alley we were in before he stepped through a door and started jogging up a staircase like a fucking soldier doing drills, climbing five floors faster than I ever could have managed even without carrying a whole person on my shoulder.

He pushed through a door and I blinked at the dark red carpet and opulent hallway that must have belonged to a hotel before he strode purposefully down to room 505 and opened it with a key card.

A beat later, he dumped me on a huge bed with cream sheets and I sat up, finding three women and a muscular man with a shaved head wearing light pink eyeshadow descending on me.

"Ah!" I kicked at them as they pulled me to my feet and Frank gave me a stern look, his lips moving in a command I couldn't hear as my music drowned him out.

One of the women tried to pull the headphones from my ears and I slapped her forcefully, making her head wheel sideways and a red mark blossom on her skin.

I got free of their grabby hands, getting to my feet and baring my teeth at them. "Get the hell away from me!"

Frank pushed through them, barking another command as he pointed at my headphones and I glared at him for two long seconds before tugging them down to hang around my neck.

"These are your stylists for the wedding," he snarled, clearly irritated by me and the feeling was mutual.

"Oh my god, she's like a wild antelope with the eyes of an angry bear. I simply adore her," the eyeshadow guy said in a theatrical tone.

"Well I'm going to shoot this antelope and bake it in a pie Sweeney Todd style if it's not put in a dress and made ready for the boss, Dylan," Frank growled and Dylan blanched, nodding quickly.

"Yes, sir," he said, reaching for me and cupping his hand around his mouth. "Don't worry about him, honey, he's a puppy dog when you tickle him in the right spots."

"Just get on with it," Frank snapped, moving to the door and stepping outside. "I'll be right out here."

"You heard the man," Dylan said. "You're in safe hands. They don't call me the Fairy Godmother for nothing. I'm about to bibbity-bobbity-boo your fine arse."

I let him guide me off the bed, serving Frank a cold look about the pie comment before he shut the door between us and I was relieved of his intense company. I was seated in front of a mirror and the group of stylists clustered around me, the one I'd smacked looking pissed. Dylan directed the girls with flamboyant hand gestures and though he was hench and looked like he could snap my neck with one hand, he gave off a vibe that said he wasn't a total psycho like my previous company.

"What's your star sign, honey? I'm a Leo, can you tell?" Dylan did a pirouette beside me and my eyebrows jumped up in surprise. "Wait, don't tell me. You're a Scorpio, aren't you? You're just oozing don't-mess-with-me-I'm-a-hot-bitch vibes."

"I'm an Aquarius," I said, amusement flickering through me. "And I don't believe in star signs."

"Oh my god, that's such an Aquarius thing to say," he laughed, snatching up some foundation and dabbing it on my cheeks. "Wow, your pores are like tiny little ant's anuses, how do you get them so tight?"

"Err – moisturiser?" I guessed and he laughed again like I'd made a joke. The girls all giggled too, none of them having much to say, but seeming to know exactly what Dylan wanted them to do at the slightest look or gesture from him. One of them started putting heated rollers in my hair and my heart worked a little harder as the weight of this day descended on me.

"Do you know Danny Butcher?" I asked, eyeing Dylan closely as he did a dramatic head roll at the mention of his name.

"He's like a tiger with a diamond stuffed up its arse," he said, his green eyes glinting with fear as they darted left and right. "Or like a badger poked with hot sticks and starved for a year." He jabbed at the air with a make-up brush in his grip then leaned down, holding the arms of my chair as he spun me to face him. "Don't anger him, honey. He'll eat you up." He gnashed his teeth in front of my face. "He ate a man's ear once because the guy called him crazy. But he's worse than crazy, he's gasoline poured on a hive of bees and set on fire."

"Perfect," I bit out.

"Oh poor, sweet thing," he said with half a sob in his throat as he took hold of my face. "I didn't mean to frighten you."

"I'm not frightened," I snarled, but I was. Not of Danny, but of failing in my plan to kill him. Or of having nowhere to run when I did. But worse than all that, of finding out my brothers really expected me to belong to him and not fight back. Because I was not going to be the meek little wife to some mobster with no heart. I wasn't the submissive type and if he thought I was going to allow him to own me, he was fast going to be proved wrong.

"There's no shame in fear. He looks like sin for a reason, and that's because he's the Devil incarnate." Dylan shuddered full bodily then continued with my makeup, shaking his head and clucking his tongue. "Pretty, pretty little American bride. He's going to devour you."

"Not if I eat him first," I muttered and he grinned.

"I like riling you, honey, it makes your eyes twinkle. At least you'll look ravishing walking down the aisle. Mmhmm, all that rage is gonna make you sparkle like a unicorn fart."

I released a breath of amusement and he continued painting on my makeup with skilful strokes of every brush he used.

"Are you part of The Firm?" I asked him curiously.

"Part of it? Honey, I've been in it, on top of it, and under it," he said with a wink.

"Which means?" I pressed.

"I'm a bitch for hire, Anya. I'm the hands on help in a beauty crisis like this. You'd be surprised how often a dirty, rotten gang need someone looking pretty. I tidy up corpses too. For the right price, I can make a bullet hole look like a beauty spot. And when a stiff needs disposing of, I can make them go poof like a rabbit in a hat." He smirked and I snorted.

"How do you know my name?" I asked curiously and he leaned closer.

"Everyone knows your name, honey. Miss Anya Volkov is the talk of the underworld. There's a lot of bets being placed on how – well, never mind," he cut himself off mid-sentence and I frowned as the girls giggled.

"On what?" I demanded.

He stole a few seconds combing my eyebrows, and I got the feeling he was building suspense. *Side note, who combs an eyebrow?*

"Well some people are betting on how quickly Danny will start, you know, slipping other women his deadly dick after he ties the knot with you." He gave me an innocent look.

"People like you?" I narrowed my eyes and he fluttered his lashes.

"If it helps, I'm betting it'll take three entire months, honey," he said. "And now I'm looking at you I might even stretch it to six because you're a whole eyeful, Anya."

My heart descended into a cold pit in my gut as my upper lip curled. "He's welcome to fuck whoever he wants, whenever he wants, and preferably not me," the words slipped out before I could stop them and Dylan slammed a hand to my mouth, shaking his head anxiously and giving the other girls firm looks.

"Watch your wild tongue, honey, it'll get you into trouble. The violent kind." I shrugged and he dropped his hand, a heavy breath leaving him. "None of us heard you say that anyway, did we girls?"

They all nodded in agreement, though I hardly cared, but I wasn't really sure why they were bothering to cover for my ass. Why would Danny Butcher expect me to be happy about this arrangement? I was hardly going to be singing his damn praises.

It took over an hour for them to finish my hair and makeup, and when I was led into the bathroom and found my wedding dress hanging in there on the back of the door, all the air was crushed out of my lungs.

It was huge. A princess dress straight out of a fairy tale, the bodice encrusted with diamonds with delicate straps to hold it up. Something I would never have chosen to wear for all the money in the world. It was also so low cut it was basically a sin to wear it to church.

"Ergh, for the love of fuck," I groaned.

Dylan took hold of my hand, giving it a squeeze before guiding me closer to the dress, my feet not wanting to move me anywhere near it.

"It's a monster," I breathed.

"It's your monster," Dylan tried, wiggling his brows at me, lifting my hand to lay it on the diamantes. "Tame it, Anya. Battle the beast."

"I hate it," I hissed.

"Hate's a strong word," he said, rubbing his chin as he stepped back to admire it.

"It's the only word for this white, flouncy, fucking *frock*," I said in disgust.

"Well you probably won't be too happy about the next part then, honey," he said, a note of apology in his voice.

"What's the next part?" I bit out and he turned me around, taking a jewellery box from beside the basin and opening it for me to see.

I grimaced as I spotted the silver collar inside, a delicate yet very obvious padlock at the back of it.

"No," I spat, rage rising in my veins. "Fuck no."

"Choices are for people who aren't engaged to Danny Butcher, I'm afraid honey," he said, a warning to his tone.

"Oh yeah? Do you wanna place another bet on that?" I grabbed the collar from the box, striding to the toilet and dropping it straight down into the water.

"No!" he cried, springing over to me as I pushed the flush button. The thing was too fucking heavy to go down easily though, so I grabbed the toilet brush and shoved it into the bowl as Dylan locked his arms around me.

"Anya – no!" he wailed just as the door flew open behind us.

Dylan instantly released me, backing up fast as horror fell over his features.

I turned, brandishing the toilet brush at the newcomer and finding a man there with piercing brown eyes that were full of endless malice, paired with a face that was harsh and beautiful at once. He wore a black suit which was fitted to his broad shoulders and tapered in at his waist. Deadly tattoos crept up out of the collar of his shirt to adorn his neck in lines of black ink and slipped from the cuffs to paint his hands too. Without a single introduction needing to leave his lips, I knew that this was Danny Butcher. It was obvious from the power filling the air and the way my soul seemed to reject everything about his presence. He was my end, my captor, my fucking fiancé.

"Anya Volkov," my name dripped from his lips in his rough, British accent as his eyes drank me in, every inch, from my bare feet scrunching on the cold tiles, to Church's boxers and shirt, settling on my mouth for a lingering moment before finding my eyes.

"What's in the toilet?" he asked me in a tone filled with the most lethal venom known to man.

"Nothing, Mr Butcher," Dylan answered for me in a panic. "We just need a moment alone to get Anya dressed and then-"

"Get the fuck out of this room," Danny commanded him in a sharp voice that cut deep into my chest.

Dylan bowed his head and scarpered from the bathroom, shooting me an apologetic look before the door clicked shut and I was left alone with my husband to be.

Danny stepped closer, straightening the blood red cravat at his throat as he swallowed up the distance parting us. He was the kind of handsome that reminded me of the sun, too intense to look at for too long without your eyes melting in their sockets.

I raised my chin, my hand fisting tighter around the toilet brush as I refused to cower and glared at the man I'd been sold to. I was the daughter of the Russian don. My father had been a ruthless, cold hearted man and his blood ran thick in my veins. I'd hated him, but his strength was built into me, and it was the one piece of him I didn't reject. I could stand before any enemy and defy them with everything I was. This one was no different. And I'd show him how sharp a Russian princess's claws were when she was backed into a corner.

He prowled closer and my skin heated with a warning to move, run, hide, but I was a Volkov, and I'd face a dragon with a pen knife if I had to – or a mobster with a toilet brush as it so happened.

He stole away all the space between us and caught a lock of my curled platinum hair between his fingers, inhaling in a way that seemed to drag the oxygen from my lungs. His fingers took a smooth path along my chin, his touch rough and speaking of weapons and tools gripped in that hand, the skin of a murderer. I still had the toilet brush raised but until he made a move against me, I didn't really have a reason to whack him with it. Though it was seriously fucking tempting.

His fingers reached my throat then slid firmly around it, his grip sharpening in a move that made my heart jolt. His face remained calm and his eyes were so empty, I was sure this man's soul had long since left his body. I swung the toilet brush toward his head as I bared my teeth, but he caught it without even looking that way, peeling it from my fingers and tossing it across the room.

He peered over my shoulder, his towering height allowing him to do so with ease and I knew without looking where his attention had fallen.

"Did someone forget to tell you that collars are for dogs, not wives?" I asked in a hiss.

His fingers locked harder around my throat as he saw what lay in the toilet bowl, cutting off my air supply. I took hold of his hand, tugging at his fingers to try and loosen them, not showing any sign of panic as my lungs began to burn and my eyes watered. And all the while I continued to glare at my nemesis, filled to the brim with hate.

"Rejecting your place already, I see. And you're right, Anya. Collars are for dogs. And you just so happen to be a dirty fuckin' mutt like the rest of your family." He swung me around and shoved me to my knees before the toilet bowl and I swallowed a lungful of air as my knees impacted with the hard tiles.

I tried to get up, but his hands shoved down on my shoulders to keep me there and I suddenly felt the cold kiss of a blade against my throat.

"Fetch your collar and wear it like the leashed bitch you are," he commanded and I found my face reflected in the water beneath me.

"Fuck you," I spat.

The blade pressed a little harder in warning and I wondered if he really was crazy enough to kill me over this.

"Watch your fucking mouth," he drawled.

His hand fisted in my hair and in the next second he forced me face first into the water. The moment my head went under, my mother's screams found me and I locked my jaw tight to ensure my own screams didn't join hers. I kicked and thrashed, fighting to get up as hard as I could as I struggled not to swallow a drop of the water in this fucking toilet bowl.

When I thought I was going to black out, he yanked my head back out and water streamed off of me as I coughed down a lungful of air and his laughter filled the room. It reminded me of my father, the joy he'd taken in hurting me and my brothers. Even after all these years, the thought of him still sent a chill sweeping through my body. But I wasn't a little girl anymore, I was a void. A lifeless, detached void who couldn't be broken.

"Put your collar on or the only drinking water you'll be getting for the next month will be from a toilet bowl, love," Danny said, his fingers knotting in my hair until my scalp ached.

I reached back, my nails digging into his hand and he cursed, throwing me to the floor with a snarl. Acid seeped through my flesh as I scrambled to my feet, hunting for a weapon but finding nothing of use around me.

Danny sneered at me as he shoved his hand into the toilet, taking the collar out and whipping his hand to send the water flying off of it.

"Do you know who I am?" he barked, looking like a wild man as he stretched out his arms wide. "I'm Danny motherfucking Butcher. And I'm the bloody governor of your life now."

He came at me, smiling a twisted smile and I did the opposite of what a sane person would do and ran to meet him. I wrapped my leg around his, slamming my hands to his chest in a bid to uproot him, but he was so fucking strong and he already had a fistful of my hair, driving me back into the basin and cracking my head against the mirror.

I saw stars, bile rising in my throat as he took advantage of my daze and slid the collar around my throat, locking it in place. It was tight. Too fucking tight.

"You're my bitch, Anya Volkov," he hissed, his eyes glittering as he drank in my expression.

He may have thought I was his captive, but I was plotting his imminent death and picturing the moment his blood splashed hot and thick against my flesh. *I'm your end, you piece of shit. Just you wait and see.*

He pressed his thumb to my right eye, smearing my make up down my cheek and making me grimace. "You're pretty, Anya. Real pretty, in fact. Thing is, I can get pretty on the corner of every street in London. But you know what ain't cheap?" He leaned down to speak in my ear, his breath hot on my neck and sending a horrid shudder down my spine. "Tears ain't cheap, love. And I want all of yours. Every last one."

He stepped back and for a moment I thought he was done before he snatched hold of my arm, hauling me after him and dragging me out into the bedroom. Dylan and the girls scattered, their eyes wide at the sight of me before Danny barked, "OUT!" and they ran to comply.

Frank's eyes met mine beyond the door for half a heartbeat, a frown pinching his brow before Danny threw the door shut in his face and locked it.

My heart thrashed wildly as Danny shoved me down on the bed and strode over to a leather bag by the door. I got up, grabbing the lamp from the nightstand as a snarl pulled at my lips. I was done. I'd kill him here and now. And fuck the consequences.

Danny took four lengths of rope from his bag and I dove at him with a shriek of fury, bringing the lamp down hard enough to crush his skull. He dodged it, his fist slamming into my stomach in the next second and I hit the floor on my knees, a curse falling from my lips as the pain made me wheeze.

He lifted me up, throwing me onto the bed again and his fingers latched hard around my leg as I rolled onto my front, trying to get up as I started to recover from the punch. I kicked and thrashed and fought, but he managed to secure it in place and capture my other leg in the next second, tethering my other ankle to the parallel bed post with a fierce speed.

My pulse went haywire before he moved to the top of the bed and I twisted around, punching him hard in the thigh. He growled as he moved to kneel over me and forced my hands into place one at a time, tying them to the headboard and immobilising me completely.

"Let me go, you motherfucker!" I bellowed as he got up, striding back to his bag and I craned my neck to try and see what he was getting. I yanked at my binds, struggling harder as I feared what was about to happen. I wanted my music. I needed it. I could get through anything so long as I could shut him out.

I tried to slide into that empty place within me again, but I couldn't grasp it now. My pulse was skipping and fear was coiling through my veins like a wicked serpent.

Danny took a short iron poker from his bag that had the word Butcher on one end of it and as he produced a blowtorch too, my stomach churned.

"What are you gonna do?" I demanded, but he ignored me, a manic gleam in his eyes as he lit up the blowtorch and heated the poker in it until the name Butcher was glowing red.

My throat dried out as he approached the bed, placing the blowtorch down on the nightstand and my muscles bunched up.

His hand ran down the length of my back, and he licked his lips. "You're mine, Anya Volkov," he said darkly, hooking his fingers into the waistband of the boxers I was wearing and dragging them down to my thighs.

"*Stop*," I ordered him, using the authority of the Volkov name. But what good did it do me now? I wasn't even going to be a Volkov in a few hours. I'd be a Butcher, bound to this man who could do anything he pleased to me.

He clenched a handful of my right ass cheek in his hand until it hurt then let go and slammed the poker down there instead, making me scream bloody murder as the brand seared my flesh. I yanked so hard against the binds that held my ankles and wrists, and panic blossomed through my chest as I screamed every curse I knew in English and Russian at this monster of a man.

He finally took it from my flesh and it somehow hurt even more as the burn met with the air, a pained groan tearing from my throat as the scent of burning skin filled the air.

Danny leaned over me, his breaths heavy in my ear like he was getting off on this.

"I'm the only one with a key to that collar around your neck, love. There's no breaking it either. So I guess you'll be wearing it forever unless someone lops that pretty head from your shoulders." He laid a kiss on my temple which felt like a promise of more terrible things to come then withdrew from me, moving to the bathroom and running water sounded as he cooled down the brand.

My heart pattered unevenly and the echoes of my mother's death replayed in my mind, the memory disjointed and full of terrors that drew me into the darkest place I knew. Panic was flourishing, chaos reigning as I tried to break out of its grasp, but it was impossible without my music.

"Please Vadim, no!" my mom begged and Zakhar gripped my arm, trying to turn me away from the horrors before me. But I wanted to see Mom, I wanted Daddy to stop hurting her. "Not in front of the children. Please."

I didn't know what Daddy was doing, but I wanted him to stop. He kept hitting her. He kept making her cry. And I didn't want her to cry.

"Anya, listen to this," Zakhar said, pushing the headphones over my ears and holding my chin so I looked at him. Only him.

Danny's hand slapped down onto my ass over the brand, forcing me back to the room as I swallowed a cry of agony and the tears rising in my eyes from the stinging, searing pain spilled down my cheeks. "See you at the church, wife. I'd put some Savlon on that burn, it'll hurt like a motherfucker when I'm pounding into that nice arse of yours later on tonight otherwise." He laughed callously, marching from the room with his bag over his shoulder, leaving the door wide.

I stared after him, my mind a turbulent storm full of death and the endless pain of grief. I wanted him dead. No, I *needed* him dead. I'd bleed him dry and hear him scream for this.

"You're officially her personal guard, Frank," I heard Danny saying out in the hall. "She doesn't take a shit without you knowing about it, got it? And any crap she needs, you sort it out. You own her arse when I'm not riding it. That girl is your one and only."

"Got it, boss," Frank replied and a beat later he moved into the room, tossing the door shut behind him. I wanted to look away, to crawl into the blackness of my soul and wither there. But I was trapped, my mind a rising tide of bad memories and I was on the verge of drowning in its waters.

Frank took a flick knife from inside his jacket, opening it up and I just stared at him, wondering if it would be the worst thing in the world to feel that knife slide into my heart and hand me into death's arms. Maybe I'd find my mom waiting for me there. Maybe death wasn't as hateful as life.

His eyes seemed to search mine for an eternity before he let his gaze move down my body to the brand that must have been more than fucking clear on my bare ass cheek.

I wanted my tongue to be sharp, to throw curses at him and demand he free me, but there was no way out of the heaviness descending on me now. It was a dark cloud consuming every piece of light in me it could find.

I was half aware I was shaking as the adrenaline that preceded a panic attack crashed through me, but before it came on in full force, Frank walked over and cut the binds tying me to the bed. I didn't move, lying there as my muscles remained rigid and the violation of Danny's touch seemed to lick beneath my flesh.

Frank disappeared into the bathroom, returning a moment later and sitting on the bed beside me, the weight of him pressing the mattress down hard.

He had something in his hand, but I didn't know what it was until he started massaging the cool cream into the brand on my ass. I winced from the pain, my eyes shifting to him in confusion.

"This will help," he said stiffly, not looking at me.

Frank was no doubt as heartless as his boss, but he was still helping me when he didn't need to. Somehow the firm strokes of his fingers kept the panic from getting its claws in me any deeper. That wasn't going to warm me towards him though. He was the enemy, as clear as his boss was.

"I don't want your help," I hissed.

"The harder you fight, the worse this will be," he warned and I nodded, accepting that.

But that didn't mean I wasn't going to fight. No, it meant the exact opposite. Because I was going to take down that son of a bitch Butcher before I was forced to endure more of his depravity. And I needed to get it together fast and be ready for tonight, because in a couple of hours, I was going to agree to be his wife till death do us part. And I planned on keeping my word on that particular vow as soon as I goddamn could.

CHAPTER FOUR

A low buzz sounded the beginning of the first day of my life starting all over again.

I pushed myself upright in the uncomfortable cot they'd given me for a bed the last eight years, and raised my chin to look outa the barred window and see a glint of sunshine brightening the sky. Today was gonna be a beautiful day.

"I guess that's it then," Boyd said from his own cot on the other side of the cell we shared and I nodded, my gaze still on that sliver of sunlight.

"What'll you do without me, eh?" I muttered, though in all honesty, I couldn't give a flying fuck about the answer to that. The only thing that mattered to me was that he kept his word to me. But with the amount of money I was paying him, and the less than subtle threat I'd made against his family, I was certain he would.

I'd ruled over this concrete kingdom since the day I'd been locked up in here, but there was no joy to be taken from presiding over a place without freedom. It was what it was. I'd walked through those gates and left my freedom behind, but now it was finally out there, like a faithful wife who'd remained celibate for all these years just waiting for me to return and wet my dick.

That errant thought drew my attention to the morning hard on I was sporting and I fisted my cock irritably as I rearranged it in my boxers. Christ, I needed the attentions of a good woman tonight. No, fuck that, I just needed the attention of any goddamn woman after all these fucking years. And it just so happened I had one in mind - I had to hope she could live up to the fantasies I'd been painting in my head because I'd been hungering for a taste of pretty flesh almost as ravenously as I'd been hungering for revenge.

I wasn't a bitter man by nature. I tended to deal with any source of rage or irritation swiftly and brutally then go on to forget all about it. But not this time. Because this I couldn't forgive and the rot of it had been eating into my soul and tarnishing all it touched for eight long years, ever since the night I'd taken the fall for a crime I didn't commit. My brother had set me up so that he could steal my crown and now I was coming back to claim it. It was just kismet that my early release happened to fall on the same day as his wedding to the girl who shoulda been my bride.

Not that he knew that. Oh no, so far as Danny Butcher was concerned, I was still due to stay locked up in here for seven more years - I guessed he'd be surprised to find out what a bunch of appeals and a whole load of good behaviour had gotten me. Not that I'd been good a damn day of my life, let alone in here. But I did have a knack for not getting caught, and a few loyal followers who had protected my name from slander. Danny had men watching me in here of course, but Boyd was the only one of them still breathing and he was gonna keep reporting back to anyone who wanted to check in on me, faithfully sending word of my continued incarceration to the people I'd once called family. My ma and Church were the only visitors I ever got anyway and I'd made Ma stop visiting six months ago in preparation for this, refusing her requests and telling her I hadn't wanted her seeing me like this anymore. I had it all wrapped up in a tidy little bow.

So here I was, packed up and ready to get the fuck outa here while my dear twin brother had no fucking idea that a storm was headed his way.

I got to my feet, dressing in baggy grey sweats and scratching at the latest tattoo which had been inked along my ribs for a moment before pulling the jumper down to cover it. I'd gotten a whole lot of ink during my incarceration and I'd paid a fucking mountain of bribes to ensure I managed to get each and every one of them done to perfection. Most people thought I had some addiction to going under the needle or maybe they thought I was losing my mind in this place and obsessing over the tattoos because I was cracked in the head.

I didn't really give a fuck what they thought because the truth behind them was a secret shared between very few people and each one of them held more importance than I cared to admit to anyone else. Anyway, all that really mattered was that I had them all before I left this place and with that final addition to my skin, it was safe to say I did.

"What's the first thing you're gonna do when you get out there?" Boyd asked wistfully, sitting up in his own cot as the sounds of the guards moving about reached us through the iron doors.

I ran a hand over the dark stubble which coated my jaw and turned back to face him, leaning my arse against the sink.

"I got debts that need paying," I said darkly. "And a prize to reclaim."

Boyd looked inclined to ask me more on that, but the door to our cell buzzed loudly again and it swung open before he could get the words out.

"You ready, Butcher?" Officer Hollands asked me. He was a big lad with deep eyes and even deeper pockets which he'd more than enjoyed having me line during my time here. I almost could have called him a friend if it weren't for him being a screw - fuck the establishment and all that.

"Yeah," I said firmly, pushing offa the sink and stalking towards him, not bothering to say anything else to Boyd. He was a part of my life in here, but that was done now. He knew where to find me when he got out if he wanted to be part of something bigger. Something that mattered a whole lot more.

Hollands led the way down metal gangways and I followed him while the rest of the prisoners headed the other way towards the mess and breakfast.

There wasn't a chorus of goodbyes or any emotional bullshit. Mostly because hardly any of the fuckers in here even knew I was getting out, but also because they were a bunch of hardened criminals and soft and fuzzy really wasn't our thing.

I kept walking, feeling the metaphorical shackles lifting from my limbs with each step and fighting against the big fucking grin which wanted to spread its way across my face.

We went through the motions, signing shit and heading through doors which had always been locked to me before now. Hollands even got all soppy and told me he'd miss me. He'd miss my money more like, but I just grunted some form of acknowledgement and turned my face towards the exit.

When I stepped out at last, I found the sun shining down on me and I paused, closing my eyes and tipping my face to the sky while the heavy metal gates rattled closed at my back and I remained firmly on the outside of them.

Free.

And oh how fucking sweet it tasted.

"You gonna stand about there all day or what?" Church's voice broke my peace, and I grinned the first true smile I'd grinned since the day my twin brother had set me up.

I opened my eyes and looked to the side of the prison where he stood leaning against his classic Mini Cooper with a smoke between his lips and mischief dancing in his grey eyes.

"Come here, you ugly fucker," I called, striding forwards with my arms wide and pulling him into an embrace strong enough to crush bones.

Church laughed and slapped my back before grasping my face between his hands and pushing me away so he could look at me.

"Fuck, I could kiss you right now," he growled, smiling so widely that his smoke fell from the corner of his lips and went tumbling to the ground where it hissed out of life in a puddle.

"Well don't," I said, shoving him back with a laugh which resulted in him lunging at me and managing to get me in a headlock.

We tussled like that for a few minutes while I drove my fist into his kidney, and he scrubbed his knuckles against the top of my head until we broke apart again.

Raindrops began to patter down from the heavens as my taste of the sun was stolen away and Church looked up at the sky with a frown.

“Thought we were gonna get a clear day for a moment there,” he sighed, heading around to the other side of the car so that he could drop down behind the wheel.

“Not likely,” I muttered, more than used to the joys of British weather patterns and their tendency to result in fucking rain more often than not.

I climbed into the little car, pushing my seat back as far as it would go and smelling passionfruit on the air as I leaned back against the upholstery.

“You had a girl in here?” I asked as Church started up the car.

“Yeah,” he replied, shooting me a smirk. “The one who’s all set to marry Danny today in fact.”

“And?” I asked, curiosity over the Russian bride pricking my attention as we began to drive away down twisting streets. Once upon a time that girl had been destined for me after all, so my curiosity only made sense.

“She’s hot, mate. Like scorch you to death hot. And she’s got a smart mouth on her too, the kind with full pouty lips and a wicked tongue perfectly designed to rile you up and make you want to fuck it all at once. I definitely wouldn’t be kicking her outa bed.” Church winked at me, looking away from the road despite how fast he was driving and the way the bends made it impossible to tell what was up ahead of us.

Green trees and hedgerows created a kind of tunnel for the road to pass through and as the rain picked up, the grey day only seemed to grow darker, but it was bright as fuck to me. Just seeing something other than cold concrete and desperate souls was like lighting a damn torch in my heart. So I’d take a gloomy day and a race through the English countryside quite happily, thank you very much.

“Sounds like my brother is a lucky man,” I muttered, unable to stifle the way Church’s description of that girl made my cock throb. It had been so fucking long. I needed a woman almost as bad as I needed to stain my hands in blood tonight. Eight long years without a taste of pussy. I was gonna blow my damn load like a virgin with a hooker the moment I got close to one.

“That he is,” Church agreed with amusement.

“Any word about Dahlia?” I asked, my mood souring somewhat as I thought of my baby sister who was currently in New York City, awaiting her own marriage to Lucien Rossi, the future head of the Cosa Nostra.

When we’d agreed to the terms of the peace deal all those years ago, it had seemed unlikely this day would ever come. Me and Danny had just lost our Pa and had taken over The Firm, we’d come to the meeting fresh from a kill and to be honest, I hadn’t truly taken on the fact that she would be forced to bear the cost of this too. Of course, in the years that had passed since that day, I’d wanted to try and do something to get her out of her side of the arrangement, but there was very little I could do from behind bars and I had my hands full with plotting my own moves for when I was released.

It was just my fucking luck that she'd flown out a few days before I got out of lock up though. I never even got to have a proper conversation with her. And though I'd spoken to her about my plans to take the crown of our family back from my fuck up of a twin brother, I knew she was of the opinion that it was too little too late.

My relationship with her had ended up becoming yet another casualty of my unjust incarceration and now I had no choice but to accept the hand fate had dealt her and hope to fuck that she would be okay with that pack of heathens. Dahlia was the baby of our family, not least because there was a whole fourteen years between her and us. Ma thought she'd done her dues giving birth to a pair of demons but then lo and behold, Dahlia decided to come into the world. Right around the time when me and Danny had started getting a taste for bloodshed, we found ourselves becoming big brothers for the first time.

Danny of course had never really taken to our little sister, jealous of the attention her arrival supposedly stole from him, but me? I'd fallen in love with her the moment I'd first laid eyes on those big baby blues and she'd curled those tiny fingers of hers around my thumb.

I'd been there for her as much as I could while she grew up, teaching her to throw a punch after her ballet lessons and making sure she never took any shit from any of the posh bitches in that fancy arse boarding school our Pa had sent her to.

But it had become a whole lot harder for me to be there for her once I was sent away, and I couldn't help but feel like I'd failed her during that time. Church had stepped up as best he could, making sure she knew how to fight and hold her own, but it wasn't ever meant to be his place. And now she was gone, set to marry some fucker who I'd been brought up to hate and I couldn't even walk her down the fucking aisle like a decent brother would.

"I checked that her plane got in okay," Church said, casting me a look like he could tell how pissed I was feeling over her being all the way across the pond in New York City with a bunch of wankers she didn't know from Adam. "And I told her you'd call once you were out."

Church offered me his phone and I brought up my little sister's number, listening to the phone ring and ring until it cut out.

Just as I went to call her again, Church swerved the car violently and a curse spilled from my lips as we almost spun out, the tyres skidding in the mud as some motherfucker in a Land Rover almost ran us off the road.

I twisted in my seat as the prick yelled some abuse at us, thrusting his hand out of the window and holding his middle finger up like we were a pair of little cunts before speeding away down the road.

I exchanged a look with Church as the Mini Cooper came to a halt, neither of us quite believing the balls on that bastard.

"We ain't letting him get away with that shit, are we?" Church asked, arching a brow at me to try and tempt me into trouble. But he knew full fucking well that I didn't need tempting into any such thing.

"Of course we aren't."

Church grinned as he revved the engine, yanking the steering wheel around and hitting the accelerator as he tore back up the road at full speed, chasing down the Land Rover, flashing his lights on off as the two of us laughed wildly over the hunt.

The arsehole who had damn near run us off the road tried to speed away as we chased him down, but this car was Church's baby and despite its small size, it was faster than a rabbit with a carrot jammed up its arse when it needed to be.

I whooped in excitement as my heart began to pound to a violent tune, watching the fear in the fella's eyes as he kept glancing back in his mirror at us, finally seeing what he should have the first time he looked our way – a pair of hungry dogs just looking for an excuse to spill blood.

Church swerved onto the righthand side of the road, overtaking the Land Rover before yanking the wheel hard and slamming on the brakes as he blocked the road and forced Mr Road Rage to skid to a halt before us. Unlike Church's little car, his big heap of metal had no chance of making a quick U turn in the middle of the lane and as the two of us leapt out of the car, I was pretty sure the fucker pissed himself.

"What was that you said to us back there?" I called, striding towards his car with my arms held wide in a challenge as Church casually grabbed a heavy branch from the side of the road and hefted it in his grip.

"I didn't quite hear ya," Church agreed. "So why don't you step on out here and say it a little louder?"

"I'm sorry," the fella gasped, jamming his finger on the button to close his window just as the sound of his doors locking rang through the air.

"Sorry?" I asked, cocking my head. "Maybe you should try saying that again. Out here…on your knees."

He shook his head profusely, holding his hands up in surrender and showing me exactly what kind of prick he was. The type who liked to talk loud but didn't have the balls to back it up. Yeah, road rage made him feel like a big man when he was tearing off down the road like some entitled cunt in his Chelsea tractor, but right here and now, when faced with a man of substance he was reduced to the trouser pissing little bitch he clearly was.

I broke into a sprint suddenly, causing an honest to fuck scream to tear from his lips as I ran straight at his car before leaping up onto the bonnet and crouching down to look through the windscreen at him with a wide grin.

He stared at me like he thought he was seeing his death and another scream poured from him as Church smashed his back window with the branch.

"Please, take my wallet, whatever you want! Just don't hurt me!" he wailed and I laughed loudly before reaching out and snapping his windscreen wiper off, pointing it straight at him through the glass. I was half tempted to stab him with the thing just to hear what pitch he could reach with that scream given the right motivation, but it seemed a little extreme, even for me.

"Next time, try not driving like a prick and you won't find yourself in such a pickle in the future," I warned him before punching the windscreen right in front of his face and causing cracks to splinter all over it.

It hurt like a motherfucker, but I just barked a laugh as I shook my hand out and leapt back down onto the road. I stabbed his front wheel with the broken windscreen wiper then strode back to Church's car with my boy at my side, not even bothering to look back.

My blood was up and my breathing came heavier from the little thrill of that tangle. I laughed with the man I loved like a brother as he tossed the branch in the back of the car, started the Mini up again and we drove off, leaving the wanker to deal with his fucked up vehicle and learn a life lesson he'd do well not to forget: Never start something you can't fucking finish.

Church's phone started ringing and I snatched it as I spotted Dahlia's name on the screen, still a little breathless from our fun.

"Hey," I said, hoping to fuck she would sound okay when she replied.

"Lucian's delayed the wedding by two weeks," Dahlia announced, not mucking about with any pretence that she wasn't pissed at me. And I couldn't really blame her – I was pretty pissed at me too. I shoulda been there to stop this from coming together, or at least to see her off, explain it, do…well fuck knew what really because our hands were all tied by this damn peace treaty, but I knew in my heart that I'd failed that beautiful little baby girl who I'd sworn to protect all those years ago and I hated myself for that, even if I couldn't change it.

I frowned as I took in her words, wondering what the bastard was playing at by making her wait.

"That fucker better not be pulling out. The last thing I need right now is to have to come to New York and kill someone," I said, wondering if she'd hear the mixture of a joke and a promise in my tone. Because treaty or not, if she said the word, if he wasn't treating her right or even if he was just plain old insulting her, I was more than happy to follow through on that threat. I'd figure out the part where every other ruling family around the world came for my head after the fact.

Church jerked the car around a corner a little violently and the huge branch he'd used as a weapon fell from his backseat into the footwell with a bang which made him wince. He promptly grabbed the thing and hurled it out his window. We were far enough from the scene of the crime for us not to have to worry about it being found now anyway.

"I don't think you need to worry about that," Dahlia said with a half laugh, almost sounding like herself, though I was certain there was more than a little resentment for me there. But she wasn't sobbing or begging me to rescue her. She sounded pissed but I was hoping she was alright where she was, that this deal wasn't causing her too much misery. But was that just a fool's hope because I knew it would be damn hard to undo it now?

"How are you?" I asked after a long pause in which it became clear that she wasn't looking for some lengthy catch up despite all the shit we were both knee deep in right now.

Dahlia hummed in a way which I knew meant she was rolling her eyes at me, ever the brat, never willing to let me off the hook for my bullshit.

“Since when have you cared about that?” she finally answered and there was enough bite to that question that it cut me, making it clear she blamed me for this situation, at least in part.

“Dahlia...” I sighed, pinching the bridge of my nose as I tried to figure out what the fuck I was supposed to say to my baby sister after allowing her to be sent off into some arranged marriage with a man she’d never even laid eyes on before. It was a shitty fate for all of us, but there wasn’t an alternative now and she was a single thing on one whole pig of a list of problems which I needed to deal with sharpish. And as much as it pained me, unless she called begging me to rescue her because her life was in danger, I just couldn’t prioritise her right now.

“I’ll make sure the wedding goes through,” she barked, clearly misreading my frustration and taking it the wrong way but she hung up on me before I could correct her, causing me to curse loudly.

“I’m gonna guess you’re not her favourite person right now?” Church asked as I tossed his phone in the cup holder and swiped a hand down my face.

“I have eight years of failing her to make up for at some point,” I muttered. “But I feel like anything I try to do for her in this moment will seem empty.”

Church nodded, his brow furrowing as he thought about her too and I knew he felt almost as protective over my little sister as I did. But she was in the clutches of the Cosa Nostra now and short of bringing a war down on all of our heads, that was where she was going to have to stay.

I let the subject drop and Church caught me up on as much as he could about what had been happening at home while I was in prison as we continued the long drive back towards London. I’d been getting plenty of updates while I’d been banged up, but we always had to watch our words in there in case some nosey fucker was listening in, and it was damn liberating to be able to talk candidly about everything that had been going on within The Firm while I’d been gone.

As expected, Danny had been letting things slip. The construction company which was our biggest front and by far our most lucrative business was in trouble thanks to his lack of attention, and the restaurants, pubs, casinos and other businesses we ran needed a healthy dose of my attention too. We had good people running the various branches of our empire, but without the top dog checking everything was going smoothly and making the big decisions, the whole thing could end up crumbling just like any other enterprise.

I cursed as Church filled me in on the various instances of disrespect and flouting the rules which had been overlooked among the smaller gangs that ruled over chunks of our city too. I blew out a harsh breath as I decided to park the endless list of problems I had to deal with now that I was back in favour of focusing on the most important one.

“Is the wedding still on for this afternoon?” I asked as we finally began to head into the London traffic, the green fields that had been consuming the view outa my window now fully replaced by the concrete jungle.

There were people everywhere, heading this way and that, ducking between gaps in the traffic and filling the pavements. Church navigated the carnage on the roads like a pro, pulling in and out of the different lanes like a cab driver with his tip riding on a fast drop off time. He swore at the cabbies and came damn close to taking out more than one cyclist before racing down the bus lane behind a red double decker then cutting across a roundabout and causing a cacophony of horns to blare out in anger at him.

“Good thing I got fake plates on this baby,” he joked as he managed to somehow set off a speed camera despite the traffic practically being at a standstill all around us.

“Yeah, not to mention how subtle the car is in general,” I mocked because how many cherry red classic Minis with a British flag on the roof could there even be roaming around the streets of London? But that was Church, always taking unnecessary risks and somehow managing to never get caught out either.

He made it off of the main roads while still laughing and driving like a maniac, and we bumped up a curb on a side street before he yanked on the handbrake and killed the engine.

“You parked on a double yellow,” I pointed out.

“We won’t be here long enough to get a ticket,” he said with a shrug, pushing his door open and stepping out of the car.

I followed him, looking around and taking in our surroundings. The road ended just ahead of us, turning into an alley which wound away between the buildings that towered overhead. The rain had petered out during our drive, but heavy clouds still hung overhead which cast the alley in shadow, promising another downpour soon.

“This ain’t our patch, is it?” I asked, wondering if I’d just missed the memo on the expansion or if we were here for some other reason.

“You worried, mate?” Church mocked, slamming his car door and heading around to the boot which he popped open before taking out a black police jacket and quickly putting it on.

“What’s the fancy dress for?” I asked, distracted as he finished buttoning it and added the flat, black cap to the uniform too. At a glance, he looked like a regular bobby on the beat.

“I think I pull it off quite nicely,” Church said, brushing his jacket down then taking a baton from the boot too and twirling it in his fist, drawing my attention to the church tattoo on the back of his right hand with its spires running up onto his fingers, a cross topping it on the central knuckle of his middle finger.

He slammed the boot, locking it as he led the way down the narrow street with a swagger in his step. There weren’t many people down here, but the bustle and noise from the surrounding city still lit the air like a backing song to whatever chaos he clearly had in mind.

"So are you gonna tell me why we aren't on our own patch?" I asked again as I followed him.

"I thought the Butchers ruled London Town?" Church mocked.

"We do," I growled as we stalked between alleyways, heading into the thick of the buildings. "But that don't mean every street belongs solely to us. At least while we aren't wearing the mask of The Firm. And the last I checked, this right here was the Candlestick Maker's turf."

Church paused beside a metal door set into the side of one of the buildings which loomed over us and shot me a smile that set adrenaline pulsing through my veins.

"And what if it is?" he asked, raising his hand to knock, but waiting on my agreement before he did so.

I paused, looking around at the grimy alleyway we were in and wondering if I was mad for considering this. There was a vague stench of piss in the air from whatever drunken arsehole had stumbled home this way last night as a credit to the lack of public toilets around here, and several bags of trash were piled outside other doors which backed onto this cobbled walkway. It took me a few moments to spot the graffiti tag up on the corner of the building opposite us and I pursed my lips at the black candelabra with three red flames. Yeah, this was definitely the Candlestick Maker's patch.

"I always did hate that prick," I mused.

The Butchers had been running these streets for years but there were some jobs we liked to farm out - hence the arrival of the Bakers into our little organisation. They were fixers really, the people we went to when something needed sorting, be it a dead body or an alibi, the Bakers would pull through. It had been a little joke between my grandpa and the men surrounding him that all they needed now was a Candlestick Maker, and that had been just fine until this motherfucker showed up and crowned himself with the title.

It had been a clear challenge from the day he'd started using the alias, a mockery of our name and what it meant to us. He was saying he was on our level even though he never would be. But he'd also managed to surround himself with enough muscle and align himself with people we didn't want to offend while accruing enough money to force us to accept that he really was a player on the board.

His go to was sex trafficking and we could thank him for the drug addicted hookers who lined the streets of this fair town like a plague. But much to my disgust, my pa had gone and made a deal with him, letting him run his operation in our city in return for a cut. But ever since my dear old dad had dropped dead while taking a shit, I'd been fully intending to get rid of him. In fact, he was just lucky I'd been banged up or he likely woulda taken a bullet to the skull a long time ago.

London itself was divided into countless turfs run by countless gangs, all of them thinking the Butchers were simply one of the biggest and the baddest, none of them realising the truth about The Firm and who ran it. In fact, most of them didn't know The Firm even existed, only the men and women at the very top of their individual organisations were privy to the information, and they had to pay tribute to us. They didn't fuck us about either because we were the masked and unknown men of substance who made brutal and bloody examples out of anyone stupid enough not to pay their monthly tythe.

"Fuck it, let's go then," I agreed. "What are we here for?"

"I heard he keeps a safe here," Church said with an innocent shrug. "Can't hurt to take a look inside it."

He pulled a flick knife from his pocket and tossed it to me so that I was armed, then knocked heavily on the metal door while I moved to stand to the side of it where I wouldn't be seen.

"Who's there?" someone called a moment later.

"Constable Hardcock," Church called back. "I got a few questions about a fight that happened out in this alley late last night. I'm going door to door hoping to find a witness."

"I didn't see nothin'," the voice grunted.

"All the same, if I could show you a few photos, see if any of them ring any bells..."

A heavy sigh followed and the door swung open.

"I already told you, I didn't-"

Church swung his baton at the fella's head and a harsh crack sounded a moment before he hit the ground.

I stepped out from behind the door, releasing a low whistle at the sight of the big bastard on the ground before us with blood slowly spreading around him and the kind of dent in his skull that wasn't exactly fixable.

"What's got your blood pumping, Church?" I asked, following his lead as he stepped over the body and hooked the door shut behind us.

I made sure not to step in the pooling blood as I went, and we made our way down the dark corridor inside the building.

"I'm just sick of this bastard pushing in on our turf while Danny does fuck all to stop him. The last eight years have been one helluva test of my patience, Butch, and I'm telling you, it's wearing thin these days."

"Good thing I'm back then, ain't it?" I said in a low purr as we moved deeper into the dark building.

"That it is," Church replied, his voice thick with malice, though we both knew it wasn't going to be as simple as me just striding on into my old life. No, Danny had done a damn good job of making sure as many of our gang hated me as possible for what I'd supposedly done. So there wouldn't be a welcoming committee laying out the red carpet for me upon my return, but then again, with the plan me and Church had come up with, we wouldn't be needing one.

There were several doors leading off of the corridor we crept down and we fell silent as we drew closer to a room where a loud droning sound filled the air.

Church turned towards a staircase, but I ignored him, moving towards the door where the sound was coming from. It was cracked open and I tilted my head, lifting the flick knife so that I held it ready to strike if anyone appeared.

I nudged the door a little to get a better look into the room, my brows raising as I spotted the rows of girls sitting around long tables, cutting and packing cocaine under the watchful gaze of a couple of armed assholes. The girls were young, mostly teenagers or in their early twenties by the look of them, and most of them had a deadened look in their eyes which said they were either traumatised or hooked on something which was numbing them to the world around them.

Church's hand landed on my shoulder and I tensed, letting him tug me back while my jaw gritted with the desire to take option B, but I was willing to bet my flick knife wouldn't do me a whole lot of good against the guns the fuckers in that room were carrying.

Church stayed silent as he wheeled me around towards the stairs and I let him despite the demon in me wanting to head back down to that room.

We reached the upper level and Church gave me a shove towards the closest door which earned him an elbow to the ribs.

I turned the handle, finding it locked, but Church just nudged me aside and dropped to one knee, tugging some picks from his pocket as he began to work on the problem.

I kept an eye out for him while he worked the lock over, and within a few moments the door was swinging wide and we were stepping into an office which was lit through a grimy window with broken blinds hanging over it.

Church made a straight path for the rear wall where a large safe stood in the shadows, but I paused as I heard a soft whimper from somewhere. Or did I?

I turned back to look towards the door, but there wasn't any more noise so I headed to the desk instead. The scent of stale sweat and expensive booze hung in the air and I wrinkled my nose as I looked down at the well-worn leather desk chair where I guessed the Candlestick Maker liked to sit.

There was a monitor on the desk and a full ash tray with butts overflowing from it alongside a half-consumed bottle of fancy whiskey. I tilted my head as I looked it over, dropping to one knee in front of the drawers beneath the desk and trying to open the top one. It was locked, but it wasn't anything a little bit of force couldn't handle. With a sharp tug and the sound of splintering wood, it popped open.

Church threw me a glare over his shoulder and I shrugged innocently as he pressed his ear to the door of the safe again and continued his attempts to crack it.

I turned my attention back to the newly open drawer before me. There was a pistol inside it along with a bit of paperwork written out in some kind of code, no doubt to do with his less than legal business dealings.

I took the gun from the drawer, checking the magazine and finding it fully loaded with seventeen pretty bullets just for me.

There didn't seem to be a whole lot else of interest in there, so I stuck the gun in the back of my belt and knocked the drawer closed again. But as I did so, the mouse sitting on the desk was jolted and the monitor before me illuminated as the computer came to life.

"Jackpot, motherfucker," Church announced in an excited whisper behind me, but I didn't even spare him a glance, instead placing my hands flat on the desk and leaning forward to look at the recording which was playing out on the screen.

There was no sound, but I could tell the girl in it was sobbing, her face painted with tears as she thrashed against the restraints tying her wrists to the headboard above her and tried to move away from the man who was closing in on the bed.

The pig of a man's chest heaved as he pumped his cock while watching her, moving onto the end of the bed, his hairy arse crack aimed at the camera and bald spot gleaming. I didn't need to see the Candlestick Maker's sweaty face to recognise him and my lip curled back in hatred as I looked on.

The girl's mouth parted in a scream and my head snapped up as I heard it from somewhere deeper in the building. This wasn't some sick sex tape that motherfucker had made of himself, it was a live stream. Which meant that girl was within reach, crying out for help.

"Butch," Church said in a low voice. "Why have you got that fucking look on your face?"

"Have you got what you came for?" I asked, turning to him.

"Yeah," he admitted, holding up a crystal duck which looked like it was worth exactly two pound fifty. What the fuck was that about? I had no fucking idea and no time to question it.

"Then I say we let the Candlestick Maker know that a member of The Firm paid a visit to his house and that I don't take kindly to him branching out into the drugs trade." I rolled my shoulders back and Church sighed but the gleam in his eyes said he was all kinds of up for this plan.

"Let's hear it then?" he asked, stepping closer and revealing the stacks of cash heaped up inside the safe.

I moved forward, hooking the bottle of whiskey and a lighter from the desk and pouring the contents of the bottle into the safe all over the cash. I grabbed a few wedges of fifty pound notes, winking at the Queen in her pretty pink glory before shoving them into my pockets.

"You ready to cause a ruckus, mate?" I asked and Church grinned as he headed for the door.

"Seems like it," he agreed.

"Just like old times," I murmured before sparking the lighter and holding it out to the pile of cash. There was a good mixture of old and new notes in there and the paper currency took to the flames more willingly than the new plastic fuckers did, but with the encouragement of the booze, the whole lot soon went up.

I jogged for the door, tugging it wide and leading the way into the dim corridor a moment before the shriek of a fire alarm rang out and the sprinkler system kicked in.

I grabbed a door handle at random and threw the door open, ducking inside with Church on my heels a moment before the shouts and thundering footfalls of the Candlestick Maker and his men came charging our way.

Church was practically bouncing beside me, the police hat pulled down low over his brow and shadowing the bloodlust in his eyes. But it was there alright. The urge to fight instead of hide, to step out of the dark and rain down bloody murder on everyone here. And I was feeling it too. But I could admit it probably wasn't the best shout in a building full of armed thugs where we were hopelessly outnumbered.

"What the fuck is going on?" a thick voice bellowed as footsteps pounded past our hiding place and I cracked the door open to look just as the Candlestick Maker stormed past with his shirt flapping open and his pants half hanging off of that hairy fucking arse.

My upper lip curled back and I tugged the pistol from the back of my pants but I held myself in check on account of the ten men who all came running up the stairs to meet him at the office door.

I jerked my chin in command and slipped back into the corridor as they all disappeared into the office, yelling about the cash and falling into panic as they tried to figure out what was going on.

We broke into a run, going in the opposite direction to the office and I started throwing doors open as I hunted for the girl.

"What are you doing?" Church hissed, throwing a look back over his shoulder as the sound of the goons hunting for us filled the building behind us.

"Just looking for a damsel in distress," I muttered and Church cursed.

"Always gotta play the hero, don't ya, Butch?" he muttered.

"You know me, Church, regular Prince Charming right here."

He scoffed, knowing that held no truth to it whatsoever and I shoved open the door I was looking for at last.

The girl screamed at the sight of us and I shushed her with a finger to my lips. I grabbed hold of the camera which was mounted on the wall above my head and ripped it free, breaking it and making certain no one caught sight of me on it. I pulled the flick knife from my pocket and quickly cut through the bonds tying her to the bed. The skimpy underwear she was in was thankfully still in place and I could only hope that had been the first time that sick fuck had brought her to a room like this.

She cried out again, but then her gaze landed on Church in his police getup, and she lunged at him with a sob of relief.

"Help me," she begged and he caught her looking awkwardly to me.

"It's alright love," he muttered, pushing her back a little and shrugging out of his black police jacket before wrapping it around her near naked body.

"Come here," I caught her arm and tugged her towards the window, glancing out at the alleyway below where a couple of dumpsters had been parked up. "I'm gonna lower you down there and then you're gonna start running and screaming for help, got it? Head that way." I pointed to the left of the alley where I knew she'd quickly find herself out on the busy London streets again, and no doubt some helpful little cherub would make sure she got to the real coppers. And if she wanted to start singing like a canary about the Candlestick Maker then that really had fuck all to do with me.

"How am I supposed to get down there?" she gasped, eyes wide with fright, but there wasn't time for that.

"Simple really." I grabbed hold of her and tossed her out of the window before she had time to do more than shriek in alarm. I kept hold of her hand, grunting as her weight fell to hang beneath me and leaning forward outa the window. "Ready?" I called as she kicked and flailed but the dumpster was only a few feet below her now, so she'd be just fine when I let go.

"Wait," she gasped but I just offered her a wink and dropped her.

She landed on her feet like a cat, dropping into a crouch with a yell of alarm before staring back up at us in fright. I shooed her away and she seemed to realise that was her cue to run, taking off down the alley the way I'd told her to and screaming like a goddamn banshee as her bare feet pounded down the cobblestones.

"Now what?" Church asked.

"Now I imagine we're in for some drama."

"No one can see us here, Butch," Church reminded me as I if I needed to have that little sausage rammed down my throat.

"Yeah, yeah. Anyone who lays eyes on me is gonna end up dead. Does that soothe your blackened soul?"

"It definitely doesn't hurt," he admitted just before the door flew open and two ugly fuckers stormed inside, their eyes widening in surprise as they spotted us.

Church slammed into the one closest to him, swinging his baton with ruthless ferocity as I threw my flick knife straight at the second fucker. The blade sank into his shoulder and he roared a challenge at me as he barrelled forward, yanking a gun from his belt.

I leapt into the fray, my fist colliding with his square jaw and my other hand locking around his wrist as I fought to stop him firing that gun.

We fell to the floor with a crash and I cursed as he managed to get on top of me, swinging my forehead at his nose and breaking it with a move I'd perfected during my incarceration. The fella reared back as his blood splattered my face and in the next moment we were rolling and I was tearing the gun from his fingers.

I didn't shoot him though, turning the cold metal into a bludgeon and slamming it down into his face over and over and over again until my arm was aching and there was little left of his features aside from pooling blood and shattered bone.

I sat back on him, panting as I yanked the switch knife from his shoulder then drove it into his chest to make sure he was definitely dead and wouldn't be telling anyone about seeing me here.

"I think you're getting rusty, Butch," Church said, drawing my attention to him where he stood, leaning against the door and covered in blood, examining his nails like he had nothing to do and nowhere to go while the corpse at his feet spread blood across the floorboards.

"Fuck you," I grunted, shoving myself upright and stepping over the body he'd left behind as he opened the door to the corridor with mischief in his silver eyes and blood staining his blonde curls.

I tossed him the gun I'd taken from my corpse and he caught it with a nod of thanks, letting me take the lead as we headed out into the dark corridor beneath the rushing water from the sprinklers.

"Protect the product! And I want the girl back here in the next ten minutes or heads will fucking roll!" the Candlestick Maker yelled from somewhere downstairs.

I jogged that way with my blood pumping, wondering how far I should take this game and if I might just have been in the mood to take that fucker off of the playing field for good.

I was back now after all. And I intended to take control of these streets the way my pa had always intended, which meant there was only room for one tradesman around here and that was sure as fuck gonna be a Butcher.

But as I crept back down the stairs and spotted the glutenous motherfucker striding away from me in the middle of a crowd of armed men, I had to admit it wasn't a fight I was likely to walk away from today.

Church gave me a nudge to get me moving in the opposite direction and I reluctantly darted across the corridor and shoved through the closest door.

Screams and chaos met us as we made it into the room where they'd been sorting the drugs, and a laugh fell from my lips as I took in the sight of the sprinklers washing it from the tables while men ran back and forth trying to rescue it.

The girls who had been working to separate it were all huddled together in the far corner of the room, but I barely had time to do more than take in the sight of them all cowering there before Church fired a shot so close to my ear that I was damn near deafened.

"Fuck!" I bellowed, aiming my own gun as the men in the room all turned to us at once, looking our way and forcing us to duck into cover behind the closest table as we shot back at them.

Bullets flew, girls screamed and my pulse pounded so thickly I felt it echoing inside my skull alongside the sound of that shot Church had fired.

I chanced a look over the table and fired off a shot that hit one guy in the chest before aiming into the corner where another was firing our way.

"Move your ass, Butch!"

Church bellowed and I whirled towards him as I shoved one of the heavy tables towards the door behind us, barricading it a moment before bodies collided with it on the other side.

I fired off a few more rounds, hitting the guy who had been shooting back at us and I looked around again in search of anyone else who might be aiming our way.

"I think we got 'em," Church said through gritted teeth as he worked to hold the table against the door.

"I'll get the exit clear," I said, shoving to my feet and racing past him towards the crowd of girls who all screamed louder as I forced my way through them.

There was a door behind them but it was locked up tight, so I aimed my gun at the lock and fired off the rest of my rounds.

"Hurry up!" Church roared, making me look around at him as the door he was trying to hold bucked and trembled with the promise of giving way any minute.

"On it!" I replied, trying the door again but the bullets hadn't done a fucking thing to help our predicament.

I backed up and kicked it as hard as I could, slamming my boot against it three times before it burst open and crashed against the wall on the far side.

Cold light and drizzle met me in the alleyway beyond and I shooed the girls towards it. "Fucking run then!" I bellowed, making them all scream again, but they weren't stupid at least and a stampede of terrified girls raced out into the rain a moment before Church took off too.

I waited for him to cross the room, ducking as the door was forced open against the table he'd used as a barricade and the men on the other side tried to force their way through.

Church aimed back over his shoulder, firing wildly and making them pull back just long enough for him to make it to the door with me and then we were off.

The girls had taken the obvious path, turning right at the end of the alley but we hooked left, vaulting over a line of dumpsters before scaling a wall and dropping into another alley beyond it.

We hid the guns in our waistbands and I thanked whatever god who liked to look after heathens and scoundrels that the water from the sprinklers had washed the blood from us too. We just looked like a couple of silly fuckers who had gotten caught out in the rain to anyone who cared to look our way now.

We ran on, ducking down alleys and crossing main roads and I drank in the feeling of the familiar streets closing in around me. I'd been born and bred right here in this city and breathing in its air was like sucking on the teat of life itself for my blackened soul.

We took another few sharp turns, completing our circular route without any sign of the Candlestick Maker's men catching up to us and before I knew it, we were dropping back into Church's obnoxious little Mini and tearing onto the congested streets of the city I loved with all my heart.

"You gonna tell me what that crystal duck is about?" I asked as I looked out past the racing windscreen wipers while we tore across Tower Bridge.

"No idea. I just heard he loves the fucking thing so I took a fancy to it is all," Church replied, shooting me a grin.

The two of us burst into laughter as he swerved around red buses and black cabs and I sighed as I leaned back into my seat.

"Fuck I missed this. The rush. The life. Even your ugly mug."

"Don't go getting soppy on me, princess," Church warned though his continuing smile said he felt the same. "We still got a whole lot of shit to get through today."

"Here comes the bride," I cooed, my heart fully charged with adrenaline which only made my anticipation for the rest of this day more potent. "Let's go crash a wedding then."

CHAPTER FIVE

I was preened to perfection once more as Dylan danced around me, straightening out the skirt of the huge dress I was caged within. The bodice dug into my hips and the weight of the skirt made my flesh ache, but I didn't feel much of anything as Band On The Run by Wings filled the room. After I'd put on my headphones and lashed out at anyone who came close to me, Frank had stepped in. He'd connected my iPod to the Bluetooth speakers in the room and confiscated my headphones by force.

Dylan had tried to get me to talk, but had given up after my continued silent vigil as I vibed out to the music and instead had settled on monologuing about various actresses and models he'd worked with.

"-this bitch Queenie J thought she was the bee's knees, you see honey?" he was saying. "But she was more like the cat's arsehole with her puckered up lips always aimed at me like they were about to take a shit. She was *always* bragging to me about her Jimmy Choo heels that she said Cristiano Ronaldo gifted her." He threw his head back on a laugh. "Honey, ain't no Cristiano Ronaldo gifting you anything when you walk in heels like a Muppet without the strings. Honest to god, I saw her coming down the street once and almost called Jim Henson to come pick up Kermit the Frog." He finished whatever he was doing with my dress, stepping back to admire it as his crew of girls all looked to him hopefully like dogs waiting for praise.

"You look fucking fabulous, Anya. I've painted on your face so good, I almost can't see your deadened soul in your eyes," he announced.

I blinked back to the room, my chest swimming in good vibes from the song and the killer in me purring in anticipation of what was to come tonight.

"If you painted away my deadened soul, then how would my husband know what I think of him?" I teased and Dylan grinned wickedly then snapped his fingers at his girls.

"Out of the room, I want to do the finishing touch alone with her."

They ran to obey and Dylan cried, "Posture, Linda!" at one of them and her back straightened instantly, making him clap in praise.

They slipped outside and Frank tried to look inside but Dylan threw the door shut in his face and locked it tight.

"*Hey*," Frank barked.

"We're not finished!" Dylan shrieked and Frank didn't respond. Dylan composed himself, tucking a pretend lock of hair behind his ear as he stepped closer to me, looking down at me from his impressive height. "Honestly, Frank is beautiful, but that man has the personality of a Chihuahua that's been rattled in a box, I don't know how he puts up with himself."

I snorted a surprised laugh. "You never know, maybe he goes home and cuddles up with his old grandma while sobbing over chick flicks."

Dylan beamed at that idea. "Oh no, honey, Frank's more likely to squeeze a tear out of his arsehole than his eyes. Now let me look at you..." He took hold of my chin, tilting my face up to examine my makeup. "Listen Anya, I don't like many people. But you have a certain quality. It's like rage and beauty and pain all wrapped into something very unique. You've been listening to music for the past two hours without saying a single word in response to anything I've said, and I just absolutely adore that. I don't know many people in London who don't give a blind fuck about what anyone else thinks, but you are an expert at it. And that makes you just exquisite on a bagel, honey. It's absolutely chef's kiss." He drew his fingers together and kissed the ends of them with a dramatic arm gesture and my lips twitched up at the corner.

"Thanks, I guess," I said with a shrug.

"You're welcome. And don't worry, when Linda slags you off later I'm going to roast her like the parsnip she is." He winked, doing some sort of dance move spin as he gasped. "Oh my god! I forgot about the best bit." He ran to the many, many glittery bags he had piled beside the dressing table, taking out a gleaming tiara and falling to his knees as he held it out to me like I was a freaking queen about to be coronated.

"Do I really have to wear that?" I deadpanned, reaching up to tug at the collar around my throat with a scowl.

"Yes, honey, and not because Danny chose it, because he didn't. This is mine. It belonged to a true queen – a drag queen, but still. She was the baddest bitch in London and I just know she'd want you to wear this today because you're not going to walk down that aisle without a little defiance in tow, are you?" His eyes glinted with rebellion and I stepped closer to him, chewing on my lower lip as a thrill danced through me. "You're a queen and Beyonce is going to be there with you in spirit today – not the actual Beyonce, that was the name of the drag queen who owned this crown. My partner," he choked out the last word and I had the terrible feeling Beyonce was dead. "She'd be so honoured if you'd wear it and showed Danny Butcher that you're a boss bitch."

I reached for it, figuring that didn't sound so bad and he leapt to his feet, placing it on my head for me instead.

Dylan slapped the back of his hand to his forehead as he gasped. "It's a masterpiece."

He turned me around to face the long mirror on the wall and I took in my outfit for the first time. The dress was so low cut that it dipped down deep between my tits which looked twice their normal size because of the magic Dylan had worked on them. The bodice glittered with gemstones and the skirt was big enough for an entire family to camp in, but with the crown on my head, I did feel sort of…powerful. The collar didn't help, but it sat above the line of musical notes inked along the right side of my collarbone and they were what I focused on instead, taking a moment to brush my fingers over them as I remembered my mom, drawing on the monster born in me the day she'd died. I looked like a princess, my hair styled into a fancy updo with loose tendrils hanging down from it to tickle my back.

The one good thing about this giant skirt was that I had miles of material to hide a weapon in. Now all I needed to do was find one.

"We need to leave," Frank snapped beyond the door then the light above the handle turned green as he let himself in.

"Wait!" Dylan dove in front of me like he was taking a bullet, his arms outstretched and Frank glared at him with his teeth bared.

"What can possibly take this long?" Frank snarled.

"There's just one last thing," Dylan insisted, whipping around to face me and blocking me from view with his impressive shoulders. He reached out and teased another tendril loose from my hair then nodded his approval.

"That's it?" I asked.

"For now, Anya. I'll be doing the *final* final touches for you at the church." His jaw flexed and I got the feeling he didn't want to let me go. But my music was still playing and I wasn't afraid. I was in numb bliss, ready to spill blood and paint this dress as red as the Queen of Hearts' roses.

"See you there then, Fairy Godmother," I said with a quirk of my lips and he nodded several times.

Dylan stepped away with a spin as he spread his arms like he was unveiling me to Frank.

Frank's eyes widened ever so slightly as they fell on me, moving from my crown, to my ruby red lips, to the collar at my throat, my tits, my waist, all the way down and all the way back up again.

Despite the miles of dress I was housed in, I felt naked under his scrutiny and the way his throat bobbed said he liked what he saw. Something about that set my heart racing. But any lust I thought I'd seen in his eyes extinguished in an instant as he grabbed my iPod, cutting the music off before putting it in his pocket. At some point, he'd changed into a suit with a red cravat that matched Danny's and fuck did he look fine. James Bond eat your fucking heart out *fine*.

My headphones peaked out of his jacket pocket too and I scowled as I realised he was now the keeper of all my things. I realised I'd left my Van Halen tee in his stupid van too, so I was officially going to go klepto on his ass when I reclaimed my shit.

"Let's go, Cash," he demanded, jerking his chin at the door in an order.

I offered him a cold scowl, refusing to bite and ask what he'd just called me, offering a two fingered wave in goodbye to Dylan as I stepped past my moody faced companion into the hallway. He immediately followed, taking my arm and holding on tight as he led me toward the elevator. My flesh burned beneath the grip of his hand on my arm and I swallowed thickly as I stole a look up at him from beneath my lashes, while my heart sprinted around my chest like it was hunting for an escape.

"Question, what's it like being a henchman?" I asked lightly as we stepped through the steel doors into the elevator. He ignored me so I went on. "Like, does your evil boss give you vacation time? Or is it more of a non-stop job?"

Nothing.

"How does one get into this line of work? Do you have to apply to be a big, bad henchman? And if you die, do you just get replaced by another lump of muscle like in the movies? And no one even blinks when you go down because you're just a nameless bad guy and all anyone really cares about is the main bad guy who-"

"Quiet," he snarled, but I hardly saw that I had anything to lose by continuing. So I did.

"Or maybe you think you're a good guy, fighting for the right team. It sucks to have to tell you this, but the bad guys always have British accents in movies. Like Hannibal Lecter, Scar, Voldemort. And Sean Bean. Sean Bean plays a bad guy in everything. Even when you think he's not evil, that's when he most definitely is. Beware the Bean."

"Anya," he snapped my name and my pussy liked the sound of that on his lips way too much.

"Yes, Frank?" I asked sweetly. This reminded me of annoying Adrik, and for a second it felt so familiar that I wasn't even thinking about where this asshole was taking me.

"If you don't stop talking, I'll gag you and mess up that pretty lipstick of yours."

"Wow, it's like you think I actually care what I look like for the wedding," I said, unenthused. "Seems like you'd be the one to get in trouble if I turned up looking like you'd just stuffed your dick in my mouth and had a good time with your boss's fiancé. I wonder who he'd believe if I gave him that sob story…"

He fell quiet, his eyes sharp on me and I wetted my lips on instinct, drawing his attention to them as the image of having this guy's rock hard cock in my mouth made dark and twisted thoughts ignite in my head. He was definitely thinking about the same thing as he watched my lips closely then his features twisted into a sneer.

"I've been Danny's right hand man for years, as if he'd believe his enemy over me. Besides, Cash, I doubt he'd give a fuck what I did with you so long as I handed you to him in one piece."

"Bullshit," I challenged, wondering if I could lure him in to doing something bad. If I could get my jacked escort fired by his boss (AKA dead) before tonight, it might be easier to run the hell away once I'd killed Danny Butcher. So I took a step closer, batting my lashes as I looked up at him and confusion rippled across his brow as I placed my hand on his chest. Heated flesh and solid muscle awaited me beneath it and I was surprised at how much I wanted to move closer to him, how much I didn't mind playing this game...

I let my fingers slide lower, our eyes locked as I waited for him to act against his boss, to give me some ammo for this weapon I was forging.

Just as my fingers skimmed his waistband, he caught my wrist in a grip that was so tight it made me wince.

"You must think I'm a fucking fool, sweetheart," he growled, his tone so deep it seemed to rumble into every corner of my body.

"All men are fools," I whispered and he laughed in a low, mocking way, yanking me hard against him and I gasped as I felt his dick stiffening, driving into my stomach.

"No, just our cocks are fools. But my mind is sharp. And I wouldn't lay a hand on you if you were home to the last pussy on earth, Anya Volkov."

"How loyal of you," I said dryly, the size of that thing making my core clench traitorously. "I really hope being Danny Butcher's bitch is worth the blue balls."

The air frayed and my breaths came more furiously as he remained pressed to me and I fell into the void in his eyes. He looked empty enough to crawl inside, but I imagined I'd only find a trail of wicked deeds painted on his hollow interior if I did. Even so, I wanted to look. Wanted to claw my way into the cavity of his chest and find out what beast had ripped out his black heart.

If Church was a Siren's song who lured me in, Frank was the drum beating in time with it, every thump furious enough to send a quake through my bones. But something still seemed to be missing from that tune, something I couldn't place.

The elevator doors opened and time seemed to start again as fresh air gusted in around us, sharpening my thoughts in an instant. Frank shoved me away from him, marching me out into an alley where a gleaming black Rolls-Royce was waiting for us. He opened the back door, pushing me into it and knocking me across the back seats with force. I cursed as he gathered up handfuls of my huge skirt and shoved it unceremoniously on top of me before slamming the door shut.

He got in the passenger side of the car in the front and the driver handed him a gun which he casually checked was loaded as I scrambled upright in my seat.

I opened my mouth to curse him out, but he hit a button and a divider closed between us which I punched hard enough to bruise my knuckles.

"Asshole," I spat, shaking my fingers out and turning my attention to the view beyond my window with a snarl on my lips.

As we turned down street after street, my breath suddenly snagged in my throat as the River Thames came into view, the water grey beneath the clouds as it wound through the heart of London under bridges, carrying ferries on its back like a giant python coiling through the city. Red buses broke up the monotone colours of the traffic and as we turned onto a bridge, my gaze fell on the golden walls of the Houses of Parliament ahead of us and the imposing clock tower of Big Ben. The air rushed out of my lungs and my heart swooped like I was on a rollercoaster as I fell in love for the first time in my life. Struck fucking dumb with instalove as grit and beauty collided before my eyes and I fully appreciated where I was for the first time. London. Beautiful, dirty London. And I fucking adored it.

I forgot the fate awaiting me at the end of this journey as I stared out unblinking at the past and present twisting together before my eyes. Ancient buildings sitting in the shadow of glass towers, hipsters leaning on iron lampposts, the giant Ferris wheel of the London Eye turning slowly above the river which had served the people of this city for centuries.

Suddenly the sun spilled through the clouds and colour bled into the world, the gleaming walls of the parliament buildings turning to liquid gold and as we reached the other side of the bridge, the clock of Big Ben rang out to mark the time and I felt the vibrations of the bells right through to my soul.

This wasn't Vegas, nothing was fake or a mimicry of anything. The buildings were steeped in so much history, I could practically feel the power of them all, the weight of so many decisions that had once built Britain into an empire.

"Holy shit," I breathed. If Vegas was the City of Sin, then this was the City of Power. And I liked the way it made me feel, the way it seemed to welcome me home like a queen arriving in her court.

I lost sight of the river and the monuments that London was famous for as we headed down winding streets and had to queue for half a mile in solid traffic while angry drivers beeped their horns. But I enjoyed the chance to study the people who were sitting outside cafes, laughing, drinking coffee, reading newspapers. It didn't even look warm out there, but they sat outside like the cold couldn't touch them, basking in the sliver of sun peeking through the clouds as if they knew it would soon be gone. And within a few minutes it was, the sky blanketed in grey once more. And for some reason I liked that, the way the clouds hung there as a constant threat, the rain like a loaded gun it could fire at any moment.

We eventually made it out of the traffic and arrived on some interesting streets, some of them coloured with graffiti, others with pristine courtyard gardens, every turn we took seeming to land us in a whole new world.

We finally arrived on a bustling road with old grey stone buildings on either side of it, and along it was an imposing white church with ivy crawling up the walls and a tower which seemed tall enough to pierce the sky.

My tongue weighed heavier in my mouth and my fingers itched for my headphones as the driver pulled up outside the church and the walls of fate closed in around me.

Frank got out of the car, opening the door for me and offering me his hand. I took it, letting him guide me out, surprised by the warmth that passed from him to me as he kept a tight hold of my fingers. I looked up at him as I made it outside, all jibing abandoning my tongue as I felt the weight of what was about to happen pressing down on me. Thunder cracked in the dark clouds overhead and my pulse flickered as adrenaline coursed through my veins.

Frank checked his watch then towed me into the church and we arrived in a short entrance hall before the main doors just as the rain started pouring down outside. He pulled me along to a door to our left, pushing through it and I found Dylan already there with the small space set up like a beauty salon, his girls no longer with him. Wasn't I preened enough as it was? How could he possibly do any more to me?

"You've got twenty minutes before you become the property of Danny Butcher," Frank announced with a scowl that could have cracked glass then he stepped out of the room.

"Is he always so smiley or is he just particularly merry at weddings?" I asked Dylan, not really expecting an answer but he laughed wildly, bouncing up and down on the balls of his feet.

"Oh *stop* it. You're so bad, honey," he said through a wide grin.

I cracked a smile, which was something considering I was now living in the final moments of my unmarried life.

"Frank might be a brooding, miserable git who enjoys killing as much as your regular psychopath, but do you know what? I'd still let him bend me over and call me his little princess."

I snorted a laugh. "Why are raging motherfuckers so hot?"

"Because nice guys will judge you if you ask them to choke you, a bad guy does it for free," he said with a smirk and I had to admit he had a point. Dylan caught hold of my hand, making me do a spin then tutting loudly. "Your dress is creased. Turn around, honey, I'll get the steamer." He headed over to where the thing was plugged in by the wall and he picked it up, resting it on his shoulder like a damn shotgun.

"Any chance that thing fires bullets? I think I'd look good with one right here." I pointed between my eyes and Dylan chuckled.

"You're funny, Anya. But that mouth's gonna get you in trouble."

"Lucky I like trouble then, I guess."

He shot me a mischievous look as he knelt down to start steaming the hem of my dress. "Don't let that demon Butcher out there eat your soul, kay?"

"Kay," I agreed. *I'll just have to get my teeth in his soul first.*

CHAPTER SIX

We pulled up in the shadow of the big white church which Danny had chosen for the wedding. I wasn't quite sure how he'd managed to convince the vicar that he was a pious man, deserving of a union in the house of God, but I had the feeling a few fat donations had a fair bit to do with it.

We were a stone's throw from the Tower of London and I spotted The Gherkin as I looked out into the rain through the crowds of people hurrying down the street beneath a sea of umbrellas. Fuck, I loved this city.

"Fucking hazardous out there for tall fuckers like us," I pointed out, watching a short woman jog past with her umbrella spikes right on fucking eye level.

"Even more hazardous for my brother," Benny muttered, his gaze firmly fixed on the white church tower.

He'd gone quiet on me on the drive over here and I knew he was caught up in our plans for today. They'd been a long time in the making and they had to go right, or everything would be fucked.

"You sure he's here?" Benny asked and I tugged my phone from my pocket, shooting Danny a quick text to make sure.

Church:
Had a job to run, but I'm here. Where do you want me?

Danny:
Inside. You need to get dressed. Hurry the fuck up about it.

I flashed Benny a look at the message and he nodded.

"What about the bride? She gonna be any trouble?" he asked.

"Trouble? Oh yeah, Miss America is a whole big bundle of trouble alright. But I ditched her suitcase at the airport so as far as I can be sure there's no chance of her having any bugs or weapons on her from her little Russian friends. I gave her a strip search in the shower too just to make sure." I winked at him and he arched an eyebrow at me.

"You fucked her?"

"Nah." I shrugged innocently. "She's the boss's bride. Besides, I didn't have time - I had to come get your sorry arse outa jail."

Benny snorted then jerked his chin towards the front of the church, drawing my gaze to his ma as she climbed the steps in a pale blue frock with a big fucking hat to match while trying to avoid the downpour beneath a big black umbrella.

"Fuck, I wish I could go give her a hug," Benny muttered.

"In time," I said. "She's doing alright. Better now that you're out, no doubt. Once you start getting the family business back on track, she'll have a whole lot less to stress about come nightfall."

"We'll see about that." Benny sighed and turned away as his ma made it into the church. "Looks like it's time then. You go on in and I'll shadow you."

"Just like old times. How do you think Danny is gonna like his surprise?" I asked, rubbing my hands together excitedly as a little shot of adrenaline found its way to my heart in anticipation of what would come next. I'd been waiting on this for a long damn time, and I was seriously looking forward to watching it play out - I wouldn't object to getting my own hands dirty too.

"Oh I'd say he'll be fucking flabbergasted," Benny replied, shooting me a grin that was all malice and dark intentions. What a perfect fucking day for revenge.

I tossed him a black hoodie and he tugged it on, pulling the hood up to conceal his features and retreating into the shadows within it so no one would recognise him if they caught a glimpse. This cat wasn't coming outa the bag until the opportune moment when Danny would be getting a nice big surprise.

I threw my car door open - ignoring the curses of the fucker who I almost took out with it as he hurried down the street - and stepping into the sleeting rain. What a fucking August we were having. Apparently summer had just decided to skip over good old England this year and we were in a perpetual winter instead - which was a damn shame because I'd been looking forward to striding around shirtless and causing old ladies to gasp at the scandal as I wandered into fancy shops like I owned the fucking place. It was my summer tradition and at this rate, the only shirtless cream tea I'd be enjoying would be one which included goosebumps and my nipples taking someone's eye out.

I jogged around to the back of the church, feeling Benny following me and moving off the main street into an alley which led to the back entrance of the huge white building.

I hurried up the stairs, finding the heavy wooden door unlocked and tugging it open before walking to the antechamber the vicar had told us to use to get ready when we'd come for the rehearsal a couple of days ago. Not that Danny had rehearsed shit. He'd just strutted about like a peacock with the balls of a prime bull while checking all around the place for signs that anyone might have been fucking with things. The man was paranoid as fuck which was probably on account of him being a backstabbing motherfucker who had accrued more enemies than I could count over the last eight years, but seeing as he was also the scariest fucker in London, so far not many of them had tried to come at him. Still, it was only a matter of time and he knew it.

I headed across flagstones older than the Queen herself and pushed a hand into my blonde curls to swipe some of the rainwater out of them before shoving open a smaller door into the little antechamber there.

A girl squeaked in surprise as she spotted me, hooking the strap of her dress over her shoulder and putting her tit away as she glanced nervously towards Danny.

"Unless you're looking to suck his cock too, you can fuck off now," Danny barked at her. "It's worth bearing in mind in future that the moment you find yourself swallowing my cum is the moment I'm fucking done with you."

"Got it," she muttered, swiping her swollen lips with the back of her hand before sidestepping me and hurrying away.

I didn't bother calling him out on the fact that he was fucking around on his wedding day, though I happily called him a cunt from within the confines of my own mind.

Danny started pacing as I entered the room, his black trousers on and white shirt hanging open to reveal his tattooed chest. His ink was all violent deeds and sinful acts, beautiful in its own way but the only tribute he was paying with it was to his own personal vices. I let the love of my country shine bright on my flesh, the heart and soul of who I was and where I came from. It was what made me, me, and I was damn proud of my noble heritage.

"Where the fuck have you been?" he barked at me as I strode in and I arched a brow at him.

I knew he fucking hated me despite the fake smiles and bullshit he offered up. He never had gotten over the fact that me, Frank, Olly and Benny had been tight as kids and he hadn't been included in our bond. Then again, that really had more to do with him mutilating pets for a hobby and being an all-around psychopath than it had to do with us cutting him out or whatever bullshit he liked to believe.

Still, he hadn't tried to kill me yet. Not because I believed for one second that he wouldn't like to see my blood spilled all over the fucking place. But because he knew I was irreplaceable. My family were powerful around here - almost as powerful as the Butchers themselves, and our loyalty had a price which was far too steep for him to cover if he ever crossed me. I was the biggest player on his board whether he liked it or not and his empire would quickly topple if he turned on me. So we played this bullshit game of being best buddies while secretly enjoying the thought of gutting one another if ever the opportunity arose.

"I told you, I had a job," I replied with a shrug, making a show of closing the door behind me and turning the key in the lock - only I half turned it then turned it back again so that we weren't locked in at all.

Danny's gaze darkened as I failed to offer up more of an explanation, but he seemed to realise we didn't have time for a dick measuring contest, so he just tutted irritably and turned away from me.

"I want this shit over and done with," he said. "We'll do the vows, the cake and the fucking mingling for an hour max. Then I wanna take my bride home and see how tough the Russian's really are when you push them to their limits."

"You made a promise not to hurt the girl you were offered in the peace treaty," I pointed out, moving towards the suit which was hanging on a rail to the side of the stone chamber and pulling off my wet t-shirt as I went.

"Yeah? Well what are they gonna do about it?" Danny asked. "Besides, I didn't promise shit. That was all Benny. But now he's not here and their precious little princess has found her way to me instead. And I fully intend to show her what it's liked to be owned by the king of London."

I scoffed at his self appointed title and he shot me a barely veiled scowl. The thought of him making my little Miss America into his latest plaything sent a shiver of rage chasing down my spine and I unbuckled my belt a little more violently than I meant to, snapping it out of the loops so forcefully that it cracked against the stone wall beside me, drawing Danny's curious gaze my way again. I didn't turn to meet it, only feeling the burn of it against my skin. I forced myself to rein in my anger though, only needing to remember the plan to let it slip away. I just had to keep my eye on the prize.

"Shouldn't we be getting down there?" I asked, dropping my jeans and kicking them off along with my shoes while leaving my back to him.

"If I want the world to wait for me then they'll fucking wait," he snapped, but he started buttoning his shirt all the same.

I took the blood red cravat from the clothes which were waiting for me and casually wrapped one end of it around my fist, shooting a look Danny's way from the corner of my eye as my pulse thumped a little harder, the thrill of the hunt injecting adrenaline into my veins. He had no fucking clue what was coming next and that made me all kinds of giddy.

The door creaked as it was pushed open and Danny whirled around. "What the-" he began as his gaze locked on his twin brother, but his words were cut off sharply as I flung the untied cravat over his head and jerked it tight around his neck.

"Hello, brother." Benny tossed the door closed behind him as Danny kicked and flailed, reaching back to punch me as best he could at the awkward angle I held him at, while my arms strained with the effort of trying to strangle him.

Danny grunted, his fingernails biting into the backs of my hands as he tried to force me off of him and his foot collided with the edge of the large mirror, knocking the whole thing crashing to the ground with a large smash as shattered glass flew everywhere.

I shoved him away from me and Benny's fist connected with his jaw, sending him tumbling to the ground amid the broken glass as he gasped for breath.

"Last time I saw you, you were stabbing me in the back, brother," Benny hissed, pulling a knife from his pocket as he closed in on Danny while he tried to scramble upright again. "Let me return the favour."

Benny leapt on him, fisting his shirt and shoving it up before driving the knife into Danny's back. I managed to slap a hand over his mouth as a roar of pain escaped him, muffling the sound.

A heavy knock came at the door. "Is everything alright in there, gentlemen?" the vicar called.

"Yeah, we're all dandy!" I yelled back. Danny tried to sink his teeth into my fucking hand, and me and Benny fought to keep him restrained between us while the knife remained lodged in his back. "Just a few last-minute nerves, don't worry vicar man, we'll be out shortly."

The vicar muttered something else as he moved away and I threw a couple of punches into Danny's side just for the fun of it.

I'd managed to keep hold of the cravat and I quickly switched out my hand in favour of making a gag for him, stuffing it into his mouth while Benny wrestled him upright and shoved him face first against the stone wall.

"Did you miss me, brother?" Benny hissed, his hand fisted in Danny's black hair as he drove his cheek against the pale grey stones which made up the church wall. "Because I'm back now. Back to reclaim the life you stole from me eight long years ago."

Danny tried to say something from beneath the confines of his gag, but it came out muffled and I had no fucking idea what it was. Probably a death threat or some bullshit like that. A crazy laugh escaped me as I bathed in this moment, the culmination of all our planning and plotting. How many times had I been forced to listen to Danny's bullshit or stand and watch him make a fucking pig's ear of the work we did while I daydreamed about this very moment? The moment when we took it all back. Set things fucking straight at long last.

I tugged a loaded syringe from my pocket, flicking it like a psycho doctor and making sure Danny got a nice, long look at the needle as I offered up a maniacal grin.

"Don't worry," I said as I moved closer and he tried to thrash furiously against his brother's hold. But between the knife still lodged in his back and the fact that Benny was actually a good few pounds heavier in the muscle department than him now, he couldn't break free. "I asked daft Barry to cook me up something strong enough to knock out a buffalo - so this should see you off to La La Land for a nice long while," I said with a grin.

Danny thrashed harder, his eyes all wild and killer crazy but I just grinned even bigger, relishing the moment as I sunk the needle into his neck and pushed down on the plunger, giving him every last drop of whatever the fuck Barry had mixed up for me. He liked to experiment with all kinds of ungodly concoctions and fuck knew I wouldn't have wanted a single drop of that shit in my bloodstream.

It hit him fast, his eyes rolling up into the back of his head within less than a minute and as the tension went out of his muscles, Benny dropped him so that he slumped to the floor, face down.

"Well that came together nicely," I said, plucking my cravat back out of Danny's mouth and shaking it to get the saliva off. Didn't really work, but the thought was there.

"Yeah," Benny grunted, looking down at his brother with a frown.

He tugged his hoody and shirt off and began to inspect the tattoos lining his flesh to make sure they all matched up perfectly to his twin's ink.

As far as I could tell he was all good - aside from the forget-me-not flower he had inked on his ribs. It matched mine. And Frank's. And Olly's once upon a time too.

I bit my cheek against the pain of that old wound and glanced at the spot on Danny's ribs which had no ink marking it, but there wasn't much that could be done about that. There weren't many people who would notice it and Benny was just going to have to make sure Frank never laid eyes on it. Aside from that, there wouldn't be a single fucker who would have the faintest idea that we'd just pulled a Parent Trap on the whole damn world.

"It might have been a good shout to get a van or something," Benny muttered as he tugged the white shirt off of his brother's unconscious body and inspected it for bloodstains. There were a couple on the back of it, the main one at the bottom in line with the stab wound he'd given him, but he'd managed to avoid putting the knife through the damn thing at least. It actually looked pretty fucking tidy, all things considered. "Because I don't see us sneaking him outa here in the back of your Mini, Church."

"Ah. Good point." I snapped my fingers as a plan came together. "Got it - some of the Bakers are here. I'll have them fix this mess and deliver him to the warehouse during the ceremony."

"No one can know about this," Benny growled and I rolled my eyes at him.

"I know, Butch, but the Bakers aren't fucking stupid. We can just stick a bag over his head and cover him up good then get them to take him back to the warehouse for us while the celebrations are still going on. They won't dare look under his hood, so no one will be any the wiser," I said.

Benny looked less than convinced about bringing anyone else in on this, but it was either that or leave him lying here until we could sneak back tonight. I was guessing bringing a Baker in was less risky than that.

"Alright," he sighed heavily. "I'll work on covering up who he is and you go find one."

I grinned as I quickly grabbed my suit and pulled it on, fastening my waistcoat and leaving my damp cravat hanging open around my neck before finding a big shard of the broken mirror so that I could fix my hair in it, pushing my tattooed fingers through the blonde strands until they sat right.

Benny already had Danny stripped down to his boxers, the flick-knife still sticking outa his back as he lay face down on the flagstones, dribbling a little through the drug induced coma I'd gifted him. He was probably tripping right up to the moon at the moment, which was a damn sight nicer than his reality would be when he came crashing back down to earth.

"How's that wound? Is he gonna bleed out when you pull the knife out or what?" I asked curiously.

"Not likely, but I'll leave it there for now just in case," Benny muttered as he started to dress in his brother's suit.

"I'll go find us a Baker then. He had Dylan working on the bride, so I'll probably find him with her," I said.

"Shit, I haven't seen him in...well I guess I haven't seen anyone in a long damn time," Benny muttered and I paused, placing a hand on his shoulder as he pulled the bloody shirt on.

"I know, mate. But you can't let them know that when they see you. You ain't Benny no more. Not yet. You've gotta embody that asshole." I tossed a look filled with disdain at Danny where he lay on the floor. "Which means there won't be a whole lotta people who are pleased to see you."

"Yeah, yeah, I know," he replied and I caught his face between my hands as I forced him to look at me.

"Have you got this?" I asked. "Because from this moment on we're running this play. You ain't gonna have time to take a moment off. Eight years is a hell of a long time to be stuck outa the game, and this is one mind fuck of a way to get back into it. Intense don't even come close. It's all in."

"I got this," he swore to me and I could see that steely Butcher glint in his eyes which made me believe it. "You don't need to worry about me. I've been waiting eight long years to take back my crown, and I've gone above and beyond to make it happen. I didn't cover my fucking body in tattoos to impersonate this son of a bitch just to let it fail at the first moment. I'm all over it."

"Alright then. And if you need something good to focus on before we walk down the aisle then I suggest you start thinking about how hard you're gonna fuck that wife of yours when we get out of here."

"You don't need to remind me, I've been jerking off over the thought of her pussy for months and I still don't have a fucking clue what she even looks like. Though at this point I'm so pussy starved that I don't think it would even matter if she was a fucking troll," he joked.

"Believe me, she ain't a troll," I promised with a grin, though my gut twisted as I thought about her being in his bed tonight for reasons I wasn't gonna give my attention to. I wasn't going soft for Miss America. I wasn't dumb enough to do that.

"Thank fuck for that," he breathed, his eyes lighting with desire at the mere thought of her and he hadn't even had a glimpse of her beauty yet. He was one lucky fucker alright.

"Good. Then I say we fuck off outa here and ditch the reception. Your new bride isn't gonna want to have to meet every member of your family and I don't think you're ready to face all of them with your Danny mask on yet either. So let's just get the fuck outa here the moment you say 'I do' and we can make your apologies later."

"Yeah," Benny agreed, his eyes lighting at that idea. "I'm still worried Ma will know the difference as it is and if I'm being honest, I could do with a few days to get my head straight. It's a big old world out here and I've been locked up for a long time."

"You got it, mate. Game face on, play the part and you'll be balls deep in Miss America before you know it." I slapped his cheek twice and strode from the room, waiting to hear the lock click before I walked off in search of Dylan and the bride.

I scrubbed a hand across the stubble on my jaw as I gave myself a few moments to think about that reality and wondered just how faithful of a husband Benny was really planning on being. Everyone knew Danny had a reputation for fucking anything that stayed still long enough so it wasn't like anyone expected him to go all monogamous. So if Benny decided to make up for lost time after being on cockdown for eight years then maybe me and Anya could fill a little time of our own...

I was deep into a fantasy of her lips wrapped tight around my dick as I stepped out into the body of the church, and I cursed as I almost walked face first into Old Lady Butcher's hat.

"Sorry, Ma," I said as I caught her, making sure she was steady on her feet as she swatted me half-heartedly and called me out on not watching where I was walking.

Benny's mum was a proper fine woman, all class with a dollop of East London charm heaped in. She had her short blonde hair curled up beneath the monstrosity of a hat she wore and her warm eyes crinkled as she smiled. Me own ma had left this earth well before her time and I'd been calling Mrs Butcher Ma for as long as I could remember, seeing as she was the closest thing I had to one.

"How's the groom?" she asked. "Not getting cold feet, I hope? That poor gal won't be left high and dry at the altar, will she?"

"Not a fucking chance," I swore and she swatted me again for cursing in church. "Sorry, sorry! I'm just off to find the bride now. Danny wanted me to tell her how excited he is to be making an honest man of himself at last."

"I had been worried he'd end up on the shelf," Ma admitted, moving aside to let me pass. "He's not getting any younger and I need grand babies. Have you seen the Russian? Does she look well suited to birthing?"

I barked a laugh as I started backing away through the congregation. “Calm down, Ma, he’s only thirty-four! Plenty of time for all that.”

“You need a nice young lady too, Jeffrey!” she cried as I made my escape and I cringed at the use of that fucking name. No one else dared to use it, but I couldn’t ever get her to just call me Church like every other fucker I knew.

I tossed her a salute, skirted the vicar while ignoring his request for information on the groom and hurried out of the room to find the bride.

I found Frank standing guard outside a door which led to an antechamber beside the exit to the church and grinned at him in greeting.

“Hey, Frankie boy, how’s our beautiful bride doing?” I called and his scowl somehow deepened. Yeah, there were some big wounds between me and him, but now really wasn’t the time to be worrying about that.

“Shouldn’t you be waiting at the altar with Danny?” he grunted, staying firmly in the way of the door.

“All good things come to those who wait,” I said. “But right now, Danny needs me to get him a Baker and I heard you got one locked up in there with the bride?”

Frank looked inclined to tell me to get fucked, but Danny’s word was law around here, so he reluctantly stepped aside and opened the door for me. I clapped him on the shoulder in thanks and he shrugged me off with a look of hatred that felt something akin to a stab wound. My lips parted as I looked at the man I thought of as a brother and I felt his hatred landing on me with the weight of all he’d lost crushing me to the flagstones at my feet. But it wasn’t just *his* loss. Problem was, he refused to allow the rest of us to claim any of that grief.

I closed my mouth again, knowing this wasn’t the time and that he wouldn’t wanna hear it anyway and I stepped through the door instead.

I fell still as my gaze landed on Anya and the breath I’d been in the middle of inhaling got trapped somewhere on its way to my lungs.

“Lord have mercy,” I breathed, drinking her in. This girl looked good enough to devour while wearing a scowl and a baggy band tee, right about now she looked like Helen of Troy and I was willing to go launch a thousand ships for her right down the River Thames.

I studied every damn inch of her and I swear a possessive growl built in my throat as I just stood there staring like some dumb fuck virgin.

“Shut your damn mouth, Churchy sweet, or I’ll have to go fetch a mop for all that drool,” Dylan said, stealing my attention as he strode in front of Anya and blocked my view of her in his playsuit and killer heels combo which was apparently his wedding outfit.

I tried to look past him, but he was a big fucker so I was just left with swathes of white skirt to look at and a seriously disappointed cock which was trying to stretch out the crotch of my trousers.

“Any chance you really are a virgin all dressed in white like that?” I called to my girl, ignoring the Baker in favour of her for a few extra moments.

"Why do you care?" she asked, that American twang outa place in this east end hidden kingdom.

"Just trying to figure out if I like the idea of popping your cherry more than I like the idea of fucking the memory of all other fellas clean outa your tight pussy."

Anya choked out some kind of gasp, mixed with a surprised laugh and Dylan arched one finely pencilled brow at me.

"Why are you sniffing around the boss's bride, Church?" he asked, giving me a look like I was a dog trying to piss up the wrong lamppost.

"I'm just figuring out what I'll be imagining when I'm jerking off over her - not offering to actually fuck her," I said innocently. "Besides, she's not what I'm in the mood for right now, big boy - you are."

"Is that so?" Dylan purred but I knew he didn't buy that shit for a moment. Never hurt to flirt with him though - he was a damn sucker for a compliment and he'd be all the happier to help me out if I got in his good books.

"Yeah. Danny needs you - in an official capacity."

Dylan sighed dramatically. "These heels aren't meant for hard labour. Does it seriously have to be now?"

"Yeah...we had a bit of an incident with an uninvited guest and we need a little clean up before the vicar finds the mess we made and joins his almighty before his time." I shrugged apologetically and Dylan huffed.

"Fine." He turned his back on me and fiddled with Anya's hair for a moment. "Chin up, honey - no matter how bad things seem they can always be worse. And on the plus side, I've got it on good authority that Danny Butcher has one hell of a cock, so at least you've got that to comfort you."

"That helps so much," Anya deadpanned and I snorted as Dylan swept from the room.

I shoulda followed right after him, but I couldn't resist the temptation to step forward and breathe in the air surrounding the girl who was all set to marry my best friend. The succulent scent of passionfruit carried from her and I was half tempted to take a juicy bite out of her.

"You look all kinds of sinful, Miss America," I breathed in her ear, my mouth grazing the soft skin of her neck and I coulda sworn a shiver passed over her flesh. "Try not to break too many hearts out there."

"I didn't have the impression that Englishmen had hearts, Church," she replied coolly, tilting her head towards me so that those lips were a mere breath away. "You all seem like soulless villains to me."

"That we are," I agreed. "But on occasion we've been known to fall hard and fast for a beauty such as yours. And you know what they say about being loved by a Brit, don't you?"

"Is it some kind of Prince Charming bullshit?" she asked.

"Nah. None of that."

"Tell me then," she demanded and Christ, I didn't hate being on the receiving end of her glare.

"We fuck hard and we love harder. So if you wanna catch yourself one, you'd better hold on tight and get ready for one hell of a ride." I winked at her as her lips parted in surprise, drinking in the blush that rose in her cheeks and wondering if she might just like it if I tried to prove the first part of that claim.

I stepped back, pulling out my phone and snapping a picture before giving myself a mental slap and quickly striding from the room.

"How much longer?" Frank asked as I passed him, using as few words as he could get away with just to make sure I knew how much he despised having to speak to me.

"Ten minutes," I called over my shoulder as I joined Dylan and headed back into the church. "If we're not waiting at the altar by then, he's done a runner and you'll have to marry her instead."

"I could think of worse fates," he muttered and I smirked to myself because he was right about that. Marrying the creature in that room was the kind of hell I could get onboard with.

Dylan gave me an appraising look as we cut back through the church, but I didn't offer him anything and he didn't ask whatever question was clearly perched on his pursed lips.

We made it back to the room where Benny and Danny were locked away and I knocked on it, calling out to let him know it was me.

The door cracked open and Benny tossed a sweeping look down the corridor beyond us before opening it fully to let us in.

Dylan released a low whistle. "Well, I guess it wouldn't be a Butcher's wedding if no one ended up getting stabbed," he said, moving towards Danny's unconscious body.

Benny had managed to wrestle his brother into the clothes he'd worn here from prison, the flick knife still on show protruding from his lower back where the hem of his hoody was pushed up. He'd also tied a black sack over Danny's head and tied his hands behind his back with enough duct tape to hide the tattoos which crawled onto his hands too, concealing everything that could have given away his identity. It was a bloody beautiful job.

Benny was fully dressed in the wedding suit now and from the outside he looked utterly like the man he was impersonating.

"I didn't ask for a commentary, just a clean up," Benny ground out, sounding just like his arsehole of a brother and damn near making me shed a tear with pride.

"Keep your hair on, honey, you know there's no judgement here," Dylan said, raising his hands dramatically. "But I have to say, you've done a bad job of killing him so far because he's still breathing like a fish gasping on the riverbank. So do you want me to finish him off for you before I dispose of him or-"

"No. I don't want him dead yet so I'm not after a disposal, just a removal. I want him put in the lockup beneath the warehouse. Don't fuck about with food or water, just give him a bucket to shit in and make sure he doesn't bleed out," Benny said firmly.

“Is that all?” Dylan asked, yawning dramatically and waving his pink tipped nails before his mouth.

“No actually. I want my fucking knife back. So you can patch up this hole in him too.” Benny bent down and yanked the switchblade out of Danny’s back, causing blood to start pissing out of him.

“Oh for the love of all that’s sacred,” Dylan huffed, dropping his sparkly pink bag and opening it up as he began to rummage around inside it. He quickly emerged with a wad of cotton wool which he promptly stuffed into the bleeding wound to staunch it then he grabbed a curling iron and plugged it in at the wall.

“What’s the curling iron for?” I asked curiously.

“And that, my dear, is why you are the muscle and I’m the one they call in to clean up after you,” Dylan replied, giving me a disdainful look before pulling a spray bottle out of his bag along with some ziplock bags and a cloth.

I exchanged a look with Benny while Dylan quickly sent a text out on his phone and the next thing I knew, the blood had been cleaned from the floor, Benny’s switchblade had been sprayed down with bleach and cleaned off and every bloodstained cloth was neatly tucked away inside a ziplock bag.

“Don’t take that bag off of his head,” Benny growled as Dylan’s phone began to ring. “This fucker’s identity is best left a secret, you got that? I don’t care how long we’ve known you or what allegiance you think we hold to you - I’ll tear your head clean offa your body if you go looking at things you got no business knowing.”

“Please,” Dylan huffed. “As if I want to be privy to any more of your sordid secrets than I already am, Danny Butcher. I’m quite happy in ignorant, well-paid bliss, thank you very much.” He picked up the curling iron, tugged the bloodstained cotton wool out of Danny’s stab wound and promptly jammed the curling iron inside it instead.

“Jesus,” I muttered as the stench of burning flesh reached us and Danny jerked beneath him. The drugs must have been fucking strong though, because that was all the reaction he gave.

“What’s the matter, Church? You never seen a wound get cauterised before?” Dylan mocked as he tugged the curling iron free again to reveal a blackened, no longer bleeding stab wound. “I’m just glad you didn’t hit anything important because it is way too early in the day for me to be sewing a man’s insides up in the house of god.”

“That was fucking Savage, Dylan,” I said.

“You’d better believe it,” he replied with a cocky grin. “Don’t you boys have a wedding to get to?”

“Yeah,” Benny agreed. “I take it you’ve got this handled?”

“You know I do, honey.”

Benny nodded and the two of us headed to the door, leaving Dylan to finish up the job of moving Danny and cleaning this place up. He had it well in hand and we knew we could trust him, so I focused on the more pressing issue as I closed the door behind us and led Benny towards his fate.

“Cheer up, fella,” I said as he held back a little. “You’re about to marry one hell of a girl.”

“Oh yeah?” he asked, not seeming convinced of that, so I took my phone from my pocket and quickly showed him the snapshot I’d taken of Anya just a few minutes ago. She looked fucking breath-taking in it and that didn’t have a patch on the real deal.

“Fucking hell, I’m gonna come the second I get my cock near her, let alone inside her,” Benny muttered as he stared at the photo like a starving animal.

“Well I’d be happy to step in if you need a little help,” I said, slapping him on the back and ignoring the hint of truth those words left on my tongue.

“I’ll bet,” Benny said, tearing his eyes from the screen and looking through the door to the church filled with members of his family and other associates who he hadn’t seen in eight long years, all of whom would assume he was his brother. “I wish this wasn’t necessary,” he muttered and I knew he meant the deception and having to pretend to be Danny.

“I know, mate. But we gotta be smart about this. We gotta prove that Danny set you up and you weren’t responsible for none of that shit before they’ll ever trust you again.”

“I know,” he sighed, swiping a hand over his dark features, “Let’s just get on with it then, shall we?”

“Yeah,” I agreed. “Once you’re a married man, it’ll all just get easier from there.”

CHAPTER SEVEN

Music started up in the church, someone playing a violin to the tune of Something by The Beatles and a breath of relief passed my lips at that song reaching me right now.

"Ready?" Frank asked as he stepped into the small room and I frowned, surprised he was even bothering to ask.

"Ready to sell my soul to Lucifer?" I clarified and his jaw ticked.

"Come on." He led me into the entrance chamber in front of an arching wooden door and I drowned in the song carrying to me. The brand on my ass stung like a bitch as the heavy material rubbed against it, but there wasn't much I could do about that. I'd just have to take it as a mark of victory against Danny when I slit his throat.

Frank shifted his hold on me, taking the crook of my arm instead as he guided me forward towards my destiny.

"Guess you're giving me away then, Daddy," I whispered and he looked at me with a deep note of laughter leaving him, the sound making my stomach squeeze.

He flattened his lips so fast I almost could have been convinced he hadn't laughed at all and had actually witnessed someone murdering his mother instead.

He pushed through the door and I held my breath as he guided me out into the aisle and I was dazzled by a hundred faces turning my way, staring, muttering, pointing. I was a collared dog being paraded in a show, all of them judging the sleekness of my coat, hunting for good breeding.

But then my eyes landed on the man waiting for me at the end of the aisle and all of their stares paled by comparison to the one he was giving me. Danny Butcher had his hands clasped behind his back, his brow low as his intense and forbidding gaze ate directly through flesh and bone to gaze at the very essence of what I was. His face seemed somehow more beautiful now, looking more like a god than a demon as I approached him, and my heart fluttered a mad and furious tune.

As I arrived at the head of the aisle, I spotted Church standing just beyond him, not even trying to hide the filthy smirk he was angling my way as he openly stared at me. I fought my eyes away from him and back onto the monster who was about to claim me and Frank passed my hand into his.

For an insane second, I almost held onto him, but Frank was no angel, and nothing and no one was going to save me from this marriage but me.

Danny's eyes travelled over me like he'd never seen a woman before, this potent, animal hunger in his gaze that made my whole body flush with heat and as his fingers tightened on mine, a bolt of energy passed between us that made some insane part of me hunger for this man.

But then I remembered what he'd done to me, the collar he'd strapped to my neck and the name he'd branded on my ass. My features settled into a cold glare. If he thought I was going to play pretend that I was a happy, willing bride, then he was more stupid than I'd thought.

"Well fuck me, the Russians produced a damn bombshell when they made you, Anya Volkov," he said in a low voice meant for only me.

"You're right. And I'll be sure to make a crater out of you, Danny Butcher," I said flatly and his eyes lit up as he grinned. That smile wasn't like the psychotic one he'd aimed at me earlier, it was the smile of a kid with a new toy and it threw me off a little.

"I'd love to see you try," he said like he was thrilled by the prospect, then the vicar spoke loudly, grabbing our attention along with the congregation's.

"Dearly beloved, we are gathered here today to celebrate the union of these two-"

He went on and I zoned him out as I examined my husband-to-be, picturing his throat cut and bleeding as he pawed at my feet. It helped me get through this a little, reminding me it wasn't just me being bound to a creature of destruction, he was being bound to one in return. I was a force of chaos and death, and he'd soon find out what the Volkovs were capable of.

A twisted smile curled my lips at the image of his bloody corpse and his brows arched as he took in my expression, trying to suss me out. It felt pretty good to be confusing him, but I knew the danger he posed, and maybe this inviting expression he was wearing had more to do with the people watching us than it did with me. He'd collared and branded me after all. And I was hardly going to forget that in a hurry. I was pretty sure I'd feel better about it once I slashed up that godly face of his though.

"Do you, Danny Butcher, take this woman to be your wife? Do you promise to be faithful to her in good times and in bad, in sickness and in health, to love her and to honour her all the days of your life?" the vicar asked.

Are you gonna love and honour the burn on my ass back to health, you motherfucker?

"I do," Danny said smoothly, his fingers tightening on my hand possessively, making my heart bunch up into my throat. Those hands had wounded me already, what more were they capable of?

"And do you, Anya Natalya Volkov, take this man to be your husband? Do you promise to be faithful to him in good times and in bad, in sickness and in health, to love him and to honour him all the days of your life?"

I hesitated, my tongue not wanting to wrap around the words which would chain me to this gangster. But I knew there was no choice in this. I had to wait until I had a chance to kill him, and I couldn't do it in front of a room of mobsters and violent criminals.

"I do," I forced out and Danny smirked like an asshole.

I made my way through the rest of the vows in a bland tone, my heart screaming as I tried to figure out how I was going to get my hands on a weapon to kill this piece of shit.

Church suddenly stepped forward with the rings, jolting my mind away from the murder fest I'd been having in my brain as he passed us one each.

His fingers skimmed over my palm as he placed Danny's one in it and I locked eyes with him for a moment as a tremor wracked the foundations of my body. There was something about this asshole who pulled on the chords of my lust far too easily and as he stepped away, rubbing his thumb over the corner of his mouth to cover a grin, I could have sworn he'd felt it too.

When the vicar instructed Danny to put the ring on me, he gripped my wrist with one hand and slid the ring onto my finger with the other. His fingertips stroked against the inside of my wrist in a way that made my clit tingle, and I yanked my hand away the moment he had the ring in place, causing mutters to break out in the congregation.

The vicar cleared his throat and Danny's eyes danced with amusement as he watched me like a hungry animal.

I swear to god, my clit had absolutely no bar for the type of man it wanted attention from. But I was extra horrified by its interest in Danny Butcher.

He shoved my head in a fucking toilet.

Hatred coursed deeper inside me and I held onto it tight, wielding it like a blade. I knew what this man was, and I knew he was going to hurt me again the moment he got a chance.

The vicar directed me to put the ring on Danny's finger and I took some joy in shoving it on as hard as I could, making him curse under his breath as I looked up at him with an overacted bat of my lashes. Then my eyes fell back to his hand and I frowned, realising there were no scratches there. I could have sworn I'd ripped his skin open when he'd shoved me onto the bathroom floor in the hotel. But I was disappointed to find I hadn't even left a mark on this devil. No doubt his black heart lay dormant in his chest, so it wasn't beating any blood around his body for me to spill it anyway.

I drawled out the words the vicar asked me to repeat then experienced a pang of horror as he announced us husband and wife.

It wasn't like I hadn't known it was coming, but somehow the shock of it hit me like a hurricane all at once and I wasn't remotely prepared for Danny grabbing my waist, yanking me against the hard planes of his body and sinking his tongue deep into my mouth.

Hellfire and brimstone blazed in my chest as he gripped the back of my head with his free hand so I had no chance of getting free. He kissed me like no one was watching, his lips moving on mine in a filthy, possessive, sinful kiss that would have been X rated in a movie. And it took me three whole seconds to realise I was kissing him back, my body betraying me once again as I tasted his tongue, meeting the rampant starvation in his kiss with all the fury overflowing in my body. I said 'I'll kill you' in that kiss, while he said 'I'll fuck you raw' with his.

It was a battle of wills of who was going to pull away first, my fingers finding the bare skin at the back of his neck and my nails raking down it as a growl escaped me which he swallowed with an answering laugh. *So you are able to bleed, Danny Butcher. I'll make sure to claim every drop of it from you.*

Firm hands suddenly accosted us, yanking us apart and I found Church there, pressing Danny back and slapping his face playfully. "You've got an audience, mate. You'll give poor old Aunt Tilda another heart attack," he said and a woman in the congregation laughed loudly, making the rest of the onlookers join in.

Danny was still staring at me over his shoulder and I watched intently as my heart raced a thousand miles an hour in my chest. He lifted a hand, wiping my lipstick from his lips with his thumb and smiling fiendishly. I should have feared his interest in me, but there was something blazing between us in that second which I couldn't deny. Lust. Pure and simple.

Confusion rattled my brain as I quickly rebuilt my defences and bolstered the hatred in me towards him. He was vile. A fucking barbarian. And I wasn't going to be distracted by a monster's kiss.

Besides, one good thing had come of it. While he'd been pressed against me, I'd felt something hard digging into my chest which simply had to be a switch blade. It was in his inside pocket. A temptation too hard to ignore. Because I was pretty damn sure I'd just found my murder weapon. *Now how can I get my hands on it without him noticing…*

Danny suddenly grabbed my hand, towing me to the side of the aisle where a table was set up for us to sign the marriage register. I sat down carefully, resting my weight on my good ass cheek and clenching my jaw through the pain of the other. Then I went numbly through the motions, my fingers branding my name beside his and binding us once and for all. But our marriage would be a short one, hours at most, because I planned on being a widow by midnight.

I kept feeling Danny's eyes on me, but I refused to meet a single one of his stares as I concentrated on the task before me. I could feel his desire rolling off of him like he was a furnace and the heat of it was baking my flesh.

I clenched my thighs together, feeling like a sinner in this house of God, because holy shit my body was reacting to him like it really did belong to him now. But fuck that. He'd collared me and I wasn't going to be an obedient bitch. Of course, maybe it wouldn't be the worst thing in the world to use this heat between us. Manipulate him, draw him closer until my fingers found that blade and I had a chance to swipe it clean and deep across his throat. I'd make sure it looked like an outside attack, play the terrified victim, I might even cut myself too so Danny's men would buy the lie. Anything it took to pull it off.

My lips hooked up at the corners and I let myself glance his way at last, finding his whole body turned towards me and a wild man in his eyes. The ink peeking out from his collar and cuffs looked almost metallic against his bronze skin and my fingers tingled with the urge to see if it felt as hard and cold as it looked. His shoulders were built to break down doors and his eyes were the colour of chestnuts, looking somehow richer than they had before, and I swear there was something haunted in his gaze. Something that made me question whether this man actually did have a soul. But I guessed if he did, it was a twisted, rotten thing that the Devil already had stocks and shares in.

We finished signing the paperwork then Danny took hold of my hand, drawing me to my feet and that same potent rush of energy seemed to dance between us. It made no sense. These hands had shoved me to my knees, forced my head in a toilet, tied me to a bed, branded his fucking name on my ass.

I tried to tug my fingers free, but his grip told me I was his prisoner and adrenaline buzzed beneath my skin as I set my mind on the knife in his pocket, going to the darkest place I knew. I thought of my brothers, of their betrayal and of the fucking treaty which had placed an unthinkable price on my head. My life, my body. And that was all it took for me to find the determination I needed to pull this off.

My eyes found Frank as he circled the congregation and paused by the exit, clearly waiting for us and my gaze hooked on his pocket where my stuff was stashed. I was itching for my music again, but I didn't know when I'd be getting it back. Maybe he'd keep it from me. Maybe I'd have to run from this place without it and track more down elsewhere. The thought made anxiety dance in my chest and I forced my mind off of it. It wasn't important. I had to do this without it.

We headed down the aisle hand in hand while people cheered and my fingers were crushed in the grip of my new husband's fingers. It was surreal to attend a wedding where none of my own family were here. It wasn't like I'd ever really thought about marriage, but I guessed if I had it would have looked a lot different to this. I'd have been marrying someone I loved for a start, not some villainous stranger who was going to torture me just for being my father's daughter.

He tugged me outside and Frank fell in to step behind us like a diligent little guard dog and Danny took out a pack of cigarettes, lighting one up as he turned us to face his man.

"Fetch the car," he ordered and Frank nodded, trotting off to do as he bid and I glared after him as he took my stuff with him.

Church appeared, looking like the kind of best man who'd fuck every bridesmaid in the wedding party on any other day, but unluckily for him, I didn't have any.

"Nice dress, Miss America," he said with a wink. "Or I guess I'll have to call you Mrs Butcher now." He clapped Danny on the shoulder who grinned then Church jerked his head with a mischievous look.

Danny tugged me after him and we were soon moving at a swift pace around the side of the building to where Church's Mini Cooper was parked.

I dug in my heels as we made it there and Church popped the door open, folding the passenger seat forward and gesturing for us to get in.

"I thought we were going with Frank," I said in confusion, backing up and looking over my shoulder for him.

"Change of plans, bombshell," Danny said, giving me a shove towards the opening as smoke poured from his lips.

"He has my shit," I growled in refusal.

"Well, you can get your shit later. Get in," Danny commanded.

"No," I snapped, trying to get my fingers free of his. "I won't fit in there in this dress."

"Wanna bet?" Danny grinned.

"Ten quid says she fits," Church agreed, the two of them sharing a wicked look and my upper lip curled.

"Twenty *dollars* says she'll stuff that nodding bulldog up your ass if you try," I warned, pointing to the obnoxious thing on the dashboard.

"Why have you got it in for Barkley so bad, huh?" Church demanded but as I opened my mouth to tell him why the plastic monstrosity offended me, Danny tossed his cigarette away, picked me up and shoved me through onto the back seat.

I yelled in anger as my dress went over my head and the noise turned into a pained scream as his hands landed on my ass and he shoved me harder so I fell into the back seat. The burn on my right ass cheek flared with agony and I cursed as I tried to turn around, feeling a huge body shoving itself in beside me. I was lost to a sea of netting and silk, trying to find my way out of it as Danny and Church's laughter filled the air.

The sound of the doors slamming and the engine starting reached me and with a burst of speed, the car shot off down the road.

I fought my way out of the material I was drowning in, cursing in every colourful word I knew, emerging to find the streets of London zipping past the windows as we sped away from the church.

"Fuck me, is that tongue as filthy when it's sucking cock?" Danny asked and a snarl rolled from my lips.

"As if you'll ever find out, you prick," I hissed and he roared a laugh.

"Told you she was a livewire, mate," Church said, glancing at us in the rear view mirror, his silver eyes full of mirth.

"You were panting all over me in the church, love, you don't need to play the innocent virgin with me. I'm your husband now and wives are allowed to fuck their husbands. It's kind of the point actually, ain't it?" Danny said, flashing a set of wolf's teeth at me and acid poured through my chest. He was half buried in my huge skirt and was taking up so much of the room back here, I couldn't quite believe we'd both fit in.

I bit down on my tongue, almost drawing blood with how much I wanted to bite and snap at him. But I had to keep my head if I was going to get hold of the knife stashed in his pocket. And it seemed like there was one obvious way to do that. Though I didn't have to drool all over him, I'd just goad him in to doing exactly as I wanted. Men were easy like that.

"You couldn't satisfy a whore who'd been paid good money to come for you," I said dismissively, turning to look out the window beside me.

Church barked a laugh. "I've seen Butcher fuck three girls at once and make them come like it's his God-given gift, darlin' – though he might be a bit rusty these days. What do you reckon, mate?"

"Fuck off," Danny said through a smirk, looking to me and wetting his lips in a way that made my pussy throb. *Shit.*

I turned away again, trying to shift to get more comfortable, but if I wasn't leaning on my burned ass, the bodice of the dress was digging in instead.

"Are you a virgin?" Danny asked curiously, his assessing gaze moving over me while I scowled at him. "Because I know a few of the families were garbling on about keeping the brides pure or some shit, so if the Russian's kept your pussy under lock and key-"

"Sorry to disappoint," I hissed, glad I could steal this one victory from him. "But I've fucked plenty of men and tasted enough cock too. So you won't be able to claim any firsts from me."

"Oh bombshell," Danny chuckled, licking his bottom lip as he looked at me in a way that shouldn't have been legal. "I'd have been disappointed if you *were* a virgin. I don't need the questionable accolade of breaking your seal, I can handle the pressure of being the best you've ever had without needing to know there was never any competition for the title. And I'm sure there's one or two firsts I can come up with if you feel like gettin' creative, love."

Danny shed his blazer, tossing it into the footwell before us and my heart hammered as my gaze locked on it for half a second. That knife was so close. I *had* to get my hands on it.

Danny's phone started ringing and he causally slid it from his pants' pocket, checking the caller ID before putting it away again.

"Frank's gonna be pissed," he sniggered and Church chuckled.

"He'll find us eventually," Church said. "Poor fucker might be looking for a while though."

"I thought you wanted him hounding my ass," I said and Danny's eyes snapped to me.

"I did? Right, yeah, I did. But not while you're with me, bombshell." He somehow found my ankle among all the material, taking hold of it and skimming his thumb around it in a circle, the movement making me draw in a sharp breath.

Why did his touch feel like the best kind of sin when just hours ago it had felt like razors on my flesh?

"Now about that dare," Danny said darkly, his gaze full of wicked intention.

"What dare?" I scoffed and his fingers sailed higher up my leg, caressing the smooth fabric of my stocking before reaching the top of it and groaning softly as his fingers moved onto the skin he found there as lust hooded his gaze.

"The one where you dared me to make you come," he said, shifting forward in his seat and driving his knee between my legs to force them wider.

My heart thrashed over my enemy moving closer, but a fucked up part of me wanted this almost as much as I wanted to get my hands on that knife. And luckily for me, those two wants were currently aligning.

My gaze flicked to Church in the front seat as I remembered he was here and heat blazed up my spine in a fiery path.

"Don't look at him," Danny growled, reaching out to grab my chin and turn my head to face him. "Look at your husband like a good wife."

"Oh yeah, I'm a real angel of a wife," I said dryly and his knee pressed deeper between my thighs, making my breathing hitch.

He fisted handfuls of my skirt and I felt the energy shift between us as I realised I was actually going to allow this. And worse than that, I wanted it.

Danny raised his left hand, curling down all of his fingers except the one with the ring on it that marked him as mine. Then he slid his hands between my legs, peeling my panties aside and finding me soaked for him.

"Fuck, you seem like a pretty good wife so far, look how wet you are for your husband," he growled, pushing that finger inside me, the ring cool against my burning flesh as I gasped. He pumped it in and out of me as he watched my expression, his eyes hooding as a merciless kind of hunger filled his gaze.

"I'm not wet for you, I just have a thing for that hideous plastic bobbing head dog," I said breathlessly.

"Why have you got it in for Barkley?" Church demanded and I smirked a second before Danny grazed his thumb over my clit and I swallowed a moan, not letting him know how fucking amazing that felt.

"You're a liar, bombshell," Danny accused and fuck that name did something sinful to me.

He slowly drew his finger out of me, bringing it to his lips and sucking the taste of me off of it in a display hot enough to make me ache.

"How does she taste?" Church asked in a rough voice, making my heart jolt as I was once again reminded that he was right fucking there and Danny didn't seem to give a shit.

"Like my dinner," Danny said brutishly, then took his knee from between my legs and buried his head beneath the material instead. My hips bucked in surprise, but he wrapped his arms around the backs of my legs, tugging me forward and the moment his mouth landed on my clit, my will crumbled and a wanton moan broke free of my lips.

He laughed against my pussy, sucking and teasing my clit as I braced myself against the back of Church's seat, all my thoughts scattering. Danny's tongue worked me up into a frenzy as he growled and groaned into my flesh like he couldn't get enough of me and despite hating him with all of my being, I never wanted him to stop.

I panted as he moved his mouth lower, licking away my arousal before driving his tongue into me in a hard and dirty move that had me almost coming apart already.

"Oh my god," I moaned, my fingers clawing into the seat and suddenly Church's hand was on mine, pulling it forward and pressing it to his shoulder instead.

"Don't fuck up the upholstery, darlin'," he said in a deep tone that sent another wave of pleasure through my pussy. I dug my nails into Church's skin through his shirt, my eyes locking with his in the rear view mirror as he stared at me, his gaze fully off the road.

I opened my mouth to tell him to pay attention to driving, but Danny shoved two fingers inside me at that second and what came out was closer to a fucking howl. I'd never made noises like that during sex. But this…this was a skilled tongue that belonged to a man who looked like an inked demon. Not to mention the fact that we were being watched by a man who set my soul alight.

I'd always been adventurous in bed, but I hadn't ever had anyone watch me get off with another man. And the way Church's gaze kept meeting mine in the mirror, full of lust and a blazing heat that said he was desperate to join in with the party told me I officially had a voyeur fetish.

Danny pushed a third finger into me, showing me no fucking mercy and making my back arch as his tongue slid onto my clit again and started working me up into a complete fever. The hot, wet pad of his tongue moved in perfect, endless strokes, circling and circling while I panted and shamelessly ground my pussy against his hot mouth.

I wrapped my legs around him, digging the heels of my stilettos into his back and making him growl at the pain, responding with a nip to my clit that nearly sent me over the edge.

Oh fuck, the knife.

I drew back the tide of pleasure that was threatening to crash through me, trying to focus on the suit jacket Danny had discarded on the floor. I dropped my hand from Church's shoulder and reached for it with grasping fingers, covering the movement with a layer of my dress as my hand slid under it.

My fingertips grazed the knife through the material of the inner pocket and I stretched further, trying to reach the entrance to it. Danny's fingers moved faster and my head started spinning. I could barely see straight, so I gave up on trying and just tried to feel my way to that knife instead.

Danny's merciless touch had me right at the edge of ecstasy and it took everything I had to hold it off.

He growled in frustration, clearly sensing what I was doing as his tongue started riding my clit with such skill I swear he was taking control of my body entirely, possessing me, demanding I bow to the pleasure he was forcing me to take.

"Come for me, wife," he commanded, but I refused, my toes scrunching as I continued to hold off.

"Havin' a little trouble there, mate?" Church taunted and Danny cursed in anger, curling his fingers inside me and pressing into that perfect spot as he assaulted my clit with his tongue once more.

The windows were steaming up and I swear I was melting as I started losing control of my limbs. I was half in the footwell, my legs latched around Danny and the dress a sea of white we were drowning in.

Church suddenly reached back into the footwell and panic reared in me for a second before his hand found mine, dragging it through to the front of the car and pressing it against his solid abs.

I came, my fingers tearing across his stomach as Danny's mouth forced me to surrender and pleasure poured through me in wave after violent wave. Having held off for so long made the orgasm all the more powerful and Danny kept fucking me with his hand to prolong the tide of ecstasy. It was the best thing I'd ever experienced, but that made it the worst too, because I'd just let my enemy do this to me. And I hadn't even gotten the fucking knife.

I lost all strength in my body, going slack as my cheek pressed to the back of Church's chair, every one of my limbs wound awkwardly through the space.

Danny emerged from my skirt with his lips wet, his hair fucked up and a gleam in his eyes that made my heart judder. Fuck, he looked powerful, the creator of my ruin. He'd set an entire forest fire in my flesh, reducing me to ash.

"What's that Winston Churchill quote about victory?" Danny called to Church without taking his eyes from me.

"As long as we have faith in our own cause and an unconquerable will to win, victory will not be denied us," Church answered, those words sending a tremor through me.

"That's the one," Danny purred, leaning forward and whispering to me. "Victory won't ever be denied me, love."

I swallowed down the razor in my throat as our eyes remained locked and my defiance rose up like a cobra in my chest.

"We'll see about that," I hissed, though the bite to my words was somewhat lost considering I was still twitching with the aftershocks of his fingers and tongue on me.

"We're here," Church said in a voice that was tainted with sex and he yanked up the parking brake hard enough to make my head whip against the seat.

"Motherfucker," I cursed as Danny hauled me upright, staring at me with an intensity that said he wasn't even close to done with me.

Church jumped out of the car, pushing the lever to make his chair fall forward and grabbed hold of me, dragging me out onto the concrete. His eyes glinted like moonlight as he pressed me back against the side of the Mini with both hands on my hips, making my tongue weigh heavily in my mouth.

Danny stepped out after me with his suit jacket in his fist and I glanced at it with my heart sinking. *Well that was a fucking fail.*

Danny shoved Church's hands off of me, claiming me for himself and I swear for a second Church looked disappointed as Danny dragged me away from him, his arm locking tight around my waist.

I took in my surroundings as he led me to the doors of a huge warehouse and I frowned in confusion as he unlocked them and whipped me into his arms as he carried me over the threshold. The cavernous place had been converted into a home with the huge space of the lower floor all open and full of light which poured in through the black framed, double height windows. Exposed red brick walls and black beams reached up to the ceiling, the faded colour of the brickwork telling a thousand stories of years long since past.

The upper level only ran along the right side of the enormous space, leaving vaulted ceilings to the left and I took in the long walkway which gave access to the rooms up there from the black staircase just beyond the kitchen which took up the space to our right. There was a heavy wooden table beyond that and a large seating area with comfortable looking black couches at the far end of the space, all set close to a fireplace which looked like it was used often, the whole warehouse practically making my jaw drop.

Danny kept me in his arms as he headed straight for the iron staircase, carrying me up it with ease and he strode along the balcony with intention as he made a beeline for a door halfway along it. As he made it there, he cursed, swerving away and carrying on instead towards another door at the end of the walkway like he'd changed his mind.

He shoved through it and I found us in a large bedroom with iron furnishings and black curtains blocking out the light from tall windows on the other side of the room. I stared around at it, but found my new husband's attention much more focused on me as the weight of his stare made my blood heat and forced me to look up at him instead where I found myself devoured by his dark gaze.

Danny placed me down, fisting a hand in my hair and tugging the pins free of it as his mouth fell to my ear. "I'm not sure if you're the most beautiful woman I've ever wanted to fuck or if I've been starved of pussy too long."

"I thought you said you could pick up girls like me on every street in London," I hissed bitterly and he grunted at that.

"Not every street," he muttered then his mouth dropped to my shoulder and his teeth grazed my flesh, sending goosebumps down my spine in a waterfall.

He tossed his suit jacket onto a black leather couch beside us and my eyes snagged on it, but my attention was lost again as his hands moved to grip the top of my dress and he ripped it hard enough to make my tits spill out of it and a gasp caught in my throat.

"I wanted to do this the second you said I do, bombshell," he growled in my ear palming my breasts and teasing my nipples between his fingers and thumbs, causing an earthquake at the centre of my body. *Oh fuck, why is he so good at this?*

"That might have given the vicar a heart attack." I reached behind me, grasping his solid dick through his pants and he swore, grinding into the movement as I felt every inch of him. He was huge, thick and throbbing in my hand already, like he was desperate to be inside me. And I knew in that second, I was going to let him. As a distraction, obviously.

"Nah he'd have jerked himself off while I fucked you on the altar," he chuckled then slid his hand up to lock around my throat, his tongue raking over my ear as his fingers pressed the metal of the collar against my flesh more firmly. "Now let's find out if enemy pussy feels as good as I expect it to." His fingers tightened on my throat and I jerked in his hold as he all but dragged me to the couch and bent me over the arm of it, his hands moving to hold me down.

"Asshole," I gritted out as he kept one palm flat on my back while flipping up the miles of skirt covering my ass and freeing his cock from his pants.

My gaze settled on the suit jacket just ahead of me and my mind slotted together with a *totally* reasonable plan. The moment he came, I'd get hold of that knife and give myself a happy ending. One where he died at my hand. I'd be the last woman to find out if Danny Butcher fucked like the heathen he was and if I stole another orgasm along the way, then that seemed like a perk worth spreading my legs for.

Danny found the edge of my panties beneath my skirt and a shiver danced over my flesh in anticipation as he tugged on them, pulling them over the curve of my ass and making me hiss at the pain of them passing over the brand there. They fell to my ankles and I stepped out of them obligingly, a breath fluttering past my lips as desire pooled in me and I gave in to the fucked up need of my flesh as I waited for him to take what he was aching for from me.

His bare cock suddenly rutted between my thighs and he groaned as he circled the head of it in my wetness, kicking my ankles wider as he lined himself up with my entrance. His palm remained on my back, keeping me down and my clit throbbed at being held at his mercy, a wanton moan escaping me which let me know that I was going to enjoy this no matter what my intentions were.

"You were always meant to be mine," he growled almost to himself then thrust into me with an unforgiving move that filled me deeper than I'd ever been filled, my fingers biting into the couch as I held myself up and took all he had to offer.

I cried out as his thighs slammed into the backs of mine and his hand slid up to fist in my hair as he groaned.

"You're so tight," he panted before drawing back out of me torturously slowly, making my pussy squeeze with the need for him to fill me again.

With another drive of his hips, his cock buried in me once more and the noise that left me was pure animal as he hit some deeply sensitive place inside me.

"Oh fuck, I've missed this," he groaned.

Before I could question that weird ass statement, he started fucking me with the fury and wildness of a caveman, his fingers digging into my flesh as he took complete control, using my body for his own pleasure while I tried to chase down my own. But his thrusts were too powerful and my clit wasn't getting the attention it needed as he reared over me, taking and taking and taking.

I reached for the suit jacket as I felt him somehow hardening even more inside me, on the brink of finishing already. But then he slowed his pace and he grabbed a cushion from the couch, lifting my hips and shoving it underneath them to change the angle his cock drove into me.

My fingers clawed against the leather instead of reaching the jacket as his huge cock filled me at a different angle, hitting my g-spot over and over, making me cry out as my clit ground against the pillow too. And yep, it turned out Danny Butcher was a seriously good fuck.

I pushed my hips back, meeting every one of his earth-shattering thrusts as I started building towards an inevitable tsunami of pleasure and all thoughts of the knife were forgotten.

When his hands moved to grip my hips, I turned my head to look at him, finding his cravat loose at his throat, his dark hair in his eyes and a look of absolute carnal desire in his gaze that made a shiver tumble through my skin. He was achingly hot to look at and as he caught me watching, he smirked like a cocky asshole.

"How's your mortal enemy feel inside you, bombshell?" he asked with a menacing glint in his gaze, his hips pistoning more furiously as he worked to make me fall apart for him.

"Fucking awful," I gritted out and he laughed loudly, his hand slapping down hard on my ass through the netting bunched up around it. I cried out as his palm hit the brand and pain ricocheted across my flesh, but as he kept up the furious rhythm of his thrusts, I found myself coming, the pain consumed by pleasure as my pussy tightened around him.

"Fuck yes," he panted as he drove his cock in deep and came with a masculine groan that sent a shiver through my whole body. He spilled himself inside me and I felt the heat of his cum filling me up with a curse as I realised we hadn't used protection. *Fuck.*

He pumped his hips a few more times then drew himself out of me with a heavy sigh of relief and his zipper sounded as the weight of his palm on my back lifted.

I remained there as I caught my breath, my gaze on the jacket ahead of me which I hadn't even tried to get a hold of. I was the worst fucking assassin ever. But that needed to end now. I had to make my move. And fast.

I leaned forward and caught hold of it, but my lungs froze as Danny said, "What the fuck?"

I looked back at him, ready to snatch the knife and drive it into his throat as fast as I possibly could. But his gaze wasn't on the jacket, it was on my ass. He caught hold of the dress, shoving it up further to fully expose the reddened brand there of his name.

"Who did this?" he growled, his voice taking on a deadly tone and his brows pulling sharply together.

"Very funny," I spat, my hatred for him spinning a furious web in my chest.

I slid my hand fast into the jacket pocket, my fingers wrapping around the switch blade as my heart beat to a rampant tune. Enough of this. He might have been a good fuck, but that was the only thing good about him. And I was done being distracted by his dick.

I shoved myself upright, keeping the knife hidden in my palm as my dress fell down to conceal the brand.

His eyes widened as he stared at me and I crept closer, a viper about to strike.

"Oh…I did it," he said darkly and I sneered.

"Yeah, you did. After you shoved my head in the toilet and locked this fucking collar around my throat." I tugged at the horrid thing, my hatred rising faster, keener. Was he on drugs or something? Probably. He certainly wouldn't be the first gangster I'd known to be hooked on his own product. It would explain a fucking lot.

I blew out a breath. How could I have been so dumb as to let him fuck me to the point of distraction? He was my enemy. A fucking psycho. And as it was only me, him and Church in this big old warehouse, it seemed like the perfect time for him to die. I'd figure out the details after.

"Well, where's the key?" he asked, his dark gaze on the collar now, anger in his expression which only made it clearer to me that he was using.

"I don't fucking know, Danny," I snapped and he sighed, turning to look vaguely around the room. And that was it. My moment, burningly bright, his throat exposed, his guard down. But as I twisted the knife around in my hand, ready to spill his blood, a knock came at the door.

"Everything okay, boss?" Frank called, apparently having found us and Danny looked back at me, my moment dying just like that.

"Fine," he called to Frank. "Nice pussy, wife." He winked at me, striding to the door and a snarl peeled my lips back as he left just like that and the door swung shut behind him.

I stood there with my hand trembling around the knife and a sense of utter failure descending on me.

When you added up all the actions I'd just taken, I looked like the biggest fool in the history of fools. I could still feel his heated cum between my thighs and shame sent a hot flash across my cheeks as I stared at the door and wished for a song I had no way to listen to.

I was a cock blinded wife who'd let her monstrous husband fuck the senses clean out of her. And I could never, ever let it happen again.

CHAPTER EIGHT

A frustrated scream cut the air from behind the door to Danny's bedroom and he paused, looking back at it as the sound of his new wife smashing something followed.

"She's got a Russian temper alright," he joked, running his tongue over his bottom lip and my gaze fell to his unbuckled belt for a moment before Anya's angry snarling drew my attention to the door again.

"Is she still pissed about the wedding?" I asked, wondering if he'd gotten a better read on the girl than I had while his cock was buried between her thighs.

"I guess she isn't a fan of English hospitality," Danny replied dryly, his gaze moving back to me as he buckled his belt and pushed a hand through his dishevelled hair. "But she wasn't complaining all that much during the consummation, so I think we'll figure this marriage thing out well enough."

I grunted a noise of agreement, my mind trailing back over the sounds I'd been listening to through the door when I'd first gotten back here. I'd decided it was best not to announce myself while they were clearly in the middle of fucking, so I'd stood out here listening to the sounds of her coming all over his cock instead. I wasn't entirely sure if that was what he'd meant when he'd told me to guard her at all times, but as he clearly wasn't telling me to fuck off, I had to assume he wanted me here now.

"Are you going somewhere?" I asked, my gaze flicking to his face for a moment before I looked off to the side. Looking at him always made me think of his fucking twin for obvious reasons, but tonight the resemblance seemed even more potent, and the thought of that motherfucker had bile rising in my throat and tension lining my muscles.

"Well I should probably show my face at the reception - Ma will be doing her nut," Danny replied, fiddling with his cravat which was tugged loose and half hanging from his neck. He gave up after a few seconds and just yanked the thing off, tossing it aside with a sigh.

"Without the bride?" I asked curiously.

Danny smirked at me. "I think she's too worn out to attend actually. Besides, I'm pretty certain she doesn't wanna come." I said nothing but he seemed to read into that, so he thumped on the door at his back and called out to her. "Hey, bombshell? When you finish wiping my cum from between those silky thighs of yours, do you fancy heading back to the wedding reception to meet the rest of my family?"

"Get fucked!" Anya yelled back and I had to suppress the twitch of my lips that would have betrayed my amusement over that. I might have hated Benny Butcher with a vehemence to rival all things, but I didn't much care for Danny either – the man was a fucking unpredictable psychopath with no goddamn limits. He was the boss though, and I knew my place.

"I already did, thanks," Danny called back. "It was a fairly good first round, but I'll be expecting more from you on the next turn."

Something smashed inside the room again and Danny laughed.

"I'm gonna enjoy letting her take that anger out on me later," he said, taking a step away from me but then he fell still and looked my way again. "I didn't happen to give you a key by any chance, did I?"

"What key?" I asked curiously.

"The one to her collar," he said, his expression ironing out and a glimmer of some darkness showing in his brown eyes.

"No boss. You just gave me my orders. No keys," I replied with a shrug.

"Right...and those orders were to..."

I frowned at him, wondering why he was questioning me like this. He knew I was perfectly capable of doing this job without fucking it up and it wasn't his usual style to micromanage me. More likely he'd give out vague commands then start cutting off heads if they weren't followed to perfection.

"You told me I own her arse when you're not riding it," I said slowly, looking for the catch here. "You wanted me with her at all times."

"Right," he replied, raising his chin and arching a brow at me. "And am I currently riding her arse?"

"No, boss," I said, seeing where he was going with this.

"So maybe you should do your job then, yeah?"

I nodded in agreement and he strode away quickly, his fancy shoes thumping along the wooden mezzanine as he headed towards the iron staircase which led back into the main body of the warehouse. Danny had told me I'd have to stay here once the Russian girl arrived, and I guessed that meant babysitting was officially my full-time occupation.

Church laughed obnoxiously at something Danny said downstairs then the sound of the door banging closed signalled the two of them leaving.

I sighed as I looked back to the door where Anya had gone suspiciously quiet then pushed it open and stepped into the dark space.

A frown pinched my brow as I found the room empty but as I opened my mouth to call out for her, a feral snarl sounded from my left and the flash of a blade caught my eye as she swung it for me.

I ducked aside with the assistance of instincts built from surviving years on the dark streets of this city and wrapped an arm around her waist as she collided with me, her stiletto connecting with the side of my knee.

A grunt of pain escaped me as my leg buckled from the impact and I hurled her towards the bed, her small physique making her light enough to toss clean across the room.

An explosion of white taffeta and silk erupted around her from the huge wedding dress she still wore and I dove on top of her as she struggled to free herself from it.

Anya screamed something at me as my weight crushed her down onto the bed and I fought to grab her arms between the folds of white fabric. I found one of them, but her forehead swung towards my nose before I could grab the other, making me jerk back and the knife slammed into my shoulder a second later.

"Jesus," I snapped in pain, twisting away from her so that she lost her grip on the knife, managing to catch her other hand so that I could slam it down to the bed above her head with the first.

I drove her down beneath me, the two of us panting and making the layers of her wedding dress flutter in the space dividing us as we glared at one another.

"What now then?" she hissed, her onyx eyes glittering with fury as she practically begged me to do my damn worst.

I licked my lips, transferring both of her wrists into one of my hands and gritting my teeth as I reached up to yank the knife from my fucking shoulder.

Blood splattered her white dress and splashed against her cheek, making her flinch, but the wound wasn't too deep, it just stung like a bitch.

"Were you aiming for my throat?" I growled, knowing I'd only avoided that because I'd been rearing away from her when she'd tried to break my fucking nose with her forehead.

"No, I was just trying to butter some bread and my knife slipped," she deadpanned.

I stared at her for a long moment before a laugh spilled from my lips and I leaned back, releasing my grip on her wrists as I knelt over her hips. She shoved the skirt of the dress aside so that she could glare up at me better and my gaze fell to her bare tits as she exposed them, the front of her dress torn open and her nipples like diamond points on the fullness of her flesh. Fuck, those were nice tits.

"Like what you see?" she snarled, fire flaring in those dark eyes which made me think of her brother and her family name.

Any hint of desire I might have been feeling banished as the sound of my own agony echoed in my ears and I was momentarily forced back into that place, reminded of what she was and who she was no matter how hot she might have looked pinned beneath me. She was a Volkov and there was nothing running in her veins but poison.

"Problem with your outfit?" I tossed back, moving to stand and letting her push herself upright.

I was surprised when she made no attempt to cover herself, simply raising her chin and glaring at me despite her tits being out and the fact that we'd just had a fight in which she would have killed me given half a chance.

"So what now?" she demanded.

"You tell me, my job is to watch you, not entertain you."

Her eyes narrowed suspiciously. "Where's my shit then?"

"To my knowledge you have no shit," I replied with a shrug, turning the flick knife she'd used against me over in my hand before dropping it into my pocket. "Aside from the dress you're currently wearing."

"I have my iPod and my music," she growled, pointing at my jacket where the bulge of those items showed through the material. "And you'll have to find me something else to wear."

"Will I now? And what if I'm perfectly happy to leave you like that with your tits out and that fancy skirt hanging offa your arse?" I tilted my head at her, wondering what she was going to try and do about these little demands of hers now that she didn't have a knife to back them up with.

Anya pouted then turned her back on me, storming across the room to the wardrobe standing against the wall and tugging it open. She rummaged around and pulled out a black t-shirt, tossing it down on the bed before reaching around behind her and trying to unhook the complicated fastenings which were still holding the heavy fabric of the wedding dress up.

I folded my arms as I watched her, the damp heat trickling along my shoulder letting me know that I was still bleeding, but I wasn't any kind of stranger to pain, and it was hardly a life-threatening wound.

She cursed and snarled, huffing and even stomping her foot dramatically as she tried and failed to unhook the buttons before finally whirling on me with a furious expression which I looked away from in favour of checking out her tits again. She might have been born of the Devil, but he sure had known what he was doing when he designed her.

"Are you just going to stand there?" she demanded.

"I was planning on it," I agreed.

"Well how about some help getting this fucking thing off of me?"

I considered that for a moment then stalked forward, taking the bloody blade from my pocket and flicking it open.

Anya sucked in a breath as I closed in on her, her gaze zeroing in on the weapon I held and she backed up a step before I caught hold of her wrist and spun her around.

She stumbled forward and grasped the wardrobe door to steady herself, looking up at me in the mirror which lined the inside of it. I took hold of the back of the dress and quickly sliced the blade into the white fabric, cutting it off of her and staining it red with my blood as I did so, ignoring the countless tiny buttons in favour of a more effective method.

The dress fell to the floor at her feet and I was gifted a view of her standing before me in nothing but a pair of white stilettos with tan stockings held in place by a white lace suspender belt. I had to guess Danny had done away with her underwear to gain access to her cunt and as my mind considered that, I spotted the unmistakable trail of cum running down the inside of her thigh. She smelled of sex and passionfruit, her perfectly styled hair all fucked up from her new husband fisting it, and I couldn't help but linger on that mental image as she stared back at me in the mirror.

I remained there for a moment, looking at her when I should have been stepping away again and she straightened suddenly, her glare darkening.

"Getting a good look at the prize pig?" she hissed as she tugged at the diamond studded collar around her neck and turned to face me. I caught a look at the angry brand on her right arse cheek in the mirror for a moment, gritting my jaw in anger over it before shoving the emotion aside. "Because I'm telling you now, if you lay a hand on me I'll rip your fucking dick o-"

"You should have a shower," I interrupted her, leaning in so close I could have tasted her lips if I licked my own. "Maybe try and wash some of those dirty thoughts out of your pretty little head while you're at it. I'm not here to fuck you, Cash. I'm here to watch you. And I think it's a little conceited of you to believe every man who sees you naked automatically wants to sink his cock into you."

Embarrassment flickered through her eyes, but she stamped it down and glared back defiantly.

"I'm not conceited, Frank," she hissed, saying my name with as much disdain as she could muster. "I'm just not blind and I don't need you to *tell* me you want to fuck me when your cock is shouting it loud enough for the whole world to hear." She reached out and gripped my swollen dick through the fabric of my trousers, squeezing hard to try and get a rise from me.

I wasn't sure what she expected to get from that move, but I doubted it was what I did.

I dropped my hand between her thighs and pushed the tip of the switchblade into the cum running down the inside of her leg, slowly moving it higher and causing her to gasp as I closed in on her pussy.

"Go clean up, Cash, and stop trying to get something from me which I'm never going to give you. You think you can manipulate me with sex? Go ahead and try, but I've got my orders and I have no intention of risking my neck for a taste of your greedy pussy."

I tugged my hand away before the blade could touch her cunt, knocking her hand from my dick in the same movement and I stepped back so fast that she blinked at me in surprise.

"Bathroom is this way." I turned and walked out of the room, not bothering to check if she was following me as I headed back down the mezzanine to the furthest door and I pushed it open for her. There was an en suite in Danny's room, but I knew he was precious about his space. He'd had me kick women out of his room before they could enter that sacred room, so I wasn't gonna bother risking his wrath tonight by letting her touch his precious shower gel or whatever the fuck it was he coveted in there. The arsehole had gutted men for less.

In the bathroom, there was an old copper claw foot bathtub below a long run of windows which stretched across the far wall by the ceiling. The end walls in here were exposed red brick like the rest of the warehouse coupled with the black wood of the stud work that had been erected to divide the space into rooms. There was a waterfall shower in the far corner and white tiles lining the floor. I grabbed a dark grey towel from the pile beside the sink and held it out for her as she followed me inside with the black t-shirt now covering her body.

"How old is this building?" she murmured, looking at the original features with wide eyes that made me think she actually appreciated the history.

"It was built in the early eighteen hundreds, used for tobacco mostly," I supplied. "The Butchers snapped it up when it fell into disrepair and had it all converted. Now it serves as the centre of their kingdom as well as a storage facility for other products."

"Such as..."

"Same kinds of things the Russians deal in, I'd imagine. We've got our fingers in so many pies that you can't even tell what flavour you're tasting when you lick 'em," I replied, giving her a flat look which let her know I wasn't going to be handing out any little secrets about The Firm for her to report home on. It was up to Danny to tell her about that shit if he wanted to and so far as I knew, he didn't plan on giving her a crash course.

She rolled her eyes, moving away from me and I expected her to head for the shower, but instead she moved to the copper bathtub and reached out to set the water running.

A drip of blood ran down my forearm and I huffed out a frustrated breath as I looked at the still bleeding wound on my shoulder which was steadily soaking through the white shirt I'd worn to the wedding.

I crossed the room and opened the unit which sat above the Victorian style sinks, grabbing the first aid kit from the shelf inside and closing the unit again so that I could use the mirror to see what I was doing.

I shrugged out of my suit jacket then yanked my tie loose and unhooked the buttons of my shirt, yanking the shoulder down while keeping the thing on so that she didn't get a look at my back as I inspected the wound which was doing a good job of painting my dark skin red.

"So I guess you're going to tell your boss about me almost killing you?" Anya asked, raising her voice over the sound of running water.

"It's sweet that you think you almost killed me with this little scratch,"

I replied dismissively.

"That little scratch would have been a whole lot more serious if it had hit your neck," she replied.

"Well if I let myself be concerned over all the occasions when someone had *almost* given me a fatal injury then I'd spend a lot of my time worrying about shit that never came to anything."

I ran some cold water into the sink and splashed it over the wound to wash the blood away, ignoring the sting as I did so.

"And is Danny similarly unconcerned over his men nearly dying, or..."

"Or?" I glanced over at her and caught her chewing the side of her lip, but she stopped it the moment my gaze found hers.

"Don't go thinking I'm afraid of violent men," Anya growled, seeming to see something in my gaze that got her back up. "I've lived my whole life surrounded by them, living at the mercy of their whims."

"No doubt," I agreed, wondering what exactly it was like for a Russian mob boss's daughter to grow up surrounded by the kinds of bullshit I found myself drowning in daily. But if she was anything like the monsters who had raised her then I was willing to bet she wasn't just unafraid of violence, but thrived in it as well, thirsted for it even.

"I'd just like a heads up, that's all. If he's going to be pissed at me for stealing that knife and attacking you then I want to be ready for him." She started pulling pins from her blonde hair, releasing the last of it from the style it had been put in for the wedding.

"So that you can try to kill him too? Or was that who your blade was really intended for?" I asked, turning back to the mirror as I pressed a towel to my shoulder to dry it before slapping a self-adhesive dressing down on top of it. It probably could have done with stitches, but what was one more scar to me at this point?

"He collared me like a dog," she hissed so low that I could hardly hear her over the running water.

"Shame you forgot about that when he was driving his cock into you then, isn't it?" I mocked.

I tugged the bloody arm of my shirt back up over my shoulder and moved across the room, closing the toilet seat before making myself comfortable on top of it.

Anya looked about ready to try and murder me again, but she could hardly deny the cries of pure pleasure I'd heard spilling from her pretty lips while she fucked him, so we both knew the truth of that. I didn't really want this argument to drag on, so I folded my arms over my bare chest and leaned back against the cold toilet as I fixed her with a stare.

"I ain't gonna tell him shit about you stabbing me, alright? I've got a job to do and it isn't to fuck you over at every given opportunity. I'm not looking to get you in a fiddle over some nothin' flesh wound."

Anya seemed suspicious of that statement, but she'd figure out fast enough that I meant it. I had no desire to give Danny more reasons to inflict his twisted attention on her no matter what I thought of her or the people she called kin.

"What are you here for then?" She shut off the water as it reached the brim of the tub and the bubbles threatened to overflow.

"To watch you," I replied. "And protect you. That's it."

"To watch me? As in, you're staying in here while I have a bath?" She didn't look all that pleased about that, but it really wasn't my problem.

"Boss's orders, you heard him. When he's not riding your arse, I own it. So get used to it, Cash."

"Are you going to explain that little nickname at any point?" she muttered irritably and a smile touched my lips for the briefest of moments.

"You were listening to Johnny Cash when I first laid eyes on you. Hurt specifically. Can't say I've ever thought a song matched a person's soul quite so well as that one seemed to fit you in that moment. I guess you could say it left an impression."

Her brow dipped like she wasn't sure if she liked that assessment or not but there was something there in her eternally dark eyes, some glimmer of truth which she couldn't deny. Because as beautiful as that song was, it was lonely and vengeful and powerful too. That was what I saw in her when I looked and it sure as fuck wasn't a bad thing.

"So…you're staying?" she surmised, seeming not to want to discuss my name for her any further.

"I am," I agreed, no room for compromise.

Anya looked inclined to argue but then that fire in her eyes went out like someone had blown it clean out of existence and she just shrugged like she didn't give a fuck before tugging the shirt off and exposing her body to me again. What was that? Where had she gone off to? 'Cause it sure as fuck seemed like she'd just checked the hell out of here.

I kept my face impassive while I drank in the sight of her bare skin, ignoring the way all of the blood in my body instantly started heading south without my permission as she unhooked her stockings from the suspender belt and rolled them off of her tanned legs.

She was…well, fuck me, if she'd been any other woman, anyone aside from Danny's wife and a fucking Volkov, I doubted my resolve would have held. The sight of her bending over like that, her hands sliding down her legs as she peeled the stockings off, it was more than a little temptation. It was enough to fill me with an animal kind of need, the type that demanded I bend her to my will and spend hours proving to her how good it would feel to be owned by me. But I didn't move, not one inch.

When she was fully naked, she stepped into the bath and sank into the bubbles with a soft hiss of pain which I guessed was in reaction to the brand meeting with the hot water and closed her eyes.

"I'm just going to pretend you don't exist then."

"Fine by me," I agreed, still watching her, my eyes on the bubbly water that hid most of her body, my dick throbbing every time she shifted and I caught a glimpse of her pink nipples between them. If she'd been any other woman I'd have been buried deep inside her right now, making her scream for me until she lost her voice before jerking out of her and coming all over those tits, marking them as mine.

As it was, I knew my job. And that was to watch her, not touch. So that's what I'd do.

"You wanna give me an overview of how The Firm works then?" she asked after several minutes of silence where I indulged in fantasies of her flesh which I knew I'd never act on. Looked like she wasn't going to ignore me after all then.

"Not particularly," I hedged.

"Because your boss hasn't specified what I'm allowed to know?" she guessed a little too accurately and I shrugged, knowing that was a confirmation of its own.

"If you won't tell me anything about The Firm, then tell me something about you," she said, changing lanes.

"There's not a lot to tell," I replied in that same flat tone.

"How about the tattoo? Tell me what it means?" She still hadn't opened her eyes, but I was guessing she must have gotten a good look at my chest piece before she got into the tub.

"It's Latin."

"Wow, how riveting."

I swiped a hand down my face, wondering how much more of this infuriating girl I could take.

"Vivamus, moriendum est," I quoted for her, not needing to look down at the swirling script which ran across my chest surrounded by the feathers of large angel wings to know it by heart.

"My latin is a little rusty, big fella."

"It basically means, 'let us live, since we must die.'"

She was silent for several long minutes and I thought she might have dropped it, but of course she hadn't.

"Who did you lose?" she asked softly and the pain of my grief twisted inside my heart as my mind was flooded with all I'd lost. I felt the darkness in me rising at those memories, but I kept it quiet inside my soul like I did so often out of pure force of will.

I almost didn't answer her, almost told her to mind her own business. But then I found myself just telling her instead, because it wasn't like it would be hard for her to find out this story and I would rather it came from me.

"My brother. He was killed because of a man we both loved. A man who I thought of as a brother too once." There was a whole lot more to that story, but she didn't need those details, at least not now.

"I'm sorry," she breathed, her obsidian eyes opening at my words and seeming to swallow me whole as I fell into their depths. Eyes like that shouldn't have been possible, they were too big, too deep, and they were as dark as every sin I'd ever committed.

"That kind of loss and betrayal does things to a man," I went on, my fist tightening as I thought of Benny Butcher and all the ways I'd make him suffer through when he finally got out of that prison. "Things I can't undo. So don't go thinking of me as a friend or a saviour in this little arrangement, Cash. I'm nothing more than eyes on your flesh and a body between you and danger when your husband isn't here to keep you occupied himself."

"And what if my husband *is* the danger?" she asked, her gaze roaming my features for something she wasn't going to find.

"Then I suggest you figure out how to handle him. Danny Butcher is a god to the rest of us. We serve at his desire and that's all there is to it," I replied.

Shutters slammed down between us in her dark eyes and I felt myself drawing back too. Pulling away from the temptation of her and reminding myself of the only thing I kept drawing breath for in this monotonous fucking life. One day Benny Butcher would finish serving his sentence for killing my kin and when he was done rotting away inside for it, I'd be waiting for him, ready to offer up a ticket straight into hell by my own hands in the most agonising, lingering way I could imagine.

"I want my music back," Anya said sharply.

"Why?" I questioned.

"I need it," she growled and for a moment I could see that pain in her too. The agony which lived in me at the detriment of all else. She knew the taste of it well.

I stood and picked my jacket up from where I'd left it on the floor and took her iPod and headphones from the pocket. Anya watched me as I strode towards her, her grip on the edge of the tub tightening like she thought I might shove her beneath the water.

But I had no desire to hurt her. Despite all the reasons I had to offer some pain up to her family, I wasn't going to lay my hands on her in some twisted kind of vengeance.

I leaned down and placed the headphones over her ears, my scarred knuckles brushing against the softness of her skin for the briefest of moments as she looked up at me with barely parted lips which were still stained deepest red.

I backed up, taking her iPod with me and opening up her playlists before selecting a song for her myself. Otherside by Red Hot Chilli Peppers.

Her eyes widened as the music found her and I watched as the tension in her posture noticeably loosened and she slowly relaxed back into her bath.

After a few moments she let her eyes fall closed once more and I studied her as she continued to listen to her music, lost in a world of her own. A world I stole a piece of by selecting song after song for her, my gaze staying fixed on her expression as I read every twitch of her lips or pinch of her brow and figured out exactly how each song spoke to her without being able to hear a beat of it myself.

I hadn't met many people in this life we led who felt that same kind of connection to music as I did, but the longer I watched her while the music took her soul captive, the more apparent it became that she and I had that in common. Lyrics and rhythms and the steady beat of a drum were a language which everyone spoke, but only a few breathed. And in that moment we were sharing oxygen, letting the songs consume us while all I did was watch her as she listened to it, my own music playing in my head as the songs came to life through those small reactions on her face which spoke so clearly to me.

In that silence, I saw her, and I found myself enraptured as I stole the freedom to look.

CHAPTER NINE

The worst part of having a shadow appointed to me by my new husband was the way his eyes felt like lasers on my skin. Blocking him out was much harder than blocking out most people, and as I lay in the huge bed meant for the self-appointed ruler of my new world and Frank sat quietly in a chair in the corner, sleep wasn't my friend.

It rose up slowly, drowning me in the dark only to spit me back out again on an endless loop during the night. I swear every time I stirred, every time my body shifted against the mattress and my fingers reached for some non-existent safety within the sheets, Frank stirred too.

It was like his boss's order had bound him to me in some deeply tangible way and his body now had invisible threads connected to mine. Whenever I peeked out at him, hunting the shadows and finding the large silhouette of him in the armchair across the room, I swear he looked back.

My headphones were still firmly on my ears, playing all my favourite tunes as I slid in and out of consciousness. It was like a fever dream, shivers tap-dancing down my spine and my skin erupting in goosebumps only to wake again and find myself burningly hot and aching. But the ache wasn't in my bones, it was between my thighs, because every dream I fell into contained my ever-observant guardian, the one who'd watched me bathe, who'd picked out song after song for me to listen to while I fell into my own private world. A world I had never once shared, and yet it felt like I had with this stranger now.

Why had I done that? I had no answer. So I was putting it down to the fact that I was alone in a foreign country, my world spinning violently as everything familiar melted before my eyes, leaving me trying to hold onto anything solid I could find. Maybe I'd been looking for a companion in him just for a second, and maybe I could wield that as an advantage.

If Frank was going to be hounding me every time Danny wasn't around, then we'd have plenty of opportunity to talk, and if anyone knew Danny's weaknesses then it was surely one of his right hand men.

Sometime around dawn, I pushed my headphones off my ears and realised the raucous laughter that had been carrying from downstairs every now and then had finally fallen silent. Danny had probably been drinking away the night with his cronies and I was all for him passing out on the couch and leaving me the fuck alone.

But just as I was about to pull my headphones back on, the door opened and I stiffened as light spilled over the bed, clamping my eyes shut as I feigned sleep. My breaths came quicker as I heard him move deeper into the room.

"You can fuck off now, Frankie boy," Danny growled and I heard Frank stand from his chair, making my heart pound faster.

My fingers slid onto the collar around my neck and the brand on my ass tingled with the memory of what Danny Butcher had done to me. He might have been a good fuck, but that didn't change anything about the venomous hatred I felt toward him. And as I'd had his guard dog's eyes on me since he'd left me here, I hadn't had a chance to get hold of another weapon.

"Why are you still standing there?" Danny growled and I cracked an eye, finding Frank's huge frame silhouetted in the doorway. I swear for a second, he glanced my way, but then he bowed his head like an obedient little mutt and walked away. So much for thinking I might have been able to claim an ally in him.

Danny shoved the door shut and the distinct click of a lock made my spine prickle. My muscles tensed and my whole body wound up like a coiled spring. If he touched me, I'd fight. I'd fucking bite and kick and tear at his skin until I ripped open an artery and bled him out.

"Oh I do like to be beside the seaside, oh I do like to be beside the sea," Danny sang as my hands curled into fists and I waited for him to strike, but instead he walked into the bathroom and the sound of him showering carried to me. "Oh, I do like to stroll along the prom, prom, prom where the brass bands play tiddley-om-pom-pom."

I peeked out momentarily as I looked towards the door which he'd left wide open, steam billowing out of it as he showered and I was gifted a mental image of him in there, water running down his muscular frame…

After a while, the water shut off and I clamped my eyes shut a beat before he walked into the bedroom.

Silence rang dully around my head as I put on the best sleeping show of my life, my features perfectly calm, my breaths rising and falling in a steady lull. The light from the bathroom burned against my eyelids, but it was his gaze that burned deeper. I could feel him observing me, and I had to wonder what he was thinking.

What did the big, bad British mob boss think of his unwilling Russian bride? Was I a thorn twisting in his side? An irritation easy enough to ignore? Or one he'd stage an accident for eventually? Maybe Danny was planning my death in this very second, figuring out how he could do it without breaking the treaty. Or maybe he was just going to use my body time and again in any way he liked. Maybe now he'd fucked me, he was thinking of other ways he could derive pleasure from my flesh. Like watching it split and bleed.

The light in the bathroom went out then footsteps carried towards me, slow and measured, every one of them making it harder to feign sleep. This place was so cavernous, every thump of his bare feet sounded like a gunshot ringing through the room, echoing up to the high ceiling and bouncing back down again.

He was in front of me, I was certain. A monster of a man leering over me, deciding my fate. But if he wanted to watch me hurt again, I was going to fight like a demon from the inner rings of hell and draw some blood of my own.

"I know you're awake, bombshell," he said, his voice gruff and so close that it made every atom in my body crackle with electricity.

I remained still, silent, forcing my breaths to rise and fall evenly. He didn't know shit; he was probably blind drunk from the party and I was going to pretend I was a heavy ass sleeper despite the fact that I slept lighter than a feather on the breeze.

Danny leaned down and his breath fanned over my ear, hot and scented with peppermint toothpaste. He smelled like scotch and leather too, the intoxicating aroma of him laced with absolute danger.

"When monsters come to the edge of your bed, it's a good idea to look 'em in the eye. That way, they're less likely to eat you up."

Those words triggered a memory of my father coming to me in the night, gripping my arm in a bruising hold while his sweaty palm slapped down over my mouth. He'd drag me out of earshot of my brothers and use his belt or fists on me. The only chance I'd ever had of him leaving me to sleep was if I managed not to release a single murmur of fear, if I kept my eyes closed and pretended he wasn't there. But I wasn't a child cowering in her bed anymore, I was a woman sired by violence, a beast in my own right.

"Not in my experience," I whispered to Danny, poison coating my words.

"Well you've never had a monster like me before." He took hold of the comforter, sliding it off of me in a slow movement, drawing it down all the way to my bare legs so the cold air found me, making me shiver. But still, I didn't open my eyes, instead I reached for my headphones and pulled them on, but they were only there for a second before Danny knocked them off my head. In the next moment, he climbed over me and moved under the covers behind me, spooning me and drawing me tight back against his hard body, his mouth going to my ear as I stiffened in his hold. He'd had the grace to put some boxers on, but the thin material did nothing to stop the hard ridge of his cock grinding against my ass. I growled out a curse as his body grazed against the brand of his name where it was burned into my skin and he shifted back a little like he actually gave a fuck. *Unlikely*.

"I wanna talk," he said in a gruff tone as he pulled the comforter over us again, the taste of whiskey on the air from his breath. "And maybe I wanna fuck my wife again."

"Get your hands off of me or I'll snap your fingers one by one," I warned, but he didn't let go, only tightening his grip on me while pulling up the covers and locking his bare leg over both of mine. I was in the cage of his body, his heat like a balm against the biting cold of this room, but it didn't do anything to ease the chill inside my chest.

"I'm gonna make you come so hard you divorce Russia *and* America then pledge your allegiance to all things British," he said, chuckling darkly.

"I'm gonna knee you in the balls so hard, they divorce your cock," I hissed, ignoring the heat which rushed through my body at his words.

He laughed and his hands roamed all over my body, but didn't stray to my tits or pussy, he just felt me, dragging his hands everywhere like I was the first woman he'd ever touched. His rough fingers carved up my side, along the curve of my neck, twisted into my hair, every touch like a worshipping kind of caress which made my flesh prickle and goosebumps spread all over me.

It had my breathing hitching, but every time I tried to wriggle free and get some distance between us, he just pulled me back against his chest with impossible strength.

It should have felt like a cage, and I should have wanted to break free of it, but it wasn't like that somehow. He held me like I was…important to him. And though I could feel the hard press of his cock driving against me and his words had clearly suggested he wanted more than this from me, he was still just touching me in this impossibly ardent way, like he wanted to commit every piece of me to memory for reasons I couldn't even begin to fathom.

Whenever his fingers trailed close to the burn of the brand on my ass, he shifted them carefully away again, almost as if he was making a conscious effort not to aggravate the tender skin, though the idea of that made no sense to me at all.

His hand brushed down my arm, his tattooed fingers running over the back of mine and pushing between them, linking with my own as he pushed them down into the sheets before my face, giving me time to study the old fashioned pocket watch he had inked there. The chain of it tumbled over his fingers, making it look like it was threaded between mine, tying us together, and I licked my lips as I considered the reality of that image. We were bound now. Willingly or not, I was his wife.

Danny shifted at my back, breathing in so deeply it was like he was trying to inhale me and as he ran his hand back up my arm once more, tingles scattered all over my skin, some defiant, wildly idiotic part of me almost wanting him to take more than this. But there was no fucking chance of that happening again.

He ran his fingers down to my knee, his big hand hooking around my leg and making it bend more as he rolled me a little further onto my side, inching the burn on my ass further away from him with the movement as his back stayed flush with mine.

"God, this feels so much better than hugging a pillow," he murmured, his stubble grazing the sensitive skin of my neck and making my nipples harden with the rough grit of his voice. "I don't have to come in a pillowcase tonight."

What the fuck? Maybe he was on drugs again.

"C'mere you beautiful…fucking…pillow wife." His face pressed against my neck as his hand ran back up the side of my body, once again skirting the burn before it fell to brush against my tit.

I readied to attack, refusing to be some dick hole for him to satisfy his drunk ass with, but then he released a soft snore and I realised he'd passed the fuck out.

I relaxed, exhaling a long breath and trying to slip free of his arms, planning to search the room for a weapon. But dammit even in sleep his grip hadn't gone slack, his body like an iron cage as I fought to get free, finding myself somehow locked against him even tighter, his solid cock making itself very much known.

I eventually gave up trying to escape him, deciding to take advantage of his drunken state and not wanting to wake him up in case I found myself the victim of his anger or he tried to push for a sloppy fuck. I reached for my headphones instead, sliding them on and immediately slipping into a world of calm between the lyrics of Free Bird by Lynyrd Skynyrd.

Nothing could touch me here. I was gone, a million miles away in a land where only the rhythm existed and I could almost forget that I lay in the arms of my enemy and my life was no longer my own.

I woke to someone ripping my headphones off and a sharp flick to the ear.

"Up. If you wanna eat, you'd better get your arse downstairs before the boys polish off the grub."

I sat upright, finding Danny standing there in a long sleeved white t-shirt and a pair of black jeans which hung low enough on his hips to give me a glimpse of the sharp V diving beneath his waistband where a slice of tattooed skin was on show. My gaze caught on a little cluster of blue flowers amongst the thorny roses and I frowned curiously at the forget-me-nots before lifting my gaze to my headphones which were dangling on his outstretched finger. He was smirking too. His head tilted to one side as he regarded me.

I snatched my headphones even though he clearly wasn't trying to keep them from me, but the fact that he'd taken them set my blood sizzling. I eyed his irritatingly good looking face, hunting for the signs of a hangover and hoping he felt like a half-baked turd right now. But he looked as fresh faced as if he'd slept for ten hours and been on week-long fucking yoga retreat, the dark stubble lining his jaw a little thicker than before but only accentuating the line of his strong cheekbones and the depth of his brown eyes.

"You look like shit, I guess even the king of London isn't immune to drinking himself half blind," I tossed at him anyway, picking up my iPod and getting out of bed, bumping straight into him when he didn't get out of my way. *Um, ow? That was like walking into a fucking wall.*

He arched a brow in vague amusement as I tilted my chin up to look him in the eye.

"I was out on business all night, so I'm as fresh as a daisy, bombshell. Especially since I woke up and had a real nice morning wank into the back of that t-shirt you're wearing."

I gasped in horror, gripping the shirt and twisting it around to try and see the back of it, but Danny barked an obnoxious laugh, clearly having been joking and my blood boiled.

I dropped the hem of the shirt, shoulder checking him as I marched out of the room, heading along to the bathroom and throwing the door shut behind me.

"Hurry up, bombshell. The food won't last long," Danny called to me beyond the door, apparently having followed me.

"I guess you'll be skipping breakfast then, right husband?"

"Why's that?" he indulged me.

"Because you're already full of shit."

I drowned out his reply as I switched my music on full blast and stripped out of my clothes. I didn't bother to hurry up. I was hungry, but I'd rather my belly stayed empty than do anything my beloved husband asked of me. Even if that was petty.

The water stung as it trailed over the brand and I forced myself to inspect the angry skin in the mirror, relieved to see that it didn't seem to be getting infected at least, but I could already tell that it was gonna take nothing short of a skin graft to remove that fucking name from my skin.

By the time I was done, I headed back to the bedroom wrapped in a towel, shivering in the cold air and finding a cream dress left out for me which looked like something a rich housewife would wear for brunch with her girlfriends.

"Er, that'd be a fuck no," I muttered, walking over to the black set of drawers which housed Danny's clothes, taking out a pair of blue jeans and pulling them on. I winced a little at the scrape of the rough material on my burn but I definitely wasn't going to be wearing any of Danny's boxers, so I'd just have to grin and bear it.

They were way too big, but with a bit of work, I managed to roll up the ankles and cinch a belt around my waist to keep them on. Then I pulled on a plain white t-shirt and tied a knot in it before pulling on a warm pair of socks too. It was the best I could do, and I felt more myself in this than I would have in a dress that offended my soul. The very least I could do in this place was hold onto the last pieces of me which hadn't been ripped from my grasp.

Though as I ran my fingers over the metal collar around my neck, I felt like I was weaving an illusion for myself. I didn't belong to myself anymore. I was the property of Danny Butcher. But not for long.

I slipped my headphones around my neck, tucking my iPod into my pocket before doing a sweep of the room for anything sharp that I could stick Danny in the gut with. But sadly, I came up short and had to admit defeat as I walked out of the room and moved along the metal walkway, the thick socks muffling my movements.

Light streamed in through huge glass panels in the warehouse roof above me, the sky bright today and reminding me a little of home as the sound of chatter carried from downstairs.

I set my gaze on the doors further along from me, my mind whirring with thoughts of escape.

My fingers itched for a weapon and my heart thudded harder, urging me on as I moved towards the nearest room, turning the handle and slipping into it. It was another bedroom, vast and looking unslept in. A quick root around in it turned up nothing and the trend continued as I searched the other rooms too.

When I stepped out of the last one, my heart jerked at the sight of Church standing at the edge of the walkway, leaning on the railing and watching me with a grin pulling at his mouth.

"Mornin', Miss America. Find anything sharp?" he asked curiously. He always had a look about him as if he was amused, his silvery eyes all twinkly and shit. But I supposed that made him slightly more likeable than the others.

"Nothing at all," I said lightly. "All I could find was your wit which is as blunt as a butter knife."

"Ouch." He held a hand to his chest like I'd wounded him and I rolled my eyes, heading for the stairs beside him.

He swung around, falling into step with me, his arm rubbing mine over familiarly and his blonde curls falling into his eyes in a way that almost made me want to push them aside. I made a point of side stepping to put some space between us, but he just closed it again like a dog trying to bother some affection out of me.

"The food's all gone," Church announced just as I reached the bottom step and found a room full of strangers staring at me.

The kitchen island was more like an actual island considering the size of the thing. I swear it could have housed a whole village and their livestock. But all it actually contained was a bunch of empty plates, takeaway boxes and coffee cups.

Danny was missing, but Frank's blue eyes immediately moved to mine, sending a jolt through my body like the weight of his gaze was a physical thing. He was wearing a pale grey tank top and my eyes skimmed over the way his arms bulged with muscle beneath his impossibly smooth looking dark skin, tempting me to draw closer even though the violence in his expression warned me to stay away.

I wasn't sure why he seemed to hate me so adamantly, but the connection that had been forged between us and the music we'd shared still hung in the space dividing us too, it just hummed with the potency of his dark emotions in the pale light of day.

I tore my attention from that beast of a man and let my gaze drift to the four other tattooed assholes to his right. One of them was skinnier than the others and he was smiling at me with a couple of gold teeth glinting out of his mouth – do people still have those?? – his head was shaved and a tattoo ran along one whole side of it of the numbers 2/4/84.

"Well ain't she a sight," the gold-toothed guy said overly sweetly. "I'm Sikes. C'mere, angel. Have a seat next to me." He shoved a guy off of the stool beside him, smiling encouragingly at me while the other man cursed him out.

"Yeah…no." I walked straight over to the huge fridge that dominated the space behind them and whipped it open, stilling as I found the whole thing fucking empty. Like, not even an unwanted onion rolling in the bottom drawer or a half forgotten yoghurt awaiting its divine moment in a back corner. Not a scrap.

"Food's gone," Church reiterated and I sighed, giving up my plight and looking around for what was next on my priority list.

"Where's the coffee machine?" I demanded, confused as I hunted for it.

"We drink tea in this house, darlin', so you can put the kettle on if you like." He pointed to a pot marked *Tea* and I whipped the lid off of it, finding it empty. "Ah, never mind. Guess we're all out."

The men started to laugh at me and I gave up, tossing the lid into the sink in annoyance and leaning back against the counter instead.

All of their eyes were on me and Sikes's gaze fell to my tits, his tongue slicking his lips in a way that reminded me of a slug slithering between a pair of rotten cucumbers as the rest of the cronies beside him looked too.

I glanced down, finding my nipples hard as fucking diamonds in this freezing place and I fought the urge to fold my arms over my chest, my hands balling into fists at my sides.

"That's such a clever idea," I said, jerking my chin at Sikes's tattooed head to get the attention off of my tits. "It must really help you to remember your birthday."

Church barked a laugh and Sikes grimaced, his scarred fingers raising to touch the mark.

"Are you mockin' me?"

"No," I gasped, holding a hand to my chest like I was offended he'd even think such a thing, laying on the sarcasm thick. But it didn't look like this guy was picking up on it.

"It ain't my birthday, angel," Sikes said, his tone softening again as he gave me a patient look like I was just a dumb little dodo at his mercy.

"Oh of course it isn't," I said in mock realisation. "You couldn't have been born in nineteen eighty-four. You're clearly *much* older than that."

The men beside him laughed at his expense, catcalling him and slapping him on the back as he was called out and Sikes's ears turned red as he stared at me like he was trying to work out if I was intending to insult him, the little cogs in his eyes whirring on overdrive. But apparently his small brain couldn't comprehend the idea of a girl cutting him down to size, so he settled on what he clearly knew best. Being a creep.

"You look cold, angel. Maybe you need a seat that's a little warmer. C'mere and I'll tell you all about the date marked on my skin. It's the day I made my first kill." Sikes patted his knee and Frank suddenly moved so fast, I barely caught it. His hand locked around the back of Sikes's head and in the next second his face was being slammed into the kitchen island.

"Watch your mouth," Frank snarled in his ear, pinning him there and snarling down at his prey like a beast ready for the kill. My heart leapt at the sudden brutality, though in my home I'd been no stranger to it. But there was something about the way of these men, how their laughter turned to violence on the turn of a dime which set me on edge. Back home my brothers wore their dark intentions like armour, never once letting anyone believe anything other of them so it was never a surprise when they struck. But Frank's sudden attack had my heart skittering and the mood of the room plummeting so fast I wasn't sure of my footing anymore.

"She's the boss's wife," Frank growled, somehow making it look easy to pin a full grown man beneath him with a single arm.

Sikes jerked against the strength of Frank's hold and my eyebrows arched as I watched in delight, a thrill buzzing through my skin. Frank's muscles bulged against his grey shirt, the dark skin of his neck looking good enough to lick as his tendons strained against it.

"Alright, alright," Sikes grunted and Frank released him just as fast as he'd struck, staying on his feet as his eyes flicked my way.

My breaths were coming a little too heavily and my nipples were hardening for a whole different reason as this mountain of a man dripped testosterone all over the kitchen floor. Fuck me leftways, rightways and backways. He really was edible.

"We were just going anyway, weren't we boys?" Sikes said, trying to regain some respect even as the reddened fingerprints on the back of his neck deepened. His friends sniggered at him, but nodded and I was relieved when the lot of them got up and headed for the exit. Some still threw curious glances my way as they left and one of them grasped his junk through his sweatpants as he bit down on his bottom lip before Frank's murderous gaze made him turn and scamper away, the door banging closed behind them.

These men weren't the stoic mercenaries I was used to, they were wild, untamed and utterly unpredictable and I wasn't certain what to make of that. How did they maintain their power with such volatile soldiers holding up their empire?

I took Frank's seat, balancing my weight to one side to avoid the brand and found Church drifting closer to me with a raw energy in his eyes which spoke of the untamed beast that lived within him. I felt Frank at my back, the two of them boxing me in and I had to admit I didn't entirely hate feeling the heat of their muscles surrounding me. Especially as I was in danger of getting nip frost in this cold ass place.

"Have you assholes ever heard of heating?" I muttered.

"It ain't cold, darlin'," Church said with a smirk. "This is actually our summer, though I'll grant you that the heat wave hasn't arrived yet."

"There's a heat wave coming?" I asked, unable to hide my desire for that.

Frank snorted behind me and Church's lips curled up like we were sharing a joke.

"Damn straight there is. There's always one coming. Though now that we're heading into the arse end of August, the papers are saying an 'Indian summer' is coming our way."

"What's that?" I asked, my brow furrowing in confusion.

"You know, when the summer heat comes in autumn instead of the actual summer," Church replied.

"You get summer weather in fall?" I asked, liking the sound of that because I'd been expecting it to be cold from here on out. "When does the snow arrive?" I asked suddenly, changing lanes as I thought of one of the few things I was actually looking forward to about being in this country. We hardly ever got snow in Vegas but I'd seen the Christmas cards of foot high snowfall coating the UK and I wanted to experience that at least once in my life.

"We're expecting nearly three foot of snow just in time for Christmas," Church replied, grinning broadly.

"Really?" I breathed in astonishment, but Frank burst my bubble by snorting derisively behind me.

"No. Not really," he said, making the hairs raise along the back of my neck as I realised how close he was standing to me. "British people are always talking shit about heat waves, Indian summers and record snowfall. The truth is, ninety five percent of the time it won't happen. It just pisses rain instead."

"Oh," my heart sank and I shot Church a glare as he shrugged innocently.

"I'm an optimist," he said. "But you'll get used to the temperatures soon enough. You've just got desert blood in ya. Britain will change that. She's a country forged in pain and glory, her soil is tainted with the blood of those who fought and died for her. She's the conqueror of the old world and the streets of this here London Town weave spells around those from foreign lands. She's opportunity and history and culture. She's beauty and fucking grace, darlin', and she'll leave her mark on you forever now, because you've already placed your feet upon her pavements, and once you walk in the footsteps of the people who've lived here, it'll alter you in ways you can't even imagine yet. This city was a kingdom of brutality, from the cutthroat royals who publicly executed countless unfortunate sods at Tower Hill, to louts like

Jack the Ripper who spilled the guts of his victims all over Whitechapel - the very place you find yourself in right now. This city's been burned to the ground, bombed by the Luftwaffe, and still she stands. It's survived plagues and winters cold enough to freeze your heart in your very chest. It ain't easy to leave a mark on this place, but it sure leaves a mark on you. And you're marked Anya Volkov, it's already too late for you."

My lips had parted and my heart was rioting to a beat that begged to be answered. His words made me ache to know every piece of this merciless world he described, it was the feeling I had when my music was playing and everything just seemed…right. Because I may have been raised in the sun in a city that never slept, but it had never felt like home.

Las Vegas was a city where a person could be made or destroyed, every spin of the roulette wheel deciding the fates of men. It was a playground of sin, and the Devil slept in its doorways, hunting for new victims night after night. But all the glitz of the hotels and high rises cast giant shadows over the victims of that place like gods standing atop a mountain of fallen warriors. The rich did rise, but hell did the poor fall deep.

London didn't hide its savagery. It wore it like battle scars, every street steeped in history, in blood. The Tower of London was a monument of death and chaos and it stood as proudly on the banks of the River Thames as it had for nearly a thousand years with no attempt to hide the cruelty which had lived within it. The truth of this place lay in plain sight, and I had known so little of that growing up in a city which promised you that your wildest dreams could be granted at the throw of a dice. It was a pretty lie. One that desperate people fell prey to time and again. London promised me nothing. She was a sleeping dragon, her claws still wet with the blood she'd claimed, and the treasures she lay upon were just waiting to be discovered.

Church's silver eyes darkened as they fell over my expression, some silent, mirrored desire in us echoing between our souls. I could feel his love of his country in a way I had never truly loved anything that wasn't family. And I wanted to prise that love from his chest and take it for myself.

My mind shifted to the man missing from this room and I swallowed away the burning lump in my throat, forcing my gaze to break from Church's.

"So, where's my beloved husband gotten to?" I asked.

"Underground," Frank answered for me and my head snapped around as I found him a hair's breadth away, towering over me with his impossible height.

"What?" I questioned in confusion.

"Danny likes to spend time in the old tunnels down there. He calls it his quiet place," Church explained and my ears pricked up at that.

"Tunnels?" I pressed.

"An abandoned tube station is under this warehouse," Church went on, offering up secrets like he was tossing crumbs to a pigeon and cared nothing for them.

"She don't need to know shit about that," Frank growled.

"Pfft, what's she gonna do about it? Danny's the only one who has a key anyways. Ain't like she can go play hide and seek down there, is it?" Church said dismissively and Frank released an irritated breath through his teeth like he thought that was exactly what I might do.

There was a metallic clunk and I leaned back in my seat so I could see into the large, open plan living space. Danny was there, shutting a door sharply behind him and locking it tight with a large iron key. He dropped it smoothly into his pocket and I took note of that as he approached, his dominating aura sucking away all the air in the echoing room.

I wasn't sure how he managed it, but when Danny Butcher walked into a space he somehow became the only thing that mattered within it, every eye turning to him, every sense taking note of what he was doing. Perhaps it was the evil in him making itself known, calling out to the subconscious instincts of those surrounding him and warning them to beware incurring his wrath.

His dark eyes ran over my outfit curiously, making my skin prickle at his attention then he snapped his fingers at Church. "Take her shopping today. She looks homeless."

Asshole.

"Yes, boss." Church stood up straighter.

"I'll bring the van around front," Frank said, stepping forward, but Danny held up a hand to stop him.

"Was that an order for you or Church?"

Frank paused at that, a frown lining his brow. "You told me to hound her, boss."

"And I'm tellin' Church to do it too. She doesn't need two arseholes following her around London, and *frankly*, Frank, I don't think she likes you very much."

Frank seemed unsure of what to do for a second before he nodded and dropped onto a stool at the island, taking his phone from his pocket and giving it all of his attention like I was no longer there.

"I like him more than you," I told Danny then pointed to Church. "And I like *him* the most."

Church beamed, his chest puffing out.

"But I still like him less than a turd on a hot summer's day, so take that how you will," I finished, dropping the little nuclear bomb on Church's head and watching as his smile fell to ruin in the blast.

Danny tossed Church a credit card and he caught it out of the air, eyeing the name on it with a snigger before putting it in his wallet. I noticed a sizeable wedge of cash sitting in there before he tucked it away and grabbed hold of my t-shirt by the sleeve.

"Let's go, Miss America. First stop will be the bra shop."

"It's not called a bra shop, douchebag." I rolled my eyes. "And my tits are freer than I am right now, so I'm good with not caging them again any time soon. Plus I'm pretty sure if I get one degree colder, I'll be able to use my nipples to slit your throat, Churchy."

Church burst out laughing, slinging an arm around my shoulders and guiding me towards the door like we were oh such good friends. I tried to duck out of his hold, but he held on until his grip was almost painful, his mouth falling to my ear and whispering so the others couldn't hear. "I'm willing to test out that theory if you are."

"Can we try with a knife first?" I replied sweetly and he laughed louder.

He led me outside and straight to his red Mini Cooper, nudging me into the front passenger seat for once instead of the back. I had no shoes on, but okay cool. At least it wasn't raining.

He got in the driver's seat and took off, driving like the maniac he was as I strapped my seatbelt on firmly and plugged my iPod into the dash to control the music. Church didn't complain as I set The Beatles playing and I found my excitement rising as I gazed out the window and soaked in the views of London as he drove me who knew where.

I realised I was practically pressed up against the glass as I stared at the grey streets which seemed to be reflected by the sky. There was colour though. Pops of red mailboxes and old phone boxes too, black cabs zoomed past us in their own lanes followed by red double decker buses and cyclists who seemed to take their life into their hands as they wound between the endless traffic.

Graffiti coloured some of the high stone walls in places where I couldn't even fathom how someone had reached them, and there were murals too, enormous pieces of art scrawled on brick walls, so beautiful they stole my breath with the stories they told. With the twang of The Beatles in my ears, I was in freaking heaven. I was living, breathing, *hearing* London and I wanted more, all of it, every damn piece.

We eventually arrived on a busy street lined with boutique clothes stores and Church pulled up on some double yellow lines, pulling the parking brake so hard that I was thrown forward in my seat.

"Watch it, asshole." I punched his arm but he ignored me, jumping out of the car and hurrying around to open my door like he was some eighteenth century gentleman.

I gave him a suspicious look before popping my seatbelt and stepping out, glancing at the signs which explicitly said he couldn't park here on penalty of large fines.

"Won't you like, get in trouble or some shit for parking there?" I asked, not massively caring either way.

"Someone sure will, darlin', but it won't be me." He winked and walked away like a mysterious cat and I frowned at him.

"Meaning?" I pushed.

"I change my plates every other week," he said with a shrug. "Those numbers on the front and back of my baby ain't mine. I sure as fuck don't know whose they are, but if anyone's getting a ticket in the post, it ain't me."

"And what if they clamp your wheel, smartass?"

"I keep an angle grinder in the boot." He shrugged, glancing back at me and slowing his pace until we were walking together. "Don't get me wrong, it doesn't always go to plan. The last time I was in court for 'perverting the course of justice' I had to fuck every member of the jury to get myself declared innocent. I'm not sure if the ninety-year-old grandma or the hairy-backed biker dude haunt me most these days, but I'm a free man so I guess it was worth it." He gave me a harrowed look and I stared at him in shock for a second before I realised he was joking and I rammed an elbow into his gut hard enough to make him cough.

"Jesus, you're fighty today, Miss America. You wanna sack off the shopping and go for a wrestle in the mud at Finsbury Park? I bet you look good all dirty."

"Fuck you," I said, warring with a grin before he guided me through a doorway and I found myself being corralled into some fancy ass boutique.

There were no customers inside and it was eerily quiet as the store assistant looked over at us, her upper lip curling in distaste at the clothes I was wearing and the fact my feet were bare. *Well I don't like your ugly ass purple pantsuit either.*

"No," I said decisively before I was barely two steps inside the store. I turned back, trying to fight my way past Church's huge body while he opened his arms wide to block my way further and moved me towards the lingerie section like some sort of smirking sheepdog.

He was keeping me in my own personal hell of snooty tea dresses and god forbidden tummy-tucking pantyhose. Panic was rising in me and suddenly I wanted my music, because this place represented something I feared more than being married to a psychopath. It represented my personality being stripped away, the root of me cut out, stamped on and left to die in the gutter. Danny wanted me to be his dolled up little housewife, his obedient bitch who'd been so easily brought to heel, a wife he was going to parade around on a leash attached to this fucking collar on my throat.

"Church, move," I growled as he pushed me back, and I gripped his arms, my nails digging into his shoulders as I stared up at him, my breaths coming too heavily as I felt the walls closing in all around me.

Church may have seemed friendly at times, but he was just Danny's henchman, he had his orders, and it was clear what they were now. Dress me up for Danny's pleasure. Mould me into the woman he really wanted in his bed at night. But if I gave in to that, then what would he take next? My music? My fucking soul?

"Madam," the store attendant said sharply. "Please desist."

"I'm trying to fucking desist. I want to desist your whole ugly store," I snarled, shoving at Church again and he grabbed hold of my jaw, forcing my chin up so I looked him in the eye.

"Anya," he hissed and something in his voice made me freeze in his hold as I sank into the silvery pools of his eyes. "What's going on in your head? Don't bullshit me."

I answered him truthfully because what did it matter? I didn't need to lie. "He wants a trophy and I'm not going to be one. I'm not putting on those disgusting dresses, I'm not becoming some pantsuit asshole in high heels either."

The attendant gasped dramatically at the dig, but I didn't give a fuck. That pantsuit was an insult to pants *and* suits.

"I know he'll hate what I like to dress in," I continued. "I know he didn't want some grungy rock chick, but that's who I am. And he can't take who I am. I won't fucking let him."

My eyes darted to the window and the street beyond. If I could get out, I could run. Maybe running was the only answer I really had. It would fuck the treaty, but who cared? My brothers had abandoned me. Why should I uphold the end of a bargain I'd never had a choice in?

But without money I'd get nowhere. And I'd need a lot of cash if I was going to survive, if I was going to disappear forever.

"Easy, darlin'." Church's hand slid up to cup my cheek and my eyes snapped back to his as his thumb brushed along my cheekbone. "No one's tryin' to take that from you."

My throat tightened, burning with a retort and my disbelief of those words, but he went on before I could say anything more.

"If you want to buy some more band shirts then we'll go to Camden and get you what you want. *Anything* you want."

"Anything," I echoed bitterly, but I could feel myself relaxing, I could see the promise in his eyes and some foolish part of me was falling for it. "What I want is to get back the shirts you ruined. Do you know how many years I've been collecting those? Do you know how fucking rare some of them were? They don't even make them anymore." I sighed, trying to pull out of his hold, but he suddenly drew me even closer and I heard the store attendant clucking her tongue in irritation.

"I'm going to call my manager," she announced.

"Keep your knickers on, Karen," Church growled without looking her. Because he was looking at me. So hard it felt like he was staring right through my eyes directly into the essence of my being. And I could honestly say I had never been looked at like that in my entire life. It made me feel starkly present in the world. I spent so much time checking out or drifting into my music whenever things got too loud or too hard to face, and it never seemed like anyone cared that much when I disappeared. I was just 'Anya being Anya'. But that wasn't who I was, not really. And it looked like Church knew it.

"I'm sorry," he exhaled. "For the shirts."

Surprise radiated through me as his thumb brushed up to my temple, his hand so big it encompassed the entire left side of my face. It was warm where I was cold and his heat soaked into my flesh, awakening it like I was a zombie coming back to life.

"You're not," I countered, too stubborn to allow that apology in.

"I am. It was the boss's orders. We couldn't risk you bringing in a little bug from your Russian pals," he threw back. "I shouldn't have really let you keep the iPod either…"

I sucked in a sharp breath in horror at that suggestion, but he just shrugged.

"Don't panic. I figured technology that old barely even came with a colour screen, so I left it be."

"It's not that old," I grumbled protectively and the corner of his lips turned up in amusement.

"Come on, I'll make it right." He dropped his hand, taking my fingers between his and – dumb fuck that I was – I let him lead me out the door, looking up at him in surprise as he guided me back to his car in silence.

I spotted a parking warden in a navy uniform standing behind his Mini, printing him out a ticket on a bright yellow piece of paper.

"Excuse me, mate," Church called out to him as he quickened his pace. "Can I see that for a sec?"

"You can see it when I'm finished," the warden grumbled. "If you wanna challenge it, you can fill out the form online. I don't wanna hear your bullshit story about how your girlfriend's grandfather's dying or some other crap. You broke the law, so that's that."

He signed the ticket and Church swiped it from him, stuffing it straight in his mouth, making my lips part as he chewed his way through it and swallowed it in a way that looked like it had been painful.

"Have a great day, mate." Church flicked the warden's peaked hat hard enough to send it flying off his head and as the man scrambled to pick it up, Church yanked the passenger door open, shoving me into the car.

A laugh escaped me as he dove over the hood like an action hero, pretending to shoot a gun with his fingers before falling right on his ass and leaping back up to get in the driver's seat.

"Oi!" the warden barked, lifting his little parking warden device to snap a photo and I opened the window, leaning out of it and flashing my tits just as he took the picture.

Church grabbed the back of my jeans, yanking me down into my seat just before he took off at speed down the road, laughing his ass off as I dropped my shirt and cracked up too.

I pulled my seatbelt on and closed the window, my pulse skittering as Church dropped a hand casually onto my knee and squeezed, glancing over at me with darkness twisting through his eyes. His gaze dipped to my mouth for the briefest moment, but it was enough to make my veins burst with adrenaline.

"Put some music on, darlin'. Play something which makes you roar inside."

I picked out Basket Case by Greenday as his hand slid from my knee and I was relieved to get some space between us. Church was a bad idea with mistake written all over it. And I wasn't going to fall for the playful side of him which seemed so inviting, because I knew what he really was, and that was a sinner under the rule of a wicked king. A king who happened to be my goddamn husband.

He drove us along through narrow streets, seeming to know the whole city without needing a map as he took endless turns without hesitation and I became endlessly lost.

As we rounded another corner, my eyes locked on a vintage clothes store with a green rimmed window. A mannequin stood among a display reminiscent of the nineteen sixties with a record player set up to one side of it and an old record box full of music. The mannequin wore a pair of chunky biker boots, some ripped jeans, a Dire Straits cropped t-shirt and a leather jacket which screamed old school.

"Stop the car!" I cried and Church slammed on the brakes so hard, I was thrown forward in my seat again.

"What is it?!" he barked, looking left and right along the street, a gun somehow in his hand which he'd plucked from fuck knew where, but I was already undoing my belt and getting out of the car. "Hey!" he shouted, pulling up on the curb and following me out onto the road as he tucked the gun into the back of his pants and concealed it with his shirt. "We can't stay here. It's the Candlestick Maker's turf. There's not many places in London where my mug ain't welcome, but this here isn't safe."

I ignored him, moving to the window and staring in at all the cute shit in the store before my eyes locked on that mannequin again.

"Anya," Church said seriously, catching hold of my arm and I glanced up at him.

"I want to try this on." I pointed at the outfit and he looked about to refuse before his expression melted and he nodded, guiding me inside, casting a wary look down the road before ducking into the store.

I wriggled out of his hold, feeling like a kid in a candy store as I bounded up to the mannequin and tried to pull the jacket off of it, half climbing up onto the display.

"Oh, um, miss?" the store attendant called awkwardly.

Church locked an arm around the whole mannequin, lifting it off of the window shelf and carrying it straight over to the attendant as I got distracted by all the vintage clothes surrounding me on tiny racks and rails, the place jam-packed with the most amazing stuff I'd ever seen.

It had been so hard to get hold of things like this in the US and this stuff could have been worn to some of the most famous gigs in British history. I half squealed as I started piling shirts and rocker dresses in my arms along with a bunch of cute mini skirts. I was definitely getting carried away, but I'd had a shitty couple of days and Church didn't seem to be complaining as I hurried over to him with a mountain of clothes in my arms as he stripped the mannequin bare as it lay on the counter before a stunned looking girl in some cute ass red plaid shorts and an Aerosmith shirt.

"Nice tats." I nodded to the colourful tattoos she had swirling down one arm and she broke a grin.

"Thanks, I like your um…" She looked at what I was wearing, glancing at my bare feet and I laughed.

"Don't worry, I totally stole these clothes from a douchebag. You don't have to force a compliment on them. Is it okay to try all of this on?" I asked and she nodded, helping Church to get the boots off of the mannequin. "Please tell me they're my size," I groaned, tilting my head to try and see the sole of one of them and I frowned in disappointment when I found they were a six. "Oh."

"That's a UK size, darlin'," Church reminded me.

"What's your American size?" the girl asked.

"An eight," I offered hopefully.

"Then it's your lucky day." She pushed the boots towards me and I bounced up and down. I wasn't often a peppy kind of person, but I was in my element right here in this awesome place, and I could tell by the looks Church kept shooting me that he was surprised by my reaction.

I tried to pick the boots up in my too-full arms, and went to grab them with my teeth failing that. Church snorted and knocked me aside, bundling up the last of the stuff in his own arms and leading the way to the changing room at the back of the store.

Church shouldered through the door and I followed, finding a pokey space with just one changing cubicle inside. I hurried into it and Church and I tossed the pile of clothes down on a chair beside the mirror along with my headphones. I pulled my top off excitedly and Church's breath fanned against the back of my neck, reminding me I wasn't alone. I inhaled sharply, knowing how close he was as goosebumps tumbled down my spine.

A moment fell between us as we both just stood there, the reality that this wasn't okay hanging in the silence while a charge built in the atmosphere which asked, why not?

He broke it first, backing up to give me some space and I glanced over my shoulder after him. I could have just closed the curtain between us, but the reckless girl in me wanted to play with him. Besides, it wasn't like he hadn't seen me naked already when he'd hijacked my shower yesterday, but this was on my terms.

He dropped down onto the chair opposite the changing cubicle, waiting to see what I was going to do as I kept my back to him. There was a look in his eyes like he expected me to hide, to run like a little mouse down a hole and not go through with what I'd started. But I was Anya Volkov. Daughter of one of the most ruthless Russian mafia bosses to have ever lived. I didn't back down from anything.

"I still didn't get any underwear," I said breathily.

Church reached into his pocket, tugging out a bunch of lacy panties in his fist. "That ugly dress store had something worth taking."

"What about bras?" I asked, wanting to crack a joke to break the heightening tension between us, but I couldn't do anything but stare at the beautiful stolen garments wrapped around his big, tattooed hand, imagining how good those fingers might feel inside me.

"I'm officially joining the free tits movement," he said, his eyes dancing with mirth but his mouth didn't lift with a smile.

My tongue felt leaden as I nodded, liking that idea. Maybe I'd say fuck you to the bras for good, keep my tits uncaged until I followed them into freedom. It was stupid, but it felt like a little secret between us, like he was quietly joining my rebellion. And perhaps it was worth trying to see how far I could get under his skin. Maybe he really would help me rebel if I made him want me enough.

I turned slowly to face him, exposing myself as I unbuckled the belt pulled tight around my waist and let the jeans fall to my feet, kicking them off, leaving me totally naked in front of him except for those big cosy socks on my feet. Then I walked towards him and held out my hand for the panties.

His pupils dilated and his throat bobbed as he stared at me, unashamedly looking at my body, taking his time to drink it all in, his gaze lingering on the musical notes I had inked along my collar bone like he was trying to read them before looking me in the eye.

"Pick a colour," he commanded, something in his tone making me want to obey.

I looked through the array of panties in his hand then settled on one. "Red."

"Now why'd you have to go and pick my favourite colour?" he asked, and my gaze fell to the Union Jack flag he had inked on his bicep.

"What about white and blue?"

"Joint second," he said.

He placed the panties on his lap then captured my knee, tugging my leg up so my foot rested on his thigh. I sucked in a breath from the shock of his touch and the way he looked right at my pussy had me practically quivering as he pushed his tongue into his cheek then slowly dragged the sock off my foot and tossed it away.

He held the back of my knee again, lowering my leg back down before lifting up the other one and repeating the action. But this time he didn't let me go. His fingers caressed the sensitive skin at the back of my knee and I wobbled on one leg before fisting a hand in his rugged blonde hair to stop myself from stumbling back.

"Give me the panties," I commanded and the corner of his mouth twisted up, like the idea of me bossing him around was amusing.

"Turn around," he ordered in response.

"No," I said immediately, trying to tug my ankle from his grip but he locked his fingers tight so I couldn't escape.

"Careful, darlin', you wouldn't wanna fall," he taunted. "Now turn around."

He released my ankle and as my foot hit the ground, he caught my hips and flipped me around to face away from him. My back straightened, my gut knotting because now he'd see exactly what I hadn't wanted him to see.

The brand placed there by Danny still stung sharply, but what hurt the most was the shame I felt from Church finding it.

I tried to twist around but he was suddenly on his feet at my back, his hand latching around my wrist to keep me from turning.

"Danny," he growled like that name was as worthy as soot on his tongue.

"What's the matter, Church?" I asked bitterly. "Surprised your friend is a piece of shit? Or did he already gloat about this to you last night? Did you enjoy hearing him tell the story?"

His fingers suddenly traced the brand, not touching the wound but circling it all the same and making me stiffen with the almost pain of it. There was tension in him as he held his tongue for once, a tightness in his grip which I swear could have been anger, though that made no sense at all. When he finally broke the silence again, I swear he was working to keep himself in check, fighting against the violence in him as he restrained himself.

"The Danny who did this to you is gone, Anya, I swear it," Church spoke at last in a voice dipped in rage.

"What the fuck is that supposed to mean?" I growled, trying to jerk out of his hold but he continued to keep me there.

He paused before he answered. "He made his wedding vows and he'll keep 'em. To honour and protect."

"Bullshit," I snapped, glancing back at him and finding him dropping down to kneel behind me, my heart lurching into my throat at the sight. He reared forward and pressed his mouth to the brand, the kiss hurting as much as it soothed. It was wrong, forbidden, and it made me so wet that I nearly moaned.

"Church," I rasped.

He reached around me with the panties I'd chosen, his stubble grazing my thigh as he leaned past me and gestured for me to step into them. I had no fucking idea what he was thinking, but I did as he asked and he dragged the panties up my legs, his fingers grazing the outer sides of my thighs all the way up until he was standing behind me again, fixing them in place.

He dropped his mouth to my ear, his rough fingers lingering on the skin below my hips. "Whether he takes that vow seriously or not, I'm his man. And I always keep to my word. So I'll keep that vow for him if I have to, darlin'."

His declaration left me confused and my head spun as he shifted his right hand, his fingers sliding just below the line of my panties and running smoothly around to graze the skin above my pussy.

I arched back into him, knowing I was playing a deadly game, but Church brought out my wild side and I wanted so much to feel something that it didn't matter to me how stupid this was.

His fingers lingered there and I felt his cock swelling against my ass as I pressed back into him, the air in this room seeming too thin to breathe.

"You have entered my life like a fuckin' meteorite, Anya Volkov. I can still count the hours I've known you and somehow you've possessed my thoughts in every single one of them," he said with grit to his tone.

"Butcher," I corrected on a breath. "My name is Butcher now."

For a single, maddening moment, I was certain both of us were going to break. That we'd collide and fuck and give in to this maddening tension between us. But almost instantaneously, I felt us both pulling away from one another, knowing we couldn't cross this line, that it could be as good as a death sentence for both of us. Or maybe Church really was just that loyal to his boss.

His fingers skimmed my flesh as he drew back and I missed the feel of his touch on my skin the moment I lost it.

I walked into the changing room and ripped the curtain shut so hard I almost pulled it down, sagging back against the wall for a second as I caught my breath. Then slowly, I regained my self control and I started internally berating myself.

He's the Devil with a pretty smile. So fuck him. And fuck his gang.

I had to keep my head. Maybe I could play this desire between us to my advantage if I did that, because if I didn't, I might be securing myself a bullet between the eyes, or maybe I was securing one for Church. And though on paper he was a bloodthirsty criminal who was aligned with my enemies, I still didn't want him dead for this.

I snatched up some of the clothes a little aggressively and spent some time trying them on. I didn't bother to show Church, using the mirror in the stall with me to check out how I looked in my new attire. And when I was done, I kept on the outfit I'd seen on the mannequin and scooped the rest of the clothes up in my arms, leaving Danny's clothes behind as a little middle finger to his empire, then I held my chin high and walked out of the changing room.

Church was gone, and as I returned to the store, I found him handing a bunch of cash over to the attendant. "Bag it up fast and keep the change."

The happy-go-lucky guy was nowhere to be seen in his expression as he gestured for me to pass the clothes over and the girl helped bag it up for me.

"I thought Danny gave you a credit card?" I questioned.

"This one's on me, seeing as I'm the reason you have no clothes," Church said, but there was no warmth in his voice anymore.

A little jingle of the bell ringing as someone entered the store made me look over and I spotted a thuggish guy in a leather jacket and a baseball cap. He walked straight up behind the counter, leaning down and possessively kissing the girl serving us before tossing a glance my way. She accepted his mouth against hers but there was a tension to her posture which made me uneasy. Something about him set my instincts blazing as the girl handed the bags over to me with a small tremble to her fingers and said goodbye with a tight smile.

I nodded to her, heading away and glancing back at the grimacing dude as I followed Church onto the street.

He popped the trunk of the car and I placed the bags in the back before he swung it shut.

The street was empty now and a distant siren wailed, making the hairs on the back of my neck prickle.

Church didn't look at me as he walked around to get in the driver's seat, dropping into the car and jerking the door shut behind him.

I was about to step off the sidewalk to circle the car when the bell on the door to the store sounded behind me and the heat in my blood rose.

I swung around, sensing the attack before it landed and narrowly missing the swing of a knife, setting my heart thundering. I gasped as the man from the store came at me again and I dodged sideways, letting out a yell of anger as I threw my shoulder into his chest, trying to unbalance him to give myself a chance to get that knife. I'd trained for this a hundred times, I knew how to fight, how to kill if I had to. But rarely had I had to put my skills to the test like this.

The man caught a fistful of my hair, yanking my head back and the knife came at me once more, but I was already throwing my own fist towards his arm, slamming into it hard.

He cried out as his wrist snapped back and the knife clattered to the ground, but in the next second he was on me with brute force, throwing me to the ground, his fist slamming into the side of my head and setting my whole world wheeling and fear blossoming in my chest.

A roar that seemed to come from an animal filled my head and suddenly the shadow looming over me was wrenched back and I blinked away the haze around my vision, adrenaline blooming in my blood as Church wrestled the guy backwards into a narrow alleyway beside the store.

I shoved to my feet fast, snatching up the blade and running after them, but I came to a sudden halt as I found Church cracking the man's head against the wall over and over, blood splattering his shirt, his eyes alight with a vicious savagery. Church released him and the man crumpled dead at his feet, the knife going slack in my grip as Church wiped a line of blood droplets from his brow, his chest heaving with exertion.

"Why didn't you just shoot him?" I asked huskily, eyeing the bulge of the gun in the back of his jeans.

"You don't just pop off bullets in England unless you fucking have to," Church said darkly. "This ain't the wild west you come from, Miss America. I'd get nicked before we could make it halfway down the street."

"Nicked?" I questioned in confusion. His accent was the hottest one I'd ever encountered, but fuck if I knew what him and his friends were saying half the time.

"Arrested, darlin'."

A gasp behind me made me turn and I found the girl from the store there, her shoulders shuddering. I lunged towards her, clapping a hand to her mouth before she could scream and she looked to me with terror in her eyes.

"I'm not going to hurt you," I swore. "He attacked us."

She nodded and I slowly lowered my hand, allowing her to speak.

"Thank you," she said breathlessly. "He's the Candlestick Maker's man."

"What do you know about him?" Church demanded, pulling his bloodied shirt off and wiping his bloody arms with it to clean them as best he could.

I stared at his tattooed body, still fresh from a kill and the darkness I'd been born into sank deeper into my veins. It was no news to me that I was a depraved fucking soul. How could I not be after the way I'd been raised? But seeing someone die had never turned me on before. Not until Church.

"He runs cash through my store. He always sends that guy with the money…but he always wanted something from me in return," she admitted shakily. "I-I can't stay here now. What if the Candlestick Maker finds out about this?"

"How many cameras are on this street?" Church demanded, tossing his bloody shirt down onto the body and walking towards us.

"J-just mine," the girl said.

"Then erase the footage. You didn't see us tonight, and you certainly didn't see that asshole. If anyone asks, he didn't show up."

She nodded quickly.

"Do you know who I am, sweetheart?" Church asked her and she hesitated before nodding. "Did you tip off that asshole that I was here today?"

"No, I swear I didn't. I swear," she begged, looking to me like I might save her. I knew liars, and I didn't think this chick was one.

"Alright, well if you know who I am, you know what I'll do to someone who rats me out to the cops, you got that?" he growled and the power in his voice sent a tremor rolling through me. Call me smitten, but Church had gone from dangerous hot guy to rockstar psycho in my books.

"I promise," the girl said and Church took his phone out of his pocket, nudging her towards the dead body and snapping a photo.

"If you don't keep that promise, I'll leak this image to the old bill." He smirked and sent her scurrying off back to her store.

"What's the old bill?" I asked in confusion.

"The police, darlin'," he answered.

"Right…well what now?" I looked to the bloody body, pushing a hand into my hair anxiously. I suddenly came down from the high of watching Church kill, crashing back into earth with a healthy dose of reality smacking me in the head for good measure.

Fuck, we were in the middle of one of the most populated cities in the world. How the hell were we going to hide this? I couldn't go to fucking prison. If this was my own city, I'd be able to come up with a plan of my own, but I didn't know how shit worked in The Firm.

"Stay here," Church ordered and seeing as I had no better options, I did.

A minute later his Mini appeared, reversing into the narrow alley. He jumped out, squeezing through the small space between the open door and the alley wall before flipping open the trunk.

I grabbed my shopping, tossing it into the back of the car instead and by the time I got back to the trunk, Church had shoved the guy into it, somehow having folded him up like a fucking pretzel to make him fit.

Church shoved the trunk shut then headed out of sight in the direction of the store, reappearing a beat later with a large bottle of bleach. He headed over to the splatters of blood on the ground and washed them away as best he could, emptying out every last drop. The blood was barely visible as it mixed with the grime at the edge of the alley and one good downpour of rain would likely wash it all away – something we could definitely count on soon by the looks of the dark clouds in the night sky. He moved to the car, popping the trunk again and tossing the empty bottle in with the body before snapping it shut once more.

"You good?" Church looked to me and I nodded, my teeth clenching in determination.

"Yeah. How are we disposing of the body?"

His eyebrows arched as he moved towards me, looking me over like he was inspecting me for bruises. But one punch to the head was nothing compared to the pain I'd endured at the hands of my father for years.

"I'm good," I reiterated. "What's the plan? We bury our bodies in the desert, what do you Brits do?"

"You really would help me bury that body, wouldn't you Miss America?" he mused.

"I'd bake it in a pie and feed it to your momma if it got the job done, Churchy," I said sweetly.

"Good thing my mum's dead then, ain't it?" He chuckled then pointed to the car and my gut tugged at those words, not smiling at his dark joke. "In. We're going to see one of the Bakers."

I had no clue what that meant, but I got into the car and we both held our breath for a second as a siren sounded close by, but it passed away into the distance and Church switched the engine on.

"You didn't tell me you could fight," he commented as he reached into the back of the car and produced a spare shirt from somewhere, pulling it on before driving back onto the road.

"There's a lot you don't know about me, Church," I said coolly.

"That's the problem, Anya," he said seriously and I studied him from the corner of my eye as his hands tightened on the wheel. "I think I wanna know everything."

CHAPTER TEN

I strode through the warehouse that me and Danny had bought once upon a time to be the crown jewel in our empire.

Right after dear old Pa had kicked the bucket, we'd decided it was best to start things fresh within The Firm. Make changes. Check allegiances, root out any rot and most importantly of all, be certain that our high standards were met at all times. Alright, maybe they were more *my* high standards than that prick's, but he'd gone along with the plans because he knew full well that I'd always been the fucking brains of this outfit. I was the brawn and the looker too, so I guessed that only left him with the position of psycho in chief, but it wasn't my fault he'd never measured up.

Of course back then, I'd been cocky. Too fucking cocky. I'd thought his love for me would always outweigh his jealousy. I'd thought I had him in hand. Hell, I'd thought a lot of things that turned out to be utter bollocks when I came to think of it.

But this place. This fucking beauty of a place in the heart of Whitechapel, the centre of our empire, just a stone's throw from the Tower of London and the history which had brought us here. It was a palace for the king of the real men of this city. Not the fancy lords with their low morals and corruptible souls. No. This here was the home of the hellions who truly ruled the city, through the underground networks of our criminal empire and beyond.

And I was finally back to reclaim my crown.

It had been a mad few days, getting my head around so much open sky, so many people and so many changes. I'd been in business meetings, trying to figure out the shit show my brother had made of our fronts. Luckily most of the pubs, clubs and restaurants were still running well, the men and women who ran them more than capable of handling their shit. But there were messes in a lot of the other companies. Not least in Horizon Construction – our biggest fucking front and the most important jewel in our goddamn crown. The company needed the firm hand of its CEO, and Danny had not been taking his role there seriously at all. In fact, he'd only been to a handful of board meetings in the last few years and the numbers spoke for themselves. The company was dancing the line of going bust and it was a damn stroke of luck that I'd returned when I had, or I may not have had a fucking empire to return to.

Fortunately, Danny wasn't completely incompetent and he had been working on a deal which would see the company back on its feet and give me the breathing room I needed to fix the rest of the issues with its management. I was still figuring out all of the facts about it but so far as I could tell, we were getting into bed with a Russian billionaire who went by the self-appointed title of The Czar. He wanted to invest millions in the construction of a massive housing development in Soho and between our hold on the city, our sway over the politicians and our construction company, we were the only ones who could make that happen for him. Which meant one hell of a pay day for us, and the salvation of our empire. So yeah, I had a whole heap of shit to wade through and problems to figure out.

Not to mention my new bride.

Fuck she was something else. Her body was hot, tight and had felt like a living miracle around my cock. So yeah, I meant her looks in that statement, but it was somehow more than that too. I'd wanted to claim Anya Volkov from the moment she'd walked up the aisle looking like a gift handcrafted for me by a fucking angel right out of heaven, but I hadn't expected to be intrigued by her beyond that. Guess I'd been alone too long, because intrigued I damn well was, and I intended on discovering a whole lot more about my wife, preferably while I was inside her again.

Not that I'd be fucking her again any time soon. Not now I'd seen what my fuck up of a brother had done to her, what she thought *I'd* done to her.

I'd known a lot of women before my incarceration and none of them had been able to look at me the way she did; like she could cut right through my bullshit with one sweeping glance of her endlessly dark eyes and see the very bones of who I was. The only problem there was that as far as I could tell, she didn't much like what she saw.

I was pretty certain Danny's use of a fucking brand on her arse, alongside snapping a collar around her throat didn't help with that either.

But I'd come up with a plan to deal with that. The heat between us was undeniable, even through the haze of hatred she clearly felt towards me. She still hungered for me. The bad and the good. And I could be *so* fucking good to her if that was what it took to make her forget the sins of my twin against her flesh. I'd replace the memory of that pain he'd inflicted upon her with so much pleasure that she'd be coming apart at the seams from it.

I planned on worshipping her body with everything but my dick, learning every inch of it and finding out all the ways she best liked to come for me as many times as I could convince her to let me. As much and as often as I could, I'd make her fall apart for me until it was enough, until she forgot that hatred she felt and the need for me outweighed it. Until she begged me to use my cock as well as my hands and mouth to destroy her and I could see in those deep, dark eyes of hers that she desired that more than anything.

Until then I'd suffer in abstinence for the sins of my brother and focus my efforts on winning her over.

My upper lip pulled back as I thought on that, and I couldn't help but wonder for the hundredth time what hell my twin had wreaked all these years he'd gone unchecked. Church had told me some of it of course, but I could tell I barely knew a fraction of Danny's depravity.

I swung the paper bag I held in my fist and headed across the room to the black door which led down to the abandoned underground tube station which lay beneath this building, taking the key from my pocket and placing it in the lock.

It turned somewhat reluctantly, the heavy thump of the lock sounding a moment before the door swung wide to admit me.

I took the tightly twisting metal staircase down into the dark, using the torch on my phone to light the way. Church had spent over an hour showing me how to use the fucking thing when he gave it to me and I was still getting used to it, but I had the basics down now. Technology had moved on a whole bunch while I was rotting away, that was for sure. Technically the phone was Danny's, but as he'd stolen my life by getting me sent down, I felt no guilt in stealing his right back in return.

It got colder the further I descended, the bare skin of my arms speckling with goosebumps as I headed down and down, until I finally met the bottom of the stairs and could see the faint light of the station up ahead of me. Faded signs for Krays End were painted on the walls in red and blue, the old name of this place now eradicated from the new tube line maps, but it still stood here in the dark, waiting for a train that would never come.

I shut the phone off and dropped it into my back pocket, striding through the narrow tunnel towards the station which was lit with a single bulb that hung from an extension cable I'd run down here years ago when we first bought the place.

Since then, it had been used on more than one occasion to house motherfuckers who needed to be interrogated before they died, and the disused tracks had seen a whole load of blood and gore. If the walls here could talk then both me and my brother would easily gain several life sentences just for the acts committed down here alone – and that was before I'd gone to prison. Fuck knew what else he'd used this place for since then.

I hoped the memories were giving him nightmares.

I paused at the heavy gate which blocked the way on, twisting the numbers on the padlock to open it, my jaw hardening at the sight of the date when my own brother had turned on me. The night he'd taken my life from me and caused the death of one of the few men I loved in this miserable world. I had to admit I'd enjoyed snapping this padlock shut on his sorry arse and leaving him down here on my wedding night.

I swung the gate wide and stepped through it, heading down the tunnel to the platform with a heady feeling bringing a twisted smile to my lips.

The last two times I'd come here to check on him, he'd still been off his fucking rocker, garbling about the hallucinations the shit Church had injected him with had provided, but the silence which awaited me now made me think he was lucid at last.

My heart began to pound at the thought of that. Of finally facing him and letting him look upon the face of the brother he'd betrayed.

White tiles lined the curved walls of the tube station ahead of me, posters for movies which came out before my birth peeling from the walls and the distinct scent of rot and dust hung in the air.

This station had once been the end of the line here. It was called Krays End and it was an oddity stuck between a bunch of far more useful stations which never got a lot of passengers passing through it even before its closure. And when the elevators had needed maintenance to keep them functioning, the cost had outweighed the value, meaning the decision was taken to close the station down and forget it had ever been there at all.

The tracks led one way, to the left of where I was about to step out onto the platform, but they'd been barred off when the station was decommissioned and all that was left was this subterranean memory of a time long passed. There was a way out through a maintenance passage further back up the stairs, a secret escape route if we ever got cornered in our own home.

I stepped out onto the grey stone of the platform, turning towards my brother and finding him sitting on one of the benches meant for passengers, his dark eyes hollow and his hands resting in his lap, a chain attached to his left wrist.

The chain was secured to a metal pipe which wasn't going anywhere and had just enough slack in it to allow him use of the single disabled toilet which sat to the left of the uncomfortable looking bench. It even still flushed and everything which was a damn brilliant stroke of luck – none of us wanted to be cleaning up his shit after all.

"Good to see you awake, brother," I said, offering a devil's smile as I closed in on him and he bared his teeth at me.

"So it *was* you," he replied, his gaze full of violence as I came to stand before him, just at the point where I knew his chains would snap taut if he decided to lunge at me. I was all for beating the shit out of him again if he was after that, but right now I was more interested in gloating. And I didn't feel a single bead of shame about that.

"Who else?" I taunted as his gaze moved over the new ink I had coating my arms and creeping up my neck. I'd only had one tattoo before I'd taken on the decision to imitate him, so getting the rest had been a simple enough disguise to orchestrate and it sold my lie all the better. Who would ever think I'd paint my flesh in ink to match his? Who would ever guess the lengths I'd go to for this revenge? No one. And that was precisely why I was going to get away with it. "You had to know I'd come for you one of these days."

"I thought I had a little longer before then," he muttered, looking like he was nursing one hell of a hangover. The scent of piss and vomit hung around him, the evidence of both staining the clothes he wore as well as the ground a little way from us. I guessed he hadn't made it to the toilet in his drugged state.

"Was the high not to your liking?" I asked, not bothering to hide my disgust from him as he flexed his fingers, clearly working damn hard at trying to keep his head. I had to admit, I was impressed by the amount of self-control he was showing – that had really never been his strong suit.

"That shit was fucked up. It made me see and think and feel things that no man ever should," he replied. "But you knew that. So why not ask me about something you *don't* know?"

I cocked my head to one side as I considered that. "Where's the key to the collar you put on my wife?" I asked, wondering if he might save me more hours of hunting for the fucking thing by just giving it up. If not, I was going to have to get a pair of bolt cutters involved, though I didn't much like the thought of that so close to her flawless skin.

Danny tossed his head back and laughed, slumping against the wall behind him as his gaze fell on me again and he looked me up and down.

"Why? Is she having trouble swallowing your cock with it on? I will admit it was a little tight."

"It's just so fucking tacky," I shot back. "Which is exactly what I'd expect from you, but I'm hoping to reinstate some of our reputation while I keep you out of the fucking way and we have a chance to reclaim it."

"Fuck me, have you gone soft on her?" Danny taunted, a wicked smile breaking across his face. "Is her pussy that good? Or has it just been so long since you got a taste of any that desperation is making you vulnerable to the call of it?"

I knew what he was doing, but that shit wouldn't work on me. I took a step forward, then another, towering over him so he was forced to tip his chin back to keep maintaining my stare.

"It's that good," I confirmed, my lips lifting in a smirk as I thought of the way her body had felt clasped tightly around me, of how her cries of pleasure had coloured the air and how fucking exhilarating it had felt to spill myself deep inside her and mark her as mine. That was one thing he was never gonna take from me. "And all the better for knowing I took it from you. Just like I took your car and wrapped it 'round a lamppost right outside Buckingham Palace. Just like I took the watch Pa left you and stamped on it repeatedly until all the little bits inside it were nothing more than dust on the floor." Danny's expression was descending into nothing but savage rage but I just kept going, my smile growing as I told him everything I'd done to topple his empire in just the few short days I'd been back. "Just like I took your cocaine and flushed it down the fucking bog this morning too-"

"You what?!" Danny roared, lunging at me so fast that I almost flinched as he ran straight towards me, his chained hands curled into fists before him.

The chain jerked tight and I slammed my head down on the bridge of his nose in the moment when he was snapped back a step by it, laughing loudly as he was knocked on his arse, cursing me venomously.

I took a step away as he came for me again, snarling like a beast as he tried to get to me and the chain yanked tight.

I grinned wider, taking a little blow torch and the cattle branding iron out of my paper bag. I'd gotten the brand from Bermondsey Market just for him and I took my time heating it up as he yanked against his chains, the metal cutting into his wrists as he yelled challenges at me and I ignored every fucking word. He called my wife a whore a whole hell of a lot though and I had to say that only made me hungrier to dose out this little lesson to him.

I waited until the number two began to glow, waiting until the cherry red colour of it flared in his eyes as he watched, and I could practically see his thirst for my blood in his gaze.

"You shoulda killed me," I warned, rolling my sleeves back one at a time and tossing the blowtorch aside as I adjusted my grip on the brand. "And I think deep down, you know that. Don't ya?"

"Nah," Danny replied, that cocky look on his face which I'd always hated so goddamn much. "I wanted you rotting away in there, knowing I'd beat ya. Knowing which one of us came out on top in the end."

"Well that's your mistake, Danny boy," I said, rolling my shoulders back as I prepared for this fight. "Because you should have accepted a long time ago that you were always destined to be the number two amongst us. You never did have what it took to beat me man to man. Never will. So let this be a lesson and lifelong reminder of that fact."

Danny's eyes lit with the challenge as he backed up a little, gaining some slack on his chain and jerking his chin to encourage me into the circle of his reach.

I stepped closer, walking to the bench and placing the brand down on it, watching the way he tracked the move, knowing he'd be aching to place the mark on me instead. And I wanted that. I wanted him to know he'd had every chance to win this. That he'd been given the opportunity to test his mettle against mine and that the outcome was down to who the better man was and nothing else.

I stepped closer, opening my arms and offering him a free shot, just the way I always had to mouthy little fuckers who had made the mistake of thinking they were good enough to take me on back in the day. And Danny knew as well as I did that no one had ever come out of a fight with me still standing.

Danny ran at me with a feral snarl, swinging a fist at my face which I swerved half a second before his shoulder slammed into my gut and the power of his strike sent the two of us crashing to the floor.

I threw my fist into his side as he reared over me, a wild look in his eyes that spoke of all the petty jealousies he'd stacked up over the years and the bitterness he harboured because of them.

He threw a fist at my face and I let him land the blow, using the opening to strike him with an uppercut that snapped his mouth shut so hard I wouldn't have been surprised if he'd lost a few teeth. The rattling blow stunned him for a fraction of a second but that was all I needed to rear up and roll us over, straddling him beneath me as I hit him again.

Danny bucked and thrashed beneath me, sending vicious blows my way in return as we fought like the pair of black hearted dogs we were and my blood sang to the tune of violence.

I had him at my mercy, the power of my blows greater than his and the venom of my wrath so much more potent an emotion than any jealousy could ever hope to match.

I grinned down at him as I laid into him, spitting insults at him for his cowardly bullshit and all he'd stolen from me as I did so.

But just as I was getting too fucking into the power I held, Danny swung the fist held by the chain at me and somehow managed to loop it around my neck.

I lurched back as he fought to yank it tight, the two of us throwing desperate blows at one another as I tried to force myself off of him and he yanked on the chain like he was hoping the damn thing would decapitate me.

I managed to roll away but he followed, grasping the other side of the chain with his free hand and laughing as he cinched it tight, the weight of his body pressing to my back.

Panic didn't come for me. Nah, I wasn't the type for that. So in the moment of my need, the only thing I felt was an uptick in my pulse and the most ferocious thirst for bloodshed that I could muster.

I threw my elbow back into his gut, slamming it into him over and over with all the strength I had as he cursed and grunted and fought to maintain his grip on me.

But as my elbow slammed into him for the fifth time, his hold slipped and that was all I needed.

I ripped the chain from my throat and bucked him off of me, sending him crashing into the wall with a smack that sounded loudly as his head collided with it.

I was on him within seconds, punching him so hard that he almost blacked out before ripping his top down and grabbing the brand.

I bared my teeth at him as I pushed the number two against his flesh, the scent of burning skin filling the air as he tried to thrash beneath me and I marked him just like he'd marked my fucking wife.

"I was always the top dog, Danny. Your only problem was that you could never just accept it," I spat, the taste of my own blood lining my tongue. "But I think this will help you to remember."

He roared in pain as he fought to buck me off and I shoved to my feet, tossing the brand away where it clattered down onto the unused train tracks and disappeared into the dark.

"You not finishing the job then?" he called as I backed out of his reach once more and stooped to pick up the paper bag I'd brought down here with me. "Not gonna kill me?"

"Not today," I said, tossing the paper bag at his feet where it tore open from the impact, letting one of the bottles of water roll away from him while the loaf of brown bread just looked kind of pathetic, sagging in the middle where it had been squashed a little.

"Enjoy," I said, backing up some more while the insults he hurled at me echoed off the curved walls and bounced right back at him.

I took the stairs two at a time, a grin biting into my cheeks as I didn't even bother to light my way with the phone, enjoying the dark as my brother's furious screams chased me away and loving the fact that they weren't loud enough to reach me by the time I made it to the top of them. It was too fucking good. Too fucking poetic.

I tugged the door wide and locked it up securely behind me, my smile falling as the heaviness of all I'd lost weighed down on me once more. It was all well and good making that bastard's life hell, but it wouldn't return my reputation to me, it wouldn't grant me my position back and it sure as fuck wouldn't do anything to help Olly.

"Are you sure about this, boss?" Olly's voice echoed in my memory from that fucking night and I wished with all I had that I could change the answer I'd given him.

"Of course I am. When have I ever been wrong?"

"Fuck," I breathed, the weight of that lie hanging heavy on my tongue and tasting bitter as I was forced to swallow it all over again. Just like I had night after night since it had happened. Alright, I hadn't known it was a lie then. But it turned out to be the worst one I'd ever told.

I swiped a hand over my face, banishing those demons with a force of will and heading upstairs to try my luck looking for the key one final time. If it came to it, I'd just cut the fucking collar off of her, but the key would seem less obvious if only I could find it.

I headed back into the room which had been my brother's until I'd come to steal his life, my gaze straying to the couch where I'd fucked the girl destined to be his bride, and I chewed the inside of my cheek as I gave myself a few moments to fantasise over those memories.

When I'd gotten out of the nick I'd been suffering from the world's most severe form of blue balls and I'd been fucking aching to sink my cock into his bride no matter what she'd been like, but fuck me, I hadn't been even a bit prepared for the reality of my little Russian bombshell. She was like every filthy fantasy I'd ever had given flesh alongside a wicked tongue and feral spirit which called to my own like it recognised the animal in me just as I did hers.

I couldn't get her outa my damn head. And I couldn't stop cursing my fucking luck at the fact that Danny had managed to get to her before the wedding. I hadn't anticipated that. I'd assumed he'd have waited for the ceremony and she never would have had to get to see the asshole I was being forced to impersonate. But it was irritatingly clear that the brief interaction they'd had had been more than enough to ruin her opinion of me.

I needed to try and fix it. No matter how fucking desperate I was to feel her body beneath mine once more, I needed to get that fucking collar off of her first and fix what Danny had broken between us. But the brand… even thinking about the brand sent a rage through me so powerfully that I had trouble containing myself over it. But I'd figure that out. I'd make her body feel so much good for me that eventually she'd have the memories of that pain replaced by nothing but how much pleasure I could make her feel.

I yanked the curtains wide, letting the pale daylight filter in and frowning at the clouds, wondering if they'd cut us a fucking break and let the sun peek out any time soon.

Danny's room was a boring kind of neat and tidy, but I knew better than that. Fucker had always been one for trophies.

I moved around the room slowly, stomping my foot on the floorboards and knocking my fist against the walls until I heard an echoing thump that signalled a hidden space below my right foot.

I dropped down and dug my fingernails into the edge of the floorboard, popping it out of its position and finding exactly what I'd been hunting for within it.

There were watches and bits of jewellery, a couple of pairs of knickers from girls he'd no doubt fucked in more ways than one and even a little jar with several teeth rattling around in the bottom of it.

My upper lip pulled back as I lifted it out, but a smile dug into my cheeks a moment later as I spotted the small silver key keeping the bloody teeth company.

I scooped it out, ignoring the sick feeling in my gut as I tried to avoid touching the teeth then dropped the jar back into the hiding place.

I made a move to pull my hand back out, but my fingers brushed something soft which was hidden beneath the next floorboard and I tugged it out on instinct, wondering what else he had stashed down here.

A pale green stuffed bunny flopped over in my hand, loose threads of stitching hanging from the places that should have held his button eyes and his little waistcoat missing all of its buttons too.

"Shit, Mr Buttons," I muttered, taking in the childhood toy I'd loved so fucking much when I was knee high to a grasshopper. I ran my thumb over the eyeless face with the ache of the old wound of losing him echoing on in my memory.

"Where's your buttons, mate?" I asked him, realisation sinking in. Danny had taken him from me when we couldn't have been more than four years old. He'd taken him and watched me cry to my ma for weeks over him while our pa told me it was best I learned the meaning of loss early on.

"You always hated that motherfucker when we were kids," I muttered, shaking my head as I stood and kicked the floorboard back into place. "Now look what he's gone and done to ya."

The sad little bunny toy said nothing in reply, and I blew out a breath of irritation for the childhood trauma my arsehole of a twin had caused me before sitting him in the windowsill with a view of the city below. It was a shame he couldn't see it on account of his eyes being gone and him being a stuffed toy and all, but the little kid in me was soothed somewhat by the pointless gesture.

I dropped the little key down beside my phone and headed into the shower to wash the blood and muck from my fight with Danny offa my skin and I closed my eyes as I let the scalding water rush over me. It was a fucking novelty to do so without twenty other fellas all lining up around me and the possibility of taking a shank to the back while trying to get clean.

My phone was buzzing as I strode back out into the room and I scrubbed a towel through my dark hair to dry it as I answered.

"Yeah?"

"Alright, mate?" Church's voice came down the line and I waited for him to go on. "Nothin' to get your knickers in a twist over, but we ran into a bit of a problem on our day trip and I need to get my car valeted."

My lips twisted as I took that in, understanding what he was saying and wondering who he'd had to kill.

"Is my wife alright?" I asked.

"Course she fucking is," Church replied. "She's made of fire and iron that one. Any chance you could come pick us up? We're having tea at the Bakery."

"Yeah. I'll be there in ten." I cut the call and headed across the room to get dressed.

Irritation prickled at me as I pulled open Danny's drawers and I made a mental note to go shopping for some shit of my own as I chose a pair of jeans and a shirt to wear. I didn't like sleeping in his fucking room either, especially knowing mine was right next door.

I'd looked into my old room the night I'd first come back here and of course none of my shit was there anymore. It was just an empty room with a bed in it now, but maybe it didn't have to be. I could play it off as a gift to my new wife. Let her decorate it if she wanted and make it ours so I didn't have to keep on being surrounded by his shit day in, day out.

With that thought in mind, I grabbed the keys to the new car I'd bought to replace the one I'd murdered outside Buckingham Palace, dropped the phone and the key to Anya's collar in my pocket and headed on outa the house to go pick them up.

I strode outa the warehouse, nodding to Frank who was standing outside, casually eyeing the street for any sign of trouble. I wanted to say a whole hell of a lot of things to the man who I still looked on as a brother, but I knew the time for that hadn't come. He'd kill me if he knew I was back. Pure and simple. And I couldn't even blame him, knowing what he believed of me.

"I'll be back in a bit," I called to him. "Can you get some of the boys to stock the fridge while I'm gone? I don't think my wife appreciated the lack of options this morning."

Frank arched a brow at me and I paused, seeing the words he was choking back flaring in his eyes.

"Spit it out," I commanded.

"I just didn't think you gave a fuck if the Russian was comfortable here," he said blandly and I had to force myself to pause, wondering what Danny would have been saying about his bride in the lead up to the nuptials and knowing I couldn't fuck this up by having too many sudden changes of heart. I also knew full well that Frank had more than enough reason to hate Anya's entire family and that he wasn't all too thrilled about being tasked with watching her. No doubt Danny chose him for the job for that fact, knowing she wouldn't gain any comfort being watched by a man who hated her.

"It ain't about comfort," I said dismissively. "It's about her keeping her energy up for when I wanna fuck her all night long. So how about you just do as I ask and don't question me on shit, yeah?"

"Yes, boss," he replied, the dislike in his tone clear, though I doubted Danny had ever caught it.

I hesitated a moment, wanting to say something more, to see some of the man I loved like a brother in him and…

I blew out a harsh breath, tipped him a salute then turned and strode away. It didn't matter how I felt about Frank or the current state of our relationship. All the time he believed the lies about me and what had happened to his brother, he was never gonna see me as anything other than his enemy. I was actually surprised that he'd stuck it out with Danny all these years, but I guessed for men like us it was never really a choice anyway. This was the life we were born into and the one we'd die in when the grim reaper decided our sins had stacked up enough.

It was best I avoided him anyway. There were only a few people who knew both me and Danny well enough to be able to spot the differences between us easily, but Frank was one of them and I couldn't risk him figuring it out until I'd managed to expose the truth. He'd kill me if he learned of this lie and I couldn't even blame him for that, knowing what he believed of me.

I strode over to the gold Jag and dropped onto the leather seat, taking a smoke from the glovebox and lighting up as I started the engine. I dropped the window and took off into the London traffic with my arm hanging out of it, tapping the ash from my cigarette onto the street.

I headed out of Whitechapel, weaving through traffic towards Upper Thames Street and driving along the river as the sun began to breach the clouds overhead and light up the bustling crowds as they hurried to wherever the fuck they were going.

My gaze roamed over Tower Bridge as I passed it, the blue pillars seeming to wink at me in a welcome home as I smiled at them, eternally standing there while the world rushed by all around them.

Traffic was an utter bitch as usual and I took to the bus lanes as I passed through Blackfriars, the deep grey water of the river a constant companion to my left as I followed the curve of the water, flipping off a cab driver as he blasted his horn at me for being in the wrong lane.

I followed the river, my gaze skimming over the London Eye as it slowly turned high above the water, full of tourists who snapped photos and pointed out Big Ben from their high vantage point.

I swept past the Houses of Parliament, almost flattening some arsehole with a camera as he stepped into the road to take a photo and I cursed him out for his stupidity before flicking my cigarette at him and speeding away, heading back towards the river. I followed it all the way around to the west side of the city, turning into the fancy streets of Chelsea where the richest arseholes in London lived.

The streets were quieter here, though not by much as cyclists raced past the rows of tall white houses. They had little pillars outside their doors and fancy black iron railings to keep the riffraff at bay.

There was a general air of superiority in this place, from the upturned noses of the joggers whose designer trainers were beating the pavement, to the freshly groomed dogs with their walkers who probably lived on nothing but premium bottled water cried from the eyes of new born babies and sirloin beef cut from a cow which took its own life for the pure privilege of ending up on their plate.

I followed the route I knew like the back of my hand until I made it to Dylan's house, turning off the road and pulling up on his drive while I waited for the door to the underground garage to roll open for me.

I headed down the ramp the moment it did, spotting Church's Mini Cooper in the far corner, the boot open and two of Dylan's boys scrubbing it of all DNA evidence, making sure no one would be able to tell there had ever been a body in there.

I parked up and headed to the door which led into the house, snorting at the classical music which was playing softly through the speakers as I strode down a hallway with a marble floor and paintings on the walls which likely cost more than the car I'd driven here. Not that the Bakers had actually paid for them. But they sure did like to take payment in the form of shit like that, especially when doing side jobs for bankers or politicians who'd fucked up.

I followed the sounds of voices into a wide living room, the cream sofa curving around one side of it where Anya sat beside Church, nibbling on a tiny cucumber sandwich.

Dylan was opposite them in a huge grey chair, a pair of midnight blue harem pants tucked into some expensive as fuck looking stiletto boots while he drank from a tiny teacup decorated with red roses, his pinky extended like he was as royal as the Duchess of Canterbury herself.

"Alright, Butch," Church greeted me as I strode in and I replied in turn, my gaze falling on my wife who seemed to be more interested in the tower of tiny cakes and sandwiches sitting in the centre of the coffee table than she did in looking at me.

All I could do was look at her though. She wore ripped jeans, a cropped band t-shirt and some biker boots that looked fit for stomping heads. I liked that look a fuck lot more than even the wedding dress. This was the real her, the clothes her choice, a glimpse of what she liked, who she chose to be when she was holding the reins of her own fate. And I wanted to know this version of her more than I'd wanted to know any girl in my life.

She had that give-no-fucks look on her face again which had made me so hard for her right in a house of God, speaking my vows like a virtuous man, when all I'd been thinking were ungodly thoughts about this woman. This fucking beautiful, mouthy wife of mine. *All mine.*

"Where's the body?" I asked curiously and Dylan pointed behind me.

"Just taking a dip, honey. He'll be all done before you know it."

I arched a brow, taking a step towards the open door and finding a huge white bathroom, the clawfoot tub in the centre of it hissing and bubbling a little as the acid it contained took care of the problem.

"Nice work," I commented as I returned to the living room and Dylan gave me a bright smile.

"What has you in such a good mood?" he asked me curiously and I shrugged.

"You know me, murder and mayhem always get my blood pumping."

"Sandwich?" Dylan offered but I shook my head, not sitting down.

"Anya," I said, forcing her gaze to rise to mine and finding an endless sea of insolence there which only served to make me want her attention even more. "Are you alright?"

She blinked, seemingly taken aback by my concern but she covered it quickly.

"I've dealt with bigger, uglier bastards than him before and come out swinging," she replied, her American accent hugging the words and letting them drip from her tongue.

"I want to be certain of that," I said, not sure exactly where I was going with this, only knowing that the longer I looked at her the more I wanted her to myself.

She looked damn good and I couldn't get over it. Clearly their shopping trip had gone well before the untimely death of the fucker in the bathtub, and there was something about her dressed to kill like she didn't give a single fuck in all the world which just made me hungry for her.

"Isn't my word good enough for you?" she demanded irritably but that only made me wanna bite back.

"No. I think you're a rotten little liar, so I wanna check you out myself. Come on." I jerked my chin in a clear command and Church arched a brow at me like he was wondering what the fuck I was doing.

In all honesty, I hadn't decided that yet. All I knew was that I wanted her alone for a few minutes so that I could decide.

“There’s no need for that, honey,” Dylan said, trying to turn me from this path and I didn’t fail to notice the way my wife had gained herself these allies so quickly. “I gave her the once over when she arrived. Nothing but a little bump to the head and-”

“What happened to *you?*” Anya interrupted, her narrowed gaze dropping to the bruise I had blossoming on my jaw thanks to my dear old brother.

“I got in a fight,” I said with a shrug. “Don’t worry though, love - I won.”

“I wasn’t worried,” she replied simply. “Only disappointed you didn’t lose.”

Church released a low whistle and Dylan tried to hiss some kind of warning at her to be quiet, but I just barked a laugh.

“Let’s see how hard you hate me when we’re all alone,” I replied, striding towards her with the full intention of dragging her away if I had to, but she rose suddenly before I could make it to her.

“I can walk,” she said coolly, placing her plate on the table and brushing past me as she headed from the room.

Church gave me a questioning look, but I just shrugged.

“I can’t help myself, mate,” I replied innocently. “That woman does things to me.”

Dylan looked half tempted to say something more, but a flat look from me shut him up pronto and I strode from the room in pursuit of my bride.

“Where do you want to go?” she asked, barely sparing a glance over her shoulder at me.

“Upstairs, let’s have some privacy,” I suggested, my attention sticking to her arse in those jeans as she began to climb the stairs with some snarky comment about her not being able to think of anything worse tumbling from her lips.

“Pick a door,” I encouraged as we reached the top of the stairs and she crossed the pale landing to push open one of the white doors.

Anya hesitated as she found a small toilet there, her lips pursing at the mistake.

“Wanna pick again?” I offered but she shook her head.

“Here seems fine to me,” she replied, stepping inside defiantly, refusing to admit to the mistake. “What better place for your crap than in a bathroom?”

“There ain’t no bath in here, bombshell. So you can call this a toilet, a bog, a loo or a shitter, but a bathroom, it is not,” I pointed out as I stepped inside right behind her, making her gasp as we were forced together in the small space and I clicked the door shut after us.

Anya flicked the lights on and we found ourselves chest to chest between the navy tiles which lined the walls of the small room, nothing but a sink and toilet to keep us company in the couple of feet that divided us.

She raised her chin in challenge, waiting to see what I’d do next and I stepped forward, devouring the space between us as I reached out to run my fingers into her platinum hair, feeling the small rise of a bump there as she sucked in a breath laced with pain.

My eyes met hers as I brushed my fingers over the hurt in a gentle circle aimed to soothe it and for a moment neither of us spoke or moved or did a fucking thing but just be.

At least we did until her arm snapped out and a glint of silver sped towards my side, angled up like she was hoping to hit my blackened heart.

I snatched her wrist with reflexes born of my time in lock up, my fingers finding a pressure point which forced her to drop her hold on the blunt butter knife she'd been aiming to stab me with.

"Seriously?" I asked as I caught the thing and spun it in my fingers, before pressing it to her throat and pinning her against the wall.

"What did you expect?" she replied, her lip curling.

"A better death than this, that's for sure. That woulda been fucking embarrassing. Can you pick something a little deadlier to strike at me with next time?" I teased and her eyes flared with anger which only made my amusement grow.

"You shouldn't laugh, Danny," she said icily. "Because the moment I do get my hands on something deadlier, the first you'll know about it is when you feel yourself bleeding out and find me standing over you."

"Don't call me that," I muttered, not liking the sound of his name on her lips for me. I probably shoulda been more bothered about the death threat, but it was that name which had me out of sorts. "Call me something else. Something real. Butch if you really want to use my name, but I'll take prick, arsehole, cunt. Whatever the fuck you like so long as it holds the truth in it, but not that fucking name."

I took the butter knife from her throat and tossed it aside, releasing her as I stepped back and waited to see what she'd do next.

"That's it?" she asked, her body tense like she was expecting a strike. "I try to kill you and you just make a fucking joke then forget about it?"

"I'm in a generous mood," I shrugged. "Must be because of how hard you made me come for you when we fucked. I guess I've gone soft."

Her eyes narrowed though they heated too and I knew she was thinking about us consummating our wedding last night and how good it had been, even if the rest of it had been something of a shit show.

Anya's lips parted on an inhale which I was certain would return with an insult, but her barbed tongue didn't lash me when she finally spoke again.

"You're not Danny Butcher, are you?"

My heart stilled as her ebony eyes roamed over my face and for a moment I thought the gig was up, she'd figured it out somehow, impossibly seeing what no other fucker had managed since the moment I'd returned here, but as she went on I realised that wasn't it.

"Not when you're out of sight like this. Not when there's no act to put on, no show to perform. When there isn't anyone watching, you're not him."

"So who am I then?" I asked, wondering if she held that answer because I sure as fuck didn't.

"I haven't figured that out yet," she replied, reaching out to trail a finger over the bruise on my jaw, pressing down hard enough to make it sting, the shot of pain racing all the way through me and making my cock jerk as her eyes lit with the thrill of hurting me.

She ran her hand lower and I watched her as she dropped it to the collar of my t-shirt, tugging it aside to reveal the tattoo of a skull shrouded in smoke which I had inked on my skin, crawling up to coat my throat. I exhaled slowly as she traced it with a fingertip. Fuck, I loved the feeling of her skin against mine. There was something so damn heated about her, something so fucking wild, and yet it was like she had never been free before either. Like she was as used to a cage as I was and hadn't yet worked out how to be set loose from it.

"But I will," she added.

"Good." I caught her cheek in my grasp and claimed a kiss from her lips which I knew she hadn't been offering, tasting the fire of her as she kissed me back for one endless moment before jerking away and punching me clean in the jaw, making pain radiate through the existing bruise even more sharply.

I lurched back as the hurt spiked through my mouth, blood spilling onto my tongue and my heart leaping with the thrill of that attack.

"Fuck me, who taught you how to punch like that?" I asked, advancing on her as she backed up a step, going on the defensive like she expected to have incurred my wrath with that move. But I wasn't feeling vengeful, I was feeling all kinds of turned on. And she had nowhere to run in here with me.

"My brothers," she hissed, reminding me of exactly where she came from. "And they taught me a whole lot more than that too."

"Really?" I asked, my pulse hammering harder as I closed the distance between us and I set my gaze on her lips once more. I knew the three men she'd grown up with were demons of a very specific kind. In fact, Frank knew that best of all, having spent an extended period in the company of Nikolay a few years back, though I doubted she knew about that. I wondered if she'd studied the art of splitting skin and stealing secrets from reluctant lips like he did, the idea all kinds of alluring. I reached out to lock the door beside us and she flinched just a little at the sound of it turning. "I'd like to see that."

"Give me a proper knife and I'll give you a real show," she snarled, but her chest was heaving and her nipples were pressing through her shirt, dragging my gaze to them as she tried to front out the lust in her eyes.

"You wanna make me bleed, bombshell?" I asked, licking my lip slowly where she'd already done that and tasting the evidence of her power.

She tracked the movement hungrily and nodded.

"I want to make you bleed," she agreed.

I leaned in and kissed her again, harder this time, letting her taste the blood she claimed to be so hungry for and she snarled as she sank her teeth into my bottom lip, drawing more and forcing me to break away.

"You want me to stop?" I asked, placing a hand on the tiled wall either side of her head, boxing her in and watching her as I waited to see what she'd do next.

Her eyes flared but she didn't say the words.

"I've done a lot of bad things in my life, bombshell," I said, inching closer to her, eyeing my blood where it stained her lips red. "A whole host of bad which I haven't suffered for nearly enough."

"I can tell," she growled, her gaze tracking over me as I closed the distance until it hardly existed at all.

"So maybe I deserve a little punishment," I added and her gaze snapped back up to mine as she frowned at that statement, clearly not understanding what I was offering. "Hit me if it makes you feel something," I offered, tilting my head as I watched her reaction. "I won't stop you. I won't hit you back."

"Why?" she demanded on a breath.

"Maybe I want to feel something too."

She took a moment to process that, but I could see the light in her dark eyes at that offer.

Anya reared her hand back and swung it at me, her palm flat as she aimed to slap me, but I caught her wrist at the last second, stopping her and leaning so close that I could taste her lips as I spoke again.

"Like you mean it, or not at all," I demanded, and a snarl of rage escaped her before her other hand locked around my throat, her lips peeling back in fury as she dug her nails into my flesh and squeezed so hard my oxygen was cut off.

She shoved me back and I hit the wall beside the sink, but I didn't release my hold on her, yanking her with me and leaning into the bite of her grip as I pressed my mouth to hers once more and my pulse jackhammered with the thrill of her fingernails cutting into my flesh.

She squeezed even harder, a snarl escaping her, but she didn't break the kiss, her lips parting and tongue pushing into my mouth as I released my hold on her wrist and dropped my hand to her fly, unbuttoning her jeans.

Anya gasped at my boldness, but she didn't draw back, just kissed me harder and rocked her hips as I pushed my hand inside her knickers.

Black and white sparks began to float on the edges of my vision as she continued to choke me but as I sank my fingers into the soaking heat of her pussy, her grip slackened and a breathy moan passed between our lips.

A dark laugh escaped me as I sucked in a breath and she slapped me hard enough to make my head wheel aside while parting her thighs to give me more access.

"More," she demanded, fisting my hair and yanking hard enough to send pain through my scalp.

I groaned at the relief of it, basking in the pain as I dragged my fingers back out of her and used the wetness on them to start work on her throbbing clit.

"Give me more too," I growled and her gaze met mine before dropping to my crotch for a moment where my cock was straining against my jeans, but that wasn't what I was asking for. Not right now. And she knew it.

Anya licked those sinful lips, considering me for several achingly long seconds before her grip on my hair tightened and she yanked so hard that my head was forced back.

I swore as she moved her mouth to my neck, kissing me softly and making me shiver at the attention before biting me hard enough to break the fucking skin.

"Fuck," I gasped, moving my fingers faster, rolling her clit between them and then sinking them deep inside her as I ground the heel of my palm against it instead.

Her thighs clamped tight around my hand and she yanked my head down again, kissing me hard as I moved forward, driving her against the wall and fucking her with my hand, loving how tight she was, how wet, how fucking perfect.

Her grip on my throat increased once more, cutting off my oxygen and making me groan in pleasure. My cock throbbed with need and I felt her building and building beneath me, ready to cave in to my desire.

Blackness danced around my vision and my lungs burned with the need to draw breath, but she didn't let go, her hips rocking more urgently against my hand and the demand of her mouth against mine clear.

She was panting and moaning as she warred with me, taking from me in every way she could, and I relished in repenting like this for her. For the sins of my brother, for the collar wrapped around her throat and the Butcher name marked permanently onto her skin. I was more than happy to be the sacrifice on her altar. She could have pleasure and blood from me in equal amounts, and I was pretty sure I'd die happy so long as she was gratified.

If I wanted her to release me then I was going to have to release her first. And as my head began to spin and my limbs started to feel leaden with the need to draw a breath, I focused on that. On what I had to do to gain it. Because I wasn't going to draw back. I was going to fucking finish this on her terms.

Her hand caressed my cock and I damn near came in my pants from the contact, her fingers gripping me through the fabric of my jeans and giving me just enough friction to send my entire body haywire.

The burning in my chest intensified and I could hear oblivion calling my name, so I thrust my fingers into her harder, demanding her body to bow to mine, willing it to be so.

She cried out so fucking beautifully as she fell apart for me, breaking our kiss and dropping her head back against the wall as the strength went out of her limbs and she finally released her hold on my throat.

Her pussy gripped my fingers tightly and I pumped them a few more times as I watched her come for me, making sure she got every last drop of pleasure from me while the rush of her choking me out made my head spin.

I withdrew my hand and stumbled back to lean against my own wall, panting as I fought to catch my breath and blinking the darkness away from my vision as I looked at the stunning creature before me, watching her in her post orgasmic bliss as a smile played around those sinful lips.

“I fucking hate you,” she panted as she buttoned her fly once more and a laugh spilled from me.

“I like the taste of your hatred, bombshell,” I replied, fisting my solid cock through my jeans in an attempt to relieve a little of the pressure in it.

Her gaze tracked the movement and I could have sworn she looked tempted for a moment before she sidestepped, unlocked the door and yanked it open, taking what she’d wanted from me and leaving me aching in her wake.

Another breath of laughter spilled from my lips as I dropped my fly and tugged my cock out, closing my eyes and thinking of her brutal kisses the moment she was gone. With a few firm strokes I was coming for her in the sink with one hand pressed to the wall, her name on my lips alongside the taste of her as I groaned with the desire to do that all over again. And again and again and again.

I didn’t know much about my new bride, but one thing was for certain, she really was a bombshell and when the two of us collided, the passion between us was fucking explosive.

“Wait,” I called as I twisted the tap on to wash away my cum, putting my cock away and jogging out after her.

I caught up to her just before she made it into the room where Church and Dylan waited for us. No doubt they’d heard her coming for me and knew exactly what we’d been doing, but I doubted either of them would comment on it.

Anya turned, an icy glare falling on me but I ignored it as I moved up behind her, taking the key to her collar from my pocket and brushing her hair aside so I could unlock it.

She fell utterly still before me as the lock clicked and I tugged the ugly thing off of her to the sound of her releasing a heavy breath of relief.

“I was a cunt before,” I murmured in her ear as she just stood there for a moment, her hand on her throat as I teased my fingers along the back of her neck, feeling the goosebumps that prickled over her skin at my touch and wondering how long she would make me wait before she gave into this passion between us again. “I can’t promise I won’t be one again. But I’m throwing the fucking collar away at least.”

“I guess you want a thank you?” she asked, no inflection to her words and I swear I could see her building walls to keep me out.

“Nah, bombshell. I’m just telling you how it is.”

She gave me a once over then strode away from me without another word, leaving me with absolutely nothing to go on. But damn, I liked watching her go.

CHAPTER ELEVEN

The surreal first few days of my unchosen life slid away into weeks, and I fell into a routine with my husband and his men while I tried to figure out what to do. The more I thought on it, the more killing Danny was becoming less of a viable option. He was surrounded by too much muscle all of the time and Frank's ever watchful eyes seemed to follow me whenever I moved.

I'd even considered calling my brothers, telling them that Danny Butcher had branded his name on my ass to see what they might do about that, tempting their psychotic little tendencies into action. They might just break the treaty if they knew he'd hurt me, but I was done relying on them. I was going to handle this myself, prove I was capable of surviving without the help of my big brothers.

A few days after the wedding, Danny had told me they'd left him a message, begging me to get in touch with them to prove I was alright, so I'd taken his phone, snapped a photo of me with my middle finger up and sent it back to Zakhar. I was pissed at them. Royally fucking pissed, and I could hold a grudge longer than The Grinch, so they'd better be prepared for my wrath if I ever saw them again. The thought of *not* seeing them again suddenly made me flinch inside, my heart hurting over the possibility. I was mad, fucking furious, but dammit I'd always love them.

I'd come up with a new plan to secure my freedom, scrapping the murder plot and sticking more firmly to the idea of making a run for it. I'd started pickpocketing all of Danny's boys, taking the odd twenty or fifty pound note here and there and hiding it in the pocket of a pair of jeans I had folded in the closet. I needed enough to get out of the country, but I'd need someone to get me a fake passport if I was ever going to make it back to the US. I didn't have the contacts for that shit, but maybe if I had enough cash, I could find them. I'd just have to buy myself a few days once I made my move, so I'd leave a trail that sent my husband and his pack dogs chasing after me to a town called Bristol. I'd steal a notepad, scribble my fake plan on it then 'accidentally' leave it somewhere they'd find it.

In the meantime, I was enjoying the perks of being the wife to a guy who seemed determined to make me come as hard and as often as he could without sticking his dick inside me. And not only that, he encouraged me to hurt him too. To bite and claw at him while he used his hands to blow my mind in his bed or went down on me in the shower.

He sprang his attacks so randomly, that I was always caught off guard, days and days slipping by between one touch to the next until I was practically panting for him.

It was a mindfuck I was trying not to think about too much, because since I'd married Danny, I hadn't once seen the side to him that I'd witnessed the morning of our wedding. And sometimes it was too easy to forget that that man lived inside him when he looked at me with all the want and need of a starved creature, and I found I was starved too.

I'd lived so much of my life checking out, slipping away into the numb bliss of my music that I hadn't felt truly seen in a very long time. But Danny Butcher saw me. Our eyes were constantly locking whenever we were in a room together and all it took was one mischievous smirk from him to get my stomach fluttering and my heart pounding.

I was playing a dangerous game, because I was allowing this to continue, letting myself crave him, letting myself enjoy the burn of his body at my back at night even when he didn't lay a hand on me. The desire was driving me to madness, because his sporadic finger fucks were not enough to keep me sated, and from the raging hard ons he sported whenever he was done wrecking me, I knew it wasn't enough for him either. So why didn't he take more from me?

I never asked him. I wouldn't give him the satisfaction of knowing I wanted more. Because I did. And I was ashamed of that. Danny Butcher was a monster; I'd heard of the terrible things he'd done, but now I was starting to wonder if he was hiding his dark side from me, the monster in him only unleashed when he was elsewhere. But he'd shown me it before, so why change that? Maybe he just flipped occasionally and I'd caught him on a bad day the first time we'd met, but that shit with the brand had been calculated. It didn't seem like the whims of a madman, it was too…callous, too thought out. It just didn't make any sense.

I didn't know anything about the jobs Danny went off on with Church or where he spent his days when he left the house dressed in a suit worth more than most cars. Sometimes the two of them came home flecked in blood with dark looks in their eyes that told me all I needed to know about what they'd been up to. It didn't scare me. My brothers had come home like that countless times, and I knew it was necessary in their line of work.

That was the way of sinners…they sinned. But there were always lines drawn with my family, I knew how far they'd go. These Brits were animals, and I didn't know their limits.

They wore these carefree masks dressed in wild abandon. I swear they just seemed to spend their days doing whatever the fuck they wanted, unfettered and without rules or laws to chain them. But every now and then the dark in them slipped through the cracks of those masks and I saw it. Saw the creatures they could become at the drop of a hat, the nefarious, lawless beasts who feasted on blood and pain and relished every second of it.

I'd seen it in Church when he'd killed that man who attacked me, watched his carefree visage shatter and the monster within emerge. And as disconcerting as that was, it was exciting too, liberating, intoxicating. These men held themselves to no standard but their own and I found myself hungering for a taste of that kind of ownership of my own desires.

They saw something they wanted and they took it. And they let me have a taste of that too. They let me wear what I wanted and do what I liked within the parameters they'd set for me and of course under the watchful eye of the three of them. But I wanted more. I wanted their freedom and I planned on taking it with me when I left this place.

Maybe I was just a dumbass trying to fool myself into thinking they really weren't all that bad. Perhaps it was just my pussy talking, trying to convince me to just enjoy the perks of being Danny Butcher's wife, but it really did feel like there was something more here sometimes, a potential waiting to be realised.

It hadn't been so awful so far after all if I analysed it. I was imprisoned but I wasn't harmed. And suffering the punishment of Danny's wicked tongue and fingers was certainly no hardship. But I couldn't let myself fall into the trap of accepting this as my lot in life now.

No, I had to keep my head. Had to keep gathering money and work harder at shutting them out. That was the bigger issue. The others. Specifically, Church and Frank. When I wasn't shamelessly daydreaming about my husband's cock, I was fixated on Church's rogue mouth and Frank's hardened glare. Between the three of them, I was living in a fantasy land of hot assholes who made me ache inside. Maybe I was developing Stockholm syndrome, or maybe I'd just led a really sheltered life up until this point and hadn't realised there were men like them out there in the big wide world. But that was just it, I didn't get the feeling there were any other men like the three of them.

I lay on the grey couch downstairs in the warehouse with my headphones on and my eyes shut, my head bobbing to the music a little as I listened to Behind Blue Eyes by The Who, trying not to think of my own blue eyed man and the way Frank's stare set me alight every time I felt the weight of it on me.

I wore a denim skirt with a white Jimi Hendrix t-shirt and some knee-high black socks because the air seemed to be permanently cool in this place and was only getting more so the further into September we moved. Church's Indian summer was nowhere to be seen, though he still claimed it was on the way.

My iPod was clasped tight in my hand, my thoughts scattering and reforming around the rhythm of the music, my heart thumping in time with it until I swear I was a living embodiment of the song.

A hand smacked against my head, knocking my headphones off and my eyes snapped open, my fist flying out and slamming into the crotch of the guy beside me. The stranger's junk was crushed beneath my knuckles and I realised it was Sikes as he stumbled back, cupping it with a cry of pain.

"You fucking bitch," he gritted out between his gold capped teeth, his hand shooting out in the next minute, shoving my head forward hard before he ripped the headphones fully off of my neck.

"Hey!" I snarled, leaping up after him as he strode to the kitchen and tossed my headphones in the sink.

He reached for the tap to douse them and I sprinted at him, shrieking in rage as I dove onto his back and sank my teeth savagely into his neck. *Not my headphones, you cocksucker!*

"Argh!" he wailed, trying to get me off of him as he reached back and pulled at my arms.

I sank my teeth deeper, tasting blood and he yelled like a wounded animal, wheeling around and slamming me back against the wall to try and stop me. Bruises blossomed up my spine and I locked my ankles tight around his waist, my knees pressing into his ribs as I bit deeper.

Suddenly someone was upon us and my teeth were yanked free of Sikes's neck as they fisted their hand in my hair.

I was pulled off of Sikes kicking and flailing as I battled to get free, needing my headphones in my hands, my music back in my ears.

Frank's large hand came around my throat, twisting my chin so I looked at him and my breath caught as I found a cold, furious look on his devastatingly handsome face.

"Stop," he commanded in a fierce growl and I managed to rein it in, knowing this asshole was more likely to stomp on my headphones than let me go and get them.

"She's an animal," Sikes cursed, gripping his bloody neck as he stared at me. "Hold her still. Lemme teach her a lesson."

"She's the boss's wife," Frank snarled, all of that anger in him making his muscles flex with tension as he kept hold of me. "You touch her and I'll gut you."

Sikes spat a laugh. "Like he cares what we do with her. And he's not here, so he'd hardly give a damn if we keep his girl nice and warm for him." He took a slow breath, his eyes dragging down to my skirt which had ridden up several inches over my thighs. He licked his lips, looking like a slimy eel as he did it and stepping closer. "You'll be a good girl and say sorry to me nicely, won't you angel?"

“Get fucked,” I snapped, fighting against Frank’s hold again but he wouldn’t let me go. And as I twisted my head to look at him once more, fear dashed against my heart as I wondered if he was considering what Sikes had said, his eyes pinned firmly on the asshole in front of me.

Up until this very second, I’d felt safe in Frank’s company. I mean, he definitely seemed to hate me and my entire family, but I was sure he’d die before he did anything against the boss’s orders. But what if I’d been wrong about that? Or what if Danny really didn’t care what his men did to me?

He hadn’t come home last night, not even in the early hours like he usually did if he wasn’t there when I went to bed. I’d woken with Frank still watching me, no sign of my husband anywhere and no explanation for his absence. Had he grown bored of me? Maybe he’d expected me to beg for his cock all those times he’d teased me and played my body with that ungodly skill of his. But maybe I hadn’t measured up to the little fantasy in his head of what he’d wanted, so now he’d given his men the green light to do what they liked with me.

“If you don’t turn around and walk straight out the front door in the next five seconds, Sikes, I’m going to take a pair of pliers and rip the gold outa your face bit by bit to make myself a nice necklace,” Frank warned in a rumbling tone which I swear made the air crackle all around me as relief washed through my chest.

“Oh come on, mate, don’t be like that. I’m only messin’ about.” Sikes backed up, looking to me as his face paled. “Wasn’t I, angel? You and me were just playin’, weren’t we?”

I didn’t answer, still straining against Frank’s arms but he was as immovable as a mountain.

“Five,” Frank started counting. “Four…three.” He took a step towards Sikes and he arched his brows, a flicker of fear in his eyes before he sprinted away towards the door.

“See ya, mate,” he called, stepping outside then throwing the door shut behind him, looking as white as a sheet and making me wonder what the hell Frank was capable of to have instilled that much fear with little more than a look.

My pulse was pounding to a rampant beat and Frank’s fingers were pressed against it where they were still wrapped around my throat, feeling every erratic thump against his skin.

He had me alone now. Church and Danny had been out all day and I had no idea what time they planned on coming back. Frank was a huge guy and I didn’t like the idea of my chances against him if he decided he wanted to hurt me. I’d fight like a tigress if he did though.

He placed me down, releasing me and I took a wary step back, twisting around to face him, unsure what he was thinking.

“Don’t look at me like that,” he said, but I couldn’t work out if it was a warning or a plea.

My eyes darted towards the cutlery drawer and I wondered how fast I could get to a knife.

Frank turned and walked straight for the sink, fishing my headphones out of it and tossing them to me. I caught them out of the air in surprise, my fingers locking around them possessively. I'd left my iPod on the couch and I took a step that way, wanting it in my hand, but Frank was quicker, walking across the open space and picking it up, eyeing the song playing on the screen.

Whenever Danny was out until dawn, Frank was left to watch me, and we'd fallen into this silent routine where he took my iPod and played songs for me while I slept just like he had the first night I'd been here.

It was forming this unspoken sort of bond between us that was forged wholly in music, and sometimes I was sure he was trying to communicate to me through the songs he picked.

He played me Heroes Dress in Black by Blues Saraceno, connecting my iPod to the Bluetooth speakers and his mouth lifted at the corner.

I breathed a laugh, my shoulders dropping. "You think you're a hero?"

"It's just a song." He shrugged, but he was a damn liar.

He moved to sit on a chair opposite the couch as the twang of the song fell over me and the music poured out to fill the whole warehouse, making my pulse vibrate to the tune.

"I can handle Sikes," I told him. "I don't need saving."

He was man-spreading in the chair, his legs wide, a look on his face that said his balls were as big as watermelons and really did need all that room between his thighs. "I know that, Cash. The blood on your lips proves exactly what you are."

"And what's that?" I asked, indulging him as my hips swayed a little to the music, my body infected by it now that it was surrounding me like this. It was chasing away the shadows in this place and even the bite of the cold.

"A predator," he said roughly and I tasted my lips, sucking the blood off of them as that word seemed to dive beneath my flesh and make a home there. I liked the sound of that, but I wasn't sure it was accurate.

"Predators are at the top of the food chain, in control of their destinies. I'm just a canary in a cage." I rocked my hips in time to the beat, tilting my head back and getting lost to the music as it filled me up and brought my senses alive.

"Canaries don't need chains," he pointed out.

"I don't see any chains." I raised my hands, twisting my wrists to prove there was nothing holding me down. When Frank didn't answer, I let my eyes fall closed and just danced, almost forgetting he was there as the music tangled with my soul until it was a part of me as deeply as I was a part of it.

Frank's hands were suddenly on my hips and his gruff voice fell over me like a cresting wave. "I'm your chains, Cash. Danny might own you, but I'm the one thing stopping you from escaping. I'm the metal links locking you to this place, to your fate. And I'm never letting you go."

My breathing hitched and I kept my eyes closed as I instinctively moved towards the heat of him, finding him so close behind me that my ass pressed to his crotch and the swelling bulge within it.

My throat thickened and I continued to dance, swaying and rocking as he remained entirely still and my body seemed to take over. His hands remained on my hips, unmoving but his grip was iron tight like he was on the verge of forcing my hips to stop rolling, but he couldn't find it in himself to do it.

"Who says I want to leave?" I questioned huskily, needing to throw him off the scent of my plan, but those words had a ring of truth to them for a second that threw me for a loop.

Why would I want to stay in a house of monsters?

"You think I'm such a fucking fool," he ground out and I responded by rubbing my ass against the huge swell of his cock.

He grunted, his fingers digging into my hips before riding up beneath my shirt, skimming the skin just above the waistband of my skirt. I nearly gasped at the heat of the contact, a buzz of energy driving under my skin from that forbidden touch. I was the wife of his boss, I was the girl he'd been commanded to watch, but what if Sikes had been right, what if Danny didn't care what his men did with me? What if I was just some plaything to them now and this was all a game to see who could make use of me first? The possibility of that made bile rise in my throat, but another tide of the music stole away my hesitation. I wasn't going to fuck Frank anyway. I wasn't that stupid, so what was the harm in dancing?

I pressed firmer back against him. "Yes, I think you're a fucking fool, but I think I'm a fool too," I admitted and his fingers skimmed higher, his large hand carving up the centre of my stomach as the heat of his breath fell against my neck.

My nipples were tightening as he started to sway behind me, his chin resting to my temple and suddenly we were moving in the most seductive way I'd ever known. His fingers circled and tormented my flesh without ever straying to my tits as the music swallowed us whole and I slipped into my fantasy land with someone else for the first time in my life.

Something told me Frank needed this escape as much as I did, the burdens that weighed on him lifting for a moment as we simply became one with the rhythm.

It didn't feel like a game anymore as his fingers roamed higher under my shirt and a moan fluttered past my lips, his hands grazing the swell of my braless tits as I arched into him, drowning in the desire and want pounding through my veins.

I couldn't think straight, couldn't remember where we were or why this was wrong as his hands explored me and his thumb caressed the curve of my breast without crossing the line we couldn't come back from.

It was like the music had taken us captive and swept us away from who we were and what roles we were supposed to play. There was no one here but him and me, and in this moment we were free.

My heart rate was wild and rampant and as one song drifted into another and another, I took comfort in the fact that this was likely the least of my sins. I'd bought my ticket to hell a long time ago, and no doubt Frank would be riding the express train there with me too. So why not commit a few more devious acts before the Devil came to collect his debt?

I inhaled deeply and his thumb pushed between my tits, carving a line there that set a fire burning in my blood.

I didn't know what I wanted from him in that moment, or why I was letting him touch me like this, but between the music and his caresses, I was drowning in ecstasy.

"Is this how you treat all your enemies? Or are you just so into me that you can't help yourself?" I taunted and a huff fell from his chest, his hand dropping a little to press against my stomach.

"Don't kid yourself, Cash," he growled, but he didn't take his hands off of me.

I glanced back at him over my shoulder to meet his blue gaze, and all aggression between us fell away. I couldn't breathe as his mouth nearly touched mine, a hum of energy in the air begging us to close that tiny space parting our lips.

But instead of the kiss I expected, his words brushed against my mouth instead. "Danny doesn't give a fuck about you," he said and my heart twisted, taken off guard.

"You think I care about what my husband thinks of me?" I hissed, but some sad little part of me did. Because I was getting hooked on Danny's smiles and the way he touched me, the way he let me hurt him and seemed to relish every strike. But there wasn't a person in this world I'd admit that to.

"Yeah, I do," Frank said coldly. "I think you're gonna fall for his pretty face and paint yourself a lie that he ain't a bad man."

"You're right," I said lightly, though bitterness laced my insides. "I'm just a silly little Russian princess with nothing but rainbows and unicorns inside her tiny mind. I think the red stuff staining Danny Butcher's clothes is strawberry juice because he spends hour after hour picking strawberries on his strawberry farm in the grassy hills of Canterbury."

"Stop it," Frank commanded, his fingers digging into my stomach.

I swung around, taking control of this situation as the music faded into the background and reality became all too sharp. I glared up at Danny's bodyguard with all his muscle and stern harshness, seeing something lurking in the depths of his eyes. It was bleak, a wound bleeding right in front of me, but it was only for a second before he shut it away entirely.

"What do you care if I fall for him?" I demanded, sensing there was more to this than he was letting on.

"You don't know what them Butchers are capable of, that's all," he said darkly.

"So you're trying to protect me?" I scoffed.

"No," he said, his jaw tight, an iciness to his voice which said even the suggestion of that offended him for some reason I couldn't fathom.

"Then what?" I pushed, but he tried to turn away from me and I caught his arm, yanking him back to look at me, my fingers digging into his dark skin. "You stand in the shadows, always watching me, always obeying the pack leader, never voicing your thoughts. But I can see them in your eyes. You don't like Danny Butcher. Why?"

He hesitated a moment before he spoke again. "Danny's a sicko, but I don't hate him. Nah, all my hate is saved for the one he reminds me of."

"Who?" I breathed, but I realised who it must be. Because Danny wasn't the only Butcher brother. I'd heard about his twin, the one who was in prison. "Benny?"

Frank's jaw flexed at that name and he nodded stiffly.

"What did he do to earn the hate of a man who barely shows emotion?" I asked curiously, reaching out to touch his jaw as he ground his teeth together. The tension eased a little from his features as he stared down at me, his eyes darting to the door then back to me like he feared someone walking in on us. He was stunning in his rage, his pain, his face so harshly cut it was like the lines of it were drawn by the hand of a deity. He was captivating in a way that felt endlessly dangerous, and yet I couldn't resist the call of it.

"Benny Butcher got my brother killed," Frank snarled, a wicked hatred burning in his eyes. "And one day, when he steps outa that prison he's been rotting away in, I'm gonna take him to the deepest hole in London I can find, somewhere I can make him scream for days on end where no one can hear him. And even when he begs me to finish him, I won't. I'll make him hurt so bad, he'll beg the Devil to come riding in on a black horse and steal him away to hell."

A tingle ran down my spine at those powerful words, the force of his hate so potent I could taste it on my tongue. "What happened?"

Frank grimaced like he couldn't stand to voice it, but he didn't shy away from the grief in him, he answered me straight. "Benny did him dirty. Brought him on a job he never shoulda been on. One none of us wanted to run, that should have been dealt with different. And when it all went tits up, Benny left my brother to die in the street like he meant nothin' to no one. He was alone when he went outa this world with his guts spilling outa his body onto the dirty, shit-stained street, and the man who'd brought him there long gone, saving his own tail like the rat he is." I realised Frank was shaking and the sound of The Killing Moon by Echo & The Bunnymen echoed in my head from the past as I thought of my mother. Seeing her lifeless eyes. The music pounding in my skull and the numbness I'd been swallowed into fully, never truly letting go of me since. I had looked death in the eye and it had looked back, promising to come and claim me too one day. But that wasn't what I was afraid of, my fear had already been realised that night, because there was nothing worse than losing your family. Nothing. Especially at the hands of family.

I realised a tear was rolling down my cheek and I reached up to feel it, the warmth wetting my fingers as I looked down at it and Frank grasped my wrist, bringing my fingers to his mouth and sucking my tears from them.

I gasped at the feel of his tongue grazing over the sensitive pads of my fingertips before he released me and I dropped my hand to my side, my whole arm prickling heatedly from the contact.

"Looks like your pain is my pain now," Frank said, darkness wrapping around him like a cloud. "So are you gonna tell me who you lost, or pretend that grief I see in you doesn't exist?"

I swallowed thickly, holding his gaze, not shying away from this terrible thing I held in my chest. I released it, like a creature with claws and fangs crawling its way out of my chest into his. "My mother."

He nodded slowly, absorbing that.

"You saw it," he stated.

"Yes."

"And it was someone you know who killed her?" he stated again, recognising it all in me.

We were a mirror to each other right then and I was surprised to find someone a whole ocean away from me had somehow lived through such a familiar pain. It was something I had only ever shared with my brothers, but to find someone else who understood was like finding a fallen star among a sea of worthless pebbles.

"My father," I told him and he continued to study me, seeing me in a way that was far deeper than my flesh. His eyes prompted more from me and I found myself surrendering, giving a voice to something I had never even voiced to my brothers. Our pain had been shared, but we'd buried our grief in ways too, never discussing exactly what had happened that night, and I had the feeling that was because they hadn't wanted to upset me.

"He was violent," I admitted thickly. "One day he got too violent."

Frank didn't move, but his eyes flickered with the raging beast that lived within him. "With you?"

Of all the questions, I found that the hardest to answer. It felt like admitting to a weakness in me, even though logically I knew I'd been a child. I hadn't been able to fight back. My father's words had always been as vicious as his fists though, and they'd done the more permanent kind of damage on me. He called me weird, different. He said I was too boyish, that I would have to crush that part out of me if I was ever going to make a husband happy one day – as if that was the only thing that mattered. Like my purpose in life should be a man's happiness.

But to this day, it left me with a doubt that I didn't quite make the cut. That men wouldn't choose me because I wasn't the type of girl who dressed up in pretty things, layered my face in makeup and worked hard to look pleasing on the eye. I dressed in clothes that were pieces of my personality, but guys didn't want a girl with too much of that, right? And I didn't give a fuck. I'd never met a guy worth keeping around either, but maybe I would have tried harder to find one if I'd thought I'd be what they wanted. And that was the problem, wasn't it? I could play the part, I could pretend and lure men in when I liked, but when it came down to it, I was just too damaged, too broken to fit into anyone's life, my jagged edges too sharp and too awkward to fit anywhere.

"I think he believed he could beat the weird out of me," I said coldly, raising my chin as I dared him to see me as weak for my past. But Frank only looked at me more intently, closing up some of the space parting us.

"Well I can see he didn't succeed, Cash."

It might have hurt once, but I took those words on the chin. Yeah, I was different. I'd embraced that years ago when I realised trying to be someone you're not is akin to slicing off pieces of your soul with a mandolin. And so what if Frank agreed and judged me for it? Who cared? He wouldn't be the first to dismiss me because I didn't check society's tick boxes for what constitutes an acceptable woman. Fuck society.

"Are you disappointed I don't totter about the place in high heels and a push-up bra, boasting about my new eyebrows?" I asked dryly.

He fisted his hand in my shirt, his knuckles tight against my bare tits beneath it as he dragged me nose to nose with him, forcing me to tip-toe and making my breath halt in my lungs.

"You're the first thing I've seen in a long fucking time that makes my heart beat again, do you get that? You're far from perfect. In fact, you're so rough around the edges you chip off pieces of the people around you without even trying. But fuck perfect. I've had perfect and it tastes like nothing. Vanilla, boring, soulless and fucking empty. But you, you're so full, you're practically overflowing with life. And not just the good, you're full of the bad too. I look at you and see death and music. And sometimes I see a girl who wants happiness more than anything in the fucking world, but you decided a long time ago you couldn't have it, didn't you? You gave up on that dream, but it's still there, sleeping. And maybe it's time you woke it up."

I was overwhelmed by his words, sure it was the most he'd ever said to me at once and it was so beautiful that it made me shiver. Where the hell was this coming from? Frank hated me. He'd made it more than clear that he despised the Russians and I was the spawn of whatever evil he saw in them. And how could he think I was full when all I'd ever felt inside me was a void?

"Frank-" I started, but I was cut off as his phone started ringing and he took it out, glancing at the name on the screen before answering, his eyes meeting mine again as I tried to get air into my lungs.

"Boss?" he answered and I gave up on the air, holding my breath as I strained my ears to hear Danny's voice on the other end of the line.

"Hey, Frankie boy!" Danny cried, the sound of a man screaming in the background making my lips part. "We're just about to close ourselves a real nice deal with the Gallington Estate boys. They're gonna be keeping an ear out for the Candlestick Maker's plans for us, aint you lad?"

The screaming wherever Danny was turned to whimpering which spoke of untold pain.

"It'll be a little harder now he's only got one ear, boss," Church chipped in in the background, chuckling cruelly. And fuck did that sound do something good to my pussy. Why were all these assholes so fucking hot when they went to psycho town?

"He'll manage, won't ya fella? You owe us since you've been pocketing more than your percentage, ain't that right? And didn't I always warn ya any funny business gets dealt with in blood?" Danny pushed and the guy sobbed out a yes. "Good, lad. Now, Frankie, we wanna celebrate tonight. We should be cleaned up in a couple of hours and raring to go for a night at the pub. Bring my wife to The Duck and Dog by nine pm, and make sure she's got some grub in her belly too."

"Yes, boss," Frank agreed then Danny hung up and silence fell between me and his man.

"Well, you heard him," Frank said, stepping back and putting some distant between us. "I ain't cooking so we'll head to the pub early and eat there."

"Okay," I agreed, excited to get out of this place and see a bit more of London.

I was always being left here with nothing to do and I was living vicariously through Church's gang stories – not that he ever told me about what him and my husband got up to when they went off together. I wished I could come along on some of their jobs. I'd always been left out of gang business back at home too though, so I was used to this shit. Didn't make it any easier to swallow.

"I wanna shower and change before we go," I decided.

If we were going out then I was gonna put my favourite biker boots on and the red check dress I'd bought at the vintage store which was begging to be taken for a night out. I jogged away upstairs as Frank moved to sit on the couch to wait for me and I hurried to Danny's room, pushing inside and grabbing the clothes I wanted from the closet.

I turned to the door, about to head to the bathroom down the hall when my gaze hooked on the en suite across the room which Frank had warned me Danny was weirdly possessive about.

I wasn't sure why because he kept going on about moving into the room next door, but was waiting to do so until I'd decorated it, claiming it was some kind of gift for me to make me feel at home here. He'd instructed Frank to get me anything I needed to do it, but when Frank had refused to go and buy a bunch of Paw Patrol themed curtains, bedding and wallpaper, I'd decided I wasn't interested in playing interior designer. The decor either had to be absolutely mortifying to my husband, or I just couldn't muster the interest in it. This place was no home of mine anyway. I was just the prize cow kept here to secure the peace deal put in place by the big bad men who ruled my world.

I slipped through the door, tossing the clothes down on the white marble by the basin and looking to the black tiled shower before me. It wasn't anything special, so I wasn't sure why Danny would be so precious about it, and I was all for testing his limits anyway.

I stripped out of my clothes, tying my hair up in a scrunchie before stepping into the shower and switching on the water. It was fine, I guessed. Nothing to get dragon hoardy about, and to be honest, I actually preferred the shower in the main bathroom. *Well, you can keep your disappointing douche shower, Danny Butcher. You're welcome to it.*

When I'd dried and dressed in my vintage check dress which was short with thick straps, I used a towel to wipe the condensation off the mirror so that I could fix my hair, but something clicked as I applied pressure and the mirror suddenly popped open.

I hesitated for an intense second before swinging the secret compartment wide, my heart hammering as I did something I was sure was absolutely out of bounds. Inside the space was a slim laptop, a wedge of cash and a handful of large black buttons.

I carefully slid the laptop out of its hiding place and hurried to the toilet, sitting on it and flipping the laptop open on my knees. A screensaver of Danny was on the screen with his arm slung around his twin's shoulders as they stood in front of a grey River Thames, a black umbrella held over their heads.

The two of them were so similar it was like looking at a mirror image and I found my fingers tracing one face to the next, hunting for the differences. It was hard to find any aside from the tattoos crawling up Danny's neck and over his hands, their natural looks uncannily similar in a way that had me staring.

I quickly tapped on the keys, bringing up the screen to login and chewing on my lip. It was predictable but still annoying. I could crack passwords like a pro, but I had to know the person well enough to figure it out. What did Danny like?

I thought of everything he'd told me over the past weeks, hunting for the little details that were often used for passwords. I tried his birthday first in a few different forms, but when that went nowhere, I tried a few variations of his surname with those same numbers. Nothing.

"Cash?!" Frank yelled, making my heart nearly leap out of my chest and commit fucking suicide.

"Jesus," I cursed, snapping the laptop closed and hurrying to put it away. I left the money where it was for now, but did a quick flick through it, estimating there was nearly eight grand there. And that sounded a whole hell of a lot like a plane ticket and a fake passport out of here. The problem was, I didn't have a plan in place yet, and I couldn't risk touching that money if it was something Danny checked on regularly. No, I'd leave it for now and come back to it when I was ready.

"Cash!" Frank shouted again, his voice inside the bedroom this time and I pushed the secret compartment closed, my breaths coming heavier just as the door swung open and Frank stepped in. There was no lock on it thanks to his little suggestion to Danny that I shouldn't be able to lock myself anywhere within the warehouse. *Thanks for that, dickcheese.*

"What?" I snapped a little aggressively and his eyes narrowed sharply.

"What the fuck is taking so long?" he demanded, his eyes dropping to my bare legs.

"You got me so worked up, I had a little finger bang in the shower, okay?" I said, batting my lashes and laying it on so thick he'd know I was absolutely bullshitting him.

No need to go giving him an ego boost he didn't deserve, even if we had had a little moment downstairs. I knew that Frank was one helluva stupid idea, and I would be putting my pussy on twenty-four-hour surveillance when it was around him, guard dogs and all. I didn't need the complication of him brought into my already complicated husband situation.

"Watch it, Cash," he warned, pointing me out the door. "Three minutes and we're leaving."

"Okay, boss." I gave him the rocker sign with my fingers and he growled as he followed me out into the bedroom.

He folded his arms and waited while I grabbed some black pantyhose from the closet and started rolling them up my legs. I met his eye as I pulled them all the way up under my dress and he got a look right at my silk thong before I let the elastic snap around my waist.

"Done eye fucking me yet?" I asked sweetly as I dropped my skirt.

"Done being a brat?" he tossed back.

"Never," I answered, twisting around and knowing full well my dress was tucked up into the back of my pantyhose and my ass was on full display. I wondered how long Mr Stick-Up-The-Ass was going to go without mentioning it.

I slipped my biker boots on then grabbed my leather jacket, sliding that on too and turning to him with a smile. "Shall we go?"

"You think you're funny, don't you Cash?" he said and I swear he almost cracked a grin.

"Funny? Me?" I asked innocently, doing a twirl for him as I looked down at myself, making sure he got another good look at my exposed ass.

He released a low chuckle and I swung around to look at him, my smile widening and fuck, I realised that had been what I was aiming for all along. I liked when he smiled, he looked younger, and I guessed that was because he wasn't old at all, he just had the weight of a hundred years of loss already pressing down on him.

"Pull it out," he commanded, getting control of himself and becoming scowly once more.

"Alright, if you insist." I moved towards him, taking hold of his belt and starting to unbuckle it.

He caught my wrists, his eyes sharpening like razors and my breath caught at the strength of his grip, the pure, masculine power of this man. Frank was so big, so strong and rough around the edges and yet with me, that power in him was always held in check, his silences potent and glares deadly while never once using any of it to wound me. But as I tipped my head back to meet his gaze and the strong planes of his face captivated my attention, I couldn't help but wonder what it might be like to see that control break, to feel him shatter and use all of that power against me. Or for my pleasure.

"Enough games." He reached down the back of my pantyhose and tugged the skirt out, his fingers grazing over the back of my thigh and up my ass as he did so, leaving a tremor dancing between my thighs.

"I like games. I used to play pranks on my brothers when I was locked up all alone in our big house, supergluing their stuff to their desks, plastering toilet tissue all over their walls, and when they came home they'd laugh and hug me and tell me all about their adventures while I'd been safe at home. It feels like that here sometimes. Like I'm being protected. But protected is just another word for caged." Frank said nothing as I kept talking, his captivatingly blue eyes carving their way across my features and hesitating on the movement of my mouth as I went on, unable to stop now I'd started. "I heard this story once about an old, old man who suffocated his wife with a pillow because she was dying of cancer. He didn't want her to be in pain anymore. He tried to tell the court she died in her sleep, but they'd already found the feathers in her lungs." I gripped Frank's shirt in my fists, leaning close to him. "I may not be dead, Frank, but sometimes I can feel the feathers tickling my lungs. And maybe that old man was right. Maybe it's better to die when you're unable to live."

He regarded me and I expected him to dismiss what I was saying, but instead he nodded, unknotting my fingers from his shirt and keeping my hands within his calloused grip. "You're right. Canaries are for cages, and we've established you're not one of those. Tonight, we live."

He turned and led me out of the room, dropping one of my hands but not the other as he towed me through the house, and I stared up at him with my heart thrashing and hope blooming inside me that I might actually be able to breathe tonight.

"You do realise that story is bullshit though, right?" he asked as we walked, his gaze fixed ahead of us while I tried not to get too excited over an innocent little thing like him holding my hand, but shit, it was hard. He had big hands, the callouses on his palm and scars on his knuckles only making it more difficult for me to keep my hand still and not run my thumb across his skin to explore it.

"What part?" I asked, distracted by the feeling of his skin against mine.

"People don't breathe feathers into their lungs," he scoffed and I narrowed my eyes.

"Oh, I'm sorry, I didn't realise you were an expert in smothering people," I said, laying the sarcasm on thick.

"I'm not," he admitted. "I prefer to wrap my hands around their throat and watch the panic rise in their gaze while they thrash beneath me, holding on tight until it sparks out of existence."

Holy fuck. There wasn't a word of that dark admission which sounded like a lie. Worse than that, there wasn't a word of it that hadn't slipped beneath the barrier of my skin and made every damn inch of my body ache for him.

Nothing about that should have been a turn on, but as his grip on my hand tightened marginally in a faint echo of the act he'd described, I felt a jolt of energy crash through me which raced all the way to my core and had me battling against a whimper of desire which tried to claw its way up my throat.

Frank led me out front while I battled to hide my lust and get control of myself. We walked down the road to where his white van was parked up and he opened the passenger door for me, guiding me up into it like it was a damn horse and carriage. When his hand left mine, I gazed after him, my fingers flexing as he shut the door and walked around to get in the driver's seat.

I put my belt on half a second before I realised I'd forgotten my iPod and headphones like a fucking maniac and I unclipped it, lunging for the door just as he started the engine.

"Wait, my music," I gasped, but Frank took off down the road, leaning over and snapping my belt back into place with a sharp jerk which made my breath hitch.

"You won't need it tonight." His hand dropped to my knee for the briefest moment before he remembered himself and withdrew from me fast.

"I always need it," I growled, staring back at the warehouse as it shrunk in the wing mirror.

"There'll be music at the pub," he said. "It's open mic night, so if you want, you can sing your little American heart out and pretend you're in a Disney movie."

"I can't sing," I huffed, because that shit bothered me. I could stay in tune, but I sadly had no gifts in that department. If you wanted a flat, lifeless rendition of Hey Jude by The Beatles, I was your girl, but I wasn't gonna book any weddings anytime soon.

We pulled up again only a few streets away and I took in the old pub on the corner of the road, the dark blue exterior rising up to meet a weathered old sign with a duck and a dog sitting side by side on it. The building looked old, with wooden beams slotted between the brickwork and lead framed windows looking out onto the busy street. We didn't have buildings like that where I came from. This place had history staining every inch of it from the well-worn flagstone which stood beneath a wooden door to the tally carved into one of the windowsills, this place had seen all manner of things over countless years, and I found myself itching to know all of its forgotten secrets.

"The Duck and Dog?" I read the name with a frown, eyeing the haughty looking mallard on the sign as it looked right into the face of the brown and white dog which stood to attention, tail straight, nose extended and one paw raised. It was clear the dog was meant to be hunting the bird yet something about the fire in the duck's eyes made me think it wouldn't go down without a fight, and I found myself empathising with the painted creature in the hopelessness of its battle.

"Yeah, we don't fanny about with names over here." With that, he got out of the van, throwing the door shut behind him and before I knew what was happening, he'd rounded the hood, opened the door for me and offered his hand to help me out.

I hesitated, looking at it like it had slapped me, unsure what to make of this behaviour from a man who always seemed ready to remind me that I was his enemy.

"I can jump down just fine," I said, but he didn't remove his hand.

"I know, Cash. It's just the gentlemanly thing to do, ain't it? But forget it." He dropped his hand and I pouted, wanting it the second it was taken away from me.

Frank arched a brow at me when I didn't hop out and offered me his hand again, making a small smile pull at my lips as I took it, my fingers sliding over his rough palm and making my mouth dry out as I let him help me down.

Wow that felt…nice. Weird, but definitely nice.

Frank shut the door, letting go of my hand and locking the van before leading the way to the pub. He opened the door for me – opened the motherfucking door for me – and gestured for me to go ahead.

"Is this a British gentleman thing or a *you* thing?" I asked in confusion, stepping inside, his fingers brushing the small of my back as he followed and leaving a line of sparks darting along my spine. I'd watched Bridgerton, so I knew how that shit went, but up until this moment my impression of the Englishmen I'd met had left me with no illusions that chivalry and gallantry had died out somewhere in the last few hundred years.

"There ain't no gentlemen left in Britain, Cash," he confirmed my thoughts then led me deeper into the pub.

The place was filled with a ramshackle of different size and shape tables with antique looking wooden chairs clustered around them and a few red Chesterfield sofas and armchairs gathered around a large fireplace. The walls were red brick and covered in all kinds of old bronze pots, serving spoons and pans. It was cosy and full of character, the chatter in the place loud enough to make my ears buzz. I was instantly, unashamedly and wholeheartedly in love with it.

Frank led the way to the bar where a bunch of old guys in flat caps sat drinking beer in large glasses and a girl came jogging over in a low-cut black top with a bright smile on her face.

"Well if it ain't Frank Smith," she said. "You gonna hop on the mic tonight?"

"Not tonight," he said quickly.

I looked to Frank, my eyebrows rising and rising as a little birdie whispered *holy shit* in my ear. "You sing?"

"Oh he sings alright," the girl said. "Pulls in a nice big crowd too. We'd pay him to come in every weekend if only he'd take the job."

"I'm busy with the Butchers, ain't I?" Frank said dismissively.

"That's what I have to tell the groupies when they're sobbing over yet another missed opportunity to warm your bed night in, night out," the girl sighed wistfully and I managed to snap my open mouth shut in favour of scouring the room for any sign of said groupie bitches and wondering if I'd be needing to cut one of them tonight. Not that Frank was mine in any way. Except technically he was my bodyguard and I didn't need to end up locked in a room somewhere in this place while he tucked his dick into Groupie Gwenda and banged her against the wall. Yeah, I was going with that, ignoring the tightness in my belly that spoke of the green, green monster who was spitting hellfire into my gut.

"Fetch us a drink, Shaila." Frank looked like he was trying to hide a smile beneath that big bad asshole thing he had going on and I was tempted to punch him for holding out on me. I needed a whole lot more information on this and I needed it now.

Shaila smirked, looking to me. "What can I get you, love?"

I eyed the range of beer pumps all along the bar with intrigue and Frank noticed my line of sight and my clear lack of knowledge over any of the drinks on offer.

"Get us a couple of pints of Timmy Taylor," Frank ordered, pointing out a pale ale with some old guy on the label and Shaila took her time pumping us out a glass each. I examined the amber drink as she placed it in front of me in a large glass, sniffing it before taking a sip and the hoppy taste rolled over my tongue.

Frank took a large gulp of his, watching me the whole time as he dropped onto a stool. "Thoughts?" he prompted as I swallowed and placed the glass down.

"That's…warm," I said in surprise. It wasn't chilled like the beer I was used to and it tasted so much richer.

"And?" he pushed.

"I like it," I decided, drinking another mouthful and Frank hooked his foot around the stool closest to me, tugging it closer in an offering for me to sit down. I dropped onto it, my knees brushing his as he leaned in and pointed to something behind me with his glass. I turned, finding a girl standing before a mic as the band began playing behind her. She started singing Don't Dream It's Over by Crowded House and I fell into a trance as I listened to her beautiful voice embracing the words, her rendition of it setting my heart drumming.

When she'd finished, everyone in the pub clapped and I drained the last of my ale, finding Shaila placing another one down wordlessly in its place as she collected the old glass. A beat later, she handed over a massive plate of chunky fries and Frank quirked a grin at me that told me he'd bought them. *Alright Mr Nice Guy, what have you done with my nemesis?*

I decided not to point out the fact that he was being a gem, enjoying the perks of this warmer side to him. *Long may he reign.*

I grabbed one of the fries and took a bite, glancing at Frank as he took one for himself, his fingers brushing mine as we both went for the bowl at the same time.

Something twisted in my chest as I met his stare, a thought occurring to me as we sat here, eating together in a pub while I was all dressed up and he looked…well, he looked good enough to lick and he freaking knew it. But in any other circumstance, one where I wasn't married to a man he called 'boss' this would have seemed kinda like…a date.

My cheeks heated a little as that thought occurred to me and I turned my eyes from him, not wanting him to see. I didn't embarrass easily and I'd certainly fucked enough guys not to be shy when it came to the desires of my flesh but in my home town, with my three terrifying as hell brothers and the well known fact among the people who counted that I was already a betrothed woman, there had been no chance in hell of me going out on dates.

In fact, I was pretty certain that the only reason why I hadn't ended up coming to London with my damn hymen intact was because my brothers didn't want to give the English the privilege of being the ones to break it. My brother Alexi had as good as told me so once, reminding me that a woman could use sex as a weapon if only she wasn't afraid of it, and I knew he'd intended that to be advice for me on how to deal with my new husband. At the time I'd thought it would only have been a short-term thing before they executed the plan they'd promised to and helped me escape the chains of my matrimony. But now I knew better. They'd just wanted me to be able to use my body as a strength if I needed to, a way to temper my husband's rage if he turned it my way. And a scared virgin would have had a lot more trouble wielding that kind of manipulation. Not that I was thanking them for their so called help. Teaching me to fight and letting me fuck any man who caught my eye wasn't exactly all that great a comfort when Danny Butcher had tied me to his bed and branded his name upon my flesh.

I frowned as I thought of home. Of my brothers who were right now getting used to their own mafia bride. I wondered what my new sister-in-law was like, the girl from the Irish mob in Boston who now lived in my old home and was surrounded by the only men I loved in this world. Not that I thought for a moment her lot in life was any better than mine. My brothers may have been my whole world once, but to everyone else, they were nothing but heartless demons who dealt in death.

But even as I tried to sink into the hurt and anger I felt at my siblings, I couldn't help but miss them too. I wondered if I would be allowed to call them if I asked. Or if I even had any desire to do so after their betrayal. Perhaps I was better off leaving them in the past just as they had cut me out of their future so willingly. I'd dismissed them when they'd tried contacting me before, but every time I thought of them, I kept wondering if that had been the right thing to do. I wondered about the girl they'd married too, how she was fairing in the company of my demonic siblings. Had they treated her well? Or had they shown her how depraved they were? How dark the Russian blood could bleed. *I hope you kicked them in the balls, girl. One for me and two for you.*

"What's that look for?" Frank asked, pulling me back into the moment and drawing my attention to him.

"I was just thinking about my brothers," I said, not seeing any reason to lie. "And how much I fucking hate them now." That was a lie though, because try as I might, I really couldn't hate those boys. They had been the best things in my life for so long, I couldn't even imagine a world without them in it. Well, not until now.

Frank's eyes lit with a furious heat at the mention of my kin and I almost flinched at the hatred that danced in his pupils. But before I could question him on the sudden shift in his mood, we were interrupted by a man in a cycling helmet as he strode forward, pulling a paper bag from his backpack and calling Frank's name.

"Here you go, mate," he said, handing over the bag of takeout and making me frown in confusion.

"Why do you need takeout?" I asked as Frank accepted the bag and the guy hurried off, zipping his backpack as he went and leaping onto his bike outside, clearly in a rush to deliver his next order.

Frank seemed to consider me for a moment then shrugged, jerking his chin in a silent command before rising and leading me around the bar, nodding to Shaila as she stepped aside to let us pass and he strode right into the kitchen like he owned the damn place.

I followed hot on his heels, curiosity keeping me quiet as he let himself through another door into a small office, holding it open for me to follow.

I stepped beneath his arm and the heat of his body washed over me as I passed him before he closed the door with a loud click and shut us into the dark space together.

The light flicked on before I could question it and I took in the line of heavy wooden bookshelves and the single small desk in the windowless room.

"I'm guessing you have a whole lot of questions about the way we run things around here?" Frank asked, moving around the desk and taking a seat in the single chair, dropping the takeout bag on the surface before him as he leaned back, watching me.

"I do," I admitted.

"Danny has been saying it's time you were educated. At least about the big stuff."

I raised my brows, wondering why my husband wasn't the one telling me this, but not voicing that question, instead asking the one that had been burning on my tongue ever since I'd watched Church kill a man in a back alley and nothing more had seemed to come of it.

"If The Firm runs London then why are there other gangs crawling all over your streets? Why not just destroy them all and run the place yourselves?" I asked, wondering if I really might be about to get some clarity here.

The corner of Frank's mouth lifted and he leaned forward, patting his hand against the desk right in front of him a couple of times in what was unmistakably a command for me to sit.

I sucked on my bottom lip, tempted to deny him for no other reason than not wanting to bow to his whims, but I wanted the answer to that question a whole lot more than I cared about making some foolish powerplay with him, so I gave in instead.

Frank watched me with a hooded expression as I strode closer to him, the little dress I was wearing somehow seeming to cling to my body more than it had before, the hem shorter than I'd thought, the chest lower. It was like he was peeling the clothes from my flesh with nothing but the intensity of his stare on my body yet neither of us was admitting to that at all.

I moved in front of him, stepping between his widened legs before taking a seat on the edge of the desk like he'd commanded, resisting the urge to flatten my skirt over my thighs and not letting myself question how far he could see up it from his vantage point.

"Open the bag," he encouraged and I reached out to pick up the paper bag.

It was heavier than I expected, the scent of food absent as I placed it on my lap and uncurled the top of the bag, looking in at the burger boxes and wrappers while noticing that it was cold where it rested on my thighs.

"Keep going," Frank urged so I did.

I took a burger box from the top of the pile and flipped it open, sucking in a breath as I found a thick roll of cash inside, secured with a rubber band and heavy enough to weigh my palm down.

There had to be thousands of pounds there and it was only one box. I didn't wait for another command, tugging out box after box, grabbing cash from each of them until my eyes were widening like saucers and my lips were parted at the sheer amount of money I now had stacked in my lap.

"Did that takeout guy know this was in here?" I asked, tugging my attention from the money and placing it back on the man who held the answer to all of my questions.

"No. Do you have any idea how many takeaways those delivery drivers ferry all over this city every day? None of them have a damn clue that they're also transporting The Firm's cut from each and every one of the petty little gangs who run the various turfs on the streets. And that's just the small fry shit which comes hand in hand with lording it over those little gangs. The construction company, casinos and restaurants – including this very pub we stand in are fronts which pay in far more than this little taste."

"Why do it like this?" I asked, not understanding it. "Why not make them come to you directly?"

"And make it easy for the coppers to catch on? Or for every low level wannabe gangster in this city to know exactly who is creaming the top offa their profits? Nah. The Firm doesn't need to be seen to keep hold of our power. Our control is absolute without us ever having to reveal our identities to anyone. The more legitimate businesses don't need tarnishing with gang association either. The Butcher gang is one of the biggest and baddest in London, so our reputation there is enough to maintain the power we need day to day. But there aren't even many members of our own gang who realise the truth. That those of us at the top of the food chain run The Firm right under all of their noses."

"How does The Firm maintain its power then?" I asked, trying to get a better grasp on the way they worked. How the fuck did they manage to keep all of those rival gangs sending them a cut of the profits like this every month without rebellion?

"Simple. If some clever little Tom, Dick or Harry decides they don't need to pay their tythe, we pay them a visit and make an example outa them. We wear masks to keep our identities secret, and if we're ever seen it's game over for them." He ran his finger across his throat, making my heart patter at the bloodshed I could see in his eyes. The wickedness in him seemed to grow at that admission, the weight of it filling the room like smoke creeping over me, coiling around my limbs and luring me closer.

"And that works?" I asked. "Simple as that?"

Frank stood suddenly, making me suck in a sharp breath as I blinked up at him and he reached out for a handful of my hair, wrapping it in his fist and curling it twice around his wrist before reaching the nape of my neck and tugging hard enough to make me expose my throat to him.

"The things we do to those who defy us would make even you flinch, Anya Volkov. The Russians may be brutal, cold-blooded beasts, but they don't have a spot on the viciousness of an English Butcher."

My lips parted as I stared up at him, my heart hammering wildly as I read all of those dark and haunting deeds in his eyes and knew he was speaking the truth. The things they did to their enemies, the things *he'd* done were right out of the most terrifying kinds of nightmares. But not my nightmares. No, he was a monster built of my most twisted appetites, the kind who came to me wet with the blood of my demons and knelt before me, willing to bow, to please. Though I doubted Frank would ever submit to me in the way my imagination conjured.

Frank tugged on my hair a little more and for a single, insane moment, I wondered if he was going to push me down beneath him, force the hem of my short skirt up and show me the beast in him right here on top of this desk among the blood money and takeout boxes. Because I was pretty certain that if his mouth found mine then I would let him. I'd let him ravage and destroy me, and make me feel all of the endless emotions that were burning in his hateful, lust-filled eyes.

He released me so suddenly that I almost fell back against the desk, my chest heaving as I fought to regain my composure and he scooped up the money, opening a heavy safe that was set into the wall and tossing all of it inside.

Frank didn't look at me again as I tried to ignore the pounding of my heart, but he held his hand out for me as he strode towards the door and I let him take my fingers between his once more.

He led me back to the bar and I quickly grabbed a couple more fries from the now cold plate, giving myself something to focus on while I tried to settle the rush of electricity which was sparking through my veins.

"Please welcome Frank Smith to the mic," the girl who'd been singing called out as she finished up her set and everyone started clapping as Frank cursed.

"Shaila, I told you not tonight," he growled and Shaila shrugged innocently behind the bar.

"You can't disappoint them now," she replied.

"You have to," I insisted, turning to him hopefully and I swear the resistance in his eyes melted a little. He leaned in close, talking into my ear so only I could hear him.

"If I do this, you owe me, Cash."

Heat flared up at the back of my neck at the roughness to his voice and I nodded. "Name your price."

"You'll know when you pay it." He stood up, tipping his beer down his throat and placing the empty glass down before wiping the back of his mouth like a savage and heading over to the mic.

Excitement rattled through me as he spoke with the band, and the crowd fell quiet as they waited for him to start. Anticipation spilled through me and I was surprised when he grabbed an electric guitar from near the drums and strapped it over his muscular body. Someone brought him another beer and I watched the muscles work in his throat as he swallowed several mouthfuls of it.

Um, hello rock god, Frank.

He curled a finger at me and I frowned in confusion before he jerked his head in an order. And with that guitar strapped to his chest, I was just a groupie in heat, happy to go along with anything he asked. So I made my way up to him, winding through the sea of tables before he pulled me close to speak to me.

"Hold my beer like a good girl, Cash." He pushed it into my hand then pointed at the amplifier his guitar was plugged into and nudged me down to sit on it.

Er, what the fuck asshole?

I glared up at him, sipping his beer as a little fuck you, but then he strummed his pick across the guitar strings and the vibrations of that chord rumbled right up through my pussy and spread throughout my entire body in a shockwave from the amplifier.

Holy fucking shit.

I went to get up, but the crowd cheered as he started playing along with the band and the vibrations rolled through the amp, buzzing out through my thighs. My body trembled with how good that felt, every strum of his fingers ricocheting through me in an echo that had me nearly moaning. My thoughts snapped together as I realised what he was playing and he started singing Oh Darlin' What Have I Done by The White Buffalo.

I shuddered as he played a long chord, sure I could feel every pluck of his strings as they vibrated through my whole body and I became one with him and the music he made. He knew exactly what he was doing by making me sit here and though his back was mostly to me, there was a slight smirk on his lips as he turned his head halfway in my direction and the lyrics dripped from his tongue like liquid sin. His voice was all deep grit which set every hair on my body standing on end as the deep baritone of it trembled through the speaker and dug its way right down to my soul, every word somehow seeming to be sung just for me.

He stole a glance my way as he played a deep and powerful chord and I had to cross my ankles and squeeze my thighs together to try and hold back the pleasure tumbling through my body. It felt so good. So fucking good, I swear I was gonna come right here in front of a whole audience of people.

I took a long sip of beer, moaning into the liquid, covering my face with as much of the glass as possible as my hips rocked a little and I fought to stay still.

That fucking asshole. He was playing chicken with me, because if I got up, he'd win. He'd know what he was doing to me even more than he already knew. And I just couldn't let him get one up on me.

So I sat there, taking every deep rumble of his voice, every strum of his hand, my gaze fixated on the movement each time, feeling like those fingers were playing me, not the guitar.

Oh god.

His voice was satin soft and so deep and gritty, it set my toes curling. Fuck, he was inside my head, my pussy, fucking me with his music and I could do nothing but take it as he shot little satisfied smirks my way, only sending me into a fiercer frenzy. And as the pace of the song picked up and the vibrations got faster and more frantic, I knew I was done for.

I was panting and someone was surely gonna notice any second so I did the only thing I could think of and buried my face in my lap, the beer glass slipping from my fingers as my breaths quickened and my core tightened. His growly voice was pouring through me and the lyrics were twisting through my head, casting a spell on me. My hips rocked of their own accord as I gave in to this madness, my muscles bunching, my fingers fisting in my skirt as a final deep strum of his guitar finished me, an earthquake rumbling through the depths of my body as the whole amplifier shook with the power of his music.

Pleasure crashed through me as I came, biting down on my knee to stifle the cry that tore from my throat.

I felt it everywhere, the vibrations pounding right into the centre of my fucking soul as Frank's gruff voice continued to circle around me and the song came to a powerful end that was almost as fierce as the orgasm I was a slave to which still washed through my core.

Shaila was suddenly there, cleaning up the glass I'd broken and I garbled an apology, my cheeks flushed as she waved me off, thankfully not seeming to notice what the problem really was as I pushed myself up on shaky legs.

Frank appeared in front of me in the next second, his eyes on mine and this deep and sinful fire seeming to burn right through them.

"I think one song is enough for tonight, don't you, Cash?" he asked me and all I could do was nod as he took hold of my arm, his hand on my flesh igniting even more desire in me as he tugged me towards the bar.

I licked my parched lips as my gaze fell on Danny and Church who were just taking their seats and I worked to get my thoughts together as my husband and his best friend gave me hungry looks which only served to fluster me further.

Fuck, I'm getting in so deep here.

Frank leaned in to speak to me, my breaths still far too heavy from what he'd just done to me, and the gleam in his eyes told me he knew I'd come for him on that amplifier. His lips brushed my ear as he spoke, an aftershock of pleasure tumbling down my spine at the seemingly innocent contact.

"Your debt is paid, Anya. But the next time you wanna make a wager with me, be warned that the stakes will be even higher."

CHAPTER TWELVE

Two months with my Miss America living on English soil had done little to curb my infatuation with her and as I scrubbed a hand through my dishevelled hair, I once again found myself fantasising over the one woman in this city who I had no right to be lusting after.

A curse passed my lips as I pushed the thoughts out, focusing on the road instead as I yawned widely.

I whistled as I drove the streets of fair lady London, my knuckles peppered with blood and my muscles barking like a dog from the fatigue I felt from last night. It hadn't been much of anything really, just the Candlestick Maker sending a few of his men out to sniff around the edges of our turf.

It had just been luck that I was finishing up a pint in The Duck and Dog right as the shouts went up. It was nothing a little punch up couldn't handle, though one of the cunts had pulled a knife and given John Boy a run for his money.

But then the good old flash of red and blue and the wail of a siren had marked the cops showing up and we'd gone our separate ways, sprinting off into the night with our blood on fire and testosterone charging our limbs.

I'd run with John Boy all the way back to his flat on the farthest east end of our patch and had to lay low there for a bit. But when he'd gotten the smart idea to turn the whole thing into a party and a bunch of wasted girls had shown up at his door shrieking and stumbling about in dresses so small they left nothing to the imagination, I'd decided to cut my losses.

There was something to be said for fucking a girl right after a fight, putting all of that amped up adrenaline to damn good use by sinking it into the heat of a beautiful woman, but there hadn't been a single one of those gals who'd stolen my attention.

So I'd slipped out the back as the music started thumping, vaulted the balcony and climbed my way down the three floors to the urban jungle waiting for me below without John boy or anyone else being any the wiser.

They'd probably end up so shit faced on illegal substances that they wouldn't even remember me being there anyway.

Nah, that was a lie. No one forgot me that easily. But they sure as fuck wouldn't be able to say for certain what time I'd cut and run on them.

So after half an hour of skirting through back streets and taking in the bright nightlife of my home town, I found myself back at my faithful Mini Cooper just as dawn was cracking her eyes and the city began to wake.

I'd let my damn phone run out of juice somewhere in the melee, so I decided on heading over to give Benny the low down on the dodgy as fuck challenge to our authority. I was starting to think The Firm would have to get involved with this if it didn't get dealt with soon, but the fucker was still paying his tythe, so it was hard to justify ending him without bringing attention to the Butchers. Not to mention the fact that he was tight with The Czar, the fucker who Benny was relying on to pull through with the deal the construction company needed to stay afloat. Not that much progress had been made on that front – the Russian billionaire had been as elusive as a damn fart in a northerly breeze since Benny's return to London, sending vague messages about there being some trouble with Interpol which were keeping him in hiding while he got them sorted.

In my experience, billionaires were always at least a little cracked in the head, not to mention entitled as fuck, so there was no surprise that this one was giving us the run around. Problem was, we needed that deal to happen. Needed his fucking money to fix the mess Danny had made of the company. So now we were caught in a waiting game, trying to tempt The Czar back out of hiding so that we could seal the deal.

I pulled my car up outside the refurbished warehouse that Benny now called home again after all these years, bobbing my chin in greeting to the fellas who were casually hanging out on the street a little way from his front door. They were mostly new recruits to the Butchers gang, given these kinds of lookout tasks as a way to test their dedication and strengths. Their main job was to make one hell of ruckus to give us warning if any unfriendlies decided to darken Benny's door.

I took my key from my back pocket and let myself in, flicking the lights on in the dark space as I strolled towards the stairs, aiming for the bathroom and stripping outa my clothes as I went.

"What are you doing here at this time?" Frank's rough voice broke the silence and I nearly went for my fucking gun as my heart leapt in surprise.

It took me a moment to locate him, lurking in the shadows on the upper walkway, his own pistol in hand and a scowl on his face which said he wouldn't have much minded shooting me by accident. For a big fucker, he sure could move around like a ghost when the mood took him.

"I ran into a little trouble last night," I explained, making sure I didn't show him that he'd rattled me as I moved towards the stairs and started up them, my shirt and jacket in my fist and my belt unbuckled.

"The boss isn't here," he replied, tucking his gun into the back of his jeans. "So maybe you should just go home and check in with him later."

"I'll wait," I replied coolly, making it up to his level and falling still a few feet from him where he blocked my way onward.

I could feel his contempt for me crackling in the air between us and it put me on edge. On the one hand, I fucking hated that the man I'd grown up loving like a brother looked at me like that these days. On the other, I was sick of him being a god-awful cunt and refusing to listen to a single thing I had to say about the truth of what had happened to Olly all those years ago.

I mean, I got it, he was grieving, but grief was only an excuse I'd tolerated for so long. At this point, he was just being pig headed. But I also knew he was never gonna go on blind faith the way I'd had to when I'd come to terms with what had happened. He was never gonna hear Benny out while he thought he was responsible for all of it. But I had. I'd gone to the man I'd given my soul to when I signed up to this life when he was locked behind bars and I'd listened to every word he had to say before sharing my own suspicions with him. We'd gotten to the truth of it all eventually. The only problem was that without proof, not a soul had wanted to hear it.

So here we were.

"Mrs Butcher is sleeping," Frank rumbled, his upper lip peeling back like even this small interaction with me was painful to him.

"Well I'll make certain not to wake her," I replied, sidestepping him and just about resisting the urge to slam my shoulder into his as I went.

Frank followed in my shadow as I let myself into the bathroom then passed me by and strode away to Danny's room at the far end of the walkway.

I paused to watch him go, my gaze slipping to the wide bed which was visible in the centre of the room and catching on the girl sleeping there amid a tide of platinum hair with her headphones securely placed over her ears.

I licked my bottom lip then dragged my attention away as I headed into the room and ran myself a bath in the huge copper tub, filling it with bubbles and making sure it was hot enough to scald before dropping into it.

I scrubbed the blood from my skin and rinsed my hair out before laying back and letting my eyes fall closed, the sight of Anya all curled up in that big bed hanging around in my mind as I dozed and bringing a faint smile to my lips.

I nodded off in the hot water, catching up on some of the sleep I'd missed the night before and letting the dark have me, despite the pain I always felt when I sank into it.

I woke to the sharp snap of the door closing, jerking upright and sloshing lukewarm water over the tiled floor as I grabbed a sponge like it was a fucking knife, raising it in my fist briefly before spotting Benny and releasing it with a splash.

"Fucking hell, you shouldn't wake a man when he's in the tub," I grumbled as Benny arched a brow at me and folded his arms over his bare chest.

"How about you tell me why you're in my tub in the first place then I'll decide if it was a dick move or not," he replied.

I swiped a hand down my face to remove some of the droplets from my skin then stood, abandoning the fast cooling water and climbing out, claiming a towel to dry myself with as I spoke.

"We had a bit of a tussle with the Candlestick Maker's men out by Mile End Park last night," I explained. "Nothing too lairy, but the fuckers were trying their luck. I was thinking it might be time to send a clearer message."

Benny nodded thoughtfully, then took his phone from his pocket.

"I've been getting a few messages demanding a meet," he said, holding the phone out to show me the texts from an unknown number.

Unknown:

I thought we were above the shit that happened tonight. We need to discuss the terms of our arrangement further. I want a meet.

I frowned at it, scrubbing at my hair with the towel before tying it around my waist.

"Are you thinking Danny was up to something the rest of us didn't know about?" I asked.

"We know he was," he replied darkly. "I'm just starting to think it could be even worse than we suspected."

"So what are you gonna do? If you show up to some meeting with this mystery fucker without a scrap of knowledge on their deal then you could easily get yourself found out," I said.

"I know. Which is why I plan on getting Danny to sing like a canary for me today. I'm gonna act all merciful and let him snort as much blow as he likes. The fucker is tweaking like crazy down there since the last time I let him have some anyway, and you know how much the arsehole likes to brag. I'm thinking I can get him to spill once he's shit faced, and if that doesn't work then I'll start cutting off toes."

There was nothing but a demon living in Benny's eyes as I lifted my gaze to his, and I smirked at the darkness in him as he casually discussed torturing his twin brother like it was any other Tuesday.

"You want help with that little task?" I offered, my own blood heating at the thought of doling out a little payback on the fucker for the years I'd been forced to serve at his pleasure, but Benny just shook his head.

"Nah. Frank has been up all night watching Anya for me, so I was hoping you could keep her busy while I send him away to get some sleep. It'll be easier for me to spend the time I need in the tunnels if there isn't anyone else home while I'm down there anyway."

My lips pulled up at the corner and I had to admit to myself that that sounded like a much better way to spend my day than in the company of fucking Danny, even if I coulda had the pleasure of cutting a few of his appendages off myself.

I really shouldn't have been looking forward to having my best friend's wife all alone for the day, but I'd been working hard on not giving too much thought to all that since she'd first shown up here, so I shoved the thought aside.

"I'll take her out to do some tourist shit," I said with a nod. "The girl tries to hide it, but I've seen the way her eyes light up whenever she catches a look at the city. It's taken her hostage even more effectively than you have and she's all ready to embrace her Stockholm syndrome with it – she just needs a little push to get her there."

"Good," Benny replied and I could tell he meant that. "I don't want her to hate it here. This whole treaty is fucked up enough as it is. I keep thinking about Dahlia off married to some Cosa Nostra arsehole and it eats me up inside."

"Have you heard from her recently?" I asked, knowing that this was a sore subject. I mean sure, she wasn't my sister, but when he'd been locked up I'd made sure to visit Dahlia whenever she came home during her breaks from her fancy boarding school to spend the holidays with her mum. I made certain she kept well clear of the gang and she hadn't ever shown any interest in being involved in it, but I ensured she knew how to defend herself if ever she needed to.

I still didn't like the idea of her being sold off in this trade between the most powerful mob families in the world. They might have all sworn to protect the girl who came to them, but did that really mean shit? I knew full well what kind of life Anya would have had with Danny if we hadn't dealt with the motherfucker before he managed to marry her, and it sure as fuck wasn't wedded bliss. The Devil only knew what Dahlia had married into.

"Nah, not recently. I'll check in with her again soon."

We headed out of the bathroom to go get some breakfast and my breath caught as I found Anya already down there, leaning forward over the hob as she cooked some eggs, making the white Nirvana shirt she was wearing ride up to reveal half her ass.

I swallowed a lump in my throat as I took in the branded skin there, the name Butcher now healed, though it still looked reddened against her tanned skin.

Benny exchanged a dark look with me which said he was still fucking furious over that stunt, and I was just glad that Danny would be suffering all day today.

Anya hadn't noticed our arrival, her ass moving from side to side to the beat of the music which played through her headphones and I walked to the breakfast bar as Benny approached her, dropping onto a stool.

"Morning, bombshell," Benny said, catching hold of her waist and making her gasp as he jerked her around towards him.

His mouth landed on hers and my gut clenched as I watched them. Watched the moment where she fell into that kiss, her lips parting, eyes closing.

Her hand fell to the counter and shifted towards a knife which she'd been using to slice avocados as Benny sank his tongue between her lips and I pushed myself to my feet as I moved behind her.

My hand fell on the knife a moment before her fingers reached it and she caught my hand instead, a growl escaping her as she was forced back a step and found her back flush with my chest. I plucked the headphones from her ears to further announce myself, catching the sound of Heart of Gold by Johnny Cash playing faintly through them.

"Fuck," she hissed, breaking away from Benny and looking over her shoulder at me, those deep, coal eyes widening in surprise. "Where did you come from?"

"Your darkest desires," I replied with a grin. "You musta been thinking naughty, naughty thoughts to summon me."

Her eyes narrowed and Benny chuckled, moving his mouth to her throat and making her moan in surprise as his hands slid to her hips and lifted the t-shirt just enough to show off the lacy black knickers she was wearing beneath it.

"You wanna perch your pretty little arse on the worktop so I can eat you for breakfast, bombshell?" Benny asked, giving absolutely no fucks that I was here as he caught her hips and lifted her suddenly, placing her on the counter without waiting for an answer.

"Church is right there," she pointed out, her gaze snapping from him to me as he dropped to his knees and pushed her thighs apart.

I bit down on my bottom lip, shrugging a little as I took a step back, bringing the knife with me but keeping my gaze fixed on her.

A part of me wanted to step in. I wasn't even certain what for, or what I would do if I did. But another part wanted to get a good look at her as she came for him, the idea of watching her get off again making my pulse pound and sending a whole lot of blood rushing south.

"You didn't mind it when I did this in the back of his car," Benny commented. "In fact, you were so wet then that I'm pretty certain you enjoyed having an audience."

"Oh yeah, I just *love* the asshole parade putting on a tour while I'm-"

Anya began but he just pushed her thighs wider and kissed the inside of her knee, making her suck in a sharp breath, her eyes fully fixed on me.

The front door opened and Frank strode in, bringing a gust of cool morning air with him, though I was hopeful that the sun would hold out today. It was the perfect autumn day, a little frost on the ground, a chill in the wind and the promise of the deep, dark winter to come. A white Christmas was definitely on the cards this year.

"Does this count as you riding her arse?" Frank asked mildly, taking in the scene playing out here and looking casual as fuck, as if he had no feelings on it whatsoever.

"Not yet," Benny gritted out, snapping Anya out of her shock and causing her to fist his hair, yanking it back so violently that it just had to hurt before she snapped her thighs shut and scowled at him.

"Is that a no?" Benny asked, pushing to his feet with a huff of irritation.

"I'm making breakfast," Anya replied firmly. "And I don't want any sausage with it."

I barked a laugh while Benny grinned but as he tried to lean forward to kiss her again, she rocked back, bringing her knees up to her chest before pushing her bare feet into his abs and kicking him hard enough to make him stumble back several steps.

Benny laughed loudly as he crashed into the breakfast bar and I watched Anya ravenously as she tossed her platinum hair over her shoulder and hopped back down to plate up her food.

"What are we eating?" I asked as my stomach rumbled, but she just shrugged as she kept her back to us.

"No idea." Anya moved to take a seat as far from us as possible, placing a plate of scrambled eggs and smashed avocado on toast down for herself with a glass of orange juice beside it. "But my breakfast smells great. You could always eat Danny's ass if you're desperate."

"Arsehole," I muttered, shaking my head and moving to find myself something while Benny roared a laugh.

Frank pulled his phone from his pocket, connecting it up to the speakers and setting Mr. Brightside by The Killers playing, earning a look from my Miss America which she sure as shit had never offered to me.

I settled on a bowl of cereal, filling it to the brim with Crunchy Nut Clusters before washing milk over it and taking the seat on Anya's other side.

My towel tugged sharply at the change in angle and as Benny started frying himself up something to eat, I felt the damn thing fall open.

Anya sucked in a breath beside me and I raised my gaze to hers over my spoon, finding her eyes otherwise occupied with checking me out.

I was still sporting a semi from the thought of watching Benny eat her out and my dick only hardened further the longer she looked.

I continued to eat, letting her look if she wanted to and devouring the rest of my cereal while watching her dark eyes roam over my body.

She seemed to realise what she was doing, her gaze snapping up to meet mine suddenly before she violently speared a piece of toast on the end of her fork, making my cock jerk in alarm.

"Wow, maybe you really should go eat Danny's ass. I didn't realise you were so into the idea, Church, though maybe I should have with how much you're always kissing it."

"Fuck you," I drawled through a grin. That tongue wouldn't be so sharp when I had her bent over and screaming my name. I mean *if* I had her bent over and screaming my name. Which of course I wouldn't, seeing as she was my mate's girl.

Shit, I'm in a pickle here.

I promptly placed my empty bowl down and stood, securing my towel once more.

"What's the plan today, boss?" I asked, ignoring the feeling of Frank's eyes on my skin and the certainty that he was indulging in fantasies of doing me bodily harm.

"I got some shit to sort out," he replied, still cooking his food.

"You want me with Mrs Butcher today?" Frank asked, like he'd been expecting that, but Benny shook his head.

"Nah. You're no good to her dog tired," he replied. "You can fuck off and get some sleep at home. Church can take her sightseeing for the day."

"Really?" Anya asked, perking up at that suggestion and I knew I had her then. This city had been whispering her name so sweetly these past few weeks, offering up glimpses and teases and making her ache for all its secrets. And now she was ready for them, wanting to let them consume her, devour her and turn her into a true Londoner.

"Anywhere you wanna go, anything you wanna see," I said dutifully and she gave me an honest to shit real smile. It was brief and vanished as fast as it had come, but there it was.

I headed off to steal some clothes for the day, finding a pair of stonewashed jeans and a white long-sleeved shirt to go with them before pinching a bit of hair product to fix my blonde curls.

Anya headed into the room as I exited it, passing me wordlessly, though the bounce in her step gave away her excitement.

I waited downstairs and she reappeared before long, wearing a black Guns N Roses t-shirt dress, cinched tight around her waist with a belt and leaving a whole lot of leg on show. I ran my thumb over my bottom lip as I watched her bounding down the stairs, a pair of little white sneakers on her feet and a brightness to her eyes which made my chest swell.

"I want you all over her today, Church," Benny warned as I stood to leave. Frank must have fucked off already, because he was nowhere in sight. "She doesn't so much as take a piss without you there."

"On it, boss," I replied easily because being all over that girl was a job I could take very seriously.

I jerked my chin at Anya as I headed for the door and she jogged to catch me up, flipping Benny the finger as he called out a goodbye to her and making him laugh loudly before the door closed between us.

"Where first?" Anya asked, heading towards my Mini where it was parked up, but I shook my head.

"We're walking, Miss America. You can't fully appreciate the city properly any other way." I held my hand out for her and fuck me, she actually took it.

I turned her north first, tugging her along street after street and playing tour guide as I pointed out the different buildings, old and new, watching her as she drank in everything I said and asked countless questions.

We didn't hurry and after a while I noticed her shivering a little despite the sun, her American blood still not used to the nip of the English climate. I released her hand, dropping an arm around her shoulders instead and tugging her close to offer up some body heat. She fit right there like she'd always been made to do so and her cheeks coloured just a touch as she looked up at me almost shyly.

We headed down twisting roads, the offices spilling out as the beginning of the lunch hour rush marked the start of the carnage and the workers in the City of London all started following the call of their hungry bellies on their breaks.

I kept an arm around Anya's shoulders, caging her in at my side and started to lead her between the crowd. There was a knack to it which I'd mastered long ago – I called it 'being a big, scary fucker who didn't move aside' – and I had to say it worked damn well. The odd banker with a sense of self inflated importance would occasionally walk right at us, expecting me to move aside, but it only ever took one good look at the tattoos crawling out from beneath my clothes to the expression on my face which promised an untimely death to make them scamper outa my way instead.

Anya didn't seem to mind me touching her like this. In fact, she didn't seem to mind me at all today. She'd been all wide eyes and smiles and I had to say, I liked this side of her a whole lot. I almost felt like a normal fucker, no blood on my hands or sins on my soul, just some guy taking his girl out to see the sights and drink them in.

Not that she was my girl. But it kinda felt like she was for now. And I didn't hate it. Despite knowing what a bad fucking idea that was. Despite knowing that Benny would quite likely turn Butcher on me if he got so much as an inkling of what I was thinking. I couldn't help my damn self.

I tugged her away from the rush of the lunch time carnage, not envying those arseholes their lives of servitude to the tax man one fucking bit as I found side alleys and walkways which were lesser used and offered us some freedom from the crush.

But as we turned onto another side street, I fell still, my gaze fixing on the three men who were lurking there right outside a shop which absolutely fell under our jurisdiction.

"Shit," I muttered, half wishing I'd brought my gun out with me as I considered our odds here, but wandering the streets of the city with a gun stashed on me was a pretty dumb idea considering the police presence on every other corner.

"What is it?" Anya asked, her body tensing as she sensed the shift in me. She placed her feet in a way that told me she knew what she was doing and her hand curled into a fist.

"Trouble," I explained, my fingers twitching for the kiss of a knife, but I didn't go for it. There were too many witnesses about for that.

"More information," she demanded and I glanced at her just long enough to see that stubborn lilt to her lips taking hold fast. No fear. In fact, she looked hungry for the fight.

"Those fellas aren't allowed on our patch," I explained.

"Maybe you shouldn't hide the fact that you run The Firm then," she muttered. "They wouldn't dare defy you if they understood the full extent of your power."

"Why am I not surprised to hear that sentiment from a Russian?" I teased, raising my chin as the first of the men spotted me. "No fucking subtlety to you lot, is there?"

"When everyone knows to fear you, there's no need to be subtle," she tossed back.

"When no one knows who to fear or who they can trust, complete control is inevitable," I replied in turn. "Is there any point in me telling you to run?"

"No."

My smile grew. "Alright. But don't go doing anything silly like getting yourself stabbed."

"So long as you don't go doing anything dumb like getting your pretty face broken," she replied.

"Oh, you like my face then, do ya?"

"Mostly when you aren't speaking."

I barked a laugh and strolled forward, my shoulders back and hands held out either side of me to show them I wasn't armed. Though any fucker worth his salt would recognise me and know I didn't need a weapon to end a man's life.

"You lost, lads?" I called loudly, eyeing the three of them as they perked up.

"Just retrieving something of ours," one of them said, planting himself at the front of the group and narrowing his gaze on me before taking in Anya who had stayed at my side.

I recognised him easily enough, the three pubes he called a beard fluttering on his chin in the breeze that ran though the alley. He was one of the men higher up in the Candlestick Maker's organisation, going by the name of Slice, though I knew he was really called Peter Bronson. We didn't go in for that kind of posturing bullshit so much in the Butchers' gang. I never really saw the point of having some supposedly intimidating nickname when I could be as intimidating as fuck even if I was called Florence Fannywrangler.

"Well you ain't got permission to be this close to Whitechapel," I pointed out.

"The City of London is no man's land," Slice replied, sneering at me and turning his hand to show me the knife which he had stashed up his sleeve. "So I suggest you fuck off out of our way before we have to remind you who we are."

"And what's that?" Anya asked, cocking her head to one side as she assessed him. "A man-boy who thinks waving a knife around in the street makes it seem like his balls have finally dropped? Because believe me, asshole, no one's buying it."

Slice's dark eyes flashed with fury and he took a step forward, the other two motherfuckers moving up close behind him, having his back.

"What did your whore just say to me?" he snarled and the amusement I'd felt at Anya's comment fled at the sound of him calling her that.

My face fell into a cold, hard mask and I stalked forward, my fingers curling into a fist.

"Did you just call my girl a whore?" I asked in a low, deadly voice, a thousand murderous thoughts flashing through my skull as I pictured him bleeding before me in as many ways as possible.

"Wait a second, isn't that Danny's new wife?" one of the other fuckers piped up and my fury pumped harder as I realised they already knew too much about her.

"What the fuck are you doing running about with your boss's wife?" Slice asked. "She really is a whore, isn't she? How much for me to have a-"

I was on him before he could finish that sentence, a roar escaping me as I swung my fist into his jaw so hard that a crunch sounded followed by an agonised scream as I broke his fucking jaw.

Slice dropped to the floor like a sack of shit and my boot slammed into his face a moment later.

The other fuckers had gotten past their shock in the time it took for me to kick him several more times and as I stomped my foot down on the side of his head, one of them slammed into me.

I hit the wall beside us, a cry of alarm coming from someone down on the busier street behind me as some everyday little Karen spotted us and lost her shit. This wasn't fucking good. This shit shouldn't happen in this part of the city, there were too many coppers about and too many good Samaritans too.

I threw my shoulder into the gut of the fella who was trying to come at me with a knife, knocking him off balance just in time for Anya to clock him with a right hook which knocked him on his arse.

I looked around for the third bloke, finding him ripping open the door that they'd been guarding and yelling for whoever was in there to come out and help them.

I caught Anya's arm, yanking her behind me as I spotted six more fuckers running to the door and I realised it was time to cut our losses.

"Run," I barked, the sound of sirens in the distance sending a spike of adrenaline through me. I'd had enough run ins with the cops to know how to talk my way out of trouble, but I much preferred sleeping in my own bed to spending a night at Her Majesty's pleasure, banged up for a crime I wouldn't ever admit to.

"We can take them," Anya hissed and fuck me, that fire in her eyes got me all kinds of amped up, but as the gang of thugs shoved their way out the door, I just tightened my grip on her arm and forced her to run.

"Not before the cops show up," I pointed out. "And one of those arseholes had a gun. I wouldn't put it past them to stick a bullet in me even if it is broad daylight and, darlin', the ink on this body cost too much to end up ruined by a bullet hole."

She breathed a laugh as we took off, giving in to my demand and running with me down the alley before turning left with me and racing on away from the motherfuckers who took chase.

We sprinted down street after street, taking random turns as I used my knowledge of the city to try and lose them, but the fuckers were damn persistent.

I hooked a left, tugging Anya with me as we sprinted past the Old Bailey, sparing a glance for the ancient courthouse and hoping to fuck I never had to see the inside of it.

We were drawing too much attention running like this and as I spotted a police car up ahead, I darted down a side street, almost getting us mowed down by some arsehole in a flashy motor.

I looked around at Anya, finding her eyes wild with the thrill of the chase and I grinned big at her, tugging her around another corner and taking off towards St Paul's Cathedral.

I glanced back, finding our pursuers falling back at last, some distance spreading between us, though they didn't appear to be giving up any time soon.

The crossing ahead of us flicked to green and I sprinted across the road, my grip tight on Anya's hand as we ran down several side streets, veering away from the crowd of tourists who were congregating around the cathedral and leaping into a rickshaw lit with bright pink LEDs with fluffy seats to match.

"Get me to the river, mate," I demanded, tossing a fifty pound note the rickshaw driver's way as Anya dropped into the seat beside me and the guy grinned as he took off, cycling into the traffic at speed as we flew through the streets in the little cab behind him.

"I've always wanted to ride in one of these," Anya breathed and I turned to look at her, finding the broadest smile on her face as she gazed out at the streets of London racing by, her eyes wide with wonder as she drank it all in.

She looked so fucking beautiful, fired up on violence and adrenaline and so full of life that I wanted to catch it in a bottle and steal it all for myself.

I leaned in before I could stop myself, my mouth capturing hers and the whole world just melting away as I tasted that glorious smile on her lips.

It wasn't just any kiss, or some collision of mouths searching to steal something from one another.

No. Kissing Anya was like tasting the first lightning strike of a storm. Devouring her lips was like claiming a bite of the most beautifully forbidden poison and heading into death willingly for the pure fucking ecstasy of that taste.

She fisted my shirt and pulled me closer, her lips parting so her tongue could meet mine and my hand landed on her hip as I tugged her against me, needing every single piece of her that I could get.

My heart free fell in my chest like I'd just leapt from a cliff without a parachute and though I knew reality was gonna hurt like a bitch when it reared its ugly head again, I was so caught up in enjoying the high of her lips against mine that I couldn't summon the energy to give a fuck.

The rickshaw came to a halt and a yell forced the real world back on us like a bucket of icy water as I broke our kiss reluctantly and looked around to find the motherfuckers still chasing us from way up the street.

"There's the river, my man," the Rickshaw driver said. "The beautiful ribbon of water that runs through the heart of our great and wonderous-"

"Don't oversell it, mate, the thing was used as a sewer for hundreds of years," I said, cutting him off as I leapt out of the little pink cab and caught Anya in my arms as she followed.

Millennium Bridge winked at me from up ahead and we broke into a run once more.

A tourist vendor was on the other side of the road, selling all kinds of tourist paraphernalia from fridge magnets to snow globes with a healthy range of 'I love London' apparel to boot.

Lucky for me, he was fully occupied with a large group of tourists and I yanked Anya round the back of his wooden stall, snagging a leather jacket with a Union Jack on it and pushing it onto her before snatching a flat cap for me and running on.

Anya's laughter punctuated our footsteps as we ran faster and I led the way onto Millennium Bridge which had large steel railings twisting along either side of it, the two of us running through the tourists and heading to the far side of the water.

I spotted a white river cruise boat to our right as we went, the thing empty and clearly heading upriver to start the day's cruises. A grin found my lips as I recognised the driver and I turned abruptly, glancing back to make sure our friends hadn't caught up to us yet before grabbing hold of the railings and heaving myself up onto them.

"Do you trust me, darlin'?" I asked, looking around at Anya as she stared at me in surprise and the nose of the river cruiser passed beneath me.

"You're gonna jump?" she breathed.

"I'll catch you," I swore, only waiting long enough to see her nod before I leapt between the twisting metal which ran along the side of the bridge and landing heavily on the boat below.

Harold cried out in surprise as he spotted me, but I only grinned at him as I turned back for Anya, hoping to fuck she didn't bottle out at the last minute.

But of course she didn't disappoint, jumping from the bridge before I was even ready for her and rolling smoothly like she'd learned how to take a tumble a long time ago.

Tourists gasped from the bridge above and I quickly tugged my cap off, bowing for them and holding it out.

"Next show starts in an hour," I called. "Be generous and next time I'll add in a backflip!"

Pound coins rained down on us from above as the boat moved on and they hurried to toss their spare change our way. I even managed to catch a few coins in the hat, earning more applause and cheers before I bowed again and we made it out from beneath the bridge.

"You on the run?" Harold guessed as I caught Anya's hand and pulled her towards him.

"How'd you guess?" I asked innocently, drawing a laugh from him.

"I'm on my way to Westminster to grab today's first batch of tourists. If you wanna hide out below I can drop you at St Katherine's within half an hour."

"Deal. I'll owe ya, mate." I clapped him on the arm and jogged below deck before any of the Candlestick Maker's boys got a chance to spot us.

"You're insane, Church," Anya panted as we ran down the steps to the lower deck and I quicky tugged open the door to the engine room, ushering her inside.

"Yeah," I agreed, pulling the door shut behind her and plunging us into near complete darkness. There was a red maintenance light on in the far corner of the space though and the glow of it gave me a view of her distracting features. "But I think that's what you like about me. Ain't it?"

Her gaze scoured over me again and the air between us seemed to charge with energy as the dull roar of the engine made the floor vibrate around us. It was hot in here, too fucking hot when I was trying to catch my breath from running all over London and I could feel a bead of sweat running down the centre of my chest and over my abs beneath my shirt.

"You make me feel alive, Church," she said, pushing off the door and taking a step closer to me. "You make me feel like the world is mine for the fucking taking and there's nothing I can't have from it."

"And what is it you wanna take, Miss America?" I asked her, my attention moving down to her bare thighs as I thought on that question for myself.

Anya tilted her head, that long, endlessly blonde hair spilling down her side as she gazed at me in a way that made me fucking ache for her. I didn't know what it was about this girl, why she had me so fucking fixated, but ever since the first moment I'd laid eyes on her it had been there. Like this void inside my chest, this empty place which had been aching for her for longer than I'd even known that it was there.

I couldn't fill it with her though. She wasn't meant for me. But as I thought on the way her taste still lingered on my lips, I wondered how long I would be able to keep to my hopeless resolution to stay away from her. She was something far beyond temptation and the desire for her in me was fast outweighing the sense.

Anya shrugged out of the leather jacket I'd pinched for her, letting it fall to the floor before she pushed her sneakers off with her toes.

I watched her with this ravenous kind of need, staying utterly still like a predator waiting to strike, my hunger for her growing as she played with me like she was dangling a string before a mouse.

"Do you love your boss, Church?" she asked me, her voice low and husky, almost lost to the constant roar of the engine.

"I do," I agreed, my gaze locked on her fingers as she unbuckled the belt which cinched her dress in around her narrow waist. The material tugged tight over her tits as she did it, the hard points of her nipples making a groan catch in my throat as I looked at the way they pressed through the material. There was no way she was cold in here, which meant her body was as aware of me as I was of her.

"And are you loyal to him?" she went on, her eyes flashing with the challenge as she dropped the belt, the sound of it hitting the floor like a warning claxon blaring in my skull, but I could no sooner heed that warning than slit my own throat to escape this fate, no matter who her husband was.

"Yeah," I agreed. "I'd go to hell for that man, walk right through the fiery gates and let the Devil ram a hot poker straight through my blackened heart."

Anya drew in a slow breath, seeming to steal the very essence of who I was from me as I exhaled and let her fucking take it. She was a snake luring me out to the apple tree and I was willing to drown for this small moment of her looking at me like that.

"So tell me…" She tugged the t-shirt dress off and tossed it aside, standing there in nothing but those little lacy black knickers with her nipples like diamond points and her chest heaving with lust. "Why did you fuck his wife?"

I held myself there for all of two seconds, a tiny voice screaming at me that this was one hell of a bad idea, that I was one fully fledged cunt of a friend and that there was no fucking way back from this once I broke. But that was just it. I'd been breaking in my resolve on this from the very first second I'd spent in her company. I'd been balancing on a precipice which was always going to crumble because when I looked at her, I saw so much fucking more than I'd ever had before. And I wasn't just hungry for it. I was ravenous and I was greedy and I really would take up my place in hell if that was the cost of this too.

I was on her in a heartbeat, my mouth against hers and my hands on her arse as I lifted her up and she wound her legs around me.

A growl spilled from me that was all animal and need, this primal fucking desperation which would never be sated any other way.

She moaned for me, her head tipping back and my name spilling from her lips as I ran my mouth down and sucked her nipple into my mouth.

Anya's hands fisted in the back of my shirt and she tugged, making me release her as I stepped back and yanked it off.

"Your tattoos are such garbage," she moaned as she dropped her mouth to my neck, kissing her way down my body as she unbuckled my belt and stroked my solid cock through my jeans.

"Jealousy doesn't suit you, darlin," I replied, watching her kiss that same ink she'd been trying to insult like she was worshipping it.

My head was fucking spinning with the intensity of her lips on my flesh and I couldn't help but groan again as she moved lower. The desire to fuck that spiteful mouth of hers was so potent that I knotted a hand in her hair, the blonde strands twisting all around the ink on my fingers, tangling around the church spires which coated them.

I forced myself to slacken my grip as she tugged my belt open and she looked up at me with a flash of irritation as I licked my lips and looked right back.

"I came here as a sold woman, given to a man I hate with no choice in the matter at all," she growled, standing upright once more and looking me in the eye. "I won't have my choice stolen from me like that, Church."

"Won't you?" I asked, my cock straining as I forced myself to stay there, my muscles practically trembling from the restraint I was imposing on them.

"No," she replied darkly. "So I don't want you to be gentle with me and I don't want you to hold back. I see life in your eyes and taste freedom on your lips. So make sure I feel it when you fuck me. I'm not some English rose you need to be careful with. I was born in fire and hellstone and I want every piece of you when you claim me."

I took in what she was saying and nodded once, giving her all the warning that she was going to get before I stepped forward and kissed her hard, fisting my hand in her hair again and forcing her head back with my hold on it.

I released her lips, moving my mouth down her throat until I captured her nipple between my teeth and bit down hard enough to make her cry out. Bloody hell, I loved the free tits movement she was leading. I was gonna be head of the committee and hold tea parties every second Sunday of the month.

I pushed my hand down the front of her knickers, finding her fucking soaked for me and sucking her nipple harder as I sank three fingers straight into her, stretching and feeling her as I growled my desire into the plump skin of her breast.

Anya dug her fingers into my curls, pushing my head down in a clear demand and I dropped to my knees like a good boy, willing to serve her this once before taking what I wanted from her in kind.

I moved my mouth down her stomach, licking and nipping my way lower as I rolled her knickers down her thighs, pocketing them as she obligingly stepped out of them for me. I kept my mouth moving lower, my dick throbbing with need at the mere thought of tasting her until I was sucking her clit into my mouth and she was moaning my name like it was a damn prayer.

Her fingers twisted in my hair as she lifted a leg and hooked it over my shoulder, her heel digging into my spine while I licked and sucked at her, tasting the perfection of her pussy and tugging my cock from my jeans.

I looked up at her as I began to jerk off, relieving some of the tension in my cock and loving the way her eyes widened as she watched me.

"Shit, you look so fucking hot like that," she moaned, and I lapped at her clit more firmly, bathing in the look in her eyes while pumping my cock harder and growling into her sweet pussy.

Anya moaned louder as the sound of tourists filing onto the boat reached us and she clapped a hand over her mouth to stifle the noise, her hips gyrating against my face as I fucked her with my mouth and she chased her release.

Precum beaded on my cock and I smeared it over the head with my thumb, groaning again as I pumped my shaft and licked her sweet cunt until she was coming all over my face, her fingernails biting into my scalp and her teeth sinking into her own fist as she fought to stay quiet and failed fucking spectacularly.

I pumped my fingers in and out of her a few more times while she squeezed them tight with her inner walls then I pushed to my feet and kissed her again, swallowing down the pleasure I could see buzzing in her dark eyes.

Anya's hand met mine as she found my cock and she began to work it in time with me, her eyes widening a little as her thumb caressed my piercing and she drew back.

"Does it hurt?" she panted and I chuckled, shaking my head.

"I'm guessing you've never fucked a guy with a piercing?" I asked and she shook her head, looking fifty shades of intrigued. "I'll give you a full education," I promised her, leaning in to kiss her once more as she returned her hand to my cock and I began to guide her up and down over the piercing, letting her explore it while my whole body shuddered at the contact of her hand on me. "But we are gonna need to do something about all that noise you keep making."

"We could stop," she suggested, though the way she was still fisting my cock told me she didn't mean that at all.

"Not a chance," I growled, pulling her knickers back out of my pocket and balling them up. "We just need to keep you quiet."

Her eyes widened as I raised them to her lips and for a moment I thought she'd refuse me, but of course she didn't, she was fucking fearless. Her lips parted and I slowly pushed the balled material between them, my cock jerking at how fucking sexy that looked as she did as she was told.

Anya kept working my cock as I released my hold on it and I gave her a dark smile as I tugged my belt from its loops, creating a noose with it and arching a brow at her.

She bit her lip as she nodded and the second she did, I flipped her around, securing the belt around her wrists and tying them tightly at the base of her spine.

Anya moaned as I kicked her legs apart, pushing my jeans down so that they were hanging from my arse and moving up behind her as I crushed her against the door.

I found the brand on the full curve of her arse and caressed it gently while guiding the tip of my cock to her drenched pussy.

I hesitated there a moment, savouring the feeling of her quivering against me as I leaned in and kissed the side of her neck, breathing in the scent of passionfruit from that endless blonde hair of hers and closing my eyes as I drank her in.

I'd fucked my fair share of women in my time, but I didn't think I'd ever wanted one like I wanted her. This wasn't some itch to scratch or lust to conquer, it was need, pure and simple, and I knew that this wouldn't be the end of us. It was barely the beginning. This goddamn temptress of a woman had me in a frenzy, and I'd learned a long time ago that when something this good lands at your door, you don't question it, you don't hold back, because you don't know how fucking long it'll stick around in a world designed to gut you while you sleep. And Anya was the best thing I'd ever had the fortune to lay my hands on, so I was gonna make the most of her before she slipped from my grasp.

Anya whimpered with need as the moment stretched and I lost the last of my control as I drove my cock up into her and groaned like a beast from the perfect tightness of her sweet body.

"Fuck, yes," I growled in her ear and she moaned around her gag in the sexiest goddamn way as I began to fuck her with the wild abandon of the animal I was.

I gripped her arse and slammed her into the door, making the damn thing rattle on its hinges so hard that I was half worried it might break at any moment and send us sprawling out into the middle of a boat full of tourists. But I doubted I'd stop even if it did. Because being inside her was the most intoxicating thing I'd ever experienced, and I was pretty sure I'd just become an addict after only one hit.

Anya moaned for me as I fucked her like a man possessed, my grip on her arse bruising as I drove my cock in as hard and as deep as I could while she pressed back into me in a demand for more and more no matter how brutal I was.

Sweat rolled down my spine as my abs flexed and I bit and sucked on her neck in a desperate, barbaric way, my hips pistoning until I felt her coming for me, her whole body going rigid as her pussy clamped tight around me and her moans rang out loudly despite the gag.

I fucked her harder through her orgasm, chasing my own release with a feral desperation which had a roar spilling from my lips as I finally came deep inside her, filling her with my cum and realising far too late that I'd forgotten all about a condom.

I crushed her to the door as we panted against it, our bodies still joined and her bound hands trapped between us.

I reached up to tug the black knickers from her mouth and she turned to catch my lips in a kiss which made my whole body hum.

"I've never been religious, but I think I just found a Church I want to pay service to over and over again," she murmured, seeming drunk on the lust in the air as I smiled wickedly, kissing her once more, knowing I'd never grow tired of her lips.

"Butch is gonna fucking kill me," I muttered, a little of the pleasure I felt fading at that reality.

"You're going to tell him?" she asked in surprise.

"'Course I am. Do I look like the kind of cunt who would fuck his best friend's wife in secret?" I asked, tilting my head in question.

"Apparently not," she replied, uncertainty crossing her face alongside a trace of fear which she tried to hide. "Do you think less of me for being the kind of woman who would fuck her husband's best friend?" she asked and I breathed a laugh.

"A husband you never asked for and who you don't love? Darlin', unless you told him to his face that you were promising him fidelity, I don't even think Butch will be able to hold that against you."

"I didn't," she confirmed, though I knew that already. The uncertainty in her eyes told me she didn't believe my claims about Benny and I pressed another soft kiss to her lips, wanting to soothe that concern away.

I stroked a couple of blonde strands from her eyes and gave her a reassuring smile.

"Any fallout will come down on my head, not yours, I swear it," I said to her. "Butch won't punish you for this."

"How can you promise me that?" she asked, the doubts clear in her onyx eyes.

"Just trust me, darlin'." I eased out of her, though my cock was already growing hard again and it was damn tempting to take her once more, but we really did need to get back to the warehouse.

I tugged the belt from her wrists and she turned to look at me, biting her lip as she stood there, her fingers moving to the cum which now trailed down her thigh.

"Here." I bent to grab my shirt from the floor and knelt before her.

Our gazes met as I cleaned her gently and her fingertips brushed along my jaw in a tender caress like maybe that had been something so much more than some physical release.

Call me an arsehole, but I'd never been in love before. I didn't do all that mushy gushy shit. But for the first time, I could see the reasoning behind the madness of love. I wasn't falling for her, fuck that. But I could see exactly why a man *would* fall for this girl. She was the kind of woman you didn't let slip through your fingers, but no doubt Benny would figure that out soon enough too if he hadn't already. And I knew how that'd go. I might have been able to get girls on their backs for me whenever I liked, but Benny was the one who could keep 'em coming back for more and more. I was the pretty toy, a good lay and not much more. Probably 'cause I didn't bother to offer them more, but when I really thought about it now, maybe that was just because I didn't have any more to offer. Anya Volkov deserved the moon, the sun, fuck it, the whole damn sky. And I didn't even have a measly star to give her.

I grabbed her clothes and handed them back to her, pocketing her knickers which were too wet from a mixture of her arousal and saliva for her to wear again anyway.

Once we were both dressed – minus my shirt which I tossed in a corner and forgot all about – I took Anya's hand and guided her out of the engine room, pulling my flat cap back on and tugging the brim down over my eyes.

The bottom deck of the boat was fairly busy and the scandalised looks a few old gals shot us said our attempts to be quiet had absolutely failed, so I just tossed them a cheeky wink.

"Sorry I'm a little late, ladies and gents," I called as we made it to the upper deck which was crammed full of people taking in the sights as we sailed down the River Thames towards Waterloo Bridge. I pointed Anya towards an empty seat and she dropped into it with a confused look on her face while I strode down the aisle between the rows of plastic chairs and held my hands out wide. "I couldn't find my damn shirt. But the show must go on, so here I am."

I glanced over my shoulder towards Harold who smirked at me, falling into the role I'd perfected on this boat many times in my youth and playing tour guide.

"Anyway, I'm here now and I'll give this my best shot, even if I haven't started off on the right foot." I shot a knowing grin at a group of women who were checking me out and wondered why I'd never thought to run this scam topless before.

I started calling out facts about the landmarks we passed, explaining how Waterloo Bridge had been constructed entirely through female labour during the Second World War before pointing out more landmarks that lined the banks of the Thames. I got the crowd laughing more than once and cooing in amazement at my knowledge. I even pointed out Custom House where all the illegal contraband seized at the UK borders was brought to be burned, and I pointed out the lack of smoke pouring from the chimneys.

"Rumour has it that they don't really destroy any of it," I called. "I've heard tale that there's a secret entrance underground where it's smuggled back out again and into the hands of gangsters who sell it on the black market. Seems far-fetched, but then again, if they really are burning all of it, you'd think you'd see the smoke, wouldn't you?"

The tourists laughed but I caught Anya's gaze, winking at her knowingly as her brows rose at my brazenness, but that was the beauty of running in my line of work – no one ever believed you if you sang from the rooftops about it. Because who would be dumb enough to do something like that?

When Tower Bridge finally appeared spanning the water, I called an end to my riveting tour, apologising about not being able to continue on to Greenwich with them to see the Cutty Sark - the old English tea clipper which had been turned into a tourist attraction further along the river - because I had to head off to the hospital to visit my kids.

"We're gonna find out about the amputations today," I said, bowing my head, and taking the cap from it to hold it out before me. "Hopefully they won't be necessary, but unless I can scrape the funds for a second opinion privately, it really is impossible to say."

My cap was soon weighed down with loose change and more than a few crisp notes too for my fake children, and I thanked everyone profusely as the boat docked at St Katherine's Pier just beside Tower Bridge.

Anya shook her head at me as I moved to join her again, tipping half of my takings into Harold's palm as I passed him by and thanking him for the safe passage before leaping down the stairs and landing by the exit to the boat.

I hopped onto the pier and Anya let me take her hand as she followed, the two of us filling our pockets with the rest of the tips I'd received before I donned my cap once more and led the way back through the streets to the warehouse.

I whistled while we walked, drawing Anya under my arm once more and tracing patterns along her arm with my fingers like I might if she really was mine. I didn't really know where the fuck we stood now, but I did know that I was mighty fond of the feeling of her body against mine like this and that I was already caught up in thoughts of her naked body, wanting more of it, all of it, all of her.

I called out as I led the way inside the warehouse, noticing the hesitance in Anya's steps and squeezing her hand reassuringly as I slipped my arm from her shoulders.

Benny appeared a moment later, his brows rising at the sight of us, and I gave him a brief rundown of what had happened with the Candlestick Maker's boys too.

"Where's Frank?" I asked and Anya shifted her weight like she was preparing for an attack.

"Should be back any minute," Benny replied, checking his watch, but the door sounded behind us, solving that mystery.

"Good. Frank, would you do me a favour and take Anya out for a bite to eat or some shit?" I asked him, making my ex-friend look at me suspiciously, clearly wondering where my shirt had gone, but I was getting to that.

"Why?" he asked and I gave Anya a little nudge towards him as I rolled my shoulders back and faced Benny like a man. He was gonna lose his shit, no doubt about that.

"Because I have something else to tell Butch, and he ain't gonna like it. Anya can fill you in."

"Really?" she asked, looking less than enthused about that.

"Really," I agreed. "I might be one hell of an arsehole, but I ain't a fucking liar. Frank should know what happened too."

Anya nodded a little hesitantly then her and Frank left at a bob of Benny's head.

I waited until the door closed behind them and met my best friend's gaze as I raised my chin.

"Spit it out," he said, his expression darkening.

"You're gonna want to beat my face in," I warned him and his posture tightened but he just jerked his chin for me to go on. I wetted my lips, my pulse picking up in anticipation of what was coming, but I'd face it like I'd said I would. "Me and Anya…well, there's no easy way to say this so…I fucked her."

Benny blinked at me like the words hadn't computed and his hand curled into a fist. "Come again?"

"You heard me, Butch. I fucked her. I know it makes me a right royal prick and I know you're gonna fucking hate me for it, but…I ain't gonna leave it at that either. I like her. I dunno what it is about her but I fucking like her and I want her and now I've had a taste, I know that ain't the end of it."

"You were right," Benny snarled. "I'm gonna beat your fucking face in."

He ran at me and I let him clock me with the first punch without even trying to block it, agony rocketing through my jaw as my head snapped aside half a heartbeat before he slammed into me and the two of us went crashing to the ground.

I deserved that one, but I wasn't just gonna let him give me a kicking like a little bitch.

A curse escaped me as his fists slammed into me over and over again and I started fighting back, the two of us rolling across the hard floor and staining it with each other's blood as we let this feral, possessive bullshit play out in a dance of fists and fury.

I wasn't sure how long we fought for before he got the upper hand, slamming me down onto the floorboards and yelling in my face as his black hair spilled over his forehead and his hands closed around my throat.

"She's my fucking wife!" he bellowed, his eyes wild.

"I know," I choked out and he fell still as he met my gaze, this brutal, primal thing passing between us as we just glared at each other, both of us owning our desire for her and neither of us willing to back down.

"What now then?" he demanded, releasing his hold on my throat suddenly and sitting upright as he shoved away from me. He kept his weight on my chest though and I could only cough as I looked up at him.

"I don't wanna take her from you," I said, seeing that void in him which had been put there by prison and knowing that she was doing something to fill it for him even while she continued to hate him. But that was just it, she didn't even hate *him* – it was Danny who had earned her loathing and I knew the change in him since their marriage had confused the fuck out of her, but that was because Benny was a different man - one she clearly hungered for if the amount of times I'd listened to her coming for him was anything to go by.

"You don't fuck her again," he snarled, swiping a hand over his face as he fought to push his anger away, the need for it tempered a little by our brawl.

"I told you," I began. "I can't promise that. I-"

"Let me fucking finish, Church, honest to fuck, I've always said you don't know when to shut up."

I arched a brow at that, feeling the sting of a cut in it as blood trickled along my forehead. "Go on then."

"You don't fuck her again – unless I'm there."

"What?" I asked, needing some damn clarification on that.

"You ain't deaf, Church. If you're gonna fuck my wife then you'll be doing it out in the open, no sneaking around, no bullshit. If it fucking hurts then that's my problem and if it turns out I like it…well, then we're gonna need a new conversation on the subject. Deal?"

I thought about that, lifting a hand to swipe some of the blood from my brow. It wasn't exactly the normal way of doing things, but then again, we never had been what anyone could call normal.

"I can't say I hated watching her come for you in the back of my car," I admitted and he broke a grin, a depraved kind of a thing which set my blood pumping. "If I'm honest, I've gotten myself off over the thought of it more than once since then."

Benny spat in his palm before holding his hand out to me and I looked between his eyes before spitting in mine too.

"One condition," I said before we could shake on it. "You have to be the one to put it to her. You're her husband, it's only right it comes from you. But if she's in…" I let the implication hang there and he smiled darkly.

"Done." He slapped his hand into mine then stood, yanking me to my feet.

"So what happened with Danny?" I asked as we broke apart and I wiped my hand on my jeans, feeling the lump of Anya's knickers still inside the pocket and deciding I was more than happy to keep that little memento.

"Turns out, our problems are a whole lot worse than we thought," Benny said on a sigh. "My arsehole brother has been working with the Candlestick Maker for years – he's in business with him, taking a cut from the sex trade and letting him push his dodgy drugs on our streets too."

"Fuck," I breathed, my mind whirling with that information as I tried to figure out how the hell we were going to fix that mess.

"My thoughts exactly," Benny replied. "Fuck."

ANYA

CHAPTER THIRTEEN

Frank silently towed me along the sidewalk by the arm, turning left and right down a few narrow streets before pulling me to a halt in front of a burger van. Except instead of a standard van, it was a converted blue VW Campervan. Hipsters clustered around it, but they slunk back with their electric scooters as Frank muscled his way to the front of the line and ordered a bean burger for me along with some greasy thing for himself.

He returned a minute later, handing me my burger wrapped in some paper and I thanked him, hesitating on taking a bite as he started eating his like a furious beast, staring intently at me like he was waiting for me to say something.

He managed to eat his whole burger in what felt like two point five seconds then tossed the paper at a faraway trash can without even looking, the thing falling straight in like it would rather defy the laws of physics than disobey him.

"So, um..." *Shit, am I seriously going to tell him about what happened between me and Church? What right does Frank have to know about that?*

But if I didn't, it was clear Church was going to tell him anyway, like being honest made up for the fact that he'd fucked his best friend's wife.

Holy fuck, what the hell was Danny going to do? Was Church really going to get the sole blame for this? What if Danny lived up to his reputation and went on a gruesome murder spree? Hell, maybe I needed to think about running my ass away right now. But even as I thought it, my mind latched on Church and I released a slow breath. I couldn't leave him to face the music alone. I'd been just as responsible for what had happened and I wasn't exactly a saint, and I sure as shit didn't run when things got difficult. I especially didn't abandon others to face the punishments of my own crimes.

I took a bite of my burger just for something to do as Frank continued to stare at me with eyes that could have melted the skin from my bones.

Damn, that was good. I chewed my way through whatever delicious shit made up the plant based burger and groaned, realising how hungry I was. I'd worked up quite the appetite running around London, chased down by the Butchers' enemies, then fucking one of the most exciting men I'd ever met.

Yeah, I'd had one helluva day, and I couldn't say I was feeling even a single drop of guilt over it. I'd never chosen to be Danny Butcher's wife, so I certainly had never chosen to be a faithful wife. But even as I thought those thoughts, guilt did find me. Just a little, a tiny morsel of a crumb. But it was enough to make me wonder whether Danny might be hurting over this right now. Did he care about me enough to care if his friend railed me? Maybe not. But sometimes when he looked at me, usually in the moments right after he'd made me come so hard for him that I couldn't see straight, or those quiet few seconds when he crawled into bed with me and our gazes collided before he pulled me into his arms, I saw something there. Something which I kept trying to deny to myself because the call of it was too terrifying to even consider answering. But it had made me wonder on more than one occasion, what if?

Frank watched me eat my burger, and I didn't even care that sauce was smeared over the corner of my mouth as I finished every bite. Before I could wipe my face though, Frank stepped forward and wiped it himself, his large thumb carving over my entire lips before pushing into my mouth. I sucked obediently, watching his expression flare with a heated kind of approval at my compliance, my heart racing before he moved back, throwing a glance up the street, but the hipsters had dispersed and the burger guy wasn't paying us any attention. In fact, he was paying us so little attention that I was almost certain he was going to give himself a bad neck if he twisted any further away from us.

Frank and I had hardly spoken since our night together at The Duck and Dog, and we definitely hadn't spoken about what he'd done to me with that damn amplifier. There was a wall back in place between us since the freedom of that night which had everything to do with who I was and where I came from - even though he'd still never explained why my heritage equalled his hatred.

My skin was still tingling with the touch of another man, and yet now my pulse was rising for him. What the fuck was wrong with me? I must have been a danger whore, because I was getting myself in deep here with men who had a lot of blood on their hands. What if mine was next?

"I'm still waiting," Frank said at last, patient, though an edge to his voice told me he wasn't fucking about. He wanted answers on why Church had needed to talk to Danny in private, on why Church had told me to 'fill Frank in.'

Well, here goes. Goodbye cruel world and all that jazz.

"I had sex with Church," I said, figuring it was best to cut straight to the point.

Frank's eyes widened and his stare intensified as he just stood there absorbing that information and I decided some context might help, though I wasn't sure what difference it really made beyond me just filling the echoing silence.

"Some men chased us and we had to escape onto a boat, I guess we got caught up in the heat of the moment and one thing led to the next and, well…" I shrugged innocently, or at least as innocently as I could manage while my core still ached with the memory of another man's dick possessing every inch of me.

Frank continued to stare. And stare and stare. A pulse was working in the side of his throat and I swear his blue eyes had never looked so dark.

"Frank?" I questioned uncertainly as he continued to stand there without response.

He turned away from me abruptly, striding down the street and slamming his foot into the trash can where he'd tossed his burger wrapper. The thing was welded to the ground but he kicked again and again until a groaning, cracking noise sounded and the whole can toppled.

But he didn't stop there. Frank picked it up as the burger man gaped at him in alarm and I did the same, watching as Frank lifted it over his head and threw it with the might of a bull, the metal bending and crunching as it hit the ground, bouncing hard with a noise that reverberated inside my skull.

Frank stood there with his shoulders heaving, his back to me, but in the next second he twisted around and a gasp snagged in my throat as he came marching towards me.

I wasn't a fucking idiot with a death wish, so I turned my ass around and ran, sprinting away from him with a squeal of fright as his heavy footfalls pounded after me.

I was faster, but he was gaining on me and I didn't know where to go as I sprinted down the street, hunting for somewhere safe to run. I made a split-second decision and charged up a ramp into a parking lot, praying I could snatch some keys off someone, get in a car, get the fuck away.

"Frank – stop!" I yelled at him, throwing a glance back over my shoulder and finding him coming at me like a charging rhino.

I ducked under the ticket barrier and kept running, looking back again and finding him lifting the whole barrier up so he could get past it.

I turned into the parking lot, finding the place full of cars, but there were no people anywhere, no one to fucking steal a key from. My attention locked on an elevator on the other side of the lot and I ran for it, pushing my legs to my limits, but for every one of my steps, I could hear the long ass stride of the tank behind me getting closer.

I was only five feet away when he caught me, wheeling me around and throwing me down on the hood of a flashy white Lamborghini, setting off the alarm in an instant and making me cry out in fright.

Frank crushed me to the hood and I shoved at his huge shoulders to try and keep him back, unsure what he was going to do as my heart thrashed like a wild animal in my chest.

I was half convinced I was about to die and I fought like mad, but that only served to devour more of the space between us.

Frank caught hold of my shoulders and pushed me down, so I threw a hand out and punched him in the head as hard as I could.

His eyes widened, his head snapping up as he stared at me and I realised my legs were spread and my pussy was nearly exposed from how far my dress had ridden up, my panties still long lost to me because of Church.

I was breathless from the struggle, but it wasn't just that, and I knew it.

This was too much of a headfuck, and my body could barely keep up as I realised how wet I was for him. This was a deadly game, but shit, I'd enjoyed it. It was a terrifying way to go out, but oh to die at the hands of this black-hearted man…

He grabbed my wrists, pinning them above my head and shoving his weight down firmer, holding me entirely at the mercy of his powerful body and awakening a whole lot of sordid fantasies in me that I had for him while the car alarm kept blaring all around us.

"Frank," I rasped and he looked at me like he wanted nothing more than to lay his mouth on mine, and for a crazy, stupid moment, I actually considered leaning in to close the distance parting us.

He grunted, anger still chiselled into his dark features as he glared at me, his breath fanning over my lips and making me hungry for a taste of him. But I was already in so much trouble, why was I looking for more?

Someone started calling him and I gasped as the vibrations of the phone in his front jeans' pocket sent a tremor over my clit and a stifled moan left me.

He watched me like I was the best fucking thing he'd ever seen, not moving to answer the phone, only pressing into me harder and shifting a little until the phone was buzzing directly onto my pussy, hard. It was like he was the god of vibrating objects and apparently every time I was around him, they came to goddamn life.

"Frank," I begged as he watched me, a twisted look filling his eyes like he was punishing me, making me squirm just for him.

"What?" he asked coldly, like he didn't already fucking know, but it was clear he wanted me to say it.

"The phone," I growled.

"What about the phone?" he asked, a bite to his tone that made my heart flinch.

The call cut out but immediately started up again and I cursed, tugging at my wrists to try and get free but he kept me exactly where he wanted me.

"Say it," he demanded. "Tell me your greedy pussy can't get enough. Tell me your husband isn't enough. That's why you fucked Church, ain't it? You're a little slut who'll fuck anyone she can to get herself off. One man can't satisfy a girl like you, can he? You're an insatiable little brat."

"Fuck you," I spat, jerking hard against his hold again as the call cut out once more and I was relieved when it didn't start up again.

His weight shifted and I felt the rock solid thickness of his cock through his jeans, making my lips part.

"You're the one pinning me to a car with your fucking boner pressing into me," I hissed. "Who's really the insatiable one around here? Are you jealous, Frank?" My voice was filled with venom and his upper lip curled at my words.

"Jealous?" he laughed callously. "I'd rather fuck a dead bitch than a Volkov."

It stung, but I didn't let it show. If he hated my family, then fine. I didn't give a shit.

"Are you lying to me or your cock right now?" I asked, taunting him with a vicious smile and he bared his teeth at me in anger.

I knew I should have been terrified, screaming for help, fighting or doing something other than baiting the beast above me, but I couldn't help it, I came alive in the fight and this was one hell of an opponent. And with my thighs spread and pussy wet for him, I didn't even know which one of us would be the winner if he drove himself inside me and showed me just how insatiable I could be.

Okay, maybe I did give one percent of a shit about him hating my family, and maybe I was curious as to why his hatred seemed so personal. I hadn't done jack to him, but there were other Volkovs, and there were a lot of wicked sins tarnishing their souls too. I just had to figure out which one in particular offended Frank so deeply.

His phone started ringing again and a moan left me that made his throat bob as my back arched against the car and I gave up trying to fight against it, giving in to what my body had already decided anyway.

Frank released me suddenly, stepping away and taking the phone from his pocket, snapping me out of whatever insanity I'd just been about to indulge in.

"Yes, boss?" he answered curtly as I sat upright, hurriedly closing my legs before he could get a view up my dress. Call me the Hoover Dam, because I was hot, wet, and as high as a mountain. "We'll be back in ten." He hung up, grabbing my arm and tugging me off the hood of the car, his grip like a vice.

Frank didn't say another word to me even when I named all the reasons why he was a prick as he dragged me along behind him, and we eventually arrived back at the warehouse after earning ourselves more than a few curious stares from strangers.

We headed inside and found Church and Danny there, their hair messed up and a few bruises lining their flesh making it clear they were both fresh from a fight.

I'd been so caught up in Frank that I'd forgotten I had to face the wrath of my husband, and I regarded him nervously as he approached us. For a second, my gaze caught on the key to the underground that Danny always carried around with him, but it was currently left abandoned on a table behind him.

Frank released my wrist, but took a slight sidestep in front of me that seemed almost protective, his head lowering as he looked to Danny.

My husband regarded him for a second then beckoned me closer. "C'mere, bombshell."

"Nah, I think I'm gonna wait over here until I figure out whether you're about to slit my throat or not, kay?" I said sweetly, though my hands were twitching for a weapon and I was trying to make a mental plan. If I could grab that picture frame on the wall, swing it with enough force –

"I'm not angry," Danny said, raising his hands in a gesture of truce but that seemed all too unlikely to me. "I just want to talk."

"You can talk from over there then," I insisted, folding my arms as I remained slightly behind the towering form of Frank, though he was probably more likely to throw me to the wolves and watch while I was torn apart than protect me from them.

"Fine," Danny said and Church caught my eye, giving me a little wink that said I didn't need to worry.

I think I'll make my own mind up on that one, Churchy.

"The long and short of it is, bombshell, Church is my boy and you're my wife," Danny said, making my fists curl as I prepared to defend myself. I swear the wedding ring on my finger was growing hotter by the second, like the damn thing was trying to remind me of the vows I'd been forced to make to this monster and the fact that I'd just broken them. Was he going to walk over here and run a blade over my throat? Drive one up under my ribs? Was murder usually this calm when it came to him?

"I'm not sorry," I blurted, because apparently my grave wasn't deep enough already. But if I was going to die today, then I was going to at least let my asshole husband know that I'd made my own choices. My decisions had been stripped away from me from day one because a bunch of men had decided my fate for me, and I didn't take fucking kindly to that.

Church had wanted me just like I'd wanted him, and why shouldn't I have given in to it? Why should I have to go along with what everyone else wanted me to do just because they said so?

"I'm not a product to be bought and sold," I growled as Danny started to approach me and Church eyed me with a frown. "I'm a woman with blood in her veins and wants in her heart as important as yours, Danny Butcher. Just because I'm yours on paper, doesn't mean you earned me. You could never buy me, not really. You can steal my heart and soul from me, but it'll never be worth the same as if I offered it to you. So if you have to kill me, then fine. But know I'm not yours. I was never yours."

Frank stepped into Danny's way before he could make it to me and Danny shot a narrow eyed look at him. "Step aside, Frankie boy."

"No," Frank growled dangerously and I wondered what the fuck he was thinking. Hadn't he been the one pinning me down and calling me a slut ten minutes ago? Was this some bullshit power move against Danny which I didn't understand? It sure as shit couldn't have been about me, because despite the obvious lust Frank felt towards me, I had no doubt his hate for me ran deeper. That was clearer than ever now.

"I ain't gonna hurt her," Danny said as Frank and him remained with locked eyes before Frank slowly stepped aside, making my frown tighten.

Danny walked towards me, cupping my cheek and I shivered from his warm touch, hunting for any sign of a blade in his other hand, wondering where the strike would come from. But instead of death, he offered me a kiss, leaning down and pressing his lips to mine in the sweetest of touches.

"I know I haven't earned you, Anya," he said against my mouth. "And I'm listening to your wants. I know you want Church, but you want me too, don't you, bombshell?"

His thumb caressed my cheek and our lips broke long enough for me to look up at him, finding such warmth there that it made me feel cold right down to my bones. Because he was right, I wanted him, I wanted to find my way into that warmth and never leave, but none of this made any sense to me. He was a man I was supposed to hate, who'd branded his name on me, and yet every day since with him had been like spending it with another man. A man who made my heart skip over beats, a man who only ever seemed to want from me whatever I was willing to give.

"So what do ya say, love?" He tilted my chin up with the tips of his fingers, being gentle with me like he was trying to prove a point that his hands – which were capable of so much brutality – would never lay harm on my flesh. "You, me, him. We can work somethin' out."

My lips parted in surprise at those words, my pulse spiking at the implication he was making as I wondered if he meant what I thought he did.

"But you're my wife first," he went on, his voice taking on a firm tone, the tone of a man who expected to be listened to and obeyed no matter what, the tone of the leader of the English mob. "So if you wanna fuck Church, you do it when I'm there. Do you understand me?"

His thumb scored along the edge of my jaw as he watched me for my response, my heart thrashing at the mere suggestion of it. I'd expected rage, violence, demands, rules, punishments – but this? Was he really saying that he could see some kind of arrangement to our marriage which included bringing Church into our bed?

I cut my gaze from Danny's dark eyes, my throat thickening as I looked to Church who looked like he wanted to make good on this offer right here and now, no doubts in his silvery gaze whatsoever. But this was crazy, wasn't it? The three of us? Me, my husband…Church.

Oh my god, Church is gonna be my fucking mistress.

Danny's hand moved along my jaw once more and I fell back into the endless, brutal expanse of his eyes as I found myself nodding, agreeing to this madness which sounded so incredibly sane somehow.

"So she's your whore then, is she boss?" Frank ground out and both of us looked around, our small world shattering as I remembered we weren't the only ones in the room. Danny always had that effect when he was this close to me, seeming to eat up the oxygen in the air and reel me in.

"What the fuck did you just say?" Danny asked, a razor's edge to his voice.

"I said, is she your whore?" Frank asked, deathly calm and my blood prickled at his words.

Danny turned to me, his eyes like nightshade. "Go to our room," he ordered, but I arched a brow at being spoken to like that. *Um, come again fuckwit?*

"No," I said simply.

"Go," Church urged, but I folded my arms in refusal. I wasn't going to be dismissed like some naughty Labrador who'd just chewed up the couch.

"Go to your fucking room!" Danny barked and I gasped, taking a step back in surprise at the sudden change in him. There he was, the beast I'd seen all those weeks ago, the monster who had forced my head down a fucking toilet and branded his name into my flesh before I'd even had the chance to say 'I do'.

I bared my teeth, glancing between them all, my gaze settling on Church as I wondered if he might go upstairs with me because I sure as shit didn't want to stay in this room now. But he just turned his angry gaze on Frank, seeming more concerned with their testosterone filled bullshit than me now anyway and I sneered at them, turning away in anger and heading for the stairs. I marched up them, striding to Danny's room, throwing the door open before slamming it hard enough to make the roof rattle.

That fucking asshole, how dare he speak to me like that?

I paced the room like a caged tiger for several seconds before throwing the door to the en suite open and grabbing Danny's toothbrush holder, hurling it at the wall where it smashed. That felt good, really fucking good. And as he loved this stupid ass bathroom so much, I went to town on it, smashing everything that was breakable. Then I stood, panting in the wake of the carnage around me and my gaze locked with my own reflection in the mirror.

I clicked it open suddenly, taking out the laptop and dropping onto the toilet seat as I flipped it up, needing something to focus on before I lost my shit entirely.

I started trying new combinations of words I'd been thinking on since I'd last tried this, muttering under my breath about how Danny was a fucking asshole, Church was his little bitch and Frank was an angry motherfucker who needed to get laid.

I gave up trying combinations of Danny's name, drumming my fingers in frustration, the screensaver popping up to show Danny and Benny together in the photo. I frowned, carving my fingers over Benny's face, able to tell the difference between them because he lacked the tattoos which Danny had crawling over his neck and hands, then tapping the keys to try another password.

BennyButcher

The laptop made a musical tone as I was given access and my jaw dropped at the simplicity in that password. His brother's name. Fuck, how had I not tried that?

I was instantly disappointed when I found the thing wasn't connected to the WiFi, so if I wanted to use it for that I was gonna have to get the password off the back of the router downstairs. For now, I decided to rifle through Danny's folders instead, curious to find out what the big, bad Brit kept hidden on this thing.

I had to wade through a bunch of surface level folders which tried to make this laptop seem innocent, but I wasn't an idiot. I kept going until I found my way to a mysterious unnamed folder which had restricted access and I tried out several password combinations to get into it. A smug smile pulled at my mouth as the words *TheButcherBoys* unlocked it and I found more folders inside, one of which was marked *Anya Volkov*.

I frowned, clicking on it and finding a whole host of images inside along with plans for what looked like some sort of prison. A coldness descended on me as I scrolled through the images, finding collars, leashes, whips, chains, and an iron cage big enough to house a person. To house *me*.

The plans for the room showed where the cage would go, along with space for a rack on the wall with shackles and spikes along the length of the wood. This wasn't some kinky shit, this was a fucking torture room, and my name was linked to this folder. This was Danny's plan for me, this was what he intended to do with me. Why had he held off? Was the room not ready, or was he trying to lure me into a false sense of security before stripping it all away from me when he was ready to strike.

My hands were shaking, bile was rising in my throat and I couldn't breathe properly as I tried to process this. He was a monster. A fucking monster and I'd slept in his bed every night. I'd let him touch me. I'd looked into his eyes and convinced myself he wasn't so bad.

Oh my god. What have I done?

I exited the folder, clicking on another beside it and finding a single video inside. I opened it up, wondering if I even wanted to see more of the creature behind the mask he'd been offering me, but I couldn't stop now. I had to know. I had to look the truth of my husband in the eye and know the depths of his degeneracy.

The video started playing and I frowned, trying to work out what I was looking at as a thick fog swirled before the lens. I realised it was a dark street as whoever was holding the camera ran past a streetlight, their breaths heavy and frantic.

The mist lifted a little and a figure came into view, a man with dark skin and blood-flecked cheeks, his eyes filling with relief as he spotted whoever was behind the camera.

"Alright, Benny," he called, then a frown dug into his brow. "Oh shit, sorry Danny, you don't half look like your brother."

"That's the thing about being twins, we're identical in every way. One and the same," Danny answered from behind the camera and my throat tightened.

"What's with the phone, are you starting up a filmmaking career now, you fuckin' dipstick?" The man laughed, but in the next second Danny lunged forward and plunged a knife straight into his throat. The man's eyes widened as a small gasp left me, the man falling to his knees before him as Danny gripped his hair in his tattooed fist to stop him from hitting the ground.

Danny yanked the knife free of his neck with a groan that sounded almost sexual and he forced his victim's head back as he clasped his bloody throat.

"It ain't personal, Olly," Danny growled then he shoved him to the ground, leaving him bleeding there as he started to back up. "Alright, scrap that. Maybe it is personal." He laughed, turning and running away into the mist, swallowed by the night before the video cut out.

My stomach was as hard as iron as I stared at the blank screen, unsure what I'd just witnessed as I closed the folder and snapped the laptop shut. I'd seen enough.

I'd known that he was a killer long before I'd ever set foot in his country, I'd heard the stories and I wasn't delusional enough to disbelieve them.

Had the weeks since our marriage been nothing but a game to him? Was he working so hard to pull pleasure from my flesh and play the role of a reformed man just to drag me into some torture chamber? Was he waiting for me to crack, wanting me to beg him to fuck me, to give me all of him and do his worst so that when he revealed the monster beneath his skin once more my downfall would taste all the sweeter, coated with the taste of betrayal and heartbreak I would feel after letting myself be lured right into his trap?

I stood up, carrying the laptop to the mirror and quickly pushing it back inside as I continued to tremble. My gaze locked on the wedge of cash in there staring back at me and whispering promises of escape. My thoughts snapped together and a decision rushed over me, sending a chill sweeping through my bones. I had to run. I had to get as far away from here as I possibly could and never, ever let that monster catch up with me.

Had he been playing me all this time? Leading me into a false sense of security, ready for the day he decided to destroy me? And even if that wasn't his intention anymore, it didn't matter. I couldn't excuse what he'd been planning for me, not ever. It was barbaric, the work of a madman who should be incarcerated, not out on the streets ruling the world.

I grabbed the cash, pushing the compartment closed and leaning over the sink as I splashed my face with cold water. Fuck, I needed to go. Right fucking now. Because if that man came for my body tonight, I'd break, I'd shove him away and let him see my contempt for him. No, I couldn't let him touch me ever again.

I held the money in my fist and pushed out of the door, hurrying to the closet and tugging off my dress as I went. I put on some underwear, jeans and a black Queens of the Stone Age t-shirt before shrugging on the leather jacket Church had stolen for me.

I grabbed the cash I'd already managed to steal and shoved all of it in the inside pocket of my jacket before zipping it up tight and picking up my biker boots, tucking them under my arm. I snagged my headphones from the nightstand, hooking them around my neck before pushing my iPod into my pocket. I spotted the mini flashlight that Church had bought me in the nightstand drawer and snagged it, pushing it into my pocket too and drowning out any thoughts I had on it being a memento. I might need it, that was all. Fuck Church. He could be as psychotic as his best friend for all I knew.

I took a breath, steeling myself for what was to come. That was it, that was all I needed in the world. Just me and my music, and perhaps that was the way it should be.

I crept out onto the balcony, listening for the men who were now in a heated argument on the floor below. I dropped down to a crouch, shuffling over to the railing of the balcony and peering down at the L-shaped space.

Danny, Church and Frank had moved into the kitchen area, the sounds of their raised voices echoing off the high ceiling.

"So she's just a fucking whore to you now, is she?" Frank barked and I frowned, pausing at the emotion in his voice like he actually gave a shit. But why would he?

"Watch your fucking mouth," Danny snarled then the sound of a scuffle broke out.

"Stop it, for heaven's sake," Church snapped, clearly getting between them and I focused back on the task at hand.

They'd see me if I went for the front door, and I felt my heart sinking as I realised I might have to wait until everyone was asleep tonight to make my way out of here, but then my eyes hooked on the key Danny had left on a table which would give me access to the underground station. My heart stalled and a plan clicked together just like that. If I was quiet enough, I could get down there and into that tunnel and they wouldn't notice. I didn't know where it led, but anywhere had to be better than here, so I had to try.

I clamped the top of my boots between my teeth and stood up, swinging my leg over the balcony and climbing onto the other side of it. The din of the guys' voices continued to echo around the warehouse, but I blocked them out as I hooked my leg around one of the large iron struts holding up the balcony and I held my breath as I carefully slid myself down it as quietly as possible.

My feet hit the floor silently and I tiptoed across the room, grabbing the key and hurrying to the door that would lead to my freedom. I pushed the key into the lock, ever so carefully turning it until it clicked, the sound like a gunshot in my ears as I froze and waited for the sound of Danny and the others coming.

But they continued to argue and I slipped through the door, gently closing it behind me. I tried to lock it but there was no keyhole on this side and I gritted my teeth in frustration before hurrying down the dark stairway, not bothering to look for any lights as I went.

I kept going down, down, down, following a twisting iron staircase to the very bottom and finally pulling on my boots when I was confident I wouldn't be heard. I gazed left and right, a low glow up ahead lighting the way forward, the passage seeming to lead to an old platform for a station called Krays End.

I hurried along, catching a glimpse of the train tracks but a heavy iron gate barred my way forward. I rattled them, cursing when I found them locked tight. *Dammit.*

"Hello?" a grunting male voice sounded beyond the gate and my heart lurched into my throat as I turned back in alarm, hunting for another way on. The men Danny obviously had stationed down here had just realised they weren't alone, and I wasn't gonna hang about to be found.

Fuck, fuck, fuck.

I started to panic, fearing I'd screwed up my only chance of escape. If Danny was called down here, or if he figured out that I was gone before I could get away –

No, keep calm. Just focus and find a way out. There has to be another way out.

I climbed back up the stairs, acutely aware of the seconds ticking by, but then my gaze locked on a door marked Maintenance and I hurried toward it, breathing a sigh of relief as it swung inward. A long, dark passage swept away before me and I shut the door behind me before bolting down it, using my mini flashlight to illuminate the path in front of me.

The tunnel swept deeper underground as I ran down it and as I turned into another passage, I found a huge hole carved into the wall, a rough tunnel burrowed deep into the earth beneath it. It was the only way forward, and I didn't have much choice but to press on now.

I took a breath, my fingers tightening on the flashlight as I slipped into the darkness, running as fast as my legs could carry me.

I had to pray this tunnel led to freedom, because I couldn't go back to my Butcher husband, not now I knew for sure that he truly lived up to his name.

FRANK

CHAPTER FOURTEEN

My blood was pounding like the beat of a war drum signalling every piece of me to attention and demanding I take action, telling me to do the one thing I was put on God's green earth to do.

"You know me, Frank," Church snarled, getting in my fucking face despite how close to the edge I was. "You might hate me now, but you and me were brothers once. You know the bones of me, and you know the worst of me. And I can see that you're fucking raging right now, but you need to think clearly. Because what you're accusing us of is all kinds of fucked up and you know it."

I gritted my teeth, my gaze snapping from him to Danny as I tried to figure this out. Despite my regrets on the subject, Church was right, I had loved him like a brother once, I had known the damn essence of his soul and I knew his limitations. He'd never been the kind to hurt a woman, and Anya had told me straight that she'd wanted what had happened between them.

So why did I feel so cut up about the whole thing? Why did I feel so inclined to rip the two of these arseholes apart and coat my flesh in their blood?

Better yet, why the fuck had I lost it with her when she told me? I'd been doing so well, keeping my feelings over her and the family she was spawned from as separate as I could make them and yet in that moment it had all boiled over, the resentment, the rage, the fucking hatred.

And yeah, some of that had been hatred for myself, because she was right, I had been jealous, jealous of the men who she offered her body to and angry over the fact that I wanted her too, despite who she was. Who her fucking brother was.

She reminded me of one of the most horrendous experiences of my life every single time I looked at her, every time I caught sight of that same darkness in her eyes as he possessed. And yet…there was so much else to her too. So much more which I was fighting so fucking hard to ignore, but which I kept noticing all the same. As much as I detested the idea of wanting someone with even the vaguest kind of connection to her family, I couldn't force those feelings to stop building, or the desire to stop plaguing me.

"I know it's your job to watch out for her, mate," Danny said, his deep brown eyes raking over me in an assessing way that made my damn skin prickle. "But I made it clear to you that that's only when I'm not there to do it myself. Why the fuck are you coming at us over this? It ain't your business."

My jaw gritted hard enough to crack a tooth as I was forced to accept those words, forced to accept the real reason why I gave a shit. It wasn't just me getting up on my high horse about the idea of Danny passing his wife around, it was about her and Church. The fact that she had wanted *Church* when I'd been walking in her shadow these last few weeks and wanting *her*.

It stung, but I was no stranger to pain. I'd just gone and let myself fall into the pretty fantasy of her when I'd had no right to do so. When I knew better and had every reason not to, every reason to hate her and all she was.

"Fine," I bit out, somehow curbing the monster in me despite the hunger I felt to let it out.

Danny's phone started ringing and he snatched it from his pocket, looking down at the unknown caller ID and exchanging a look with Church before killing the call. There was something big going on between those two. Something they were keeping me out of. I didn't know if it was some new job they were running or some problem they were working on, but it irked me every time I saw them whispering together.

Church thought about as much of Danny as I did, his loyalty to The Firm keeping him here in the exact same way as it held me. But recently something had shifted between them, something which was itching at me like a scratch I couldn't reach, begging me to satiate it.

"Are you currently riding her arse, boss?" I asked, the disdain in my voice clear and forcing Danny to raise his chin at the challenge.

"No," he snapped. "So I guess you have a job to do."

I cut them a disgusted look then turned my back on them and strode away.

"You keep looking at me like that and you might find a bullet in the back of your head the next time you walk away from me, Frank," Danny called after me and knowing him, there was likely a whole lot of truth to that.

I stomped up the stairs, my fingers flexing with the need for a fight, my mind drifting to the boxing ring as I wondered how long it would be before I could alleviate some of this anger in me.

Ever since Olly had been ripped from my life, violence had become my solace, one of my few respites from the aching chasm of grief inside me. It had been that and music – though it had taken me a few years to find my way back to the latter. But they were my only forms of escape from the grief which always threatened to drown me. Or at least they had been until her.

I strode down the walkway to the room at the far end, thumping my fist against the door and sighing when silence was the only reply Anya offered me.

"It's me," I called through the wood, a heavy breath tumbling from my lips as my skin continued to buzz with that hungry energy, my pulse pounding with a need to find violence to relieve its pace. "Look, I'm sorry for what I said earlier. I was a fucking arsehole. I ain't judging you," I went on, trying to consider how she was feeling in all of this and working to focus on that instead of my desire to try my luck against the last of the Butcher boys downstairs. "I just know Danny a whole lot better than you and I'm…worried about you." I forced those last words out, not wanting to admit to them because they implied all kinds of things I wasn't ready to accept or face.

I didn't get attached to anyone. Least of all pretty little broken girls meant for greatness far beyond the likes of me. I just wasn't cut that way, not anymore, not since my brother had been lost to me because of a man I'd loved like kin.

I swallowed a lump in my throat, my hand resting on the doorknob as I hesitated on her threshold, trying to pull myself together, to take control of the rising storm in my chest and take stock of what the fuck I was doing.

It didn't matter what situation her and Danny were agreeing to with Church. Didn't make the blindest bit of difference so long as she wasn't hurt. It wasn't my place to step in. I had one job here, and that was to protect her. Nothing more than that. Nothing beyond it was my place. So I had to stop being a fucking prick every time I felt an ounce of jealousy, especially if they were serious about this because I got the feeling there would be a whole lot more for me to be jealous about soon if they were.

"Anya, you don't need to say anything else about it if you don't want to. Just tell me you're okay and I'll let it drop. Tell me this arrangement is something you've agreed to, something you *want*, and I'll leave you be on the matter."

Still nothing in reply and my irritation spiked once more. I might have been a royal cunt back in that parking lot, but I'd gone to fucking bat against my own boss down there for her and she wouldn't even do me the curtesy of a reply?

Fuck that.

I turned the handle and pushed the door wide, striding over the threshold into the dark room but coming up short as I failed to spot her between the shadows.

A frown descended on my brow like night falling in place of day and I stepped into the room, my gaze scouring the neatly made bed, the dark corners, the open en suite which had been smashed to hell in her anger.

I moved quickly, hurrying around the space and checking any dark corners where she could have conceivably hidden herself away. The windows were still shut and the drop beyond them was sheer and impassable anyway.

It quickly became clear that she wasn't in the room and the hungry beast in my chest turned feral as I raised my voice and bellowed her name.

"Anya!" I roared, looking around one last time before hurrying out onto the walkway.

I ripped open the door to Benny's old room next, checking every corner of it for her before turning back and finding Church and Danny there with wild looks in their eyes.

"I can't find her," I snapped, my anger over the fact lashing out at them, though neither seemed interested in it.

"She can't have left, we've been down by the door the whole time," Danny said tersely. "There's no other way out."

"Except the tunnels," Church breathed and Danny's eyes widened in alarm as he quickly checked his pockets for the key.

"Fuck," he cursed, turning and sprinting towards the edge of the walkway to look down at the room below while I elbowed my way past Church and started throwing open the doors to the rest of the rooms in the place, finding nothing in every one of them and cursing myself for wasting so much time on my rage.

"The key's gone," Danny called as he looked back around at us and I turned for the stairs at that declaration, taking them two at a time before vaulting the railing at the foot of them and charging across the open area to the metal door which led down to the abandoned tube station below our feet.

I made it to the door and turned the heavy handle, the dull thunk within the metal making it clear that it was unlocked before I heaved the thing open and the cool air from the tunnel washed over my cheeks.

I made a move to step through it but Danny was suddenly there, catching my arm and yanking me back a step.

"You can't go down there," he barked at me, his eyes wild and that darkness in him on the rise.

I wasn't sure what he would do in response to this betrayal, but a lump formed in my throat at the thought of him punishing that girl.

"She can't be that far ahead of us," I replied. "She doesn't even know the layout down there, we can catch her."

"You need to go to the far end of the tunnel to cut her off," Danny barked, shooting a wild look Church's way and he nodded in agreement.

"Yeah, we have to come at her from both directions. Go to The Duck and Dog and make sure she doesn't get out at that end. We don't wanna be hunting her through the streets after dark," Church agreed.

"We're right on her arse," I snapped, making a move to head on down into the darkness of the tunnel but Danny stepped into my path, blocking me off with an angry snarl.

"Just do as you're fucking told, Frank. We're gonna hunt her down like a pack. She's bound to hear me and Church chasing her through the tunnels, and she'll be running for her fucking life. So I say we let her run right into the arms of the wolf she never even knew was waiting in the long grass ahead of her."

He held my gaze for several uncomfortable seconds, his authority over me making the air crackle with tension as I fought between my desire to race after her into the dark and my duty to obey the man I'd given my worthless life to.

It was a hard won thing, but I managed to force my eyes away, a nod jerking my head stiffly before I turned and ran for the front door instead.

Danny and Church disappeared into the tunnel and I was out the door within the next heartbeat, grabbing my keys from my pocket and diving into my van with a furious noise escaping me.

I thought of Anya running scared through the dark with those two motherfuckers chasing her down, then thought of all the ways I'd witnessed Danny punishing those who defied him in the past. I punched the dashboard so hard that a crack splintered through the plastic as a bellow of rage escaped me.

I started the engine in the next breath, focusing all of my furious energy on getting to her first. If I had to place myself between her and the wrath of her husband, then I already knew I'd do it. But if I wanted any hope of doing so, I needed to get to her first.

ANYA

CHAPTER FIFTEEN

I ran into the dark, the tunnel winding and narrow, barely high enough for me to stand upright in it and the feeling of claustrophobia pressed in on me while I worked to ignore it. The Butchers must have carved out this passage, and I prayed that meant there was an exit at the end of it.

I finally reached a dead end, my heart lurching for a second as I feared there was no way out before I spotted a ladder climbing the wall and a hatch above.

I tucked my flashlight back into my pocket, catching my breath as I climbed the metal rungs and felt for the latch on the wooden door above me. My fingers brushed it and I twisted it, carefully pushing it open with my shoulders and peering out through a crack to try and figure out where I was.

The room was concrete and a bunch of beer barrels and shelves stood in front of me filled with all kinds of liquor.

I strained my ears, the distant chatter of voices carrying from somewhere above me, but there was nothing close by. So I carefully opened the hatch and climbed out before closing it quietly, the hatch melding back in with the stone floor, invisible to anyone who didn't know it was there.

I glanced around for a way out and spotted a stone stairway which led up towards what must have been a bar. I crept onto it, but the sound of footsteps thumped this way and I darted through a door beside the stairs instead, shutting it as silently as I could and holding the door handle tight in case anyone tried to come in here.

Someone walked past the door I was hiding behind and I prayed that whoever it was would hurry the fuck up as the sound of them rummaging among the bottles reached me.

I glanced over my shoulder, finding myself in a short corridor with another door at the far end of it, light glowing beneath it and the low sound of male voices beyond it.

Shit. Maybe I just needed to risk being seen and make a run for it upstairs.

But as I went to turn the handle and make a break for it, the door shoved open and I was knocked back, finding a large guy with a tattooed neck walking in, a bottle of vodka in his grip.

The guy blinked down at me in surprise, recognition filling his gaze a moment later, drawing a cruel smirk to his lips.

"Well lookie here, a Russian spy," he purred and I realised he was one of Danny's fucking cronies, the kind that hung out with that asshole Sikes.

I cleared my throat, straightening and trying to appear as if I hadn't just been hiding behind that door.

"I'm not spying," I scoffed, trying to step past him and front out the fact that I shouldn't have been here. He didn't know that, how could he? I was his boss's wife which surely meant I held some kind of power over him, but the moment I tried to slip past him, he blocked my way, pushing the door shut behind him and making my stomach knot.

He moved forward and I moved back, not wanting him to get close enough to touch me as my muscles coiled in anticipation of a fight, my instincts prickling in warning. The man was the size of a boulder and his skin looked just as tough, but I was fast and fearless, my brothers had at least done me the favour of making certain I'd never be the victim type.

"Danny will fucking destroy you if you keep me here. He's waiting for me upstairs," I growled and the guy arched an eyebrow.

"That so?" He smirked and his expression made me queasy. "'Cause I was just upstairs, and I didn't see hide nor hair of him. In fact, I heard he's at home tonight, so what's his little mouse doing scurrying around out on her own?"

"I'm not on my own," I snarled, trying to sell the lie but it was clear this asshole wasn't buying it.

My back suddenly hit the door at the far end of the corridor and the guy leaned past me, shoving it open and making me stumble backwards through it. One glance behind me told me I did not want to stay here. A poker table was laid out between Sikes and two more of his meathead friends in a room which had deer heads hanging on the walls and no windows.

Nope. Fucking no thanks.

I darted forward, throwing a hard elbow into the big guy's ribs and diving under his arm to get out.

I made it past him as he was knocked sideways but then his hand locked in a fistful of my long hair, making me cry out as he dragged me back into the room and clamped a sweaty palm over my mouth, cutting off the noise.

“One of you shut the door, and keep a tight hold of her Abe.” Sikes said excitedly rising from his seat as his tongue darted out to moisten his wide lips and one of his other buddies hurried to shut it, locking it with a key which he stashed in his pocket.

I bit down on the gross, salty palm against my mouth and the big guy who I now knew was called Abe growled but didn’t let go, only holding on tighter.

“It looks like the boss finally sent us our little bonus, boys,” Sikes purred as he walked towards me and I jammed my heel down on Abe’s foot. Nothing. He was a fucking wall, but I was a sledgehammer and I was not giving up.

“He promised you to us the day he got bored, angel,” Sikes said, getting close to my face so the scent of vodka and nightmares seeped through my nostrils.

Those words cut a hole in my chest that felt all too real, and the worst thing was, they hurt. Even after I’d seen the vile intentions of the man I was married to, even though I was starting to accept that every soft caress he’d offered me had been a trick, a lie, I was still foolishly shocked to discover how little I meant to him. And it was all too clear it was true, because I’d seen the monster he was through the sick dungeon he was planning for me, the veil had been drawn back and now I could do nothing but stare the beast of Danny Butcher in the eye. I saw him, and the truth was terrifying.

“Looks like he finally got tired of you,” Sikes continued. “But don’t worry, we’ll look after you. We’ll never get bored of your pretty flesh.”

CHAPTER SIXTEEN

"This is bad, Butch," Church muttered as we ran through the dark, using the light of our phones to illuminate the path ahead. "Really bad."

"You mentioned," I ground out. "Repeatedly in fact."

"What if she saw Danny?"

"The gate was still locked down there, she couldn't have seen him," I hissed.

"No, but she coulda spoken to him."

"He's as high as a fucking kite right now," I snapped, sick of going over and over this shit. "And if by some fucked up miracle she did speak to him and he did explain the truth of who he was and she hung around long enough to listen to his fucked up ramblings, we'll deal with it when we find her. Emphasis on the finding her part, Church. Got it?"

"Yeah," he agreed, the concern in his voice thick. "Yeah, I got it. We need to find her first."

I gritted my teeth and ran on, my pulse echoing in my ears as we passed into the roughly hewn, unofficial part of the tunnels which we had painstakingly carved out ourselves during the renovations of The Duck and Dog when we bought the place. Not that anyone knew we owned it. Officially Shaila's name was on the deed, but it was our blood money that had paid the price for it and we made good use of it while turning a tidy profit and cleaning some of our less than legal earnings through its tills too. The addition of the tunnel was just the icing on the cake. It was a beauty of a plan really, this sneaky little escape avenue for if things ever went sideways. Or at least it had been until it had backfired and been used against us by my cunning little wife.

"I'm gonna spank her arse raw when I get my hands on it," Church growled.

"Get in line, brother," I replied darkly.

We reached the end of the tunnel where we hurried up the ladder and I shoved the hatch open at the top, climbing out into the cellar of the pub. We didn't waste a second, running for the stone stairs and racing up them to the top.

But as I pushed open the door, my erratic pulse thumping in my throat and a sense of goddamn dread washing over me, I didn't find my bombshell, I found Frank fucking Smith, looking ready to rip the world apart as he flew through the doorway in front of me.

"Where is she?" we both barked at the same time while Church swore colourfully at my back.

"She musta made it out already," I snarled, striding right up to Frank like I was looking for a fight, but I forced my way past him instead, gazing out into the packed pub for any sign of our little runaway.

"She wasn't outside. Not on any of the closest streets," Frank said anxiously. "How could she have gotten out of here so fast?"

Church leapt up onto the nearest table, causing several fellas to catcall him as heads turned our way curiously.

"I can't see her," he spat, scouring the pub. "I'm gonna ask Shaila if-"

Church fell silent suddenly as the doors at either end of the pub slammed open and a group of ugly fuckers all pushed their way inside. They were dressed in black and had hoods pulled up and ski masks over their faces, a couple of them sporting baseball bats which they held at the ready too.

A woman screamed, the regular punters shitting their britches at the sight of a gang pouring in through the front doors.

My phone buzzed in my hand and I looked down at the message with a sinking feeling in my gut, because I just knew what it was going to be before I'd even looked.

Unknown:

I think you need reminding of who I am. Let this serve as a lesson. We still need to talk.

"Right, lads," I called, hopping up onto the table beside Church as more of the Candlestick Maker's men pushed into the pub. They might not have been wearing anything to identify themselves by, but it didn't take a genius to figure it out. No other fucker would dare stand against the Butchers, no other gang would be so fucking stupid. "Let's let the nice ladies and gentlemen get out of our fucking way, yeah?"

John boy stood from his spot in the corner to our left, his slim frame, brown hair and forgettable face always making it easy for him to go unnoticed, but that was the key to his power – no one ever saw him coming and he was a true savage Butcher when the occasion called for it. He threw the side door open when none of the masked fuckers so much as twitched a pinky finger and he bellowed at the punters to get the fuck out.

A stampede took place as they ran for their goddamn lives and I didn't even blame them. No fucker wanted to stand in the middle of a gang war when it kicked off because once the blood started flying, there were no promises made about who would end up bleeding out. Collateral damage was all too likely to occur.

Our gang closed in around us as the patrons escaped and the moment the last of them were gone, more of the Candlestick Maker's men swarmed in through the side door, making it more than clear that there was no way out of this mess without us all getting bloody over it.

But that was fucking fine by me.

"Looks like we're in for a good old fashioned knees up then, boys," I called loudly, my hands curling into fists as I set my gaze on the big wanker who stood at the front of the swarm of gangsters ahead of me and marked him for my own. "Let's show these motherfuckers why you don't mess with a Butcher!"

I took a running leap from the table with Church right beside me and a roar of noise broke out as the two gangs collided with blood, fists and fury.

CHAPTER SEVENTEEN

At Sikes's command, Abe threw me down on the poker table, but I'd already taken stock of everything that was on it, and the second one of my hands came free, I grabbed a glass of vodka, twisted around like a cat and smashed it against the side of Abe's head.

He roared in pain, flying backwards as he tried to pluck the pieces of glass out of his face while his friends looked to him in alarm.

In the next second, I kicked the guy sitting on my right in the face, my boot breaking his nose and sending his chair toppling backwards as he screamed.

I dove off the table and ran for the door, but I had to slow to try and get the key from the asshole who'd locked it, adrenaline coursing through my body as I set my gaze on him.

"Get hold of her, Crispin!" Sikes yelled, taking a knife from his hip that made my pulse jackhammer.

Crispin swung around just as I collided with him and my fingers hooked the key out of his pocket.

His fist slammed into my cheek before I could run, knocking me to the ground, pain ricocheting through my skull. But the key was still in my hand and all I could think about was that door as I shoved up onto my knees and scrambled towards it.

Hands fisted in my jacket, hauling me backwards and a weight pressed down on my back as someone sat on me. My lips parted on a scream for help, but Sikes rested the huge knife to my throat as his other hand locked in my hair, his bony ass pressing hard down on my back.

"Scream and you're dead, angel," he warned and a tremor rocked through my body as someone prised the key from my fingers. *No.*

Sikes's grip softened in my hair, caressing instead as he cooed his approval of my compliance.

"Now roll over nice and slow for me," he ordered, lifting his hips to let me move.

I locked my teeth together, doing as he said as I tried to figure out my next move.

"Let me at her first," Abe snarled, his towering form stepping closer as he picked the last shard of glass out of his eyebrow and blood pissed down the side of his face from his wounds.

Sikes gently stroked the blade along my chin, his gold teeth glinting at me as he smiled kindly like he wasn't about to fucking violate me.

"Patience, Abe, we'll all get a turn, but she's mine first." He slid the knife down to my shirt, sheering into the material and sitting back on my hips so he could cut it all the way open. He peeled it apart down the middle, exposing my tits and while every motherfucker's gaze fell on them, my hand snapped out, punching Sikes hard in the throat, making him wheeze and fall backwards.

I grabbed his wrist with a snarl, yanking it to my mouth as I half sat up and drove my teeth into his skin, making him scream like a baby and drop the weapon. I snatched it and Sikes had the good sense to run for his life as he scrambled away from me and crawled under the table.

I leapt to my feet, swinging the blade as Abe came at me like a battering ram, a snarl of determination leaving his lips.

I may have been far smaller than him, but I was trained by the Russian princes of the mafia in my homeland, and I could fight better than this fucking elephant could.

His fist rammed into my ribs, throwing me sideways, but I planted my feet and shoved my shoulder into his chest.

Crispin collided with me on my other side, trying to wrestle the knife from my grip, but I brought up my knee, crushing his balls and making him gasp as he stumbled back. And in that inch of space I gained, I drove the knife towards Crispin's neck and sliced it in deep.

Deep enough to stop him from screaming, deep enough to make him immediately choke on a tide of blood that rose in his throat as I twisted it sharply with a growl that made agony flare in his eyes. But with my newfound blade buried in his skin, I was momentarily vulnerable and Abe took quick advantage, yanking my hand off of the knife's handle and leaving his friend slumping to the floor, pissing blood everywhere as it spurted out around the knife.

He looked for help that wasn't coming, Sikes kicking at him from under the table as Crispin clutched his ankle and Abe suddenly shoved me up against the wall, my forehead impacting with it so hard that stars burst in front of my eyes.

I could taste Crispin's blood on my lips and it was turning me into an animal, like something within it was awakening a violent creature in me and I liked the feel of her in my veins.

But as more fight returned to my limbs and I started to thrash, Abe gripped my head and cracked it against the wall again. Music exploded into my skull which stunned me. The Killing Moon by Echo & the Bunnymen burst into my ears as if it was really playing all around us and I was captured by the worst night of my life as Abe's hands slid around to grope me between the ripped tatters of my shirt. I fell still, a paralysis seeming to claim me as I was dragged back into the past.

"I like 'em wild," Abe growled in my ear.

"She's mine first," Sikes hissed and I felt Abe obliging, bowing to the rule of the creep as he came closer and they just left their friend to die in favour of assaulting me while the other one clasped his broken nose and sobbed.

Sikes's hands were cold and clammy as they worked to pull my jacket from me, the slimy feel of him already seeming to crawl under my skin.

I just have to scream. Someone will come if I scream.

But maybe what Sikes had said had been true, maybe Danny really had said these men could have me. And if that was the case, if he really thought of me as just some whore to be passed around his gang, then who would come for me? Who would care about a girl who was nothing but a pound of flesh sold for the sake of a treaty she had no say in?

The sound was locked deep down in my chest as fear bound me in iron ribbons. The music was too loud in my ears, the darkness was closing in too tightly around me, and the strength was falling from my limbs.

Scream, Anya, fucking scream!

CHURCH

CHAPTER EIGHTEEN

Carnage sang my name in the crash of bodies against the tables and the shattering of glass which rang out like a melody designed to perfectly fit my bloodthirsty soul.

There wasn't much in this world that made sense to me the way the swing of a fist did, the strike of a blow, the bittersweet taste of pain.

Yeah, we were brutal, savage men, better suited to times long since past when our kinds of barbarity were honoured and celebrated the way they were in the courts of the kings of old. But we were the rise of a new kind of monarchy, self appointed kings of the underworld where we ruled over the dark, and paved the path of vices for the sinners lurking in plain sight.

Society liked to brush all knowledge of us aside, but they sought us out all the same. The businessmen and women with their fondness for the products we pedalled, the law-abiding husbands finding escape with the women who sold themselves on our streets. So many of our so called betters relied on us to prop up their pretence of pious living. But down here in the dirt and blood of the streets, we owned who we were and we were damn proud of it too.

So as my fists struck flesh and my muscles burned with the force of my own blows against our enemies, I was flying high on a ride of utopian purity, living in the moment between life and death where I knew one wrong move could see the end of me.

There were knives in this fight, bats and knuckle dusters too, but I had always preferred the feeling of my own bare fists cracking against hard bone to the slice of a blade or swing of a weapon.

An agonised yell made me whip around, the tang of blood on my lips and sweat rolling down my spine as I panted from the exertion of the fight.

My gaze caught on old Billy Baxter across the room as he grabbed hold of a bar stool and launched it at a fucker who had just stuck him with a kitchen knife, blood pissing down his side while he roared his allegiance to the Butchers and sent the stool crashing into the face of his opponent.

It was utter fucking mayhem in here, my gang and the enemy merging in a lump of clashing fists and pounding feet.

Minutes or hours could have passed and I wouldn't have known the difference, my heart drumming to the rhythm of the violence we were dressed in and my sinful soul humming with the thrill of the fight.

"Butch!" I yelled a warning as two arseholes tried to rush him at once, grinning as Benny turned to meet them with the look of the Devil in his dark eyes and not an ounce of fear in sight.

Agony suddenly crashed through my spine as some fucking wanker clocked me with a baseball bat and I rolled as I hit the floor, narrowly avoiding a hit to the head as he swung it at me again.

The bat hit the floor right by my temple and I grabbed it, kicking the fucker in the chest as I ripped it from his hands and flipping it over so that I caught the handle as I leapt to my feet.

I raised the bat over my shoulder, bellowing a challenge which had the little weasel turning and running like the kid he no doubt was and I charged after him, roaring the whole way and sending several more scattering in fear too.

The door swung wide and the sound of sirens called to me on the breeze, sounding the beginning of the end to this shit as I turned from the fleeing cowards and looked back to the brawl.

Another arsehole came at me, yelling a challenge as he ran for me and I threw the bat straight at his face, letting it fly away from me as he was forced to leap aside to avoid it caving his head in. A window shattered behind him and I sent a silent apology to Shaila whose pub was getting ripped to shit, but she was giving as good as she got to protect it. The rest of her staff were no doubt locked upstairs in the safe room we'd had fitted here for whenever shit went tits up like this. It didn't happen all that often, but none of us wanted their blood on our hands, so having somewhere safe to lock themselves away from the reality of our world when it came knocking at their door made sense. Shaila never did go running and hiding from a fight though, she was on the front line just like the rest of us.

I spun around, hunting for my boys in the mess and my gaze locked on a big bastard who was swinging his sledgehammer fists with abandon, keeping Frank busy as he gave as good as he got. I took a step towards them, but a scream caught my ear which had me falling all too still.

My head snapped around, my gaze falling on the stairs beyond the bar as that sound came again, the desperate, haunting plea of it filling my chest and striking fear deep into my blackened heart as I recognised the girl who was crying out for help.

"Anya!" Benny bellowed, hearing her too.

He threw his opponent away from him with a savage shove which sent his head smacking into the edge of the bar and I found myself running at his side as the two of us raced for the stairs.

The brawl was forgotten behind us as the flash of red and blue lights burst through the windows and the wails of the police sirens made every fucker in the room stop what they were doing.

The Candlestick Maker's men started to flee, yells of warning over the arrival of the police ringing in my ears while I sprinted towards those fucking stairs.

I vaulted the bar, charging along with Butch on my heels as the sound of her screaming filled the air once more.

I raced downstairs and ran on into the cellar, certain her screams had come from there. But I barely took four steps before another cry for help tore from her throat and I spun back, finding Benny charging through the door that led towards the poker room, a furious bellow escaping him as he went.

I was at his back in seconds, sprinting towards the door which led into the illegal gambling room as fast as my feet would carry me and calling out for Anya to let her know we were coming.

Benny slammed into the door, making the hinges rattle as it failed to open for him and I moved to his side, the two of us bracing ourselves before kicking it in sync, sending it crashing into the room beyond.

My eyes widened as I took in the sight before me, finding Anya in the arms of Abe as he pinned her to the wall and Sikes tugged at her destroyed t-shirt where her tits were exposed.

Sikes yelled in alarm as he realised who had just come to crash his sick party and he scrambled away from us as Benny snatched a vodka bottle from the floor and smashed it against the wall.

Abe shoved Anya at us, trying to apologise or some equally pointless shit and I caught her in my arms, dragging her against me.

Benny roared like a beast, colliding with Abe and sending him crashing back onto the poker table, chips and cards scattering everywhere before he slammed the sharp end of the shattered bottle down into his chest.

My gaze met Anya's as she sucked in a sharp breath, but it wasn't fear I found in her onyx eyes, it was a beautiful and terrifying desire for vengeance.

Two-bit Jim scrambled to his feet on the other side of the table, holding his hands out wide in surrender and revealing his bloody nose as he met my gaze and started backing up.

"I didn't do nothin'," he begged, seeing his death in my eyes as my upper lip peeled back and I took a step towards him, releasing Anya.

"Did you try an' help her?" I asked, my blood pumping hot and fast as he glanced beyond me to the girl I was gonna kill for and shook his head.

"Sikes said Danny didn't mind," he began, but I was on him before he could finish that sorry fucking excuse, colliding with him with fists and fury and enough fucking rage in me to know I would see him dead at my feet before I stopped with this.

In my periphery Benny kept stabbing and stabbing, every surface surrounding him painted red as he went to fucking town on Abe while he convulsed and thrashed beneath him, fighting to get him off while the energy faded from his limbs.

I unleashed all of my rage on Two-bit Jim as I let the worst of me shine through, my body becoming nothing more than a weapon as I felt his body crack and break beneath the power of my blows. I shoved myself back to my feet as he stopped fighting and I started kicking and stomping instead, roaring my anger to the walls as I ended his sorry excuse for a life and met Anya's heated gaze across the blood soaked room.

My attention focused on Sikes as Anya spotted him too, creeping towards the door like he thought he could escape our judgement. She was fast, snatching a knife from the throat of a fourth fucker who I hadn't even noticed while he twitched and bled out on the floor.

"The boss said we could play with her once he got bored," Sikes pleaded, backing away from me as I prowled towards him and raising his hands in surrender when he found nothing but his death in my eyes.

Yells of "Police!" and demands for people to stop beating the shit out of each other filtered down to us as the coppers made it into the pub upstairs. I knew we were running mighty short of time to finish this, but I wasn't capable of letting him live now. Not after he'd dared to lay his hands on my woman.

A wet thump sounded Abe's body falling to the floor as Benny finished with him and I glanced at my best friend as he stalked forward, soaked in blood and hungry for more.

But it wasn't either of us who got there first.

Sikes screamed as Anya shoved past me, her lips peeled back in a feral snarl as she swung her arm back and slammed the blade home in his chest.

Sikes lunged at her, his face twisted in violence, but my fist connected with his jaw, sending him crashing into the wall again as I caught Anya in my arms and hauled her away from him.

Benny surged forward though, gripping Sikes by his greasy hair as he began to slump towards the floor and swinging his head to one side before slamming it into the wall with a sickening crack.

"No one," he snarled, driving his head into the wall again and leaving a bloody splatter against it. "Lays a *fucking finger*." He smacked Sikes's skull into the wall twice more with those two words and I was pretty certain that last one did him in. "On *my* fucking-" His head cracked against the wall with such force that Benny was forced to release him that time and there was no doubt left that the fucker was dead. "Wife!" he roared, his chest heaving and blood coating his flesh.

Anya's lips parted in shock as she stared at him, this bloody demon, painted in sin just for her, and the way he looked back made my fucking heart skip a beat. Because that look right there was electric, I could feel the aftershocks of it radiating around the room even as the old bill poured through the pub upstairs and I knew we needed to fucking run.

She raised her eyes to meet mine next and that shock rattled through me as I took her in, bloody and battered and so damn beautiful it broke my heart to gaze on her.

"You're alright now," I swore to her and she nodded as she drank me in, the charge between us all so potent you could have struck a match on it.

A furious roar ripped into the silence and we looked around just as Frank charged into the room, ready to battle with a broken chair leg raised in his fist while one hell of a cut bled down the side of his arm.

Anya dashed from my arms in the blink of an eye, her hands grasping his face as she stared up into his blue eyes and the chair leg hit the floor with a rattle as he dragged her into his arms.

I could feel it again, that fucking force of nature which seemed to buzz all around us, the blood and carnage in the room only adding to its potency.

"Put your hands on the fucking ground!" a police officer yelled from somewhere above us and the spell we were caught in shattered as I looked to the exit. I was gonna guess we had all of two minutes to spare before the cops came on down here to look for stragglers and found us standing in a room with four corpses, painted bloody with all the evidence they could ever ask for to put us away for life.

I looked to Anya and my brothers, a knot forming in my throat. "Well shit, we're in one hell of a pickle here, lads."

PART TWO

BEING TOTALLY FRANK

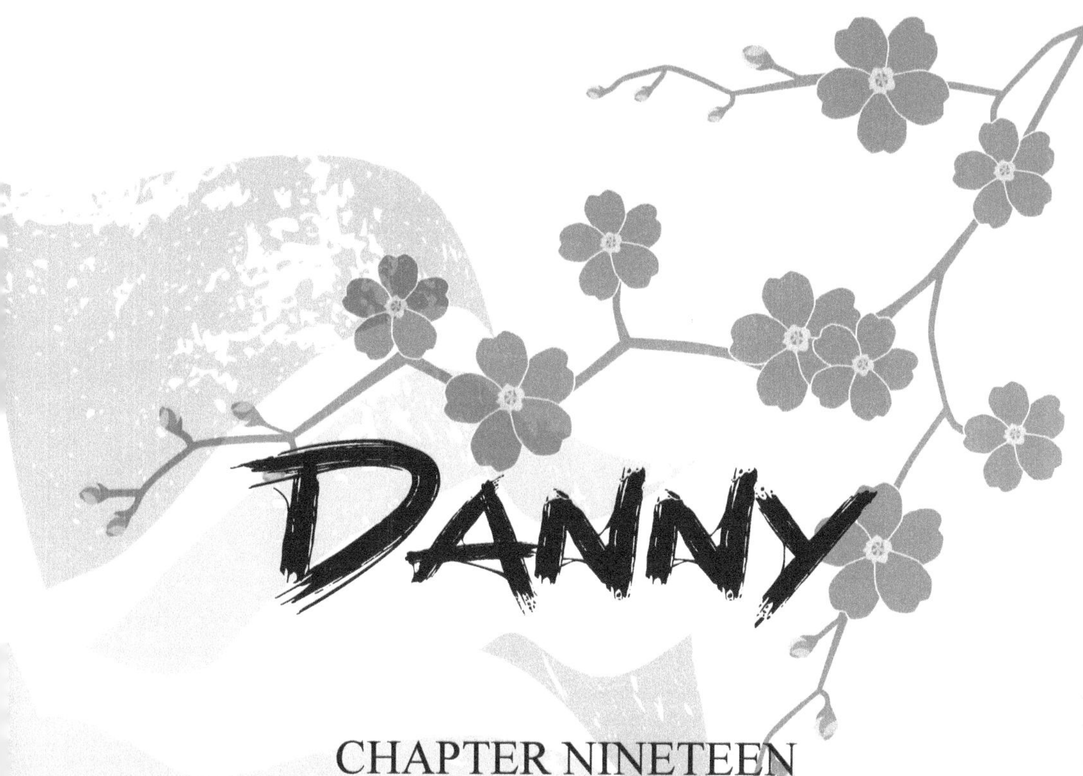

CHAPTER NINETEEN

I whistled to myself as I looked across the dimly lit platform, counting the tiles along the wall opposite me from the mattress put here for me to sleep on. I sat on my arse and perched my forearms on my knees, letting my hands hang loose before me as my fingers flexed and relaxed.

I kept losing count of the time down here, days blending into weeks in this endless monotony of darkness.

I was living between visits from my brother, acting out the life I'd thought he'd have while he was locked away. Though of course he'd stopped letting me visit after a bit. His own flesh and blood. Born of the same womb.

He'd cut me deep with that move. Made me feel anger like I'd never experienced before. Forced me to act out in an attempt to sate that rage in me, causing countless misery to unsuspecting buggers along the way.

That was all on him.

I mean, I got it. I got why he'd been so cut up over things, why he'd been salty over doing a long stretch behind bars. Men like us weren't born for cages. We were kings in our own right. But he'd had to learn.

And I could see now that he had. Despite his attempts to show me how much he wanted me broken, how much he hated me and wanted me out of the picture, I knew this was all just revenge for his time in prison. He'd been locked up and now I was suffering that fate too. I got it. I really did. But he would thank me for my intervention in the end.

I remembered the glorious days at the start of our reign, the nights we spent out on the town together, the fuckers we put down and the shit we did when it was just us. Me and him were this cohesive unit, we shared DNA, it was written right through us. We were the same.

I'd had to do what I'd done all them years back and now Benny had to do this in return. Tit for tat. But the truth was, I'd have been long dead if he really hated me the way he claimed. Men like us didn't suffer prisoners who we were plannin' on killing. What was the point?

I mighta been down in this pit for a few months, but I knew it wasn't permanent. One day soon he'd come down here and embrace me as the brother I was. We both knew it. Our time to rise was finally upon us and together we'd rule these streets with blood and iron.

Eight years ago, I hadn't had a choice in what I'd done. Those arseholes had forced my hand. They'd been stealing him from me. Bit by bit by bit, tempting him away like the snakes they were. His little crew, his band of merry men, his so called Forget-Me-Nots with their rising reputation and flare for brutality.

Benny had claimed the four of them were building something which I wouldn't understand. He'd told me their reputation would strengthen our hold on these streets we called home, that everyone would fear their name and understand that their word was law.

It was a pretty little tale of bullshit, and I knew full fucking well that they'd been whispering in his ears to make him a part of that. Murmuring pretty promises of loyalty and honour amongst the darkest men in our court of the underworld.

I'd seen them for what they were. Power hungry rats. All three of them. All tempting my brother into their fold. Tempting him away from me.

That wasn't right. Benny belonged with me. We were supposed to rule as one, killing and fucking our way to success, working our way through flesh and bone to take everything and anything we could ever desire. It was supposed to be me and him.

But they twisted him against me. I saw it. I watched from the side lines as they took and took and took. Nights out without me. Running jobs I had no part in. Laughing and joking and acting like they were fucking kings and I was nothing but a jester in their court.

Well there was no fucking way that I was ever gonna stand for that.

Benny musta known that deep down. It was a test. He wanted me to fight for him. To fight to reclaim my place at his side so that we could rule together in beautiful, chaotic anarchy.

Which meant something had to give. They had to go. Just like all the others before them had.

I coulda done it bloody. In hindsight, maybe I shoulda. But I guessed I'd felt a little pity for my brother on account of how deeply they'd drawn him in. Their bloody ends weren't enough to stamp out that love he thought he felt for them. I needed to prove the falseness of it before that.

I scoffed to myself as I sneered at the mere memory of him and his boys, acting like they were a right barrel of laughs and I was the rotten apple who always came to sour their fun. Nah, killing them all outright wouldn't have released him from that bond he thought he felt with them: he'd needed to see their true colours.

It had been a hard lesson to have to teach him, and fuck knew I hadn't expected him to go down for that long, but of course Benny had ended up at the mercy of the one judge in this fucking city who I hadn't had in my damn pocket.

I'd killed him for that of course. After Benny was sentenced, I'd snuck into the old boy's house and cut his fucking eyes out, followed by taking his fingers and toes then tugging his insides onto the outsides and letting him lie there and bleed out in his own bed. It had been an empty kind of justice, but one I'd relished all the same. Had Benny rejoiced at the news of the judge's death though? Oh no. Of course not.

The lack of gratitude I received from him was appalling. It was why I'd decided to let him rot. Let him fester away in there and think about me the way I was always thinking about him. Let him miss my company so bad he was left craving it. And I knew that when the time was right we'd be together again, ruling side by side once more.

Olly had had it coming. Benny must have been starting to see that now. I hadn't even had to kill the others in the end. Frank was practically a walking corpse after Olly anyway, the only thing that sparked something in his deadened eyes, the mention of my brother's name. I knew he planned to kill Benny the moment he saw him, and I'd been keeping that gift in reserve, waiting for the day when my twin was finally released and returned to me so that we could end Frank together. Benny would have no choice but to see the truth then, when his so called best friend tried to kill him over a lie he'd never even questioned.

It had always been like this over the years. People trying to come between me and him. Teachers tryna seat us apart, supposed friends looking for a way into the fold, working to draw Benny away from me, to steal him from me. But I wasn't ever gonna let that stand. I'd seen them all off, time and again, through violence, blackmail or fear, they'd all gone running one way or another.

I'd thought the girls were the worst of it once, back when we were younger and he used to get silly ideas in his head about fucking the same pussy over and over again, letting some bitch whisper bad things about me in his ears while his cock was buried between her thighs. I'd had my work cut out with a few of them, some of them dumb enough to think he would stand at their side over mine when I came for them, but he never had. In the end, I'd gotten rid of them all.

Tessa had been the hardest, ignoring my threats, surrounding herself with her brothers so that I couldn't get close when she was alone, all the while making Benny look at me with darkness in his eyes. I'd warned her. I'd told her not to try and get between us, but nothing I'd done had been enough to make her leave. At least not until the end, not until I found the way to break her.

I'd fucked Tessa myself, making her think I was him, waiting until I was inside her before giving her the truth. It had been a delicious kind of victory, watching the realisation merge into horror while I fucked her into her ma's bed and pointed out the camera I had set up right beside us, proving her loyalty to my dear brother to be nothing more than bullshit.

She'd gone running after that alright.

In fact, Tessa had started something of a hobby for me, a little fascination I had with the women Benny chose to fuck. She'd been the first of his women who I'd claimed for my own, but not the last. There was just something about knowing he'd had them first that made me ache to have them too. Another thing we shared, the way we'd been born to share everything.

That was just the way it was. Benny and Danny Butcher, one and the same. And we didn't need no one else getting in the way.

So today, I might have been sitting in a cell of his making, but I wasn't feeling all that cut up about it. He'd been making it progressively more comfortable for me down here, giving me a bed, clothes, some things to read - and he'd even been bringing me my drug of choice whenever the need rose too high in me.

I wasn't even a slave to the chain anymore – he'd come down here a while back and released me from it, giving me free run of this place while he wasn't here. The bars which blocked the tracks off kept me caged alongside the heavy gate which he made certain to keep locked at all times, but I was already a little freer than I had been when he'd first returned.

Those weren't the actions of a man set on murder. This was just my punishment for the years he'd spent in lock up.

So as I sat in the dark, waiting on his next visit, I just focused on all the things that counted while I bided my time.

He ain't killed me.

He still loves me.

It'll always be the Butcher boys against the motherfucking world.

CHAPTER TWENTY

My eyes flicked between the three antiheroes who had come to my rescue, but these weren't the shining armour kind, they were dark knights with a plague of death in their wakes. As my gaze settled on their leader, Danny Butcher, man-made monster and captor of my life, the strange bond that seemed to be humming between us all released me. And I turned and fucking ran for the door.

I managed to get it open and step two feet beyond it before strong hands clamped around me, three sets of arms hauling me back.

"Get your hands off of me," I snarled, twisting my head and sinking my teeth into the tattoo of a church which covered the back of the hand on my shoulder.

Church cursed but didn't let go and I was dragged back between them all, the three muscular walls of their bodies driving against me until I was trapped once more.

Danny was in front of me, his fingers locking on my jaw, though not tight enough to hurt. I flinched away from his touch and a frown deepened on his brow like he couldn't understand why I didn't want him anywhere near me. And I didn't plan on telling him I'd been through his private little laptop, that I'd seen the monstrous dungeon he was planning for me.

"We're down to a minute to get outa here," he growled. "Do you know what's gonna happen if those coppers get hold of you, love? They're gonna lock you up for good, and you'll rot away in jail until there's nothin' left of your soul."

“There’ll be no music there, Anya,” Frank added and I looked to my right, my shoulders heaving. I realised my shirt was still hanging open down the middle, barely covering my breasts and I quickly tied a knot in the loose ends. Church produced my leather jacket from somewhere, draping it around my shoulders and I pushed my arms through the sleeves.

“Come home, darlin’. We can protect you,” he insisted and I looked to him, finding the warmth of the sun in his eyes.

“We need to hurry,” Frank urged his boss and Danny nodded stiffly, taking a matchbox from his pocket and handing it to him.

“Burn it,” Danny ordered gruffly then shifted towards me all of a sudden. “Time’s up, bombshell. I ain’t gonna see my wife go down for this.”

He grabbed me, throwing me over his shoulder and I gasped as he started running with Church on his heels. Behind us, Frank poured vodka all over the poker room, lighting it up in a blaze before chasing after us.

The cops barked orders from above and they were definitely getting closer, so I kept my damn mouth shut, preferring this option to being caught.

At least if we made it out of here, I had a chance of escaping again in future. If the cops got me and I went down for murder, I was fucked.

When we made it to the hidden hatch, Church bent down and started scrambling to find the edge of it in the darkness. He growled in frustration as he searched the rough floorboards before finally locating the edge of it and yanking it open.

Danny didn’t waste a second, jumping into the hole, making my stomach soar and my heart pound, his feet hitting the floor below before he set off running into the dark.

“Put me down, asshole,” I gritted out.

Church and Frank made it through the hatch, shutting it behind them and plunging us into darkness while Frank slid a bolt into place to lock it tight. I guessed they had faith in it remaining undetected during the investigations which were bound to take place.

“We can move faster if I run on my own,” I insisted.

Danny ignored me, his grip only tightening on my legs as he pressed on into the dark.

Church appeared beside us, lighting up the path before us with the flashlight on his phone.

He glanced my way, a tautness to his brow that spoke of the dark thoughts swirling in his mind, but he said nothing, and I decided to seal my lips and try to form a plan. But as the quiet and the dark twisted around me, all I could think about was those men’s hands on my flesh, the hunger in their eyes, like carnivores closing in on fresh meat. I’d never been in a position like that before, even the wrath of my father’s fists had been preferable to what they’d been planning for me, and it made me sick to my stomach. I wanted to wash, to scrub and scrub my skin until it was raw and there was nothing left of their mark on me.

The fire in my belly was burning low, and the more the silence pressed in, the more desperate I became for my music. I fumbled for my headphones which were still somehow looped around my neck, pushing them up onto my ears and hunting for my iPod, relief inching into me as I found it still lodged in my jeans' pocket.

The light illuminated on the screen and I hooked it up to my headphones, about to press play when Danny lurched sideways down a passage and sent the iPod flying out of my hands.

"No," I gasped as it hit the ground and Danny didn't stop. "Wait." I punched him in the kidney and he snarled but didn't slow.

Frank bent down as I looked back to it hopelessly, scooping it up easily, his features set in hardened lines as he ran. But he didn't hand it back to me, he chose a song instead, letting it play.

The tension instantly went out of my shoulders as Nirvana's cover of Lake of Fire swirled around my head. *Better*.

I went slack on Danny's shoulder, my head bouncing against his back as he ran on and my eyes falling shut as the memory of Sikes's greedy eyes faded away and the music took their place. It was a balm soothing my heart and I fell into the blissful numbness of it, leaving everything behind. I was a girl lost into the night, stolen away by Kurt Cobain's voice and riding on the wings of the rhythm somewhere no one could find me.

The next real thing I knew, I was being placed on my feet and hot lips burned against my mouth. My eyes snapped open and I shoved Danny back, my heart thrashing as I took in this man painted in the blood of my enemies. There was a feral desire in his eyes which set my soul alight, but I knew who he was now. Who he truly was. And I wasn't going to forget it.

I realised I was back inside the warehouse, standing on a large plastic sheet alongside Church and Frank who were stripping out of their clothes.

Danny tapped my headphones in a demand and my teeth ground together before I reluctantly pulled them off.

"Oh honey, you look like the best train wreck I've ever seen," Dylan stepped into view beyond the sheeting, pink washing up gloves pulled up to his elbows, his muscular body squeezed into a tight black jumpsuit. "Carnage is an absolute vibe on you. If it wouldn't incriminate you and send you to prison for fifty years, I'd leave it on you for good. But needs must." He snapped his fingers at me as Danny pulled his shirt off and I realised what Dylan was asking.

"You got 'ere quick," Church commented as he unbuckled his pants, pulling his jeans off and tossing them down on the sheeting alongside his socks and shoes.

"Shaila called, honey," Dylan answered. "And we all know that the cops won't waste a second in coming to see if they can catch you red handed after a gang brawl with Butcher written all over it. Now less talking, more stripping."

The last thing I wanted to do was get naked after what I'd been through, but I clenched my jaw and kicked off my shoes then unbuttoned my jeans, shimmying out of them. I pulled off my jacket and socks next, then my panties followed and finally I took off my ripped shirt, tossing it down with the rest of my clothes, hugging my headphones, iPod and mini flashlight to my bare chest.

My eyes flicked sideways as I became overly aware of the naked men beside me. Danny tossed his boxers down with his pile of clothes and my gaze slid over the ink housed within his flesh, the violent cacophony of tattoos looking back at me before my attention fixed on a forget-me-not flower on his lower abs, almost hidden by the thorny roses which surrounded it.

I glanced up and met his gaze for a moment before ripping my eyes off of him, instead finding myself looking at Church's muscular frame, a lump forming in my throat as I stared at his body, unable to convince myself in that moment that I hated his tattoos. Because with the addition of the blood which painted his arms in flecks of red, I couldn't deny how beautifully powerful he looked.

Frank was the last to finish stripping and as he turned his back my way, my heart stalled in my chest at what I found there. All down the dark skin of his back were scars, brutal, endless scars cut painstakingly precisely into his flesh to create one huge symbol which spread right down from his shoulders to the base of his spine. They formed a mark I would have known anywhere, in any life. The huge V was created of two images, the details of the original design somewhat lost in the scarred skin, yet sickeningly accurate all the same. A blade and a gun crossed with one another to form the letter and smaller scars cut around the two weapons to represent the thorny vine which surrounded them. The skull in the background of the image looked like it had been burned into his flesh, impossibly perfect flowers carved into the space surrounding it and leaving his skin a masterpiece of agony which I couldn't even imagine. The time it must have taken someone to do that to him made my stomach turn, the pain he must have endured making my fingers tremble at the mere thought of it.

I knew that symbol. I'd seen it every day of my life before I came to this land of rain and power.

It was the mark of my family, of the Volkovs. And that could only mean one thing. Frank had been captured and tortured by the Russians, and not just any Russians. I knew the work of my brother Nikolay when I saw it.

Holy fuck.

"Here, honey. I need to take those." Dylan stepped closer, holding out a plastic bag for me to put my things in.

I clutched my headphones and iPod tighter, shaking my head in refusal, even though I knew I couldn't keep them.

"I need these. You can't destroy them," I growled.

Dylan nodded slowly in agreement. "I'll bring them back, honey, I promise."

He moved forward, trying to prise them from my fingers and I forced my hands to release them as he slipped them tenderly into the ziplock bag he had waiting.

"Now, shower. All of you," Dylan commanded. "Use the one down here, get in together. Don't waste time. We've got approximately ten minutes before the cops show up at your door and I'm gonna need as few places to clean as possible."

Danny grabbed my hand and though I tried to tug it free, he wouldn't let go as he dragged me to the bathroom a few feet away while Church and Frank followed.

Inside was a cream-tiled shower which didn't look remotely big enough for all of us, but in the next second I was being hounded into it by my husband with the two other huge guys in tow.

Danny turned the shower on and I winced at the cold water before it started to run hot, rushing over us as I was crowded in against the back wall.

Danny shifted a little and Church's arm pressed to my side while Frank's hip knocked against mine and Danny remained at my back. My pulse pattered wildly at the closeness of them but at the same time, a sense of calm seemed to fall over me. Even after the touch of those creeps, I didn't want to push these men away from me, though I had no idea why.

The water washed over us in a torrent, the blood on our skin sliding down to form a pool of red at our feet.

Danny suddenly squirted a handful of shampoo into my hair, lathering it up before letting the suds fall over my body and helping to wash every inch of blood from my skin.

The others worked to remove the blood from their own flesh, but their eyes never left my body. Not in a way that made me want to disappear like Sikes's gaze had, but like they were hunting for traces of blood, ensuring there was no scrap of evidence left on me.

I spotted a fleck of blood on Church's cheek and reached up on instinct, wiping it away and he caught my wrist, holding my hand against him for a moment.

"Are you okay, Miss America?" he asked in a low voice and I didn't want to give him a bullshit answer where I lied, but I also wasn't sure I wanted to confide in him, in any of them. So I stayed quiet, aching for my music.

"Course she's not fucking okay," Frank snarled, muscling Church aside as he moved to look at me and my hand fell back to my side.

Danny continued to work over my body, meticulously washing every inch of me and despite my horror with him over what I'd discovered, I couldn't seem to summon my disgust with him then, his touch somehow calming that raging beast inside me who had risen to the challenge of the fight and now lay dormant in my flesh, uncertain of her place.

"Say somethin', darlin'," Church begged, looking distressed by my silence and I started to notice all the blood they'd missed on themselves as they focused too heavily on me.

I took a sponge from the rack and moved forward, running it over Church's chest and scrubbing the blood away, the task helping my thoughts sharpen as I concentrated on it.

He watched me intently the whole time as I worked the sponge down his arms next, then took his tattooed hand in mine, scrubbing at the blood caked on his fingers.

I moved to Frank once I was done, glancing up at him as water collected in my lashes and I ran the sponge down the centre of his chest. We had to make sure there was no evidence, we had to go through the motions now and cover our tracks. There could be no corners cut. And though my tongue burned with unanswered questions, I didn't let a single one fall from my lips, knowing this wasn't the time.

When I was sure Frank's skin was clean, I turned to Danny, a ripple of hatred spilling through my chest before I stepped forward and worked to clean him too. It needed to be done. I wasn't going to go to prison for this.

Dylan tossed a bottle of bleach into the room and Frank caught it, taking a nail brush and dousing it in the potent liquid before scrubbing his nails clean and handing it to Church.

I watched as they splashed more bleach over their bodies before offering it to me and Danny. I followed their lead, wincing at the sting of it against my cuts before soaping up the sponge once it was done so that I could wash the strong smelling liquid away again, turning my attention back to Danny who still had blood speckling his skin.

Church and Frank stepped out of the shower, grabbing towels and drying themselves off, leaving me with the man who had claimed me for his wife while I wrung the sponge between my fingers and suds foamed over my hands.

Danny observed me as I placed the sponge on his chest, working over the ink on his body as I cleaned away the blood, focusing on it diligently like it was the only thing in my world.

"Why did you run?" he asked, his voice ringing with a note of pain.

I glanced up at him, scoring the sponge down to his stomach and rubbing it in hard circles.

"Because you're a monster," I told him icily.

"I thought you already knew that," he said, his dark brows pulling together. "What was it I did that made you fear me?"

"I don't fear you, Danny Butcher." I finished wiping away the blood and let the sponge fall from my fingers. "I hate you."

I filled those words with as much venom as I could summon then stepped out of the shower and claimed a towel for myself, hugging it to my body as I dried off.

I didn't look at the others again, descending into a deep, dark pit inside me.

Dylan stepped into the room with a pink bucket of cleaning products in his arms.

"I've left clothes for you out there. Get out so I can clean up in here. Leave the towels. Go, go, go. Time is ticking."

We followed his orders, finding some hoodies and pants waiting for us in the lounge. The plastic sheeting and our bloody clothes were long gone and panic flitted through me at the loss of my music. But I couldn't be an idiot. I had to let Dylan clean everything.

I'd get it back. I just had to wait. Had to do what needed to be done. There was no other choice now. I'd been in this situation before. When the cops came knocking, you had to be ready.

"What's the story?" I muttered to Danny as we both pulled some clothes on.

"We were here all night. The cuts and bruises are from the four of us having a little fun boxing earlier on today, the boys down at the gym will back us up. We can tell 'em we fancied trying our hand at fighting without gloves. They can't do shit about us enjoying knocking ten bells out of each other. Zoya will say she was fighting you, bombshell. She runs the gym and she's a fucking legend around here, she'll have your back," he said, and the others nodded. "Just follow my lead. Don't speak unless they directly address you. And Anya, you officially don't speak English, love – it'll save you at least a bit of time while they hunt down a translator."

"Fine by me," I said, turning away from him and feeling his stare on my back.

Dylan soon reappeared from the bathroom, pulling off his gloves and dropping them into the bucket. He held a black sack which I was guessing contained the towels and aside from that, I couldn't see a single thing which could link any of us to that brawl remaining in the house.

"That's it. I'll come back when the police are gone to clean the tunnel. I'll take the key so we can be sure they won't find their way down there. How certain are you that they won't get in from the other end?"

"That hatch is all but invisible from the cellar of The Duck and Dog and we bolted it up for good measure. They ain't gonna find it," Danny said confidently.

Dylan nodded. "You can come pick up your phones and shit in a few days."

"Thanks, Dylan," Danny said.

"Oh it's no bother, honey. I do love a spring clean. Besides, you're paying top whack for this miracle." He sashayed his way to the kitchen, hopping up onto the worktop and sliding the window open before slipping outside and disappearing into the night like some freaking cleaning ninja.

Silence fell between us, penetrating and thick, but before any of us decided to break it, a loud knock came at the door.

"Police – open up!" A voice shouted beyond it and I raised my chin, steeling myself for whatever was about to come our way.

Church pulled me down to sit on the couch while Frank leaned casually against the wall and Danny moved to answer the door.

"Well hello, boys, what have we done to deserve the pleasure of your company on this fine night?" Danny asked brightly and I knew from the accusation in all of the cops' eyes, that we were completely fucked.

CHAPTER TWENTY ONE

I leaned back in my chair, legs spread, eyes cold, lips still.

They didn't have shit on me. Not a damn thing. And they had even less on the others.

"We have witnesses," the cop tried, still looking to draw some kind of reaction from me, but I wasn't gonna be giving him one. Certainly not to this uniformed prick who didn't even seem to fully know who he was dealing with.

My gaze slid to the woman beside him, her chin held high and her dark eyes wary as she assessed me. She knew. That look said it all.

"Look," the new fella tried, softening his tone and leaning forward like we were just two pals, exchanging pleasantries. I had to give it to him, he was eager, keen to prove himself in his new job, but if he seriously thought I was about to open my mouth then he had another thing coming.

I could hear Church jabbering on in another interview room somewhere close by. Unlike me, that fucker never shut up, weaving pretty tales and talking the cops in circles while he gave them all kinds of information about his life – none of which could ever be used to incriminate him. Right now, he seemed to be in the middle of telling them all about the three best drycleaners within walking distance of his house and how great they'd been at getting bloodstains out of his clothes the last few times he'd been boxing with us. No doubt they'd be sending someone to each place, looking to see if he really was dumb enough to get bloodstained clothes laundered and checking for any incriminating evidence, but I doubted Church had ever so much as stepped through the door of any of those places, let alone given them his shit to clean.

The officer before me glanced at the door as the sound of Danny loudly singing a verse of I Fought The Law by The Clash came from somewhere down the corridor. Damn, these bastards must have hated us. My lips twitched with amusement as frustration flashed over the face of the copper who was trying and failing to question me.

"You might get out of here faster if you just answer some questions, Mr Smith," the other officer tried, making me look at her and I licked my bottom lip slowly as our gazes met and held. She wasn't so easily distracted though and she forged on. "So why don't you just tell us where you were tonight. Explain what happened. Why were you at The Duck and Dog?"

I moved forward suddenly, leaning towards her with my hands falling between my thighs, the suddenness of the move making the new fella flinch, though this one held her nerve, arching a brow at me which said she knew full well that here and now she held more power than me.

"Any chance I can grab a glass of water?" I asked her. "All this talking has me parched."

The two of them exchanged a look at the first words I'd chosen to speak which said they both very much thought of me as a cunt. I smiled, sweetly at first before letting it darken, letting them look at all the deeply fucked up and twisted pieces of the man before them and watching as the irritation in their gazes switched to caution.

"You know the deal here, Mr Smith. Just tell us where you were last night, let us get through this and you can get out of this room all the faster," she reminded me.

"Turns out, I'm not feeling chatty after all," I replied, scoring my thumb along my jaw and feeling the raw sting of the bruise there. It wasn't broken though and I'd survived a whole lot worse.

The female officer stood abruptly, announcing her intentions for the tape before striding from the room and leaving me with the new fella, the door left open to reveal a few more uniformed coppers standing outside. Anyone would think they were concerned about having us in here for some reason.

I laid my hand down on the table between us, glancing around at the small, grey interview room, wondering how many times I'd ended up sitting in one of these places by now. Enough to lose count anyway.

"It looks like you were in one hell of a fight," the new fella said, his gaze on my split knuckles and I curled my fingers into a fist, knocking on the wooden table.

"Boxing is a brutal sport," I replied.

"Especially if you don't wear gloves," he noted and I grinned at him.

"Especially then."

"Do you often fight against women?" he went on, his contempt for me burning in his eyes even though he was keeping it offa his face and out his tone. I knew he was referring to the bruises Anya bore.

I chose silence again for that one, knowing I wouldn't be able to discuss what had happened to her, lie or otherwise, not without giving away how I was really feeling about all this.

The female officer returned with Detective Saunders in tow, a woman I'd spent many an hour with locked in a small room just like this. She was tall with her dark braids pulled into a high ponytail and her black pantsuit was rumpled from what I was guessing was one bitch of a night.

The officer who had gone to collect her informed the tape of their arrival, and I waited for her to address me as they went through their procedural bullshit.

"Evening, Frank," Saunders said finally, moving to take the empty chair before me. "Why is it that whenever there's a scent of blood in the air, I know I'll be seeing you?"

"Maybe you're just taken with me," I replied. "So it's more that you're *hoping* to lay eyes on me than knowing it."

She scoffed lightly, unaffected by my bullshit and more than used to it by now.

"I hear you haven't been all that forthcoming tonight?" she asked.

"I just don't have anything to say about things I know nothing about," I replied, shrugging one shoulder and leaning back in my chair again.

An angry outburst in a language I was almost certain was Russian drew my attention towards the door as I heard Anya's voice.

"Your boss's new bride is looking to leave," Saunders explained while I schooled my expression, not wanting her to see anything of my thoughts on that.

"Aren't we all?" I asked dryly.

"We just want to know what happened at The Duck and Dog last night," she said. "You give us your side of things and we can get this all cleared up."

"My side of what? I wasn't at the pub last night," I replied, though I knew I was the weak link in that lie. But I also wasn't a dumb fuck. I'd gone there on foot, running with my hood up and my head down. Even if they had me on CCTV, they didn't have a clear shot of my face, I was confident of that.

Saunders eyed me for a long moment, the hours that she'd been trying to work this case showing in the bags beneath her eyes. They'd let us sit in our cells for a good spell before bringing us through for questioning, and I for one had spent that time sleeping. The plastic mattresses they provided might not have offered much in the way of comfort, but I'd long since learned the art of sleeping no matter where I was. Tiredness made you slow, made you sloppy, and I wasn't dumb enough to allow myself to fall prey to either of those things.

She could only hold us for twenty-four hours without charge and we both knew she didn't have shit to charge me with.

"Alright," she said abruptly. "Is there anything you'd like to clarify or add to this interview?"

"No, ma'am," I replied, giving her a cocky smile which I knew only deepened her desire to see me locked away.

"Interview concluded at eleven thirty-three am. I am now switching off the recorder."

I pushed myself to my feet, more than ready to leave as I allowed her to lead me out of the room. The new fella looked like he'd have enjoyed using the full twenty-four hours at their disposal to try and crack me, but the detective and I both knew that I'd been playing this game for too long to waste all of our time on that.

I locked eyes with Anya as she was led out to the reception at the same time as me, the fire in her gaze enough to let me know that she was seriously pissed and was most certainly still a flight risk.

She was spitting something venomous in Russian, her eyes locked on me and letting me know in no uncertain terms that those insults were aimed my way. I had to assume she hadn't much enjoyed her time in her holding cell.

The interpreter they'd gotten for her said something to her which made her huff out a breath, causing a lock of platinum hair to flutter before her eyes as she turned her attention to the officer who was telling her she was free to go.

I caught her arm as she tried to stride past me, making her dark eyes whip up to mine and take in my expression which confirmed she would be staying with me until the others got out.

"I'll take you for food while we wait for Danny," I said, my grip tight enough to let her know I wasn't fucking about.

She could scream if she wanted, she could rip her arm out of my grip and tell every police officer in earshot that she didn't want to go with me, but I was more than willing to bet she wouldn't. She was a Volkov. And just like I was a made man, she was a made woman. Our kind didn't blab to the police and we sure as fuck didn't rely on them to solve our problems for us.

Anya muttered something in Russian which made my jaw clench, memories of her brother demanding all kinds of unknown shit in that same tongue ringing in my ears. It hadn't mattered that I hadn't understood him. He hadn't wanted me to be able to answer anyway.

The moment that we were free to leave, I tugged on Anya's arm and guided her out onto the pavement.

Rain was crashing down over the streets of London and she cursed me as I drew her out into it, the icy cold droplets drenching us within moments as I pulled her along with me.

"Where are we going?" she demanded as I kept walking, my t-shirt clinging to my chest as it was saturated and water dripping from my eyelashes.

"I dunno what way the wind blew at the end of that fight last night," I said to her, drawing her down the street and squinting out at the busy road, hailing a black cab as I saw one coming our way. "So it ain't safe to go back to the warehouse right now. You can come back to mine and we'll wait for Danny to call when he's released too."

"You're sure he will be?" she asked and I looked down at her, wondering if she was hoping he wouldn't be.

"Yeah. They got nothing to link us to The Duck and Dog last night beyond a vague description of thirty odd fuckers who all went racing off into the night, not to mention however many of them they arrested. Doesn't matter what side of that fight anyone was on, not one of them will give up names. Besides, Sikes and his little bunch of cunts were Butchers. They won't be looking to us for a suspect. The gangs don't kill their own. Not unless they're betrayed."

The cab pulled up, washing more rainwater over our feet and Anya hissed her disapproval as I tugged the door open, giving the driver my address and pushing her into the back of it in front of me.

We were both dripping, the hoody she'd put on before the cops turned up for us last night soaked through and she wrapped her arms around herself as she shivered.

I cut my gaze from hers, staring at the rain drenched streets and wondering what other casualties there had been last night. With a bit of luck, our side would have pulled through fairly unscathed. The last I'd seen of the brawl, we'd been winning, so I had to assume that was how it had ended. The Candlestick Maker wouldn't be making that mistake twice, that was for sure.

Anya shifted on the other side of the cab, drawing her knees up to her chest as she continued to shiver and I looked back at her with a frown, the cold biting into my skin too, though it was clear I wasn't feeling it as intensely as she was.

"Come here," I barked, jerking my chin in command and her dark eyes fell on me, a frown pulling her brows together sharply.

"You're not the boss of me, Frank," she bit out, shivering harder.

"Let me rephrase," I said in a low tone. "Come and sit on my lap or when we get back to my place, I'll put you over my fucking knee and spank you like the little brat you are."

The driver choked out a cough, his gaze darting to the rear view mirror as he looked between the two of us then hastily gave the road his attention once more.

Anya narrowed her eyes at me, defiance sparkling in her gaze and I let her see the honesty of that threat in mine.

A single beat of hesitation passed between us before she cursed me out then scooted closer.

I hooked my arm around her waist and lifted her onto my lap without a word, holding her tight against my chest as she stiffened in my hold.

I observed her as she remained there, her posture rigid like she was expecting me to do something else, but I just wound my arms around her and gave her little body the heat I had to offer. The driver cranked up the heating too and as we headed down a few more streets she slowly began to relax.

Her head fell to lean against my shoulder and I released a slow breath as I ran my hand up and down the length of her thigh over her wet jeans, trying to warm her some more.

There were words waiting to be spoken between us, but neither of us broached them, letting the silence lay thickly over us as we headed through the crowded streets in the back of the cab and I brought her back to the place I called home.

The cab pulled up outside my flat and I paid the driver, tugging Anya back out into the rain and jogging across the street to the black door which led into the block of flats.

I took her hand and guided her to the stone steps as we skipped the lift and started up them, winding our way higher and higher in the yellow brick building as we headed for the top floor.

Anya kept pace with me in silence, looking on curiously as I used the combination lock to open my front door and let her into my space.

My grip tightened on the doorknob as she stepped over the threshold, my jaw grinding as I fought against the desire to yank her back out again and slam the door closed. No one ever came here. Not since Olly. I didn't allow anyone to pass through my door. And yet here I was, letting a girl who in all rights should have been my enemy step in as if it were nothing.

The space seemed to shrink as I followed her inside, her curious eyes falling on everything in the living room and dissecting it like she understood it all without a word.

Her gaze caught as she took in my record collection at the far side of the room, the old player set up beside it beneath a long roof window which currently filled the space with the sound of the thundering rain outside.

She toed her boots off and stepped further into the space, wrapping her arms around herself as she went to stave off the shivering of her flesh. I guessed growing up in the desert made her blood more suited for a much warmer climate, and I wondered how she'd deal with winter when it came in full force.

She drew closer to the ceiling to floor length window, looking out at the view which peered across rooftops in the direction of the river, showing a glimpse of Tower Bridge between the sheeting rain which dominated the view today. There was a balcony out there with a small curving staircase which gave access to the roof I owned too.

"I don't have a bath," I told her as I followed her into my space. "So it's a shower unless you wanna keep shivering like that."

Her attention moved to me as she stepped from the wooden floorboards onto the thick cream rug which sat in the centre of the room, her toes sinking into it as she sought out some small measure of warmth.

"Okay," she agreed simply and I nodded, striding past her towards the small bathroom and setting the hot water running over the white tiles. I got a fresh towel out for her then took one for myself and turned away without another word, leaving her to it as I headed for my bedroom.

More floor length windows stretched along the far side of my room, these ones showcasing a little of the Tower of London on a good day, though now it was mostly just giving the rain a greater stage to host its destruction.

I unbuckled my belt and stripped out of my clothes, yanking my saturated shirt off next and towelling down once I was naked. I felt the raised ridges of the scar which coated my back and dried myself, biting my tongue against the memories which accompanied it. She was going to ask me about it. I'd seen the questions in her eyes from the moment she'd first seen it and I wasn't going to shield her from the truth.

I grabbed a pair of navy sweats from my drawer and tugged them on, leaving my chest bare so that she could get her fill of looking. I wasn't afraid of her seeing them. I just hadn't wanted to offer her more pieces of me by showing them to her before now. But the time for concealing the truth of our mixed histories was gone.

I took a thick blue hoody and a pair of sweats from my drawers next and headed back into the bathroom, setting it down on the sink for her before gathering her clothes and straightening with them in my fist.

I paused as I made a move to turn away, my traitorous gaze moving to the shower curtain and the steam billowing out around it.

There was a gap at the edge of the curtain, a single inch left open and gifting me a glimpse of her drenched, soapy skin as she washed herself, her hands gliding up the side of her breast and massaging the product in better.

My cock thickened as I stood there, lusting over my enemy and fighting the urge to rip that curtain aside and show her what she did to me with that body of hers.

I turned on my heel sharply, striding from the room before I could get caught up in that foolish fantasy and heading into the kitchen to put the kettle on.

I placed a couple of slices of bread in the toaster for good measure and leaned against the black counter as I listened to the sound of the kettle boiling and the rain pounding the windows like they were fighting to take dominance of the air.

When I had a brew made, I stacked the buttered toast on a plate and headed back to the living room, placing it all on the coffee table and dropping onto the cream couch as I cocked my head at Anya where she now stood by the door, her hand latched around the doorknob like she had somewhere to be.

"That's locked with a code," I said simply, relaxing in my chair. "As are the windows."

Anya jammed her thumb against the keypad beside the door uselessly then turned to face me with a scowl.

I took a bite of my toast, letting my gaze roam up her bare legs to the base of the hoody which swamped her and hung to her mid thighs. Apparently she hadn't wanted the sweats, but then again they might have just fallen right off of her considering the difference between her size and mine.

"What is this, Fort Knox?" she hissed but I didn't bother to reply.

She moved towards me slowly, like a mouse approaching a lion. But I think we both knew by now that she was no mouse.

Anya moved to the chair opposite mine, curling her bare legs beneath her, careful not to offer me a view between her thighs as she made herself comfortable and took a slice of toast for herself.

"Tell me," she demanded as the silence stretched and I observed her for a few more moments before replying.

"What difference does it make?" I asked, the scar on my back tingling as if the mere memories of its creation were enough to summon a reaction from the damaged nerves.

"Maybe none. Maybe a lot," she replied, her curiosity clear in her endlessly dark eyes.

I considered that for a moment, wondering if I had any real reason to hide the truth from her and deciding I didn't.

"About nine years ago, a man who worked for us went missing," I said, leaning forward to pick up my mug of tea and taking a long drink before going on. "He hurt a woman who was under our protection. Hurt her bad enough that she still ain't the same now. So when I figured out where he ran to, I followed."

Understanding dawned in her eyes and she drew her bottom lip between her teeth, making me think about doing the same before I forced myself to remember who she was. What she was.

"You were a fool to go to Vegas," she said, raising her chin like the fact that I shouldn't have set foot in her family's precious city without permission somehow validated what her kin had done in retribution.

"So what does that make you for coming to London?" I retorted, wondering if she knew how easily I could take my vengeance out on her flesh for what I'd endured.

"A pawn," she replied bitterly. "One used and sacrificed for the benefit of the real power on my board."

I grazed a thumb over the corner of my mouth as I considered that then went on with my story.

"I got the fucker who I was after," I said slowly, watching the way she hung from my words like they were a lifeline which she needed to breathe. "But before I could fly back out of there, your brothers caught up to me."

Anya swallowed thickly, nodding her head as her gaze dropped to my shoulder like she was aching to get another look at the scars I'd been gifted in payment for my disrespect.

"How are you still breathing?" she asked.

"Stubbornness," I bit back. "I refused to let those fuckers have me. Though your brother Nikolay certainly gave it a good go."

"He let you go?" she asked like that made no sense to her. "I don't think anyone has ever gotten away from him once he has them in his grasp."

"He didn't let me do shit," I growled. "But luck was on my side in a way. The treaty had not long been agreed. Your other brothers didn't want evidence of a British death to be led back to them, so they tried to hide me away, tried to cover up the truth of who held me. They took me to some fucking shack out in the desert where Nikolay came calling regularly to carve me up and keep me kicking. He didn't want me to go out easy. And I'm guessing from his choice of artwork on my back that *he* didn't give much of a fuck about everyone knowing exactly who had killed me. The last time he came, he told me he was almost done, his masterpiece near completion and my death would be the culmination of his work."

"So how are you here?"

"Like I said, luck. He got a call and left in a hurry. One of the ropes he'd used to tie me wasn't tight enough and somehow, through the agony and heatstroke and the fucking mess of my head thanks to suffering his attention for weeks on end, I managed to get myself free. Fuck knows how I made it out of the desert, but eventually I found a campsite, stole a car and here I am, nine years later, still fucking kickin'."

Anya's brow furrowed at the truth of what her brother had done to me but she didn't flinch from it, didn't try to deny or excuse it. Nah, she wasn't the kind to back down from the truth that easily. She owned it, just like she owned everything else about her.

"Nikolay can be a bit…intense," she said finally. "He acts out at times."

"Acts out?" I barked a humourless laugh. "Well at least I know the violent streak runs in the family. Tell me, Cash, how did it feel when you stabbed that arsehole back in The Duck and Dog?"

She swallowed thickly, looking me dead in the eye as she gave her answer. "Good."

I held her gaze for an endless stretch of time, my lips turning up in the ghost of a smile which she returned despite how hard I could see she was willing herself to hate me.

I stood suddenly, placing my mug back on the table and turning away from her, letting her get her fill of seeing her family crest carved into my skin while I moved to the record player and took my time selecting some music for us to listen to.

Eventually I picked out Come As You Are by Nirvana, taking the record from its sleeve and carefully placing it on the player, setting the needle down and waiting for the song to start up.

As the first note of the music broke the silence, her fingers landed on my shoulder, the soft brush of her skin skimming against the top edge of my scar.

I stilled, my entire body tensing as she began to run her fingers down the jagged edges of the damaged skin, a shiver coursing through my limbs at the foreign touch as she explored the scar, moving lower in an achingly slow caress.

I closed my eyes, echoes of that pain tumbling through my chest as the sounds of my own screams mixed with the memories of my throat tearing from the roars of pain which escaped me as her brother cut me open. I could feel the heat in that fucking cabin, the oppressive thickness of the air as I panted through the agony and was dissected right beneath the monster who shared this woman's blood.

Her fingers brushed the base of my spine and I snapped, catching her in my arms and whipping her around. I pushed her face down over the back of the sofa, my chest rising and falling heavily as I panted through the memories which fought to consume me.

I wrapped her long hair around my fist, my body pressing down over hers as I forced her neck to bend back, my lips falling to her ear and the stubble on my jaw grazing her soft flesh.

"Perhaps I should send your brother a reply to the message he carved into me," I snarled, making her gasp as I drove my weight down on her back, feeling the curve of her arse pushing back against my crotch.

"Would that help?" she asked. "Would it make you feel better about what he did to you?"

"Only one way to find out," I replied, shifting away just enough to put a few inches of space between us, tugging on her hair so that her spine arched beautifully and a soft gasp escaped her lips.

I slipped my free arm beneath her and lifted her into my grip, crushing her to my chest as I carried her out of the room and into the kitchen.

"What are you doing?" she asked breathlessly, her fingers digging into my arm as she fought to force it from her body to no avail.

"You'll soon find out."

We made it into the kitchen and I dropped her to her feet, forcing her face down over the counter as I maintained my hold on her hair.

Anya snarled at me, trying to stamp on my feet and I cursed her as I kicked her legs further apart, driving my knees into the backs of hers to hold her still.

"What would your precious brothers think of you if they knew you'd made such a fucking fuss over some simple payback?" I taunted, pressing my hips against her arse and pinning her to the worktop as I flattened my palm on her back and made sure she was well aware of how much control I held over her.

"They'd mostly just be pissed that you weren't bleeding out at my feet right now," she snarled, trying to swipe at me behind her back.

I took my hand from her spine and reached over to the knife block, grabbing a wicked little blade from it and touching it to her throat.

She finally fell still, panting beneath me and blowing a lock of hair from her eyes as I allowed her to turn her head enough to glare at me.

"Good girl," I praised, earning myself another curse as I pressed the blade to her jugular a little harder, making sure she knew I wasn't fucking about.

And why should I be? She was nothing to me. Just the sister of a man who had caused me endless pain and disfigured me for life. I owed him this bloody redemption. I owed him a taste of his own passion. Danny wouldn't like it, but I didn't really give much of a fuck about that either. I only stayed here because I had nothing else. I was only loyal to him because I had to be if I wanted to be close by when Benny was finally released from prison and delivered to me for his final penance.

The only difference that this would make to my plans would be in where I waited for that fucker to be released. And maybe it was worth it to vent some of my demons on her flesh. That had been my plan after all, the one I'd come up with on the nights when I was woken by the memories of being tied up awaiting her brother's visits. When I had nothing but the torment of those twisted weeks which bled through my psyche and threatened to unhinge me. I'd thought of her. Of the Volkov who was due to be sent straight into our hands and all the things I could do to her flesh in payback for what he'd done to mine.

"Fuck you, Frank," she hissed but the way her chest was heaving beneath me said she was feeling a whole lot more than anger. And as I thought on that, I couldn't help but consider what else she might like me to do to her while I held her in this position.

"Place your hands flat either side of you," I commanded, a thrill dancing through my chest as she complied. I liked that, having the sister of the man who had tortured me compliant and at my mercy.

I moved the knife from her neck and fisted the back of the hoody I'd given her to wear, drawing the material up until her arse was bared to me alongside the flawless skin of her lower back.

I dropped the knife to the back of her thigh, pressing the tip to the sensitive skin there until she sucked in a sharp breath which I swear I felt right through my own body like a jolt of electricity.

"Are you afraid?" I asked her, unsure what answer I even wanted as I trailed the knife up the back of her leg, the tip scoring a faint mark along her skin while the pressure remained just shy of breaking it.

"I've lived my whole life surrounded by monsters," she replied, not even bitterly, just in acceptance.

I hesitated as the blade made it to the curve of her arse, the name of her husband marked clearly in red against her smooth skin. I turned my hand, my thumb scoring over the healed flesh, making her gasp as I slowly massaged the letters of his name, committing the feeling of those scars to my memory as I tried to take some pleasure from them, tried to feel some kind of relief or satisfaction. But there was nothing.

"Why Church?" I asked her, my voice rough in my demand as the question I'd been wanting to know the answer to ever since she'd told me about the two of them fell into the silence.

"Does it bother you?" she replied, not giving me my answer.

"Do you want it to?"

Silence. She gave me nothing as I continued to rub my thumb over the brand on her flesh, balancing on the edge of my desire to hurt her for what her family had done to me, or to do something far, far worse.

"Tell me," I insisted when it became clear that she wasn't planning on humouring me in this.

I turned the knife in my grip, returning the blade to her skin and trailing it over her exposed body, watching the way she shivered beneath me as the threat of the cut hung in the space between this moment and the next.

"He makes me feel alive," she breathed, her spine arching just a little as I ran the blade back down the length of it, finding my way to her arse once more and shifting my hand so that my thumb continued that trail.

"And what do I make you feel, Anya Volkov?" I asked, unable to deny the desire I felt as I looked down at her beneath me, her thighs spread and palms still flat on the worktop like I'd commanded.

She had no choice. I held her at knifepoint. And yet I got the feeling my weapon wasn't the reason for her heavy breathing and nor was the threat I posed the reason for her compliance.

"You see me," she murmured, the words almost lost to the sound of the song which still played from the living room as I slowly skimmed my thumb between her arse cheeks, following that line lower inch by inch, wondering what I might find when I got low enough.

"And what is it that you see when you look back?"

A whimper escaped her as I closed in on her arse and I relented, moving my thumb to one side and running it over her inner thigh instead, drawing soft circles on her flesh just to the right of her pussy. I didn't look down, keeping my eyes on the side of her face and my fist in her hair as I watched her press her eyes closed and fight against the moan that was building in her throat.

I was starting to think she just might have been drenched for me, aching for my cock to fill her sweet pussy and dispel my demons in the sanctuary I might find between her thighs.

"I see sadness," she said breathily. "Pain. And an echo of the loss I feel every day of my life. I see lyrics when I look at you, Frank, the thump of the bass and a melody which pulses with every kind of emotion there is. You make the world loud in all the ways that count."

A growl built in my throat and I shifted my hand again, the knife grazing the curve of her arse as I dragged my thumb towards her centre, feeling her shiver and tense beneath me before she lost the battle she was trying to wage with her own body and a moan of need escaped her full lips.

I was so close to crossing that barrier, to feeling how hot she was, how wet, how tight, but as I paused on the precipice of that divide, my cock straining inside my sweatpants, a heavy knock sounded at my front door.

"Frank?" a kid yelled from beyond it and I cursed, withdrawing my hand and releasing my hold in Anya's hair before tugging her upright and yanking her hoody back down again. "Butcher says to tell you he's home. He wants you back ASAP."

"Got it," I barked, my eyes locking with Anya's as we stared at one another and I turned the knife over in my palm.

The sound of footsteps pounding away from my door followed and I tossed the knife into the sink with a clatter, making a move to step back.

"That's it?" Anya asked, her eyes full blown with desire and a demand there which I hungered to meet more than I would ever admit to.

"No," I replied, stepping forward and stealing her oxygen, taking her wrist in my grasp and moving her hand. I bunched her hoody up over her stomach and pushed her hand between her thighs, smiling darkly as I fought to ignore the throbbing in my own cock. "Now you can take yourself to my bedroom and fuck your own hand while thinking about a man who ain't your husband. When you're done, find yourself some trousers and get back out here sharpish because we've got our orders and they need to be followed."

I expected her to blush, snarl or even call me on my own shit but instead she just lifted her chin and held my eye as I slowly exerted pressure on her wrist, circling it to make her fingers move against her clit and watching her lips as they parted in a way that was so fucking hot I almost lost my own control.

"Was that an order too?" she asked as I let go and I dropped my eyes to her hand where it remained between her legs, the hoody bunched around it obstructing the view I really wanted to gaze upon.

"Yeah," I replied in a firm tone, wondering if she really was gonna go through with that and finding nothing but a challenging kind of resolve in her dark eyes. "And hurry the fuck up about it."

Anya's lips lifted in a smile designed to make me fucking ache, and she casually looked down at the obvious swell of my dick within my sweats before slipping out from between me and the worktop, heading for my room like she owned the fucking place.

I moved to sit on the couch which faced the bedroom door as she reached it and she tossed a challenging look over her shoulder at me before heading further into my personal space and leaving me outside.

She left the door ajar as she went and I found myself staring at the small gap, my hands fisting at my sides as she moved onto my bed out of sight.

My heart leapt as a moan came tumbling from her throat a moment later, her bare toes pushing down my sheets the only thing I could see as I forced myself to remain there, locked in that position while she tried to call my bluff.

Fuck.

She moaned louder as she worked herself over and I had to fight with everything I had to stay seated where I was, watching her toes curling against my sheets through the small gap as she panted and moaned and did exactly as I'd commanded.

The need to stride into that room was overwhelming, the desire to get the full show, to join in with it and make her moan even louder for me causing my entire body to go rigid with the strength it took to hold back.

Anya moaned louder and there was no doubt in my mind that her fingers were deep inside her pussy right now, driving in and out of her wetness and caressing her clit in exactly the way she liked.

I'd been aiming to torture a Volkov in payment for what her brother had done to me. But I'd found myself at the mercy of her bloodline once again as she turned the tables on me and made me fucking burn for her.

The desire to fist my cock in my hand was damn near overwhelming and I fought it off with all I had, knowing it was pointless anyway, that at the first opportunity I got I would be fucking my hand over the thought of her in my bed and coming harder than I had in a long fucking time.

Anya's moans got louder and I could tell she was close to coming. I swear I could feel that need for release in her mirrored in my own body though I hadn't so much as touched my fucking dick.

Anya cried out as she found her release and I almost came in my boxers right as she shouted Church's motherfucking name loud enough to shake the damn rafters.

I cursed her loudly enough that I was certain she'd heard me and her laughter rang out in reply.

Thankfully, by the time she emerged from the bedroom a few minutes later with a pair of my sweats on and the strings tied tight around her waist to keep them up, I'd managed to school my expression. Through some form of miracle, I remained still as she sauntered into the room too.

Her cheeks were flushed from her orgasm and I couldn't help but imagine how much more colour I could have brought to them if I'd had her pinned beneath me instead of her playing with herself all alone.

"Happy?" she questioned innocently.

"Why wouldn't I be?" I asked, standing suddenly and moving forward so that I towered over her once more.

"I just wanted to be sure I did a good job. You told me to fuck my hand while thinking about a man who wasn't my husband." She batted her eyelashes at me in a way that said she was pretty sure she thought she'd won a point with that little show as she cried out for Church when she came, but I wasn't gonna have that.

I snatched her hand into my grip, lifting her fingers to my lips and sucking them deep into my mouth, watching the colour in her cheeks darken as she felt the caress of my tongue right down to that tingling bundle of nerves between her legs and was forced to press her thighs together in response to it.

I tasted her orgasm on her fingers and I smiled darkly at her as I released her hand and leaned in close.

"You did good, Cash. Nice to know you can follow orders when I give 'em."

Anya blinked at me like she wanted to argue some point against me there, but I just turned my back on her and strode to the door, barking an order at her to keep up. And like a real good girl, she did just that.

CHAPTER TWENTY TWO

Frank led me out onto the road and I tugged my hood up against the endless rain, his hand immediately latching around mine like he thought I was a flight risk. Which, I guessed I was.

"You haven't mentioned why you ran yet," Frank muttered as he pulled me along the road, using an overhang which ran along the side of the building to shelter us from the rain as he led me towards a sleek black Mercedes which was parked up between two iron streetlamps.

"I'm aware," I said lightly.

My skin was still buzzing with the orgasm he'd ordered me to give myself, but the ache between my thighs hadn't lessened in the slightest. My vagina was spoiled by top-of-the-range vibrators but since coming to the UK and finding myself fucked seriously well by not one, but two of the British gangsters who held me captive, I had to admit I was kinda tempted to go for the hattrick. Were all British men that good in bed? Had the American dudes missed the memo, or was it just the blackhearted kind who could fuck me the way I liked?

Frank opened the passenger door, pushing me inside, his hand moving to the top of my head as I went like I was being arrested all over again. *Douchebag*.

We were soon driving through the thrashing rain towards the warehouse and I gazed out at storm torn London, the lights burning in the windows of the skyscrapers despite it being mid-afternoon, but when the sky decided to pour here, it was like night had come early.

"Why now?" Frank growled and I kept my eyes on the view, wondering if it was worth answering or not.

Sometimes Frank looked at Danny with so much contempt, I could taste it in the air. But did that mean I could trust him with my secrets? I didn't think so. He had confided in me about what my brother had done to him though, and I had this niggling feeling that I owed him for that. My family had scarred him, and retribution was probably due. I guessed that was what I was supposed to be anyway. I was the price of peace, just like a daughter from every other family we'd been at war with. I thought of them, and of the girl who'd been sold into my own family, Iris Kelly of the Irish mob who were based in Boston. I wondered what she thought of my brothers. They were men born of hellfire, and I prayed she was made of the same stuff because no lesser creature would survive them.

"Who is Danny really? When I'm not around, when he goes on jobs, when he speaks with you and knows no one is listening, who is he?" I asked, carefully picking my words so I didn't give away too much. Even if Frank told me he'd sign up to Anya's army and attack Danny at my command, I still wouldn't be telling him about that laptop. For all I knew, Frank repeated every word I spoke to Danny – although I doubted he'd be telling him about the way I'd moaned when I'd fucked my own hand on his orders. Perhaps that was my ammunition though. I could pull the trigger on Frank if he went against me. Then again, Danny had already agreed that Church could have me, so would he allow my bodyguard the same privilege?

I thought of the words Sikes had spoken to me in that poker room and my gut tightened into a hard ball. *"He promised you to us the day he got bored, angel."*

I shuddered, my fingers threading together and twisting. What if Sikes had been telling the truth? Danny had offered me to Church, was this the beginning of me becoming some whore for his men? Did Church know? Had he just been waiting for an opportunity to get his hands on me to use the boss's Russian wife for his own pleasure?

The thought sent a burning chill down my spine and I glanced at Frank, wondering if he'd been made that same promise.

"Who is he?" Frank echoed back at me, a light scoff in his voice. "He's the Butcher King. Every bad thing you've heard about him is true, but it's the things you haven't heard that would really make your bones quake."

"I'm not afraid of him," I hissed.

"Then why'd you run?"

I twisted around to look at him. "Maybe I can see my fate coming towards me like a train in the night, Frank. What if Sikes was right? I'm just a pussy to be passed around once Danny gets bored."

Frank's head snapped sideways to look at me and a horn blared as he swerved the car in the same movement, but neither of us flinched even when a crash seemed imminent for an endless second. Somehow, the traffic seemed to dissolve out of Frank's way, like they were bowing to the true power which owned these streets right now. And I never broke Frank's gaze.

"You think I'd allow that?" he spat, fury lining his features. "You think if Danny offered you to me, I'd fuck you whether you wanted it or not?"

I stared into his eyes, about to bite back at him, but I was struck by the intensity in his gaze which vowed his words were true. I turned back to face the view, but his hand came down on my thigh, his fingers digging in and making my heart judder. I looked back at him, finding a world of untold pain in his eyes and I wondered if my brother had put it there.

"I'm your guard, and so long as there's breath in my lungs, I'll remain that way, Cash."

"You're his man," I said, shaking my head. "You'll bow down like the good guard dog you are the moment he gives the order."

His jaw flexed. "Not for this." His fingers dug in harder and I found it more difficult to draw my next breath as I stared at the raw honesty in his gaze. Maybe he really did mean it, but what good would it do against the might of the Butcher gang? Like he said, Danny was the king.

He removed his hand from me as we closed in on the warehouse, but I felt imprinted with his touch, the mark of his fingers burning deep.

An ache filled my chest as we arrived home, the absence of my music leaving a hollow space within me which was desperate to be filled. I just wanted to curl up and numb out, but as we pulled up outside the Butcher castle, I knew I was going to have to stay firmly rooted in reality, something which had always been optional up until recently.

I steeled myself as Frank stepped out of the car, moving around to open my door and offering me a hand. I took it, his skin rough against mine for a moment before his grip slid higher, locking around my wrist instead and tugging me towards the door.

"You still didn't clarify the reason why you ran," Frank said under his breath as we walked through the rain.

"I didn't sign up to be a wife willingly, Frank, isn't that reason enough?"

"No…it's more than that. Something changed," he said, his eyes narrowing on me in suspicion.

"Well, you just go put on your flat cap and puff on your little pipe, Sherlock. In the meantime, I'll go on with my life," I said airily, but I felt his gaze continue to bore into me.

We headed inside and I braced myself, unsure what to expect now that the dust had settled on last night.

We found Danny and Church in the lounge. Church shoved to his feet at the sight of me but Danny remained seated, his eyes full of the blackest night I'd ever seen as they fell on me.

Shit.

I folded my arms, hitching on a casual expression while inside, my heart rioted as I faced down the Devil's glare.

"Anya," Church breathed and I couldn't help but feel a sweeping sensation of relief that he was okay. I got a flashback of him brutally killing for me last night alongside Danny, the blood speckling their skin, the rage in their eyes. It had been for me. I'd witnessed the fury of my husband when another man touched me – well, one who apparently didn't have his consent. And my head was still too fucked to figure out what that meant.

"Delivery!" Dylan announced as he walked in behind us and I was relieved as the tension in the air split apart.

Dylan was wearing tight pink jeans which hugged his muscular thighs and a white crop top, his abs fully on show as he carried a large sparkly bag under one arm.

Danny remained quiet, but sat forward in his seat, resting his elbows on his knees as Dylan moved between us all.

"Anya, honey, will you be a gem and come help me put away everyone's clothes? I bought new ones to replace what I had to destroy." Dylan didn't wait for an answer, linking his arm through mine and pulling me away from the three men who seemed to be communicating telepathically through brooding glares alone.

None of them voiced a word of complaint, but as I glanced back, I spotted Danny beckoning Frank over to him and they started to speak in low voices. *One guess who they were talking about.*

"It's like the crack of dawn in here," Dylan whispered to me. "Cocks everywhere. If you ever need a break from the testosterone, you're always welcome at my place, honey. I've got the testosterone levels of a My Little Pony, it's a safe space, I swear it."

I snorted a laugh as we made it upstairs and he guided me down to Danny's room, pushing through the door. Even after all this time, I didn't feel like this space was mine. It was a room where Danny had fucked other women, a place made by him for him. There wasn't a single part of it which had my mark on it.

Dylan kicked the door shut with his high heeled white boot and tossed the bag on the bed, rounding on me with his hands on his hips. "You've been a bad girl and it's absolutely fabulous."

"What do you mean?" I breathed, my heart jolting as I glanced back at the door for a second.

Dylan moved to the bag, unzipping it with a dramatic flare and taking out my leather jacket which was folded within it. "I had to burn the rest of the clothes, but this was a masterpiece I couldn't let die. I worked hard to get all the DNA off of it so you could keep it."

"Thank you," I said in surprise.

"And this." My heart jolted as he produced the wedge of cash from the inside pocket, the notes looking crisper and cleaner than they had when I'd last laid my eyes on them.

Dylan waved it in his hand, arching an eyebrow at me. "Now call me a silly goose if I'm wrong, but this amount of cash just screams escape plan, Anya. Did you try to make a run from the lion's den?"

I wetted my lips, hesitating on answering as I considered whether or not confirming that could land me in trouble. I'd always liked trouble anyway, but this seemed like flirting with a bit too much of it. If Dylan showed Danny that money, he was going to figure out where I'd gotten it. And if he did that, maybe he'd realise I'd seen the laptop. Would he believe me if I told him I hadn't gotten onto it? Possibly. But from what I'd seen of Danny's rage, I didn't want to invoke more of it.

"Say no more," Dylan said before I could figure out how to answer him and he moved towards me, cupping my cheek, his eyes sparkling. "Here." He placed the cash in my hand. "Our little secret, 'kay?"

I frowned as he stepped away from me, starting to unpack the bag with little sways and rocks of his hips like he was dancing to a tune inside his own head.

"Why?" I blurted in confusion, staring down at the cash and trying to work out if this was a trap.

He frowned at me as he moved to the closet with a bundle of clothes in his arms, releasing a sigh that made his whole frame slump. "I always hated zoos...all those wild animals kept in cages. It's the tigers that broke me the most though. They pace, you see? Up and down, up and down, along tracks worn into the ground by countless days of circling, hunting for a way out. And sometimes, they find one. Sometimes they make it beyond their bars and sink their teeth into those who held them. And oh honey, what justice that is, but those poor babies end up at the end of a rifle for wanting the single thing in this world all of us deserve."

"Freedom," I whispered, my chest tightening. When was the last time I felt truly free?

Dylan nodded, a sad look in his eyes. "Those boys down there are fools, Anya, because you've got a tiger's heart, and you'll always search for a way out. I don't want to see you at the end of a gun, so keep searching." He gestured to the cash with his chin. "There are only three things that can buy you freedom in this world, the two most easy to find being money and death. I will pray for the former for you."

"What's the third thing?"

"It's rare, and there's none of it for you in this house." Dylan glanced away. "Love breaks all chains."

He moved over to the wardrobe, and I realised my fingers were locked tight around the money, my knuckles turning white. *Love*. Yeah, he was right about that. It didn't live in this house. There was only damnation.

While Dylan was busy putting the clothes away, I slipped into the en suite and popped open the secret compartment in the mirror, placing the cash back beside the laptop before shutting it firmly.

When I returned to the bedroom, I spotted my headphones and iPod on the bed and hurried forward with a squeal of excitement, gathering them up in my arms and hugging them like an idiot. But they were more than just inanimate objects, they were a portal into a world full of companions, from Johnny Cash to The Beatles, they were all here waiting for me to return into their embrace whenever I needed them. But as I considered slipping them on and disappearing for a while, I realised I had a different kind of music to face right now. And I may as well get it over with.

I headed to the wardrobe to grab some clothes and found Dylan holding the crown he'd lent me for the wedding, his brow furrowed and his eyes glazed. I felt I was intruding on something and tried to back away, but he noticed me, looking up with a gleam of grief in his eyes.

"It's funny, isn't it? The years tick by but all it takes is the right scent, the right song, or a silly little crown to bring them back to you."

My heart tugged and I stepped closer to him, resting a hand on his arm, knowing that sense of loss so deeply that it rung a bell in my heart.

"At least they visit," I whispered, though a weight of guilt burrowed into me, because I knew deep down I didn't let memories of my mother in all that often. It was too painful, too sharp, even now. And I'd hidden away from facing that pain by diving into my music, drowning out the touch of her because if I allowed her closer, I'd shatter into a thousand jagged parts.

"Yeah." Dylan smiled sadly, looking to me with emotion brimming in his gaze. "And it's how it is in this life. It's not a question of if you'll lose someone, it's when. I just wish it hadn't been him."

I squeezed his arm and he drew in a breath, pressing his shoulders back.

"Right then, I'd better go, honey. I'll see you soon." Dylan leaned in, pressing a firm kiss to my cheek then swept past me out of the room, clutching the crown to his heart and for a moment I felt my own grief circling around me, trying to break in. But I gritted my teeth and pushed it back, keeping it at bay as always.

I changed into some ripped jeans and a blue Eagles t-shirt which I tied in a knot above my midriff before putting on some sneakers. When I walked downstairs, I had my headphones around my neck and my iPod in my back pocket, promising myself a long session with my favourite bands the moment I spoke with my husband and dealt with the shitstorm I felt blowing in.

The three of them were in the exact same position I'd left them in. Church was on his feet while Frank stood near Danny, his arms folded and his expression taut, and Danny was still sitting down, his face like a hurricane set to wipe out a whole island and its people.

Danny got up at last, and the atmosphere thickened, the other two exchanging a glance like they knew something I didn't. But I'd always been an intuitive kind of bitch and in the past, a face like that had warned me to run and hide.

I didn't plan on giving in to the child crying out within me now though, today I'd stare down the hunter coming for me and sharpen my own claws in preparation of its attack.

"If you think I'm going to beg for forgiveness or come up with some bullshit excuse for why you found me in The Duck and Dog last night, you're mistaken," I said calmly while Danny strode toward me.

I wound my fingers into fists, feeling like I was a lone idiot on a beach about to be struck by a tsunami. But maybe I understood that idiot, because there was something to be said for standing your ground in the face of your own demise. It felt fucking powerful and if I had to go down, then at least I'd go down without flinching.

But the end of the world didn't come, Danny halted right in front of me, leaning in so close to my face that I could only see his deep eyes which seemed to be drowning in darkness.

"I'm a patient fella, bombshell. But when I snap, it ain't pretty."

"Aw, don't be so hard on yourself, hubs," I said dryly, patting him on the cheek – a move that made his eyes sharpen like knives. "You're a pretty boy, all the girls wanna go to the dance with you." Yep, I was toying with a demon. Seemed about right.

I side-stepped, trying to casually brush past the asshole who was definitely going to slaughter me for it. But going out in a blaze of glory seemed more my style than going quietly anyway.

I made it past him one step, finding Frank moving closer to us, shaking his head at me in a warning. Church was frowning at me in a way I'd not seen on his face before, no sign of the happy go lucky guy who lurked beneath his flesh.

Danny whirled after me, locking an arm around my shoulders and yanking me back against his chest. "Lucky you then, love, because I just picked my date for the night. And you remember how you said you didn't have any firsts to give me? I think I just thought of one to take from you."

He marched me towards the door and I started to struggle, the coldness to his tone sending a blunt knife into my chest.

"Stop – let me go," I snarled, scratching at his arm, but he held onto me tight, his other hand fisting in my hair to get better control of me. He was mad, ragingly fucking mad and as he kicked the front door open and dragged me sideways through it, I caught sight of Frank and Church hurrying towards us.

"What the fuck are you doing?" Frank barked.

"Let her go, mate," Church tried, but Danny flung the door shut in their faces as he got me out onto the street.

I screamed and I motherfucking screamed, but his hand clamped down over my mouth to shut me up. I wasn't done there though. I threw my elbow back and stamped my foot down on his, but he just growled against the pain and held me tighter, locking my arms to my sides with both of his.

A couple of men came hurrying out of the shadows in dark hoods and for half a second I thought some wannabe heroes had come to my aid, but of course that wasn't the story I'd grown up in. They were his men, and their concern was solely for him.

"Get the trunk open," Danny commanded one of them and in the next second I was being hurled into the trunk of a gold Jaguar. I had one frantic second to meet my husband's soulless gaze before the lid slammed shut in my face and I was plunged into total darkness.

I scooted backwards then threw my feet against the trunk door, kicking it as hard as I possibly could with a savage snarl leaving my lips. Again and again, I drove my feet against it, but the engine soon started and we sped off down the road towards a fate I couldn't escape. I screamed at him instead, shouting every colourful word I knew his way and demanding he free me, but he never once answered.

Danny started blasting some shitty fucking garage music in the front of the car, so loud it was all I could hear and I could feel the fuck you in him playing it. My breaths came raggedly as I slumped down on the floor, my throat ripped raw and my mind a haze of adrenaline that I couldn't put to good use.

I felt around in the space for something I could use as a weapon, but there was nothing here. It was empty. Even the little space for a toolbox beneath the lining of the trunk was empty. Like he'd known, like he'd planned this. Or like he'd done it enough times not to make a mistake like leaving me with a weapon.

His words circled in my head again. *"Remember how you said you didn't have any firsts to give me? I think I just thought of one to take from you."*

My life, that was what he was going to take, I knew it in my soul.

I'm dead. I'm fucking dead.

I calmed my breathing, trying to focus on a plan, going through everything I'd been taught about finding myself in a situation like this. My brothers had told me to fight and kick and bite and do anything within my power to escape. But my brother Zakhar's voice drifted up from the recesses of my memory about those instructions, making a cold lump of dread fill my gut. *"If they get you in a vehicle, you're done for. You'll disappear like you never existed."*

A tremor invaded my body and I shut my eyes, forcing it out as I took a deep breath. Then I did the only thing left to me as I lay there in the dark, the only thing I wanted to do anyway. I slid my headphones over my ears, pulled my iPod from my pocket and turned my music on.

Instantly, the fear fell away, I drifted into the space between the lyrics where nothing existed but a rhythm so deep it carved its magic into my bones.

Death was easy. Death was surrender. And music had taught me the gift of that. I just hoped that wherever I went beyond this life, the music followed.

High and Dry by Radiohead played its melancholy tune inside my mind and I gave myself to it in offering, a willing sacrifice on an altar of desperation. If I had to vanish as if I never was, then let me at least stay there.

An hour, two maybe. The time slipped away and I played all of my favourite songs, kissing my fingers and placing them against the screen to say thank you to each one. They were friends, the only friends I'd ever had in fact. People probably thought I was lonely back home, but they hadn't seen the endless company I'd carried in my pocket.

Once upon a time, I'd wished for real friends, the kind to tell stories to and make memories with. But where did a girl like me fit into a normal world like that? No, I was born to a family with blood on its hands and too many hidden graves in its past.

Thanks to my vagina, I was useful enough to help stop a war between our enemies which had given me a purpose to serve if nothing more. But I guessed that was fucked now. Danny could make up any lie he liked about my death, but my brothers would come, they would seek vengeance and it would be a bloody, grisly thing. The war between our families would start all over again and the first sacrifices to their unending need for violence would be the girls who had been sent against our wills to marry our enemies.

The car eventually came to a halt, the vibrations of the engine stopped rumbling through me, but I remained there, eyes closed, my soul tangled with the music, never to be released.

I was half aware of the trunk opening, the shift in the air from warm to cold as it rushed over me, but I didn't open my eyes. The song switched to Here Comes The Sun by The Beatles and a serene smile filled my lips. *Ah yes, what a song to die to.*

Someone took the headphones off of my ears and my eyes snapped open, defiance tearing up the centre of me as I reached for them. But Danny hooked them around his own neck, glaring down at me with his head haloed by a full moon.

"Let me die to The Beatles," I demanded, lunging up to snatch them from him, but Danny caught my waist, dragging me against his body and lifting me out of the trunk.

"Not a chance, bombshell," he said, shoving the trunk shut and sitting my ass on it.

I glanced around as he released me, finding myself in the middle of a dark woodland, a low fog hanging between the trees, lit by the silvery moon. It was cold. Scrap that, it was fucking freezing and I shivered as he regarded me, carving his fingers over the stubble on his jaw. There was an overnight bag sitting on the ground beside him, making it clear that he'd planned this fucking thing while I was still with Frank and making me feel even dumber for falling into his trap so easily.

I swallowed the hard lump in my throat, deciding which way I was going to run when he came at me, but before I could make that call, he spoke.

"We need to talk," Danny announced and I frowned suspiciously at him.

"Before you kill me? Seems kinda pointless, don't you think?" I tossed at him, deciding on my route at last. There was a hefty-looking branch several feet to my right, if I grabbed it and swung it hard enough, I could finish him.

One good whack to the head and that lump of muscle and tattoos would go down like a sack of shit. It was my only shot, and I was estimating a ten percent chance that I could pull it off, but ten percent was better than zero.

"I ain't gonna kill ya, love, what the fuck gave you that idea?" he asked, a lilt of mocking in his tone.

"Asshole."

"Bitch," he tossed back.

"Fuckwit."

He stepped toward me and I pressed my hands to the cold metal of the trunk, ready to push myself off and run if I needed to.

"You're a mouthy little runaway," he accused. "And you're gonna listen sharp now, wife, because I ain't fuckin' about. So do you wanna talk here in the freezin' arse woods, or do you wanna go inside?"

"Inside?" I looked around behind me as he pointed, the fog twisting and lifting for a moment to reveal a pair of large iron gates with sharp spikes on top of them. The name on the brick pillar to the left of them was Galvods Place.

"I've got a key to this here mansion," Danny said temptingly. "One of the old boys who used to run The Firm with my dad retired here when he got outa the game. Or at least as out as any of us get. He's off cruisin' the world right now, and said I can 'ave access to his house while he's gone."

Danny scooped me off of the trunk without warning, holding me with one arm under my legs and the other around my back, picking up the bag then heading towards the gate.

"I can walk," I growled and he looked down at me darkly.

"You can run too," he said then shifted his hand against my ass and shimmied my iPod out of my pocket. "I'd say you'll stay close while I have this though."

He put me on my feet and I scowled at him as he pocketed my prized possession and I was forced to follow him or abandon the thing. But as I seemed to be in the middle of nowhere and would likely freeze to death before I found civilisation, I decided staying with him was my only viable option anyway, especially as he didn't seem to be intent on murdering me anytime soon.

He unlocked the gate with a large iron key and it creaked ominously as we stepped through.

We moved up a long, gravel driveway and a house loomed out of the fog which looked like it belonged in a horror movie with ghosts lurking around every corner. The bricks were almost black and rose up high above us to where stone gargoyles sat on the roof. It must have been hundreds of years old and despite the shiver that tracked along my spine, I found myself endlessly intrigued by this place, the arching windows and the darkness beyond them sending a buzz of exhilaration through me. Fuck, if I had to die tonight then at least I was gonna go out epically.

Danny guided me to the front door which had a roaring lion on the knocker at the centre of it. He unlocked it, leading us into an entranceway with red carpet and even a suit of armour by a grand stairway that circled up towards further rooms. There was a chill in the air and my breath puffed before me as Danny worked to get some lights on in the place followed by the groan of a boiler starting up as he turned up a thermostat.

"Fuck me, my tits are gonna freeze off," he said as he rubbed his hands together vigorously then led me through to a lounge with chintz armchairs and a fireplace that took up half the wall, the thing big enough for me to walk right into it.

Danny set to work lighting a fire and I grabbed a furry blanket off the back of a wingback before moving to sit on a wide loveseat before the fire just as the first flames caught.

Danny moved to sit beside me, tucking himself under the blanket too and wedging his giant body into the loveseat with me. I was so freaking cold that I didn't even care about stealing his body heat. But it did strike me as odd that I was now snuggling with the monster who I'd thought was going to kill me tonight. I had to mentally block out the fact that he was an asshole who'd collared me like a dog and no doubt had plans to do far worse to me when he got around to it too.

He looped an arm around me beneath the blanket and I shamelessly tucked myself closer to the heat of him, stealing it away and wishing I could take so much of it that it stopped his heart.

"So are you gonna explain why you've driven me all the way out to a freezing, ghost-infested mansion?" I asked through chattering teeth.

"I told ya, we need to talk," he said and I looked up at him with narrowed eyes.

"And we couldn't have done that back in London with witnesses?"

"No," he said, his eyes turning to pitch. "This is me and you business. Husband and wife."

Something about those words made my pulse quicken and I nodded slowly. "So?"

He took a deep breath. "What you did yesterday nearly jeopardised the entire peace treaty."

"Fuck the treaty," I said, enunciating every word so he knew exactly how much of a shit I gave about it. "If all of you men want the fighting to stop, how about you marry each other rather than sacrificing your sisters to your enemies?"

"You think I wanted to send my baby sister off to some fucking Cosa Nostra arseholes?" he snarled. "I'd marry and fuck whoever I had to to save her from that fate."

"So why didn't you?" I scoffed.

"I ain't got the biology for what this is really about, love." His hand slid down, resting over my womb and I stiffened, pushing his hand off of me. "You can't tell me you didn't already know."

I shook my head in refusal, because obviously I'd known, but it hadn't mattered before. "I didn't come here to stay here."

He eyed me closely. "So you always planned to run, did you bombshell? Didn't your brothers explain to you why that was never gonna be an option?"

Bitterness laced my tongue and I decided to just be honest, figuring it couldn't do me any harm now. "They told me there was a plan to get me out of this when there wasn't. I thought…well, frankly, Danny, I thought you'd be dead by now and I'd be back in America with the rest of my family."

He frowned at that. "They knew you'd never go along with the marriage otherwise," he said in realisation and I nodded, shifting my gaze from him to look at the fire instead.

"But they lied and here I am, still trapped," I whispered, more to myself than him. "Always fucking trapped."

"You were always gonna run," he muttered.

"Yeah," I agreed, then looked back at him. "And one day I'll get away, I won't stop. I'll never stop."

He ran his tongue over his teeth. "Is it really all that bad here?"

"It's worse," I snarled, though it felt like a lie. London was perfect. My husband was the problem.

"Well here's a reality check, love, I ain't goin' anywhere. You and I are bound now whether we want it or not. I ain't breaking the treaty because I know what the world was like before it. It was a life lived in fear for everyone I loved, where blood was drawn in vengeance time and again, a cycle of tit for tat which had no end. So this answer isn't perfect, we all know that. But it is an answer."

"It's a man's answer," I sneered. "Your women are paying the price, because you're all too cowardly to pay it yourselves."

He bared his teeth and I raised my chin. Neither of us backed down for a minute but he sighed as he pushed his fingers into my hair and trailed them down my neck. "We ain't cowards, bombshell, we're businessmen. And I was sold into this just as you were. I didn't get to pick my bride any more than you got to pick your groom."

I scoffed, turning my head, but he yanked my hair to make me look back at him. He might have been given an arranged marriage too but he had agreed to it freely, he'd been allowed to remain in his home with the people he knew and loved surrounding him. That was far more than I'd been offered.

"I know what's being asked of you ain't fair, bombshell," he said. "But I'm gonna ask more of you too. Because the treaty doesn't get upheld by a ring on your finger, it gets upheld by a healthy little bundle of joy in your arms."

I jerked away from him, refusal burning through my chest. "Never."

"You know this marriage means nothing without that," he said and I was surprised when a note of apology entered his voice. "In return, I promise you this. I'll be faithful, respectful and give myself to this marriage fully as you've had to."

I continued to shake my head, trying to pull away but his grip only tightened.

"It ain't up for negotiation," he said and I jammed the heel of my palm into his chest, forcing him back and scrambling away onto my feet.

I started to pace, locking my fingers in my hair as I felt the world descending on me. I couldn't do it. I *wouldn't* do it.

All this time, I'd thought I'd just figure it out, I'd get away, make it out of here. But suddenly that didn't even seem like an option anymore. It was so much worse than being caged because now I could see my life stretching out before me, having to offer children to a man I despised. Who wanted to control me, lock me in a dungeon and turn me into some thoroughbred dog ready for breeding.

I'd been careless before now when we'd fucked, thinking the two of us had just gotten too caught up in each other to think of contraception, but of course that wasn't the case for him. He hadn't ever planned on using any. So here I was, trying to play catch up while he was stating what he wanted clear as day now and I wasn't going to give it to him. I'd seen what he was, and I wasn't going to let him chain me to him with some child. I wasn't going to just go along with what every gangster in this war wanted. *Fuck them.*

"I won't!" I shouted, my rage breaking free as I picked up the nearest object and hurled it at him. *Him.* This heinous man who was going to take everything from me.

He ducked aside so it sailed over his head and smashed on the floor beyond the chair.

"You will," he countered, rising to his feet.

My eyes locked on a poker by the fire and I picked it up, wielding it at him as my upper lip peeled back. "I'm not going to be used. If you put a baby in me I'll get rid of it!" I shrieked, anger pumping furiously through my blood.

"Anya," he said, his tone hard and imploring. "I'm not sayin' now. I'll give you time."

"Time for what?" I scoffed. "Time for me to die inside?"

"No," he said fiercely like the idea of that actually bothered him. He got up, walking toward me and I held the poker higher in warning, but he just kept coming until he was right in front of me and I pressed the tip of it up under his chin. "It's time for us to figure this all out, time for you to love me."

"I'll never love you," I told him plain and clear, because I was sure of that now I'd seen who he really was. "I know what you want, Danny. You put a collar on me the moment I arrived here. You think I can love a man who wants me chained? Who agrees to anything and everything he wants just because he demands it?"

"No, Anya. I love that fucking fire in you. I want you to push back every time I'm an arsehole, I want you to scream at me when I'm being a cunt. I don't want you to change one fucking bit."

"So it's more enjoyable for you when you force me to give in?" I spat, thinking of the cage I'd seen in those plans. How long was it going to be before he took me to that vile place? Was it already built or was he still setting it up for my future?

He released a harsh breath in frustration, taking hold of the poker that was driving up against his chin and digging it in harder, almost drawing blood on his skin.

"*I* won't demand anything from you, but *the treaty* is demanding this from both of us. It will happen. And if you hate me for it, then I can accept that, but gimme a chance, just one fucking chance, bombshell, and I promise I can be a good husband, one that makes you smile, who gives you everything you could dream of, and who makes you come harder than any other man whose ever laid a finger on you. But for now, hate me. Hate me with all the ire in your soul and the fight in your Russian blood. Punish me until I've paid for every scar on your heart, until you can bear to accept the good I offer you, because I may have thought nothing of you before you arrived at my door, but now you're here, you've taken root in every depraved fantasy in my mind and etched yourself into the fabric of my being. The Butcher King bows for no one, but I'll make an exception for you." He dropped to his knees and my hand lowered with him, keeping the poker under his chin as I absorbed his words. I didn't want them to find their way beneath my skin, but the way he was looking at me was making me really think for a second that he was being honest. That maybe he didn't want to do all those terrible things to me anymore, that for some reason he'd changed and now he was trying to be a better man. But was I a complete fool to believe that? Was I going to regret it if I gave myself to this all-consuming fire that burned between us whenever we were this close?

"Hurt me, bombshell," he commanded, his voice dropping an octave. "Take your pound of flesh from me."

I drove the poker harder up under his chin, bitter anger mixing with the sugary sweetness of my desire for this man, creating a potent cocktail inside me that caused the deepest kind of burn.

The most frightening thing, was that my desire for him was growing to something much more difficult to cut out. If it hadn't been for the evidence on that laptop and the way he'd been with me the first time we'd met, I knew I could have fallen for this man kneeling before me. He was everything I'd been craving in my life, yet what kind of woman did it make me if I let myself be persuaded by him? Was I standing on the threshold of his manipulation, about to willingly walk through the door with my eyes wide open? Somehow, confronted with him and what appeared to be the stark honesty in his eyes, it was impossible to turn away. To slam the door and lock it for good.

Whatever this thing was between us, it was hungry and demanded to be fed. But I didn't want to be a victim of this dark creature, so I'd show him the essence of me and let him feast on the darkness I possessed too. I wasn't some fool drunk on love, I was a demon at a crossroads shaking hands with a sinner. I was the one who would punish him if he broke that promise in his eyes, and I'd give him a taste of that punishment now.

I tossed the poker away, the metal clattering across the wooden floor as I took his face in my grasp instead, my nails digging in.

"If you hurt me, cage me, or deny me the world, I will be your death, Danny Butcher, do you understand me?"

"Yes," he rasped, lust flashing in his eyes.

"I'm your lawfully wedded wife and you have vowed to honour me. So will you honour my wishes, husband, even when they are bound with a ribbon of sin?"

"Especially then," he agreed and I tilted his head back, exposing his adam's apple and the stubble that coated it.

I released his jaw, reaching my hand back and anticipation built in his gaze as he watched, waiting for me to strike him. My palm smacked against his cheek and his head whipped sideways as the finger marks flourished on his skin. He released a heavy breath like he'd enjoyed every second of that and I lifted my boot, pressing it to his shoulder while our eyes remained locked.

"Shirt off and lie on your back," I growled and he smirked, shifting his legs out from beneath him and tugging his shirt off, making my gaze fall to defined muscles of his chest and the tightness of his abs as he laid himself out for me.

I moved to the fireplace, picking up a long, tapered candle out of its holder and leaning down to light it from the fire. I held it up, admiring the flame as it danced before my eyes then I turned to my husband.

"Hands locked together and clasped behind your head," I commanded and he obeyed, which sent a rush through my veins despite the cocky look in his eyes which never once faded.

I approached him again, watching his chest rise and fall with every breath he took, watching as his breaths came quicker and his cock hardened in his pants.

"Open your mouth," I commanded, lowering down to kneel over him and he did as I asked before I slotted the bottom of the candle between his teeth and smirked at him. "Hold it tight, you don't want to burn your pretty face."

He tightened his teeth around it, watching me with a look that said he could stop this game any time he liked, but he let me have my way and played along. The wax wasn't yet hot enough to drip, but it was starting to soften around the tip and the longer it was there, the more likely scalding wax was going to roll down it and burn his lips.

I stood up, unbuckling my boots and kicking them off before slowly shimmying out of my jeans. His eyes kept following my movements, but every time he lost concentration on the candle, it slipped a little and he had to tighten his jaw to keep it from falling.

When I was down to my silky blue panties and knotted up t-shirt, I moved to kick his legs apart and stand between them, pressing my bare foot against his hard on through his rough jeans.

He groaned as I flexed my toes and I watched as a bead of burning wax rolled down the long length of the candle towards his lips. I pressed down harder just as it hit his lower lip and a faint hiss sounded it hardening against his flesh. He released a deep growl in his chest and his chest flexed, his hips rising to grind his cock against the pad of my foot.

I took my foot away and the candle wobbled precariously as his hips jerked in frustration.

I smiled at him tauntingly, stepping forward so I was standing either side of his stomach and I reached down and plucked the candle from his lips just as another bead of wax ran down the side of it.

I held it over his chest, tapping the side of it and the wax fell, landing against his right pec and making him groan his approval as it hit.

"Do you get off on hurting me, bombshell?" he asked, running his tongue over the dried red wax on his lower lip before drawing it into his mouth and swallowing it like a savage.

"Yes," I admitted as I tapped the candle again and two hot droplets splashed against his chest in quick succession, making his eyes spark with the need for more.

"Show me how much," he growled, the ring of a true leader in his voice, reminding me exactly who I had at my mercy.

I raised the candle to my mouth on its side, holding it between my teeth, hot wax falling to his ribs, his body jerking as he hissed between his teeth. He was clearly enjoying every second of this, and I was too. It made me feel powerful, like I really did rule this mafia boss I had beneath me.

I slid my panties off, exposing my pussy to him and tossing them away as he watched me, transfixed and unblinking as he waited to see what I'd do next.

I took the candle from between my teeth, twisting it in my grip until the rounded base of it was against my soaking core.

"Bombshell," Danny groaned as the fire came dangerously close to my thighs, more burning wax spilling down on his stomach beneath me, red droplets hitting the forget-me-not tattoo he had inked just above his waistline. I slid the candle inside me, never breaking his gaze as I fucked myself with the item that was causing him pain, showing him how much I loved making him hurt, how much I wanted to punish him with every piece of me. But how much he turned me on too.

With the flame curling upwards, the wax was melting faster and Danny unlocked his hands from behind his head, dropping them to my ankles and tugging me forward so it splashed against his chest. It was hot and wrong and fucking twisted, but that was exactly what the two of us were. And two wrongs sure made one helluva fucking right.

I drove the candle so deep, the flame nearly burned my fingers and Danny gasped as another bead hit his chest, rolling down through the valley between his pecs before hardening against his skin.

He reared up suddenly, blowing it out and knocking my hand away, taking hold of the hot end of the candle. He pumped it in and out of me a second before his mouth closed over my clit, sending pleasure rushing through my flesh.

I cried out, my voice echoing around the huge empty house as he licked and sucked, driving the candle in and out of me as burning wax sank between his fingers. I was so hot for him already, I started falling towards bliss in an instant, a few more strokes of his tongue and pumps of the candle sending me over the edge.

My head tipped back and I panted and moaned my way through the orgasm, my pussy tightening around the hard length of the candle as he continued to suck on my clit and prolong the pleasure he was giving me.

My eyes fluttered open as the final shockwaves rippled through my body and I looked down at him, fisting my hand in his hair and yanking his mouth away from my pussy. He withdrew the candle from my body, dropping it on the floor as I tugged his head back to the point of pain.

"Are you done with me yet, love?" he asked and I knew he meant more than just right now.

"No," I admitted, accepting that this thing between us had its claws in me far too deep.

I'd see it through for now, but I wasn't promising forever, because I didn't know where I'd end up if I stayed in this beast's den. Was I destined to be consumed by him, my bones picked clean? Or was there really a place for me in this life that could offer me the freedom I'd been searching for? It seemed impossible, but the tantalising idea of this somehow working out made me want to try. Just for a little while. To see if Danny really had changed or if I was only deluding myself into thinking he could.

"But if you cross me, Danny, you know where this ends." I lifted my foot, placing it against his throat and crushing his windpipe for a second. "I'd rather sleep eternally in the dirt than end up in a cage. But I'll try to cut your throat before I decide to cut my own."

I placed my foot back down on the floor and he ran his hands up the back of my legs, caressing the soft skin behind my knees and making me shiver.

"If you ever find yourself caged by me, you only need to point it out and I'll hold a knife to my own throat, bombshell."

I sank down to straddle him, falling into the vow that kept flaring in his eyes, one I wholeheartedly wanted to believe. His fingers ran up my spine, pushing beneath my shirt and pulling it over my head, throwing it away and leaving me fully bare for him.

I reached down to unbuckle his pants as he leaned up, his mouth meeting mine in a frantic kiss that spoke of the promise he was making me. And I raised my hips a moment before he drove the full length of himself inside me, making me moan against his mouth.

He fucked me slow and deep until I was breathless and clawing my nails into his shoulders from the intensity of it. With every rock of my hips, he thrust inside me, hitting the perfect spot and forcing me towards another inevitable climax.

He watched me as I came for him, my spine arching and his hands squeezing my breasts, his thumbs carving over my nipples. He was so hard, I knew he was on the point of spilling himself too and as our eyes locked, he yanked my hips up, pulling out of me and coming between us instead of inside me with a heady groan.

I knew what he was telling me with that gesture, that he wasn't trying to get me pregnant tonight, that I could have more time. And I just had to hope that when the time came for me to fulfil the duty of our marriage and provide a child to secure the treaty, that he would have proved he was worthy of that offering. But if it turned out that he wasn't a changed man and he planned to trap me like I feared, then I would fight with all the ferocity of a warrior for my freedom. And if the king had to fall to secure it, then so be it.

CHAPTER TWENTY THREE

I kept cutting looks my wife's way as we drove through the streets of London, closing in on the warehouse and the life we'd stolen a little time away from.

She didn't hide her fascination for this place, her eyes wide and lips slightly parted as she tipped her head back to look up at monuments and skyscrapers, each sight seeming to thrill her and make that hungry look in her eyes grow more ravenous.

I perched my smoke between my lips and moved my right hand to the wheel, reaching across and dropping my left hand on her bare knee.

Anya sucked in a surprised breath as she looked around at me and I gave her a challenging smirk as I inhaled smoke and drank in the sight of her.

"Those things will kill you one day," she said, bobbing her chin at my cigarette as I was forced to glance at the road once more.

"I figure if I make it that far, I'll worry about it then," I said with a shrug. "I had to go a long damn time without vices, bombshell, this was the one which I was afforded the luxury of keeping, so you'll have to excuse the filthy habit. Though if you're in the mood for excusing filthy habits, I have a better one in mind." I shifted my hand further up her thigh and she bit her lip before turning to look out the window again.

"I'm not your keeper," she replied dismissively. "I can't stop you from enjoying whatever vices you choose to claim."

"I don't get the feeling you want me to stop enjoying this one," I pointed out, reaching the hem of her little pleated skirt and teasing my fingers beneath it just a bit.

"Well there has to be some perks to this marriage," she muttered, her thigh tipping towards me obligingly as I shifted my hand higher and smirked at the mouth on her. Sometimes, I was pretty sure she was looking to get that foul mouth of hers fucked into submission.

I turned a corner, cutting through the traffic as my hand made its way to her core and I smirked to myself as I found her pussy bare for me.

"No knickers? Naughty girl," I chastised, causing her to roll her eyes.

"Someone forgot to pack them," she accused. "So don't go getting too excited about the idea of it being anything to do with you."

"Fair enough," I conceded. "But what's the excuse for the stain you're putting on my upholstery?"

Anya shot me a scowl but I made my point by pushing two fingers straight into her soaked pussy and the only retort she managed to give me was a sexy fucking moan.

My cock hardened in my jeans as she began to rock her hips against my hand and I had to work damn hard to keep enough attention on the road to stop us from crashing.

Anya was a screamer, no exceptions, and as I pulled up to the warehouse, the beautiful chorus of her moans of pleasure filled the air even louder than the song she'd set playing on the car radio.

I parked at some wonky as fuck angle across the private drive outside our home and turned to look at her as she writhed and pawed at her tits in the seat beside me.

I smirked at her as I continued to fuck her with my fingers and she cursed me, reaching out to pluck the cigarette from my lips before ashing the damn thing on my arm, burning a hole straight through my shirt, the heat of it sending a spike of pain into my flesh.

I cursed as my cock jerked at the bite of pain, a grunt of lust escaping me which had her smirking right back at me like she was making a fucking point. And with the feeling of her pussy locked tight around my fingers, I was more than happy to let her.

I leaned forward, wanting to taste the anger on her lips while I started to get lost in all the ways I was going to enjoy fucking her once we got inside.

But before I could make good on any of those things, my door was ripped open behind me and I was hauled from the car by strong arms to the sound of a furious snarl which sent my adrenaline pumping a mile a minute.

Frank whirled me around and slammed my back against the wall of the warehouse, his forearm driving forcefully against my throat as he pinned me there and snarled in my motherfucking face.

"What did you do to her?" he demanded, the fury in him wild and unfettered.

I shoved him back hard enough to dislodge the hold he had on my neck and barked a wild laugh.

"Calm down, Frankie boy, anyone would think she was your woman instead of mine," I said, cocking my head as I looked at him and tried to figure out his angle.

Frank made a noise which sounded like an honest to shit growl as he came at me again and the amusement in me faded as I was forced to duck outa the way of his fist.

I slammed into him as I lowered my head and dropped beneath his attack, throwing him backwards so that he landed on the bonnet of my car, the whole thing bouncing on its suspension as the weight of the two of us fell down on it.

I glanced up at Anya through the windscreen where she still sat shotgun, and she arched a single brow at us a second before Frank clocked me in the goddamn jaw hard enough to make the bone crunch.

I was almost knocked offa him, but I managed to right myself, punching him in his face to see how he bloody well liked it.

Frank threw me off with his next punch and I stumbled backwards, keeping my feet and spitting a wad of blood to the cobbled street as I backed up and pointed a warning finger at him.

"Remember your place, arsehole," I warned. "You're dancing the line of pissing me the fuck off now."

"Where the hell have you been?" he demanded, shoving himself upright and straightening his jacket just as Anya stepped out of the car behind him. "I've been looking for you everywhere."

"It's true," Church's voice came from the doorway. I glanced over at him where he stood shirtless and barefoot in the biting cold of the morning drinking a cup of tea with his sweats hanging low on his hips like he was enjoying the show. "He hasn't even slept, have you Frankie boy? Got his knickers in a right twist, worrying about what you might be doing to our Miss America."

"Really?" Anya asked as she got out of the car, looking at Frank with this warmth I swear she'd never once shown me, before shuttering it off again as fast as it had ignited. "Well as you can see, I'm fine. Can't a girl spend a night away fucking her husband without the hell hounds picking up the scent and setting off on the hunt?"

Frank frowned as he took in her words and I sighed, deciding to let his little psycho attack on me slide on account of the fact that he was under the impression that I was Danny. And Danny was a fucking whack job who most likely woulda been making Anya's life hell if he'd taken her away for a night, so I could understand his concern.

Church grinned, opening his arms for Anya as she strode towards him, but instead of embracing him, she flicked him right in the cock and slipped past him as he winced and buckled in on himself, sloshing tea on the floor. "Bloody hell, what kind of person flicks a fella in the cock?"

"That one," Frank said with something of a smirk on his lips.

The three of us were left staring after my wife like a pack of hungry mutts and I pursed my lips at the clear end to the party me and her had just been about to start on.

"Well thanks for the blue balls, dickhead," I growled, slapping Frank around the back of his head before striding on inside and stalking my woman into the kitchen where she was already in the middle of making herself something to eat.

I walked to the breakfast bar and leaned my forearms on the cool worktop as I watched her, wondering what it would take to draw her attention back to me.

"We have a few things we need to discuss, boss," Church said as he moved to mimic my posture, his shoulder bumping against mine while he watched my wife with the same rampant kind of lust that I was feeling.

I gave that a little consideration before forcing my game face back on and focusing on his words.

"Trouble?" I asked, getting that question outa the way sharpish.

"There's a hold on planning permission for the Soho development," Church explained. "Probably nothing, but with the Candlestick Maker still demanding a meet and The Czar still playing chicken when it comes to coughing up the cash for the building work to get underway…"

I sighed, scrubbing a hand down my face as I forced myself to focus on that instead of the way Anya's skirt rode up to reveal the bottom of that beautifully round arse of hers whenever she leaned forward to stir her eggs.

"Seems like I'm being backed into a corner," I muttered.

"You'd think everyone would know not to do that to a feral creature like you," Anya said in a disinterested tone, but the fact that she'd been paying enough attention to make that comment only proved how much she wanted to know about it.

"Tell me, bombshell," I said slowly as the door banged shut and Frank stomped across the open space to take a seat on the other side of the room about as far from me as he could get. I ignored him and kept my focus on her. "How much of your family's business did you take part in out in Vegas?"

Anya turned to look at me over her shoulder, all of that blonde hair of hers tumbling down her spine at the movement and drawing my focus before I moved it to her obsidian eyes and got stuck there.

"Honestly?" she asked and I nodded. "None. I was just a woman after all. My father had a single use for me which was sending me to you. And even after he died, my brothers never included me in anything that mattered. I was their sweet sister. I don't know if it ever occurred to them that I was born of the same bloodline as them. That I was just as smart, just as capable. Powerful men do have an unfortunate habit of thinking of women as being little more than a decoration for their arm."

"Or entertainment for their bed," Church added, earning himself a scowl from her, but I knew he wasn't agreeing with the sentiment. "That's because they're fucking fools," he went on. "There's something so mind numbingly predictable about old men thinking they own the world, darlin'. But don't you worry; around here, we aren't so archaically inclined."

"Meaning?" She arched a brow.

"Meaning I want your input if you wanna offer it," I said, pointing to a chair opposite us and making her pause.

Anya hesitated for a beat before turning back to her food, plating it up and dropping into the seat I'd indicated.

"Come on then, don't keep us in suspense," Church said as she remained silent, looking between us like she expected some trick.

"What do you think I should do about this little conundrum?" I asked.

"You need the deal with The Czar to go through?" she asked. "As in, him suddenly finding himself without a head wouldn't work for you?"

I snorted a laugh, shaking my head. "Unfortunately not. We need this pay out, bombshell. There have been several…miscalculations over the last few years and without going into too much boring accounting bullshit, I can assure you that we want this one to go through or we could end up with some complications which I really don't need the headache of."

Church huffed out a breath in irritation at the fucking mess Danny had made of our organisation in my absence. We were just lucky we had some seriously talented people working to help run our businesses, because when my brother had decided he was more interested in getting shitfaced on blow and fucking hookers all night long than he was in overseeing that shit, things had quickly started to take a dive.

It was no fucking wonder he'd ended up involved with the Candlestick Maker and this prick of a buddy of his – he needed this job to go through otherwise our whole organisation could be at risk. Which in turn meant I needed the fucking thing to go through too. Once it did, I would have some cash to play with again, more options for the future and ways to pull us outa this hole.

"Unfortunately, my bloodthirsty little bombshell, we are stuck so far as the two of these pricks go. We need The Czar's money. We need this fucking deal. And as much as it pisses me off, he's best buddies with the fucking Candlestick Maker so killing him isn't an option either."

I'd already figured out that the tightness of their bond was likely to do with the girls the Candlestick Maker was trafficking through my town and that just pissed me off even more. These two dirty old men were running the fucked up kind of gigs which our organisation had never allowed and now that I was being forced to stay my hand, I knew it was only a matter of time before more chancers decided to take those kinds of liberties and I'd be left to run around my own fucking city, trying to put out fires as fast as they ignited, unable to stop the spread of the damn flames. If that happened, then the whole house could come burning down right on top of our heads and I couldn't allow that.

I needed to get this deal to go through and get rid of the Candlestick Maker somehow along the way without angering the man with the money.

It was one hell of a pickle.

Anya sighed like me having to keep those pricks alive was somehow inconvenient to her.

"Divide and conquer then," she said with a shrug. "What's that saying about keeping your enemies close? Seems to me like you need to find a point of contention between them. You want the Candlestick Maker dealt with? Then get The Czar to do it for you."

The corner of my lips lifted as I thought on that, liking it a whole hell of a lot. "You know, I think you might be onto something there, love," I admitted, exchanging a look with Church.

"Maybe we should take the Candlestick Maker up on his offer of a meet," Church added and I nodded, smirking at my wife as she tried to hide the triumphant look in her eyes and dropped her attention to her plate instead.

"I'm gonna need a little more information before I can agree to that meet," I said thoughtfully, glancing at Church. "Though I think I have a good idea on where to get it from."

He nodded, his thoughts clearly taking the same turn as mine and I stood abruptly, circling the breakfast bar and snatching Anya's plate before dumping her barely touched food in the trash.

"Frank!" I barked, drawing his attention so that he scowled at me across the room while Anya yelled some outraged nonsense at me. "Take my wife for a proper meal. She just gave me the idea I needed for a bit of business I'm stuck on and I'm gonna need to crack on with that for the next few hours."

"What the fuck, asshole?" Anya hissed, taking a step closer like she was gonna give me a good smack, but I caught her wrist and yanked her toward me before she could do it.

Her chest hit mine and I gripped her jaw in my hand, claiming her mouth and pressing my tongue between her snarling lips, kissing her so hard that it was almost bruising and loving the way she caved to the pressure of my mouth. I sank my tongue between her lips, devouring her outrage and feasting on her anger as I controlled the kiss and stoked the flames which burned hot between us.

I forced myself back before I could get too lost in her and ended up fucking her right here in the kitchen while my men looked on.

Anya panted harshly, snarling something at me in Russian which sounded like a host of insults and I barked a laugh.

"Save that anger for when I'm fucking you later, bombshell. I wanna feel every spark of your rage while you beg for me to satisfy you, and I promise I'll fill that angry little mouth of yours with something far more interesting than venomous words too."

Her eyes flashed with that dismissal, but I released her and backed up before she could strike at me again, grinning widely as she glared.

"Well you'd better be prepared for the reality of that little fantasy of yours," she said, raising her chin defiantly. "Because I have one hell of a bite on me."

She gave the bulge in my jeans a pointed look before turning and striding away, grabbing a coat from a hook by the door and stepping out onto the London streets without another word.

I frowned at the idea of her biting my cock, knowing without needing to test the theory that I wouldn't enjoy that particular form of pain from her and having absolutely no desire to test my accuracy in that guess.

Frank had to jog to the door to catch up with her, not even bothering to say anything to us as he went and leaving me scowling at his back until the door snapped shut behind him.

"You think I need to deal with that?" I asked, nodding after the man who had just disrespected me right to my fucking face. "He didn't even apologise for punching me in the goddamn mouth."

Church scoffed. "You know Frank. He's like a bull with a red rag always fluttering just out of reach. He pops off at anything these days. And at least now you know he gives a fuck about our girl. She literally couldn't be safer than she is in his hands if he cares for her."

I hummed my agreement then turned towards the door at the far end of the living room, my gaze fixing on the black metal as I thought about the best way for me to play this. Danny had been better behaved recently, reminiscing about the good old days when we'd run these streets together among other bullshit I didn't have much of a mind to listen to. But I had to wonder if he would be a little more forthcoming with me than he was the last time I'd asked him about his dealings with these fuckers. Because if I was going to be impersonating him to the Candlestick Maker's face then I sure as shit needed to know what deal the two of them had struck.

"I might go grab myself something to eat with Frank and Miss America," Church said, as I moved across the room to the safe where I kept my keys locked away. "The last time Danny saw the two of us together, he turned into an angry little wasp looking to ruin my tea party."

I nodded in agreement to that. "He's always been a jealous fuck over me having friends aside from him. I think he seriously used to believe that it was me and him against the world when we were younger. He never liked the idea of me letting anyone else into my inner circle."

"Yeah well, he's a fucking psycho, so that makes sense." Church kicked a pair of sneakers on then tossed a leather jacket over his bare chest and grabbed the keys to his Mini from the side.

"How do you know where they've gone?" I asked, my brow dipping in confusion.

"You know Frank, he's feeling pissy so he'll be chasing live music. There's a band doing some kind of charity gig down by the river today and I heard they aren't half bad, so I'm gonna guess he's buying her street food and they'll be in their little rocker heaven just waiting for me to show up."

"Alright. I'll go talk to my brother and then I think we'd better crack on with this. I need that deal to go through by the end of the month and if we don't get it together soon, I don't see it happening."

"It's coming along fine, Butch, don't stress."

"What about the red tape?" I asked because there was no good reason why we didn't have the little issues with the council sorted yet to make sure our development was approved.

"I've got a fella in place to get the dirt we need to secure it," Church assured me, scratching at the five pound note tattoo curling around his wrist. "He's got a date all set up for tonight – plenty of drugs on hand and cameras to catch every moment of it. He has a team of hookers chomping at the bit to make it into a real family friendly show by taking as much dirty old man dick as they can. We'll get all of the problem makers on tape having the time of their lives in the most sinful ways we can think up and we'll have any stragglers under our thumb come morning. Then all the red tape will flutter away just like that."

"Good. Check in on that situation and make sure it's all in place. I want to be able to move forward quickly once I have this shit with the Candlestick Maker sorted."

"Trust me, Butch. I'm the man who stole a Beefeater's hat and strapped it to a statue of Shakespeare so it looked like a huge fluffy cock. *And* I got away with it."

"There's still a photo of you hanging in that cathedral warning people about the Shakespeare vandal," I snorted and he roared a laugh.

"Shakespeare and me would have gotten along like a house on fire. He'd have written that hairy dick into one of his plays and called it Much Ado About A Big Hairy Cock – or maybe he'd have gone with something classier like A Midsummer Night's Penis. He was a fancy bloke that Shakespeare."

I chuckled as I opened the safe as Church left me to it, taking out the keys, a gun and a generous bag of white powder for my fuck up of a brother before locking it up tight again and heading down to the underground station where he waited for me.

I made it down the winding staircase, strolling along the tunnel which led to the platform and pausing at the gate to unlock it. Danny appeared as I was stepping through and I casually pointed my gun at him to make him stay back while I locked up.

"Morning, Ben," he said brightly, his gaze snapping to the drugs in my hand and back to my face again with a hungry kind of desperation. "Or is it evening? I lost track again."

"It's around noon," I said, nodding to the side of us in the direction of his makeshift bed and indicating for him to move that way.

Danny did so, the slight shake in his hands telling me how much he was aching for a taste of the poison I'd brought him, and I decided to use that to the fullness of my advantage.

"I need information today, Danny. No fucking around. Just cold, hard facts so that I can keep this deal with The Czar going ahead and fix the financial catastrophe your inadequacy set in motion."

Danny licked his lips, taking a seat on the far end of the row of metal seats which sat on the platform beside his bed.

I glanced at the various things I'd brought down here for him over the last few weeks, wondering if I was going fucking soft for allowing him so many luxuries. I told myself I was doing it for our Ma, knowing how upset she'd be if she knew he was down here shivering without a bed, but maybe it was a little for me too. Or at least for the kid version of me who had tried so hard to love my twin brother no matter how many times he showed his true colours and gave me more reason to hate him instead.

"I wanna know what the deal is between you and the Candlestick Maker," I said firmly as I took a seat at the far row of the chairs, leaving a wide space between us.

I laid my gun on my knee, pointing right at him and letting him see how easily I could grab it again before I slowly opened the little bag of cocaine.

Danny wetted his lips once more, eyeing the bag while I held it hostage and I almost pitied the fucker as I looked at him, seeing the need in him for this shit, the hold it had over him. We were all a slave to something in this world, but some masters were crueller than others.

"It's nothin' really," Danny said dismissively. "We just came to a bit of a ceasefire. I let him run some businesses the way he wants, crossing into our turf from time to time and he pays me for the privilege. Simple."

I reached out between us, shaking a little of the drug onto a seat close to him and he leapt up, grabbing the rolled fifty pound note I'd given him to use for his habit the last time we'd played this game. He quickly used his fingers to make a line with the white powder, rubbing the excess onto his gums before snorting it as fast as he could.

I placed my hand on the gun, watching him as his head snapped towards me once more, knowing that hit would barely be enough to take the edge off for him.

"I want to know the details, Danny. All of it, or I'm gonna leave right now and you can sweat your way through another night of withdrawals."

"No," he barked, rage flashing in his dark eyes and giving me a glimpse of the bad in him as he bared his teeth like a dog. "What do I care anyway?" he went on, working to regain his composure but that had always been a struggle for him, even before his addiction. "When you finish tryna punish me, the two of us will be dealing with him together like old times."

My brow dipped at that. It wasn't the first time he'd made a casual reference to me eventually letting him outa here and us just going back to ruling together like it was some foregone conclusion in his mind.

But that was never gonna happen. Problem was, I hadn't quite decided what way this would end. I could kill him of course. That woulda been the easiest thing to do from the start, and for a long while I had planned on it.

I was a man with a lot of blood on my hands and I had never once given pause to consider the life I'd been taking when I had to kill. I was a monster when I had to be, but I didn't find sport in ending lives. It was necessary in our line of work, that was all. I didn't lose sleep over it, and I couldn't even pretend I didn't enjoy it when my blood was pumping and I was in the flush of the kill, but I wasn't the way Danny was about it.

Danny took a twisted kind of glee in the ending of a life.

I was more practical. I could think through rage and bloodlust, especially when I'd been given the time to stew on my decisions the way I had with my plans for my brother. I just wasn't sure what conclusion I'd come to. He was a wild dog and though I'd tricked myself into believing I could control him over the years, I'd found out the hard way that that wasn't true. So what the fuck was I supposed to do with him long term?

When all things were said and done, he was still my brother. My twin. Even if he was a monster.

It would break our Ma's heart if I killed him, and I was sticking to that reasoning while I kept him locked up beneath my house and went about my business trying to reclaim my life and prove my innocence. Long term? Well, that was a problem I was going to have to deal with another day.

"I wanna learn all there is to know about you and the Candlestick Maker," I reiterated, not wanting to get into the problem of my brother right now. One thing at a time. "Everything I need to know to be able to hold a conversation with him without him wondering why the fuck I don't know what he's harping on about. Got it?"

Danny's gaze slid to the bag of blow in my grip and he nodded, fisting his hands as he fought against the desire to try and snatch it from me.

I figured that was the best I was gonna get, so I reached out and poured another measure of coke onto the bench for him, watching with a mixture of contempt and pity as he fell on it like a hyena ravaging a corpse it'd found in the desert.

Danny started talking and I absorbed every word, reading between the lines and realising the Candlestick Maker had clearly figured out who ran The Firm and that Danny had managed to create a financial pit in the middle of our empire. This deal with The Czar had come through him, dressed up like an offer of peace in return for him gaining leniency on the streets. More freedom to push his drugs and run his sex trafficking shit all over our town while Danny turned the other away and let him have at it.

It was fucking tempting to just kill the motherfucker and let the whole deal blow up in our faces, consequences be damned. But I wasn't a fool. I'd been working with our accountant and though Archie Two Times was as rotten as they came, he was a damn genius when it got down to numbers and he'd told me straight. Without this deal the construction company was gonna go bust, and that wasn't a price I was willing to pay. We ran too much of our money through that company, its reputation painstakingly built since my great, great grandpa's time.

This deal with The Czar could dig us outa the hole and set us up long enough for me to get more deals in place and sort this mess out for good. Danny never had what it took to do the real hard grind of our family's empire, but I did. This was where I fucking shone.

By the time I left my brother to his high, I had everything I needed to be able to have a face to face with the prick who had been moving in on our turf, and Danny didn't even bother to try and escape when I headed outa the gate. He just laid on the mattress I'd dragged down there for him, looking up at the tunnel roof and laughing to himself while he enjoyed his high.

His habit had increased massively since I'd been locked away and I had to wonder how the fucker wasn't dead from the amount he consumed nowadays.

I called Church when I made it back up to the warehouse, letting him know I was ready to get this shit dealt with while trying not to get all salty at the sound of Anya laughing in the background, the constant thrum of a band playing an accompaniment to our conversation.

When I hung up on Church, I opened my messages to the unanswered stream of texts I'd been receiving from the Candlestick Maker since I took on Danny's identity, blew out a harsh breath and replied to him.

Danny:
Let's have that meet. Tonight. Make it a club to keep the atmosphere light, we need to talk, not spill any more blood.

Unknown:
Agreed. Come to Vapour at ten. Bring your new wife – call it an assurance that this is a friendly interaction.

Danny:
Done.

CHAPTER TWENTY FOUR

Adrenaline hummed through me as I sat in the back of Frank's Mercedes wedged between Church and Danny, their thighs pressing hard to my legs like they didn't have an inch of room to give me. I'd been seriously fucking surprised when my husband had invited me along tonight while he spoke with the Candlestick Maker, and I was quietly satisfied that I was being included in his business for once.

I wore a black strappy dress under my leather jacket with fishnet stockings and my chunky biker boots. My hair was loose and wavy, and I'd painted my eyes with dark smoky makeup. I looked more fitting for a rock gig than a club, but Danny hadn't complained, in fact, he'd circled me like a hawk while Frank and Church had stared at me, leaving my skin prickling with the attention of so many men. Men who all seemed to have kickstarted my heart in ways I'd never even known was possible.

Danny took my hand, his fingers winding between mine and I looked down at his tattooed arm, the sleeves of his fitted grey shit rolled up to his elbows. On my other side, Church was wearing a white short sleeved shirt with fucking suspenders, and I had no idea how, but he was pulling off the look, his hair shoved back carelessly and his silver eyes constantly finding mine.

Church took my other hand and my breathing hitched as I examined the tattooed fingers of these London devils laying their claim on me.

My gaze met Frank's in the rear view mirror and my flesh tingled as I bit my lip, sensing his anger in the air like a knife held to my throat.

"I've been thinking long and hard on this, and I've decided on my payback for the dick flick," Church said and I gave him a dry look.

"What's that then, Churchy?" I asked lightly.

"One good, firm nip flick," he said, his eyes dropping to my chest. "But you're gonna need to get one tit out so I can line up my flick."

He placed his finger against his thumb in preparation and I reached into my jacket like I was actually gonna do it then pulled my hand back out and offered him my middle finger. "I didn't need your cock out to flick it, so you can have one free shot, but if you miss that's on you."

"How's that fair? Your nipple is tiny. When I put my cock away, it's like wrestling an anaconda into submission. You could see it from France on a clear day and that's with my trousers on. Without them, the astronauts would think Britain's been invaded by a giant, beautiful earthworm."

I cracked a laugh, thumping him in the chest and he lunged forward, forcing my jacket open and aiming his flick at me. Danny laughed as I pressed into him and Church flicked my tit, hitting my nipple and making me gasp. He was half on top of me, crushing me back onto Danny and suddenly the air was too thin and Church's predatory grin had me breathless.

Frank pulled over violently and we were all thrown forwards in our seats as the car slammed to a halt.

"Blimey, mate, what the fuck was that?" Danny barked, but Frank just glared straight out at the street without answering.

I realised we were at the club and I was almost relieved as Danny opened the door and towed me out after him, getting space from Church as my nipple still tingled from his strike. I breathed in the fresh air, straightening and gathering my thoughts as the intensity of that journey finally released me. Whenever I was that close to any of them, it was a headfuck, but all of them? It was like being dunked in a tank of lust and left to drown.

"I swear to fuck, he's got a right bug up his arse," Danny muttered to Church.

"I think it's eaten his personality and replaced it with a festering turd," Church replied.

The club was thumping with music, a long line of men outside it while women in skimpy boob tubes and tiny dresses with fake tans were ushered forward by the bouncer and let inside. The neon sign above the doorway named this place Vapour and I wrinkled my nose at the club which was definitely not my scene.

Church moved to my side and Danny let go of me as he patted the top of Frank's car. "See ya later, mate."

Frank glared out at him, his furious glare shifting to me for a moment before he took off down the road with a roar of his engine.

Danny strode straight up to the bouncer as a girl with fake tits looked to him and her lips popped open as she nudged her friend.

"Danny!" she called excitedly and my husband looked over at the girl who had so much fake tan on she may as well have been dressed as a slutty carrot.

"What?" Danny grunted and she frowned, shouldering her way past the bouncer, her eyes falling on me in realisation.

"Oh my days, is this your wife?" she asked, her nose wrinkling at me.

"Yeah, and who the fuck are you?" Danny tossed at her and anger crossed her features.

She glanced back at her friends before stepping close and tiptoeing up to talk into his ear, though she barely bothered to lower her voice as she spoke. "We met at Bailiff Bert's birthday party, remember? You said I had the best arse you'd ever fucked and the best tits you'd ever licked."

Her hand slid down my husband's arm possessively and the pure disrespect of this bitch made my fist snap out and smash into her nose. It cracked on impact and she screamed, stumbling backwards as blood poured and I shook out my fingers as pain shot across my knuckles.

"Now you've got the best nose I ever broke," I said airily as Danny looked to me in surprise and Church bellowed a laugh, moving to clap the bouncer on the shoulder and slide fifty pounds into his top pocket.

"You saw nothin', did ya mate? Blind as a bat in a blindfold, ain't ya?" Church said loudly.

The guy nodded obediently and stepped aside, beckoning us inside and Danny dropped his hand to my lower back, guiding me after Church. My husband spoke into my ear as we left the sobbing girl outside with her friends clustering around her.

"I'm gonna thank you for that later, bombshell." He lifted his head again as I looked up at him under my lashes, a ghost of a smile on his lips which hinted at the orgasm I'd just won myself tonight. I didn't know where that savage part of me had come from, but I was possessive over Danny tonight, and I didn't know how to slow down the momentum of that feeling.

We made our way through the club which was set on multiple levels, dance floors in every room and scantily dressed women serving shots with large pluming tail feathers attached to their asses. It kind of reminded me of Vegas, only this underworld was somehow grittier, the girl's smiles looking painted on and lacking lustre.

Church led the way to a black curtain which was manned by two muscular bouncers, but they drew the curtain aside at the sight of Danny, inclining their heads to him respectfully.

Danny kept me close as we stepped through into a room full of private booths which circled around a raised dancefloor, the thump and drone of the music more sultry here as half naked girls and guys danced and groped each other.

Danny circled around it to a booth which was filled with a glass table surrounded by pink seats where a large man was sitting alongside two girls with their tits out. He rose to his feet as he spotted Danny, spreading his arms wide and revealing two sweat patches under the arms of his floral blue shirt. His hair was thinning with a large bald spot at the centre of his head and his face was clean shaven, the rolls of his neck on show.

"Danny fucking Butcher," he boomed. "You little fucking prick."

"Alright, Gus, you cunt?" Danny moved away from me, stepping into the booth and slapping his hand into Gus's while the two of them shared an assessing look.

So this was the infamous Candlestick Maker. I wasn't really sure what I'd expected, but I was somehow both disappointed and taken aback. He was clearly a pig of a man, but he somehow failed to exude the terrifying aura of a truly dangerous gangster the way Danny and Church did.

"So you finally answered my messages," Gus growled, his eyes narrowing.

"I went on a fucking bender, mate. It weren't nothin' personal," Danny said. "You didn't have to go and kill a bunch of my men now, did ya? You fuckin' lout."

Church moved close to my side, a causal smile hitched onto his face though I could sense the tension lurking beneath this front he was portraying.

"Sit, sit," Gus encouraged. "And let me meet your lov-el-y wife." He made that word into three long syllables and something about that just plain creeped me out.

Danny beckoned me over and I walked forward, surprised when he drew my jacket from my shoulders and circled his finger in front of my face. "Give him a twirl, love."

I gave him a cool look, not wanting to play Barbie doll, but his eyes encouraged me to do it and I decided to trust him for now, giving him a twirl while the Candlestick Maker clapped his approval.

"Beautiful. They make 'em real nice in Russia, huh? Is her cunt as nice as her face?" Gus asked and horror burned a passage through my chest.

I opened my mouth to ask if his cock was as ugly as *his* face, but Danny spoke before I could.

"It's perfect, mate. Real fucking tight, just like I told you it would be." Danny winked at Gus and heat burned along my cheeks. What the actual fuck?

"Excellent," Gus laughed and I felt Church pinch the back of my dress and hold onto it like he sensed I was about to lunge like a feral animal. I looked up at him and he gave me a slight shake of his head, warning me not to. And as I glanced around, I spotted men positioned in the other booths, bulges under their jackets telling me how much heat was packed in this place. Danny had told me this guy was a real piece of shit and had asked me to play along with whatever went on tonight, but I hadn't realised this was what he'd meant.

Church pulled me down onto the seat beside him as Danny sat beside Gus who beckoned over another girl with her tits out.

"On the table, Viola," he instructed. "How Mr Butcher likes it."

I clenched my jaw, wondering what the fuck I was about to witness as Viola laid herself out on the table, her head dangling over the end of it into my husband's lap, her tits exposed before him. Danny's eyes darted to me then back to Gus as the Candlestick Maker took out a bag of coke and started making a line of it on Viola's tits.

"What the fuck is this?" I hissed under my breath and Church's hand landed firmly on my thigh beneath the table, squeezing tight.

"There we are, Danny, that's the best blow you'll 'av this side of London," Gus promised and I watched my husband intently, my stare drilling a hole in his head. But he didn't look my way again, he took a rolled up fifty pound note from his pocket, leaned forward and snorted the whole line off of Viola's flesh, letting out an obnoxious laugh as Gus did one himself.

"What's the news then, Gus?" Danny asked.

"Ivan Orlov is in town," Gus replied and for a second my thoughts jarred. Ivan Orlov? I knew that name. He'd been a friend of my father's, a Russian man with more money than he knew what to do with, and a reputation for making people disappear when they breathed a little too closely down his neck.

"Yeah, I heard The Czar was back in London, I'm hoping he will make good on that Soho development soon," Danny said and I realised The Czar was Ivan, the same guy my husband was trying to get money from for his property development.

Gus squeezed Viola's tits absentmindedly while she lay there moaning into Danny's crotch. My blood was burning hot and I wanted to punch my husband in the face as he did another line off of her tits like this was completely normal.

"He's being difficult," Gus sighed.

"How so?" Danny asked.

"Fucking interpol again. They're breathing down his neck and he's paranoid. He won't meet with me, he just keeps sending threats to my door."

"About what, mate?" Danny asked.

"He gave me something of great value for safe keeping and I've misplaced it," Gus muttered in irritation.

"What was it?" Danny asked.

"I can't say. But I'm in a predicament, Danny. I ain't got no leads on it and The Czar will have me executed if he finds out I lost it."

"Sounds like a shit show, mate," Danny said. "You sure you don't wanna talk about it? I can put some ears out for you if you tell me what it is you're missing?"

Gus looked tempted for a second, then waved him off. "Ain't worth my head, mate. Now tell me more about this wife of yours. You promised me all the juicy details, don't hold out on me." Gus moistened his lips as he looked me over. "Does she always dress like that?"

"I let her dress how she likes," Danny replied, slinging his arms along the back of the booth seat as he looked at me like I was a piece of meat. "I find it more satisfying when I rip it off of her and show her what British cock feels like between her thighs."

Gus laughed loudly, running a hand over his dick through his tight black trousers and I let him see my disgust plain and clear.

“When I can even feel it. It’s hard to tell when it’s in,” I threw at Danny with bite in my tone, wanting to embarrass him in front of his vile friend.

Danny’s jaw flexed, his eyes moving to the Candlestick Maker beside him then back to me.

“Are you going to let your woman speak to you like that?” Gus asked, a sneer on his lips. “I know how to break their spirit, it seems you’re not quite so talented. Bring her here. Let me show you.”

“No,” Danny growled. “I’ll punish her just fine myself when we get home later.”

I glared at him as Church’s fingers dug harder into my thigh.

“Fuck off, love,” Danny said casually, jerking his chin at the dance floor. “Put that tight body to use and give us some entertainment on the dancefloor. Church, go with her.”

Church got to his feet, tugging me after him as I bared my teeth at Danny, wanting to savage him for his callous fucking words, but he just leaned forward and did another line off of Viola’s tits. I didn’t want it to hurt, but it did. It cut into my heart and pulled on something vital.

Church half dragged me up onto the raised dancefloor, pulling me against his body and swaying us to the music like an obedient mutt. I growled, trying to pull free of his arms, but he held on tight, talking to me through his teeth.

“Danny’s playing a part, love,” he whispered and I frowned at him as that sank in.

“Well if that’s true, he could’ve given me more of a heads up,” I hissed. “And he’s still sucking coke off some hooker’s tits right in front of me. You think that’s part of his little act?”

“Yeah.” Church swung me around so my back was to his, presenting me to Danny and Gus as they watched and a shiver tracked down my spine at the thirst in the Candlestick Maker’s eyes. “That note he’s snorting through is lined with Vaseline. He’s barely taking a hit, darlin’. Watch, he’ll swap it for another one in a moment, he’s got a pocket of them ready to go. The coke just sticks to the inside of it.”

“He’s still sucking it off some random girl’s tits,” I growled as Danny dropped the rolled note into his right pocket before casually pulling a fresh one from his left just like Church had said he would.

“Well…yeah,” Church conceded.

He swung me back around and I leaned into him, the scent of rain surrounding me as the safety of his arms drew me in. I started to give in to the music, rocking to it and running my hand up Church’s chest as the heat of him called to me, and while my husband was busy pretending to snort coke and leaving me out of the loop of his plans tonight, I decided to leave him out of my own plans. Which now were centred entirely around Church.

I ground against him and felt his breathing quickening as I danced, letting my hands trail over his muscles and fist around his suspenders, drawing him almost close enough to kiss him.

“You’re playing a dangerous game, Miss America,” he said darkly, though it didn’t look like he wanted to stop playing it as his cock began to swell against my thigh.

“I always liked danger, Church,” I purred. “What would life be without it?”

CHURCH

CHAPTER TWENTY FIVE

Anya moved like the music was written through the fabric of her fucking soul. The beat was her heart pounding to the perfect rhythm, the melody the blood which thrummed through her veins, and the lyrics the key to her damn creation.

She gave herself to the movements, using my body as a prop for her self expression and grinding against me in a way that was bordering on pornographic.

It was no way for my boss's wife to behave, but I just couldn't summon a single fuck to give on the subject.

The lights in the club were a vibrant mix of pink and purple, the dancefloor lit up in a bright white beneath our feet and a silver confetti cannon exploding overhead more often than could have been necessary, but damn she looked good all lit up like that.

My cock had been solid from the moment she'd pulled me up to dance with her and my blood was pumping hot and fast, demanding I take hold of her, drag her from this room and claim her for my own right now.

Anya pressed her arse into my crotch, my hands tugging on her hips to emphasise the contact before she dropped low before me, her fingers in her long hair, and her head tipping back enough for me to see that her eyes were closed.

A prickle of awareness tugged at my senses and I dragged my gaze from her, looking over to the VIP booth where Benny, the Candlestick Maker and the various arseholes who accompanied him had a perfect view of the show we were putting on.

Benny's eyes were dark as he watched us, not even seeming to listen to whatever the prick beside him was saying as a mixture of jealousy and lust burned in his pupils.

A cocky smirk tugged the corner of my lips up as he watched Anya push herself back up my body again and I rocked my hips against hers, letting her feel every solid inch of my cock driving into her as I tugged her long hair aside and leaned down to speak in her ear.

"When you're done making your husband jealous enough to crack a fuckin' tooth, I'm gonna drag you off this dance floor, find a nice quiet corner and sink my cock so deep inside you that it'll steal your breath, Miss America," I growled and she moaned at that promise as she dropped her head back onto my shoulder and looked up at me.

"I thought Danny said he had to be there if we were gonna do that again?" she teased but I wasn't gonna be put off that easily.

"You want me to extend the invite to him too, greedy girl?" I asked. "Tell me, are you thinking you'll take turns with us or are you hoping to have us both at once?"

Her eyes flashed at my suggestion but as she lifted her head to look over at her husband, her jaw ticked and she shook her head.

"Let Danny suffer with his blue balls," she growled, clearly still pissed over the way he'd dismissed her and I was willing to bet the half naked hooker on the table in front of him wasn't helping the issue much either. Though I had to admit, Danny hadn't spared the girl a single look all night beyond pretending to sniff blow off of her. He was like me, utterly enraptured with this stunning creature in my arms.

"You do realise he'll probably beat the fuck out of me again if I ignore his rules?" I asked as she turned in my arms, winding her hands around my neck and pushing her fingers into my curls.

"Well I guess the only question you have to ask yourself, Church, is whether or not I'm worth the bruises?"

She leaned in so close that I was certain she was gonna kiss me, but the moment my eyes fell shut, she was gone, her hand skimming across my waist as she stepped away through the crowd and left me wanting.

My eyes snapped open and I met Benny's furious gaze across the room just as her fingers hooked into mine and she gave me a little tug.

I shrugged at him helplessly, seeing my death flash across his face for a moment before I turned and let Anya pull me away, heading off of the dance floor and straight through the curtain so that we left the VIP area behind and headed into the thick crowd.

Yeah, he might well just kill me for what I was about to do with his wife, but I was pretty sure I'd be going out with a big fucking smile on my face, so I was okay with that trade.

Anya glanced over her shoulder at me as more silver confetti fluttered down on us, metallic pieces of it sticking to her sweat slicked arms as they landed, and I reached out to pull them from her flesh.

She shivered as my fingers grazed across her skin and I pressed forward, biting down on her neck and growling with desire as she moaned beautifully for me.

My pulse hammered in my chest and I looked around frantically, hunting for somewhere to take her so that I could get her out of that little dress she'd wrapped herself in. It looked hot as fuck, but I was aching to get beneath it and see her naked before me again.

I spotted the line for the women's toilets and tightened my grip on her hand as I dragged her towards it, bypassing the queue and barking an order at the girls who were all waiting to head inside that it was closed for repairs.

A few of them got mouthy with me but I just pulled the gun from the back of my jeans and waved it around a little to make them scarper.

Anya laughed at my brazenness and I shoved her through the door, kissing her hard and vaguely pointing the weapon at the women who were reapplying lipstick and taking selfies in the mirror until they all fucked off too.

"Jesus, Church," Anya gasped against my lips and I couldn't help but grin at the way she said my name, like I owned some piece of her and she wasn't ever gonna try and take it away.

Anya's fingers started carving their way down the middle of my shirt, popping the buttons open one after another until her mouth was moving down my bare skin and she was yanking my belt open.

The urgency of her movements let me know she was just as desperate for this as I was, and I groaned as she tugged my cock free and instantly wrapped her lips around the head.

"Fucking hell, beautiful," I cursed, my hand shifting to the back of her head as I dropped my gun on the edge of the sink and pushed my hips forward, sinking my cock into the fullness of her lips and feeling that euphoric sensation as it grazed the back of her throat.

Anya moaned as she took me in and out again, her wicked tongue swirling around the piercing in the end of my cock as she explored it and I lost myself to the feeling of fucking her smart mouth as I began to thrust my hips harder, unable to hold back.

Anya's fingernails bit into my arse as she drew me in and out until I was tipping my head to the side and watching her in the mirror, loving the view of her on her knees for me so much that I was coming before I even knew it was happening.

A roar of pleasure broke from my lips as she swallowed every drop, her throat closing around the head of my dick as I spilled myself between those perfect lips and fisted her hair so hard it had to be hurting.

But as I forced myself to untangle my fingers and tugged her to her feet, the only thing I found in her expression was a smug kind of victory which made my skin buzz. This woman was hot for power. She was born for it. And taking control of me like that had clearly made her fucking night.

"Come on," she said, wiping the corner of her swollen lips with her thumb to fix her lipstick and taking a step towards the door like she thought we were done here.

I grabbed her wrist, yanking her to a halt as I tucked my dick away and looked into her midnight eyes.

"Where the fuck do you think you're going?" I demanded, watching her brow pull in as she glanced down at my body and shrugged.

"I assumed you were done," she replied and I stared at her for several seconds before realising what she meant by that.

"Oh, my poor, sweet, Miss America," I purred as I took a step forward, devouring the distance between us and backing her up against the dark tiles which lined the wall. "Have you been fucking fellas who can only go one round?" Her pupils dilated at my words, but I wasn't done. "Worse than that, have you been fucking fellas who don't make sure you come before they're finished with you?"

"Men are selfish," she muttered, but I could tell that she knew full well that I wasn't of that breed.

"Nah, darlin', not all men. They make us different this side of the water. And let me tell you, I won't ever let you walk away from me without making sure you are well and truly taken care of."

I stole a kiss from her lips, groaning as I tasted myself on them and dropping my hand to her thigh, hitching her skirt up as I sought out the centre of her, my other hand gripping her hip to stop her from squirming as my tongue invaded her mouth.

I hitched her skirt right up around her waist, my cock already at half mast as I pushed a knee between her thighs to part them. I caressed the top of her fishnet stockings, my fingers trailing over the skin that was revealed above them before finding their way to the fabric of her drenched pink knickers.

I didn't fuck about as I tugged them aside, breathing her name against her lips as I sank two fingers deep into her core and started circling them inside her, seeking out that magic spot and grinning as her cry of pleasure confirmed I'd found it.

I kissed her harder as my fingers moved inside her, my thumb finding her clit as I began to work on that too, loving the way her spine arched against the tiles and she panted for more with every breath she dragged in.

Anya's fingernails bit into my shoulders as she began to fall apart for me and I bit down on her bottom lip as I pushed her over the edge, her moans of pleasure matching the grip of her pussy as it clamped tight around my fingers and more blood found its way to my dick.

We broke our kiss and Anya's eyes widened as she felt how hard I was where my body pressed against hers.

The door banged open loudly and we both flinched, my hand flying out towards the gun I'd left perched on the sink but falling short of grabbing it as my gaze met Benny's while he stormed into the room.

"I thought I made myself clear, Church," he barked, taking his own gun from his waistband and aiming it at my head as Anya gasped in alarm. "You don't fuck my wife unless I'm in the motherfucking room!"

His voice bounced off the tiles as he ate up the distance between us in three long strides, the barrel of his gun driving into my temple as he snarled at me and his dark eyes swam with fury.

"I haven't fucked her," I replied with a shrug. "Not yet."

Benny cocked his head at me as he looked to Anya who was still sandwiched between me and the wall with her skirt hitched up over her arse, her chest heaving from the orgasm I'd just given her.

By way of further explanation, I lifted the fingers which had just been deep inside her and pressed them to his lips.

"You want a taste?" I challenged and his eyes widened in surprise for the briefest of moments before he opened his mouth and took my fingers into it, sucking hard to taste her as Anya stared on in a mixture of surprise and what was undoubtably lust.

"I think your pussy is my favourite flavour, bombshell," he growled as he released my fingers. "I'm gonna have to eat it more often."

"No chance of that," she hissed, trying to maintain her anger and I chuckled, dropping my mouth to her neck and kissing her as I reached around her and began to unzip her dress.

"I'm not fucking him," she insisted, glaring at Benny over my head as I tugged her dress down and revealed her right breast, the nipple tight and wanting.

"No one said anything about you fucking him," I replied before sucking her nipple into my mouth and making her gasp. "He's just gonna watch, isn't that right, Butch?"

I glanced over my shoulder at him as his jaw gritted before he nodded and put his gun away again.

"Yeah bombshell, I'm gonna fucking watch."

Anya made a noise which might have been some further protest but the door banged open again behind us, interrupting the party we were just starting on and making a snarl of irritation burst from my lips.

"Out!" Benny commanded and the girls in desperate need of a piss fled with startled cries, but I doubted that would stop more from appearing.

"Come on," I said, grabbing my gun before yanking Anya against me and tugging her into one of the toilet stalls. I tossed the weapon down again in the little windowsill before stamping my mouth to hers once more.

Benny followed us into the tiny space, somehow managing to lock the door behind us before his hands met mine on Anya's back and we worked together to peel the little black dress clean off of her.

Anya slapped Benny so hard that she made his already split lip start bleeding again and he smiled darkly as he licked the blood from his lip, a challenge in his eyes for her to do her worst.

"You know how much I love it when you're angry with me, wife," he growled.

"That's because you know you deserve it," she snapped in reply, but I wasn't really interested in their bullshit right now, so I just kissed her again to shut her up. Pushing her knickers down until she was stepping out of them and was left standing between the two of us in nothing but her fishnet stockings and biker boots. Bloody hell, she looked a treat.

"Take a seat, Church, I want a good view of her while she takes your cock," Benny said and I was beyond the point of caring what way we did this, only needing to be inside her as soon as I fucking could be.

I knocked the toilet lid closed and dropped down to sit on it, taking my cock from my jeans and stroking it as Anya looked between me and Benny for an endless moment before moving closer to fuck me.

"Facing me, bombshell," Benny commanded.

Anya ignored him, moving to straddle me, but I caught her hips and flipped her around, making her sit on my lap like he'd wanted and guiding the tip of my cock into her slick entrance before she could get any silly ideas about refusing.

"Let him see what he's missing," I commanded as I lifted her knees and hooked them over my own, slowly widening my legs until she was completely bared to him and a throaty moan escaped her.

"Good girl," Benny mocked and Anya hissed her annoyance, but I was already driving my hips up to start fucking her and the sound turned into a moan as I filled her.

I let her get used to the way I was fucking her for a few thrusts before her moans and my need forced me to up the pace.

My skin prickled with the feeling of Benny's eyes on us and the noises Anya was making said she was most definitely getting off on it too.

"Do you like that, bombshell?" Benny asked as he watched us and I moved my hand to her clit. "Do you like taking my best friend's cock right in front of me?"

"Yes," she moaned, defiant as ever while I could do little more than grit my teeth in an attempt not to get lost to that heavenly sensation of her body sheathing my cock as her pussy squeezed me tightly and I fucked her even harder.

"Tell me, Anya, has anyone ever fucked that round arse of yours before?" Benny went on and a curse brushed past my lips as I caught onto what he was suggesting, the idea of us both fucking her together making me impossibly harder.

"No," she panted, lifting her gaze to meet his and he gave her a devil's smile.

"I'll be sure to get some lube ready for the next time we play this game then," he said, the certainty in his voice filling my head with filthy fantasies about the ways we could destroy this beautiful woman together.

Anya moaned louder as I continued to pound into her, her pussy tightening in a way that let me know she was dancing on the edge of bliss again and as I glanced up at Benny, I could tell by the glint in his eyes that he knew it was coming too.

He unbuckled his belt as he watched us and Anya whimpered with need as he took his cock into his fist and started pumping it right in front of her.

"Look at you, bombshell," he praised, reaching out to tuck a lock of her hair behind her ear. "You're so fucking close, aren't you?"

"Yes," she panted, arching into me as I slammed my cock up into her and rotated my fingers on her clit in a demand for her to give in to her release.

"Come for me then, Miss America. Show me how much you love taking my cock," I growled in her ear, biting down on the lobe.

Anya cried out in pleasure as her body gave in and her pussy gripped my dick in a vice, damn near forcing me to follow her into her orgasm.

"Fuck," I cursed, my hand fisting in her hair as I fought the desire to come, needing to steal more of this feeling before it ended.

"Don't you dare come inside her, Church," Benny growled fiercely. "I might be okay with you fucking her, but you don't come inside her. Got it?"

"Yes, boss," I snarled, hating him a bit in that moment, though it was hard to hold on to any animosity while Anya came all over my cock and panted my name like I was a fucking god.

Benny looked inclined to say something else, but I was done with listening to him boss us around, so I tightened my grip on Anya's hair and pushed her forward.

"Make him shut up, beautiful," I begged. "Show him who's really in charge in this little party."

Anya looked over her shoulder at me in surprise and I just shrugged one shoulder as I kept my fingers twisted in her blonde hair and fucked her in slow, shallow thrusts while she recovered from her high.

"He needs to remember where the real power lies," I said and the wicked thrill that sparkled in her eyes said she agreed with that wholeheartedly.

Benny arched a brow in surprise as Anya turned back to him and I pushed her head down a little more so that she could take him into her mouth.

"Fucking hell," Benny growled as she started sucking on his dick and I couldn't help but groan at how fucking hot that was as I began to up my pace once more.

Anya moaned lustily between us as we found a rhythm together, my thrusts into her drenched pussy driving her down onto Benny's cock as she deep throated him and his hands met with mine in her hair.

I cursed as I fucked her, my cock throbbing with the need to come while I worked to hold it off, needing to feel her come around me one more time before I could give in.

I fucked her harder and Benny swore as my thrusts translated into the way she was taking him too.

Just when I was certain I couldn't hold out for a single second longer, Anya came for us, her pussy locking around my dick and bringing on my own orgasm so fast that I barely managed to jerk out of her while Benny barked commands at me not to finish inside her.

My cum spilled over her back and Benny followed us with his release, a throaty growl escaping him as she swallowed his cum and he drew back to let her catch her breath.

"Jesus," Anya panted as she fell back against me, her chest rising and falling so heavily that it was like she'd run a damn marathon.

"Come on," Benny said eventually, his eyes meeting mine as we silently communicated how fucking perfect that had just been. "The Candlestick Maker has fucked off, so we can get back to the warehouse. I might even have some lube stashed away there."

"In your dreams, asshole," Anya growled.

I breathed a laugh but as I cleaned the evidence of my desire for her from her skin and helped her back into her clothes, it was impossible to miss the lust which was painted throughout her gaze along with the hazy glow of satisfaction which clung to her.

She gave me a smile which shone so damn bright that my breath caught in my throat and my heart beat out of rhythm as I was left staring at the perfection of it.

"I think I just found my new favourite thing to do," I murmured as we followed Benny back out of the club, my fingers still tangled in hers like I just couldn't get enough.

"What's that?" she breathed, the look in her eyes making it clear she thought I meant the sex, but that wasn't it, no matter how mind blowing it had been.

"Making you smile, darlin'. And I'm gonna work on it every damn day."

CHAPTER TWENTY SIX

I woke in a haze of music, my heart thrumming in time with a song I didn't know. But as I reached for my iPod to figure out what was playing, I met warm, inviting muscles instead.

My fingers trailed along it absentmindedly, drumming out the tune which was filled with so much promise it seemed to kiss the inside of my skin. There was more warm flesh at my back too, the hot press of two large bodies surrounding me and as I came up from the depths of sleep and reached for my headphones, I found nothing on my ears.

I blinked sharply, the music fading away like it had never existed and my breath caught in my chest as I found myself face to face with my husband's best friend.

Church was sleeping soundly, the hard lines of his face softened, making him appear more boyish than usual. My hand remained on his side, my fingers itching for the feel of more skin, but I kept them still, rolling onto my back and looking to my other side as Danny rearranged himself in sleep, his arm curling around my waist and drawing me against him. Both of their heads were on my pillow, the three of us so close, there was barely any air to inhale.

Or maybe that was just how it felt considering how hard my lungs were labouring.

I remembered coming back here last night, piling into a shower with the two of them before falling into bed with them. Danny had pulled one of his shirts over my head and they'd put some boxers on at least, but now I was recalling every single thing we'd done together in that club restroom last night and my blood was rising.

Fuck, it had been something else having these two villains dominate me like that, and it had been so goddamn hot to watch the lust in Danny's eyes as Church fucked me to ecstasy.

I bit my lip, the cold light of day holding a mirror before me and reflecting back all of my bad deeds. I was in trouble. The kind I wanted more of, but I knew that if I kept going down this path, I was going to have to pay for my sins eventually. Karma was a bitch like that.

Church moved towards me in his sleep, his hand falling over my waist to lie next to Danny's, both of their fingers knotting in my shirt, bunching against my stomach like they were trying to pull me away from the other.

I felt Danny stirring and turned his way, tempted to feign sleep but knowing I'd have to face the consequences of my actions eventually. *May as well rip the damn Band-Aid off.*

His dark gaze met mine, his eyes hooded and his hair dishevelled, looking so fucking edible I was half tempted to lean in and kiss him. And maybe I would have if he hadn't been the Devil. But that was the problem, wasn't it? This man had planned to trap me, torture me, turn me into a puppet in a cage which he played with from time to time. Did it really make it okay that he'd apparently changed his mind on that? Did it excuse the truth of what he was? No. And yet…when I stared into his eyes, all I saw was a wounded man gazing back at me like I was the cure to all his pain.

"Well now ain't you a picture, love," he said in a deep growl, leaning in and stamping his mouth to mine.

I lingered there, warmth spreading into my belly before I dug my teeth into his lip hard enough to make him curse.

I snapped my head back, glaring at him, still pissed at the way he'd behaved last night. Church had said it was an act, but it had seemed all too like the man he'd been when I'd first met him. I wouldn't easily forget what he was capable of turning into.

He sucked his lip into his mouth, his eyes lighting from the pain I'd delivered him as he considered me. "What's the matter?"

Church answered, rousing beside me and curling in against me. "She's pissed at you for being a fucking plonker around the Candlestick Maker, mate. Ain't it obvious?"

"Hm," Danny grunted, cupping my cheek. "That was business. Nothin' more."

"Is that what you tell yourself? Is that the kind of business you get up to with Church when you leave me with Frank? Snorting coke and fucking hookers?"

Danny's fingers tightened on my cheek as his jaw flexed. "Look 'ere, love. I told you straight. I'm yours. I ain't gonna cheat on you, why would I want some cheap fuck when I've got you to come home to?"

My eyebrows arched at that and I couldn't look away from him until Church pressed his mouth to my neck and I felt the hard ridge of his morning glory driving against my hip.

"Lucky for you, all this fidelity shit goes one way though, eh Miss America?"

"Fuck off," Danny snarled. "You don't count. If another man lays a finger on my wife, I'll be cutting their balls off sharpish."

Church chuckled as he continued a torturous line of kisses up to my ear and I rolled my head to the side to give him more access, that delicious unknown music starting up in my mind again.

"Why doesn't he count?" I asked breathily as Danny's hand fell to my thigh and skimmed the edges of the shirt I was wearing which was only just concealing my bare pussy. Tingles rushed along my skin at the combined contact and I held back a moan as Church teased my earlobe between his teeth.

"Because you chose him. And he's Church. He's everything to me," Danny said plainly and I found that made a strange sort of sense as I looked at the clarity in his eyes.

"So you're not loaning me out to your friends like Sikes said you would?" I asked, an accusation to my tone which set Danny's eyes blazing.

Church stopped kissing me, rearing up to look down at me in horror. "Is that really what you think this is, darlin'?" There was a note of pain to his voice that cut me to the quick.

I shrugged one shoulder, unsure of my answer now they were both looking at me like that. All I knew was that I'd never felt the way I did now lying between the two of them. Like the music was playing non-stop without ever needing to switch it on. And I had the awful feeling it wasn't going to last. There were hardly any days in my life which I could remember without it, and all of those that I could were filled with darkness. Music was light and joy and peace. It was all the things I'd struggled to find in the real world, but suddenly it was here, winding around the three of us and begging me to stay.

"No," I answered Church's question at last, realising the two of them had been waiting for my response. "I don't know what this is, but it's…" I didn't have the words to finish that sentence, but apparently Church did.

"Paradise," he whispered and I reached out to paint my fingers over the inked words on his chest spoken by Winston Churchill. *If you're going through hell, keep going.*

So by that logic, if I was going through heaven, I should stay where I was.

I withdrew my hand, the intensity of his gaze and that of my husband's setting a fire in my chest which begged to be stoked. But I was afraid of what would happen if I did that, afraid to care for these men, because in the end, I couldn't stay here. I couldn't become what everyone expected me to be for the sake of the treaty. Just a good girl who did her duty. Fuck that. I wasn't anyone's good girl.

"Boss?" Frank's voice called through the door, making my heart jolt. "It's nearly eleven, shouldn't we discuss what you found out last night?"

"Yeah, yeah," Danny called back. "Come on in, we can talk about it here."

"Danny," I hissed, suddenly not liking the idea of Frank finding me here between him and Church. What would he think? *Why do I give a shit what he thinks??*

Frank opened the door, falling very still as his blue gaze fell on the three of us, the muscles in his shoulders tensing. For a second, I swear I saw hurt in his eyes before it turned to a stone cold fury.

"I'll be downstairs when you and Church are done here," he said, turning his back on us and leaving the door wide as he went.

"The fuckin' attitude on him sometimes," Danny muttered, shaking his head. "You'd think he was the boss 'round here." He pushed out of bed, grabbing some sweatpants and pulling them on as Church caged me in his arms.

He bore down on me, his leg hooking over mine and a carnivorous glint in his eyes, but Danny threw a pair of sweatpants at him that slapped him across the face.

"Up. What did I tell you about fucking my wife while I ain't present?" Danny snapped.

"You're right *there*," Church complained, holding onto me, but I pushed him off, wriggling away across the mattress and getting up.

I needed some space. And now that I was out of that bed, I was starting to need my music too.

"Well now I'm leaving, so you're leaving too." Danny strode out the door and Church gave me a pout which brought a small smile to my lips.

"Run along, Churchy," I said, and he didn't miss the implication of me speaking to him like an obedient dog.

He gnashed his teeth at me then jogged after Danny, pulling on the sweatpants as he went and I realised I had a stupid smile on my face as I stared after them. I flattened it, shaking my head at myself before bundling up some clothes with my iPod and heading down the hall to the bathroom for a session with the Eagles.

By the time I was dressed in some black jeans with rips on the knees and a pale pink Green Day shirt knotted up over my midriff, my stomach was rumbling and not even my music was enough to keep me fed.

I headed downstairs with my headphones around my neck and a fresh dose of numbness wrapped around my soul as I made it into the kitchen. The guys were talking business, all of their eyes trailing me for a moment as I headed past them to the fridge before they returned to their little man club meeting.

I got myself some eggs and started work on scrambling them as I listened to their conversation.

"Well whatever it is must be worth a lot," Danny said, taking a savage bite out of an apple.

"We need to figure it out," Frank chipped in. "Because there's a reason the Candlestick Maker is losing his shit over whatever it is he's lost. I wanna know if The Czar will kill him for losing it."

"If we're gonna rely on The Czar dropping that alliance like an old turd then we need to make sure his anger is guaranteed," Frank insisted.

"What's the news from John Boy?" Danny asked Frank, finishing his apple like it had personally offended his grandma and a smirk pulled at Frank's mouth.

"Who's John Boy?" I asked with a frown.

"You've met him before, remember? He's one of our best men," Church said. "He's got one of them faces though. Real forgettable. Blends into wallpaper, he does. It's a gift, I tell ya."

"He says the council's given us backing for the development in Soho," Frank announced and Church and Danny exchanged an excited glance. "I guess they didn't take kindly to us filming them getting their cocks sucked by a bunch of hookers."

"Or snorting our blow outa their arse cracks," Church said, grinning like a beast.

A smile tugged at my lips as I placed a couple of pieces of bread in the toaster. *Clever little shits.*

"Well The Czar will be pleased with that anyway," Danny said thoughtfully. "But it doesn't guarantee he's gonna follow through on this deal. So we need to figure out exactly how much trouble the Candlestick Maker is in. Then maybe we can *help* The Czar to recover whatever he's lost, become his new best friends and let the Maker meet his maker. Not to mention getting those millions from the fucker once he goes all in on our development."

"Too fucking right," Church agreed, slapping Danny on the back. "And when we find whatever it is, we can let on that it showed up in the pockets of The Czar's enemies."

"Yes, boys," Danny said with a grin. "We have ourselves a devious fucking plan."

I half rolled my eyes as I plated up my eggs and toast, their attention falling on me as they noticed my expression.

"What's that look for?" Danny asked as I placed my food down and sat at the island.

"You have your end game down but no way to reach it," I said simply, tucking into my food.

"We just need a way to get The Czar to tell us what he gave to the Candlestick Maker," Frank said. "And to make sure he's still interested in the investment on the Soho development, because if he's dicking us around on that we really are gonna be in trouble."

"Good luck with that," I said lightly, flashing a sardonic smile before drawing my headphones up onto my head and pulling my iPod out of my pocket. I started scrolling through the music, deciding what to play when Danny's shadow fell over me and he tugged my headphones down.

"You've got a little twinkle in your eye, bombshell," he said, arching a brow at me. "I do love a twinkle, me. So come on then, let's hear it."

“Hear what?” I scoffed, trying to tug my headphones up again, but he didn’t release them, keeping them around my neck.

“Your plan,” he offered and I frowned at him, looking for the joke. I even breathed a dry laugh, looking at Church and Frank, expecting them to snigger at me, but neither of them did.

“You’re serious?” I asked suspiciously. I was used to misogynist bullshit, of being overprotected and therefore my opinion being well and truly left out of the conversation – if I was even a part of the conversation that was. But Danny was looking at me like he really wanted to hear what I had to say, like my words were as valuable to him as those of his men. And that just left me sort of…stumped.

“We’re all ears, love,” Danny urged and I sat up a little straighter, my chest swelling at the way they were all looking at me like I was an equal. I tried not to turn into a complete kid and squeal about it, but there was a little girl prancing about inside me who had been deprived of being heard for so long that I just had to let her freaking dance.

“Well…” I started and they all shifted closer. Church rested his elbows on the island and Frank stood to his side, his head tipped down and his fingers on his chin, his elbow propped up by his other hand. Danny pressed one hand to the surface beside me, caging me in with his body as he waited for me to go on. “I know The Czar. At least, I know *of* him. I met him once when I was a kid and he creeped me out because he has these eyes that seem to wander beneath your flesh. Anyway, the point is, I grew up around men like him. I’ve learned to handle them, how to keep their advances at bay and get them talking instead by playing a little cat and mouse game. They have to think I’m the most unobtainable creature in the room and they’ll spew all their secrets to have a moment in my company. I just need to know what he likes and I could get him on a hook wriggling like a worm.”

“So you’re the fish?” Danny asked.

“I’m the fisherman, but he’d think I’m the fish.”

“I see,” Danny said thoughtfully, exchanging a look with the others. The look dragged on and I got the impression I was about to be dismissed, so I pulled my headphones on again, preferring to make my own exit, but Danny tugged them down again.

“You really think you can get him talking?” Danny asked, his eyes blazing with the idea.

“Look at the spell she’s cast on us,” Church said darkly. “Of course she can get him fucking talking.”

Frank folded his arms, his jaw tightening as he glanced between us all, clearly irritated about something.

“Alright then, how do we find out what he likes?” Danny asked me keenly and I had to admit it felt hella good being listened to by the king of London.

I knew the answer, but I hesitated, running my fingers along my fork as I stared down at my eggs which were going cold. “I need to talk to my brothers."

Fuck, I didn't want to do that almost as much as I did want to. I missed them so bad, and yet I was so angry at them that it carved out a gaping hole in my chest. But I'd put it off for so long, dodged their calls and refused to answer a single one of the messages that Danny told me they'd sent. My rage was like jet fuel and one match was all it would take to ignite it. I didn't know if I'd be able to keep my cool while I talked to them, in fact, I knew I wouldn't. But screw it.

"Gimme your phone." I held out my hand to Danny and he frowned as he picked it up from the counter.

"Are you sure, bombshell?" he asked in a low tone, placing the phone in my hand, but holding onto my fingers so I couldn't immediately take it.

"Yeah. I'm fucking sure." I gripped the phone and he let it go, allowing me to dial my brother Zakhar's number and waiting while the call connected, holding it to my ear.

"Butcher?" he growled in answer. "How is she?"

"She's just fine," I bit out and he gasped in a tell-tale sign of pain, the only one my brothers would ever emit.

"Anya. Thank fuck."

"Mudak," I snapped at him in Russian.

"I know, I know, I'm an asshole," he sighed and I could almost picture him bowing his head. "Are you safe? Tell me you're well."

"You let me think I was going to escape this, you let me believe I was safe."

"You'd never have gone otherwise," he said, an ache of apology in his tone. If it was best for my family, even if it hurt him, Zakhar would do it. He would always follow orders.

"And that makes it better?!" I yelled, all the months of rage ripping open inside me at last and pouring out. "You threw me to the wolves. I'm your flesh and blood, how could you do this? All of you?"

I realised I was on my feet, striding away from the men who had surrounded me and heading upstairs as a storm of anger swirled around me.

"You're strong, Anya. So fucking strong. I knew you could handle it," he said.

"Zhopa! Svoloch! Mudoyeb!" I started hurling every Russian insult I knew at him and he patiently waited for me to be done.

"I'm all of those things and more, but you must forgive me. All of us."

"Why?" I snarled.

"We're family. And family keep each other alive. Remember, little sister: Family First. This is how we stay alive, Anya. The mafia wars would have killed us all in the end if it weren't for this treaty. We all sacrificed for the sake of this peace."

I shook my head, bitterness coating my throat as I threw the nearest door open and marched into the room, finding myself in the spare bedroom Danny had wanted me to decorate. How was his sacrifice the same as mine?

He'd had a fucking choice.

"You sold me," I said, wanting to hurl the words at him but instead they just came out broken. "You, Alexi and Nikolay. You offered me up like a lamb to slaughter."

"You're no lamb, you know that," he said firmly and I straightened, my free hand curling into a fist.

"Yeah, I know. A lamb couldn't put you on your ass."

"That was one time and you caught me off guard," he huffed but pride leaked into his tone and a smile quirked up the corner of my lips which I quickly flattened.

I moved to sit on the end of the bed, all the breath seeming to fall out of my lungs. "How are you? How's my new sister-in-law? Nikolay killed her yet?" My middle brother had avoided me like the plague since we were kids, Alexi always told me it was to keep me from the darkness of his world. Of what he had to do for our family, to keep us safe. But I'd heard rumours from the guards of what my brother was into as he grew up, and it was enough to chill me to my core and make me feel sorry for the girl thrust upon them.

Zakhar sighed. "That's a long story." His voice lowered as if to avoid being overheard. "She calms Nikolay, I've never seen him like this, he's almost a human being. You wouldn't recognize him, Anya, he feels something other than hatred towards her, something we never thought possible after father broke him. I fear the person who ever tries to hurt her, though she would probably kill them first." He laughed and warmth filled my chest at hearing how well Nikolay was doing. And thank fuck she wasn't some meek mouse who'd been broken by my kin. She sounded like the kind of girl I could get along with and an ache filled me as I wondered if or when I'd get to meet her.

Zakhar went on, "She puts Alexi on his ass more than you can imagine... she's good for us sister. It hasn't been easy, she's not exactly a friendly sane person but then again which of us are?" There was a crash somewhere in the background along with a yelled Russian curse that sounded awfully like Nikolay and my eyebrows rose in surprise. "One second, Anya - Iris, my love please stop hitting him with the plate he said he was sorry." Some muttering followed then silence fell once more. Shit, was Nikolay really opening up to this girl? Was she helping heal the wounds in him that no one had managed to before?

"And you?" I asked, needing to hear he was happy as well. She sounded fierce but Zakhar had always been the softest of my brothers, caring, needing to treasure someone. Could she offer him what he needed too? I didn't even know how someone went about being a wife to three barbarians, but when I thought of my own situations heat burned a line along my cheeks and I realised maybe it wasn't so different to my life now. Although, I certainly didn't plan on marrying any more men.

"She makes me believe in love and family again," he said and my heart squeezed. Holy fuck, did this girl have some kind of magic because I'd never heard any of my brothers get gushy before.

I need to meet her, hug her and thank her.

A shadow stepped into the room and I glanced up, finding Frank approaching me, his gaze sharp.

"Is your husband treating you well?" Zakhar asked, a note of fear in his deep voice. "Because if he's not, I'll-"

"I handle him just fine," I said fiercely.

"Is he cruel?"

"Yes," I said immediately. "He is the cruellest man I've ever met, but only when he wants to be. He's a monster, Zakhar, but I think sometimes… that I can tame him."

"Monsters can't be tamed," he disagreed.

"Zakhar, do you think…" I trailed off, unsure I wanted his thoughts on this in case I didn't like the answer.

"What?" he pressed and I took a breath.

"Do you think people can be wicked and good at once? Sometimes I see so much darkness in my husband, sometimes I see the depths of his depravity." I thought of the things I'd seen on his laptop, of the cage he'd planned to put me in, of the first time we'd met and how he'd made me scream in pain and struck fear into my heart. "But other times, he's protective and generous – fuck, he's so generous."

"Anya," Zakhar cursed as he realised what I meant. "I seriously don't need the visual. But, yeah, I do think that people can be both. Isn't that what we are? The Volkov name is draped in blood, but good deeds live between our sins."

I nodded, sensing Frank moving closer and biting my lip as the intensity of his company surrounded me.

"Do you think people can want more than one person?" I whispered, my eyes locking with Frank's and the words falling unbidden from my lips.

Zakhar fell quiet and a beat passed like he was considering what I'd said. "I hope so, Anya."

I frowned at that, wondering how they were making it all work between them, then I remembered why I'd made this call. "Do you remember father's friend, Ivan Orlov?"

"Of course I do," he said. "What about him?"

"He's here in London. I need to know what he's like, the Butchers are pulling a job on him and I'm going to help."

"You are?" he asked in surprise.

"Don't you think I'm capable?" I tossed at him.

"It's not that, Anya. I'm just surprised you're helping the Brits."

"Aren't you happy I'm playing house?" I asked icily.

"I'm happy if you're happy," he said, but I didn't answer that, I just moved back to the subject at hand.

"So? Ivan Orlov?"

"He's paranoid as hell, doesn't let anyone near him with any kind of technology," my brother said.

"How come?" I asked.

"He's terrified of Interpol. He's afraid they're always one step behind him, though I don't know if it's even fucking true. He certainly believes it is."

"Okay…anything else?" I pressed. "What kind of woman does he like?"

I could hear the hesitation in his voice before he answered, but he clearly wanted to give me this seeing as I was still so pissed at him for selling me to The Firm. "Classy, unobtainable. If it's forbidden, then all the better."

"I guess he'd be interested in the king of London's wife then," I muttered.

"Anya, what are you planning?" he asked urgently.

Frank reached out, snatching the phone from my grip and holding it to his ear. "Hello, Volkov scum."

"Is that you, Butcher?" Zakhar's voice filled the room as Frank hit the speakerphone button, my brother's tone venomous.

"Pass on a message to your brother Nikolay for me, will you mate?" Frank said conversationally, but his eyes emitted pure hate, enough to make a tremor rack through my bones. He was fierce, terrifying in his need for vengeance and my nails bit into my palms as I stared up at the man who had been tortured by my brother. "Tell him Frank Smith's making his little sister pay his debt. Tell him the Butcher King is a fucking sweetheart to his wife compared to how his bodyguard treats her in the shadows. And tell him, she fucking loves it."

"Frank – *stop*," I growled, lunging at him, trying to get the phone from his grip, but he caught hold of me by the throat with his other hand, holding me still and Zakhar spat curses before Frank hung up and slipped the phone into his back pocket.

His upper lip curled back as he advanced on me, his strength impossible as he pushed me backwards and I fell down on the bed, staring at him as he towered above me in the dark.

The only light in the room was coming from a crack under the door. The blinds were shut and everywhere else was full of shadow. But nothing was as dark as the rage in his eyes. I could have called out, shouted for Danny and Church to come, but something kept my lips pressed together, a moment of understanding passing between us as I saw his anger for what it really was. Pain.

My brother had marked him, torn into his skin and left scars there that ran deeper than the ones still remaining on his flesh. A Volkov had done that to him. My blood. My family. My debt.

"Do you want to punish me?" I whispered and though his face was cast in shadow, I could just about see his frown deepening. "You need to, don't you?"

He said nothing and I pushed forward, raising up on my knees beneath him and offering him my wrists as if he was a cop about to cuff them. "Volkovs always pay their debts."

I didn't know why I wanted this, only that I did. That I wanted to heal some of that chaotic agony in his eyes, and I knew this was what he needed for that to happen.

"You're not my Volkov to punish," he breathed, raising a hand to grip my cheeks in his strong fingers, digging in hard.

"It can be our secret," I answered, knowing this was crazy, that Danny would kill Frank for touching me, especially for hurting me. But there was a bond forming between Frank and I over this, and it needed an outlet. It needed pain and punishment to be sated.

"Why?" he growled.

"Because I would give anything – *anything* – to seek retribution on the flesh of my enemy," I answered, the words coming to me without having to think on them at all. This was because of my father, because of what he'd done to me, my brothers, my mother. I had once been far too small to fight back, and now he was dead and it was too late for him to ever feel my hate tearing into his skin. But it wasn't too late for Frank, and I couldn't allow him to seek his vengeance on my brother via me. So I would be his willing victim, and perhaps between us we'd both find peace from the violence of our pasts.

His throat bobbed and he leaned down, knocking my hands apart and reaching for my waistband, his deft fingers quickly unbuttoning my jeans and rolling the zipper down. His face was so close to mine, all I could sense was him, and I didn't know what to expect as he shimmied my jeans down, lifting my ass to allow him to do it, but he left them in place just above my knees. He took hold of my thighs next, spreading them so I was kneeling awkwardly, my jeans digging in uncomfortably and my core feeling exposed even though I still had my blue lace panties on.

He regarded me for a moment, his head cocking to one side as my heart began to drum harder. No one made me feel vulnerable like Frank Smith did. He was like a hunter with an arrow always pointed between my eyes, and something about me fucking loved that.

He moved to my side and I followed him with my gaze, unsure what he was going to do next. He reached towards me, gripping the front of my panties and the back, pulling them up tight and making me snap my teeth together as he half wedgied me before moving his hands in a sawing motion, making my panties grind along my soaked core and over my clit.

"Frank," I gasped, the near-pain of it making me wince, but every time the material rubbed over my clit, a moan escaped me.

"Yes, Cash?" he demanded, looking to me for complaint, but I gave him none, clenching my teeth as he continued, making me so wet and so uncomfortable that I whimpered.

He hooked his finger in the material under my thigh and my back arched a little as he ran it under me, drawing it down to feel the seat of my panties, his knuckle almost grazing my core but not quite. He was avoiding touching me directly, but somehow his near touches were so hot they had me panting for him.

"Wet for Danny, wet for Church, and now she's wet for me too." He stroked his thumb along the inside of my panties, feeling my wetness and a blush rose in my cheeks as he stared at me, seeking out my reaction. He wanted to humiliate me, but it wasn't working in quite the way he hoped because as much as I was feeling exposed, I was also so turned on that all I could do was look up at him pleadingly.

"Are you just a little Volkov whore?" he asked, letting the material snap back against my pussy and making me visibly shiver. "Would you have your husband come find me here with my cock in this dripping pussy, taking what I want from you?"

"So you do want me?" I managed to latch onto those words, throwing them back at him and hitching on a taunting smirk.

"No, Cash. That would be too easy. You'd lie back and let me fuck you just like you let Church fuck you."

"I wouldn't be so sure, Frank," I said, goading him, awakening the beast in his eyes. "I fucked Church because I come alive at his touch."

"And what does my touch do to you?" he demanded, stepping back while my hips circled, the need for contact driving me crazy.

I stared at him, fighting the lump pushing at the base of my throat. "Your touch makes me feel like I could die in your hands. But it would be the most beautiful death in the world."

He brushed his fingers over his lips then marched to the door. "Stay here. Don't move."

I almost called out after him, but he disappeared just like that, leaving the door wide open so anyone could come and find me like this. I could hear Church and Danny talking loudly downstairs, laughing about something together, but I couldn't focus on what.

"What's my wife up to, Frank?" Danny shouted and my heart stopped working.

"She's on the phone, ain't she?" Frank barked.

"Alright, alright, no need for the temper, mate. It gives me a fuckin' headache," Danny replied.

I considered disobeying Frank, pulling up my jeans and heading downstairs, but the thrill of the adrenaline rolling through me made me stay there. Frank was owed this much from me, and I craved him as I craved Church. Danny had been the one to say he would deny me anything, and Frank was all I wanted in this moment.

Frank left me waiting long enough for my legs to ache, my thighs shuddering with the tension of remaining like that when he finally returned. He left the door wide as he approached me with something small in his grip.

I narrowed my eyes, trying to work out what it was, but he slid it into his fist so I couldn't see.

"Pull your panties down," he commanded on a breath as he leaned closer, nose to nose with me.

I hesitated, unsure where this was going as he stared at me like he was Zeus tempted off of Mount Olympus to come sink his teeth into a mortal.

"Are you afraid?" he asked.

I wet my achingly dry mouth, shaking my head in refusal. I wasn't afraid of anything.

"Then do as I say," he growled and I did. I rolled them down to sit against my thighs and his gaze dropped down to my pussy. He brought his hand to my core, rolling the object into his grip and a breath snagged in my throat as I realised it was a small bulldog clip.

He snapped it into place on my throbbing clit and I winced, swallowing a yelp as it locked tight around my skin.

"Fuck," I exhaled, my hand going to his shoulder and my nails digging in as I breathed my way through the pain, adjusting to it as his eyes flicked up to watch my expression. He was all I could see, all I could smell and taste and this bite of pain only made me want more of him.

My fingers knotted in the material of his shirt as I drew him closer, our mouths brushing and I swear for a second I saw his immovable façade crack.

"You look so perfect right now," he whispered against my lips and I wished those words were a kiss. One with tongue and bite and all the desire that was racing through my limbs, driving me to the point of madness.

His hands ran down my back, over the curve of my ass and I arched into him, my need for him sharpening as his roughened touch carved over my skin. But then his fingers made it to my panties and jeans and he tugged them up, dragging them into place and zipping them up fast. He buttoned the top of them and his fingers lingered on my stomach as I tried to adjust to the intense feeling of that clip around my clit, my pulse pounding between its grip.

"Go downstairs," he commanded, stepping back and I felt his walls sliding back into place between us. His hand curled around my arm, pulling me to my feet and I stumbled, the pins and needles in my legs making them tingle in discomfort.

I rested my hand to his chest to brace myself and he let me stand there, his fingers moving to my hair and coiling through it.

"You good?" he muttered and I nodded once sharply. "Then do as I told you."

I nodded, regaining my strength and walking away from him, the pain following me everywhere and only seeming to get worse as I moved. I schooled my expression as I walked downstairs, feeling Frank at my back as I joined Danny and Church once more.

"You alright, Miss America?" Church asked. "You look flushed."

"I just fought with my brother, that's all," I murmured, moving to stand opposite them at the island, figuring I was gonna be more comfortable on my feet than sitting down. I filled them in on what Zakhar had told me about The Czar while Frank stood at my side and I tried not to wince or shudder. The pain was turning to a burn now and I ached for a release from this torture, my hips shifting side to side as I tried to focus on the conversation we were having.

"Perfect," Danny clapped his hands together. "We'll invite The Czar to the races next week then and give him the best day of his fucking life."

"Look at us," Church said excitedly. "It's like the dream team back together."

"How's that?" Frank drawled and Church scratched the back of his head.

"Well it's like a new dream team uniting," he corrected. "Ain't it, darlin'?"

"Sure, yeah, whatever," I said quickly. I needed to get this thing off of me right now and as I turned to Frank and clawed my nails into his arm, I gave him a look that told him just that. But his answering little smirk told me he wasn't going to show me mercy.

I needed an excuse, any excuse and I blurted the first thing that came to mind. "I wanna decorate the spare room. Will you help me start moving the old shit out of it, Frank?"

"You do?" Danny asked excitedly and I almost felt bad, knowing he was reading into that, taking it as a sign that I wanted to make a piece of this place my own.

"Yeah, sure." *Just get me the fuck out of here.*

"Come on then," Frank gave in and I could have kissed him – right before I punched him in the junk, but still.

He took hold of my arm, half dragging me back upstairs and when we stepped into the spare room, I sagged against the wall and frantically undid my jeans.

Frank got there before I could, sliding his hand smoothly into my panties and removing the clip. I sagged against the wall while he smirked darkly at me as he withdrew it.

"Learned your lesson yet, Cash?" he asked.

The hum of adrenaline in my veins and the release I got from that clip coming off made me moan. I slid my hand into my panties, sinking two fingers into my heat, making his eyebrows arch in surprise as I worked to get myself off.

His eyes widened as I started grinding the heel of my hand on my clit and I was coming in less than a few seconds.

Frank's hand clamped down over my mouth to stifle my moans and he crushed his chest to mine, trying to keep me quiet while I came down from my high and started laughing.

He slowly peeled his hand away from my mouth and I gazed up at him through a fog of lust.

"Not even close, Frank."

CHAPTER TWENTY SEVEN

I looked my wife up and down as I took in the figure hugging electric blue dress she was wearing, my gaze roaming down her long legs to her black Louboutin stilettos with those red soles.

John Boy was driving the Bentley for us as we drew close to the racetrack and I'd been using the entirety of our journey to appreciate the beauty of the woman I'd stolen from the Russians.

"You're drooling, Danny," she said, that fucking name on her lips making me bite my tongue against the words I wanted to reply with.

"I've told you not to call me that," I said, straightening my cuff as I brushed a tiny piece of lint from my spotless tweed suit. I was channelling the old gangs of our beautiful country, the founders of our way of life today with a flat cap and pocket watch to finish the look, the whole thing costing a small fortune, but more than worth it for the way my bombshell kept looking at me despite the venom which still poured from her tongue.

"And I told you I don't take orders from you," she replied with a shrug. "What were you thinking about anyway?"

I gave her a wolf's grin as I leaned closer, speaking into her ear and letting my lips brush the shell just a little as I did so.

"I was thinking that I'd enjoy you walking those sexy fucking shoes down the length of my spine when we get home later, if you're up for inflicting pain on your undeserving wretch of a husband tonight."

"And what would I get out of that exchange?" she asked, arching a brow as she turned to meet my gaze, bringing our lips within an inch of one another and making me swallow a lump in my throat as the air around us seemed to constrict, urging me to move forward, but I didn't.

"Besides the thrill of causing me pain? I guess I could spread you out like a buffet and eat you up once your legs got tired."

Her mouth twitched in amusement as the car rolled to a stop and I wetted my lips, just enough for my tongue to brush along the seam of her smile before I pulled back and got out, leaving her blinking after me in surprise.

I circled the back of the car, opening the door for her and offering my hand before she could climb out unassisted.

She looked up at me curiously as she took my hand and I drew her to her feet, placing a kiss on her knuckles like I was a real gent even though we both knew I couldn't have been farther from that truth.

I closed the door and John Boy drove away as I wound my arm around Anya's waist and drew her close to my side, my fingers stroking back and forth over her hip while she leaned into me, presenting the newly wedded bliss which we were aiming to sell. The only thing was, it didn't feel much like a sales pitch to me. It felt raw and real and like one of the most honest things I'd ever experienced.

I led her away from the main crowd, heading towards the VIP stairs where the bouncers guarding the entrance nodded in recognition and let us pass without comment.

Anya tried to hide her curiosity, but her head kept turning as she looked all around us at the white wooden stands, an audible gasp escaping her as we reached the top of the stairs and we were gifted a view of the racetrack.

I squeezed her a little tighter, telling her about the history of this place and how almost a hundred years ago my great, great grandpa had founded the Butcher's Gang, starting off by running bets and fixing races before moving into other forms of business. Some of it legal, a lot of it not. We wrote our own laws, that was the truth of it and any politician or lawman who tried to say different usually found themselves with either a price or an ultimatum.

Yeah, we ruled with the use of fear to aid us, but it was respect which had kept us at the top of the food chain for so goddamn long.

We headed along a walkway lined with a plush blue carpet, my hand drifting a little lower as I stroked Anya's outer thigh, my lips brushing her neck every time I leaned in to tell her another fact about someone we owned or someone whose debts would be up if their horses didn't come in today.

I'd spent my time since I'd gotten out of prison reacquainting myself with everything that had happened in my absence, and I was back up to scratch on all I needed to know about the people who mattered now. There had been a fair few personal visits required to rein in the fuckers who had started taking liberties under Danny's lax rules, but it was nothing that hadn't been fixed by a couple of rolling heads and broken bones.

The Firm was living up to our reputation once more. I just needed this deal to fall into place and I would have the majority of Danny's damage fixed.

I glanced down at Anya as she continued to look around, drinking in every snippet of information I offered up, hungry for it in a way which I knew all too well.

"You were born for this life, weren't you?" I asked her, my lips brushing her skin once more and sparking goosebumps to rise all across it.

"I was born to be sold to you," she replied bitterly but I just shook my head.

"Nah, that ain't the entirety of you, Anya. You've got something not many have. Grit, fire, ambition, determination and the ability to use all of that well. You were born to rule, bombshell."

"You're the king of this world," she murmured. "The best I can ever be is a pretty queen to hang from your arm. A Russian trophy you took for a peace deal. I could have been anyone and you still would have had to have me."

"That's true," I admitted and she stiffened a little, but I didn't relax my hold. "You could have been anyone. But you're not just anyone, Anya, are you? You're a force of fucking nature. And I don't think you would ever be satisfied as some pretty queen to hang from my arm."

"What am I then?" she asked, looking up at me like she hoped I truly had an answer for that as we approached the door to The Czar's box.

"You, Anya Butcher, are the fire that burns in my chest every time I look at you. You're the passion which opens my eyes every time I want to blinker myself from the truth. You're the breath of fresh air in my lungs which shook up a life which was always going to be stagnant for me. I'm a violent, honourless man and I was content to stay as such until you."

"So what are you now?" she asked, the two of us falling still as she turned to look up at me and my other hand moved to take a possessive hold of her jaw, my thumb tracing the full curve of her lips.

"Yours," I replied simply because it was utterly true. At some point since she'd come crashing into my life, I'd fallen under the spell of her and I found I had no desire to break free of it. She wasn't just some beautiful woman I could fuck and join bloodlines with, nah, she was so much more than that. She was all I'd never known I needed and that meant I was going to stay hers until the Devil got sick of my shit and came to drag me down into the dirt where I belonged for my sins.

The double doors beside us pulled open while she remained staring up at me with those endlessly dark eyes, the windows to her soul seeming blown right open in that moment while we resisted the call of the real world which was trying to tear us back to it.

I wanted to kiss her so bad that I found myself frozen there, my grip tight on her jaw, my other hand applying pressure to her hip like I intended to drag her forward into the curve of my body.

"Mr Butcher," a man greeted from my left, his voice thick with a Russian accent and my desire to knock him the fuck out for interrupting us almost fucked up our entire plan before Anya gripped my arm to hold me back.

She tugged to make me release my hold on her cheek, a bright, fake smile flashing across her face as she turned to look at the bastard who had cut in on us and I bit my tongue as I turned my gaze to him too.

He was a big fucker, tall, muscular in that sinewy kinda way which let me know he could move fast when he wanted to, probably twenty or so years older than me with dead eyes which looked hungry for a feast of his enemies. I was pretty certain I was no enemy of his though, especially while I was paying lip service to his boss in hopes of securing this damn deal.

"I am Mr Orlov's right hand, Yuri Sokolov," he said in a clipped tone, his gaze roaming over the two of us suspiciously as he gave us The Czar's real name, but no one called him by anything other than the title which he'd either claimed for himself or had been given at some point during his rise in status. To my knowledge, he had come from a wealthy family, but he was the one who had accrued the title of billionaire for himself. If this deal - plus the countless others I knew he was taking part in around the world - was anything to go by, he was nowhere near done building on the money he had made yet either. "If you wish to proceed with this meeting, Mr Orlov has insisted that you be searched. Unfortunately, there are some…misinformed officers who work for Interpol who have decided to target him through nothing other than petty jealousy. It means we cannot be too careful, especially when conducting a business meeting."

"Right you are, fella," I said, clapping Yuri on the shoulder hard enough to give the neat salt and pepper beard which coated his chin a good shake.

He looked inclined to gut me for laying a hand on him, but Anya stepped forward to draw his attention before I had to worry about fending off the bodyguard.

"I'm not entirely sure what I could be hiding in this dress, but you're welcome to check," she said in a sultry tone, glancing back over her shoulder at me with amusement dancing in her dark eyes as she held her hands out wide for a pat down.

"Helga will see to your search, Mrs Butcher," Yuri replied, stepping back and jerking his chin to summon another bodyguard from the shadows. There was a thick curtain blocking our view any further into the box beyond these few well-armed thugs, so for the moment, they had my full attention.

Helga strode forward with a wide stride and a wider jaw, her build arguably larger than Yuri's and the dead look in her eyes pushing the limits of necrotic.

Anya murmured something to her in Russian and Helga arched a brow in surprise before replying, the two of them falling into conversation like they were the best of pals as she began to check my wife for anything concealed beneath her clothes.

My skin prickled as I sauntered into the room, my gaze locking with Yuri's as I gave him a smile which was easily a challenge and held my arms out to allow him to pat me down.

Anya and Helga kept chatting away and I pushed my tongue into my cheek, disliking the feeling of being left out of the loop on whatever they were discussing. I certainly liked the way Anya's tongue sounded wrapping around her bloodline's language though.

I may have been developing an unhealthy obsession with my wife, but that wasn't to say I trusted her implicitly. She was a cunning little thing when the mood struck her and as much as I wanted to put my full faith in her, I knew I'd be a fool to do so. It wasn't so long ago that she'd tried to run from me, and I wouldn't be letting her out of my sight while we were here.

That said, when it came to the intricacies of this plan, I had to admit I did trust her. She was excited to be a part of this. I could tell. No matter how much she tried to hide it. Her brothers had been fucking fools to keep her out of this kind of work because it was more than clear to me that she was born for it.

Yuri tugged the gun I was wearing from the holster within my suit jacket and inspected it, eyeing the silencer I had attached to it and emptying the bullets out before replacing them one by one and returning the weapon to my holster.

"You maintain your weapon well," he commented, a little of the contempt in his tone loosening at that fact while he took my phone from my pocket.

"There are two things in this world which I won't ever be letting go without due care, mate," I told him as he dropped to search my trouser legs, his firm grasp encircling my calves. "My weapons and my woman. Neglecting either one could easily get me killed."

Anya gave me a heated look at those words and I grinned at her before Yuri cupped my balls so fucking hard that I could only assume he was trying to weigh the fuckers.

"Easy there, fella," I snarled as he finished his search, but he ignored me before turning and picking up a paddle-shaped sensor and beckoning me closer.

I indulged their shit as the sensor roamed all around my body, hunting for wires or bugs and coming up empty before we were finally deemed acceptable.

My phone was placed in a black box which apparently blocked all signal from it and Yuri snapped the lid closed on it, informing me that I could have it back when we left. I had to admit it was odd to have my phone removed while being allowed to keep my weapon, but I'd expected that from what we'd learned of The Czar.

"This way." Yuri pushed through the black curtain and I took hold of my wife once more, winding my arm around her lower back and leaning in close to press a kiss to the top of her blonde hair, inhaling the scent of her.

"Ready, bombshell?" I murmured and she turned a bright smile my way as she nodded.

Her skin was fucking glowing, her eyes bright and lips naturally curving up at the corners while not a note of music played to light her up. I hadn't seen her that invigorated by anything other than sex and music up until now, and I found I really liked seeing her this way.

The private box was huge, decorated mostly in white with an ivory dressed dining table off to the far end and long, glass doors closed before the balcony which looked down on the racetrack.

A couple of waiters stood off to one side of the room and I had to resist the urge to snigger at Frank, all dressed up in his penguin suit with a tray of champagne balanced on his hand. Everything was coming together.

The Czar was standing by the glass doors, his hands clasped at the base of his spine and an ice white suit cladding his body.

He was a tall man, just into his forties and all kinds of put together. Everything about him screamed money, from the manicured fingernails to the monogramed tie pin glinting with diamonds on his tailored suit.

"Ah, Mr Butcher," he said as he turned to look at us, perfectly quaffed blonde hair pushed away from his face to reveal bright blue eyes as sharp as tacks. I was willing to bet there weren't many men who had gotten one over on this fucker. "And this must be your new bride…" His gaze turned salacious as he inspected Anya and a damn growl rose in my throat, sticking there as I forced myself to allow him to look at her like that. Any other arsehole woulda found themselves eating out of a straw for a week if they looked at my wife like that right in front of me. "I'm not sure we've met, but I was very fond of your father. I was greatly saddened by his loss."

"Tragic, wasn't it? And we have met before actually," she said. "I was just a child though."

"Ah, well children are forgettable, but you certainly have grown into a creature that is not," The Czar purred and my blood boiled.

Anya let him take her hand and as he murmured something in Russian which was clearly another compliment, she gave him a flirtatious laugh and replied in kind.

"Come, sit," The Czar said finally, releasing his hold on my woman and drawing us towards a set of plush armchairs which had a clear view of the racetrack below. There were no horses out there yet, just countless men and women moseying about in their weekend finery and gauzy hats.

"It's good to see you," I said as we dropped into our seats. "I'm sure you're as keen as we are to get this development moving along nice and quickly."

"Yes…I am keen," The Czar agreed, his eyes on my wife as she crossed her legs and accepted a glass of champagne from Frank who had appeared to play waiter.

I took one and sank it before placing the glass back down on the tray and taking another.

"I have to be very careful though," The Czar went on, tearing his gaze from Anya as he seemed to have to force himself to look at me instead. "Interpol have it out for me."

"I heard," I replied, nodding seriously. Though in all honesty, when I'd put my feelers out into the men and women I had working in law enforcement,

I hadn't been able to track down any record of any kind of major investigation taking part about him. But the paranoid fuck was clearly certain that they were after him, no doubt for a shit load of tax evasion among other things.

"It is a constant concern," he said bitterly. "But I am confident that we can find a way to conduct our business without their interference."

"As am I," I agreed.

The Czar opened his mouth to say something further then looked to Anya once more, clapping his hands suddenly.

"Enough business talk," he commanded. "I agreed to meet you here because I need to be certain that I like a man before I climb into a financial bed with them. I have it on good authority that I will like you and I'm beginning to see that the assumption is likely a correct one."

His words were aimed at me, but his eyes remained riveted to Anya in a way which was making it damn hard for me to play nice.

"Excuse me a moment," Anya said, shifting a little uncomfortably under the intense pressure of his stare. "I just need to use the bathroom."

"You won't find a bath in there," I called after her as she rose and headed towards the private toilet attached to the box.

Anya rolled her eyes at me before turning to walk away and The Czar watched her go with as much attention as I was giving her.

"So, tell me, Mr Butcher, what is it you like to do for entertainment?" The Czar asked abruptly, waving a hand to another waiter who obediently approached us with a box of Cuban cigars on his tray.

"What don't I enjoy would be a more simple question," I replied lightly, accepting a cigar as it was offered to me and clipping the end before lighting it up.

"A man of varied tastes," The Czar chuckled. "I can empathise with that. And you know…I can arrange to get that for you too, if you would like? As a gift to seal the union of our business dealings."

"Get me what?" I asked, blowing a trail of pungent smoke up towards the ceiling and draping an arm along the side of my chair as I relaxed into it.

"Anything," The Czar replied with a knowing smile. "Drugs, cars, jewels, art, anything you desire, just name the gift you want and I shall make it so."

"I'm a made man, mate," I said with a shrug. "I appreciate the sentiment but honestly, I can get any of those things for myself without you having to go to any trouble on my behalf."

"Something a little harder to come by then?" he suggested, unperturbed. "Women perhaps?"

"I have a beautiful wife and didn't ever have much problem picking up women before her," I pointed out.

"No, not those kinds of women. Your wife in particular is of a supremely high calibre. The kind of woman men like us hunger for. But we have need of more primal satisfaction too, do we not?"

"Such as?"

“Perhaps I should speak more plainly. I am offering you a woman who would satisfy those darker urges men like us suffer with. The kind no one will miss, if you catch my meaning.”

I had to force myself to take another long drink from my glass, the champagne bubbles fizzing down my throat as I swallowed and tried to hide my disgust for the man before me. I had heard rumours that his entanglement with the Candlestick Maker was steeped in the sex trafficking trade and now I had my proof. I couldn’t say I much liked the insinuation that I was like him in that regard either. But I couldn’t exactly say that outright, not while I needed his fucking money and we still had a mystery to solve surrounding him, so I placed my empty glass down and swiped the remaining taste of the drink from my lips.

“That’s a kind offer, but like I say – my wife is all the woman I need.”

“Hmm.” The Czar looked around as the woman in question stepped back into the room and my skin prickled as a thought occurred to me which set my damn hackles on end.

This man was used to getting whatever the fuck he wanted in this world, either through a transaction or by force. And as I watched him while he watched my wife, that single thought only began to grow and grow. Because the longer I stared at him, the clearer it became to me. Right now, what he wanted was her. And I had a feeling he was going to try and take her.

ANYA

CHAPTER TWENTY EIGHT

I moved back to the table and The Czar snapped his fingers at Yuri, making him pull a chair out for me beside him instead of the one I'd been aiming for beside Danny.

"Come and have a talk with me, Mrs Butcher," The Czar encouraged as he puffed on a cigar.

I met Danny's gaze for a moment, finding a tightness to his expression which I couldn't read before I dropped down beside The Czar.

I picked up my glass of champagne, sipping it as I eyed The Czar over the top of it. I knew what needed to be done here, the game I had to play, but Danny wasn't going to like it.

I placed my glass down and plucked the cigar from The Czar's lips, slipping it between my own and making his eyes bug out of his head.

"I always loved the taste of these. You don't mind, do you?" I took a puff of the cigar, letting the smoke swirl seductively out of my lips as The Czar watched my mouth. "I never could stomach a whole one. But a little taste is all I need."

"Yes, one must never be denied their tastes in the way they desire," he said, chuckling deeply.

I slipped the cigar back between his lips and felt Danny's eyes burning a hole in the side of my head as my knee grazed against The Czar's.

"So who are you betting on?" Danny asked, his fist thumping down on the table and drawing our attention to him. He picked up the booklet left out for us on the table, looking through the horses, their riders and their stats.

"How about this one?" Danny suggested, pointing to a horse. "Merry-Go-Whirler, I like the sound of him."

"Hm, perhaps I'll spread my bets today. Guarantee a win for myself," The Czar murmured and I dropped a hand to his knee as I hooked onto that nugget of potential.

"Oh, do you need some cheering up? What's the matter?" I asked sweetly, leaning in close and giving him my biggest doe eyes.

He licked his lips, leaning right back into me, having no shame about how close he was getting to another man's wife. An itch started up in my skin, the desire to move away burning at me, but I knew what I was doing. This wouldn't go further than I wanted it to.

"I left something precious in the possession of a friend, but he is taking some time on returning it to me," he admitted and I hoped I'd just struck gold.

"Oh no," I said sweetly, my fingers circling around his inner knee. "What was it?"

"Yeah, what was it mate?" Danny pushed and The Czar's head snapped around to look at him.

The moment his eyes left mine, I knew I'd lost him and I threw Danny a scathing look, finding his jaw ticking as he looked right back at me with nothing but possessive masculinity in his dark eyes.

"Nothing, nothing." The Czar waved a hand dismissively, then took the booklet from Danny and started looking through the horses for the upcoming race.

"You should go all in on one of them. Live dangerously," I encouraged. "The biggest highs in life are won through taking the highest risks."

The Czar glanced at me, his eyes glittering at my words. "Mr Butcher, your wife is rather captivating. At first it was her beauty, but now I find her spirit and zest equally enthralling too. I do not need to wonder why you married her."

"She's a catch alright," Danny agreed and I glanced at him as he leaned forward in his seat, resting his elbows on the table.

"And do you mount your catches on the wall, or do you let them roam…?" The Czar pushed and I bit down on my tongue to stop myself from speaking my mind. I wasn't some fucking animal caught from the wild.

"She roams as far as she pleases," Danny said and I cocked my head, intrigued.

"And what keeps her coming back?" The Czar questioned curiously.

"What do you reckon it is, bombshell?" Danny asked. "My winning personality, or my ten inch cock?"

I snorted in amusement and The Czar roared a laugh, slapping his hand down on the table so hard that everything on it bounced.

I realised a shadow had fallen over me and I glanced up to find Frank there with a tray of champagne glasses which he swapped for our empty ones while shooting me a look that made my pulse pound.

"Alright, I've decided. I'm going all in," The Czar said as he drank a long sip of his champagne.

"On who, sir? The bets are about to close," Frank urged.

The Czar sifted through the horses in the booklet then slammed his finger down on one. "This one."

Frank read the name and bowed his head. "The Fuzzy Duck it is, sir. And would you like to write down your bet privately, or shall I fill out the betting slip for you?"

"You do it." The Czar waved a hand again then looked to me, smiling as he ran his tongue over his teeth. "One hundred thousand pounds on The Fuzzy Duck – who doesn't love a duck?" His hand came down on mine, squeezing tightly as a desire entered his eyes which made my stomach tighten. "I am in the mood to take a risk on one of life's biggest highs, Mrs Butcher. Let us chase the high together."

CHAPTER TWENTY NINE

I strode across the room to the private bar, filling new champagne flutes and slipping the tiny listening device I'd smuggled in here out of the lining of my sleeve so that it sat ready in my palm. It wasn't actually a working device because none of us believed we could have snuck one of those in here, but the thing looked the part which was all we'd needed.

I'd already managed to slip into the toilet and retrieve the bulletproof vest we'd stashed beyond the ceiling panel in there, hiding it beneath my shirt alongside the thin blood packs which were ready to set off the moment this thing came together. The Kevlar probably wasn't necessary, but it was better to be safe than sorry, just in case any of The Czar's men got trigger happy before our plan could slot into place.

I glanced over at Danny, catching the subtle nod he shot my way as I lifted the fresh tray of drinks into my hands and made my way back over to them.

The Czar was laughing loudly at some story he was telling and Anya was putting on a convincing show of being amused by him. But I knew my little livewire well enough by now to spot the bullshit and though she played her part damn well, the darkness in her eyes told me the truth of what she thought of this particular entitled prick.

The Czar waved me away as I offered him a drink, but Anya nodded, holding her hand out as I selected a glass and carefully passed it over to her.

Our eyes met and for a moment I could see a mixture of thrill and fear in her gaze at this last chance for me to turn back. But we both knew I wouldn't do that. This plan was solid and the risks were manageable. So long as she and Danny kept control of the situation once it had gone to shit.

I turned my hand slightly before I released my hold on the glass, the tiny listening device dropping into her drink with a soft splash which was overshadowed by the dramatic gasp she gave in response.

"What the hell is this?" she demanded loudly, pointing at me and dumping her drink out on the round table which sat between the three of them.

They all leaned forward to get a better look at it and I turned to run, trying to look like I was shitting myself as all eyes in the room fell on me.

Danny was on his feet in an instant, blocking my escape and his fist swinging straight into my jaw with enough force to knock me offa my fucking feet.

I fell on my back, cursing him for not pulling that fucking punch just as The Czar yelled, "Interpol!" in alarm.

Yuri, Helga and the other bodyguards in the room all rushed towards us, one of them grabbing the other waiter and manhandling him up against the wall with a ferocious snarl.

Yuri pulled a gun with intent but Anya was suddenly there, grabbing his arm and forcing his aim aside.

"Wait," she gasped. "We can't fire weapons here – someone will hear it," she protested just like we'd planned.

"I want him dead!" The Czar yelled and Danny strode forward with a wide grin.

"I've got you covered," he said as he pulled his pistol from its holster, silencer and all. "No one will hear this."

"At least get him away from the cream carpet," Anya muttered, her lip curling in disgust while a big fucking boot pressed down on my windpipe.

"Of course, my love," Danny cooed, stepping towards me and knocking the bodyguards aside as he yanked me to my feet and started shoving me towards the fire escape.

I fought half-heartedly, begging for mercy in that pointless kind of way I'd heard far too many times in my lifetime while Danny shoved me ahead of him, a cluster of Russians at our backs.

He threw me through the door into the darkened stairwell which was completely empty and gave me a psychotic grin as he pointed the gun at me.

It was filled with blanks, the blood packs I was wearing primed to cause enough of a mess to make this believable and I raised my chin as I prepared myself to set them off.

"It's not personal, mate," Danny said, toying with his damn food as always. "I just really hate sneaky fucking Interpol bastards."

He shot the gun and a breath caught in my lungs as the force of the impact hit me so hard, I stumbled back towards the stairs.

"What the-" I began but his smile only widened as he emptied the fucking clip, one bullet after another slamming into my chest as blood flew and I was knocked right off of my feet where I began to fall fast.

I cursed as I fought to shield my head, tumbling down the stairs and hitting every motherfucking one on the way down as the agony of the bullets slamming into me combined with the rage I felt over that arsehole choosing the top of a bloody staircase to shoot me.

I finally hit the bottom of the darkened stairwell, a wheeze of pain escaping me as I found myself flat on my back, my lungs hardly able to draw breath and cold, sticky blood splattered all over me.

The clip of some fancy fucking loafers moved closer to me and I squinted up at Church as he moved to stand above me where I lay. I was unable to move through the pain in my body as my heart thrashed to a wild rhythm and I fought the urge to start groaning over my injuries.

"Problem, boss?" Church called up the stairs and the sound of Danny's reply carried back to me.

"Clean that up for me, would ya, Churchy? And if the fucker is still alive, make sure he feels every inch of his death before the end, yeah?"

"Sure thing, boss." Church gave me a kick which forced a pained curse from my lips as I continued to lay there, my chest on fire with agony and my head spinning from the knocks it had taken against the fucking stairs.

"Call that my gift to you, Czar," Danny's voice came again though it sounded like he was moving further away now.

The Czar laughed, though he still sounded kind of rattled. "Friends like you are friends indeed, Mr Butcher."

"None of that," Danny replied. "Just call me Butch."

A door snapped shut as they all left me down here and I was gifted a view of Church grinning at me from ear to ear as he leaned down and grabbed my lapels so that he could drag me out of the stairwell.

"Nice acting there, Frankie boy," he praised as he knocked a door open and dragged me out through it into the sunlight.

I squinted at the back entrance to the stands, finding no one around aside from the white catering van which was parked right in front of us with John Boy waving from the driver's seat. I almost didn't recognise him on account of his face being so fucking forgettable. Fucking gift that.

"What the fuck was that?" I hissed as I managed to get my breath back. I wanted to shove him off of me and push myself to my feet but for the sake of appearances I let him drag me all the way to the sliding door on the side of the van. "Those weren't blanks."

"Nah," Church agreed. "Me and Butch got to talking on that and we figured it wasn't worth the risk of using blanks."

"And no one thought to tell me?" I snarled.

The Kevlar might have stopped them from entering my body, but they had packed one hell of a fucking punch when they hit. And Danny had done me the favour of unloading his entire clip into me too.

"We were concerned about premature flinching," Church said with a shrug as he dumped me in the back of the van before straightening up again and taking a pack of wet wipes from John Boy so that he could clean his hands off, removing the fake blood from them.

"Fuck you," I hissed, massaging a lump on the back of my skull. "Was it really necessary to shoot me at the top of a flight of fucking stairs too? I thought the plan was for him to march me down to the bottom of them first?"

"Dramatic impact, mate," Church said, shrugging again as he tossed the wipes into the van with me. "The Russians had to believe you were a goner or one of them mighta thought to pop you between the eyes. It was a necessary sacrifice."

"Dickhead," I snarled and he grinned at me.

"Yeah," he agreed. "But it worked, didn't it? Now The Czar thinks our boss is his newest best buddy. So well done, mate. You did a good job."

With that patronising little nugget of shit, Church pushed his fingers through his hair then looked back over his shoulder towards the building he'd just exited. "You got the info I need then?"

"Yeah," I grunted, though I was more than a little tempted to withhold it in payment for that show they'd just let me be a part of without even understanding what I was in for. "He's betting on The Fuzzy Duck."

"Alright then. I've got work to do. Feel better, Frankie boy." Church slammed the sliding door in my face, patted the side of the van twice and John Boy drove us away obediently.

I sat up straighter and ripped the tattered remains of my shirt from my chest before unfastening the Kevlar to inspect the violent bruises which were already blossoming all over my skin.

But no matter how much I was cursing Danny for his bullshit plan and the way he'd gone about it, a part of me couldn't help but be pleased that everything was going so damn well. My fake death had hopefully just bought the Butcher gang lifelong loyalty from The Czar.

Danny Butcher may have been one hell of a cunt, but this plan was a real good one. Assuming it worked.

CHAPTER THIRTY

I headed back into the building, whistling a little as I went and smiling to myself at the look of pure rage on Frank's face as I'd slammed that door in his face. I knew it was petty and more than a little immature, but I was so over his shitty attitude and the way he treated me like I was a fucking pariah just because I'd chosen not to believe the lies he'd drank down so willingly about Benny.

But I had more important things to worry about than the old bitterness which hung between me and the man I'd once looked on like a brother.

I turned away from the stairs which led up to the VIP box where Benny and Anya were still buddying up to The Czar, taking a staff door into a walkway beneath the stands.

The clamour of the kitchens greeted me as I began to hurry along the brightly lit corridor, weaving past wait staff with trays laden with drinks and ignoring the yell for help with an order which someone aimed my way.

I began to move faster as I heard someone saying the race would be starting in fifteen minutes, needing to make it before the jockeys led their horses out onto the track.

I hurried through several more doors, the scent of fresh hay drawing me closer to my destination as I moved away from the stands and into the holding area for the animals, finding the jockeys all preparing to head out as I'd expected.

"I need a word," I barked loudly, drawing the attention of the lot of them while the stable hands hurried about double checking everything. "Boss's orders. No time to waste."

This here racetrack was Butcher run, though no one knew it. It was officially owned by someone called Dom Byron, but if you were a clever clogs, you might figure out that because if you rearranged those letters you'd get his real name. Mr Nobody. Total fakery, a guise to cover for the real owners. The Butcher gang.

I jerked my chin towards a small changing room which was off of the central space, striding into it without bothering to check they were all following.

"I've been training my arse off for this race," a fella by the name of Marshall muttered as they all filed in and I casually reached out to slap him round his chops.

"None of that moaning bullshit," I said firmly. "This ain't the Grand National and there's more at stake here than your pride or morals or any of that bullshit."

"What about my career?" Marshall asked irritably, clearly not put in his box by the slap.

I strode towards him, holding a finger up and pointing it right into his grumpy face.

"Now listen here, Marshall," I growled, letting my happy-go-lucky demeanour slip away until all he could see was the depths of my depravity and the seriousness of this threat. "Don't you go forgetting who pays your fuckin' wages. Who pays for your grandma to be in that lovely home down by the coast. Who put your arse in a saddle and who keeps it cosy as fuck with more back handers than I could count. I don't give a fuck if you feel salty about me calling the shots on you like this from time to time. This is the real world and the truth of it is that you aren't paid the way you are because of your fancy riding abilities or your pretty little ponies – you're paid because you're carried on a tide of lost bets and small wins. So if you like your lifestyle of prancing about all day long riding on horses and you don't enjoy the idea of me breaking your legs then you'll shut the fuck up and do as you're told."

Marshall swallowed audibly and I smirked at him, giving his face a couple of patronising slaps again. He was a little fella, in fact they all were for obvious reasons, and it did make me feel kind of big and important when I stood in a room with them, towering over the lot of them with my six foot two frame.

"Okay, so are there any more of ya who have a complaint to voice before I go on?" I asked, looking around the room, but none of them said a word. "Good. The Fuzzy Duck needs to win this one, boys."

Marshall's eyes widened as I named his horse and a blush coloured his cheeks as he realised he'd been mouthing off at me over nothing because I was giving him a free win anyway.

"I couldn't give a shit about any other positionings today," I went on. "But let me tell you now, if any horse other than his gets its nose over the finish line first, I'll be coming to see the winner this very night to cut your jockey legs off to make a pair of nunchucks outa them. Then I'll use my new weapons to beat your fucking skull in. Got it?"

A resounding chorus of agreement filled the room and I grinned as I turned and strode away from them.

"Have a good race, fellas."

CHAPTER THIRTY ONE

"I can usually smell an Interpol rat," The Czar muttered for what felt like the hundredth time.

Danny had had the other waiter escorted away by some of his men, the guy pleading his innocence as he went. He was just another Butcher plant, but he put on a good show wailing about his kids while Danny promised The Czar he'd figure out whether he was a threat or not.

The Czar's man, Yuri, kept sniffing around every corner of the room, hunting for any more devices that might have been hidden, like he suspected there could be bugs buried in the walls.

"Don't beat yourself up. All law enforcement are getting sneakier these days, I swear," I said as the new wait staff appeared, hurrying to top up our champagne glasses.

The Czar regarded me, sweeping a hand through his icy blonde hair and sighing. "Oh to be a woman with no worries in the world."

Irritation flashed through me, but I kept my smile hitched in place. I leaned in close to him as Danny lit up another cigar for himself, reclining back in his seat as his attention followed me. I lowered my voice, whispering to The Czar and he leaned towards me like he couldn't resist knowing what I had to say.

"I'm not like ordinary women. Danny lets me play gangster sometimes."

"Does he, indeed?" he asked, his sky blue gaze dragging across my mouth. "And what games does Mrs Butcher like to play?"

"He's let me in the torture room before," I whispered, sensing Danny leaning closer now like he was curious as fuck as to where I was going with this. "I've played with agents before. *Interpol* agents."

The Czar visibly shivered, a low groan passing his lips and he reached out to tuck a lock of hair behind my ear.

"You really are one of a kind, aren't you Mrs Butcher?"

"Hands off, mate," Danny growled and I glanced at him, finding him practically twitching in his seat like he could hardly keep himself there.

The Czar withdrew his hands, raising them in innocence to Danny, but a challenge sparked in his eyes too. They shared an intent look which was all secret man talk and I rose from my seat, picking up my champagne flute and heading to the balcony doors with my hips swaying. I hated this dress on principle because I looked like a posh bitch, and these heels were pinching my toes like the Devil himself lived within them, but I could walk like I was drifting on a cloud, and I knew my ass was drawing all the eyes in the room as I went.

"The race is about to start," I called, sliding the balcony door open and glancing back over my shoulder.

My husband and The Czar were already on their feet and Danny made it to me first, looping an arm around my waist and pulling me close enough to feel his breath on my neck.

"Rein it in a little, bombshell," he murmured, but I just offered him a sweet smile in reply.

I know what I'm doing, asshole.

We moved to the railing and I broke away from Danny's hold as The Czar stood on my other side, the three of us gazing out over the packed stands to the lush green track beyond. We were right near the starting point and my heart raced as a buzzer sounded and the doors to the stalls flew open, freeing the racehorses.

They galloped out of them, tearing down the track as the commentator's voice filled the stands, but my eyes were glued to The Fuzzy Duck as I cheered him on, crying out as Danny bashed his fist down on the railing and The Czar clutched it tightly beside me.

"Go on – go on!" I cried, and despite knowing this race was rigged, the exhilaration still had me on a high as the horses galloped and closed in on the finish line.

The Fuzzy Duck was in fourth place and I shot an anxious glance at Danny, but he had the biggest grin on his face, his confidence pouring from him as he yelled out encouragements. I was captured by that moment, staring at him as light seemed to burst within his dark eyes and there was such a wildness about him that it made my stomach flip over. He was beautiful this man, this husband of mine, and it wasn't just his exterior, there was something that shone within him from the darkness encasing his soul. He may have been a blackhearted king, but he was also the most intoxicating man to be in the company of. He brought excitement to every moment, electrifying the air and charging it so potently that I could feel it crackling under my skin.

I was so distracted by staring at him that it took me a second to realise he was throwing his fist in the air and crying out The Fuzzy Duck's victory. He turned to me and I leapt at him, stamping my mouth to his as I lost myself, drunk on him as his tongue sank between my lips and I kissed him with all the passion of a wife who had chosen to say I do.

The Czar laughed loudly behind us and Danny carved his hand down my back, gripping my ass and squeezing unashamedly as he claimed me with every possessive stroke of his tongue against mine.

When we parted, we were breathless and staring at one another like if we looked away, the world would end.

"Mr Butcher, you must allow me to thank your wife properly," The Czar said firmly as he moved towards us, his hand slamming down on Danny's shoulder.

"Butch," he corrected, a smirk on his lips, but his eyes were a treasure trove of sin. "You can thank her right now." He gestured to me.

"No, no." The Czar shook his head. "Let me take her for dinner tonight. Then I can have Yuri drop her home tomorrow morning. I assure you, I will look after her well."

I tried to ignore the clawing sensation running up and down my spine, despising the way this man spoke about me to Danny as if I wasn't even here. As if I was some commodity to be bought.

"Nah, I've got plans for her tonight," Danny said dismissively, grabbing my hand and towing me inside.

"Tomorrow then?" The Czar called after us as he followed.

"I don't mind," I told Danny in a low voice, sure I could get more information from The Czar if I had him alone. I could handle the creep and there was no way I'd let him take what he wanted from me anyway.

"I said no," Danny hissed at me, slapping his smile back on as we reclaimed our seats. He didn't let me sit beside The Czar this time though, he drew me down onto his lap and placed his hand on my knee in a clear alpha move.

The Czar watched us closely, not seeming to be remotely put off by Danny's behaviour, in fact, he seemed more enraptured by me than ever.

"So why are those Interpol bastards after you?" Danny asked The Czar, his knuckles running up and down my spine in a motion that was designed to make me shiver.

The Czar clucked his tongue, draining another glass of champagne before gesturing for it to be refilled. Yuri stood watching the waiters closely, his arms folded and his eyes narrowed as he assessed any possible threats in the room.

"They think I have something," he said, his tongue loosening at last.

"Oh?" I questioned gently.

"Something very valuable," he added. "I'm a collector of rare and beautiful things. And some of those things must be acquired through certain means."

"Got ya, mate," Danny said. "So what did you collect that pissed them off?"

The Czar opened his mouth, then shut it again, chuckling softly. "Something I shouldn't speak of in public, Mr Butcher."

"Butch," Danny corrected firmly.

"Butch," The Czar agreed, leaning closer, his fingers grazing my bare calf in a move that was definitely deliberate. "Speaking of beautiful things… are you sure I can't offer you something for a night with Mrs Butcher. Just one night. I need to…experience her fully."

Disgust raced through me and it took all of my willpower not to snap my fist out and clock this guy in his smarmy face. His fingers caressed my leg in long strokes, and I knew Danny couldn't see it from the angle he was at while The Czar looked me in the eye, daring me to say something.

Danny shifted me on his lap, one hand sliding tightly around my waist as he kept a perfectly casual smile on his face. "Nah, mate. She ain't for sale. This one's all mine."

Frustration flickered over The Czar's features then he sat back in his seat, relieving me from the contact of his hand. "I would offer you a great distraction while she was with me, of course. Remember the special shipments I mentioned before, hm? I assure you, you would not be disappointed. A man of your status really should taste all the fruits of our bountiful place in the world."

I frowned, glancing between them. "What shipment?"

"Nothin', love." Danny squeezed my side then looked back at The Czar. "Tell you what, mate. I'll think about your offer. Both of them, in fact."

The Czar's eyes brightened and he nodded keenly. "Absolutely. I will have Yuri arrange the delivery if you would like to take me up on my other offer. Now, enough business. Let us drink and celebrate our win." He beckoned the waiters over and while he was ordering some ridiculously expensive bottle of whiskey, I turned to Danny, leaning in close to him and whispering in his ear.

"I can get it out of him if I have a night with him. I won't let him touch me, I know how to keep men like that distracted long enough for him to talk, and I know how to slip a guy a sedative or two to make sure he falls asleep."

A growl rumbled through his chest that was purely animal. "I said no. Do you need a reminder of who you belong to, bombshell?"

I leaned back enough to look into his eyes, my heart thumping out of rhythm.

"I don't belong to anyone," I whispered defiantly in reply and he smirked, leaning in close, but instead of offering a kiss, he spoke against my lips.

"I'll take that as a yes."

"Is your one braincell lonely in your head, or are there a few dumbass lumps of testosterone floating around in there to keep it company?" I asked lightly as I stepped back into the warehouse, reaching for the zip at my back to try and get this dress straight off. I couldn't get hold of it though, so I started struggling with both hands to seize it.

Danny strode past me, ripping his jacket off and tossing it on the couch. "You really think I'd let you spend a night with that fucking cunt?" he snapped.

"I can handle him," I growled, cursing as I got hold of the zipper, but it wouldn't budge.

"You don't know that," he snarled, throwing his flat cap onto the coffee table, leaving his inky hair distractingly mussed in its wake and striding into the kitchen as I followed, kicking off my heels as I went.

"I do know actually. Because I've handled men like him before," I growled. "I've killed men, you know? Before you. Before all of this. I can look after myself."

"He's a fucking billionaire, bombshell," Danny barked, yanking open the cutlery drawer and taking out a butcher knife. "We don't know how many men he has stationed at his house. Once you went in there, you wouldn't come out until he'd gotten what he wanted from you. And if you've forgotten we don't want the arsehole dead because we are relying on his money to dig us out of the fucking hole that D- *I* put us in."

"Then how else are we supposed to get the information we need to separate him from the Candlestick Maker? Or don't you care about that anymore? Because you said that you wanted to divide them so that you could kill that creep and stop the sex trafficking shit he's been running through your city. Or don't you care about all of the poor girls who are suffering because of him anymore?"

"You know I do," he snarled. "But I care about you, Anya, don't you get that? I care about you going into a house with some arsehole who thinks he has the right to fuck you just because you crossed his threshold. And if you kill him then we're fucked. Hell, I might end up killing him if he hurts so much as a hair on your head."

"I don't have to kill him, but I can sure as shit drug him to make him fall asleep, then I'll slip away in the morning. If it was you he wanted to buy for a night, you'd go with that plan." I picked up one of my shoes, hurling it at him and he ducked it, swearing as it hit a mug behind him on the counter and it smashed against the wall, ceramic pieces flying everywhere.

"Yeah, I would," he admitted. "But you're not me. And I'm your husband. I say no."

"Oh you say no, do you?" I scoffed. "You know what, Danny, you're just like every fucking guy I've ever known. The big man, with his big house and his big fucking balls, treating his woman like she's his possession instead of someone with their own goddamn free will."

"I'm trying to protect you," he growled, marching around the island towards me with that huge knife in his hand. I glanced at it, uncertain for a second of what he was going to do, but I didn't back up, raising my chin to face whatever fate he had in store for me.

"Poor innocent me in my little high tower, please protect me oh scary dragon of mine," I mocked him and he grabbed my wrist, his features twisting into a ruthless expression. My heart juddered as he raised that knife and his face dropped into a frown as he realised where my attention was fixed.

"This is the problem, ain't it?" He raised the knife, pointing it at my neck. "There's no trust between us. There's just lust and rage. But sometimes there's more than that and you know it, bombshell. Deep down, you know, you feel this thing writhing between us growing stronger every day. You feel it right here." He pressed the tip of the blade to my heart and my lungs ceased to work. "You're gonna give in to me. You're gonna give me this beating organ in your chest, because it wants me and mine wants you back."

"So cut it out, Danny," I hissed. "It's the only way I'll give it to you. That's what you Butchers do, isn't it? You take and take, but this is one thing you can't steal or demand. So the only way you can have it from me is bloody and raw."

He bared his teeth, anger flashing in his eyes. "You're in denial, love. I've tasted the truth on you. You can't lie when you kiss me, when you come for me. You seek out my soul in my eyes because when I touch you, you burn inside. The treaty may have brought you to my door, but I woulda found you despite it one way or another. We're inevitable. At least I have the balls to admit it."

"I like fucking you, Danny, you're deluding yourself with the rest of it," I growled the lie, hating the way it made my insides knot. But I was far too stubborn to admit that maybe he was right, that when I was with him I was starting to feel my hate for him twisting into something much sweeter, like cocaine into sugar. I wanted him so bad it hurt, but love? Fuck love. He didn't deserve my love. Love was a shackle I refused to wear, because when all was said and done, I had still been sold to this man, and I was not going to relent and trot neatly into some bullshit happily ever after. Why should I? When I'd never chosen this life for myself? Why should all the men who'd decided my fate get to watch me submit and get to clap each other on the back for their marvellous choices?

Hurt coiled through Danny's eyes, but it hardened to steel in the next instant. "Liar."

He swung me around, knotting my dress in one hand while slicing into it with the knife, cutting it straight open. His mouth fell to my shoulder and I released a small gasp as he tossed the knife away, letting it clatter across the floor.

He fisted the material, tearing it open and pulling it down my arms, freeing them and pushing my hair away from my neck before kissing that too.

"You're allowed to hate me," Danny said against my skin, kissing it again and again as he pushed the dress down over my hips and let it fall to my feet. "But you're allowed to love me too."

"Danny," I said heavily, the fight going out of me as I hung my head and he unclipped the bra I'd had to wear with that stupid dress.

"Shh, don't say that name," he begged, but I didn't know why he cared.

He peeled it off of me, throwing it away then walked me towards the kitchen island, pressing me forward until I was splayed over it face down, his mouth pressing between my shoulder blades, the sensitive spot making goosebumps rush along my skin. His stubble grazed me as he worked, kissing his way down my spine and leaving me trembling with the anticipation of him. My cheek was pressed to the cool counter and platinum hair veiled my vision as he tormented me.

He nipped the skin of my ass then worked his way back up my body, pressing the hard and urgent ridge of his cock against me as he leaned forward and brushed the locks of hair away from my face

"I'm so tired, Danny," I admitted. "Tired of men controlling everything about my life. You may want to love me, but you can never offer me some fairy tale love story. When it comes down to it, I'm always just going to be your belonging, a gold coin pressed into your palm in payment for peace. That's why I'm here, and I'm never going to forget that."

He stopped kissing me and silence pooled between us for a moment. "If life were perfect, what is it you'd want, Anya?"

"Freedom," I exhaled, not needing to think on it. It was all I'd ever wanted. "Freedom to be whoever I choose to be."

"And who would you be?"

"I'd be the ruler of my own underworld," I said, the idea making my heart feel like it was going to burst with excitement. "I'd be at the top of the food chain, ruler of my own destiny. I'd fight and plot and thieve, and do whatever made my soul ignite."

Danny's breaths came quicker like he was excited by that idea too and he slowly drew away from me, taking my hand and pulling me upright. I glanced back at him, finding him sliding his shirt from his own back and offering it to me. I pushed my arms into the sleeves and let him turn me around, the material covering my tits, but leaving a line of skin exposed down the centre of me.

The masterpiece of his body was right before me, the ink sprawling across his flesh and looking somehow alive tonight. His muscles were an artwork of their own and his olive skin looked more fitting for some Mediterranean climate than a place where the rain was always waiting to fall.

"How's this then…" he said thoughtfully. "You can be a part of The Firm, you can have the same opportunity anyone under my rule gets, which is a chance to prove themselves, a chance to claim power and to make what they wanna make of themselves. And you'll be cut into the jobs too so you can earn your own cash."

My brows arched in surprise, but he went on before I could respond.

"Once we finish up this job with The Czar and you prove your mettle, I'll let you go where you like unsupervised. You can have a key, even a fucking passport if you want it. And you know why, bombshell?" He stepped closer to me, forcing me to tilt my head back so I could keep looking at him. I shook my head, confused as fuck over why he'd give me any of those things. "Because you won't run. You'll realise what we have, and yeah, it's not ever gonna be a fairy tale, love. It's gonna be real and ruinous. It's gonna push us to the brink of insanity, and there might be times when we wanna walk away from each other, but we won't. Because Lucifer himself crafted me from brimstone and hellfire, he made me irredeemable, bombshell, but I guess the daft fucker decided to make me a mate in you and didn't realise you'd save my fucking soul." He laughed, pushing his fingers into my hair and kissing my forehead. "So what d'ya say, love?"

"Yes," I said, excitement brimming in my chest and overflowing. "Yes – yes – yes!" I threw my arms around his neck, kissing him hard and he groaned against my mouth, hitching my thighs up and planting my ass on the counter.

"Oh shit, is this what I get when I make you happy?" he panted against my mouth and I dug my ankles into his back, drawing him against me. Dammit, he was getting so deep under my skin and I knew I shouldn't let him, but if he was really going to offer me this, really give me a chance at freedom then I'd snatch it up with both hands.

"Yeah, and this." I slapped him hard across the face and he groaned as I dropped my hands to his pants, unbuckling them fast and freeing the thick length of his cock, my eyes catching on the forget-me-not flower inked below his hip. But I didn't have long to study it before he'd ripped my panties clean off of me and was sinking deep inside me with a powerful thrust that made me cry out.

"Hit me again," he demanded and I did, smacking him hard enough to imprint my palm on his cheek, making his eyes spark with desire and his cock grow even bigger inside me. "Do you know how much I wanted to drag you away from that fucking arsehole today and stake my claim on you?"

"You're such a caveman," I panted as he pounded into me without mercy.

"I know you don't wanna be owned, but let me fuckin' try at least, bombshell," he growled and I tipped my head back as his mouth came down on my throat.

"You're wasting your time, husband," I said, but my taunt was lost as he drove into me deeper and I moaned, my head falling back and my hair tumbling out behind me.

He watched me with the passion of a wild beast, a grin lighting up his face. "Well if I have to waste my time on something, wife, let it always be this."

DANNY

CHAPTER THIRTY TWO

I lay on my back with my head hanging over the edge of the unused platform, my eyes turned towards the tracks as my hair spilled down towards them and I counted the slow and endless beats of my heart.

I wasn't a patient man. Not at the best of times. And though I was working hard to accept my brother's need to punish me for his years behind bars, I was also tired of this endless game. I wasn't a creature suited to an empty cage. I was a predator in need of prey and I was thirsting for the hunt.

I shifted upright at the sound of heavy shoes thumping down the tunnel beyond the metal gate which locked me away down here, blood rushing back out of my head from the time I'd spent with it upside down.

I got to my feet in a rush, stumbling a little as my fucking body betrayed me and the shakes I'd been suffering with for the last few days set in with more ferocity.

My stomach grumbled loudly, reminding me of the furious rage which had seen me hurl the last of my food out onto the tracks after the last time I'd been locked down here. It had been a mistake, but my anger was growing beyond reason and out of spite I'd done myself out of food for the past few days. I'd tried to head down onto the tracks after a day, shamefully hunting for the lumps of bread and fruit I'd discarded, but the rats had already taken all of it, leaving me to starve until Benny chose to return.

Three fucking days. He'd given me a clock so I was able to keep track and I knew that was how long it had been since his last visit.

I wasn't sure how he was able to stay away for so long. If I had been the one holding him down here, I would have been spending every waking hour visiting him, working to repair the rift between us. He was my fucking soul and yet he acted like I was nothing more than an inconvenience to him. I knew he was punishing me. I knew it. But I was so sick of being apart from him after all these years that I just needed this shit to end.

"Where have you been?" I barked as Benny strode into my space, wearing designer trousers with his chest bare.

"Busy," he grunted, tossing a bag my way which I could see was brimming with food.

I dropped down and grabbed a bar of dairy milk chocolate from the top of it, ripping it open and stuffing a huge lump into my mouth to shut up my growling stomach.

"What?" I demanded of Benny as he watched me. "No questions for me today?"

"Nah. I think I've got all the information I need from you at this point. And I can tell you, Dan, you left me one hell of a fuckin' mess to clean up with the way you've been running our businesses."

"The businesses run themselves," I said dismissively, still stuffing my face with chocolate though I knew I was really hungering for something else. "I had better things to do with my time than check up on a bunch of incompetent managers. If they'd failed me, I'd have gutted them for it – I figured that was motivation enough."

"Well you were wrong," he spat irritably. "And what better things did you have to do anyway? Snorting blow and fucking whores? Maybe a little bit of senseless violence sprinkled in here and there just so you could get your kicks?"

I shoved to my feet, forgetting the food and letting the empty chocolate wrapper fall from my hand as I swallowed the last of it.

"I forgot how fucking big your superiority complex can be, Ben," I sneered, moving towards him and raising my chin in challenge as I took in the sight of him. Deep red lipstick stained his skin in places, not to mention the teeth marks bruising his neck. "Besides, it looks to me like you've been spending more than a little time with a whore or two yourself tonight."

Benny ran a thumb over the bite mark on his skin before grazing it against the lipstick marked along his chest.

"Why would I need a whore when I have a beautiful wife waiting for me at home?" he tossed back, dropping his hand once more.

I frowned at the implication in those words, a taste of suspicion glazing my tongue as I cocked my head and tried to suss him out.

"Anya Volkov," I said her name slowly, watching his eyes for his reaction.

"You mean Butcher," he replied in a low tone. "I made her mine in front of all we love and hold dear. And I don't plan on letting her go either."

"Does she scream while you fuck her?" I asked, inching closer to him. "Does she beg for more of your cock with every thrust? Or are they screams of fear? Does she beg you to stop while you force her down beneath you and show her exactly what we think of Russian sc-"

Benny clocked me with a right hook so suddenly that I was knocked on my arse beneath the force of his attack, my jaw ringing with agony as my head hit the stone of the platform and damn near dislodged my brain from my skull.

Before I could gather my wits, he was on me, his entire demeanour turning feral as he threw his fists into my sides several more times, making my ribs rattle at the impact before his hand knotted in my shirt and he dragged me so close that our noses were brushing.

"You don't fucking talk about her like that," he snarled, a look of pure violence and a promise of death in his dark eyes. "You hear me, you fucking junky arsehole? You don't speak a fucking word about her to me again!" he roared.

My lips parted as I stared up at my brother, my best friend, my fucking soul and I took in the reality of that poison in him.

He was looking at me like he would kill me for that whore. Me. His fucking flesh and blood, the man who had shared a womb with him, his motherfucking twin.

"You love her," I stated, the twisted fucking fact of it as clear as the poison she'd tainted him with.

This was why he hadn't been spending much time down here with me. This was why he wasn't letting me go. This was why he persisted in this fucking punishment.

Not because he still believed I deserved it, but because some whore had come to steal him away from me with her beguiling cunt.

"She's mine," he said possessively, irrefutably, challengingly. Not even denying what I'd accused him of as he snarled down at me like he really would kill me for her, and I saw it then. The real problem here. The thing that was keeping this divide in place between me and him.

Her.

Benny shoved himself to his feet, spitting on me before turning and striding away without another word.

"Wait!" I bellowed, scrambling upright and breaking into a sprint as he made it to the gate.

But Benny was faster than me, slamming the gate closed between us and snapping the heavy padlock into place before twisting the numbers to secure it once more.

"Stop!" I demanded as I crashed into the wrought iron dividing us, making it clang violently as he backed away from me with a look of contempt. "I need my fix," I called, panic finding me as he continued to retreat without so much as a glint of regret in his darkened expression.

"Oh, you mean this?" he asked, pulling a bag of pure, white cocaine from his pocket and holding it out as if he was gonna offer it to me.

I slammed into the gate again, shoving my arm through it and reaching for the bag with a desperation so potent that it was making my heart thunder and my pulse pound deafeningly in my ears.

Benny took a single step closer to me, the bag brushing the tips of my fingers and making a desperate kind of whimper rise up in my throat before he tugged it out of reach again.

"I think you can go a little longer without your precious blow," he said coldly. "You can sit down here and sweat and shake and puke your fucking guts up all alone in the dark while you learn to think of my wife with the respect I demand from you."

"No," I gasped as he began to back away. "Benny!" I roared so loud that my throat seemed to splinter and tear from the sound.

My twin ignored me, turning away and striding off into the darkness of the tunnel while panic gripped me in a vice and I cried his name again.

I threw myself into the gate, shaking its hinges and bellowing at the top of my lungs, demanding he come back, that he give me what I fucking needed.

But he didn't return. Not even as minutes became hours and still I screamed for him to come back to me.

And I knew why he wasn't thinking of me. I knew why he wasn't at my side.

That whore had come between me and the man I was bound to. That fucking Volkov had done this. And so fucking help me, when I got out of this place, I was going to have to make it my mission to get her out of the fucking way.

CHAPTER THIRTY THREE

"We have a problem," Danny said loudly as he strode down the stairs to where I was sitting at the breakfast bar with Church as Anya cooked herself some food.

Somehow, this had become something of a routine for the four of us, to congregate here at the start of the day. And despite the fact that I didn't much like either of the men I was in the company of, something about it seemed oddly…nice. Like in some twisted way we were acting like a family, all linked to one another by this single meal which we ended up together for daily, no matter what else the days held.

"If it's your hard on then I already told Church that's a you guys issue, not a me issue," Anya said as she placed her plate of toast down and moved to take her seat.

But before she could move more than a few steps, Danny caught hold of her hips and drove her up against the breakfast bar, directly opposite me.

A gasp escaped her as he pinned her there with his crotch against her arse and pushed the oversized shirt she'd slept in up over her back.

"Fuck, Danny…" she protested breathily as he revealed her bare flesh and I swallowed a lump in my throat as I watched them.

"That sounds more like a plea than a denial, bombshell," he pointed out, running his hands down the sides of her arse as she looked up and met my gaze, biting down on her bottom lip. But if that was an attempt to hide how turned on she clearly was, it wasn't fucking working, all it did was make my cock swell as I watched her.

"Has the tit liberation front moved south?" Church asked curiously as he stood and shifted around the breakfast bar towards the two of them. "Because it sure seems like it from how infrequently you wear your knickers these days."

"Fuck you," Anya growled and Danny laughed.

"Is that what you want, love? For me to make you come while Frank watches on like an unblinking robot?"

Church barked a laugh and I scowled, but Danny was already shifting backwards, releasing Anya and swatting her arse playfully while she cursed him.

She tugged her shirt back down to cover herself again and Danny dropped into a chair before tugging her down on his lap.

"So, back to our problem," he said, waiting for Anya to select a piece of toast before slipping his hand under her shirt and sliding it up her body beneath it. Anya scowled at him but as his hand made it to her breast and I watched his grip shift to tug on her nipple through the fabric, she seemed to forget about making him stop. "The Czar has been in touch and he is insistent on sending me the gift of a girl who he's clearly bought via the Candlestick Maker through the sex trade. He wants to send her over to me with Yuri tonight. I can't even refuse him because he's made a whole fucking fuss about how important it is to him that we exchange gifts to seal this new deal between us, and while we continue to wait on him coughing up the construction money, I have to dance to his tune."

"So you're just going to let him gift you some poor girl to abuse?" Anya asked in disgust, trying to push Danny's hand off of her, but he just growled low in the back of his throat, twisting his fingers beneath her shirt and leaning in to speak in her ear.

"No, bombshell. Would you ever let me fuckin' finish?"

"Go on then," Anya muttered but her words turned into a gasp as Danny continued to torment her nipple, the sight of them together like that beginning to torment me too.

"I figure I have to accept the girl, but maybe that's not all bad. I can just set her free and no harm done."

"Yeah, that makes sense," Church piped up.

"What does The Czar want as a gift from you?" I asked, my gaze moving to the woman in his lap as she squirmed in his arms.

Danny pushed his tongue into his cheek and shook his head. "He's made a few insinuations, but I'm not biting. I'll figure something else out instead."

"He wants me," Anya said knowingly.

"Doesn't matter," Danny replied.

"It does," she insisted. "I can get him talking. I know I can find out what he gave to the Candlestick Maker, plus I bet I can get him to start paying up on the construction deal."

"He wants a full night in your company, bombshell. Talking isn't what he has in mind," Danny hissed, his grip on her tightening possessively.

"But-" she began to protest but Church and I both spoke at once, cutting her off.

"No," we barked and Anya scowled at us.

"There's a simpler way to find out about whatever the Candlestick Maker has lost," I said, turning my mind to the most important thing about our dealings with that fucker. "I can kidnap Yuri and make him tell us all about it."

"I like it," Church announced while Danny nodded thoughtfully. "You can show him the old English torture treatment. Tie him to the rack then he'll sing like he's starring in a West End show, and Bob's your uncle, Fanny's your aunt, we have ourselves the information."

I fought back a laugh at Church's wild imagination and nodded stiffly instead. "I can grab him on route here. Then you just say he never showed up."

"And what is The Czar going to think happened to him?" Danny asked. "Yuri has been his right hand man for years. He won't just ignore his disappearance."

"Interpol," Church supplied with a grin. "He will definitely believe it if we make it look like Interpol."

Danny thought on that for a few moments, his hand shifting back down within Anya's shirt and moving to her thigh instead.

"I like it too," he said finally.

"I want to help Frank do it," Anya announced and I frowned at her.

"No," I said simply.

I knew how to make a man talk, how to make him scream and beg for death, and I would have to do all of those things to ensure this went to plan. It wasn't pretty. And she didn't need to see a single piece of it.

"Yes," she replied instantly, turning her head to look at Danny who still hadn't voiced his opinion on this. "You said you wouldn't deny me anything," she said to him in a low tone. "You promised I wouldn't be caged here, kept from the brutal reality of our world. Or is your word as deceitful as I first assumed?"

"You're a wicked wife," Danny groaned, moving his hand beneath her shirt once more and making her gasp as he sought out her core. "A wicked, wicked wife." He huffed a sigh as Anya's spine arched and a soft whimper escaped her which made me want to drop to my knees and look beneath the table at exactly what he was doing to her.

"So is that a yes?" she demanded, her chest heaving as Church licked his lips and shifted closer to the two of them, none of them seeming to have even remembered I was here, or maybe they just didn't give a fuck that I was.

"Yes," Danny ground out, his gaze snapping up to meet mine. "So you'd better take damn good care of her, arsehole."

"I will," I replied, too fixed on the sight of her writhing in his lap as he fucked her with his hand right in front of me to put up any further argument.

Church dropped his mouth to Anya's neck on her other side and I took that as my cue to leave.

I shoved my chair back and got to my feet, but before I could turn from them, my gaze locked with hers, the darkness within them seeming to beg me to come closer, to join in their depravity. And for the briefest of moments, I almost wondered what would happen if I did.

But as I looked at their hands on her body and a potent mixture of jealousy and frustration coiled together in my blood, I came up with a far better idea than that.

Tonight, I would have Anya all to myself while I worked. I had a man to torture and blood to spill, but after that task was complete, I was beginning to think up ways I might torture her too. And if the way she was looking at me was anything to go by, then she was hoping for the exact same thing.

So as I turned and strode from the warehouse to go get everything in place for tonight's plans and the sounds of her pleasure followed me from the room, I couldn't help the way my pulse raced for her. Nor could I deny that I was once again going to be crossing a line which I really, really shouldn't.

"So what's the plan?" Anya asked, practically bouncing in her seat beside me as we sat in the dark in my van, waiting for our prey to arrive. You'd have thought we were on our way to a Led Zeppelin gig by the way her eyes sparkled with excitement, not to ruthlessly torture a man. She was a fucking enigma, and I had the feeling my mind was going to be puzzled by her for a long time yet.

John Boy had text me just three minutes ago saying he was headed this way and my grip on the steering wheel tightened as I kept my focus fixed on the road.

"Are we gonna drive him off the road, get out of the car then smash his window in while he's still recovering from the shock and drag him out by the scruff of his neck while he curses you out and-"

"Sometimes, I forget how American you are," I muttered, shaking my head.

"What does my idea have to do with being American? Besides, I thought you hated me for being Russian, so make your mind up."

I cut her a look. "I don't hate you for being Russian, I hate you for being a Volkov," I said, though the words sounded like a lie even to me, so I doubted she was buying it.

My phone pinged and I looked down at it, finding another message from John Boy confirming Yuri was turning onto the road ahead of us and I quickly shot a message to Two Bit Bob, telling him to go ahead.

I turned my head to the left, spotting the roadworks vehicle Two Bit Bob had taken for a joyride pulling out onto the street, orange lights flashing and several lower ranking gang members jumping from the back of it with traffic cones and road closed signs.

Yuri's dark SUV turned onto the road not a moment after they'd finished setting up the closure and I leaned over to Anya, tugging the riot helmet down onto her head and snapping the visor over her face before doing the same with my own.

Between the darkness and the shadows, there would be no recognising us until it was far too late, and with our black trousers and jackets heavily emblazoned with the word Interpol, anyone who saw us snatching the fucker would have a clear story to tell.

I got out of the van and strode onto the street just as Yuri was forced to bring the car to a halt at the road closure.

Anya's door shut behind me and I felt her drawing near to me as I broke into a jog, hugging the shadows and drawing my gun before stepping out suddenly beside Yuri's window.

"Hands on the wheel," I barked as I tapped my gun against the glass to announce myself.

To Yuri's credit, he didn't even flinch, just turned a sneer my way as he was forced to do as I'd instructed.

Anya pushed up against me, her own gun in hand as she reached out to open the door. I moved aside only enough to allow the door to open, keeping my aim steady and my focus clear while Yuri scowled at us.

"Fucking Interpol," he snarled, spitting at my feet as I grabbed a handful of his jacket and wrenched him out of the car before forcing him down arse up over the bonnet.

"Hands behind your back," I commanded, my gun pressing into the base of his skull as he was forced to do as I said. "Secure him, Cash."

Anya took the looped cable ties from my pocket and made quick work of snapping them closed around his wrists, making him curse as she tightened them sharply.

"Now the bag."

She pushed her fingers into my back pocket, pinching my fucking arse before she tugged the black linen bag free of it and obediently forced it over Yuri's head.

"You're looking for trouble tonight, Cash," I warned her as I yanked Yuri to his feet and slammed him against the side of the car.

Anya shrugged, keeping her voice hidden from our captive or any nosey fuckers who might have been listening from a darkened corner somewhere.

She moved around to open the boot of the car just as John Boy pulled up in a black ford which sure as fuck didn't belong to him, a cap pulled down low over his face.

A girl screamed in alarm as Anya opened the boot and I shifted to get a look at the terrified creature who this fucker had been sending to Danny as a gift. I had to admit that I was surprised by how quick my boss had been to decline. The Danny Butcher I knew would have been only too keen to have his fun with a new victim. Then again, ever since Anya had blasted her way into all of our lives, he'd been different. Maybe he really was all in with her. I couldn't say I'd blame him for the choice.

"There's a women's shelter a couple streets over from The Duck and Dog, you know it?" I asked John Boy as he raised his brows at the dishevelled, terrified looking girl, swiping a hand over his forgettable face.

"Yeah, I know it."

"Drop her off, make sure there's someone there to help her then ditch the car and lay low for a week or two."

"Got it." John Boy moved forward, talking in a low voice to the clearly terrified girl and I yanked Yuri into motion as I turned away from them and made him walk towards my van.

Anya strode ahead of us, opening the back of the van for me and I forced Yuri into it while he started up a stream of Russian which I had to assume was insulting. There was fuck all in the van aside from him so I didn't bother to do any more to secure him, slamming the door closed as he fell to the floor before catching hold of Anya's waist and guiding her back around to the cab.

She let me lift her in and I pushed her visor up, gazing into her dark eyes as I reached around her and yanked her seatbelt tight.

She sucked in a sharp breath and I smirked to myself, turning away and rounding the van to the driver's side before starting it up and pulling away.

Yuri's car was gone along with the fake road workers, John Boy and the girl who had been intended as a fucking gift. There was no sign at all of what had happened or what we'd done. Beautifully done, that.

"Who was that guy who took the girl?" Anya asked in confusion.

"That was John Boy," I said.

"Oh shit, seriously? How do I keep forgetting what he looks like?"

"Cause he's like a fucking stick insect among sticks, Cash. Fucking gift that."

I turned away from the city centre, heading east and staying silent as I took us through the heavily populated streets before turning off and driving us down a ramp that led into an underground parking lot.

I followed the curving ramp all the way down to the bottom floor then drove up to a garage door to the far right of a long row of them.

Anya looked around as I hit the button on my key fob and we waited for the door to open for us.

A short passage, big enough for the van to fit through led into a wider space beyond the door and I parked up at the edge of it, getting out while the door rattled closed behind us and rounding the van before tugging a thick, sound-muffling curtain into place before it.

Down here was where I took the people who had wronged The Firm. Down here, no man ever came out alive. Down here, no one could hear them scream.

Anya appeared at my side, a wild look in her dark eyes as she watched me open the door and drag Yuri out.

He kicked and fought a bit, but with the bag over his head and his hands tied, I was easily able to force him into submission.

I dragged him across the room while Anya followed along at a slower pace, her attention caught by the tools I kept down here as she moved along the walls curiously.

I yanked Yuri's tied hands up over his head and forced a metal hook through the bindings, hitting a button on the wall which retracted the chain attached to it until he was hoisted off of his feet, just high enough to make sure he was suspended there like that. Then he wriggled and bucked like a shark hauled outa the sea by its tail.

"What the fuck is this?" Yuri roared through the confines of the bag covering his head.

"We've got a few questions for you, Yuri," I said in a calm tone, moving to take a roll of knuckle wrap from the closest shelf and slowly binding my fists with it.

"I want my lawyer," he hissed like he was still clinging onto the hope that I was from Interpol.

Anya shifted to my side, glancing at me for permission as she reached for his hood and I nodded, letting her tug it from his head.

Yuri blinked at us in surprise, his gaze falling on her and widening before shifting to me. With a furious yell, he began to scream at the two of us in Russian, the tone of his words enough to let me know that he wasn't exactly offering up useful information.

"We wanna know about the thing The Czar gave the Candlestick Maker to look after," I said loudly, over his yells.

"Fuck you," he spat.

"I had a feeling you mighta been reluctant to talk," I replied, nudging Anya back before I laid into him with my fists.

Yuri coughed and thrashed as I struck him with brutal punches, the sound of his ribs cracking and flesh bruising filling the air as I used him like my own personal punch bag.

By the time I finally let up on him, sweat was rolling down my spine within my shirt and my blood was pumping ferociously.

"Tell us what we want to know," Anya said sweetly before switching to Russian, presumably repeating the same question.

Yuri blinked down at her as she casually twisted a knife between her fingers. For a moment I thought he was going to say something to her which would earn him another beating from me, but instead of that he jerked violently where he hung.

A frown bit into my brow as he jerked again and again, the convulsions rattling his body as he began to thrash like a fish on a fucking line and I cursed as I smacked the button to lower the chain and drop him to the ground.

Yuri crumpled as he hit the stone floor and I rolled him out, tugging his hands free of the chain and laying him flat on his back so that I could check for a pulse as he continued to convulse beneath me.

"What's happening?" Anya asked in shock and I cursed as I shoved to my feet and ran to the other side of the room.

"He must have a weak heart," I ground out, as I grabbed a shot of adrenaline from the box we kept there and hurried back to the bastard on the floor.

"What's that?" Anya asked, her eyes widening at the sight of the large needle as I clamped the syringe between my teeth and ripped Yuri's shirt open.

"Adrenaline," I supplied. "This'll make his heart beat right again."

I didn't give her any further explanation before finding a vein on Yuri's arm and shoving the needle into it, depressing the plunger to wake him the fuck up.

Yuri jerked more violently as the adrenaline worked its way into his body but within another few moments, it was clear that the seizures were only growing worse. His neck twisted at an unnatural looking angle and froth began to spill from his lips.

"What the fuck?" I growled as Anya's hand locked on my shoulder and she tugged to make me back up.

I gave in to her request, regaining my feet and retreating as the two of us watched the motherfucker spasm until all of a sudden, he fell still, his unseeing eyes staring blankly at the far wall.

"Cyanide," Anya breathed in realisation and a roar of frustration left me as all of my pent-up energy and thirst for violence was left with no fucking outlet. Not to mention the fact that the arsehole hadn't given us a goddamn thing before he up and killed himself.

"Who the fuck goes around with hidden cyanide capsules in their mouths?" I demanded angrily while Anya shrugged.

"Insane billionaires and their employees who are convinced that Interpol are after them?" she suggested dryly and I whirled on her angrily for the snarky fucking comment.

"Well now this whole thing has been for nothing," I snarled, taking my phone from my back pocket and shooting a text to Dylan to tell him I needed a fucking Baker.

I stiffened as Anya's hand fell on my arm, looking up at her through the haze of anger which had fallen over me and damn near baring my teeth at her.

"You need an outlet for that feeling," she murmured, biting down on her bottom lip in the most seductive fucking way.

I hesitated for a moment and I realised what she was suggesting, my heart thrashing impossibly harder as I turned towards her fully, reaching out and slowly wrapping my hand around her throat.

Anya held her ground, her chin rising to give me more access as I moved in closer, my body dwarfing hers.

"What is it with you and danger?" I asked her in a low tone.

"It wakes me up," she replied on a breath and the honesty in her onyx eyes had me nodding my agreement to this insanity once more. But I'd already crossed this fucking line and we both knew that her family owed me my pound of flesh.

"Take everything off apart from your underwear," I said firmly, giving her a little shove backwards so that she took a step away from me as I released her throat.

I turned around and grabbed Yuri's ankles, hauling him away from the wall towards the exit and dropping him again once he was out of the way. Then I strode over to the van and turned the ignition on, connecting my phone to it and playing Dogs of War by Blues Saraceno over the speakers, drawing a sharp inhale from my girl as she pulled off the fake Interpol jacket.

I shrugged out of my own jacket, tugging my shirt over my head for good measure so that she could see my scars, so that she could be absolutely certain of why I was doing this to her.

I strode back across the room, watching Anya as she shimmied out of her trousers and kicked them aside along with her boots before turning back to me just as she tugged her t-shirt off too.

She wore a pair of little black knickers but her tits were gloriously free beneath her shirt, leaving me with a view of her tight nipples and the goosebumps lining her tanned skin.

I took a coil of rope from the shelf beside me and advanced on her, the corner of my lips twitching as she obediently offered up her wrists for me to bind.

I took more care tying the knots than I ever had with any of the people I'd held at my mercy down here before, and I could practically feel her anticipation filling the air as she allowed me to restrain her, putting her life in my hands despite knowing I had all the reason in the world to want her dead.

My fingers trailed down her sides, making a breath flutter past her lips as I reached her waist and began to walk her backwards.

Anya raised her hands for the hook as we reached the wall and I linked it through the rope before hitting the button to suspend her from the floor, her bare toes curling as she was lifted just high enough to be on eye level with me.

"Look at you," I purred, my fingers brushing her navel and making her shiver as I slowly drew a line up the centre of her body, between her tits and onto her neck before scoring the length of her lips with my thumb.

Her body reacted to mine in such a clear way, shivers dancing over her skin, her nipples tight and wanting, her thighs clenching together like she was having trouble holding her desire in.

I'd made an effort to draw a line between me and her, trying to maintain a distance, but with her strung up for me like that, it was impossible to deny that I'd already stepped far over it.

I forced myself to draw back, moving to the closest shelf and taking a pair of little bulldog clips from it, holding them up for her to see and watching her pupils dilate as she remembered the last time I'd used one of these beasties on her flesh.

I closed in on her, my eyes on her hard nipples and my intention clear as she fought to stay still where she hung from the wall.

"Make it hurt, Frank," she breathed, licking her lips as I stood in front of her and the desire to lick them too damn near consumed me.

I'd been hungering for a kiss from that smart mouth of hers for far too fucking long at this point. I needed a taste of her. A real fucking taste. And if I wasn't careful, I knew I was in danger of stealing one tonight.

I dropped my mouth to her breast, my tongue painting a line around the curve of her full flesh and a soft moan escaped her as I ran my fingers up and down her side. I placed a kiss to her skin, licking her again, my mouth inching closer to her nipple with every move but never quite making it there as she began to pant and arch against the wall where I'd tied her.

"Please," she gasped as I skimmed the very edge of that pert flesh, my tongue almost tasting it before I shifted back and snapped the bulldog clip down on it instead.

Anya cried out, her bare feet pressing to the wall as she bent her knees and arched against the cold bricks, the pain taking her off guard, though from the sounds she was making, I could tell she liked it all the same.

I looked into her eyes as I trailed the other clip up her body and over her right nipple, her lips parting in anticipation before I let that one tighten over the bud of her flesh too.

"Fuck," Anya gasped, her back bowing once more as I stepped away and picked up an electrical wire which was attached to a battery, turning the voltage down to its lowest setting as I switched it on and closed in on her again.

The scarred flesh on my back seemed to tingle with the memories of being held at her brother's mercy and my heart thrashed with the need to pay him back for his violence. The mere thought of him knowing what I was doing to his sister had a dark smile tugging at my lips.

But as I closed in on Anya once more and her bright gaze met mine, all thoughts of vengeance and her psychotic family fell away.

Her platinum hair was tied up in a bun to hide it while she'd been impersonating an Interpol officer, but a few loose tendrils had escaped to caress her neck. I moved closer to brush a lock of it back, my hand cupping her jaw and lifting her eyes to mine just as I brushed the cable along her thigh.

Anya cried out as the shock rolled through her body, my palm tingling with it where I maintained the contact with her as I watched every beautiful second of her pain reflected back to me in her dark eyes.

My cock was solid and aching in my trousers, my need for her rising with every passing moment.

I brushed the wire over her flesh again but this time as her spine arched, her pelvis pressed to mine and the friction mixed with the current of electricity made my cock jerk with need.

I stepped back suddenly, needing to put some distance between us as I tossed the wire aside and took a riding crop from the shelf instead.

"Do it," Anya begged as she eyed the whip and I couldn't deny that want in her as I swung the whip and let it crack against her thigh.

Anya cried out, a mixture of pleasure and pain in her voice and I instantly struck her again, keeping the cracks of the whip just firm enough for her to feel that spike of pain without risking causing her any real harm.

And as I watched her pant and writhe before me with my cock throbbing desperately and my heart thundering with want, I knew I didn't really want to hurt her at all.

She wasn't responsible for my suffering. But she might just have been responsible for my salvation.

Anya's feet pressed back to the wall as I struck her the fifth time, her thighs parting and letting me see how wet her knickers were and suddenly I was tossing the whip aside, striding forward and wrapping my hands around the soft material of those little knickers as I dragged them off of her.

I released my cock in the next move, my gaze meeting hers as I stroked it, drinking in the fucking sight of her and watching her pant for me.

"Look at what you do to me," I growled. "You were supposed to be the answer to my vengeance."

"And I'm not?" she asked, her chest heaving, those clips on her nipples still in place and looking so fucking hot I could barely look at anything else.

"No," I growled pumping my cock more firmly as my head spun with want for her. "You're my temptation, Anya Butcher. Sent to torture me ever more."

"It's only torture while you deny yourself," she said, her eyes on my dick as she wetted her lips like she was hungry for it. "While you deny *me*," she added.

I swallowed thickly, watching her closely while I fought against the need I felt to give in, to take her, claim her, make her scream my fucking name.

But Anya had clearly decided that she was done letting me call all of the shots. She braced one foot against the wall behind her then hooked her other foot around my back, tugging me closer, her wanting eyes on my dick as I stroked it for her.

"Give in," she begged and the sound of her begging for me had me seriously turned on. The moment she'd done it, our fate was fucking sealed.

I released my cock and took hold of her thighs instead, lifting her higher and pressing her back against the wall, my fingers digging into her skin as I met her eyes once more.

My dick slid through the wet heat of her core, a soft plea escaping her as she tried to rock her hips and draw it inside her.

My pulse was thundering in my ears far louder than the music which continued to play from the van speakers and with a crash of bass and a thundering crescendo in my chest, I gave in and thrust forward with an animalistic growl.

My cock plunged deep inside her slick pussy, every inch buried deep within her all at once as she cried out and tightened her thighs around my waist, begging for more.

I didn't hold back, these months of pent up need and frustration, of fucking my hand and thinking of her, of watching her with Danny and Church and needing to make her mine all culminating with this primal, savage pairing as I fucked her into the cold wall of my torture chamber and watched her fall apart for me with every thrust of my hips.

My hips pistoned into hers, my hands digging into her arse as I dropped my mouth to her neck and started to kiss my way down her body while she arched her spine to give me access.

My mouth made it to the bulldog clip on her left nipple and I clasped it between my teeth, loving the way she whimpered for me just before I yanked it off.

Anya cried out as I spat the clip aside and I sucked her throbbing nipple into my mouth a moment later, kissing away the hurt while her pussy clamped tight around my cock and she came for me with a cry of ecstasy.

I didn't slow down, fucking her even harder as I fought against my own need to come and I moved my mouth over to her other nipple, repeating the process and feeling her come for me again while nothing but a garbled stream of Russian spilled from her lips that time.

My dick was pulsing with the desperate need to finish but I jerked out of her before I could, hitting the button to lower the chain and lifting her into my arms as I unhooked the chain from the rope which bound her arms.

Anya shivered in my hold as I carried her to the van, pushing her face down over the bonnet and leaving her there as I moved to amp up the volume of the music, making sure she could feel it vibrating through her body where she lay.

Anya looked over her shoulder at me as I moved behind her again and I began to slide my cock back and forth through her wetness, coating her clit and angling her hips so that I was sure she would be grinding against the vibrating metal the moment I was inside her again.

"Kiss me, Frank," she panted, looking back at me where I stood over her and I frowned at the request, wanting to, needing to, yet somehow hesitant all the same.

I gave her my cock instead of my mouth, plunging into her drenched pussy once more and fucking her deep and hard, my hands splayed on the bonnet either side of her while she forgot about kissing me and was consumed with me fucking her.

Her pussy was so wet and hot, wrapped around me like a fucking dream and making it damn near impossible to hold off my release as I fought to get her there one last time before I gave in.

Anya pushed her arse back against me with every thrust, giving as good as she got while I fucked her with everything I had until she was coming again, her pussy locking around me and making a growl spill from my lips.

I yanked out of her, flipping her onto her back and coming all over her tits with a groan of pure ecstasy before dropping down over her and taking her lips at last.

She tasted just like the piece of heaven I'd known she would be.

Anya shivered in my arms as I kissed her, her mouth parting, tongue caressing, soul rising up and claiming a chunk of mine in that one simple meeting of our mouths. I kissed her like a man possessed, my hands sliding under her back so that I could draw her closer and taste more of her and I finally gave in to what I'd already known for far too long, but had been denying with a vehemence to myself.

Because I was captured by this creature in my arms. I was owned by her and leashed by her and made undone in her embrace. And now that I'd given in to the temptation of her once, I knew there was no way that I was going to be able to hold back with her ever again.

CHAPTER THIRTY FOUR

"Frank Broderick Smith!" A voice cut through the music still buzzing through every inch of my skin. I wasn't sure if it was still coming from the speakers in the van or if it lived within my bones, but when it cut out abruptly, I had to accept it was probably the van.

Dylan appeared around the side of it in an off the shoulder glittery top and high waisted jeans, paired with knee high leather boots.

Frank clutched me harder against his chest, the cum he'd left on my skin rubbing onto him too and Dylan rolled his eyes dramatically.

"What the fuck are you doing just letting yourself in here?" Frank snarled as he untied my hands, tossing the rope away and caressing the sensitive skin with his thumbs.

"You're the one who messaged for a clean up. Presumably you forgot that while you were…busy sowing your wild oats," Dylan snarked back, arching an eyebrow at us while Frank glared at him. "Oh, don't you dare shoot me those wicked thoughts, you absolutely imbecilic muscle man." He threw his head back, rolling it as he pressed his fingers to his temples like he was having a moment then straightened and clapped at someone I couldn't see.

A host of women came into view with cleaning products in their arms, all six of them looking to us in surprise.

"Clean them up, girls," he commanded and the women descended on us, tugging us apart and setting to work scrubbing us down with cloths and potent smelling products.

"I came here to clean a crime scene, not to be an extra on the set of a low budget porno," Dylan huffed, pinching the bridge of his nose and taking in several long breaths.

When he'd regained his composure, he shut his eyes and did a seriously good pirouette with his leg extended to one side then he strode towards me, knocking away two women who were finishing their work on me by shoving their heads aside and stepping between them.

"Alright, let's get our story straight, Anya." He gripped my chin, examining my neck then looking down at my nipples which were still reddened from the bulldog clips. He tutted, rolling his neck again then dropping his head, speaking so close to my face that all I could see was his bright eyes and the blue sparkly mascara he was wearing on the tips of his lashes. "We're all going to die if you don't sell the story, honey. So how about this-" He whirled away from me, spreading his hands before him dramatically like he could see a vision hanging in front of his eyes. "There was a lot of blood. The torturing took a long time." He looked over at the dead body which was barely marked thanks to the fact that Yuri had killed himself with cyanide. "Things got messy. Then I ordered you to take your clothes off and bagged them up." He grabbed our clothes, snapping his fingers at the women who forced Frank fully out of his pants, leaving him standing there cupping his junk in his hands with a scowl on his face as they started to scrub his legs down.

"It was a blood bath." Dylan slashed his hand left and right as if he had a knife in it. "The clean-up took hours." Some of the women bagged up our clothes, throwing it in the back of Frank's van. "Anya's nips nearly got frostbite." Dylan twisted towards me, pointing an accusing finger at my nipples.

"Look I…don't want to lie," I admitted, glancing at Frank whose jaw tightened.

Dylan came at me fast, holding my cheeks with both of his hands as he shook his head several times. "But you must, honey. Danny will kill us. All of us. Do you know what he does to people who betray him?" He leaned in closer as I shook my head. "He rips their tongues out and slices their bellies open. He watches them bleed as they try to beg, but all they can do is choke on their own blood. I've baked for him too many times. I've seen what he can do. You have no idea, you really don't."

"We have an understanding," I said in refusal. "He wouldn't do that. He said he won't deny me anything."

Dylan's throat bobbed and his eyes blazed. "Anya, I've known Danny Butcher since he was just a teenager butchering animals for fun."

My lips parted, disgust and refusal colliding inside me. That wasn't the man I knew. That wasn't Danny.

"He wouldn't," I rasped, yanking my head from his grip and looking to Frank, his brows descending as I saw the truth in his eyes about that. "He's changed," I growled, and I hated myself, because I sounded like some stupid woman, defending my monstrous husband because he'd convinced me to believe he wasn't what everyone else thought of him.

"Honey," Dylan sighed, looking like he really did care about his words hurting me. "Danny will pick and choose what he deems to be okay. Maybe he's let you think you can do what you like as a test. To see what you really will do. You may have gotten away with things up until now, but that's the game, that's when you're at your most vulnerable. He will snap-" He clicked his fingers before my eyes "-and you will rue the day you ever thought he had an ounce of good in him. You'll see the darkness, and you'll never be able to unsee it." He shuddered, some horrors entering his eyes which I knew my husband had placed there.

Dylan released me and I stepped back, shaking my head, still wanting to refuse what he was saying but Frank gave me a firm look. "What he's offered you and Church, he'll never offer me, Cash. I'm sorry…I should have stopped. I shouldn't have-"

"Don't you dare, Frank," I growled. "This is on me as much as it's on you."

The women moved to give us spare clothes and I wordlessly pulled on the plain cotton panties with a pair of jeans and a warm black sweater. When I slipped on some sneakers, I looked over at Frank who was dressed similarly to me and I saw the regret in his eyes rising up like a storm.

Dylan hugged me tight, crushing me into his chest. "Don't worry, honey. Your secret is safe with me. We won't breathe a word." He turned to the girls who worked for him. "Did anyone here see Frank Smith dicking Danny's wife?"

They all shook their heads and Dylan looked back to me with a bright smile, though fear was still simmering in his gaze. "See? No harm done. You and Frank head out, go to Edgar Street and wait for Mickey Hairpiece to pick you up, alright?"

"Alright," I agreed and he ushered us away.

Frank moved to my side, staying close but not touching me as we strode out through the exit and clung to the shadows as he led the way to Edgar Street. We had to walk up the winding ramps which led the way back up out of the underground parking lot, but we were soon out in the night air where the thick clouds above veiled the moon.

I kept glancing at Frank, expecting him to look at me, to say something, but he just remained resolutely silent as my chest constricted.

"Do you regret it?" I whispered.

Nothing.

"Frank?" I pushed.

Silence. And maybe my answer lived within that silence, maybe it was as plain as day and I was just a stray mutt begging for scraps I wasn't going to get. Of course he regretted it. His life was on the line if this got out, but I still had to believe that Danny would understand, that he would act as he'd acted when he'd found out about Church.

"I really think he'd be okay with it," I said eventually and Frank launched towards me, shoving me back against a dark wall beside a dumpster and caging me in with his arms.

"Dylan's right, Anya. You don't know him. You wanna think he's got a good heart, that he's not so bad, that maybe your pussy has saved him like it's blessed by the Holy Mother Mary, huh? Well you're fucking deluded. Danny Butcher is the most terrible man I have ever known, there is no crime he won't commit. Do you understand what I'm sayin'? Every rumour you've ever heard about him is true. He might be acting like he's drunk on you, but it'll pass. There's only one vice that Danny will ever be loyal to and that's coke. If the choice was you or it, he'd pick blow every time."

"Fuck you. You don't know anything." I shoved my hands against his chest, but he pressed his weight against me.

"I'm not saying it to hurt you," he said, his voice lowering. "I'm trying to protect you."

"I don't need protecting," I growled. "He's my husband, I know how to handle him. I know who he is. He may have been a monster once, but he's different now."

"Men are defined by their acts. So maybe you should be asking me to tell you what he's done, all the things I know, all the things I've seen, and then you can tell me if you care that he's changed. Because even if he has, it wouldn't matter. Your toes would curl and your skin would crawl knowing what his hands have done."

"Stop," I rasped, pressing my palms to his chest, wanting to run, to find my music and hide away from the thoughts burrowing into my skull. "I don't want to hear it."

"That's the problem, Cash," he sighed, trailing his thumb up my jaw. "But this monster isn't one you can run from. He lies in your bed at night and one day he will crack and you'll see him do something you can't forget."

"He isn't who you say he is," I insisted, knowing I sounded completely insane, but some part of me was entirely convinced by this. That somehow, I knew Danny's soul, I saw the good in him and it didn't match up with anything Frank or Dylan said about him. But logically, I knew I must be in denial, because Danny Butcher's reputation was enough to prove he was evil through and through.

Frank pushed away from the wall, jerking his head in an order for me to follow and I trailed after him, the cold wind seeming to find its way into my chest and turn my heart to ice.

We found a black cab waiting for us on Edgar Street and Mickey nodded to us as we got in the car, adjusting the hairpiece on his obviously bald head before taking off down the road.

I shut my eyes and tried to play a song within my mind, needing the embrace of my music. It had been far too long since I'd had a full session with my bands, and I'd been so damn excited that I hadn't needed it lately. Every waking moment in this life seemed so full, so vibrant, and the music had become more of a bonus than a necessity. But now I was sinking again, losing my grip on that slice of heaven I'd been riding on in the real world and descending fast back into the bottomless void inside me.

I felt my brow pinching, my concentration breaking time and again as I tried to summon music into existence, but it evaded me, like it was betrayed by how few times I'd come to it recently.

I need you. Please come back.

But the only song that came in answer was The Killing Moon by Echo & the Bunnymen and a whimper of fear coiled in my throat as I heard my mother's screams echoing beyond it. I felt the grip of Zakhar's hand on mine and I felt the life leaving the room as my father stole away the woman who'd brought me into this world.

Frank's hand suddenly closed around mine and I was jolted out of the dark, looking to him in the gloom in the back of the cab, his eyes burning like a candle in the night. He said nothing, but his gaze said everything. *I'm here. It's alright.*

I slowly pulled my hand from his, not wanting Mickey to notice but the touch had awakened me again, keeping me in the present moment rather than the terrors of my past.

"Oh hey," Mickey said, pointing out to the street. "It's the boss man!"

My heart pushed up into my throat as my gaze found Danny on the sidewalk as he stepped out of The Duck and Dog. The pub was still closed and taped off from the police investigation into the bloody brawl which had taken place there, but my husband apparently didn't give a damn.

"Better pull over," Frank grunted and Mickey stopped beside Danny as Frank dropped the window to look out at him.

I tried to calm my thrashing heart, telling myself that Dylan and Frank were wrong, convincing myself of it. Because Danny had told me straight and I'd seen the truth in his eyes. He wanted me to be happy, he wanted my desires fulfilled.

"I thought you were going to The Duck and Dive tonight with Church?" Frank called and Danny looked around in surprise as he spotted us. Church had told me all about the chain of pubs the Butcher gang owned across London to run money through, all of them called The Duck and something. There was even a Duck and Dick in Cheapside.

"Oh yeah, well, I had a headache so I figured I'd come down here and see the lay of the land on this place." He gestured to the pub and Frank nodded.

"You want a lift back then?" he asked and Danny's brows arched before he nodded and jogged over to the cab, opening the back door and sliding in between us.

"Hello, love," he growled, leaning in to kiss my cheek, his hand dropping onto my thigh and squeezing. His fingers seemed twitchy and his breaths came a little unevenly like he'd been running.

Mickey took off down the road and I sat crushed between the two of them, my heart pounding and palms slick, that feeling of purpose and belonging I was started to get used to when I was with Danny absent in the presence of this secret.

My skin still felt like it was wrung out from the pleasure Frank had delivered to it and despite the thorough cleaning job Dylan had executed on the two of us, I swear I could still smell the sex on us, and I was certain Danny would notice it at any moment.

But he didn't say a word, his gaze fixed on the view beyond the window, his knee bobbing up and down alongside mine like he was anxious about something, and I had to thank fortune for whatever had him distracted as it bought me some extra time to try and compose myself.

Frank remained rigid and silent on my other side which wasn't unusual for him, but there was something in the hard lines of his body where it was pressed against mine which felt like a solid wall intended to block me out.

I tried not to let that sting, to ignore the twist in my gut which made the idea of this lie feel a whole lot like rejection. Like Frank was happy to keep the truth between us because he'd gotten what he wanted already. He'd had me and now he didn't want the drama involved with trying to keep any part of me because the appeal had faded with the taking of what he'd wanted.

I chewed on my bottom lip and kept my attention fixed on my lap as we wound through the streets, choosing silence over the alternative of trying to break it.

It wasn't long before we made it back home, my pulse skipping all over the place as I considered telling Danny what had happened. I really didn't want to lie to him, but I didn't want to put Frank in danger either, even if I didn't believe my husband would hurt him. It wasn't my decision to make for him, so I kept my lips sealed as I stepped out of the cab.

Danny looked at me as we stood before the warehouse, a sharp accusation in his eyes which made my breath catch before it seemed to disappear just as quickly as it had come. He slid his arm around me and drew me closer, making a shiver of unease run down my spine as the secret I was keeping seemed to burn along my skin, screaming for him to notice it.

"I left Church with the keys," he said abruptly, holding his hand out to Frank in a demand for his as he moved to follow us out of the cab, and Frank obediently pulled his set from his pocket, tossing them to him.

"Do you want me here tonight?" Frank asked, his eyes never once moving to me, and I tried to ignore the tightness that left in my chest as Danny's fingers dug into my hip possessively and he considered that question.

"Nah. Fuck off, Frank," Danny snapped, his fingers twitching against my skin and making me wonder what had him so worked up. "I want my wife alone tonight."

Frank gave me an intent look before sliding back into the cab and tugging the door shut behind him. Mickey drove away down the road and my chest knotted with tension as Frank left, instantly missing him and wishing things didn't have to be this way.

I looked up at Danny, finding him running his tongue over his teeth and flexing his jaw.

"Are you alright?" I asked and he glanced down at me, his eyes full of shadows tonight. Had something happened?

"Yeah." He licked his lips, his eyes trailing all over my face. "Did you and Frank have fun?"

There was an edge to his tone and my throat tightened as he led me inside, the thought that he'd somehow figured out what had happened flickering through my head.

"Well, if you can call torturing a man fun. Frank made him hurt for a while but then he killed himself with cyanide before he breathed a word of what we wanted. He must have had it in a fake tooth in his mouth."

"I see," Danny said thoughtfully, kicking the door shut behind us and locking it for good measure before walking away from me across the lounge. He tossed his keys aside and moved to a cupboard by the television, opening it and reaching into a compartment hidden in the back of it, taking out a gun and a large knife.

I frowned at him, watching as he rummaged deeper in it before cursing and heading across the room with the weapons, laying them on the coffee table. He took a bag from the coat rack and began filling it with weapons he found from compartments all around the place.

"Um, what are you doing?" I asked in confusion.

"Business, sweetheart," he said dismissively.

"I thought I was part of the business now," I said in irritation and he glanced at me, his eyebrows arching.

"Oh yeah? Well not this sort of business," he added, scratching a little too hard at his neck for a second before continuing to fill his bag. I didn't know what was up with him tonight, but I found myself unable to summon a fuck to give. I had my own shit to deal with and if he was in the mood to be a prick then I was gonna leave him to that.

"I'm gonna shower and go to bed," I told him, not bothering to hide my annoyance with his attitude as I strode to the stairs and marched up them, leaving Danny to his weapons hunt.

I slipped into the bathroom, stripping off, wanting to get the chemical smell off of my skin. I tied my hair up in a knot, tossing my clothes into the hamper before I stepped into the shower and switched it on. The heated water rushed over me and I soaked it in before lathering up some body wash in my hands and scrubbing it everywhere.

My thoughts lingered on the memory of Frank's hands on my body, his mouth, his cock, every intense and unforgettable moment, right up until that kiss which had said so much more than he had ever put into words. He'd been trying to act like it was nothing since the moment Dylan had caught us together, but there was no way that had been nothing. That was a whole lot of everything if ever I felt it, and he could try and deny it all he liked, but there was never going to be a way back from this for us. Which meant I needed to convince him to tell Danny and Church.

I didn't know what kind of crazy mess I was getting myself into with these dangerous men, but I did know that there was no escape for me now.

Even if I ran, they'd each remain as the keepers of a piece of me they'd stolen one by one. And the funny thing was, I didn't even think I wanted to run anymore.

After a while, I felt eyes on me and I turned, spotting Danny standing in the doorway with the door half cracked open as he stared at me, taking in every inch of my body. I slowed my movements, caressing my flesh with soapy hands, waiting for that fire to ignite in his eyes which always made me burn too.

"You can join me if you tell me what business you're up to," I offered as steam billowed between us and he cocked his head to one side. My skin prickled at the way he was looking at me and goosebumps peppered my skin despite the heat of the water.

"Come to the bedroom when you're done." He turned, walking away and sinking back into the shadows as he headed down the hall.

I offered him my middle finger a little too late, gritting my teeth as I finished washing and stepped out of the shower, grabbing a towel. Once I was dry, I wrapped it tight around my body and walked to Danny's bedroom, knocking the door open and finding him sitting on the end of the bed with his fingers flexing and the room in complete darkness.

I moved to switch the light on but he snapped, "Leave it off," and a tremor tracked down my spine.

I stilled, not moving any further into the room, trying not to let my mind go haywire as I wondered if he somehow knew about Frank. But surely he would have said something by now?

"What's up with you?" I demanded, taking a step towards the exit, but he was suddenly on his feet, striding towards me and grabbing hold of my arm.

"Let's see then," he hissed, taking hold of the towel wrapped around me.

I gasped, trying to hold onto it but he tore it away from me and tossed it on the floor, his eyes falling down my body as his fingers dug deeper into my wrist to keep me there.

"You're hurting me," I growled as I tried to get my wrist free, but he didn't seem to be listening as he knocked my other arm away from my body and took in every scrap of my flesh. I didn't like the way he was looking at me, the way his gaze was curtained with something forbidding and cruel.

"Danny," I tried again. "Let go of me."

I tugged at my wrist again and his nails dug into my skin, making me growl a curse. I lost it, done with this bullshit. I threw my fist at his face, slamming it into his jaw and he stumbled back, still not letting go of me.

"Bitch," he spat, hurling me around and throwing me onto the bed face first.

I was so taken by surprise, that it took me a second to roll over onto my back and try to get up, and by the time I did, he was already there, shoving me down onto the bed beneath him, kneeling over me and latching his hands around my throat. He squeezed hard, shutting off my airway entirely and I clawed at his arms in fright, terrified of what the fuck was happening as he leered at me, his teeth bared and a madman in his eyes.

"You're nothing but his whore. You mean nothing to him," he spat as my heart pounded up into my throat. "Do you get that? He's my boy. *My* fucking boy."

He knew, oh god, he fucking knew about me and Frank and they'd been right, he wasn't okay, he wasn't going to just allow it like he had with Church. Dylan had warned me about him snapping, and now it was happening and it was too late to do anything about it.

I clawed frantically at his arms, bucking my hips and trying to unseat him from my body, but I wasn't strong enough to shift him.

My lungs burned and darkness pressed in on me as my gaze locked with his and I found myself face to face with the demon in him, a disgusted sneer drawing his upper lip back as he choked the life out of me and my struggles began to grow weaker.

Death crawled into my mind like it had always lived there, ready to come for me. There was no music, no strum of guitar strings or sweet cry of lyrics. It was silent and lonely and fucking terrifying. And I suddenly realised how desperately I wanted to stay in a life that wasn't numb, where my heart beat and warmth kissed my skin. Even when it was brutal and painful, it was still living. Church and Frank and even Danny had shown me that. But now my husband's true colours were unveiled and he was painting the blackest of fates for me.

Just as I started to pass out, he released me, his palm smacking hard against my face in the next second and making my ears ring so loud it was like a bell chiming in my head. Awareness sped through my skull once more as I drew in a desperate breath.

"You said I could have what I desired," I croaked, wondering if I could speak him down off of this ledge of violence he was on and save my life tonight, but the look in his eyes said it might be too late for that. "I didn't know he was off limits."

He gazed at me, a frown on his brow then he started laughing loudly, shaking his head at me. "I said that, did I? What a fuckin' idiot."

He raised his hips, leaning over to the nightstand and yanking the drawer open. While his weight was lifted from me, I scrambled up, trying to get out from under him and throwing my fist hard into his balls. He roared in anger as I escaped, half falling off the bed in my haste and running for the door as terror carved a line up my back.

"No, no, no, little whore!" he barked, the sound of his footfalls pounding after me as he followed.

I wasn't quick enough and his arm locked around my shoulders, dragging me back against him as I fought to throw an elbow into his gut. He pressed a blade to my throat, forcing me to freeze and touching it there as his breaths fell heavily against my ear.

"That's it, nice and still," he purred, dragging me backwards into his room as my pulse rioted in my ears.

"Danny, listen to me-" I tried.

"No, you listen to me," he cut me off. "You can't have him, Anya. You think I'd just let you take him from me?"

"Take him from you?" I panted, wanting to keep him talking as I waited for another opportunity to try and run, because I knew I was in the company of the beast Dylan had warned me about now. And I felt like a fucking idiot for ever thinking Danny could be a good husband, someone who truly adored me without any catches. That wasn't the life I was lucky enough to live. No, Danny Butcher was exactly who I'd first feared he was, all the sweetness vanishing from him like it had never been there at all.

"You know exactly what I mean," he snarled.

"I don't want to take anything. I like Frank. Tonight was the first time we fucked, I swear. It's the same with him as it is with Church," I said in a panic, praying I could get through to him.

There was a pause as he took those words in and for a moment I let hope find me as I let myself believe that he was listening, that he was trying to understand, but as the blade drove into my skin almost enough to make me bleed, that hope fled even faster than it had sparked.

"You little slut." He barked a laugh, but it was void of humour and full of nothing but darkness. "You've been playing with them all, spreading your thighs like a dirty little Russian whore. You don't even care about him, do you?" He ran the blade down to my chest, slashing it across my left breast and I cried out as pain flared and blood spilled.

"I care about all of you," I swore, meaning it with every fibre of my soul. "I don't understand it, but I swear I do, Danny, I do."

He lowered the blade, slicing it into my belly instead, slashing the skin open and making a scream tear from my throat at the shallow cut.

He threw me onto the bed on my back, rearing over me, anger and chaos in his dark eyes as he leaned down and held the knife to my pussy in a threat. "Here's my answer. One deep slice and this pussy won't cast any more spells, how about that, huh?"

"No," I gasped in terror, wriggling further up the bed to get away, shaking all over.

I reached for the lamp on the bedstand, hurling it at him and he narrowly missed it as he lurched aside.

He pointed the knife at me, my blood still wetting the edge. "You're just like the rest of them. Getting in his head, drawing him away from me, trying to keep him from me."

"I don't want to take anyone from you," I insisted, needing him to stop his attack while his words only made my head spin.

He grabbed my ankle, yanking me down the bed and slashing it towards my pussy. I got my other leg up, slamming my foot into his face and the blade missed, slicing into my thigh instead.

I groaned in agony, kicking again and striking his throat, making him growl and fall back onto his ass on the floor as he coughed.

I got up again, grabbing a half drunk glass of water from the nightstand and rushing at him, shrieking as I went to smash it on his head. He lunged at me before I could do it, tackling me to the floor and pinning me down with his body, the knife falling from his hand as he yanked on a handful of my hair and cracked my head down on the hardwood floor.

"Fuck you!" he shouted.

My thoughts scattered but I started throwing punches into his sides, fighting with all the fury of the Russian mafia, nothing but an untameable creature in that moment.

Danny growled, trying to pin me down more firmly, but my strikes kept landing, kept bruising until he reached over my head, producing the knife once more and pointing it at my temple.

"Hold still," he commanded, tonguing his teeth, his right eye twitching. "Just fucking hold still. You're making me dizzy."

My breaths came heavily and I felt the wet heat of my blood burning against the wounds he'd given me, shame pooling in my gut that I'd ever trusted him, that I'd really thought he had changed for me. I'd always been his plaything, just a toy he'd enjoyed fucking with and now I saw the truth of the game. Had he been laughing at me all this time, watching as I started to fall in love with him, knowing he was just offering me a lie?

Danny sat up on my hips, twitching again and rubbing his palm over his face. "Stop – just stop it," he spat.

"I'm not doing anything," I said breathlessly, eyeing the knife in his hand as he rubbed his eyes again.

My fingers itched for it, but as I lunged, he got up, standing and muttering under his breath. "I just need a hit. A little sniff, that's all. Then I can do this proper. You wait there. Just fucking wait there." He grabbed a black silk robe off the back of the door, yanking the belt out of it and kneeling down. I tried to get away, but he got hold of my wrist, tying it with one end of the belt before securing the other end to the radiator beside me on the wall.

Then he backed out of the room, slamming the door behind him and I lay there shaking for a few endless seconds as the sound of his footsteps carried downstairs.

I touched the wounds on my body with my free hand, trying to focus to figure out how much trouble I was in and concluding I'd be alright. They hadn't been deep enough to cut any arteries, the blood was thick but not continuous, and I knew that meant it wasn't life threatening no matter how painful they felt. But it was little comfort as I lay there cut open by a man who had sworn to love and protect me.

It wasn't the flesh wounds that hurt though, it was the deeper wound he'd inflicted. Because as much as I hadn't wanted to give my heart to him, he'd taken it all the same. And now my heart was sliced open, raw and unhealable, throbbing with all the agony of an arrow to my chest. From that bloody hole crawled a creature born of hate and malice, a hungry, insatiable thing that ached for vengeance. And I would feed it if it was the last act I ever committed on this earth.

CHAPTER THIRTY FIVE

I stumbled on my way down the fucking stairs, my hands shaking and sweat beading on my brow while I shivered.

It was a fucking curse. A curse I'd inflicted on myself and never wanted to stop treating.

I licked my cracked lips as I fought to keep my head straight, reminding myself of what I was doing and what I needed.

A hit. I needed a fucking hit and then I'd be able to think straight again. I could deal with my little Russian problem upstairs and get Benny back where he belonged, with me and only me. No fancy foreign tarts, no fuckin' friends, none of that shit.

Just me and him. The way it always shoulda been.

My hands were a fucking mess from rattling that damn cage door for so long, but it had paid off in the end. That pain had been worth it for that hinge ripping free of the brickwork. That was all I'd needed to set me free; one broken hinge. I'd climbed over that busted gate and scrambled up the stairs before taking the tunnel to The Duck and Dog and getting myself the fuck out of the jail my brother had built for me.

I had to think it was a test. Just a test to see how long it'd take me to get out. And here I was, back where I belonged, back on the outside. So I'd passed it. Passed with flying colours.

I just…I just…

I swiped a hand down my face before shaking my head, trying to figure out what the fuck I'd been thinking about while the need in me grew and grew like a starving beast.

I had to feed it.

Had to.

I stumbled just a little as I made it to the foot of the stairs and I looked around desperately, trying to think of somewhere I hadn't searched yet. All of my regular stashes were empty but Benny had been bringing it to me. It had to be here. Where the fuck was it though? I scowled around the dark building, unable to bear the thought of switching on the lights as I tried to force my brain to think before spotting the safe on the far side of the room. My heart leapt as I looked at it. That. There.

I headed over to it, my heart thrashing as I licked my cracked lips again and again, needing some fucking relief from the pain in them. Needing my damn hit.

I dropped the bloody knife in my grip and entered the number wrong the first time, my hands were shaking so bad, but the second time, the light flashed green and the safe unlocked.

A laugh tumbled from my chest. He hadn't changed it. Hadn't fucking changed it.

I yanked the door open, shoving Cash outa my way as I hunted for what I needed, panic finding me as I searched without luck, the thought of not having any making my head spin and a furious yell escape my lips.

But then it was there, brushing against my fingertips, calling my name with the sweetest fucking voice.

I grabbed the bag of cocaine outa the safe, knocking more cash to the floor haphazardly and burying the knife within it for a moment before I dug it free again. I scrambled over to the coffee table and dropped to my knees, my heart thrashing wildly as I fought to go as fast as I could.

I stabbed the bloody blade into the brick of coke, my fucking hands shaking so much that it spilled all over the damn place as I cut it open. I cursed as I shoved my fingers into it and started rubbing it over my gums, a groan escaping me at the relief of it before I scrambled back across the room and snatched a fifty pound note up from the money I'd knocked to the floor there.

I rolled it quickly and dropped to my knees once more, forming messy lines with the blow as I hurried to get my fix, snorting down several lines before drawing in a deep breath and falling back onto my arse as the world began to right itself around me at long last.

My thoughts snapped back together, my heart began to hammer to that violent tune I knew so well and I sucked in a deep breath which felt a whole lot like sanity as I fell into the embrace of my one and only friend.

I wasn't sure how long I let myself linger in that place of bliss, seconds or minutes, but it was all too short lived as the sound of a car pulling up outside forced my attention towards the front door.

I got to my feet as the sound of men laughing beyond it drew my attention, moving closer to the door as I listened, my heart leaping as I recognised my brother's voice.

"I can't believe John Boy just got shot down like that," Church laughed. "It was fucking savage – did you hear him?"

"Nah, what did he say?" Benny asked, laughing too.

"I'd rather fuck a day old baguette than take a tumble in your rotten sheets," Church replied, laughter peeling from his lips and making a snarl form on mine as my brother joined in.

"Ah well, he can hit on that guy again later when he forgets his face," Benny said.

Church laughed. "Fucking gift that."

Their footsteps drew closer and I looked back towards the stairs where I'd left my little project, but I was out of time and out of luck. I knew that if the two of them came in here and caught me now I'd end up right back in that fucking underground tube station all over again before I knew it.

I needed a little more time. Just a bit to let the dust settle and for me to clear the obstacles placed between me and my twin before I could reclaim my place at his side. I shoved the knife into my pocket as I began to back up, looking for an easy escape and settling on one as the sound of keys jingled outside.

I cursed as I ran away from the door, crossing through the kitchen and opening the window there which led out onto the side alley just as the sound of them unlocking the door reached me.

With a final hiss of annoyance, I heaved myself up and outa the window, shoving it closed behind me just as they stepped through the door.

I had unfinished business in this fucking house. But for right now, it would keep.

BENNY

CHAPTER THIRTY SIX

I stepped into the warehouse, glancing back at Church as he hesitated, swiping a hand down the back of his neck.

"I really wanna be here when Frank brings Anya home," he said, the words seeming to pain him as he went on. "But I've got a loan that was called in a few weeks back and the arsehole is past the cut off point now. I've got eyes on him but there's whispers he's gonna try and flee the city, so I've really gotta go deal with him."

"How about I fuck our girl twice to make up for your disappearing act?" I offered with a taunting grin and he scowled back at me.

"How about I come back here when I'm done with this shit and we give her a morning to remember?" he countered.

"Well I guess it can be both," I said, laughing as he cursed me out before turning and striding away down the street.

I headed inside, not bothering with the lights beyond the lamp which lit the kitchen area and moving to hunt myself down something to eat, finding half a takeaway pizza in the fridge from last night.

I poured myself a glass of whiskey too, taking a sip then deciding I wanted the company of my wife before I finished it. I was aching for the taste of her lips against mine tonight and I planned on convincing her to spend several hours pinned beneath me before she retired for the night. I glanced at the time on my phone, irritated to find nothing from Frank but I was sure they'd be back soon.

The house was weirdly quiet and it took me a few moments of chewing on my somewhat pathetic dinner to realise that I was missing the sound of Anya being in the house. Of her music playing or her voice drawing my attention. I'd been away from this place for so long that it had practically felt alien to me when I'd finally returned to it after my stint in prison. I'd thought that the time I'd spent here was what had made it feel like home once more, but as I stood in the cold silence of the building, it was clear that that wasn't it.

Anya was what had made this my home. And the words my brother had spat at me in jealousy filtered through my mind once more, the echo of them having taken root after they sprung from his lips. *You love her.*

My phone rang, interrupting my thoughts as I tugged it from my back pocket and looked at the name on the caller ID.

Ella with the big tits

Nice.

I cancelled what I had to assume was a booty call intended for my twin brother, wondering when I could just stop playing this fucking part and ditch the stigma of his reputation.

I was sick of having to pretend I was responsible for his fuck ups. For having to lie my way through business meetings about my sudden change in attitude to wanting the fucking companies run right. Not to mention having to bear the burden of people thinking I was responsible for the sick games he liked to play. Including the way he'd treated Anya on the day I'd married her.

Fuck, I hated myself for not getting to him before he'd gotten close to her.

The way she looked at me sometimes, the distrust, the hate, the anger, so much of it was due to what he'd done to her that day.

I'd been tempted on more than one occasion to just fucking tell her the truth. She wouldn't give a fuck anyway. It wasn't like she had anything to do with that shit eight years ago which saw me sent away. She didn't know anything about Olly or whatever the fuck had happened to get half of the oldest and most respected members of The Firm locked up. She didn't have any reason to hate or blame Benny Butcher for anything at all, especially if she realised I wasn't the one who had branded her with my name.

But I'd held back on offering her that truth because despite the way I felt about her, the hunger in my body for hers and how damn insatiably in need of her I was, I still wasn't certain I could trust her. Then again, that was exactly what I'd been asking her to work on offering me. So maybe it was time I took my own advice.

The phone started ringing again and I cut Ella off once more, but it only started up instantly.

"What?" I barked as I answered it, realising this one was going to need it spelled out to her.

"Danny?" a husky voice came in reply and I clucked my tongue.

"Look, Emma or whatever the fuck your name is, I'm not interested in fucking you tonight or ever again for that-"

"I did a cleaning job with Dylan tonight," she interrupted me and I frowned, my scathing speech cut off mid flow and making me pause at the odd subject she was offering as an alternative.

"Why would I wanna hear about that?" I demanded, guessing this big tits girl must have been a Baker, though I had to assume she was fairly new as I didn't know her. A lot had changed while I was locked up and even with Church to help catch me up, there were still a lot of gaps in my knowledge. Luckily, Danny's well known abuse of substances gave me a good excuse for having slips of memory and so far any odd behaviour I'd displayed had been put down to that.

"Because when I got there, I saw something. Something Dylan banned us from telling you about."

"Go on," I said, my interest piqued. Dylan was loyal to a fault. Always had been. I couldn't even think of a reason he might have had to conceal the truth of something from me and now that I knew he had, I was eager to find out what the fuck it had been.

"When we got there, music was playing real loud, so I guess they didn't hear us coming in."

"Who didn't?"

"Frank Smith," she breathed, sounding hesitant to go on but she did all the same. "And your new wife."

"I know they were doing a job together tonight," I said dismissively, realising she clearly thought Anya shouldn't have been there.

"No. It wasn't that. They weren't...I mean they were... Well, he was fucking her on the bonnet of his truck while she panted his name like he was the best thing since sliced bread. I saw it all, watched him fuck her dirty and come all over her tits and kiss her like she was his instead of-"

I hurled the phone across the room with a furious roar, the thing smashing against the far wall, and thumping down onto the carpet before I turned and punched the fridge hard enough to put a fucking dent in it.

What the fuck?

What in the ever loving fuck???

I paced back and forth as my head spun with those words, every time I'd left her alone in his company, every time they'd ended a conversation when I'd entered a room, the way she'd looked when she'd watched him fucking singing for a crowd in The Duck and Dog. All of it. Every moment coming into crystal clear focus as I realised why he'd lost his shit when he found out about her fucking Church and why he always looked pissed off whenever he'd had to listen to me make her scream for me.

It wasn't because she was the sister of the man who had sliced his back to pieces. It wasn't disgust over who she was or what family she represented. It was jealousy pure and fucking simple. Whether that was because he'd already been fucking her or because he'd been wanting to I had no idea, but the knowledge that she had once again been lying to me bit into my insides and buried deep.

I was done. So fucking done with all the lies and bullshit between us. When she got back here tonight, I was locking her in a room with me and we were gonna have one hell of a confessional.

She would find out the truth about who I was and why I'd ended up in prison. I'd make her judge me on who I was without my twin brother's foul reputation clouding her opinion of me. Then she was gonna give me all of her deep dark secrets, her sordid little fantasies about me and the men I kept closest to me, and we were gonna figure this the fuck out.

I didn't care what it took to do it. Because Anya Volkov was the one thing in this life that I was utterly clear on now. I wanted her. So I was gonna have to figure out how I could keep her.

I tossed the half eaten pizza in the bin then turned and took the stairs two at a time, needing a shower to help me think straight so that I could face her with a calm head when she returned.

And as the hot water poured down over my skin, I focused on that one task. I was going to give her the truth and I was going to accept hers too. Once we'd done that, we'd find a way to become what I knew we could be. I might not have wanted a bride before I met her, but I'd made a vow to that woman, and so help me, I was going to uphold it.

ANYA

CHAPTER THIRTY SEVEN

After what felt like a lifetime, I finally managed to get the robe belt free of my wrist, using my teeth and fingers to untie the tight knot. I got to my feet, still shaken, but I was falling into a place of darkness within me. I'd been tainted from birth, born to a man who'd offered me up his demons and left them living within me. They were here now, baying for blood and begging for retribution. And I'd serve it to them on a silver platter.

I hissed against the pain of my wounds as I picked up the robe discarded on the floor, tying the belt around it and concealing as much of my flesh as I could as I crept to the door, pressing my ear to it and listening for Danny. He'd made a lot of noise downstairs for a while, but now everything had gone quiet apart from the running water of the shower down the hall.

I silently opened the door, tiptoeing out on bare feet along the balcony, passing by the bathroom door and hurrying downstairs. I moved into the lounge, eyeing the bag of weapons left discarded on the table and hesitating. If I shot him or stabbed him, there'd be an investigation. There was no way I'd get away with it. I'd be arrested, and even if I ran, how far could I really get when I didn't even know where I'd go?

My gaze shifted to the mess of cocaine on the coffee table and I moved to grab the half brick of it which was still in its wrapper, a plan coming together in my mind. I grabbed a knife from the bag too, sliding it quickly into my pocket as a backup plan and glancing up towards the bathroom door which still remained closed, the faint sound of running water coming from within it.

I returned to the kitchen and my gaze fell on a glass of whiskey left on the side.

Cocaine may have given a high in the right doses, but in the wrong doses…it was lethal.

No one would question Danny dying of an overdose. I'd been told time and again that he was known for liking blow, and I had to believe his reputation would be enough of a cover story for it to be believable - even if I hadn't ever seen him indulging in the habit myself. Then again, if he used it as much as I'd been told he did, he was probably taking it with breakfast lunch and dinner just to be able to function normally.

I hurried forward, rage and fear snaking through me as I solidified the decision and wincing as my wounds blazed beneath my robe. I grabbed a spoon from the cutlery drawer and chipped off a sizeable lump of cocaine, letting it drop into his glass before stirring it in until it dissolved. Then I added another, and another until there was enough in that drink to take down a kraken.

I thought of Danny's kisses, his sweet words and the promises he'd made me, tears pricking my eyes at the pain he caused me now in discarding all of it. Like they had meant nothing, like I had meant nothing. It all made too much sense in this cruel world I knew too well.

I should have known I was always going to mean nothing to him, because that was how real life worked. I was his enemies' sister, of course he'd done this. Of course it had all been a lie.

I hurriedly returned the remaining cocaine to the lounge where he'd left it, planning to run back upstairs and disappear again before he reappeared. But the door sounded to the bathroom up on the balcony and every blood cell in my body froze solid.

Too late.

I scrambled back into the kitchen, quickly grabbed a glass and the bottle to pour myself a drink of whiskey too, needing a cover story for why I was down here.

I was going to have to play the game of my life here, and pray I'd win. Because if he saw through me, I had no doubt I was dead, so it looked like I was betting my life on pulling this off.

BENNY

CHAPTER THIRTY EIGHT

I tied a knot in the cord which held my sweats up as they slipped down over my hips, pausing at the top of the stairs as my gaze fell on Anya in the kitchen as she got herself a glass from the cupboard and poured a measure of whiskey to match the one I'd left myself earlier.

"You," I stated, covering my surprise at her abrupt arrival and glancing around for any sign of Frank accompanying her.

Maybe he'd been given a tip off about me knowing what he'd been doing with my wife earlier on though, because for once he wasn't lurking in her shadow and it appeared she was alone here.

Good. I needed her to myself if we were gonna sort this out.

"You," she replied in a flat voice, sliding my drink across the breakfast bar towards me as I began to descend the stairs.

"What are you up to?" I questioned, unsure if she'd had a chance to eat yet and wondering if I had the patience to wait for her to fill her stomach before we got into it.

Anya shifted her weight, her fingers moving to the knot which secured the robe she was wearing, and I had to assume that Dylan had taken her clothes to scrub them for the evidence of whatever she'd done to Yuri with Frank, but I didn't want to get into that. And I didn't want to discuss what she was wearing. It didn't fucking matter right now.

"I…thought we should have a drink before we continue," she said bitterly, her chin rising in that defiant way of hers which always made my cock throb.

I smirked at her as I reached for my glass, lifting it to my lips and watching her over the rim.

"Continue?" I asked, wondering what my little temptress had in mind because if the malevolent look in her eyes was anything to go by, I was willing to bet she thought fucking me would rescue her from this conversation. And I was also willing to bet that she was in the mood to dole out some serious punishment on my unworthy flesh.

I licked my lips, lowering the glass without taking a sip as I bobbed my chin at her own drink.

"It's bad luck to make your husband drink alone," I said and she nodded, taking hold of her own glass and picking it up in a hand which shook just a little.

"Something wrong?" I asked, a frown pulling at my brow. "Look, if what happened tonight was a bit too full on for you-" I began, wondering if she'd been traumatised by whatever the fuck Frank had done to Yuri. Maybe that was what had driven her into his arms, maybe that was why she'd fucked him. Though I got the feeling there was a whole lot more to her motivations than just seeking comfort in the nearest warm body.

"A bit too full on?" she asked, arching a brow at me like I was a fucking arsehole, and I knew I'd pissed her off.

"Alright, alright," I conceded, holding my hands up, my drink sloshing a little in my glass as I protested my innocence. "I take it back. I knew you could take it. You're fucking bombproof, ain't ya?"

"Is that what you think?" she asked coldly.

"Yeah," I agreed, rounding the breakfast bar towards her but she shifted in the same direction, keeping it between us like we were playing cat and mouse.

"So you play sick games with me because you assume I can handle it?" she pushed.

I cocked my head to one side, realising she already knew that I knew. She thought I was toying with her, and maybe I was a bit. Then again, she was the one who insisted on fucking the men closest to me and leaving me to deal with the fallout of that bombshell going off in my fucking lap.

"I know you can," I agreed. "But we don't have to keep playing tonight if you don't want to." I fell still, leaving the breakfast bar between us if that was how she wanted it, even if it did bother me that she still gave me that look from time to time, like she thought she had to fear me, like I might do something bad. Like the kinda thing she thought I'd done the morning of our wedding. But I had a cure to that fearful look in her eyes. The truth would set us free.

"I'll drink to that," she agreed icily, raising her glass.

"To no more games," I agreed, raising mine once more too.

She knocked hers back and I followed her lead, a bitter taste coating the back of my throat alongside the burn as I swallowed it down and Anya sucked in a sharp breath, her eyes widening like she hadn't really thought I'd toast to that. But I was done with the bullshit and it was time she knew the truth of me.

"Right then," I said, slamming my glass down on the kitchen island and huffing out a long breath. "Before we get into why you spent at least a part of your evening fucking yet another one of the men I hold closest to me, I think it's time I told you the truth of me."

"What truth?" she asked, her brow furrowing as she looked at me like she was expecting something from me, but I couldn't for the life of me understand what.

"Eight years ago, my twin brother fucked me over, set me up and got me sent away for years in payment for the lies which he made almost everyone I know and love believe about me."

My heart started pounding harder as the truth of me came to my lips and my palms grew sweaty, my mouth dry too while my brain tried to come up with the simplest way of exposing this to her.

"I spent a long, long time paying for my trust in him," I went on. "And in my absence he only grew worse, his darkest traits going unchecked without me there to stifle them."

"Danny, I don't understand," Anya began but I shook my head.

"I've told you not to call me that, bombshell. Didn't you ever wonder why?"

Her frown deepened and I reached for her, wanting to smooth that look from her face, but she was too far from me for that to be possible and my hand just thumped down on the breakfast bar between us uselessly while my heart only raced faster.

"The day I married you was the day I got out of prison," I explained. "I was hoping you would never have had to meet the man I shared a womb with. I thought I'd at least spared *you* from his cruelty, but of course, I soon realised I'd been too late for that."

"What are you saying?" Anya demanded, still looking confused as fuck and I licked my dry lips, my mouth tingling and something tugging at the corners of my mind while my heart thundered in my chest and the room seemed to spin for several seconds, the only thing solid in it her.

"I'm saying you only met Danny Butcher that one time," I said. "When he collared you and branded you and *fuck*...I've tried to make up for what he did that day, bombshell. I've really fuckin' tried. I hate that he got his claws in you before I managed to get to him."

"You're high," she muttered, shaking her head a little as I rounded the breakfast bar and advanced on her once more but she backed away, maintaining that distance between us and revealing a flash of silver in her hand. A knife. She had been hiding a knife from me.

I blinked at the blade in confusion, my gaze trailing to her bare legs and noticing a line of blood running down one of them, dripping red onto the kitchen floor. Was she hurt?

"I'm not high," I snapped, sick of being judged for my brother's habit while my brain tried to connect dots which seemed intent on dancing away from one another. “I don’t touch that shit. That’s Danny. Not me. Do you get what I’m saying?” It had seemed so easy to say in my head, but somehow my words were coming out jumbled and unclear now and she wasn’t fucking getting it. “I’m not Danny. I’m Benny. My brother set me up and made everyone in The Firm and my family hate me for some bullshit I never did. There were lies and cops and…death.” I blew out a sigh at the stab of grief which found me over that truth, but that wasn’t what she needed to hear right now. “I swear, bombshell, I didn’t do the shit they said I did. Church knows. Church was the only one who would listen. Me and him came up with this. No one knew I was due to get out – good behaviour if you can believe it? I dunno how they never caught me for all the shit I was up to in there, but I had people who took the fall for me and I-”

“What the fuck are you trying to say?” Anya asked me, a look of utter confusion in her eyes. “You’re telling me that you’re Benny? That you aren’t the man who tied me up and branded his name into my flesh? How? How could you have pulled off a switch like that? Even identical twins have differences, surely the people who knew you best would have-”

“Not me and Dan,” I said but my words came out kinda slurred and my head was spinning again while my frantic heart thundered like I was running a race against a thousand speeding horses and I had to win. Had to. A breath of laughter escaped me. “He had the ink. That was the one thing. But I just got my own copies done. All of them. All but this because this was mine before I became him and no one can know I kept it and no one can see it, but I couldn’t just cover it up because it was for Olly too. You know?”

I looked down at the forget-me-not tattoo which was hidden among the roses on my lower abs and realised I wasn’t even pointing at it, so I did.

“You see?” I demanded. “Danny never had one of these. He wasn’t one of us.”

“A flower?” Anya asked, her confusion still clear while a pounding seemed to be starting up in the back of my skull and I sucked in a deep breath which did nothing to make it level out.

“Not just any flower,” I slurred but she wasn’t looking at it anymore, her eyes were on me again and I was staring at her mouth and thinking about all the things I wanted to do it.

“You fucked Frank,” I mumbled, but I was pretty sure the words didn’t even make sense.

“Where is he then?” she asked me, not sounding at all convinced. “If you took Danny’s place at the wedding then where is he now?”

A laugh fell from my lips and I pointed at the floor beneath our feet, shushing her like she might wake him. But he was far, far, far away down there so there was no chance of that.

Anya didn’t seem to understand that and as I reached for her, she backed up a step, making me stumble and drop to one knee. My heart wasn’t just racing anymore, it was stampeding, hurtling along at breakneck speed and the rest of me couldn’t keep up. Sweat slicked my brow, my arms, my chest and no matter how deeply I drew in air, it didn't seem to be enough to sooth the rampant sensations.

There was something to that. Something happening which I should have figured out already, but the room was spinning and she was the only point of focus I could fix on.

"He's down there," I said, trying to clarify my response. "Locked up where he can't hurt anyone. Safe and sound."

"The underground?" Anya asked with a tight frown. "I heard someone down there when I ran. I thought…"

"I need to feel you in my arms," I muttered, reaching for her and grasping the edge of her robe as I lost my balance.

Anya cried out like I'd hurt her and it took me several seconds to understand what I was looking at as her robe fell open and revealed several long cuts marking her perfect flesh, blood staining her skin.

I stared at the red on her, stared at it while I shook my head and my heart thundered to the point of bursting. Something was wrong. So fucking wrong.

"Who did that to you?" I asked her, my words somehow coming out clearer despite the way everything else was getting worse, my body trembling, my world spinning, my fucking heart beating too fast. Far too fast.

"You did," she accused and pain and confusion flashed through me.

"Never. I'd never hurt you. Not ever," I said in a tumble of words.

"Are you trying to say you can't even remember cutting me?" she sneered. "That your knife slicing into my skin half an hour ago wasn't memorable at all?"

"I was with Church," I blurted, shaking my head because I hadn't done that. I would never do that and I didn't understand why she thought I had. "I didn't. I weren't here. I'd never…" A fog descended on my head and I lost my train of thought.

She seemed to understand something though because clarity dawned in her onyx gaze.

"Shit," she cursed, her eyes roaming over my face like she was hunting the truth and finding it even though it was lost on me. "Danny did it," she breathed, her eyes widening in horror as I stared at her. "He must have escaped. The tunnel let him out in The Duck and Dog and…oh fuck…what have I done?"

My lips parted on a reply, but she was getting further away from me, whatever I'd wanted to say slipping from me and blackness closing in all around me as my body began to convulse, my heart racing and racing as I fell onto the floor at her feet.

The room was spinning, the air was stifling. And it was so fucking dark as I left her behind.

My pulse thundered violently as my body jerked and thrashed, the sound of it consuming me as I lost my hold on her and everything else, the echoing beat rattling through my skull, faster and faster, too fucking fast, on and on and on…

And then it stopped.

I tried to stay there, to reach for her, for anything at all but there was nothing left to me beyond the dark, nothing at all but the endless silence left behind in the wake of the final beat of my heart.

PART THREE

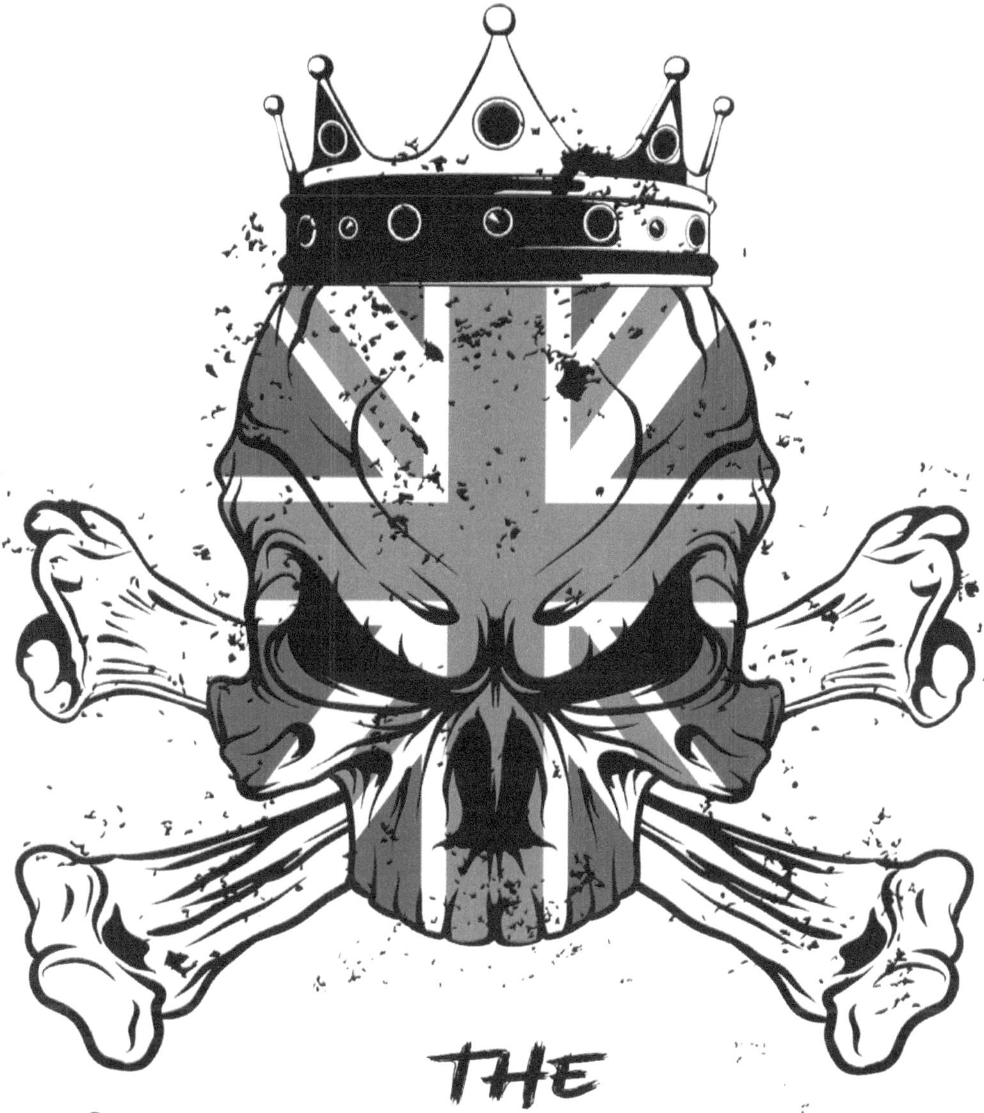

THE BUTCHER,

THE BAKER

THE CANDLESTICK MAKER

CHURCH

CHAPTER THIRTY NINE

I strode up Fenchurch Street between the party girls and club goers who had taken over the city now that it was passing midnight and the businessmen and women had retired for the night.

There were a lot of excitable shrieks and cat calling as well as brightly lit rickshaws flying up and down the streets blasting music on their loudspeakers which clashed in a disjointed way as they passed each other by.

I pushed my split knuckles deep into the pockets of my coat as I walked, breathing in that frosty bite of winter air as it blew around us and thanking any god who might have been close enough to listen for the fact that I wasn't out in the country right now freezing my arse off.

Winter was making itself known tonight and there was a chill in the air sharp enough to give a nun's arse frostbite.

I turned off of the busy street, away from the twinkle of Christmas lights, cutting down a smaller road to avoid the crowd while losing myself in fantasies about all the things I planned on doing to my Miss America when I got back to the warehouse.

I slipped down a narrow passageway between two buildings, cutting my journey down with the little shortcut, but I stopped as I spotted a figure moving towards me through the shadows.

"Butch?" I frowned as I recognised Benny, moving closer as he paused at the sight of me.

"Oh there you are, Churchy," he replied, stepping towards me once more. "I've got something for ya actually."

"What's that then?" I asked, walking straight up to him as he paused by the side entrance to one of the buildings we were passing between.

"I think it's overdue actually," he added.

A car drove up the street at the far end of the little alleyway and in that brief moment of illumination, I caught a glimpse of something silver which he held in his fist.

My arm snapped up to block the blow half a second before he swung the blade at me with a savage thrust intended for my fucking heart.

I yelled in alarm and realisation as I knocked his arm aside, the hot flash of pain biting into my skin letting me know he'd cut me, though I doubted that one was as fatal as the one he'd intended.

My fist snapped out and crashed into his face, knocking him back into the wall and giving me the room I needed to slam into him and send him flying to the ground.

"How the fuck did you get out?" I yelled as Danny laughed beneath me, swinging the hand which held the blade at my back while I pinned him down.

I cursed as I was forced to throw my weight to the side, making the knife skim over my spine instead of plunging into it before crushing my weight down onto his arm and managing to grab hold of his wrist.

"Shoulda realised he'd let me out one of these days, Churchy," Danny mocked as we fought over the weapon and the warm feel of my blood trickled beneath my coat along my back. "Me and Ben are destined. Meant to be together. He was never gonna leave me to rot down in that fucking hole in the ground."

"You make it sound like you wanna fuck him, you twisted shit."

Danny roared like a feral beast, releasing his grip on the knife in favour of throwing his entire body weight at me as the thing hit the pavement and skittered away from us.

"That was always your problem, wasn't it Church? Fucking jealous of what you couldn't understand."

Danny managed to propel himself on top of me, his fist colliding with my jaw and making my head ricochet off the pavement beneath me.

I fought him back, cursing as he pressed his weight down on me and snarling my reply at his deluded fucking face.

"I wasn't jealous of you, mate," I spat. "Who'd be jealous of someone with a coke addiction and a fucking screw or twelve loose? Your problem was always that you were so fucking obsessed with the idea of you and Benny being this unbreakable force of nature that you couldn't see what was right in front of you."

"And what was that?" Danny taunted as he slammed a fist down into my gut.

"That Benny outgrew you a long time ago," I wheezed out. "He passed you by and left you in his dust and it was only his love for you because you're his blood that stopped him from making that clearer to you back then."

"Me and Benny are the kings of this city!" Danny roared, his fury making him rear back enough for me to throw my forehead into his face.

He swore as he was knocked offa me and I scrambled to my feet, sparing half a glance around for the knife but it was long lost in some dark corner.

"The only thing that ever got in our way was you and all the others like ya," Danny spat as he gripped the wall and pulled himself upright, the two of us eyeing each other like a pair of lions just looking for an in to strike. "You and Frank and poor, dead, Olly. All of you thinking you could take him from me, whispering in his ear, tryna turn him on me."

"You did a good enough job of that yourself without ever needing us to do shit," I replied, swallowing down the pain I felt at the memory of Olly's death.

"And now that Russian whore is trying to take him from me too," he went on, the flash of headlights from cars passing on the street momentarily lighting up the manic look on his face.

"Watch your mouth if you're gonna talk about her," I warned him and Danny smiled wickedly as he raised his hand out to one side, letting me see the knife which he'd somehow found again, the silver now stained with my blood.

"Careful, Churchy," he hissed. "Anyone would think that fucking the whore has made you go soft on her."

My upper lip pulled back as my muscles coiled with an ache for violence, but with Danny holding that knife I was forced to restrain myself.

"I went home tonight you know?" he added, his eyes lighting with an eager cruelty. "Managed to get her all to myself for a little playdate."

My gut bottomed out at his words and I bared my teeth in warning. "What did you do to her?" I demanded.

"Oh, nothing much." He shrugged. "But I have to say, she bleeds so fuckin' beautifully and that scream on her – I can see why you like ramming your dick into-"

He didn't get a chance to finish that sentence because I'd already collided with him, my body slamming into his and sending the two of us flying out onto the street at his back.

We crashed down on the bonnet of a car as the sound of screeching brakes and the glare of headlights consumed us.

The car skidded to a halt and we were thrown off of it into the street. We rolled across the tarmac to the sound of onlooker's screams and we jarred to a halt. Danny was firmly on top of me and the car's headlights lit us up for all to see as he brandished the knife at me.

The shock of what had happened made us both whip around to look at the car even as Danny pinned me to the ground and held the bloody knife above me in his fist.

My gaze met with the startled expressions of the two uniformed cops who sat inside their vehicle taking in what was happening right before their eyes.

"Fuck," I cursed just as Danny swung the blade for my face.

A flash of red and blue lights was punctuated by the whoop of the police sirens as I jerked aside, the knife barely missing me and clinking against the tarmac right beside my ear.

I fought to get free of the arsehole on top of me, managing to get a foot between us and kicking him hard enough to send him sprawling onto his back.

The police got out of their car, yelling at us to remain where we were but I was already shoving to my feet, ignoring every word they spoke as I scrambled to the opposite side of the road to Danny.

I locked eyes with the motherfucker and he grinned at me before turning and bolting away down the street.

The police officers looked between him and me, clearly unsure of who to go for and I took off too, ignoring their yells to stop as I sprinted away from them at breakneck speed, heading away from Danny and back towards home.

I didn't know what the fuck he'd done to Anya, but my gut was knotting something fierce as panic rose up in me and the need to bellow her name at the top of my lungs pushed at me.

I'm coming darlin'. I'm fucking coming.

CHAPTER FORTY

Panic seared the inside of my flesh and scalded my bones as I stared at Benny on the floor. He didn't fit, he didn't convulse, he just fucking laid there so still that terror stole through my chest and fell from my lungs in the form of a pitchy scream.

I crashed to my knees at his side, my head still rattling with all he'd told me and the details still adding up, painting a picture which finally made fucking sense. And yet what kind of insane person would do this?

"Wake up," I commanded, lurching forward and holding my ear above his mouth, trying to feel for a pulse on his neck. But there was nothing, not a flicker, not any sign that the man I loved was still housed within his body.

Fear was my only company as I started to shake him, then I forced my fingers into his mouth and to the back of his throat.

"Throw up for me, please, please," I begged, frantic as I tried to get a response from him, but he wasn't here.

"Help!" the word tore from my chest and reverberated through the air, but my voice only echoed uselessly back at me throughout the empty building.

I patted down Benny's pants, hunting for his phone with shaking hands, but finding nothing as desperation clawed at me.

"Fuck, fuck," I gasped, my hands still patting his empty pockets as I looked all around me, hunting for it on the kitchen surfaces before suddenly spotting it laying on the floor beside the far wall.

I shoved to my feet, racing for it and snatching it into my hand, finding the screen cracked but thankfully still illuminating as I turned it towards me.

I ran back to Benny, dropping down beside him once more and holding it up to his face to unlock it, a sob lodging in my throat as it worked. I made my way to his call list, finding Frank's number near the top of it and pressing my thumb down on it. It rang three times before he answered, his voice clipped and formal.

"Boss?"

"Frank, it's me. He's dead. He's fucking dead, you have to help me. Please help me!" My voice didn't even sound like my own anymore, it was a broken thing with sharpened edges.

"What's happened?" Frank barked.

"Danny – he -he-" I stammered, knowing I'd gotten the wrong name, but it was too much of a headfuck to even try and explain that part of this story. "He's overdosed on cocaine. He ingested it. Far too fucking much, and now he's not breathing."

"Fuck," Frank hissed. "I'll be right there. Do you know CPR?"

"I – er-" My thoughts were jarred, struggling to focus as the agony of grief threatened to overwhelm me.

"Do you or do you not know it, Cash?" Frank demanded and my thoughts snapped together like a rubber band against the inside of my skull.

"Yes," I exhaled hard as I remembered my brother Zakhar teaching me.

"Hurry."

I tossed the phone away and shifted closer to Benny, trembling all over as I leaned forward, clasped my hands one on top of the other and pressed down on his chest. Then I started pumping in a rhythmic motion as hard as I could, wishing every breath I released I could give to him instead.

This whole thing was so fucked up, so insane and yet it made so much sense too. How I had been able to fall for the man who I'd thought branded his name on my flesh. How I'd questioned the brutality I'd felt at his hands and had found it so hard to marry those two men together as one. It was because they weren't one. They never had been, and this man beneath me hadn't deserved the vengeance I'd dealt him. He'd done nothing to me but work to earn my forgiveness for a crime he hadn't even committed, and now I might not even get the chance to offer him it.

Tears were running down my cheeks, dripping onto his still body as I worked in an endless motion, up and down, my eyes riveted to his face as I prayed I'd see a glimmer of life within his features at any moment. Every thirty or so pumps of my hands, I tilted his head back and breathed deep into his lungs.

"Please, you fucking asshole," I sobbed. "Please come back. I didn't know, I didn't fucking know. Why didn't you tell me?" Tears continued to flow until all I could taste was salt and agony on my lips. Everything was painfully quiet, all music in the world officially stopped, the silence so loud it hurt. And I had a feeling, if I lost Benny here on this kitchen floor, I'd never find music again.

"I love you," I admitted, knowing it might be my only chance to say the words I'd denied were true to myself for too long. "I tried to hate you, and I think I succeeded sometimes."

Our love was a rosebush in winter, the thorns sharp enough to draw blood, but the roses had bloomed in the end. It was like he'd said, we were inevitable. But he'd been right about another thing too, our love story was no fairy tale. It was ruinous, and here we were at the brink of our ruin, torn apart before we'd barely had a chance to love each other.

"The king of London doesn't die on some cold tiled floor," I growled through my teeth. "He dies after he's conquered the world. Come back and conquer it, Benny Butcher. This city doesn't even know who rules it yet."

His face was too still and as I leaned in close to check for his breaths again, I felt no flutter of life against my cheek. I breathed deep into his mouth again a couple more times, feeling his lungs fill with air, but he didn't respond.

A noise of pain left me as I continued the torturous effort of pumping his chest, over and over as my arms burned, but I didn't stop. I'd never stop. I was the only thing keeping his heart working, keeping blood moving around his body. But what if he really was gone? Lost to me forever…

I wouldn't give up. I'd pump his heart until someone found a way to bring him back to me, until life offered us another chance.

"Give him back!" I screamed to the Devil, because there was no doubt in my mind that if an afterlife awaited people like us, then it was Lucifer who had him now. But even that horned demon of nightmares couldn't keep him from me. I was Anya Butcher, the girl who'd toppled the Butcher king, and now I demanded further fucking use of him.

The front door flew open with a bang and I glanced over my shoulder, finding Church racing into the warehouse with a bruised face and his arm bleeding.

"Danny's escaped!" he shouted, but then his eyes fell on me and Benny on the floor and terror crossed his features. "What's happening?" he gasped.

"He's fucking overdosed," I snapped.

"Nah, he wouldn't." Church shook his head in absolute denial even as he ran to me. "He doesn't do that shit."

"*I* did it. I fucking did it because Danny attacked me," I admitted in a croak. "But then Benny was here and I didn't realise they'd switched. I thought he was still Danny – the real Danny. Then Benny told me everything, but it was too late. I'd already overdosed him. I slipped it in his drink, Church." I looked Benny's best friend in the eye as he fell to his knees beside me. "I swear I didn't know. Not until after he'd drank it and he told me the truth."

Church nodded, his face ashen pale as he clasped his hands together, placing them down right beside mine. "Take a break, Anya."

"No," I growled. "I did this. I'll bring him back."

"You need a break. You can't go on forever like this. On three." There was such a ring of command in his voice that I was forced to listen, and my fear over my arms failing Benny made me nod my head in agreement.

Church pumped Benny's chest with me for three counts and my arms went slack as Church took over, my muscles burning as I sat back on my heels and stared on in fear.

"Why isn't he waking up?" I choked out, knowing this was on me. That I'd fucked up everything, but I was furious too. Why had Benny kept this from me? If he'd loved me, why had he kept up the lie? Who had he thought I'd tell? I had no one in this place but him and his men, so why keep me in the dark?

"Come on, mate," Church said through his teeth, his blonde curls falling forward into his eyes, his biceps flexing with every pump of Benny's chest. "Anya's here, she's waiting to see ya. She wants to hear all about your crazy fucking plot to take down your brother. Don't disappoint her, Benny. You gotta wake up." His brow creased and fear sparked in his eyes when Benny didn't respond.

"Please," I rasped, cupping Benny's face and giving him mouth to mouth as Church paused. "Tell me all about it. I'll punch you for this, but I'll get over it, I promise."

Church looked up at me, his throat bobbing with emotion while he continued to pump Benny's chest for him. "I'm sorry," he breathed. "We shoulda told you."

"Just bring him back, Church, and I'll forgive all of it," I said fiercely, touching his jaw with shaking fingers. "Please."

He nodded and silence fell between us as he pumped Benny's chest, but every jolt of his body now seemed to confirm he wasn't coming back to us. He was already gone, disappearing into the dark to somewhere I couldn't follow.

"I shouldn't've left," Church muttered. "I shoulda come in. I shoulda-"

"It's not your fault," I sobbed. "It's mine. I did this."

Church went on and on, working to keep Benny's heart going while I breathed into his mouth every time he paused, but I could see the crease of anxiety between his eyes, the hopelessness starting to creep into his expression, and the way his hands were beginning to slow. He looked to me and I saw reality staring back at me in his eyes, the cold, harsh truth of what was about to happen. It was over.

"He's gone, Anya," Church whispered, like he couldn't bear to say the words any louder than that.

"No," I snarled, refusing it with all my might as a weight of guilt and loss nearly crushed me. "No!"

I fell on Benny, pressing my mouth to his, feeling for his breath, but all was still. My tears washed down onto his cheeks and a noise of utter grief left me as I pressed my forehead to his while Church continued to work his chest with weaker and weaker pumps.

"I'm sorry," I said against Benny's lips. "I'm so sorry."

"Keep fucking going," Frank's voice suddenly cut through the air and I lifted my head, finding him running in with a leather bag in his grip and a look of furious intention about him.

Church glanced back at him, nodding mutely as he picked up his pace again, but I could see he was getting tired and I pressed my hands beside his, locking eyes with him as we silently communicated three pumps before he sat back and released a heavy breath.

Frank dropped down beside Church, opening his bag and taking out a small vile and a syringe, drawing some clear liquid into it.

"What is that?" I breathed, desperation lacing my voice as I worked to keep my husband's heart beating.

"Adrenaline," Frank answered, passing the syringe to Church. "Hold this."

Church nodded, looking from the syringe to Benny's chest. "Don't we need a bigger needle?"

"For what?" Frank grunted, grabbing hold of Benny's sweatpants and ripping them off of him, leaving him in his boxers between us.

"For stabbing his heart with this." Church reached towards Benny's chest like he was planning to do just that and Frank caught hold of the back of his shirt, yanking him away.

"This ain't Pulp Fiction, you fucking plonker," he snapped, snatching the adrenaline from Church's grip. "And it's got about one percent chance of working so just shut the fuck up and let me do it."

He rolled Benny's thigh out to the side, his fingers digging into his skin as he sought out what I guessed was a vein before holding the needle to his skin, angling it just so and sliding it into his flesh as he slowly depressed the plunger.

I watched Benny's face, hunting for signs of life as Frank injected the adrenaline and I breathed deep into my husband's lungs again. The time seemed to tick on and on and my arms started to burn again as I kept giving Benny CPR.

"Why's it not working?" I begged of Frank.

"Come on you junkie, coke-sniffing cunt," Frank snarled as he stared at his boss and Benny suddenly took a breath, his lungs heaving beneath my hands and I all but screamed as I stared down at him in shock.

Benny breathed again, inhaling deep and sharp then his eyes fluttered open. My hands were still pumping as his dark brown gaze met mine and the smallest of smiles quirked up his lips before his head lolled and he passed out again. But his chest continued to rise and fall beneath my hands and Church took hold of them, drawing them away from Benny's chest.

"You can stop now, Miss America," he said then slid his arm behind Benny's back, forcing him to sit up and shoving his fingers down his throat.

At last, Benny responded, heaving and bringing up the whiskey he'd drunk as Church just let him throw up in his lap, clearly giving no fucks about it as he shoved his fingers in his mouth again. "That's it, mate. Get it all out."

I trembled as I sat watching, wanting to reach out and touch him, but I didn't deserve that for what I'd done to him.

When Benny was done vomiting, Church patted his back, helping him to his feet and slinging his friend's arm across his shoulders. "I'll put him in the shower. Anya, get him a cup of Rosy Lee with lots of sugar."

"A what?" I asked in confusion, hurrying to my feet, ready to get anything Benny needed, but I didn't know what the hell that was.

"A cuppa, darlin'," he called back.

"Like one of those Cup a Soup things?" I asked.

"No, Jesus Christ, a hot brew, Anya," Church replied and I stared after him in dismay. "A builder's."

"A fucking tea," Frank cut in, getting to his feet and the breath went out of me at last as I nodded and ran to the kettle, filling it up in the sink before switching it on.

My hands were still shaking like crazy and as I grabbed a mug, I dropped it, the thing bouncing across the counter and smashing in the sink.

Frank came up behind me, his arms closing around me. "It's alright. Breathe, Cash."

I did, leaning back against him, fighting a wince from the pain in my wounds. "Do you want your music, beautiful?" he asked gently.

I almost said yes, but I bit my tongue, shaking my head in refusal instead. We stood there like that for so long, it felt like a whole eternity passed, and Frank just held me as the shaking within my body final ceased.

"Better?" he asked at last.

"No. But I deserve to feel every piece of this pain," I admitted. "I did this to him."

"He's a coke head, Anya. It ain't the first time I've found him laid out on the floor, even if it is the first time I've seen the arsehole rise from the fucking dead."

"You don't understand," I croaked. Or maybe he did, maybe Frank knew the truth of all this. Why wouldn't he after all? He was probably in on the whole thing. "I know everything now," I said, a shudder running down my spine as I wrapped my arms around myself.

I spotted Church helping Benny down the stairs even though my husband looked less pale now, the two of them wearing fresh sweatpants, their hair damp and skin clean. Both of their chests were on show and I eyed the forget-me-not tattoo on Benny's lower abs before looking him in the eyes, hating myself for this whole mess.

"What do you know?" Frank asked me, drawing my attention back to him and I swallowed the lump in my throat.

"That Danny's not Danny at all. He's Benny. He's been impersonating him this whole time," I said and Frank withdrew from me, his brows pulling sharply together.

"Come again?" Frank hissed.

"Oh fuck," Church muttered. "Frankie boy, come sit down. Let's talk this out like proper gentlemen, yeah?"

Benny swiped a hand down his face, still seeming kind of out of it and I glanced at Frank as he suddenly barrelled away from me towards the two of them.

"Is this true?!" he bellowed at Church who took a step in front of Benny as they made it to the bottom of the stairs.

"Yeah, mate," Church admitted and I bit my lip, confused for a second before I remembered what Frank had told me about his feelings towards Benny. That he'd been responsible for getting his brother killed, that he despised him.

Shit.

Frank lunged like a feral dog, knocking Church aside and throwing his weight on Benny, the two of them crashing onto the stairs.

"Stop!" I cried in fright as Frank's hands locked around Benny's throat and my husband could barely fight back after the shit he'd just been through.

Church fell on him with an animal snarl, throwing furious punches at Frank, but Frank was a machine, pure fury cut into his features as he fought to kill Benny.

"Stop it!" I cried, leaping on them and trying to claw Frank's hands off of Benny. "Let go of him – let go!"

Church shoved and punched with mighty blows that nearly uprooted Frank, but he didn't let go of my husband, choking him so hard that his biceps bulged.

Church smashed a fist into his head, knocking him sideways and forcing his hands off of Benny, but as Frank turned on him, his elbow smashed back into my gut and I fell on my ass with a yelp as he struck the wound on my stomach. I clutched it as my robe fell wide and Frank turned to look at me the same moment Church did, their eyes falling on my injuries.

"Anya," Church gasped and he lurched towards me with Frank, the two of them examining my wounds as I fought to get past them and see Benny.

My husband was on the stairs, sitting half upright with a dazed look about him and as I reached for his hand, his fingers found mine.

"You alright, bombshell?" he rasped.

"No," I croaked, losing my grip on him as Frank scooped me up and carried me to the kitchen island, placing me down on it.

"What the fuck happened?" Frank demanded as Church grabbed a first aid kit out of a cupboard, dousing some cotton pads in antiseptic. He held one to the wound across my breast first, his jaw ticking and his muscles taut as he worked from one cut to the next, the pain barely registering. I started to explain what had happened, how Danny must have escaped and attacked me.

Benny made it over to me, clutching my hand and watching intently as the others tended to my wounds.

I blinked through tears at him, angry and sad and hollow inside. Frank shot a furious glare at him, his teeth baring as he knocked his hand away from mine. "You can have a free pass tonight, motherfucker, but all bets are off tomorrow." He looked to me. "You can come with me if you want, Cash. You don't have to stay here with this lying scum."

I looked from Benny to Frank, my heart cleaving in two, but I couldn't leave Benny tonight, not after everything that had happened between us.

"Stay," I begged of Frank but he just sneered at Benny, looking like he was working hard to restrain himself from lunging at him again.

"Tomorrow," he confirmed in a snarl then stalked away, picking up his bag as he left and I saw him checking a gun within it before sliding it into the back of his jeans and stepping out into the night. Something told me he wasn't going home, and I wondered if Danny had bought himself a hunter in the dark.

Benny moved in front of me, leaning in to kiss me as the strength of him seemed to fail, his body sagging towards mine.

"Sleep," he begged of me and I nodded.

"Anything," I agreed.

He tried to lift me into his arms, failing and gesturing for Church to step in instead. Church held me against his chest and clapped a hand to Benny's shoulder, guiding him upstairs as I pressed my face to Church's neck and took comfort in the closeness of him.

Benny didn't go to Danny's room, he pushed into the spare one I'd been decorating and fell down on the bed like he was dog tired. Church placed me down beside him and pulled the covers up around us, pushing his fingers into Benny's hair and giving him a tight smile.

"Don't ever fucking die on me again, mate." He walked back out of the room and I wrapped my arms around Benny from behind, burying my face between his shoulder blades and placing a kiss there. "I'm sorry."

"Don't be sorry, love. How many men get to say they were murdered by their wife and lived to tell the tale?" He reached back, hooking my thigh over his legs and squeezing it. "I'm a living fucking legend, me."

A bemused noise left me as I held him tighter, still thoroughly shaken by everything that had happened, and I knew I wasn't going to sleep a wink while the image of Benny's lifeless body was still so fresh in my mind. I'd be staying awake and checking his breathing all night long.

Church returned with three cups of tea, placing them down on the nightstand before pulling a chair close to the bed and dropping onto it.

Benny pulled the covers back in front of him, patting the sheets. "No you don't. C'mere, you fucker."

Church climbed into the bed, hugging his friend and drawing me into the embrace too. Benny rolled onto his back between us and I nestled against his chest, running my fingers up his neck to his pulse, comforted by the furious pounding of it.

"It ain't gonna stop ticking now, bombshell," Benny promised. "While I was out of it, I swear I felt a demon slide his hand into my chest and turn my heart to steel, like a grenade with the pin pulled. But the explosion ain't in here." He held a hand to his heart. "It's right here in front of me." He stroked my hair. "My wild, forget-me-not bombshell." He passed out and I met Church's gaze across his chest.

"He's lost his fuckin' mind," he whispered.

"Do you think we should take him to a hospital?" I asked anxiously but he shook his head.

"Trust me, Benny Butcher would rather I gutted him here and now than get a police report over this bullshit tonight. I'll call Rodney Quack in the mornin', he can check you over too."

I nodded, my fingers threading with Church's over Benny's heart, the pounding of it beneath our hands making the knot in my stomach loosen a little.

"He won't hold this against you, darlin'," Church said, eyeing my expression. "What Danny did to ya... I'd have force-fed him that blow myself if I'd seen him. You didn't know it weren't him, how could ya have known?"

I let those words settle over me, knowing they were true yet still feeling terrible about it. I'd almost destroyed one of the best things to ever happen to me, and as much as I hadn't wanted to fall for my husband, I knew clearer than ever that I had. When I separated the moment Danny had branded his name onto my flesh from all I'd felt in the company of my husband, I knew I had nothing left to cling to keep me from tumbling into this precipice.

I'd fallen for him like Troy to the Greeks, love sneaking into my chest like a wooden horse and cutting me down in the night. My heart was the conquered land of a fierce king, and I'd never seen the invasion coming.

CHAPTER FORTY ONE

Waking up felt like rising from the dead. My mouth was thick and my throat raw, my body feeling like I'd gone ten rounds in the ring then been flattened by a truck on my way home. Everything just kinda ached and my brain felt heavy and overused.

The facts of everything that had happened last night came back to me slowly, each of them slotting into place like I was creating some macabre puzzle which only made me feel worse with every piece I connected.

I was only wearing a pair of boxers but the scent of something floral made me remember Church washing me before collapsing into the bed last night.

I groaned as I tried to bring myself back to the real world and somewhere beside me, a body shifted in the bed, a hand finding mine, her fingers curling around my thumb and squeezing lightly before drawing away again.

I turned my hand over and caught hers before it could retreat, rolling onto my side and cracking my eyes open to look at her.

The room was dark but around the edges of the blinds, enough light crept in to let me know it had to be past midday. I scrunched my eyes shut against the onslaught of that small amount of brightness.

"Here." Anya drew the covers up over our heads, shielding me from the light so that I could open my eyes again. "There are some painkillers on the nightstand," she said from somewhere within the confines of our little hideaway and I vaguely remembered the doctor coming several hours ago, shining a light in my eyes and taking Anya from me to patch her up. I hadn't been in any state to say a whole lot of anything then, but I felt a little more like myself now. "But I wasn't sure if you'd want to take anything so soon after…"

"After you tried to kill me with an overdose," I supplied for her and she sucked in a sharp breath before nodding, the movement just visible in the dark.

"No more drugs for me right now," I said decisively when she failed to add anything else.

"Benny," she murmured and I released a long breath at the sound of her finally calling me by my real name.

"Anya," I replied, my voice rough.

"I'm sorry."

I let her apology hang in the air between us for several long seconds then drew the covers back off of us, squinting against the onslaught of the light and propping my head on my hand as I looked down at her.

Her eyes were puffy and the dark circles beneath them made me think she hadn't gotten much sleep despite clearly staying in the bed with me all night and for half the day. Her blonde hair was tangled around her face, some strands sticking to her mouth and tempting me to brush them aside.

Anya shivered as my fingers grazed her skin and I licked my lips as I looked down at her, this hopeless kind of vulnerability in her gaze.

"I'm sorry too," I said softly, cupping her cheek in my hand. "I should have told you the truth about me sooner. I shouldn't have let you believe you were married to the man who had branded and collared you. I thought…well I guess I thought I could make you forget about that man if I gave you enough else to judge me by. But really what I shoulda done was trust you."

"Benny, I almost killed you last night. I…I don't know how we come back from that. How can we ever build trust between us after that?" she asked, worrying her bottom lip between her teeth and I gently tugged it free.

I pushed myself to sit up, seeking out the tall glass of water which was waiting at my bedside and draining every drop of it in an attempt to remove the cotton wool feeling from my mouth.

"I'm glad you did it, bombshell," I said as I set the glass back on the table and looked down at her while I stayed sitting up. "Because I know it wasn't meant for me. It was meant for the man who hurt you."

I gently pulled the bed covers off her, finding her in one of my business shirts, the buttons done up to her throat but her golden legs peeking out beneath the hem of it.

"You did it to the man who did this to you," I said, gritting my teeth against the rage I felt at my brother for hurting her while I pushed the hem of the shirt up just high enough to reveal the cut on her thigh.

I circled my fingers around the newly stitched wound, making a mental note to thank Rodney Quack for tending to all of us.

Anya sucked in a breath as I trailed my fingers around the edges of the wound and I knew I was dancing along the line of pain and pleasure in her flesh as I did so.

"Anyone who lays a hand on you in anger deserves your wrath, Anya,"

I said to her firmly. "Even me. I don't care what the treaty says about it. If I ever did something like this to you then I'd want you to kill me for it. I'm just sorry I didn't kill him before he could get to you again."

"He's your brother," she protested.

"He's a demon," I replied with a shake of my head. "I'm bad, bombshell. Real fucking bad. Some of the things I've done would make your toes curl and your stomach churn. But compared to him? I'm a saint. I shouldn't have let my sentimentality about his blood stop me from ending him. I should have made the world a better place when I had the chance."

"There are stains on all of our hands," she said, reaching up to brush her fingers along the line of my jaw. "But some blood won't wash off. If you killed him, Benny, I don't think you'd ever get the stain out."

I swallowed thickly, leaning down until my lips were a mere breath from hers, the taste of her calling to me like I was starving for it as I waited there, wondering if she still wanted me now, if she still felt this need between us like I did.

"I want a fresh start for you and me, bombshell. A clean slate. Trust."

"Even after all I did?" she breathed and I nodded, my nose brushing hers as I looked deep into her dark eyes and found the truth of her waiting for me there.

"No more lies, Anya."

"No more lies," she agreed before tipping her chin up and meeting my mouth.

I groaned as my lips began to move against hers, her tongue rising up to press against mine, our pace unhurried and our intention clear. This was the real apology between us, the real end to our feuding, and as I kissed her I felt like a piece of me just slotted right into place.

I skimmed my fingers down the side of her neck as I continued to kiss her, finding the button which was fastened at her throat and carefully undoing it before letting my fingers trail down to the next.

Anya moaned softly into my mouth as her fingers pushed into my hair and our kiss deepened.

I continued to unbutton her shirt as I lost myself in her kiss and when I finally had it open I drew back, parting the fabric and looking down at her nakedness beneath me.

My attention fixed on the wounds which had been sewn up along her flesh, one over her left breast, another on her stomach before the last on her thigh.

The rage I felt at the sight of those injuries was unlike anything I'd ever known. I wanted to hunt down the animal who had done that to her and rip him apart, brother of mine or not.

"They'll probably scar," she muttered, seeming embarrassed as she tried to cover herself up once more and I realised she was interpreting the look on my face as disgust or distaste or something equally inaccurate.

I caught her wrists in my hands, forcing her to part the shirt once more and pressing them softly down onto the pillow either side of her head.

"All warriors have scars, bombshell," I said roughly, leaning down to speak into her ear as I shifted to kneel with one of my legs between her thighs. "There's true beauty in that."

I moved my mouth to her neck and kissed her softly, making her spine arch beneath me from that simple touch as my cock swelled in my boxers and my ever-present need for her let itself be known.

I moved my mouth lower, carving a line over her collar bone and down until I found the cut which curved over her breast.

I kissed my way around it, still keeping her hands pinned either side of her as I let her see how much I wanted to worship her. When I placed a soft kiss on the wound itself Anya hissed in pain, but as I dropped my mouth to capture her nipple between my lips and sucked gently, the noise turned into a moan.

I continued down her body, giving the cut on her stomach the same adoration, following each kiss to the injuries with a lingering caress to her nipples, making them peak and harden while she writhed and moaned for me.

When I made it down to the cut on her thigh, I released my grip on her wrists, easing her legs apart so that I had a full view of her nakedness and groaning with need as I drank her in.

Anya gasped as I kissed that wound too and this time I countered the pain with a kiss to her core, not wasting any time as I ran my tongue through her centre and lapped at the wetness I found awaiting me there.

I kept my pace slow as I sucked and licked her, circling my tongue and working her up while her fingers pushed through my hair and her back arched against the sheets for me.

She tasted divine, like my own personal summer's day and the sound of her moaning my name, my real fucking name, had me so turned on that by the time she came for me, my cock was throbbing so hard I was surprised I didn't come with her.

I kissed my way back up her body, rolling my boxers off as I settled my weight between her thighs, careful not to press down on her injuries.

My cock drove against the wetness of her core and she widened her thighs, rocking her hips and urging me forward while I kept her hanging in suspense.

"Please, Benny," she begged and that fucking name on her lips was enough to make me certain she owned me.

I gave in to her plea, sinking into her slowly and feeling every single inch of my cock slide deep into her slick heat with a groan of pure pleasure passing my lips.

"My brother accused me of something when it came to you," I murmured as I paused there, filling her, stretching her, loving the tightness of her wrapped all around me.

"What?" she gasped, her hands on my shoulders and her chest heaving with the feeling of me inside her.

"He said I loved you."

"He did?" Her eyes bounced between mine and it was impossible for me to tell what she thought of that, but I knew that I did. It had been true when he'd said it and it was all the truer now that all the lies had been peeled away from us and I was holding her in my arms, her body merged with mine.

"Yeah. So I guess he got one thing right."

Her lips popped open at that admission and I smiled at her as a look of panic formed in her eyes.

Before she could take away what I'd said with the words I could see forming on her lips, I kissed her.

I rolled my hips against hers as I sank my tongue into her mouth, drawing my cock almost the whole way out of her before sliding it back in again at an achingly slow pace.

We moved together like that, our mouths locked and hips grinding to this slow and heady rhythm which had me lost in her as we took our time devouring one another.

I kept myself in check, fucking her slow and deep while she moaned and whimpered into my mouth and when I finally felt her coming all over my cock, I drew back, observing her as her head tipped back and she cried out in pleasure.

"I love you, Anya Butcher," I said simply as I watched her. "I love you and I'm gonna fucking keep you forever just like this."

Her orgasm began to fade and I rolled my hips again, watching her as she stared up at me, clearly unable to deny my words while struggling to accept them too.

"How can you love me after what I did to you?" she asked eventually, her obsidian eyes wet with tears at the thought of what had almost happened, what she'd almost done, but I reached down to brush them away before they could even fall. I had my own share of blame to harbour in this fucked up little love story of ours.

"You didn't do it to me," I replied simply because it was true. She did it to the man who had harmed her. I wasn't gonna blame her for that.

"How can you love me if you can't trust me?" she pushed and I shook my head, needing her to see that I did.

I gripped her hips and rolled us, falling onto my back beneath her and sinking her down onto my cock as she straddled me, the two of us moaning softly at the full feeling of our joined bodies.

"I do trust you," I said, taking her hands in mine and moving them up my chest before laying them around my throat.

"What are you doing?" she asked, making a move to pull back, but I held on tight.

"I want to put my life in your hands. I want you to see how much I trust you," I replied firmly, squeezing her fingers to tighten them on my neck and her brows rose as she took in the seriousness of my words.

"Benny…when we did this stuff before I was punishing you for what I thought you'd done to me. But now-"

"I always knew I hadn't done those things, bombshell," I replied. "But there's a whole lot of bad that I've done in this world which I need punishing for, love. Besides, this isn't about that. It's about me trusting you."

I took my hands from hers and she kept her own in place, biting down on her bottom lip as I moved to grasp her arse in my hands and shift her up and down the length of my cock.

A gasp escaped her as I lifted my hips into the movement, keeping our pace slow and my thrusts deep while I watched her pupils dilate and I knew I was hitting the perfect spot.

"Come on, bombshell, don't back down on me now. You've never run from a fight before."

Anya's eyes narrowed and her grip on my throat tightened, making me grin as I thrust into her a little harder, showing her my appreciation. Her hesitation lasted a few more moments but as I kept encouraging more from her, daring her with my eyes to give me what I wanted, she finally gave in. Her grip tightened further, cutting off my breath and a growl of pleasure rumbled through my chest as I upped my pace a little, my eyes locked on hers as she bit her lip to try and stifle her moans.

My heart pounded harder as my lungs began to burn and I cupped her arse in my hands, rolling my thumb over the brand on her skin as I drove myself up and into her, hunting for my release and demanding hers in return.

Anya gave up on trying to hold back as she cried out for me, the sound of her pleasure filling the air while dark spots danced around the corners of my vision and my cock throbbed with need deep inside her.

Anya's fingers flexed around my neck but I gave her a slight shake of my head, loving the feeling of her holding my damn life in her hands even as my ears began to ring and my chest swelled with the urgent need to draw breath.

I focused on what I needed to reach that point, what I demanded of her to get me there as I slid my thumb onto her clit and began circling it in time with my thrusts while she rolled her hips seductively and pushed me to the edge of oblivion.

Darkness pressed in around the edges of my vision until the only thing I could see was her above me and the only thing I could focus on was keeping my thrusts deep and hard as I danced with the line of consciousness and my lungs burned with need.

Anya rode my cock harder, her lips parting as her head tipped back as far as it could while still keeping her gaze fixed with mine. I was going to come. Both of us knew it and she had made it clear that she didn't want me knocking her up any time soon. But as I slowed my pace a touch, the offer there in my eyes for me to pull out of her, she shook her head.

"I want to feel your cum inside me," she panted. "I want all of you, Benny. I know you now. You're mine. So give me all of you."

My dick swelled at those words, my hips thrusting harder as the dark closed in evermore around me and I lost myself in the sensation of her body wrapped around mine. And as a cry of ecstasy finally escaped her, the feeling of her pussy locking tight around my shaft made me explode for her.

I came so hard that the darkness took the rest of my vision, my back arching against the sheets as I thrust in deep one final time, filling her with my seed and feeling the most intense high of my fucking life as I swear I brushed against the gates of heaven in her arms.

Anya collapsed onto my chest, releasing my throat so that I could drag in a shuddering breath and my arms went around her trembling body as we just lay there like that, her hair spilling over my chest and our bodies heaving with the evidence of what we'd just done.

"I love you, Benny," she whispered against my skin, her lips brushing over my heart and a smile filling my mouth.

I tightened my hold on her and stared up at the ceiling, basking in the afterglow of us.

"Yeah you fucking do," I agreed, drawing a breath of laughter from her as I let my eyes fall closed once more, drinking in the moment and letting it sweep me away on a tide of exhaustion as my body demanded more sleep.

I tossed and turned in my sleep, unease finding me in the dark as I found myself reliving the night that had ruined my life, which had changed everything and seen me sent away from everyone I knew and loved for years. My empire was stolen from me, my crown toppled. All because of that one night which I still didn't fully understand.

Soft lips met mine, dragging me from the dark and I followed the call of them, letting them pull me back to consciousness as I worked to leave that night behind me and find my way to her.

"I think you were having a nightmare," Anya murmured and for a moment it was like I was there, crouched in an alleyway at the arse crack of dawn with fog swirling all around us and my brothers at my back, waiting on my orders.

"Are you sure about this, boss?" Olly asked me and I turned to glance at him where he crouched behind me alongside Frank and Church.

"Of course I am. When have I ever been wrong?" I asked in reply, cocky as ever while we eyed the warehouse we were planning to hit. The Candlestick Maker had been causing waves for our gang for far too long and though I'd been all for taking him out, Danny had fought hard against that plan, enjoying his contribution to the tythe all too much despite my distaste for his method of earning the money.

This was a compromise, a lesson I was willing to teach the fucker for getting greedy with his power and trying to push into Whitechapel. At times like this, I often wondered if it would just be better for us to own the fact that we were the real power in London. Hell, we were the real power in the whole of Europe if not beyond too. The anonymity of The Firm's identity had served us well on occasion and it kept the threats against our lives to a minimum, but it also meant cheeky fuckers like the Candlestick Maker thought they could take liberties with the Butcher gang. It made them think they had a shot at pushing us out. They wouldn't make such dumb choices if they knew the full truth.

Then again, I always had liked getting my own hands dirty.

"Danny and his men should be in position 'round back right about now," I said, looking for anyone who had eyes on the street and finding none too obvious. "We'll just make this quick, we get in, grab the payment he has ready for the next container full of poor souls he's expecting tonight, then get out again."

"Like taking candy from a baby," Church replied, grinning darkly.

"This should remind the arsehole who he's messing with," I said.

"How bloody are we willing to get?" Frank asked and Olly looked to me for the answer, not looking anywhere near as bloodthirsty as his brother, though I knew he was capable of killing a man if he had to.

"No more than we must," I replied. "This lesson can be financial. It'll buy us the time we need for me to get Danny on board with ending this shit for good. I dunno why he's causing such a fucking fuss over this, but I don't wanna push him if I don't have to. Give me a couple of weeks and I'll have him thinking he was the one who had wanted to kill the Candlestick Maker in the first place. Hell, I might even let him strike the blow."

Church sniggered while the others nodded and I jerked my chin towards the warehouse, shooting Danny a quick message to tell him we were in position before pointing Church and Frank off to the right while me and Olly headed left.

Anya shook me lightly and I sucked in a deep breath as I blinked my eyes open, trying to force those memories from my mind.

"Tell me about it," she urged.

I glanced over at the clock, my stomach rumbling as I realised I'd slept the entire day away.

I swiped a hand over my face before looking back to my wife, finding her now dressed in one of my t-shirts with her hair slightly damp from a shower as she knelt on the bed at my side.

I placed a hand on her bare thigh, careful to avoid the cut there as I stroked her smooth skin and tried to anchor myself in the present.

"There's a reason why I couldn't just return to this place with my own identity when I was released from prison," I said slowly, wondering if I should just skim over this whole thing before reminding myself that I had wanted honesty between us, which meant she needed to know. "I was set up," I added.

"By who?" she asked, though I was willing to bet that look in her dark eyes said she already knew.

"Danny," I confirmed. "Though to this day I still don't know exactly what happened."

"So what do you know?" she pressed and I sighed, pushing myself upright and leaning back against the headboard.

"We went to hit the Candlestick Maker one night," I explained. "He'd been taking liberties and causing issues for us. I wanted him dead for it, but Danny resisted. We argued it back and forth a lot before I was forced to concede and we made the plan to steal from him instead of outright assassinating him."

"Why didn't Danny want him dead?"

"Not really sure on that one," I admitted. "Though knowing that they have some dealings now makes me wonder if they were already friendly back then. That alone wouldn't have been enough to persuade Danny away from violence, but if he was getting something from the Candlestick Maker which he couldn't get from us…probably blow if I'm being totally honest. I had been working to make it harder for Danny to feed his habit for a year or more by that point, and if that arsehole was making it readily available to him then maybe that explains it. I dunno really."

"So you tried to rob him?" she prompted and I nodded.

"That was the plan, then I thought I'd be able to convince Danny on the assassination once the dust had settled. Either that or I woulda just carried it out anyway and let him pitch a fit. I guess one of the biggest mistakes I used to make back then was in trying to allow Danny some semblance of power. He was always playing the big I am. Always shouting about how important he was and I didn't think he'd ever noticed that I was the one who was really pulling all the strings."

"But he had?"

"I assume so," I said. "And I guess he didn't like that. Which was why he decided to set me up."

"How?" Anya reached out to brush her fingers over mine and I snared her hand, keeping hold of it as I went on.

"I still don't really know how much of it was him, how much was bad luck or how much was the Candlestick Maker," I admitted. "Back then me and Danny had our own little groups of right hand men. I had Church, Frank and Olly. The four of us were like peas in a fuckin' pod, thick as thieves. We'd built up a reputation of our own. People knew us as the forget-me-nots on account of the memories we left haunting them. We embraced the name when it stuck and we all got tattoos of that flower too. The only ink I had once upon a time."

Anya's fingers moved over the tattoos on my hands and she tilted her head as she looked to the others which coated my chest, arms and neck.

"At least Danny had good taste in ink," she murmured. "How pissed would you have been if it was all garbage like Church's?"

I barked a laugh and she grinned, but I also knew she didn't think his ink was shit at all. I'd watched her licking her way along the lines of it and coming all over his fingers which were dressed in it. Nah, she didn't hate his tattoos, she was just looking to bait him with her mockery.

"The tattoos were a small price to pay in the face of clearing my name," I murmured and she raised her dark eyes to mine once more.

"And have you?" she asked but I sighed, shaking my head.

"I still can't prove what he did," I said bitterly. "Me and Church have spent every spare minute trying to. Hell, Church spent the last eight years playing house with that motherfucker to try and find what we needed, but I'm beginning to think he was too thorough in his disposal of everything that could have linked him back to the truth."

"A lot of men who I knew back in Vegas served years in prison," she pointed out. "They weren't ostracised for it. So what did he do to make it impossible for you to return to your own kingdom?"

"The Butchers don't know much of anything. The gang probably woulda accepted my return, though there would have been some bad blood on account of Olly." I sighed. "It wasn't them I had to hide from though. It was The Firm. Danny cut the fat on the members of our true organisation when he set me up. Our father ran this empire for years before we rose into our power, and he had a whole host of men who he had known and worked with for years within our organisation. Problem was, those fellas had a preference for his way of doing things. They questioned us a lot, made things difficult, resisted the change in the power dynamic and basically made things harder during our rise. I was handling it, winning them around, proving what I was made of and earning their support – but Danny? Danny is like a bull in a china shop who's seen a shiny red something at the far end of it. He's volatile and unpredictable and to be perfectly honest, the older generation fuckin' hated him. So when I was arrested, he gave evidence against them. All of them."

"He ratted them out?" Anya gasped, her eyes wide with horror and I nodded darkly knowing she understood how serious that was. In our circles, talking to the police was akin to offering yourself up for death willingly. No matter what. No one talked to the cops. Except Danny had. I knew it. I fucking knew it. But I couldn't prove it. "How the hell is he still alive?" she asked and I just tilted my head at her, waiting for her to put it all together. "He made everyone think you'd done it?" she gasped.

"Yeah," I gritted out. "After I was arrested, while my trial was being conducted, one by one, all twelve of the oldest members of The Firm were rounded up and charged for all kinds of crimes which they had committed over the years. And then the whispers started, filtering through The Firm from ear to ear that Benny Butcher had sold them all out to buy himself a shorter sentence."

"No," Anya pressed her fingers to her lips in horror and I squeezed her other hand reassuringly. "But Danny is out now. What if he tells? What will happen to you if the people who believe you did that find out you're back here?"

"Honestly? I have no fucking idea. But I don't think he'll tell just yet."

"Why not?" she pushed, the fear she clearly felt over this warming something inside me as I shrugged.

"He loves me. For all his flaws and all he's done, I know that might be hard to understand, but it's true. Danny is all kinds of fucked up in the head, but his love for me has never wavered. He doesn't want me dead."

Anya looked like she was about to object to that but then she frowned, nodding slowly.

"When he attacked me, he kept saying stuff about me getting in the way, coming between him and someone. I thought it was about Frank, but…"

A growl rumbled through my throat at the thought of him hurting her because of me and I pushed my fingers into her hair, gripping the side of her face and drawing her close. "He won't ever lay a hand on you again," I swore.

Anya nodded slowly, her lips meeting mine as she melted into me and I groaned as the desire to tug her into my lap and lose myself in her again rose in me, but I knew she needed to hear all of this, so I managed to find some way to draw back.

"Danny has always hated me having other people I care about. He chased off any girlfriends who ever tried to hang around too long and even begrudged me spending time with our ma or sister too often. He hated it when I formed the forget-me-nots and he about lost his shit when he saw our tattoos. He never could understand how I could love him and love others too. For him, it was us against the world and I guess that was why I never expected him to stab me in the back the way he did."

"So why were you arrested?" Anya asked and I knew I'd danced around that part too long.

I closed my eyes, remembering the moment when I'd kicked down the door to the side of the building, hurrying inside with Olly right on my heels and racing into the depths of the Candlestick Maker's holding warehouse. It had seemed so easy at first, the way clear, the path empty.

"The Candlestick Maker must have figured out that we were coming," I explained. "We were all heading in from different directions and there was no one blocking our way there. We knew there would be people guarding the money, but aside from that we hadn't come equipped for a huge fight. The lights went out all of a sudden and the next thing we knew, we were being fired on from all around. We fought back but it was impossible to do more than just maintain our position and it quickly became clear that we were outnumbered. I sent a message to the others, telling them all to run before turning tail and getting the fuck outa there myself. Olly was right there with me as we ran outa that place, right beside me, not a scratch on him."

"Fuck me, that was close," Olly laughed as we rounded a building and pressed our spines to the cold brickwork. "Who the hell tipped them off?"

"Beats me," I replied, gritting my teeth in irritation and making my mind up to end this shit the way I'd wanted to. The Candlestick Maker would be getting a visit from The Firm and I was gonna get rid of him for good.

The fog pressed in so close around us that it was hard to see much of anything within it and I shot a text to Church, telling him and Frank to meet us down by the river where we'd all agreed to reconvene.

But as I moved to text my twin next, my phone started to ring.

"Benny!" Danny gasped as I answered, gunshots ringing out behind him. "Fuck, Benny, I think we're done for. They've got me cornered, Big Terry is dead. Fuck, fuck..."

"I'm coming," I barked, my heart leaping in fear as I turned to look back towards the warehouse where I could still make out the sound of gunfire. I ended the call and whirled back to Olly.

"Danny needs me," I told him, taking a step away and he moved to follow. "No," I barked, realising he was planning to come with me. "There are too many of them. Just go meet up with Frank and Church. I can handle this, but I'm not putting you in the firing line too."

"But-"

"I mean it, Olly. That was a fucking order," I snapped before turning away and racing back into the fog, leaving him behind me.

"We got out," I explained to Anya. "We were clear. But then Danny called me from inside that fucking warehouse, surrounded and needing me."

"You went back?" she asked and I nodded, regretting that decision more than any other in my life.

"Yeah. I went back and I told Olly to go catch up with Frank and Church…that was the last time I ever saw him alive."

"What happened?"

"I don't know. Me and Church have been trying to hunt down whoever killed him for eight long years, and we've got nothing. We had a rule in our little crew – no man left behind. We never split down into groups lower than pairs when we were working a job together. It meant someone always had your back. But I left Olly behind when I went back for Danny. I left him and someone killed him while he was on his own. That's why Frank hates me. He blames me. Hell, I blame my fucking self."

"It doesn't sound like that was your fault," Anya breathed but I just shook my head.

"It was. We had a rule and I broke it. I left him behind and now he's dead. I can't ever undo that."

The grief I always felt at the loss of one of my closest friends pressed in on me until I found it hard to draw breath and the only comfort I found was in the tightness of my grip around Anya's fingers.

"Did you save Danny?" she asked and I was surprised at the tenderness in her voice as she mentioned him. No doubt she hated my brother with a passion for all he'd done to her, and yet in that moment she was clearly more concerned with me and what I'd done that night.

"I never even made it back inside," I admitted. "I was on my way, trying to find a way in where they wouldn't just gun me down when Danny called again to say he'd made it out. I ran to meet up with him and together we fled that place. We ran all the way back to The Duck and Dog, but when we got there, the police were already waiting for us, like they'd known we were coming."

"Danny?" she asked, her brow dropping.

"Yeah," I grunted. "We'd ditched the weapons we'd been carrying before we got there so I wasn't all that worried when they demanded to search me. I didn't have any blood on me, I wasn't carrying anything I shouldn't have been – or at least I didn't think I was. But when I'd reunited with Danny he'd embraced me and looking back I'm pretty certain that that was when he'd dropped the knife into my jacket pocket."

"What knife?"

"One that was used to kill some Candlestick piece of shit by the name of Darren Kerrington. They had me with the murder weapon right after he'd been killed and even my lawyers couldn't do shit about that. So off I went to rot for fifteen years while Danny stole my empire out from under me and made sure no one believed a word I had to say on the subject by making them think I'd ratted out my father's generation to buy myself time off my sentence."

"But you couldn't ever prove any of it to be lies?" Anya asked, her eyes shining with tears. "You still haven't found anything to clear your name?"

"Not yet." I blew out a breath. "In all honesty, I'm starting to doubt I ever will."

Her brow creased but then she looked up suddenly, her gaze moving to the door as she sucked in a sharp breath.

"Benny…I think I might have found something that will help," she said, pushing to her feet. "Something that you really need to see."

CHAPTER FORTY TWO

I hurried out of the room and jogged along to the bedroom which had been Danny's, moving into the en suite and popping open the compartment in the mirror, finding the laptop waiting for me inside. I took it out and headed back to the room down the hall where my husband was waiting for me.

Although…maybe he wasn't even my husband now. I'd married Danny Butcher, not Benny. The name he'd signed on the marriage certificate had been a lie, but as I looked into the eyes of the man who had claimed me that day, I knew our bond ran deeper than marriage anyway. We were bound to each other with unbreakable threads, ties that held us together regardless of rings or names.

"I think Church should see this too," I said and Benny nodded, rising from the bed, groaning a little as he ran a hand over his face, leaving me with another wave of guilt crashing against my heart at what I'd done to him last night.

We got dressed for the day and were soon heading downstairs, my favourite Beatles t-shirt tucked into some high waisted ripped jeans and my biker boots in place.

Church was in the lounge, lying on the couch with his arm slung across his face and his blue shirt riding up to expose his abs. I moved to his side, brushing my fingers over his hand and he jerked awake, sitting up abruptly and breathing in deeply. "Is it Danny? Is he back? Is it Frank? Do I need to knock his head against a wall?"

"No one's here. But I found something a while ago and I think you both need to see it," I said, dropping down beside him and biting my tongue on a curse as my injuries stung. Benny sat down on my other side as I opened the laptop on my knees and Church and Benny leaned in close to look.

I navigated to the folder where the video I'd seen of Olly was hidden, my gut clenching as I realised the terrible weight of this footage. This was their friend, Frank's brother. And I didn't want to cause them pain by playing this, but it had to be done.

I hit play and they watched Olly be cut down, both of them gasping in horror as Danny drew blood and left him to die.

"No, fuck, oh god, Olly." Church gripped his hair in his fist, standing and starting to pace while Benny hid his face in his hands, shaking his head in horror at what he'd watched.

"I'm sorry," I said, hating having had to show them this. I could see how much they'd loved their friend and I didn't know what to do as Benny's shoulders started to shake. I crawled closer to my husband, wrapping myself around him and begging Church to join us with my eyes. He gave in to the demand in my expression, dropping down beside me and the three of us coiled up tight together as I shared in their grief.

"Fuck," Benny spat and I felt the sudden shift in him and Church as their sadness sharpened to rage.

"That fucking prick," Church hissed, launching to his feet and throwing his fist into the nearest wall. I jumped up, catching hold of his arm before he could do it again, making him look at me and a world of hurt stared back at me in his eyes.

"He was one of my boys," Church lamented, scrubbing at his hair with a look of distress about him. "And Danny fucking took him from us."

I moved forward, wrapping my arms around him, having nothing else to offer. "I'm sorry."

His arms closed around me and he rested his chin on my head as the fight went out of him. "Don't ever say sorry for things that ain't your fault, darlin'."

Benny drew closer and I looked up at him as he rested a hand on Church's shoulder.

"Can you show this to The Firm to clear you name?" I asked Benny, but he shook his head.

"It won't be enough. They hate me because of all the people I got locked up in prison. They think I'm a fuckin' snitch regardless of this."

Church clenched his jaw, his eyes brightening a little. "Don't worry, we'll find a way to get your crown reinstated, mate."

"There's someone who needs to see this before we do anything else," Benny said darkly.

"Frank," I breathed and the two of them nodded as Church's arms tightened on me.

"He was in one hell of a foul mood last night," Church pointed out. "And knowing him, he's been out all night picking fights and drawing blood to feed that rage in him. But nothing's gonna sate him like your blood. Anya and I should head to his place, see if we can get him to watch that video, make him see the truth of where he should have been aiming that hatred all these years."

"Nah," Benny said, shadows entering his eyes. "Me and him have a score to settle, so I'm coming with you on the hunt."

"What score?" Church asked in confusion and Benny's gaze settled on me.

"You wanna fill him in, bombshell, or should I?" A razor's edge lined his voice and I could see he still wasn't over what he'd found out.

"Me and Frank kinda…hooked up," I admitted and Church released me, his eyebrows raising.

"Where?"

"That's your question?" Benny hissed. "It don't matter where, it matters how many times while I was oblivious."

"In one session or…" Church frowned and Benny punched him in the shoulder.

"It was one time. Last night after we took Yuri," I said firmly. "And I'm not sorry," I added, because dammit yesterday might have been a shit show of mass proportions, but Frank lit up my soul in a way I couldn't deny. It was different to Church, different to Benny, but all three of them somehow were designed to make me feel alive. And I'd spent so long feeling muted, numbed out, that it was impossible to deny my heart and body to these men, I could easier stop the blood from pumping through my veins.

Benny scowled. "You're gonna start givin' me a complex if you keep adding men to this situation, bombshell. Is there anyone else I should know about, have you been letting John Boy in your backdoor? Has Mickey Hairpiece been finger diddlin' my missus?"

"No," I growled, staring from him to Church and letting them see the honesty in me. "It's the three of you. That's it. And that's plenty, trust me. I'm not trying to overcomplicate my life, it just keeps happening because something about you guys keeps getting under my skin. The way I feel when I'm with each of you is the way I have wished I could feel my entire life. It's live music thrumming through my veins and I'm awake while it's playing. I can feel it vibrating through my bones, and I don't want it to stop, because I'll disappear again, I'll vanish just like I vanished for so many years. And I want to stay, Benny." I lurched towards him. "Don't take them away from me. Either of them. I demand it."

Benny observed me, his arms folded as he stared down his nose at me, a crease between his eyes. "I ain't denying you anything, love. But from this second forward, none of us lie to each other, even if the truth cuts us open and leaves us to rot. I'd rather fester in the truth than die with a veil pulled over my eyes."

I nodded my agreement, holding out my hand to him and he slid his palm around mine, clutching it tight as we made the deal. Church placed his hand over ours and I looked to him with my heart thundering, sensing some sort of power at work in the air, like this promise ran deeper than just words.

"No more lies," Benny said.

Church and I agreed and we released each other, my fingers tingling from the contact.

"Now let's go catch us an angry little Frank." Benny strode to the door and I picked up the laptop, walking after him as Church fell into step with me.

We were soon piled into Benny's Jaguar with me in the back beside Church while Benny drove, heading off in the direction of Frank's apartment.

I flipped the laptop open, searching through more of Danny's files and Church tapped on the screen when he spotted a folder called Danny's Wins.

"What's that?" he murmured and I clicked on it, finding a bunch of video clips inside.

I frowned as I brought up a feed of what looked like someone's bedroom. Danny was holding the phone which recorded it while he pinned a guy on the bed, severing his fingers from his hand and making my nose wrinkle as I clicked onto another video instead.

They were all of Danny mutilating people, recording himself as he plunged knives into chests and stomachs and I grimaced as I found one of him carving the word *whore* into a woman's breasts while she screamed and begged for mercy. The videos continued and I watched as he broke into an old man's home, terrorising him and hunting him through his own house.

Realisation burned through me as more and more of the attacks played out before my eyes. Danny wasn't asking them for information, they didn't seem to know him at all. And that left me with the gut-wrenching feeling that none of this was gang related. It was cruelty for the sake of cruelty and it left me feeling sick.

Danny's laughter rang out from the speakers, cold and full of hate and I flinched at the inhuman sound of it. I hurriedly closed down the video and looked to Church in disgust. Those people weren't victims of the world we lived in. They clearly weren't a part of this way of life, of the gangs or the mafia or any of that. No. They were the targets in some twisted sport being played by a hunter whose only goal was his own sick enjoyment of their destruction. It wasn't the work of a man fulfilling his duties as the leader of his empire. It wasn't even the work of a thug lost to bloodlust while carrying out his job. It was depraved. Fucked up. Wrong on so many levels and I couldn't help but think what he might have done to me last night if Benny had never come home.

I wondered how my husband would deal with this. There were punishments Benny could deliver his twin which disregarded the law along with morality. When it came down to justice, it was usually dealt with in blood where I came from. And I'd wait to see which path my husband chose to deliver his vengeance on his kin, though I was certain it would be paved with unmerciful choices.

Benny parked up near to Frank's apartment, the car mostly concealed by a low row of bushes that lined the closest houses, but we could just see through to the entrance.

"Gimme your phone, I'll play bait," I said, holding my hand out for it as Church took it from his pocket and gave it to me.

I found Frank's number and dialled it, not liking that I had to lie so soon after I'd just pledged to be truthful to Benny and Church. Maybe I'd cut Frank in on that deal just as soon as all of this was cleared up.

"What?" Frank snarled, clearly expecting Church.

"It's me," I said, sounding frantic. "I want to see you. I'm walking up the street now towards your place, I'll be there in two minutes. Can you come meet me?"

Frank fell quiet for a moment then grunted in affirmation. "I'm coming down."

He hung up and I tossed the phone back to Church with a smirk.

He leaned in, stealing a kiss from my lips that set my pulse racing. "Dirty little liar," he murmured.

"Pay attention," Benny growled.

"I'll distract him," I said, opening the door and diving out over Church's lap before he could catch me.

I jogged towards Frank's apartment, biting my lip in anticipation of seeing him. He stepped out of the door and my stomach swooped, my excitement growing as I found myself suddenly running towards him, so grateful to him for saving Benny last night and so damn happy to see him that I didn't even hesitate as I threw my arms around him and pressed my lips to his.

He stiffened then melted, dragging me hard against him and pushing his tongue into my mouth. I hummed in delight, kissing him deeper and carving my fingers up the back of his neck as our kiss became completely inappropriate for a public display, but I didn't really give a fuck.

He was abruptly ripped away from me and I gasped as Benny and Church shoved him in the open trunk of the Jaguar, punching him and forcing him inside without mercy. Frank's eyes met mine half a second before they snapped the trunk shut, betrayal blazing in his gaze.

A bunch of people had seen the attack in broad daylight and Church started bowing. "The next show is at half four!"

Some people clapped, but others looked concerned so we ran for it, dropping into the car as Benny sped off down the road.

Frank was thrashing like crazy in the trunk, swearing and snarling and I shared a concerned look with Church beside me.

"I'm kinda thinking this was a bad idea," I said.

"Nahhh," Church said dismissively. "You're alright, aren't you Frankie boy?"

"I'm gonna fucking gut you, Church," he barked from the trunk. "I'll rip your liver out and eat it raw."

"Woah, you won't see that on the British Bake-Off," Church laughed.

Benny drove us through the city, eventually pulling up by a large boxing gym which sat on the river's edge, built inside a converted old storage unit.

Benny backed the car right up to a side door and we all exited, rounding the vehicle to look at the trunk which held a beast inside it.

"You ready, mate?" Church muttered.

"Yeah." Benny rolled up his sleeves, looking all business and I couldn't deny how hot the two of them were when they went all gangster like that. "Anya, get the door, will you love?"

I nodded, opening the door to the gym and holding it wide as they moved forward to open the trunk. The second it popped up, Frank leapt out and went full attack dog, swinging fists and promising death as Benny and Church accosted him.

"I'm gonna fucking gut you, you worthless piece of shit," he snarled, lunging at Benny as Church leapt on his back and locked him in a choke hold.

"Easy now, big fella, we just need a little chat is all, okay?" Church spoke placatingly as Frank choked and spluttered, swinging around to slam them both against the wall. I winced as Church's head smacked against the brickwork and his grip loosened a little, giving Frank the space he needed to lunge at Benny again.

Benny used Frank's momentum against him, whirling him around and managing to pin his arm to his back just as Church collided with him too and they worked together to get control of him.

Their combined might managed to overwhelm him and they hauled him through the door which I snapped shut behind us.

"I'll fucking kill you, Benny. You're gonna die screaming with your entrails sprayed across this room," Frank snarled and I sucked my lip as I followed them, eyeing their bulging muscles and sinister expressions while finding this whole situation strangely hot.

Church and Benny managed to get him through another door and I hurried after them, finding a girl there in a fitted hijab sparring in a boxing ring before us against a tall guy who had so many tattoos I could hardly make out his skin beneath them.

"We need the ring for a bit, Zoya," Benny called and the girl gazed over at us without seeming remotely phased by them manhandling someone into what I guessed was her gym.

"No worries, boss." She pointed the man she'd been sparring with out of the gym through a door on the other side of the room, heading after him and snapping the door shut behind her without so much as a backwards glance. I had to wonder how often she was interrupted like that by the Butcher boys and how involved she was in the gang, but my attention was soon snared by the wrestling men once again.

Church and Benny hauled Frank into the ring, shoving him down onto the floor and working to keep him there while he bucked and thrashed.

"There's some rope and a chair in that supply closet, would you fetch them bombshell?" Benny asked, jerking his chin towards a door behind me and I hurried to get them, carrying them into the ring and placing the chair down before handing Benny the rope.

They wrestled Frank onto the chair and tied him in place so tightly, it looked painful before finally stepping back, breathing heavily as they admired their work.

Church smeared some blood from his busted lip across his knuckles as he rubbed it away and Benny whooped like that whole thing had been fun. His shirt was ripped half off of him - not that I minded the free look at his painted abs - but he was definitely in need of a wardrobe change.

Frank bared his teeth at Benny, a chasm of rage and hate in his eyes. "You think this will save you?" he snapped. "Are you gonna kill me before I kill you? Because you'd better, or else I'm gonna get hold of you, Benny. I'm gonna cut your pretty face to ribbons, gouge your eyeballs from their sockets and watch you plead for me to end you."

"Calm down, mate," Benny said. "We just wanna talk. No one needs to get their eyes gouged out."

Frank sneered and as I moved closer, his eyes shifted to me. "You've fallen for his bullshit. He's spoon fed you it. He's a fucking liar, a traitor and a snitch."

"You need to hear him out," I tried.

"I'm not hearing fucking shit!" Frank bellowed, his voice filling up the whole space as the ropes strained beneath the force of his muscles.

"Church, fetch the laptop," Benny ordered before glancing down at his ruined shirt, tugging the remains off and tossing them aside.

"Both of you go," I demanded and Benny looked to me in surprise. "I'll get him to calm down before we start."

"Frank only has two settings, darlin'," Church protested. "Calm ocean of deadly injustice and raging storm of murder. The wind don't blow often, but when it does change he gets stuck that way, don't ya, mate?"

"Fuck you, you arse licking cunt. I shoulda realised Benny was back from the moment I saw you looking at him like the sun shone outa his fucking backside at that damn wedding. You mighta been cosy with Danny all these years but you never wanted to suck his cock the way you did Benny's," Frank snarled, spitting at Church's feet.

"Er, I think it has been long since established that my over active gag reflex makes me ill suited to deep throating any dick – even Benny's," Church replied scathingly. "Besides, I'm not the one who has spent the last eight years blinded by lies and drowning in self pity, am I, you wanker?"

"Stop it," I snapped, moving between Frank and the others before any of them could add any further insults to this pile of shit. "This isn't helping. Let me speak to Frank alone. He won't listen to either of you, and you being here is just making things worse."

Benny and Church exchanged a look and for a moment I thought my husband was about to pull alpha male bullshit on me, but he just gave Church a firm stare like he was warning him not to argue then turned to answer me.

"Alright," Benny said, nodding to me with a small smirk on his lips before him and Church left Frank and I alone together, though Church continued to mutter insults on his way out.

I was surprised at how easily my husband listened to me, my chest swirling with warmth over having the Butcher King answer my demands.

Frank seethed as I drew closer, looking more animal than man as I reached out for him and cupped his jaw in my hand. He didn't flinch away and I had to hope that meant he was going to at least try and hear me out.

"He's deceived you, Cash," he hissed. "Let me go. I'll get rid of him for both of us. No more husband, no more cage. We can run together."

I traced my fingers over his brow. "I thought he was a monster too. I know why you feel this way, Frank, I promise you I do. But you need to see something. All I'm asking is for you to give Benny five minutes to explain himself. That's it."

"Never," he spat and I lowered myself onto his lap, kissing one cheek then the other, wishing I could heal this tear in his chest over losing his brother.

He relaxed a little as I looked into his eyes. "I swear I wouldn't ask this of you if I didn't truly believe it could make a difference. I know what it's like to lose someone you love, to lose family." My throat thickened as emotion welled inside me. "But what if everything you've believed all these years isn't how it seemed? What if there was proof, undeniable proof, Frank, that Benny isn't deserving of your hatred?"

His jaw flexed, and something shifted in his gaze, just a tiny amount of curiosity.

"Will you please give him five minutes?" I asked of him. "And if it changes nothing, then I'll free you, I swear it."

Frank exhaled a low breath then after what felt like an eternity, he nodded.

"Thank you." I kissed him firmly then stepped away, turning to go and get the guys, hoping that this video could free Frank in some way. That maybe the love lost between him and Benny could be reforged once the truth was finally revealed to him.

CHAPTER FORTY THREE

It took all I had not to start yelling insults the moment Benny strode back into the room, his arm casually draped around Anya's shoulders like they really were the king and queen of our world, come to pay a visit to the common folk.

I could see it now. That obvious thing I'd been missing before. The way that he walked, something in his gaze. Benny and Danny really were fucking identical so far as looks went, there was no doubt about that, but they'd always carried themselves a little differently. I guessed Benny had been putting on an act with more than just his new tattoos since he'd stolen his brother's place here, but he'd dropped that now and I saw him at last.

Benny had a way of looking at the world like it was a problem he could solve if only he had the right key. Some obstacles had additional locks to them, but one way or another, he always figured out exactly what was needed to open them to him. It was what made him so fucking good at his job, what I'd once admired in him, why I'd thrown my lot in with him so many years ago. But it was a weapon as clearly as it was a gift. He could turn that knowledge and cunning against a man as easily as he could use it to grant wishes. And I refused to be fooled by him the way Church and Anya had clearly been.

"I know you've had a bit of a shock, fella," Benny said casually as Church strode away to grab another chair and he climbed up into the ring once more. "But you need to hear us out on this."

"I'll hear you out on one condition," I growled, watching as Benny lifted the rope and held a hand out for Anya, tugging her up into the ring behind him like he was drawing her into a fucking horse and carriage. "When it's done, you untie me and face me in this ring like a man. We end this here in blood and dirt and if only one of us steps outa here when it's done then so be it. I need this over."

"Done," Benny agreed, taking a cigarette from his pocket and lighting it with a match as he watched me with an intent gaze. "I need it over too."

Church hopped up into the ring, placing the other chair down in front of me and opening a laptop which he perched on top of it.

"I found that laptop hidden in Danny's room," Anya said, stepping across the ring until she was standing just behind me, the weight of her presence pressing against my back. "I didn't understand the things I found on it until Benny told me the truth about who he was. I didn't realise what I'd already seen and that you needed to see it too."

I remained silent as she leaned around me, unlocking the laptop and selecting a video before clicking play and standing upright again.

"I wish you didn't have to see this," she breathed, her hand falling to my shoulder as I frowned at the footage, watching as a misty night in London was revealed to me and swallowing a lump in my throat as my brother's voice rang out from the past.

I stiffened in my seat because I knew, I already knew that this was that night. The last night of his life. When Benny had left him alone despite us all swearing to stick together and he'd found himself on the end of some scum's knife.

But it wasn't some random gangster I saw approaching my kin through the fog, it was a man who I had spent the last eight years alongside, a man I'd disliked but hadn't bothered to hate. A man who had looked me in the eyes and often given me this odd little smirk like he was in on some joke that I wasn't a party to. I'd put that down to Danny being as cracked as an egg before an omelette. But what if there was more to that? What if I was about to see the more?

"Alright, Benny," my brother called out and I sucked in a breath as he was revealed on the screen, bloody and fresh from the fight, but alive, whole. A frown drew his brow down as he realised his mistake. A mistake we all made from time to time because the Butcher twins were like mirror fucking images. "Oh shit, sorry Danny, you don't half look like your brother."

"That's the thing about being twins, we're identical in every way. One and the same," Danny answered and my pulse picked up as he moved closer to Olly, raising his phone to get a clearer look at his face.

"What's with the phone, are you starting up a filmmaking career now, you fuckin' dipstick?" Olly laughed, though I could tell Danny's odd behaviour was throwing him off the way it always had. He'd been the one who was most concerned about Benny's twin brother and the problems he was causing us back then. He'd been urging Benny to rein him in, looking into rumours about the shit he'd been getting up to when he thought no one was looking. And as I watched the way the camera jerked forward, I knew that Danny had figured that out. He'd seen the mistrust and he'd feared it and he'd dealt with it the way he always dealt with his problems. In bloody, brutal, violence.

Pain lanced through my chest as I watched the blow fall, the blade driving through my brother's throat so suddenly that he hadn't even seen it coming.

A strangled noise escaped me as I stared into Olly's eyes and I swear I felt his pain and his fear as he realised his time was up.

He dropped to his knees as he started choking on his own blood and Danny fisted his hair in his hand, forcing him to look up at him as he died, making him look at the monster who had stolen his life while his blood spilled to the pavement between them.

Danny yanked the knife back out of Olly's neck with a groan of pleasure and he forced his head back while Olly desperately clasped his throat, trying to stem the endless flow of blood as death came for him on swift and certain wings.

I felt my own throat closing up as I stared at the scene before me, a painful, hopeless need to crawl right into the past and save the man I'd loved my entire life filling me as a line of salt water tracked down my cheek.

"It ain't personal, Olly," Danny said, shoving him to the ground like he was fucking nothing, leaving him bleeding out and alone as he backed away. "Alright, scrap that. Maybe it is personal." He laughed, and a bellow of rage and pain escaped me which was so intense that I felt it burning through every infinitesimal piece of me.

Agony over the full truth of that night speared me in the chest and left me bleeding just as my brother had been left bleeding on that freezing street, full of fear and all alone in his final moments.

It all made sense now. All of it clicking together bit by bit until this puzzle I'd been looking at for so long made such a fucking awful kind of sense that I was left unable to deny it. Benny had always sworn that he only left Olly on his own because Danny had called him in desperate need of help. He hadn't wanted to drag my brother back into that fight. But instead of saving him by forcing him to remain behind, we'd all just fallen into the trap that Danny had laid.

Anya dropped onto my lap, her arms winding around me and her tears wetting my cheek as she pressed her face against mine, our pain melding as one while I broke over the truth of my brother's death and she felt every stab of agony along with me.

The ropes securing me were cut away while she remained there and for several long seconds, I didn't even move.

But then Church was behind her, lifting her from my lap and pulling her away from me so that Benny could step into my line of sight instead.

He tossed a pair of boxing gloves into my chest, letting them fall to lay on my knees and I looked up at him blankly.

"I never snitched on anyone either. But I haven't got the proof on that one yet," he said roughly and I could see his own grief over Olly reflected in his dark eyes. "You wanted to settle this bad blood between us in the ring?"

Benny waited patiently, taking a long drag on his cigarette as he watched me, a haze of smoke hanging above him as he exhaled.

"I still shouldn't have left him," he added, another note of hurt to his words. "If I hadn't left him…"

"Then Danny woulda just got him some other way," Church muttered bitterly and I had to agree with him. Danny had had it out for the four of us before that night. He hated us having our own bond which didn't include him. He hated the tattoos we'd all gotten to represent that. He hated it because he hated anything that threatened what he had with Benny. Or what he thought he had.

I made myself look at Benny where he stood before me. Really look. I took in the scars which shone in his dark eyes, the years which had been stolen from him that night, the truth of what he'd come back here to reclaim, and the sight of the man I'd once loved like family.

I cut my gaze to Church where he was now standing outside the ring with Anya at his side, his heavily inked forearms leaning on the rope as he watched me, a sad kind of hope in his eyes.

"I ain't apologising," I ground out, pushing to my feet as I slowly put the gloves on.

Benny nodded, taking a final drag on his cigarette before flicking the butt aside and catching a pair of gloves which Church tossed him.

"I ain't asking you to. None of us are innocent men here."

Benny rolled his shoulders back as he gloved up, his inked body on show as he prepared for the fight, and I took in the levels he'd gone to to exact this plan. But even through all of that, even while he needed to dress his body in those tattoos to pass himself off as his brother, he hadn't covered the forget-me-not he'd gotten to match the rest of us all those years ago. He'd risked his entire plan on preserving that one remaining piece of the bond we'd once shared. And there was something in that. Something that mattered.

I tossed the chair I'd been sitting on outa the ring and eyed my opponent, the furious energy which was rolling through my body demanding this outlet.

My eyes had been opened to a whole new world, an enemy who had been in plain sight for so fucking long. And my wrath might have been misplaced before now, but it hadn't lessened for that revelation. I still planned on getting my revenge.

I tightened my gloves and eyed Benny as he took up his position across the ring from me.

He dropped his guard and raised his chin.

"I'll give you one shot for free," he said. "But you'd better make it count, because after that hit, you and me are gonna work our issues out in this ring and we'll come out of it with our bond back in place again whether you like it or not. Got it?"

I eyed him for a long moment, wondering if I could really accept those terms, but even as I looked at him it became clear to me that I could, because my hatred had always been reserved for the man who had taken my brother from me. And I still had someone who was going to answer for that.

I raised my fists and closed in on the man I'd once seen as a brother. He was going to regret offering me a free hit, because this one was gonna hurt like a bitch.

CHAPTER FORTY FOUR

We spilled into the warehouse with weary bodies and wearier hearts, all of us unsure of how to proceed with this new version of our lives where all of our dirty little secrets were out in the open and our feuds with one another had been laid to rest at last.

The moment we'd done a sweep of the place, making certain that Danny hadn't found his way back inside, Frank moved a chair beside the front door and took up position there, insisting the rest of us sleep.

It was beyond clear that he needed a bit of time to process everything, so we gave in to his demand, though as we turned to head upstairs, Anya leaned down and pressed a kiss to Frank's lips which made both Benny and I pause.

"We need to talk on this," Benny said as she drew back.

"Is it any different to me and Church?" Anya challenged, her gaze meeting mine as she wetted her lips and I smirked at her lustfully as I bit down on mine in reply.

"I dunno," Benny said. "Is it?"

Anya glanced at Frank who had gone stoic on us, his brow lowering as he was forced to confront this issue despite the fact that he clearly didn't want to.

"We don't have to talk about this now," Anya said, seeming to pick up on Frank's discomfort. "It can keep."

"No it can't, bombshell," Benny disagreed. "We said the bullshit was done. Which means this right here is the start of a new chapter. We all need to hear it straight and understand it clearly. You told me you love me, but what about them?"

Anya's cheeks burned with colour and I couldn't deny the stab of jealousy that went through me as I heard that news. My gut twisted and I had to fight to keep my expression neutral as I looked between my best friend and his wife, wondering what the fuck that meant for me.

"Did you now?" I asked, cocking my head to one side in an attempt to look nonchalant, but I got the feeling I was managing something closer to a kicked puppy.

"I did," she said, owning it like I knew she would, but that still didn't give me any answers on where I stood.

Frank tongued his cheek but still remained silent, and I blew out a frustrated breath as I looked from him to Benny and back to our girl.

"So this is what we need to establish," Benny went on like he couldn't even sense the awkward in the room. "Are you in love with them too? Or headed that way? Or is it just about the sex? Because I can handle it either way, but fucking and loving are two very different things, bombshell."

"Fuck you," I bit out before she even had to reply to that. "You can't force her to spill all of her feelings just like that."

"Why not? I'm her husband and she's fucking two other fellas. Don't I have the right to know whether her heart is in it alongside her body?"

"I just think-"

"I'm falling in love with them," Anya barked before we could get any further into it and I perked right up like a Labrador with a sniff of cheese on the wind as I turned to look at her. "I mean…" She fought a blush then raised her chin. "It's not just sex. I'm not some sex starved heathen who needs multiple dicks to fulfil me. We have our own connections. I know it sounds crazy, but-"

"Doesn't sound all that crazy to me," Benny cut in, moving a step closer to her. "Me and these boys had a connection long before you came crashing into our lives, love. There's power in our bond. Always has been. It's something animal and intrinsic and fucking vital. Problem was, the heart of us stopped beating when we lost Olly all those years ago. But it looks to me like you just came and kickstarted it all over again."

Benny took another step towards her but I moved faster, grasping her chin in my inked fingers and lifting her mouth towards mine, pausing there with our gazes locked and her pulse pounding against my fingertips.

"Is that what you want, Miss America?" I asked her in a low voice. "To be the owner of all three of us?"

Anya glanced from me to Benny before finally turning her eyes towards Frank. I couldn't help but turn to look at the brooding bastard too, curious over how the hell he felt about all of this. It had been a bit of a wildcard for me but then again, I was always up for trying anything at least once. A few rounds in the bedroom with my best mate and his wife had made it all too clear that this was exactly my kind of poison, and I was gonna drink my fill of it as often as I could. Frank wasn't the same kind of creature as me though.

“Yes,” Anya breathed, her eyes on Frank.

“Watching you with the two of them makes me wanna kill something,” Frank said slowly, his eyes dragging across the three of us. “I’m not a man built for sharing.”

“Well, you haven’t actually watched her with either of us to make a true judgement on that,” Benny replied with a shrug. “I’d have thought seeing her ride Church’s cock would make me wanna cut the fucking thing off until I actually saw her with him. But believe me, Frankie boy, there is something so beautifully raw about that pain, something so damn sexy about seeing her own another man the way she owns me that I found my opinion on the matter changing.”

Frank tongued his cheek but said nothing more and Anya frowned like his uncertainty pained her.

“It doesn’t have to be like that with us,” she said to him. “If you would rather we spent our time alone then-”

“No,” Benny snapped, stepping between the two of them to block the intense look they were sharing. “You’re still my wife and I ain’t gonna have you dancing from bed to bed like you’re hopping on and off a merry go round. Same rules apply for him as they do Church. You only fuck him while I’m present. This thing is done out in the open or not at all. I won’t be made a fuckin’ cuckold.”

“Technically, I married Danny, not you,” Anya replied, arching a brow at him. “So I’m pretty sure we aren’t married at all.”

“That’s where you’d be wrong, bombshell,” Benny replied with smirk. “You signed your name right next to mine just like the treaty said you should. You may have spoken Danny’s name in your vows, but I will happily swear blue that you said mine if you wanna try and make out you didn’t to the other mafia families. And as for the marriage certificate-”

He strode away to the safe and I offered Anya a grin as I backed away enough to let her watch him, knowing what he was about to show her as I was the one who’d orchestrated it. Benny unlocked the safe and pulled the rolled certificate out of it, striding back to her as he unfurled it and pointing at his name printed there right alongside hers. “I think if you give that a proper look, you’ll see my name is written there plain as day.”

Anya reached for the certificate, her lips parting as she read Benny’s name and her eyes flicking back up to look at him in surprise.

“How did you manage to do that without anyone noticing?” she asked.

“Simple. The vicar was the only one who knew about it and he took a healthy donation in payment for his cooperation on the fact. No one else got a look at the certificate besides you and me, and while you were signing, I let my hand rest just over the part where it says my name. Besides, Benny and Danny are only a couple of letters apart and you were so caught up on how drenched your knickers were getting in anticipation of the consummation that you barely even looked at what you were signing.”

“Why take that risk though?” Anya asked, not rising to his quip about how wet she'd been or maybe it was just the truth, I'd watched how quickly she'd come for him in the back of my car after all. "If someone else had seen it. If you'd been found out-"

Benny stepped right into her personal space, his chest pressing to hers as the marriage certificate was crushed between them and he looked down at her with this fire about him that made even my skin heat.

"I told you then and I'll tell you now, bombshell. The treaty demanded a wedding between your family and my own. And I demanded a wife who was mine in all the ways that counted. I didn't want you coming to my bed as my brother's wife, I wanted you coming to it in the way you always should have done. Because I was the one who was meant to marry you. Not him. And you were *always* destined to be mine."

Anya drew in a ragged breath, her chin tilted back in anticipation of the kiss that he left hanging in the tiny distance which separated their lips and I was almost as hungry for it as the two of them had to be.

But Benny didn't lean down to close that distance. Instead, he turned his head to look first towards me then to Frank.

"You see this?" he asked us in a low and deadly voice. "You see what there is between me and her?"

"Yes, boss," I replied, my pulse thumping recklessly in my chest and my hands throbbed with the desire to reach for her, for the both of them actually.

Benny arched a brow at Frank as he remained silent and the big fella finally caved to his position.

"Yes, boss," he ground out.

"Good," Benny replied. "Because I won't have you forgettin' who butters your bread. If you're in this, then this is how it is. You're not just in with her, you're in with me too. I ain't looking to get my cock sucked by either of ya, but I won't have you thinking she's for stealing. This is what you're taking part in. Me and her. So are you in or what?"

"I'm in," I replied, drawing a finger across my bottom lip as I looked between the two of them, wanting to move closer, to feel her body crushed between both of ours and listen to the sound of her pleasure colouring the air as we worked together to bring her to ruin.

"Frank?" Anya breathed, turning her attention to him as he considered her, running his thumb across his knuckles while the hunger in his eyes made me fucking ravenous on his behalf.

"Fuck it," he muttered, lifting his chin in a nod. "I haven't wanted anything the way I want you in a long damn time, Cash. So I guess if this is the only way that I can have you then I'm in too."

Benny grinned cockily as Anya looked like her Christmases had all just come at once and he finally took that kiss from her, sinking his tongue between her lips and grasping her throat in his hand while she melted for him.

I watched them with an ache in me to join them, fighting the urge to touch her and feel her body shiver at my touch while she bowed to his desire.

Benny drew back long before it seemed like he was done, a groan of frustration escaping him as he released her and stepped away, swiping a hand down his face.

"As much as I really wanna dwell on this particular issue, there are some things which might just get us all killed if we don't deal with them sharpish," Benny said, moving further from Anya and giving me the opportunity to drop my arm around her shoulders and feel the warmth of her body against mine. I let my fingers stroke up and down her arm in lazy circles and finally got to feel her shiver for me as she leaned in to the touch.

"You mean like the motherfucker who laid his hands on our woman and tried to kill Church last night?" Frank asked darkly, his voice filled with the clear intentions he had to rip Danny apart the moment he got the opportunity.

"Yeah, like him," Benny replied. "The Firm still don't know I'm back, but we can't rely on Danny to stay hidden for long, which means I need to up my game on proving my innocence so far as the older generation are concerned. Me and Church have been trying to get hold of proof that I wasn't the one to sell those boys down the river eight years ago, but it looks like our time is up on finding it ourselves."

"Which means what exactly?" Anya asked.

I huffed out a breath. "We have one final option which we didn't really wanna resort to," I explained. "But I'm guessing at this point we just have to suck it up?"

Benny nodded his agreement, the irritation in his expression clear. "We are gonna have to ask the Irish for a favour."

"The Irish?" Anya questioned with a cute little frown on her face. "How can they help?"

"They have a man on their payroll in the police here. We've never been able to figure out who it is, but any time one of theirs gets into a sticky bit of bother 'round our parts they always seem to miraculously get off with little to no punishment. It's fuckin' infuriating," I said. "And we know they're laughing their arses off at us over it every time their man pulls through."

"Or woman," Anya pointed out with a smirk. "If the cop is clever enough to avoid your attempts to root them out then it's probably a woman."

"Yeah, you're likely right on that," I agreed with a grin.

"Well, whether the fucker has a cock or a cunt it doesn't much matter," Benny said. "Point is, I need proof that Danny was the one to sell the older generation down the river and we've exhausted every other possibility. We're out of options so now we're gonna have to go cap in hand to those fuckers in Boston and ask for their help, or we will have a whole lot more shit to deal with really fucking soon."

"Tiernan Kelly is gonna love that," Frank muttered with a snort of amusement.

"Don't I fuckin' know it," Benny grumbled, taking his phone from his pocket and dialling the leader of the Irish Mob with a scowl on his face like he'd just eaten something rotten.

"Butcher," Tiernan's clipped voice came in answer, loud enough for all of us to hear. “To what do I owe this…well, it’s not exactly a pleasure.”

“Aren’t we supposed to all be on the same side now?” Benny asked. “Seems to me like a pleasure is exactly what it is.”

“Ending the war and being on the same side aren’t exactly the same thing.”

“Nah, I guess not,” Benny said, closing his eyes briefly like the words he was about to speak were causing him physical pain. “Still, I figured it puts us in a position to help each other out from time to time.”

Silence. Tiernan didn’t offer up a single word as he waited for Benny to go on and I had to fight a wince as he was forced to continue.

“So, I could do with a little tit for tat,” Benny said. “You’ve got a fella in the police here-”

“What makes you think that?” Tiernan asked, a cocky edge to his tone which was its own kind of admission and made me wanna punch him.

“It’s got something to do with all the Irish fellas who never quite make it to prison when they get caught on our turf. Or the cases against your organisation which conveniently fall apart before coming to trial,” Benny went on, his jaw tight while he forced himself to keep his cool. “Anyway, I find myself in need of some information which has proven to be a little tricky to get hold of.”

Tiernan burst into laughter, the sound grating against my eardrums and making Benny grip the phone so fucking hard it looked like it might break.

“Oh, Butcher, this is gonna cost you a pretty penny,” Tiernan cooed. “I’m starting to think this alliance is worth it after all.”

“Arsehole,” I grunted and Anya squeezed my hand, urging me to remain quiet while Benny went on.

“Let’s hash it out then,” Benny growled. “I’ll send over the details on what I need and we can negotiate the cost of it once you’ve got it for me.”

“Done,” Tiernan agreed. “But, Butcher, you might wanna prepare yourself for one part of the price, because I’m gonna wanna hear you beg. I’m gonna put you on loudspeaker in front of my men and I will hear you ask me oh so sweetly for my help, while admitting that no matter how big and powerful you claim The Firm may be, you still had to come to me for this, like a little orphan boy begging for scraps from my table.”

Benny cursed him colourfully while Tiernan snickered and the call cut off abruptly.

“Fucking arsehole,” Benny snapped, shoving the phone into his pocket angrily and stalking away from us towards the door.

“Where are you going?” I asked.

“I’m gonna call a meeting with The Firm,” he replied as he started typing out the details of what he needed to send over to Tiernan to get the job done. “The two of you don’t need to be there. Tiernan Kelly may be an utter fucking cunt, but he will come through on this. I need to clear my name and make sure the threat hanging over us from Danny’s set up is finally gone. Then we can focus on finding my arsehole of a brother, killing the Candlestick

Maker and dicking The Czar over like we've been planning without having to worry about anyone else trying to show up and kill me while my back is turned."

"You sure you don't want us with you?" I asked, moving after him with anxiety knotting up my chest. If the other members of The Firm didn't believe him even with this evidence, then they might turn on him. He could be walking towards his own death by arranging to meet them and reveal himself.

"No. I need to show them a little faith if I expect them to have the same in me. I'll be fine. Just watch our girl and make sure my fucking brother doesn't get the chance to get anywhere near her again."

"On it, boss," Frank agreed readily, his eyes on Anya as he stood from his position by the door to let Benny leave. "I won't let her out of my sight."

"Good."

"Are you sure this is a good idea?" Anya asked, her concern clear as she took a step after Benny like she wanted to go with him.

"Positive, bombshell. You stay here where it's safe and I'll get this cleared up in no time. Besides, if I'm gonna have to beg that Irish motherfucker for his help, I'd sooner do it away from any witnesses so that I can scrub the memory from my brain more effectively."

I snorted a laugh and he tossed me a dark smile before heading out of the warehouse and leaving the three of us in his wake as Frank locked up behind him.

"Do you think he'll be alright?" Anya asked nervously.

"Yeah," I replied. "Benny is fucking bombproof, darlin'. You don't need to worry about him. He could talk his way into a whelk convention while dressed as a kipper. He's got this."

"A whelk…what the fuck are you talking about?" Anya asked, her brow pinching and I moved forward to kiss the crease away.

"Just chattin' shit as usual, Miss America. But it got your mind offa worrying, didn't it?"

She breathed a laugh and I smiled, looking towards Frank as an idea occurred to me.

"I think our girl needs further distraction, don't you, Frankie boy?" I urged, watching his blue eyes light with interest at that suggestion before he shook his head in refusal.

"We need to stay alert in case Danny comes sniffing around again."

"What's he gonna do? Crawl up the drainpipe and outa the toilet? The doors are locked and bolted, the windows too. So it seems to me like we're safe and sound tucked away in here and Anya needs taking care of."

"Maybe you're the one who needs distracting," Anya pointed out, slipping away from me and moving towards the sofa where she flicked the TV on and started searching Netflix for a film we could all watch.

I sighed, moving away to grab some snacks and calling back to Anya. "You want some salt and vinegar?"

"Some what?" she replied, her eyes still on the screen while Frank prowled the room checking windows and closing blinds like we were in some spy movie where the bad guy was about to appear at any moment.

"Prawn cocktail then? Worcester sauce? Cheese and onion?" I offered as I stared rifling.

"What the hell are you talking about?" Anya asked with a frown as she looked over her shoulder at me.

"Pickled onion?" I suggested, holding up the purple bag for her to see and she huffed out a breath.

"Oh, you and your weird ass flavours. Just give me some normal chips."

"You sure?" I asked.

"Yeah. None of your weird flavours. Just normal chips." She turned her attention back to picking a film and I shrugged, tossing the crisps back in the cupboard and heading to the freezer, rummaging about until I found some oven chips and filling a tray with them before tossing it in the oven and putting a timer on for when they'd be done.

I headed back across the room, flicking the lights off just as Frank dropped down on the sofa beside Anya.

I took the place on her other side, tossing an arm around the back of her seat just as she set the film running and she looked around at me curiously.

"Where's the chips?"

"They aren't ready yet," I replied with a shake of my head. What did she expect me to do? Run down the chippy and get some ready cooked for her? I mean, I woulda done it, but I preferred being right where I was with the heat of her body so enticingly close to mine.

Anya seemed about to protest on behalf of her empty stomach, but I just leaned in to steal a kiss from those sweet lips, grabbing a blanket from the back of the sofa and tossing it over the three of us as I broke away again.

Some action film started up, but I found myself unable to concentrate even as the fella on the screen jumped between rooftops and did a bunch of parkour shit. Not with my beautiful girl sitting so close to me and the darkness of the room just crying out for someone to break a rule or two.

I casually rearranged myself so that my arm was under the blanket and inched my fingers onto her knee, finding a hole in her jeans and stroking the exposed skin of her thigh in little circular motions.

Anya shifted beside me, her leg tilting into my touch and I smirked to myself as I tiptoed my fingers higher, finding another hole and exploring that one too, feeling the goosebumps which rose across her skin at my touch with a surge of satisfaction.

"Church," she breathed in warning, but I never had been the best at taking warnings.

"Yeah, Miss America?"

"Benny said…"

Frank perked up on her other side at those words and I looked over her head to meet his eye, wondering how strictly he felt like following our boss's orders on this one.

"He said we can't fuck you while he's not here," I agreed, moving my hand higher until I found the seat of her jeans and ran my thumb up the seam between her legs, pressing it against her clit and making her suck in a sharp breath. "He didn't say anything about not making you come."

"I…" Anya glanced at Frank too and his brow lowered as his attention dropped to the blanket where the movement of my hand between her thighs was clear to see as I kept caressing that seam and making her squirm for me.

"What was that you said about not wanting to watch her with me, Frank?" I asked provocatively.

"It makes me want to rip your fuckin' arm off," he replied darkly, that murderous glint present in his eyes once more while I just grinned and ground my thumb down harder, making Anya moan between us.

"Is that so?"

"Yeah," Frank agreed, his glare boring into me with a clear demand for me to stop but I really wasn't the kind to back down from a challenge.

"Pity, that." I held his gaze as I continued to rub Anya's clit through the rough material of her jeans and she moaned again, her head tipping back against the sofa and her thighs widening as I drove her closer to her release.

Frank growled something unintelligible and made a move to shove me off, but her hand snapped out, gripping his forearm to stop him and her fingernails digging into his flesh hard enough to draw blood.

I rubbed her clit once more and like a firecracker going off right between us, her spine arched, and her lips parted on a throaty moan which got my cock so fucking hard it hurt.

Frank's chest heaved as he watched her, that violence clearly present in him and my death lurking in his eyes but I just sat back in my seat, shrugging innocently.

"Your turn, Frankie boy, let's see if you can make her scream even louder," I challenged.

Anya bit her lip as she looked between us, holding her tongue while she waited on his response and for the longest moment he just held us in suspense.

"Please," she panted as his resolve looked on the brink of shattering and suddenly she was being pushed face first across my lap as the blanket tumbled to the floor and Frank positioned her on her knees, unbuttoning her fly and tugging her jeans down to bunch around her thighs.

I twisted my fingers into her long blonde hair as she looked up at me, her pupils full blown and lips parted in need of a kiss.

"Have you ever met a girl so endlessly needy, Church?" Frank asked me as he looped his finger through the fabric of her blue thong and slowly began to run it down the length of her arse crack, his knuckle pushing between her cheeks and making her gasp while I gently massaged her scalp and settled in for the show. "A girl who wants three men to satisfy her? A girl who is always so wet and willing?" His knuckle made it to her centre and she whimpered as he began to rotate his hand, coating his fingers in her wetness without pushing into it or giving her clit any attention at all.

"Can't say I have," I replied, watching the show with my pulse jackhammering. "I think our Miss America is one of a kind."

"Mmm," Frank agreed. "But I have to wonder, if you want all three of us, then are you planning to take us all at once? Or were you hoping we'd run a train on you, fuck you one after another and make you come so many times that you couldn't even take any more if you wanted to?"

"I haven't really thought about that," Anya panted and I chuckled.

"Filthy little liar," I teased. "You're trying to tell me that the idea hasn't even entered this pretty head of yours?"

"Oh she's thought about it alright," Frank agreed. "She's thought about the three of us fucking her together, worshipping her body and filling every single hole."

He shifted his hand back up between her arse cheeks and Anya whimpered as he began to massage her own wetness against her arse, pressing his fingers to it lightly and testing the waters as she whimpered again.

"Relax, darlin'," I purred, stroking my fingers through her hair and looking right into the depths of those dark eyes. "Let him show you how good that fantasy could feel."

Anya's lips parted and for a moment I thought she might refuse but she bit her lip and nodded instead, making my cock stiffen with need as I shifted my eyes to Frank's hand once more, wanting to watch him push into her.

"Say the words, Cash," he growled, not letting her get away with a simple nod. "Tell me what you want me to do to this tight arse of yours."

Anya's spine straightened at the challenge, her fingers digging into my thigh as she gripped me to steady herself and her voice firm as she gave her answer.

"I want to feel you in my ass, Frank," she said. "I want you to show me how good that could feel."

Frank's lips hooked up at the corner and he gave her exactly what she'd asked for, his fingers uncurling and stroking down to her core once more, gathering more wetness onto them before he slowly eased one into her arse.

"Fuck," Anya gasped, her grip on me tightening before she forced herself to relax and Frank pushed a second finger into her with a groan.

"You're so fucking tight back here," he said, rotating his hand and making her pant as she got used to the sensation.

My cock was throbbing in my jeans as I watched them and I gave up on trying to fight the urge to relieve the tension in it, unbuckling my belt and dropping my fly so that I could tug it free.

Anya moaned as she took in the sight of how hard I was for her, my dick bobbing with want as I took it in my fist and began to stroke it, a deep breath falling from my lungs as I did so.

"Give me your belt," Frank demanded and I raised my eyes from Anya to him, a frown forming on my brow as the fog of lust I was lost in made my thoughts slow to respond.

"Your belt, Church," he barked again, pushing a third finger into Anya's arse as he did so and making her moan loudly.

I licked my lips, wondering what the hell he had in mind before realising I didn't give a fuck and yanking my belt free of my jeans, tossing it to him to catch.

I tugged my shirt off while my hands were free, wanting a whole lot less material between me and my girl than we currently had.

"Stand up, Anya," Frank said and she pushed herself upright as he took his fingers back out of her, reaching out to steady herself on me as her legs trembled precariously. "Jeans off."

She obediently kicked them off and I fisted my dick again as I sat back in my chair, getting myself off while looking at her standing there with her nipples pressing through her white band tee and her little panties drenched for us like a perfect wet dream.

Frank moved close behind her, my belt folded over in his fist as he ran his hands up the outsides of her thighs until he found the hem of her shirt and started rolling it up and off of her body.

"Fuck me," I murmured as he unveiled her tits, the bra free movement still very much in place and her nipples hard and wanting for us, demanding I ease the need in them.

I moved forward, perching on the edge of the sofa as Frank rolled the t-shirt over her face. The moment she was blinded by the fabric, I leaned in and sucked her nipple into my mouth, the moan that tumbled from her making me pump my cock harder, the need for release consuming me like it was the air I needed to fill my lungs.

Frank tossed the t-shirt aside, letting all that blonde hair come tumbling down around her shoulders, the strands tickling my cheeks as I moved my attention to her other nipple, sucking and tugging on that one too.

A sharp crack filled the air and Anya gasped a moan, her fingers knotting into my hair as she jerked toward me and I pulled back, finding Frank raising the belt again behind her.

I stilled as he swung it, the strike clapping down across her arse cheeks and making her cry out.

"Tell me how wet that made her, Church," Frank demanded before I could question that and I instantly pushed my fingers into her panties, finding them utterly drenched while Anya swayed above me, her eyes focused on my hand and a plea in them which had me undone.

"She's fucking soaked," I replied hungrily. "Her cunt is aching to be filled, isn't it, darlin'?"

"Yes," she whimpered. "Please, Church-"

"Pity you let your husband call the shots on that one, isn't it?" Frank replied before I could cave and give her what she needed. "Maybe you shoulda told him that this isn't gonna work like that. Then you could have your pick of us, hell you could have both of us inside that tight pussy of yours at once if you wanted, but as it stands…"

"I'll tell him," she said quickly. "I'll tell him he can't control this like that. Please, Frank. Church, I need-"

"I don't think so," Frank said and I damn near cursed him out for that decision, preparing to sink my cock into her no matter what Benny had to say on the matter but he wasn't done there. "If your husband says we can't have your cunt without him present then so be it. Church is going to have your mouth instead."

"Am I now?" I asked, wondering if I was going to be telling Frank to stop bossing me the fuck around or if I was just going to accept this, because having her sweet lips wrapped tight around my cock didn't exactly sound like a bad thing.

"Yeah. And I'm going to take your arse." Frank clapped the belt down across Anya's arse cheeks and she moaned again, forcing my head to the side and feeding me her nipple in a clear demand which I obediently gave in to.

"Keep her busy, Church," Frank said, his footsteps moving away from us as I tugged her nipple between my teeth and Anya moaned with need.

"Please, Church, fuck me," she begged in a low voice as the sound of Frank's footsteps reached us from the stairs.

I pulled back with a devilish grin, gripping her arse in my hands while I considered that, but Frank had a point, if we were all in on this then allowing Benny to call the shots on what we could or couldn't do wasn't gonna work long term. Though I had to think what we were doing right now already broke his fuckin' rules even if we didn't take her pussy.

"You want me to make you come, Miss America?" I teased, hooking my fingers in the sides of her knickers while her hands moved to my shoulders to help her balance herself.

"Yes," she agreed, letting me slip her underwear all the way off until she was standing fully naked before me.

I gave her a devil's grin, standing suddenly so that I was towering over her and shoving my jeans the rest of the way off, joining her in her nudity and loving the way her attention fixed on my cock.

Her hand reached out to caress me, her thumb rolling over my piercing as she began to pump my shaft and I groaned in pleasure, my head tipping back as she slicked my precum around the head of my cock.

"Fuck me, Church," she commanded again and I was so damn tempted to give in that I couldn't help but jerk my hips forward into her hand, my dick throbbing with the need for release.

"You're a bad, bad influence, Anya," I warned her, stepping back suddenly to remove her hand before grabbing hold of her and tossing her down on the sofa beneath me.

I crawled onto it with her, burying my head between her thighs without wasting a single second more and tasting her wetness with a growl of pure pleasure as she cried out and gripped my hair.

I fucked her with my mouth, lapping and sucking and rolling her clit between my teeth while her hips gyrated and her heels drove into my shoulders, her cries of pleasure so loud and desperate that I was in danger of coming with her.

I gave in to what I knew she so desperately needed as I felt her thighs tightening around my head and I drove three fingers deep into her drenched core, pumping them twice while sucking on her clit and feeling her explode for me as she screamed her pleasure to the rooftops.

Before I could get lost in the idea of sinking my dick into her, Frank's hand landed on my shoulder and he tugged me upright again, a snarl of anger escaping me as I rounded on him.

"Don't make me spank you too, Churchy," he taunted, his blue eyes alight with this feral kind of need and a breath of laughter escaped me as I forced myself to shift aside and let him tug Anya upright once more.

"What's that?" Anya breathed, looking at the bottle of lube in his hand and he offered her a dark laugh.

"You know what it is, beautiful. Now tell me you want me to claim that arse of yours and stop dicking us about." Frank yanked his shirt off while he waited for her response and my heart hammered wildly in my chest as I waited too.

"I want you to fuck my ass," she panted, her eyes wide as she skipped them back to me again. "And I want you to fuck my mouth."

"That's gonna be a fuck yes from me, darlin," I agreed as Frank grabbed her and whipped her off of her feet, pushing her down over the arm of the sofa with her arse in the air and her hands bracing her.

I obligingly moved to sit in the spot where her hands were resting, moving them onto my thighs and eyeing Frank as he moved up behind her and dropped his jeans to the floor.

I twisted my fingers into her hair as he slicked his cock and her arse with the lube and Anya bit her lip in anticipation, her eyes on mine as he slowly drove himself into her.

"Fucking hell," Frank groaned, pushing in deeper while Anya's nails bit into my skin and she panted through the feeling of him taking her like that.

I leaned forward to kiss her, devouring the moan that escaped her as he drove into her. Anya bit down on my lip as he pushed all the way in, and I growled in the back of my throat, tasting blood.

"Tell me when you want me to move," Frank said, his voice strained as he let her get used to the feeling, his hand moving down to massage her clit and give her body what it needed.

"Move," Anya begged as she broke our kiss and Frank obliged, his hips shifting back and forth in slow thrusts while she moaned and panted, her fingernails biting into my skin hard enough to draw blood.

My cock throbbed as I watched her, the sounds she was making filling me with need and when she finally lowered her head and took me into her mouth, a groan of pure relief escaped me.

I lifted my hips as we found a rhythm like that, Frank's thrusts driving her mouth down onto my cock while I fought against my need to finish, wanting to relish in this feeling, in the sounds she was making and the pleasure I could feel building throughout my body.

I found her nipple and toyed with it expertly, rolling and tugging it between my fingers just enough to make her moan, and I knew that we were all pushing the edge of how much of this we could take.

"That's it," Frank praised, his hand still circling her clit as her moans got louder, the sound vibrating through my cock. "Come for us, beautiful."

"Do it," I growled in agreement, my own release so close that I knew I only had a few more seconds left in me.

Anya moaned loudly as she drew closer to the edge but I was so far gone that I knew I couldn't wait another second.

With a bark of command, I smacked my hand down on her arse cheek just as Frank drove into her a final time. "Now."

Anya's cry of pleasure was muted by my cum filling her throat as I fell apart too and the growl of ecstasy which escaped Frank said he'd followed along right behind us.

I dragged her up to kiss her, feeling the way her body trembled for us with a surge of satisfaction as I sank my tongue between her lips and tasted myself on her.

Frank pulled out of her and I drew her into my lap as he dropped onto the sofa beside us, the three of us panting so hard that we didn't even say anything at all.

The sound of the oven timer interrupted our moment of bliss and Anya looked up in confusion.

"What's cooking?" she asked sleepily.

"Your chips," I replied, knocking my knuckles against her jaw gently.

"Why would you cook chips?" she frowned.

"Well you wouldn't wanna eat them frozen would ya?"

"She thinks you mean crisps, idiot," Frank muttered, punching me in the bicep way harder than was necessary.

"Why the fuck would I cook crisps?" I asked and Anya groaned.

"You made me fries didn't you?" she asked.

"Fries, chips, whatever the fuck you wanna call them, they're ready. So are we eating or what? I for one have worked up one hell of an appetite."

Anya looked ready to protest further but then she just shrugged. "Yeah, fuck it, I could eat some fries."

"Good." I lifted her from my lap and deposited her in Frank's, grabbing my clothes from the floor as I stood.

I strode across the room to get our food and the sound of their voices carried to me as I went.

"Do you still hate the idea of me with them?" Anya murmured and I paused, wanting to hear the answer to that question too because if this thing was gonna work then we needed to be all in on it, no jealousy bullshit screwing it up.

Frank hesitated for several seconds, keeping us all in suspense before he finally replied. "I think I could get used to it," he replied and the grin that spread across my face was enough to light the entire city of London up even on the gloomiest of days.

CHAPTER FORTY FIVE

"What in the actual fuck?" Benny snapped as he walked in the front door.

I mean, technically I should have seen this coming. After my fries, I'd gotten dick hungry again and I was currently jerking off Frank while Church sucked on my neck and pumped his fingers inside me. So, maybe this was the story of how Anya Volkov died. But I didn't mind it so much because I was teetering on the edge of ecstasy and although this probably wasn't going to end in a cheesy freeze frame moment where I winked at the camera before the screen faded to black, I was pretty sure I still wanted to stay for the fallout.

"I can explain," I moaned as Church continued to finger fuck me while staring at Benny in shock, his hand apparently on autopilot because he really needed to fucking stop.

Frank pushed my hand off of him, tugging up his boxers and squaring his shoulders like he was about to go to battle for me if Benny snapped over this.

"Church," I pleaded, my core tightening around his fingers.

Frank slapped him around the face and Church realised what he was doing and pulled his fingers out of me, drawing the blanket up around us instead like he was concealing the scene of the crime. But it was a bit too fucking late for that.

"Benny, listen," I said, getting to my feet and taking the blanket with me as I hugged it to my body, which on reflection wasn't the best plan because

Church was left stark naked with his raging boner on display and Frank wasn't faring much better even with his boxers on.

"I gave you one fucking rule!" Benny pointed at Church and Frank. "And you broke it the second I walked out the door."

"Benny," I growled, planting myself in front of him with a glare worthy of all my brothers combined. "I'm theirs as much as I am yours. You don't have the right to tell me I can't be with them when you're not around. That's like asking the sun to set every time you turn your back on it."

"I'm your husband, love," he snapped. "Ain't that worth some respect?"

"You said you're okay with me being with them, and if that's true, you can't put rules on it. It's not simple. Just like you and me aren't simple. I want them. And I won't be forced to keep my want for them only for when your eyes are on us."

"But you're mine," he growled, stepping forward.

"And I'm theirs. Do you understand?"

"Ours," Church said firmly, that word resounding through my body and feeling like the deepest truth to ever been spoken.

Benny's eyes flicked over my head towards Church and he cursed under his breath. "For fuck's sake, put your cock away, Church."

"Sorry, boss," Church muttered and I sniggered as Church scrambled to get some clothes on.

"And what've you got to say on the matter? You're being awfully quiet there for a man who just had my wife's hand wrapped around his cock, Frankie boy." Benny folded his arms.

"In the sake of total transparency, Benny, I fucked her in the arse too," Frank said and a blush coursed through my cheeks.

"Right, well that's just fuckin' fantastic then, ain't it?" Benny huffed and I realised what he was really feeling about this, moving forward and gripping his forearm to make him look at me.

"You're jealous. That's why you don't wanna miss a second with me and them," I said in realisation and his lips parted indignantly before he thought on that and frowned like he'd just realised that might be the case.

"Well yeah…maybe I am a bit, come to think of it," he murmured, unfolding his arms and pulling me against his chest. "If you're with them, you ain't with me."

"But being with them doesn't take away from how I feel about you," I said earnestly.

He brushed a lock of hair away from my face, considering that. "So this thing, it really works for ya?"

"It does. But not if you're going to restrict it, Benny. I have to be free. No chains," I said, not blinking as I let him see how much I needed this.

Slowly, he relaxed, nodding as he seemed to find some understanding in that. "Okay," he said at last.

"Okay?" I asked excitedly.

"Okay," he repeated. "So long as you always come back to me, then I think I can do this. If it'll make ya happy."

"It will," I said, feeling Church and Frank coming up behind me.

"She's ours then?" Frank asked in his deep voice, laying a hand on my shoulder and Church laid a hand on my back.

"Ours," Benny agreed and my heart beat rampantly as a smile lifted my lips.

"Yours," I promised them all.

"But it wouldn't kill you arseholes to video call me or even just make me a tape to watch when I got home from time to time."

I laughed, biting my lip and nodding in agreement to that.

"There is one rule you all have to follow though, me included," he went on, cutting a look between the three of us and I narrowed my gaze at him, ready to make a fight out of this if he was being serious. "It's about the treaty. You know, the end to the mafia wars and the deal we struck. The bargain we made-"

"The baby," I breathed in realisation and he nodded tightly.

"You understand we haven't upheld our end until we mix our blood, don't you, bombshell?" Benny asked, the meaning to his words clear.

"If I get pregnant it has to be yours," I said, glancing back at the others, wondering how they would take that.

"Yeah. Which means you fuckers need to either wrap your cocks or pull the fuck out of her before you come. Got it?"

Frank tutted irritably and Church sighed.

"Yes, boss," Church agreed, looking more than a little put out by that, and I breathed a laugh.

"Fine," Frank agreed and there really wasn't much else to say on the subject. The deal that had been struck between the mafia families had to be upheld and we were all equally bound by those ties. Not that the reality of me becoming pregnant seemed all that real while I was trapped in this bubble of bliss.

"How did it go with The Firm?" Church asked Benny.

"Fuckin' perfect actually, mate," he said, all signs of anger vanishing just like that. "Looks like I'm the king of this town once again."

Three men.

Three barbaric, cutthroat men.

And somehow, they were mine.

I was sitting at the kitchen island while Church brewed tea and my husband made cheese sandwiches for everyone. Frank was at my back, his watchful eyes always seeming to delve so deeply under my skin.

When Church laid out the tea in little floral teacups, he leaned down and brushed his lips against my neck. Benny turned to me at that exact moment and the heat in his eyes as he watched us made me bite down on my lip. He laid a sandwich in front of me before placing three more down for the rest of them and beckoning Frank over.

I felt him close in at my back then lean around and kiss the corner of my mouth, his eyes darting to Benny in a challenge for him to say something. But my husband drank it all in as a tremor rolled down my spine. This thing between us was really exciting, but we were still figuring out how it all worked.

Church took the seat to my left, his hand falling to my knee and squeezing, drawing my legs open as Frank's knuckles brushed down the length of my spine.

"Let the woman eat," Benny growled, though amusement danced beneath his tone as his friends backed up.

This arrangement should have felt strange, but for some reason it felt oddly right. Like the four of us together caused some kind of chemical reaction that made peace wash right through my body. It didn't make a whole lot of sense and I decided not to look much further into it because for now, I just wanted to enjoy it after going so long without feeling anything close to peace.

Frank dropped onto the seat beyond Church and when we were finished with our lunch, Benny rapped his inked knuckles on the surface.

"We need a new plan to deal with The Czar. Who's got something viable?"

"I go to him and get it out of him," I said simply.

"Nope. Next?" Benny shut me down and anger spiked in my chest.

"We could capture the Candlestick Maker and make him tell us what The Czar gave him then gut him good," Church suggested.

"But that doesn't buy us any favour with The Czar, it only deals with the Candlestick Maker and we need the money for the construction to go through sharpish or we are gonna be in a whole heap of shit," Frank pointed out.

"So let me go to him and find out what the Candlestick Maker has lost. I can figure out if we can make any use out of that information and convince him to pay up on his investment at the same time," I insisted.

"No," Benny said. "Any other ideas?"

"Yeah, how about you eat a dick and choke on it?" I shoved out of my seat, walking away from their little gang. I'd been an idiot to think I was a part of it. Of course Benny wouldn't let me actually play a role in their jobs. They were the big men with their big balls playing with the big boys. Well fuck their balls.

I stalked into the lounge, picking up my headphones and iPod from the coffee table and dropping down onto the couch. I was quickly lost to my own world, slipping away to More Than a Feeling by Boston and shutting my eyes as I let the oblivion of the music take me.

But before I could get truly lost, someone ripped my headphones off of me and I looked up, finding Benny there with an eyebrow arched. "You don't get to just zone out on me, bombshell. I want you present."

"Well, I want my music."

"Listen to it on the main speakers then," he said, tossing the iPod to Frank who was lurking a few steps behind him.

Church dropped down onto the couch beside me, slinging an arm over my shoulders. "This conversation includes you, darlin'."

"Like hell it does," I scoffed as Frank hooked up my iPod to the Bluetooth speakers then stared thumbing through my music. "My idea is the best one we've got, and the only reason you won't let me do it is because I'm your precious little wifey. If I was anyone else, you'd let me go and you know it."

"She's got a point, mate," Church said, his fingers tip-toeing down my arm.

"The moment you're in that man's house, I won't be able to protect ya," Benny snapped. "And I ain't putting you in risk of being fuckin' raped."

"I can look after myself," I hissed. "And I know men like him, he'll make a parade of the whole night, dinner, drinks, entertainment. He'll think he's winning me from you, which was what he really wants. And long before he ever lays a finger on me, I'll slip a sedative in his drink and get the fuck out along with the information we need."

"I think she can do it," Church said and Benny bared his teeth.

"Don't you fuckin' side with her," he warned.

"Too late, Benny boy," Church said, kicking his feet up on the coffee table. "She's our ace in the hole, this one. Let her get in the hole."

"No," Benny said. "I'm the boss and that's my answer."

"Technically, Danny's still the boss," I said lightly, wanting to piss him off. "I mean, I know you have The Firm back on side but you haven't done your grand reveal to The Butcher gang yet, have you?"

Benny stepped closer, tilting his chin down to glare at me. "I am the boss, mark my words, love. When I crow at dawn, the world stirs to life because they sense their true king is fuckin' home."

"I always knew you were a cock."

Church snorted a laugh.

"Careful, bombshell," Benny inched closer, darkness sweeping though his gaze. "Or I'll have to think of something better for that mouth to do than insult me."

"She needs a firm hand," Frank added. "She can be a little brat."

Heat stirred in my core as Frank and Benny shared a look that was full of wicked promises, and I didn't think I'd mind their punishment so much. But on principle, I'd be kicking dicks if either of them came near me right now.

Church on the other hand…

I turned to kiss him, fisting my hand in his blonde curls and relishing the way his tongue met mine and he hmmed his approval against my lips. His own hand fisted in my hair too and my breath caught at the powerful feel of his chest pressing against mine, his muscular arms snaring me in an instant.

“Back it up,” Benny barked, shoving his palm against Church’s head and he laughed as he slumped back against the couch.

“I can’t help if I’m her favourite,” Church taunted and right now he was right.

I ran my thumb over my tingling lips as I sat back too, looking up at Benny as he shook his head at both of us.

“No fucking my wife during business meetings,” Benny announced.

“I left the business meeting,” I said with a shrug. “I’m off duty.”

“Don’t get smart with me, bombshell,” Benny said.

Frank picked out a new song and a chill swept down my spine, every muscle in my body going rigid as he chose The Killing Moon by Echo & the Bunnymen. I no longer heard a word Benny said as he started berating me because the whole world was crushing me in a vice, my lungs were turning to two heavy lumps of iron in my chest and the piercing cry of a woman’s scream tangled with my thoughts.

I tried to speak, to beg for it to stop, but no sound came out as I fell into the worst memory of my life and found myself bound and chained to it. There was no way out, my mom was dying, begging for help and Zakhar was there pushing the headphones onto my ears. The music always helped, always, but not this time. Because this time every note that fell against my ears was another time my mother’s head was dashed against the floor, the lyrics were her yelling out and begging for mercy. I was helpless, forced away by my brothers while they tried to stop the inevitable from happening, but I felt the Grim Reaper at my back and knew her time had come. That the sweet, gentle light of my mother was going to be ripped away from me into the beyond.

I became aware that I was screaming, my fingernails tearing into flesh and as I thought of my father’s strong hands, I sliced them deeper, fighting him with all I had.

I’d always been so small, so incapable of stopping him, but not anymore. I was grown now, with the ferocity of a scorned goddess harboured in my body. I might not win this fight, but I’d go out drawing blood and making him feel my hate.

“Anya!” someone shouted as more hands took hold of me.

I was in a cage of flesh and muscle, pressing in on me on all sides. There was no escape. My heart was going to burst in my chest and I’d die here, never knowing what freedom tasted like.

“Open your eyes, darlin’,” a deep voice commanded, a voice I knew, a voice that wasn’t my father’s.

Through sheer force of will, I opened them, finding myself looking at a man I knew with bright silver eyes and tousled blonde hair.

“Turn it off,” I rasped, surfacing from the depths of the past for a second, but I knew it was going to steal me away again at any moment. “Please turn it off.”

“The music, Frank,” Church cried and silence pounded into my skull a heartbeat later.

I was trembling, my nails bloody from the scratches I'd torn into Church's arms and neck, but he didn't look at them, he looked at me, clutching me tight to his chest. I was on my feet, but I had no recollection of ever getting up, and as I turned my head I found Benny there, crushing his lips to my temple.

"What happened?" he asked in fear as Frank drew closer on my other side, his fingers knotted in my shirt.

"That song," I rasped.

"What about it, Cash?" Frank asked like he was going to wipe that song from the face of the earth if that was what he needed to do to make sure I was alright again.

"My mother died to that song," I whispered and I felt them tighten ranks around me.

Church rested his forehead to mine, his gaze full of pain. "Tell us about it, Anya."

I nodded, letting them draw me down onto the couch and I curled up on Church and Benny's laps while Frank sat before me on the coffee table, his elbows on his knees and his brow drawn low.

"My mom always tried to protect us from him, from my father. She took the blows from him which were meant for us, and one day he went too far." I swallowed the ice cold lump in my throat. "We were there, my brothers and I. Zakhar put my headphones over my ears, he used to do that, to help me drown out the sounds of my father beating the others. I'd disappear, slip into a world of music with nothing there but numbness to steal away my terror, my pain." I shut my eyes but Benny tracked his thumb up my cheek.

"Eyes open, bombshell," he said. "Stay here with us. You're safe here."

I did as he asked, wondering how this place of danger and uncertainty had become a place of such safety. It felt like somewhere I'd been searching for my whole life without ever really realising it.

"He killed her in front of us, and that song is the one which played when she died. It's tainted. A death march. Because as much as my music could always block out most of this world, it couldn't steal away the terror I felt at seeing my mother's life be so brutally stolen from her."

Church brushed his fingers through my hair in soothing strokes and my heart rate slowly came down.

"It's this song. Inked here because it's a part of me I can never escape." I pulled down my shirt, showing them the line of music notes tattooed across my collarbone.

"I'm sorry, Anya, I didn't know," Frank said, reaching out to caress my cheek.

"No one knows," I admitted. "Well I guess…they didn't until now."

"Your secrets are coveted between these four walls. We'll protect them, won't we fellas?" Benny demanded and the others nodded firmly.

"Are you okay?" I looked up at Church, trailing my fingers over the scratches on his arms.

“I’m good, darlin’. If you ever need to draw blood on someone, I’m your man.” He winked at me and I leaned forward to kiss one of the scratches, hating that I’d marked him like that.

“One hour,” Benny announced and I looked to him with a frown.

“What?” I questioned.

“One hour with The Czar,” he clarified. “That’s what you get. Then we’re coming in guns a-fucking-blazing to get you out.”

My lips parted and I shoved myself upright, wrapping my arms around his neck. He was agreeing to my plan, letting me really be a part of this gang. And that was enough to banish all the shadows from my heart.

“But so help him, if he lays a single fucking finger on you, wife,” Benny growled in my ear. “I’ll come in swinging like an executioner and cut his head from his shoulders before mounting it at my gates.”

I sat in a huge dining room to the right of The Czar in a red dress which was tight all over and had a dramatic slit up one leg. Absolutely not my kinda thing, but I had to admit I looked shit hot in it. The Czar seemed to agree too because his hungry little eyes kept crawling all over me.

I eyed the expensive old paintings on the wall depicting scenes of war and misery, the bloody battles and people crying on their knees giving me the creeps. The whole house was decorated as if The Czar was some sixteenth century monarch with red carpets, sweeping staircases and even a massive stuffed polar bear which stood staring at me now, the dark pit behind its dead eyes making my spine prickle and distaste curl my lip back though I fought to flatten it before he could see.

“You have a fine collection of…things,” I said.

“Indeed,” he agreed, patting his lips with a napkin as he finished up his main course which had been the rarest steak I’d ever witnessed. I’d stuck to a garden salad and picked my way through it like a true lady – something I was absolutely not. “Yuri always had a great eye for them.” He sighed. “Now fucking Interpol have taken him away, probably shoved him in a black hole somewhere where the light will never shine again. Poor Yuri. I think perhaps he was one of my most prized possessions. Such a gifted manservant is so difficult to come by.”

“That’s terrible. Yuri must have been very special to you. What’s the rarest thing he helped you acquire?” I asked, leaning forward and placing a hand on top of his. It was meaty and he had stubby fingers with glitzy gold rings on them, and the contact made my own skin shudder, but I didn’t remove it. I was already thirty-eight minutes into my one-hour time slot and I seriously needed to get this guy talking about the Candlestick Maker and the investment.

But every time I tried to turn the conversation in that direction, he deflected.

He eyed my hand where it touched his with a rampant hunger in his gaze. "The rarest thing? Hm…" He sipped on a large glass of wine, four already drained by now and surely his tongue had to be loosening? "Well perhaps it will be you after tonight." He chuckled and I laughed flirtatiously, withdrawing my hand from his and getting to my feet.

Fuck it, I had twenty-two minutes and counting. I was getting this information out of The Czar one way or another and it looked like it was going to be another.

"You'll give me a tour, won't you?" I asked, heading toward the door in a clear demand of what I wanted, giving him the perfect view of my ass as his eyes followed me.

He nodded keenly, tossing his napkin down and heading after me. We passed by several security men as we walked out into the grand hallway and The Czar's hand fell to my lower back as he turned me towards the stairs and led me up them.

His hand slid lower as we walked, riding the top of my ass before fully dropping to take a squeeze.

I twisted towards him as we made it to the top of the stairs, crowding him against the wall and pressing my hand flat to his chest.

"Have you ever been dominated by a woman before?" I asked, playing my most risky card. But I didn't have much choice now.

"Dominated?" he croaked in surprise.

"Yes…made to be the absolute centre of a woman's desires?"

"No," he admitted as my hand travelled lower to his belt and I gave him a look of complete lust.

I grabbed his junk in my fist, squeezing tight and making him squeak in surprise.

"I want this, you dirty man. Are you going to give it to me how I want it?" I demanded and he gaped at me.

I was either a dead bitch walking or I'd played this just right and he was intrigued.

"Yes, Mrs Butcher, you wicked woman," he said in a heavy breath, his cock hardening in my grip even though it was like a vice. I didn't take any pleasure in feeling his tiny dick jerking in my grasp, and it was a miracle it didn't show on my face as I stepped back.

"Take me to your bedroom," I commanded and he nodded keenly as he practically ran past me and led me down the hall.

We soon entered a huge bedroom with a fourposter bed at the heart of it and I pointed to it. "Get on it. Take your pants off and lie on your back."

The Czar yanked his pants down along with his boxers, revealing his very hairy dick before hurrying to the bed and lying on it. I opened his closet, finding a couple of ties and striding to the bed.

"Hands either side of your head," I instructed, but he hesitated, glancing at the door.

"I would prefer to remain untethered," he said and I tossed the ties down, unzipping my dress and letting it fall down to pool at my feet. I had a lacy black one piece on beneath it which pushed up my tits and clung to my figure perfectly.

The Czar let out a noise of desperation then shoved his hands above his head in compliance. I leaned over him as he panted like a pig in the sun, and I tied his hands tightly to each post of the headboard so he couldn't get free.

Then I stroked his face and smiled wickedly. "Tell me about your precious things, Czar. I want to know what I'm worth more than."

I ran my hand down his chest, peeling open the buttons of his shirt as he started to name things.

"I have a very rare Chinese vase, a beautiful piece which sits in my entrance hall, but it has nothing on you," he said, squirming as I ran my hand beneath his shirt. I tweaked his nipple so hard he yelled out but it turned to a deep, sexual moan, and I had to assume that was the only reason a bunch of his men didn't come storming in here.

"Not good enough. Of course I am more beautiful than a vase," I spat. "What else?"

"I have a sapphire ring which belonged to Queen Mary the first kept in that drawer over there – you exceed it in every way, I would throw it into the ocean for your company," he said quickly and I tutted, turning away from him in disgust. "Wait – I possess an original Van Gogh painting!"

"Paintings are dull," I said in disappointment, knowing it wouldn't be what the Candlestick Maker had in his possession. I moved around to where he'd discarded his trousers and yanked the belt out of the loops.

I curled the leather around one hand and approached him again, slapping it down hard on his thigh.

"Oh, mercy," he gasped, but it didn't sound like he wanted that at all.

"You're a bad, filthy man," I growled.

"I'm so bad, so filthy," he agreed and I whipped him across his stomach, enjoying the shriek of pain he let out, but the moan that followed made my upper lip want to curl back.

"My beauty is clearly nothing to you," I scoffed. "You don't deserve my time. You don't deserve to have a release from me."

"No - wait," he stammered as I stepped back. "A diamond," he blurted. "I possess a diamond worth more than you can imagine, Mrs Butcher. It is radiant. It is unlike anything you have ever seen before."

I paused, threading the belt between my fingers. "Go on."

"It is also of deeper value because I took it from my enemy. I have had to hide it well because it is so badly sought after. I stole it, you see? And now Interpol is after it, they want to prove I was responsible, but I won't ever let them pin the murder on me and let them take my diamond away. It is mine. It represents succession over my lifelong enemy, a man who gained my trust, posed as my friend then conned me out of millions. Then that piece of shit bought the diamond with my money, Mrs Butcher. But I got him back in the end, Yuri made him pay for all he'd taken from me before he killed him. The diamond is rare for that reason alone, but it also glitters like all the rays of the sun. It has nothing on you though, my dear. Nothing at all."

I considered him, aware that me and my boys were wrapped up in a con of our own here and I was sure The Czar would want our blood for it too if he ever figured it out.

"Then let me see it," I said, sensing I was onto something here.

"I can't," he croaked and I whipped him across his thigh so hard it almost split skin.

"Oh, Mrs Butcher," he groaned, his hips jerking and his little cock flapping. "I can't say another word."

"How disappointing," I said, whipping him again and again as he wailed.

"Don't stop," he moaned, and I realised he was actually close to coming, something I absolutely did not want to witness. So I whipped his cock instead, again and again, making him shriek like a baby. It was both gross and fucking hilarious.

"Mrs Butcher!" he cried. "Please, have mercy."

"That diamond probably doesn't even exist. You're just a dirty liar," I accused, whipping his cock again and trying not to laugh my ass off as the thing shrivelled from the onslaught.

"It does, I swear it. But I cannot show you," he panted. "It's hidden. But not here, I gave it to a friend to safeguard it while Interpol did searches of my manor.

Jackpot.

"Then where is it?" I pushed, sensing he was about to crack as I whipped his junk again.

"I- I placed it in a crystal duck," he blurted.

I paused, triumph pouring through my chest. "How clever of you," I purred.

"Yes," he agreed, looking at me with an intense need in his eyes while my gaze flicked to the clock on his nightstand. One minute to go. I prayed my boys would be on time, because I needed a reason to get out of here before The Czar blew his load. And from the look of his reddened, sweaty face, I was running out of time.

CHAPTER FORTY SIX

"Now?" I asked, my fingers flexing and my blood pumping as I adjusted the riot mask on my head.

"She's still got thirty seconds," Benny replied, twirling the baton he held while he watched the seconds count down on his watch. "I'm nothing if not a man of my word."

"I need her back with us," Frank growled, his eyes on the manor house at the end of the street and his jaw gritting with the agony of the wait.

"Twenty, nineteen, eighteen…" Benny continued counting and I whistled to John Boy, jerking my chin to draw him closer and casting a look over the swarm of Butchers beyond him.

Practically the whole gang had turned out for this job, all of us decked out in black outfits with 'Interpol' emblazoned in white letters across our backs, guns and batons at our hips and riot masks to complete the look. The Czar and his men were gonna shit a brick when we busted our way into his fancy mansion. Benny had shared the news of who he really was with the Butcher gang and they'd been over the fucking moon about it after he'd explained. Turned out, no one liked Danny bossing them around and making an ugly mess of what had once been a great empire. And the gang were firmly back in line behind the true ruler at last.

"You got this?" I asked as John Boy moved to stand before me, swiping a hand down his forgettable face while he tried to school the grin on his lips.

"Yeah, fella, I got you," he swore, moving to head up the line as Benny's countdown made it to single figures. We didn't wanna risk anyone recognising me, Benny or Frank so we were letting our own personal Mr Invisible lead the charge.

"Four, three, two, one." Benny's watch started bleeping and he cut off the noise sharply, giving John Boy a shove to get him moving.

"With us, boys!" I commanded, stepping out onto the street and falling into line with Frank and Benny as the rest of the gang clustered behind us, the excitement in the air clear.

John Boy broke into a run and we raced after him, all of us pouring down the darkened road and racing towards the fancy manor house The Czar had bought for himself with its black gates and high walls.

John Boy shoved through the gate and jogged up the steps, his fist hammering on the door as he called out. "Interpol! Open up!"

There was a whole lot of Russian shouting beyond the door, but no one opened it, so Benny turned and whistled at Mickey Hairpiece who hurried forward with the battering ram.

I yanked it out of his arms, letting Benny grab the other side and between us, we used it to knock the fuckin' door offa its hinges.

Frank leapt inside as we tossed the battering ram outa the way and John Boy yelled out "Interpol!" again.

The rest of the gang all started yelling it too and we poured into the fancy fuckin' house like a tide of pigs on the hunt. But we weren't no coppers, we were just a bunch of wolves dressed up all pretty in their clothing.

"Find her," Benny barked at me and Frank and the three of us all took off in different directions.

The sound of yelling and cursing came from the Russian guards and our gang members alike as they poured through the house in a wave, the word 'Interpol' being yelled so damn much that it was makin' my fuckin' skull rattle.

I took off up the stairs as fast as I could, aiming for the bedrooms and hoping to fuck I wasn't gonna find her in one of them because I was likely to kill a bastard if I did.

My heart was thundering to the tune of my girl's name, the need to find her and make certain she was alright eating at me like a nest of rats caught in a flooding pipe.

"Interpol!" I bellowed in place of calling her name, sure she'd recognise me and hoping she'd let me know if she could hear me.

"Run!" Anya gasped from somewhere up ahead and as I rounded a corner, I saw her wearing a sexy as fuck little black one piece and shoving The Czar ahead of her out of a bedroom as his men swarmed around them.

The Czar wore an unbuttoned shirt and a pair of boxers, two ties hanging from his wrists as his wild eyes took me in.

"They aren't here for me, get away while you can – I'll hold him off!" she cried dramatically.

"I can get you out of here," The Czar insisted as his men started shoving him away, one of them aiming a gun my way and firing off a warning shot which forced me to take cover around the corner once more.

"No. Save yourself," Anya insisted and amid a lot of Russian shouting, I got the impression The Czar was moving away from me again.

I chanced a look out and found Anya pushing between his bodyguards, running towards me with her arms outstretched as she yelled at him to run once more, and he was ushered out of sight at the far end of the corridor.

The endless yells of 'Interpol' filled the house below us but as Anya made it to me, I just grinned, tossing my riot helmet aside and whipping her up into my arms as she leapt at me.

"Did you do it?" I asked, stamping my lips to hers before she could even answer me and hooking her legs around my waist, driving her up against the wall.

"What do you think?" she breathed as I dropped my mouth to her neck and her spine arched as my cock pressed firmly to her core.

"Of course you fuckin' did," I growled, gripping her arse in my hands and wondering how pissed Benny would be if I fucked his wife against this wall before letting him know she was alright.

"You never doubted me, did you?" she gasped, rocking her hips against mine and making me groan.

I lifted my head to look her in the eye, telling her straight because for some reason she needed to hear this.

"No, Anya Butcher, I didn't doubt you for a fuckin' second. You're unstoppable when you wanna be and no billionaire prick was ever gonna get one up on you."

I moved my mouth to her neck again, but she fisted my hair in her hand and made me look at her once more.

"Say that again," she panted, her tits heaving in that little black scrap of nothing, and I was pretty sure I was gonna be putting my cock in her within the next thirty seconds regardless of what Benny might have to say on it.

"What? The bit where I called you unstoppable, or the bit where I looked at you and saw a goddess set to take over the entire fuckin' world?" I asked, the side of my mouth lifting into a grin as I let my eyes roam all over this beautiful creature who had come crashing into my life and flipped it all the way on its axis. "Or do you wanna hear the best bit of all?" I asked, my voice dipping seductively as my hold on her arse tightened and her thighs gripped my waist like she never wanted to be anywhere but in my arms.

"What's that?" she asked, biting her lip and making me groan as the distant sound of a helicopter taking off reached us alongside the continued yells of 'Interpol!'

"That you own me now, darlin'. Every black and rotten piece of my soul has found salvation in my dedication to you. I was up all night thinkin' on it. On how you light me up and make me burn unlike anything I've ever known. And you know what I realised?"

"What?" she breathed, her eyes smouldering with that same fire I was burning up in.

"That I love the fucking bones of you, Miss America. For better or worse, I'm your creature now. So do with me what you will because there's no you without me anymore."

"Church," she murmured, a hand lifting to caress my jaw as she looked at me in a way that made my heart race and my body hum with every kind of need for her.

"Stop manhandling my fucking wife," Benny barked from somewhere behind me and I swear to fuck, I woulda turned and knocked him clean out if Anya hadn't ignored his interrupting arse and finished that thought she was having.

"I love you, too."

I crushed my mouth to hers so that I could taste those fucking words while my heart catapulted in my chest and a laugh of pure joy bubbled up within me.

Before I could get too carried away with that feeling and fuck her against the wall like I'd been intending to, Benny collided with us, knocking me aside and ripping her outa my arms before stealing my kiss and tasting her lips himself.

"Arsehole," I snarled, half tempted to punch him for that bullshit before he released her and rounded on me.

"The Czar is gone and it's time for us to fuck off too. I dunno who told the rest of those pricks to yell Interpol so fucking much, but I think every arsehole in a ten mile vicinity got the damn message. What did they think this was, a game of Marco Inter-Polo or some shit?"

Anya breathed a laugh, making his gaze zero in on her and he let his eyes run all down her body in that little black scrap of nothing.

"You got what we need?" he asked and she nodded proudly, accepting another kiss as he stole one from her. "Damn right you did."

"I told you she would," I added like a prick because I was happy to get all the rewards Anya felt like offering out on account of my faith in her, and I was more than happy to milk the situation to my advantage.

"I never doubted it," Benny snapped, turning for the stairs with Anya's hand locked in his. "Come on, wife, the four of us have got some celebrating to do at home and if you decided on wearing that because you were hoping it would result in you getting thoroughly fucked by a pack of heathens, then I'm willing to bet your luck is in."

I barked a laugh, making Anya glance my way and I slapped her arse before offering her my jacket as we started down the stairs to where Frank was waiting, trying to look like he hadn't been the least bit worried about anything during all of this. And as the four of us made it out of The Czar's house and started hurrying back down the street to where we'd left the cars, I felt the happiest I had in eight long years. Anya Volkov hadn't known what she was walking into when she'd arrived in our beautiful city, and it turned out none of us had been the least bit prepared for her either.

CHAPTER FORTY SEVEN

"That crystal duck isn't worth shit, I had it checked by Bobby Jeweller and he says it's value amounts to a packet of crisps and a lacklustre hand job at best," Church said and I looked to him in surprise as Frank kicked the door to the warehouse shut behind us.

"Hang on, you *have* the duck?" I asked in shock, tugging the jacket Church had given me closer to my body as I shivered in the thin black one piece I was still wearing.

"Church pinched it the last time we had a little poke around the Candlestick Maker's turf," Benny explained, shrugging out of his fake Interpol jacket and giving me a good view of his biceps.

"Pinched it?" I asked in confusion.

"Half inched it," Church supplied as if that was any clearer, his silvery eyes travelling down the lacy bodysuit I was wearing.

"They stole it, Cash," Frank had mercy on my fucking soul and a smile spilled across my face.

"So where is it?" I asked, glancing around as if expecting to spot it in the room.

"It's at your place, ain't it?" Benny asked Church.

Church gave him an apologetic look, shoving his fingers into his hair. "Well…not exactly, no. See, when I got it back from Bobby Jeweller, I almost considered keeping the little fella. He had such a twinkle in his eye, but then I thought. No, this little ducky deserves better than that. He should be displayed in a nice cabinet, and where better to find a home like that than from the local charity shop?"

"You gave a priceless diamond to the fuckin' charity shop?" Frank barked, lunging for Church and fisting his hand in his shirt.

Church shoved him off just as I caught Frank's arm. "Well can't we just go get it back? Maybe it's still there?" I suggested anxiously while Benny pursed his lips at Church.

"Pretty little fella like that? No chance. He's old biddy candy that ducky," Church said with a morose head shake.

"Well you're gonna track that ducky down, mate, because I want it in my hand as a weapon against The Czar and his merry Candlestick Maker," Benny growled and Church nodded, bowing his head.

"I'll go there when it opens in the mornin'," he promised. "Ain't no point busting in there tonight if it's gone already."

"I'll go with you," I said immediately.

"We're all going," Benny decided. "Because we're all responsible for each other's messes, got that? That's how it always was, and that's how it's gonna be if we're all in with each other. We're the Forget-Me-Nots, ain't that right Frankie boy?" He moved to drop his arm over Frank's shoulders and the two of them shared an intent look that made my heart squeeze.

"That's right, Benny," he said with a firm nod and Church moved to clap Frank on the arm. My gaze travelled over the three of them, their eyes sparking like a match had been struck within them.

Frank looked more relaxed than I'd seen him in all the time I'd known him, like he'd been waiting to return to his rightful place in the world. I could see the bond between them forged over years of fighting through grit and war together. They weren't just friends, they were brothers in arms, bonded by countless secrets and a thirst for darkness that only this kind of life could quench. My skin hummed with the proximity of them, their unit of absolute power seeming to charge the air around me.

I realised all three of them were staring back at me and I felt like a leopard amongst wolves. We were the same at our core, predators who thrived in the thrill of the hunt, but they were a pack, and I was the lone creature who'd come wandering into their den. Although it was starting to feel like I was a part of their pack, a wolf in my own right.

"C'mere, bombshell," Benny ordered, but I didn't move an inch, my shoulders pressing back as I defied a command from the boss.

"She wants to play," Church murmured, scoring a thumb across the stubble on his jaw.

"Her games get her in trouble," Frank added.

"I wanna know what it's like to be hunted by the Forget-Me-Nots," I said, a thrill dancing under my flesh.

The three of them exchanged hungry looks and Benny nodded his approval.

"If you find me, you can have me. All of me. But you have to share," I said, my breaths falling heavily from my chest as I considered what I was offering. But I wanted this, all of them made me come to life and I might just short-circuit myself entirely if I took them all on at once, but what a way to fucking die.

Church cocked his head to one side, the playful smirk on his lips not matching the darkness in his eyes. Monsters, all of them. But who was I to complain?

"Shut your eyes," I instructed. "And count to fifty loudly. If you can't find me after fifteen minutes, you lose the chance to touch me again until tomorrow evening."

"And what do we win if we find you?" Benny asked, taking a step towards me.

"You don't stop touching me until all of you are sated," I said, a wicked smile curling my lips as their expressions heated.

"Fuck yes," Church growled, covering his eyes with his palm.

"You in, Frankie boy?" Benny asked him and Frank stared at me closely before raising his hand and covering his eyes in answer, leaving a tremor rushing down my spine.

Benny grinned at me with devious intent then covered his own eyes, leading the count. "One – two -three-"

I kicked off my shoes and ran, padding silently upstairs as fast as I could and slipping into the spare room I'd been decorating. I knew there was a place in here they probably wouldn't think of and though I did kinda wanna be caught, I was also too proud to lose this game easily.

Beneath the large window at the back of the room was a low wooden cabinet and there was a space behind it that I could wriggle into. I dropped to my knees, squeezing through the gap and tucking myself into the darkness. The cabinet had a lip on it that met with the wall above my head so no one would see me unless they were really trying to look behind this thing.

The sound of Benny counting filled the whole warehouse. "Forty-Eight, Forty-Nine, Fifty. Ready or not, here we come, bombshell."

The pounding of heavy footfalls followed and I held my breath as they immediately carried upstairs. A search broke out in every room, furniture being violently shifted around and the quiet determination of all of them made my skin prickle with how seriously they were taking this game.

When someone flung the door open to the room I was in and flicked the light on, I stilled, not drawing a single breath.

Footsteps thumped into the room and the sound of a search broke out followed by more footsteps joining the first set. They pillaged the room while I barely sucked in any air and my pulse drummed in my ears.

"Fuck, where is she?" Frank's gruff voice filled the room, so close it made my heart jolt.

"Let's check Danny's room," Benny suggested then their footsteps moved away and the door clunked.

I slowly let the air out of my chest and drew in another breath, my legs cramping up as I tried to shift a little to alleviate the pain in them. But the moment I did that, my elbow knocked the wall and a deep voice came in response.

"Gotcha," Church said, the cabinet shoved aside in the next second and I squealed as he grabbed my ankle and hauled me out on my stomach.

He flipped me up into his arms in the next second and tossed me onto the bed. Benny and Frank were in the doorway, watching us like they'd never left and I cursed as Church fell over me, trying to catch hold of my wrists to pin me down.

"She's a wild thing," Church laughed.

"You have a promise to uphold, Cash," Frank said as he prowled closer. "Volkovs always pay their debts, right?"

I fell still beneath Church as he grasped my wrists in one of his large hands and drew them above my head, my eyes flicking to Frank then Benny as they came into view beside him.

Church released my wrists and his hands travelled down my body as his knees pressed my thighs apart. I bit my lip as he worked to unbutton the bodysuit between my thighs, but he couldn't get it open. "What the fuck are these lock picker knickers? How do I get in?"

Frank leaned over me, producing a knife and slicing through the material without warning, making me gasp in surprise as he exposed my bare pussy. I realised how turned on I was already as Church rubbed his knuckles in my wetness and a moan left me.

"Is this all for us, darlin'?" Church asked, his eyes hooded.

"Only for you three," I swore.

"Don't leave my wife wanting, Church," Benny warned, moving forward to fist his friend's hair and shove his head down to my pussy.

Church obliged, his tongue lapping over my clit and making a cry fall from my lips as my eyes locked with Benny's.

My hips bucked as Church feasted on me and my husband held his hand against the back of his head, the swell in his pants telling me how much he was enjoying the show.

"Get the bodysuit off her," Benny commanded Frank and he moved to the other side of the bed, reaching over my head and taking hold of the material. He didn't pull it over my head though, he ripped it wide, sheering it from my body with his knife and tossing it away. He dropped the blade and his large palms came down on my tits, his thumbs scoring over my nipples and Benny groaned his approval as he watched my body writhe between the feral desire of his friends.

"Keep doing that. Don't stop," Benny demanded then turned and walked out of the room, leaving me missing him. But I got lost in the touch of my other two demons, Church's tongue gliding over my clit in a perfect figure of eight as Frank tormented my nipples. I was building towards climax so fast my head was in a fog, and I wrapped my legs around Church, my heels driving into his back as Frank's touch sent electricity firing through my flesh.

Benny returned just as I came, my head tipping back and my body arching between them as they worked to hold me still and wring more pleasure from me.

Benny was just in his boxers now with a bottle of lube in his hand and a dirty as fuck grin on his face. “Both of you step back.”

Church did so, wiping his glistening lips with the back of his hand as he smirked, but Frank was slower to respond, one hand sliding down to my pussy to feel how wet I was, making me moan and grind into him.

“That was an order, Frankie boy,” Benny said with an edge to his tone and Frank reluctantly withdrew his hand and stepped aside.

Benny knelt on the bed, lying down beside me and hooking an arm beneath me. He rolled me on top of him and I settled my weight down on the bulge of his huge cock, the thin material of his boxers doing nothing to hide his arousal. I rocked my hips down on him and he groaned, lifting the bottle of lube and pouring it all over his right hand.

“Boxers, Church,” Benny ordered and Church pressed up right behind me, yanking Benny’s boxers off half a second before Benny thrust inside me. I was so wet that he slid in to the hilt and I cried out, locking my hands around his throat for support and squeezing when his eyes glittered for more.

I rode him hard for a few seconds and he gripped my ass with his left hand, squeezing and caressing before sliding the fingers of his right between my cheeks and pressing two of them into my tight hole. I gasped as he got me ready for one of his friends and moaned louder and louder at the idea of what we were about to do.

My eyes darted up to meet Frank’s gaze and I found him naked, fisting his huge dick and stroking it as he watched us.

“C’mere, Church,” Benny instructed, tossing the lube in his direction and I felt Church move up behind me as he took the bottle in his tattooed hand.

Church’s fingers replaced Benny’s in my ass and my hips rolled in time with them as Benny slowed his pace beneath me to a heady rhythm.

“Are you ready, Miss America?” Church asked against my shoulder, his stubble grazing my skin and making my heart race.

“Yes,” I encouraged and he lined the head of his cock up with my ass, the tip slick with lube before he slowly pushed into me. I moaned loudly as the two of them filled me up and started moving in time with one another, making my body theirs with deep, possessive thrusts.

Frank shifted closer and I watched him as he stroked his impressive length and took in what his friends were doing to me.

I reached for him and he moved forward without hesitation, positioning himself in front of me a second before I took his cock between my lips.

“Watch where you put your fucking balls, Frankie,” Benny snapped and I choked a laugh around Frank’s cock before he shifted sideways a little and I tilted my head to follow him.

All my amusement was lost as Benny fucked me harder from below and Church upped his pace to match him, sending my whole world spinning into chaos. It was so intense, but so fucking good too and I couldn’t get enough of owning these three men at once. It was a thrill unlike anything I'd experienced before and as my clit ground against my husband's pubic bone, I was already coming apart again, whimpering as pleasure rocketed through my body.

Frank's dick swelled in my mouth and he growled, withdrawing it from my lips and giving me a chance to breathe as Church and Benny fucked me even harder, my body oversensitive as they didn't give me a second to recover.

Church spanked my ass hard and my core clenched, making both him and Benny groan loudly, the combined sound such a fucking turn on that I groaned too. In the next second, both of them were coming, filling me up as they squeezed my hips and sides bruisingly, holding me right where they wanted me as their seed dripped between my thighs and left me feeling as high as if I was on drugs.

Church eased out of me first and Benny stole a lingering kiss from my lips before speaking against my mouth. "Show Frankie boy a good time for us, bombshell. He's owed a smile or two."

Frank's large hands yanked me off of him in a heartbeat and I found myself tossed on my back with Frank bearing over me. He swirled his cock around the mess between my legs, his gaze full of lust like he was surprised how much he liked the feel of that.

He drove himself inside me and I cried out, my back arching against the sheets as he fucked me hard and fast, one hand fisted in my hair and yanking tight. He placed rough kisses against my neck, my ear and the music notes inked along my collar bone, grinding his cock into a sensitive spot deep inside me with every furious thrust of his hips. He knew exactly what he was doing and my body was so weak and at his mercy that he seemed to mould it like clay. Somehow, he made me come again, forcing more pleasure from my body like he was determined to show me how much power he had over me and my pussy squeezed his thick shaft as I gave him what he wanted.

"Good girl," he said gruffly, his hips still pistoning and I felt the head of his cock swelling as he reached the brink of explosion.

Benny was suddenly there behind him, grabbing his hips and forcing them back so his cock was drawn out of me and Frank snarled as he came all over my pussy instead of inside me.

Frank knocked him away, pumping his cock and enjoying the last of his climax as he watched me paw at my breasts and writhe with all the aftershocks of their claiming.

Benny slid a hand between my thighs, swirling his fingers there before bringing them up to my lips and making me suck them clean, the combined taste of all three of them making me moan.

"All ours," he growled and the other two echoed that sentiment.

I didn't know how the fuck we'd gotten to this point, because it sure as shit hadn't been what I'd had in mind when I'd boarded a plane to England. But the four of us were in this relationship together and it was making me happier than I'd realised was possible. It was filthy and wicked, but it was just as sweet and unconquerable too. And as Benny scooped me into his arms and the four of us headed for the shower, I knew I was right where I needed to be, in an underworld that belonged to me as much as it belonged to them.

I stepped into the charity shop - which I realised meant a thrift store – and I stared around at the tiny place which was full of shelves and cabinets overflowing with all kinds of items. And it wasn't just ornaments, there were clothes, books, tableware, jewellery, toys, everything stacked up to the roof and turning the place into a maze of wonders.

Benny and Frank waited in the car while Church and I strode up to the counter where an elderly man in a green woolly sweater was standing.

"Afternoon, mate," Church said. "You don't still happen to have that crystal duck I donated a couple of month's back, do ya?"

The guy lifted a pair of spectacles from his head and slid them onto his nose as he got a better look at Church. "A crystal duck, you say? Well there's only been one of those in here recently and I just sold it to Mrs Watson not five minutes ago. She was quite taken with the item."

"Fuck," Church barked, making the man jump.

"I do beg your pardon," the old man said in shock.

"Pardon permitted," Church said, tipping an imaginary hat to him and sliding an arm around my shoulders, guiding me from the shop.

"What are you doing?" I hissed at him.

"Going old biddy hunting," he muttered back as we stepped out into the frosty air.

Benny and Frank gazed out at us from Frank's Mercedes and I shook my head, letting them know we hadn't found it.

We dropped into the backseats and Church snapped the door closed behind us with a huff of frustration.

"Frank, get driving. We're lookin' for an old bird who's gone and bought our duck," Church commanded as he lowered the window beside him and stuck his head out. As Frank drove along, he shouted, "Mrs Watson!" to any older woman we passed and I shared a look with Benny who's expression said we should trust Church's wild methods. So I opened my window too, stuck my head out and joined him.

"Mrs Watson!" I cried.

"Mrs Watson?!" Church shouted at an older lady drinking tea outside a café and she nearly spilled it all over herself.

"Maybe we need a better plan," Frank said thoughtfully.

"How about her?" I pointed over his shoulder as I spotted an old lady towing a pull-along bag behind her as she tottered slowly along the street.

"Mrs Watson!" Church cried at her, but she didn't turn around. "Mrs

Watson!" He tried again as we pulled up beside her, Frank slowing down to meet her pace.

"Mrs Watson!" Church roared and the woman looked around curiously, her face heavily wrinkled and her hair curly and grey.

"Yes, my dear?" she asked kindly.

"You're Mrs Watson?" I asked, half climbing into Church's lap as I looked out at her.

"Yes, I'm Mrs Watson. Did I leave something at the shop? Silly me, I'm always leaving things places. I'd leave my head behind if it wasn't screwed on. Did Andrew send you? Andrew's a lovely man. A lovely, lovely man."

"Andrew sent us to help you home with your things," Church said, turning on the charm and slapping Frank around the ear when he didn't immediately pull over.

Benny tossed Frank a look that told him to comply and Frank stopped beside Mrs Watson while Church leapt out of the car and offered to take her bag for her. He towered over her by nearly three feet, but she didn't blink an eye as she batted him away from her.

"No, no, I'm not letting go of that. You never know where the crooks are lurking in this city, I have to keep a close eye on my things. Now come on dear, let me in the car." She rapped her knuckles on the window of the front passenger seat and Benny looked out at her in surprise. "Out you get, sonny Jim," she instructed. "My legs don't bend like they used to, I can't ride in the back."

Benny opened the door and she shuffled back to let him by, bustling past him as Church offered her his hand to help lower her into the seat while she tucked her bag in by her feet.

"Just nick it," Benny hissed at Church but he shook his head.

"I ain't thieving from an old lady," he growled in reply and I couldn't deny his standards were kinda hot.

The two of them climbed into the back of the car with me and Frank took off down the road, adjusting the rear view mirror and stealing a look at me.

"Where to, Mrs Watson?" Frank asked politely, making a smile pull at my lips.

"Edward Street," she said. "And don't dilly dally, Sandra is coming over to play backgammon in an hour."

"There's time for us to come in for tea though, right Mrs Watson?" Church asked hopefully.

"Oh there's always time for tea," she said. I had to admit, I was growing kind of fond of English tea, and even though I loved coffee, I was starting to be converted. Especially when Church made it for me. Dammit, there was something in that guy's touch that was pure magic. If I wasn't careful, I'd end up sipping from a teacup with my little pinky finger extended next, making small talk about the weather before excusing myself to use the 'loo'.

Mrs Watson directed us back to her house and we arrived outside the little cottage which was wedged between a row of them on a cobbled street. It was cute as hell and I found myself excited to look inside as we followed her to her door, especially because it took nearly five minutes for us walk three feet. The anticipation was killing me.

She fumbled with her keys, trying them one at a time in the little blue door and muttering about how the keys were cursed and always kept muddling themselves up to confuse her.

When she finally got it open, we followed her into the tiny house and my three boys had to duck to make it down the hallway. Porcelain plates with all kinds of British birds on them adorned the walls and Church kept knocking them off, catching them before they hit the floor and hurrying to put them back in their place. He caught one an inch before it smashed on the floor, standing upright as his eyebrows raised. "Nice tits."

I frowned at him in confusion, figuring he was talking about my tits which were definitely not on display in my leather coat, but then he turned the plate around and showed me a pair of bluetits on it.

"Nice pecker," I replied, nodding to the woodpecker on the plate on the wall to his right and he grinned at me like the Cheshire Cat.

"Nice cock," Frank muttered and I looked to him in surprise as he pointed a finger to a plate featuring a rooster – which I remembered the Brits called a cockerel – and all three of us shared a stupid look before Frank flattened his boyish grin. I seriously liked this softer side of him which seemed to be showing more and more since he'd settled his issues with Benny and Church. It was like they'd been keeping a piece of his heart captive all these years and had finally handed it back.

We shuffled past a narrow stairway as Mrs Watson led us into her lounge, my breath catching at the sight of the ornate wooden cabinets she had around the room displaying all kinds of crystal items. The carpet had a swirling pattern on it and the sofa and armchairs were a deep magenta colour, worn on the sides where a cat's claws had ripped into them.

"Oh, Branston, for heaven's sake, you must use your litter box!" Mrs Watson shrieked just as a pungent scent hit me. "It's not his fault, I suppose. I haven't been able to clean it out recently with this dodgy hip of mine. It must be full of his little kitty droppings. He can go outside, of course, but he doesn't like the rain, see? Or too much sun. Or even a light fog."

I noticed the huge ginger cat sitting by the window, staring at Mrs Watson with a look of disinterest while she pointed at a steaming cat turd sitting on top of the litter box. The old girl tried to bend down to pick up the box, but she groaned and clutched her hip.

"Oh do forgive the mess, it's tricky getting things done," she said. "Did I mention my bad hip?"

"Don't worry, Mrs Watson," Church said, slapping Frank on the arm. "Frank 'ere loves a cat. He'll have that litter box cleaned up in no time, won't you mate?" He gave Frank a bright smile and Frank glared coldly back at him.

"Oh will ya really?" Mrs Watson turned to Frank with a hopeful desperation and I gave Frank that very same look, making him glance between us and sigh heavily.

"Fine," he grunted, moving to grab the box while Mrs Watson directed him away to the kitchen to clean it.

Benny had drifted over to the nearest cabinet, examining some of Mrs Watson's collection.

"I'll get the hoover and give this place a bit of a spruce for ya, how about that, darlin'?" Church offered and Mrs Watson gasped, patting his arm.

"Well bless your heart, you are a good boy, aren't you?" she cooed and Church grinned like a kid before heading off to get the vacuum cleaner.

Mrs Watson towed her bag over to what was clearly her favourite seat by the window, slowly lowering herself down onto it and rummaging in the bag. She took out a bag of cat treats, opening them up and Branston jumped onto the arm of her chair, purring loudly as she poured some out for him.

"Did you get anything nice at the store?" I asked her, drifting closer as I eyed her bag.

"Something lovely for my collection actually," she said excitedly.

"Can I see?" I asked.

"Yes, yes, just as soon as your other friend fetches some tea," she said, glancing at Benny who turned our way with a frown.

"Off you go then," I encouraged and Benny pushed his tongue into his cheek before heading off to do as I asked.

Mrs Watson moved to put the cat treats away and Branston suddenly flipped, savagely attacking her hand and making me gasp in alarm.

"Stop that, you angry little man," she commanded, swatting at him lightly even though his claws were drawing blood not to mention the way he was chomping on her thumb.

I tried to intervene, but she flapped a hand in my face to keep me back and Branston sat upright, mewling grumpily as Mrs Watson petted his ears.

"You naughty man, now look what you've done to mummy." Mrs Watson turned to me, lowering her voice like the cat would overhear her if she didn't. "He has mood swings, poor thing."

I wasn't sure how he was the poor thing in this situation, but alright.

Benny returned with the tea as the sound of Church vacuuming the house carried to us and it wasn't until we'd eaten our way through half a pack of some sort of strawberry jelly-filled cookies called Jammie Dodgers that Mrs Watson finally took the crystal duck out of her bag. She unwrapped it from the tissue paper it was nestled in and my heart beat harder as she held it up to the light to admire it. I had no idea where the diamond was hidden within that thing, but I could practically sense it in there, that happy little duck's face definitely hiding something.

"That's quite the item there, Mrs Watson," Benny commented.

"Isn't it just?" she cooed. "He's gonna live right here with me alongside all his new friends." She gestured to the closest cabinet which was full of crystal animals. "Be a dear and put it in there for me, will you?" She handed the duck to me and Benny cocked his head, giving me a look that told me to run. But Mrs Watson's eyes were glittering and I just didn't have the heart to steal from an old woman.

"How much would you want for this?" I asked.

"Oh no, it's not for sale, my dear." She shook her head, a serious frown on her brow.

I realised the vacuuming had stopped and the sound of Frank retching carried from afar. I fought a snort of laughter as Church sauntered back into the room with a screwdriver in his grip.

"That door on the cupboard under the stairs was nearly falling off, so I've fixed it for you, darlin'. It was coming right offa the hinges," he said and Mrs Watson beamed.

"Ain't he a dote?" she said, patting my hand. "Is that one your boyfriend?"

"He is actually," I said and Church beamed with pride.

"And I'm her husband," Benny interjected, making Mrs Watson's eyes widen. "Frank's her bit on the side too."

"Is that so?" she gasped. "Goodness, that's a lot of filling for one muffin," she said under breath.

"So the duck?" I asked. "Are you sure there's no price for it? My husband will pay anything you want."

"Will he now?" Benny deadpanned, clearly more willing to just steal the damn thing, but that wasn't going to happen while me and Church got a say in it.

"Forty pounds and a spring clean 'ere once a month, how's that for an offer?" Church said, taking out his wallet and thumbing through some cash.

"Forty pounds?" Mrs Watson balked. "My Duncan here is worth more than forty pounds."

"Duncan?" I breathed.

"Yes, that's his name, of course. Isn't it obvious?" Mrs Watson chastised. "Now pop him in the cabinet and drop this nonsense about buying him. He's not for sale."

"I'll pay for a cleaner to come 'ere once a week, fresh meals brought here daily and I'll give ya two hundred quid," Church offered, but Mrs Watson was already shaking her head just as the sound of Frank saying, "Oh fuckin' hell, it's all over me trousers now," carried to us from the kitchen.

"Duncan isn't for sale," she insisted, sitting up straighter in her chair.

"We could always just take him," Benny muttered, leaning casually against the wall.

"You heathen," she spat, reaching down beyond her chair, picking up a large black umbrella and pointing it at him. "You just try it and see what happens to ya."

"We're not going to take it," I said firmly, giving Benny a pointed look as Church nodded his agreement.

"Cleaner, fresh meals, five hundred quid and another crystal duck to replace Duncan," Church tried and Mrs Watson paused, narrowing her eyes at him.

Frank retched again and the words "Cunt" and "Bollocks" reached us along with him lamenting, "Oh god, there's a nugget of shit in my shoe."

"A bigger crystal duck? With more of a twinkle in its eye?" Mrs Watson asked.

"Done," Church said. "And I'll throw in a crystal fuckin' goose to boot."

"You are a sweetheart," she said, giving in. "Go on then, take him. I always thought he was a bit of an ugly one anyway."

Church took out five hundred pounds, handing it to Mrs Watson as I tucked the crystal duck into my pocket and Benny glanced between the two of us appraisingly.

"Alright then. Thanks for the tea, love," Benny said. "We'd better be going."

"Hang the fuck on, I ain't even had a Jammie Dodger yet." Church strode forward, taking two out of the bag and stuffing them both into his mouth.

Frank reappeared in the doorway at that moment with his pants balled in one hand and the litter box in the other. He placed the box down with a furious grimace on his face and Mrs Watson gushed in thanks.

I tried not to laugh as I followed Frank to the door, but I failed and he glanced back at me with a warning look. As we made it outside, he tossed his pants into Mrs Watson's garbage can and dropped into the car with a scowl.

I slid into the backseat with Church and waved at Mrs Watson out the window, taking the duck from my pocket and admiring it with a satisfied grin.

"Well that went rather well actually," Church commented.

"Rather well?" Frank scoffed. "*You* didn't have to clean ten day old shit out of a litter box."

"That I didn't, mate," Church agreed. "I ain't got the constitution for cleaning up cat shit. But you've cleaned a man's guts from your shoes in the past, so I figured you were just the fella for the job."

"I'd take the guts over that any day. That cat is either violently ill or Satan himself came outa its arsehole in shit form. I'll never get the burn outa my eyes," Frank growled.

My fingers caught on a little roughened patch of crystal against the duck's ass and as I applied pressure, it clicked and slid open. A diamond fell out of a secret compartment which was the size of a large pebble and a gasp hitched in my throat.

"Well there she fucking blows. How'd Bobby Jeweller miss that?" Church took it from my hand, holding it up to the light as the others glanced back to see it.

"Because he's half blind and I've been tellin' ya we need to start using Ugly Christopher's boy for months now," Frank said in frustration.

"Oh well, it all worked out in the end," Church said. "And I think I've got a plan brewing."

"What plan?" Benny asked, his eyes alight as he stared at that diamond and a thrill danced through my blood.

"We just found out where the duck is, and it wasn't in some old biddy's house. No, I'd say the Candlestick Maker sold it on to some dodgy folk and now they've put it up for auction on the black market, so our little Czar friend is gonna have to bid to get it back. He can pay up for it and we can make a tidy little profit while he sings our praises for helping him find it."

"You're a clever asshole sometimes, aren't you?" I purred, leaning forward to kiss Church, my hand sliding up his thigh and squeezing.

I leaned back and he placed the diamond against my collar bone as if he was imagining what it might look like hanging there.

"Yeah, that's me, darlin'. A real clever clogs. Now what's my reward?"

I let my fingers run higher, caressing his cock as it swelled beneath my palm and sucking on my lower lip. "I'm sure I can think of something."

CHAPTER FORTY EIGHT

There was something about tweed that just fucking tickled me. I wasn't sure what it was or why I liked it so damn much, but if I was gonna be dressing up in some fancy fucker suit then tweed just called to me unlike any other. Today's choice was a grey three piece which I had donned a flat cap with, and I was running a little late on account of Anya jumping me on my way outa the door to show her appreciation of my wardrobe choice.

My mind was still all caught up on the feeling of my cock buried deep inside her and the way she'd panted my name before punching me hard enough to bruise my jaw. It was fucking electric what passed between me and her, and I was all for tasting more of it just as soon as I got back home and had this done. But for now, I had to settle for the lingering scent of her on my skin after kissing her breathless before I'd walked out the door.

I strode through the hotel lobby, tipping my chin at the man who shoulda stopped me as I passed him by, ignoring security protocols as I headed in for my meeting with The Czar. It had taken over a week for him to feel comfortable showing his face in London again after the supposed raid on his home by Interpol, but I'd managed to convince him to return by offering him up the use of my lawyer who had miraculously gotten Interpol to back off. Seeing as Interpol had never been involved in the raid on his house in the first place, it had been easy enough to convince him that their attention lay elsewhere at the moment, and now he was finally meeting me.

This situation was bordering on dire, and I needed him to put his money where his bloody mouth was so that we could get this construction underway, but he was still pussyfooting around the issue and seemed intent on leading me on a merry dance. He claimed he just needed to be certain of what kind of man he was getting into bed with before he gave the final nod on the investment, but I was getting beyond the point of tolerance for his hesitation.

The hotel was grand, with wood panelled walls and pretentiously small tables laid out in the restaurant with chintzy tablecloths and imposing armchairs. It looked like a gentlemen's club outa Downton Abbey or one of them old timey shows that Church liked to watch when he thought no one was paying attention. There were fat old white men everywhere, each of them so inflated on their sense of self-importance that it was a wonder there was any more air left in the room for the rest of us to breathe.

I noticed The Czar at the rear of the room, reading a broadsheet newspaper like he thought he was a fuckin' prince among paupers while sitting alone at a table. I spotted his personal security from a mile off though, eight of them in all, taking up tables close enough to protect him if needed, but far enough to offer up some semblance of privacy for him all the same.

A waiter spotted me and headed over as I strode through the room and I pointed my fingers at him like I was aiming a gun.

"I'll have a whiskey, mate. Top shelf, none of that ice rubbish and make sure it's from the highlands or some shit like that. I don't want no foreign knock offs, yeah?"

"Sir, this is the breakfast menu," he began but I cut him off.

"Oh, in that case, I'll have a full English and all. You can toss a cuppa in with it, but I'll have the whiskey now. And before you offer up any more objections, you might wanna go have a word with your boss before he pisses himself because *he* knows who I am even if you seem to be about as aware as a house sparrow with a grain allergy, peckin' away at the bird feeder." I pointed at the fella across the room who was trying to wave the waiter away from me, a look of horror painted across his features as I tipped him a salute and the fucker finally seemed to realise he was dicing with the wrong duck.

"As you wish, sir," he said apologetically, bobbing his head to me and I carried on my way to join The Czar at his table. Luckily, as the Candlestick Maker was avoiding him like the plague and The Czar didn't have any reason to go snooping about in gang business that had nothing to do with him, he hadn't heard anything about the swap I'd pulled on Danny. So he still fully believed I was my brother, and I didn't see the need to correct him.

"Mornin'," I greeted as I dropped into the deep green wingback opposite him and pulled a cigarette from my pocket.

An old dear a few tables away looked utterly scandalised as I pulled my matchbook out next and lit up. I gave her a taunting grin as I took a drag, blowing the smoke in her direction on my exhale.

"No Mrs Butcher today?" The Czar asked as he folded his newspaper and looked around with a disappointed expression as he hunted for Anya in the crowd.

"Nah. I thought a business meeting would be best conducted between businessmen. Besides, you had your night with her, you don't get more than that." I took a drag on my smoke as I leaned back in my chair, watching him as he frowned, his eyes darting towards the door again like she might wander in despite me telling him straight that she wouldn't.

"I'm sure your wife informed you that we were unfortunately interrupted before we managed to er…fully enjoy our evening together," he began but I cut him off.

"She mentioned the way you almost got her arrested and ran for it in your chopper without her, yeah," I agreed and he winced.

"It wasn't like that. She insisted she stay to help me get away. But unfortunately we didn't get to conclude our business, and I have been most caught up on the need for that conclusion."

"You mean you never got to blow your load while she whipped you senseless?" I asked, cocking my head at him. "She told me how much you liked that."

"Mr Butcher," The Czar began in a firm tone, clearly taking offence to the fact that she'd shared that little story with me, so I was willing to bet he didn't wanna hear about the way we'd all laughed ourselves silly over it either.

"Don't worry, mate," I said, waving him down and trailing smoke from my cigarette between us as I did so. "She's my wife. Believe me, she's done a whole lot worse than that to me more times than I can count. But we had a deal. One night. I ain't a man to share easily and she ain't a library book looking to take another stamp."

"Please, Danny," The Czar began, leaning forward and lowering his voice. "I am willing to offer you any price. I just need-"

"Hold that thought," I said as my phone began to ring and I answered it without giving him the option to object. "Yeah?"

"I have the latest catalogue ready for you, sir," Church's voice came down the speaker, his accent all kinds of fake posh just in case The Czar was listening in. "Would you like me to send it over now?"

"Yeah. You do that. When is the auction?" I asked, toking on my cigarette and giving The Czar a little smile.

"In three days. Bids are anonymous as always. I'll send it now." Church hung up and I let my phone hang from my fingertips.

"Sorry, mate," I said, offering up a half apologetic smile to The Czar. "But you know what it's like; when you get the call about the bids opening, you gotta take it or you might miss your chance to get your hands on what you want."

"You have an invitation to The Marketplace?" he asked, perking up just like I'd hoped he would and I grinned at him.

"Don't you?"

"I did, but recently I haven't been able to take part as often as I would like. I was in hiding for a few months and had to keep travelling from country to country. I missed a few too many calls and so far, I haven't received a new invite," he replied bitterly which made this next part of my plan all too easy.

I knew for a fact that the reason he hadn't been hearing from The Marketplace recently was because it had been shut down after a police raid almost caught a bunch of the major players, and they'd been working on making everything secure against the police hackers again before going live once more. But that was hard knowledge to come by and for most of the usual attendees to The Marketplace auctions – a highly selective auction which was held every few months selling only the most illicit and illegal of things to only the best connected and most dangerous men and women on the criminal side of the law – they were currently in the dark over what was going on. And luckily for me, The Czar was one of them. But I'd also managed to convince them to bring forward their re-launch and forget his invitation to the party for a tasty ten grand. Now I just had to hope our play would pay off.

"Well if you wanna take a gander, the catalogue is gonna be sent my way any minute," I offered, knowing we had him now.

"That would be most generous of you." I had to hide a grin at the eager look which filled The Czar's eyes as he scooted his chair closer to mine.

"Anything for a mate of mine," I replied easily, reaching out for the glass of whiskey which the waiter had just appeared with. I held a finger up to the fella in his penguin suit while I downed the entire contents of the glass before tossing the end of my smoke into it and handing it back to him. "I'll have another of those," I said, meeting his eye as he shifted uncomfortably, clearly wanting to reprimand me over the smoking thing, but eventually he picked right, ducked his head and left without a word.

My phone pinged and I opened up the message, holding my phone out for The Czar to see as I began scrolling through the list of items which ranged from stolen Egyptian artifacts to endangered animals, priceless art and far more besides. Basically anything and everything an over entitled cunt might want to get his hands on despite the morals of the acquisition.

I muttered the odd comment on the things I saw, taking my second drink from the waiter without a word and hiding my smile under the guise of taking a sip from it just as I scrolled onto one very familiar looking image of a crystal duck.

"What in the hell is that!?" The Czar cried, his face paling and arm trembling as he pointed the thing out, and I lifted my phone closer to my face as I placed my glass down.

"Says here it's a cheap crystal duck with some massive fuckin' diamond hidden in the middle of it," I surmised, acting like I had no idea why he was interested in it. "They reckon the thing is worth in excess of-"

"I know what it is worth, Mr Butcher! That duck is mine!"

"Alright, mate, if you like the look of it that much then why don't you just bid on-"

"You are not understanding," The Czar hissed, snatching the phone from my hand and looking around the room like he thought every fucker in here was listening to him. "It is *already* mine. I gave that to someone I trusted to keep it safe while Interpol were hunting for it. I have been asking for it back for some time while receiving excuse after excuse and now…now-"

I clapped a hand down on his shoulder, leaning in close as he looked inclined to leap from his chair at any moment and storm from the room in a fit of rage.

"Are you sayin' someone's done you dirty, fella?" I asked him, my brow lowering in well acted outrage. "On my turf? In my town?"

"Yes," he snarled, looking to me desperately. "And that is no mere trinket, Butch, it is immeasurably valuable to me. I earned it in blood and vengeance. It holds far greater value than the price of the diamond alone. I must get it back. The man who did this is going to pay for it most severely."

The Czar made a move to stand but I increased the pressure of my hand on his shoulder, forcing him to remain in his seat and causing several of his men to shove to their feet from the tables surrounding us as they reached for their weapons.

"Calm it, mate, you gotta think clearly. It was only a few days ago that Interpol tried to grab ya. Are you sure they ain't watching you now?"

The Czar slowly lowered himself back into his chair, shaking his head at his men to get them to relax too as he shot suspicious glances around the room.

"I have it on good authority that their investigations into me have been suspended, but…"

"But they're sneaky motherfuckers," I finished for him. "So you can never be too careful."

He cursed, swiping a hand down his face and glaring at the image of the crystal duck on my phone once more.

I gave him a few minutes to simmer and just as I was pretty certain he was about to bubble over the edge of his boiling brain pan, I leaned in to turn down the heat with an offer I was pretty certain he wouldn't be able to refuse.

"Look, I'm feeling all kinds of cut up over this for ya, mate. Especially with it happening here in my town. You and me have a good thing going. You're investing in the Soho development with me, you and my wife hit it off, we've had some great banter and I'm being totally honest when I tell you I think of you as a true friend of mine now. So if you like, I could deal with this little mess for ya. Just give me a name and I'll see them dead for this. I can hunt down your little ducky too, no bother."

"You'd do that?" he asked, his expression clearing a little as he looked to me like I was his salvation and damn, I liked that look. It was nice. Made me feel like I wasn't some rotten hearted bastard out to fuck him over. I mean, that was precisely what I was, but it was nice to feel like a better man even if it was fleeting and built on bullshit.

"We're friends, ain't we?" I replied, acting all offended as I leaned back in my chair. "You're investing in this development with me. I'm hurt that you'd be surprised by my offer."

"No, no, I'm not surprised," The Czar said hastily and I arched a brow at him. "Truly. But it is a lot to ask."

“Nothing is too much to ask of a friend. Besides, I’m offering. So come on then, who do I need to deal with for you?”

The Czar looked around once more, leaning closer as he kept his voice low while his expression darkened.

“Gus Trotter,” he hissed. “I gave him that duck to protect for me. And now he is trying to pull the rug out from under me and sell it like I’m some fucking chump.” His fist smacked down on the table just as the waiter arrived with my food and I let out a low whistle, picking up my knife and fork.

“The Candlestick Maker?” I asked, cutting into my fried tomato and piling it onto a lump of toast alongside some egg and mushrooms. “Old Gussy? For real?”

“Yes,” he hissed.

“Cor blimey,” I muttered, shooing the waiter away with my knife as he returned with a pot of tea for me and he scarpered nice and quick once he’d set it down.

“I realise you too thought of him as a friend, but it is clear to me now that he is nothing but a snake in the grass. No doubt he would be just as willing to fuck you over given half a chance.”

“No doubt,” I agreed, chewing thoughtfully while The Czar practically vibrated with the desire to hear my next words.

I took my time, eating another few mouthfuls of my meal and letting him squirm before raising a fancy napkin to the corner of my mouth and wiping it thoughtfully.

“Well, there’s no use beating about the mulberry bush on a diddler like this, is there, fella?” I asked, tossing the napkin down on my half-eaten meal and placing a fresh cigarette between my lips.

“What is this mulberry bush?” he asked with a frown and I gave him a wolf’s grin around my smoke as I struck a match and lit it up.

“Don’t you worry your head on that. I’ll be bringing the lighter fluid to set the whole thing on fire and burn all the rats out from inside it. Just hold tight, mate, I’ll have his head and your duck for you within the week. Then maybe we can crack on with this investment business? Though, to be honest, I did come here expecting a payment…”

“Yes, of course,” he agreed. “I’ll have four million transferred to you today so that work can get started on our development. The rest will follow shortly,” he agreed eagerly and I hid my smug smile as I pushed to my feet. *Thank fuck for that.*

I clapped him on the shoulder a couple of times before turning and striding away.

“Consider it done,” I called back to him as I headed for the exit, toking on my cigarette and feeling the sweet taste of victory filling my lungs alongside the smoke.

“Sir, I’m sorry but you really can’t smoke in here,” the helpful little jobsworth waiter called as I closed in on him and I gave him a look that would make bigger, badder men shit their britches.

“Apologies, friend, it won’t happen again.” I plucked the cigarette from my lips and flicked it straight at his chest.

He swore, dropping the tray he’d been holding and catching the smoke before cursing loudly and dropping that too, stamping on the hard wood floor in a panic as he fought to put it out and managing to crush one of the broken glasses even more with his heel.

A laugh bubbled from my lips as I left that little bit of carnage in my wake, and I strode out onto the streets of the town I owned with a spring in my step and murder on my mind, because this little bit of fun had only just begun.

ANYA

CHAPTER FORTY NINE

I was squeezed into the back of Church's Mini next to Frank's huge frame, his hand placed casually on my knee, while he twirled a knife between his fingers with his other hand. We were all dressed in black, though the Mini was a bit of a giveaway, but Church insisted it was worth bringing because it was the best getaway car in the city. That was probably bullshit, but he'd been damn persuasive with his roguish smirk and cocky attitude.

"John Boy's on standby," Benny confirmed from the front passenger seat as he checked his phone. "He'll have the gang start a fight if we get ourselves into a pickle. They're staying outa sight until then though – we can't be caught on this patch of turf without a promise of death to follow."

The tower block we were aiming for loomed ahead of us, a huge concrete pillar filled with apartments, sticking up into the sky defiantly in the middle of an endless expanse of concrete. Church got as close to it as possible before parking in the shadows, the ugly plastic Bulldog on his dashboard bobbing its head for several seconds after we'd stopped.

"Let's keep this clean, boys," Benny murmured, addressing me like I was a part of the gang just like the others, and I couldn't help but grin at that. "In and out."

We got out of the car and my heart pounded with anticipation as I brushed my fingers over the knife strapped to my hip. I had a small gun hidden in my boot too, but that was for worst case scenarios only. This block of apartments was riddled with the Candlestick Maker's men, this was his turf, the heart of his power, and the plan was to kill him quietly and slip away into the night once it was done. We were working as The Firm tonight, not the Butcher gang. And this was how they cleaned house.

I was excited to see Gus die, that gross animal of a man who traded women like they were nothing more than commodities. It was sick. I'd gladly watch the light go out of his eyes for it. And knowing my boys, they were going to make it hurt too.

Benny beckoned us to follow him and we remained in the shadows, falling into single file as Frank took up the rear and Church moved in front of me behind Benny. I was a part of this pack now and we were wolves on a hunt, ready to wet our muzzles in blood.

John Boy had done a full surveillance on this place and assured us there were no CCTV cameras that we needed to worry about. The Candlestick Maker obviously didn't want to go around incriminating himself or his men, but that left him exposed if we could just have the balls to pull off this plan. It was genius really. Walk right up to his door, break inside and gut him before anyone realised his enemies had come knocking. I was starting to get a taste for this subtlety thing they had going on.

John Boy said his guards were lazy, rarely sticking to their posts, and I guessed that was because this place was swarming with the Candlestick Maker's men. No one would suspect we'd come here, it was suicide. But only if you got caught.

Benny hugged a wall, gesturing for us to do the same before throwing a glance out in the direction of the entranceway. We watched it closely for several more seconds before Benny gave Church a signal and he walked straight out of hiding, swaggering up to the door without a hint of concern in his posture. He tapped in the keycode John Boy had managed to note down and the door buzzed, making my heart buzz with it.

I shared a grin with Benny and we moved forward as one, Frank keeping close to my back, the presence of his large body feeling like a moving wall behind me.

We crept into the stairwell and motion sensor lights flickered on around us, though some of them were busted and the faded yellow walls covered in questionable stains told me all I needed to know about this place.

We hurried up the quiet stairwell, passing entranceways to open air walkways that led to all the apartments, but we didn't slow at any of them, continuing to climb towards the top of this place where the Candlestick Maker had taken up court.

Loud voices sounded around the next corner in the stairwell and I yanked Benny backwards by his shirt half a second before he was seen.

We turned, darting back down the stairs as the male voices grew louder, the four of us slipping out onto the closest walkway as Frank quietly closed the door behind us. There was no one out on the balcony here and I realised how high we were already as the wind swept around us and the single barren tree in the centre of the courtyard below swayed back and forth.

The hard plane of Frank's chest pressed to my back while Church and

Benny closed in around me from the front, their combined scents making me inhale deeply. I wasn't afraid here on this job, it felt like I'd been placed exactly where I should be. I was made for this life, and I was finally able to prove my worth within it. I'd fight alongside my men as an equal, and I'd die as an equal too if it came to it. All I'd ever wanted was to choose my own destiny, and now that I could, I was choosing danger and risk, but I'd rather live on the edge than die with my feet still planted on the ground.

The group of men headed down the stairwell, the windows in the mottled doors allowing us a view at the back of their shaved heads and the tattoos creeping along their necks. They didn't even glance our way and I wondered if we might just pull this off without a hitch.

When they were out of earshot, Benny tugged the door open and led the way forward again, the four of us falling easily back into a natural formation as we hurried on upstairs.

My breaths came heavier by the time we made it to the thirtieth floor all the way at the top of the tower block and Benny paused as we reached the door, peering out through the window to the walkway.

In a sudden movement, he yanked the door open, catching hold of a guy positioned to the right of it and slapping a hand to his mouth, driving a knife up between his shoulder blades, a gun falling from the guy's fingertips and clattering to the floor.

Church hooked it up and pocketed it, tapping his foot lightly as he waited for the man to stop kicking and I stared at my husband with a rush rolling through my limbs as he finished the kill. Frank moved forward, throwing the body over his shoulder and popping open a supply closet across the stairwell, shoving the man inside like he weighed nothing more than paper.

I bit my lip and Frank gave me a dark look, knocking his knuckles against my cheek as he returned to my side.

"Dirty, twisted girl," he murmured in my ear as we followed Church and Benny out onto the top floor and a smirk pulled at my lips. He wasn't wrong.

The wide walkway stretched out before us, cigarette butts lining the metal railing and piles of them on the ground too, alongside the remnants of countless joints as well. The sound of a TV carried loudly from the closest apartment, but the curtains were closed as we snuck past it, heading towards the next door.

John Boy had confirmed the Candlestick Maker took up residence in all the apartments up here, but we had to work out which door he was currently behind before making our move. Apparently John Boy's forgettable face made him perfect for jobs like scoping out enemy turf – Church said he just popped a hat on and it was like some entirely new person was born. No one ever recognised him. It seemed kinda odd, but I still had trouble recognising him myself, even after all these months, so I guessed there was truth to it.

Church moved ahead of us, carefully peering in windows and I drew the knife into my grip as my men did the same.

A bang sounded behind us and I flung around, the door closest to the stairwell hitting the wall as it crashed open. The Candlestick Maker appeared, raising a gun and firing, taking us off guard with his sudden appearance and drawing a curse to my lips as my heart leapt with shock.

Frank collided with me, taking me to the ground as Benny yelled a warning and adrenaline surged in my veins.

I hit the hard floor with Frank on top of me, shielding my body with his own and the breath was forced from my lungs as I craned my neck to check that him and the others were alright.

Church leapt over us as another door flew open to our right and he stabbed the man who came at him so fast that his enemy was dead before he'd realised what was happening. Church shoved his body back into the apartment, flinging the door closed once more.

Frank got up, pulling me after him and I just caught sight of the Candlestick Maker tearing into the stairwell before Danny Butcher darted out of the door that the Candlestick Maker had emerged from with a manic look on his face.

"Ben!" he cried, waving to his brother.

Another huge gangster charged out of the apartment behind him, raising a gun and aiming straight at Church while Benny was distracted by his brother, yelling demands at him to give up and let us take him.

I pulled Frank's gun from the back of his pants and fired at the newcomer in quick succession, a growl of pure defiance leaving me in the face of Church's death.

The asshole fell as three shots impacted with his chest, slumping to the ground like a sack of shit and making Danny look to me in surprise, almost like he hadn't even noticed I was here until that moment.

"Well, well, if it isn't the whore out for a little day trip," Danny purred, his eyes lighting with a hatred so potent that it made me flinch.

Benny charged at him with a roar of anger tearing from his throat and Danny's eyes widened as he took in his brother's fury. His hesitation didn't last long and he turned and bolted.

Frank and I took chase after Benny just as Church ran to my side with a look of gratitude in his eyes. But I didn't need thank yous, none of us did. It was clear we'd all die for one another now. We were bound as one.

"Danny!" Benny bellowed, demanding he stop, though his brother ignored him as he hurtled away down the stairs after the Candlestick Maker.

"We can beat them in the lift," Church barked, staggering to a halt and pointing to the other end of the walkway. I glanced back, spotting a set of elevator doors in the shadows.

"We don't have time for that bollocks," Frank barked, dragging me after him towards the stairwell instead.

I glanced back at Church in concern and he tossed me a wink as he turned and ran for the elevator despite the clear intention for the rest of us to take the stairs.

"I'll let John Boy know he needs to start a ruckus!" he called over his shoulder, skidding to a halt in front of the elevator doors and jamming his finger against the button while pulling his phone from his pocket to do as he'd said.

I looked between him and the others as they hesitated but then Benny shook his head, jerking his chin towards the stairs once more and Frank towed me along after him, leaving me to look back over my shoulder fearfully while Church just stood there like a sitting duck.

"See ya down there, Miss America," he called, not seeming the least bit concerned, and I shook my head at him before racing on, adrenaline bursting through my veins like starlight.

I tightened my grip on the gun as I ran, the sound of cries going up all over the tower block making my heart skip a few beats as John Boy started the promised brawl down on the street. But fear didn't exist for me tonight. I was part of the Forget-Me-Nots, and we were reapers come to deal out death. Only the Devil had the power to call us off.

CHAPTER FIFTY

I cursed Church out as he stayed where he was, aiming his gun down the walkway behind him and firing off warning shots to keep the arseholes away while he waited for his fucking lift.

But there was no way he would beat us to the ground waiting for that piss stained metal box, so I continued on in the direction of the stairs.

Frank charged ahead of us, racing along the concrete walkway while me and Anya ran side by side, knowing Danny and the Candlestick Maker's lead was growing with every passing second.

A door swung open as I made a move to pass it and I grabbed it, slamming it back the other way again and knocking the man behind it on his arse.

Anya leapt over his legs and passed me by, raising her gun and firing it at the fuckers who were shoving out of the Candlestick Maker's flat and trying to put themselves between us and the stairs.

Frank barrelled through the lot of them with a bellow of rage, knocking a couple to the ground and taking a cut to his arm as one of them swung a knife, but then he was through and leaping onto the stairs as he kept up the hunt.

"You got that, Benny?" he yelled over his shoulder.

"Easy," I replied, giving him the green light to run on while I sized up our new foes.

I skidded to a halt and yanked Anya aside as one of them pulled a gun, slamming my shoulder into a door beside me a couple of times until it gave way and we tumbled inside, escaping the gunfire.

"The back windows," I commanded, pushing Anya ahead of me as the fucker outside fired off a shot and the people in the flat we'd just broken into screamed and ducked for cover.

We charged through their hallway and into their living room, finding the sliding door which opened onto their balcony cracked to let the smoke from their joints out, and I ripped it wide.

"Gimme your hand," I commanded and Anya looked at me in alarm as she realised what I was planning before shoving her gun into her waistband and climbing up onto the railing.

I gripped her hand in mine and she met my gaze as I grinned at her.

"Is your heart pumping yet, bombshell?"

"Only a little," she replied. "You'll have to work harder to make it race."

My smile widened and she released her grip on the railing as I lurched forward, keeping a tight hold on her hand as I swung her down to the balcony below and ignored the thirty-floor drop waiting for her if I fucked up.

My stomach hit the railing and I leaned over it as far as I could go, the sound of the Candlestick Maker's gang finding me as they busted into the flat at my back.

I swung Anya onto the balcony below us and released her, throwing my leg over the railing next and getting a free adrenaline hit as my hands slipped and I damn near fell to my death.

I dropped to the balcony below with a grunt of effort, Anya's hand fisting in my shirt as she yanked me towards her and made sure I didn't fall.

I stumbled forward a few steps as I got my balance then threw the sliding door open and burst in on another group of unsuspecting fuckers who all yelled in alarm at our sudden appearance.

"Don't mind us," I called, leading the way through their flat and leaping over a violent little dog as it came racing outa the kitchen and tried to savage my ankles.

I shoved the front door open and raced out onto the walkway with Anya on my heels and the little dog charging after us, snarling and barking furiously.

I looked out over the wall which lined the walkway, spotting Frank as he ran down the stairs through the barred windows a couple of floors below us, Danny and Gus just a couple of floors lower than him.

"Come on, big brother!" Danny shouted as he spotted me too, firing a shot without bothering to even aim properly. "Keep up!"

A curse spilled from my lips and we ran on, shoving past people on their way in and out of their flats and making it to the stairs just as more of the Candlestick Maker's gang began to pour down them from above.

The insane little dog changed targets and ran for one of the gangsters, savaging his ankles and buying us a few seconds to escape.

Anya fired a shot up the stairs at them, making them back off further, a wild laugh escaping her as she snatched my hand into her grip and picked up the pace. We sprinted down the stairs, leaping around the corners and gaining on Frank and the others as they exchanged pot shots and insults which slowed them down.

The heavy pounding of footfalls chased after us, but as we made it halfway down the stairs, some of The Butcher gang appeared with a challenging roar, three of them hurling Molotov cocktails over our heads to shatter against the stairs and spread a wall of fire between us and our pursuers.

I barked a laugh, running on as Mickey Hairpiece led the charge against the other gang and we focused on catching our prey.

My legs burned as we made it to the bottom of the stairwell, and I cursed as we found the fight continuing at the foot of the tower block, barring our way to Gus and Danny who had made it to the far side of the courtyard.

"John Boy," Anya gasped, pointing to a fella who looked deader than dead, likely fallen from somewhere above us, but before I could get too concerned over it, I got a better look at his face.

"Nah, that's not John Boy," I said, bobbing my chin across the courtyard which separated us from the road to point out the forgettable fucker where he was balls deep in the middle of the brawl taking place there. "That's him over there."

"Oh…I keep forgetting his face," she muttered with a frown and to be fair to her, he did have a new hat on.

"Yeah, everyone does, bombshell. Fuckin' gift that."

I spotted Frank racing towards the road in hot pursuit of my brother and the Candlestick Maker and yanked on Anya's arm to get her running again.

We broke out of the cover of the stairwell, but we only got a few steps before a big fucker with a face tattoo of a shrunken head on his cheek slammed into me.

I hit the ground hard with his weight on top of me, finding a knife swinging for my throat as I got my bearings and only just managing to block the strike with my own arm.

My blood spilled but I twisted into the movement, grabbing his wrist and lunging for it, sinking my teeth in deep and ripping a chunk of flesh right outa it.

The big fucker howled in pain as I spat the chunk of his skin from my mouth and he dropped the knife, giving me all the room I needed to knock it away from us.

A fist slammed into my jaw as he remembered the fight and my head ricocheted offa the concrete with a crunch that sounded all kinds of fucked up.

My vision swum but I wasn't one to go down easy and I was already swinging my fists into his sides with a challenging roar, throwing my head forward and cracking it into the bridge of his nose.

He reared back and ripped another knife from his belt, but before he could swing it at me, a little Russian bombshell wrapped one arm around his meaty neck and drove a knife into his chest before he could even react to her presence.

She ripped the blade free and stabbed him again and again, his blood splattering onto me where I was pinned beneath them before she whirled him around and shoved him away from us. She yanked the knife out and blood sprayed over her, painting her red and staining her face so that she looked every bit the savage she was.

Before I could say a single word, the lift arrived just behind her and the doors slid open to reveal Church looking smug as fuck with a baseball bat slung over his shoulder which he'd gotten from fuck knows where and an arched eyebrow as he took in the carnage.

"Told you we shoulda waited for the lift," he said, stepping out as I got to my feet.

"Fuck you," I grunted, pointing towards the road without a further word and breaking into a run once more with the two of them right behind me.

We sprinted through the brawl taking place between the two gangs, John Boy's cries of encouragement colouring the air as he howled like a heathen and gave himself fully to the joy of the fight.

Frank had Danny and the Candlestick Maker pinned down as he fired shots towards them and the two of them took cover behind a wall, but as we caught up to him, his gun rang empty and Danny's laughter filled the air.

"You got slow in prison, brother," he called. "Or is it just that you don't really wanna hurt me?"

A burst of movement saved me from answering as the Candlestick Maker made a break for it, racing towards the road and unlocking a little Smart car as he went.

"Don't let him get away!" I bellowed, knowing the fucker would go into hiding if we didn't end this now.

Danny bolted in the opposite direction and Frank didn't even hesitate as he chased him on foot, snarling promises of vengeance as he raced after his brother's killer.

"I've got this," Church said, noticing my indecision. "Me and Miss America can take down that ugly pig. You make sure Danny don't kill Frank."

I looked to Anya, not wanting to part from her while there was so much danger surrounding us, but we didn't have time to argue the toss and I couldn't risk Danny getting Frank alone and ending him like he'd done Olly.

"Alright. Make him bleed for me," I agreed, exchanging a dark look with Church before locking eyes with Anya and nodding in goodbye.

There wasn't time for any sappy shit, and she didn't need it from me anyway. She knew she was my everything without me needing to spell it out just because I might die before I got to see her again.

I took off down the street while Church and Anya raced for his Mini Cooper and all I could hope for was an end to this day which saw us alive and well away from the cops.

CHAPTER FIFTY ONE

I dove into the passenger seat of Church's Mini as he fell into the front seat and threw the engine into gear. My heart stumbled as he took off down the road at high speed and I clipped my seat belt into place before reaching across to do his for him too.

"Thanks, darlin'," he said through a grin, the thrill of the chase lighting his eyes up like he'd just walked into a carnival.

I yanked my sweater off, wiping my face to get the blood off of it as best I could before throwing it in the backseat.

Church's gaze dropped to my tits which were showing through the little Guns and Roses cami I had beneath it, my nipples pressing against the white fabric.

"Focus, Churchy. You can play with those later if you catch us a bad guy." I shoved his face to force him to look back at the road and he let out a whoop of exhilaration, his biceps flexing as he tightened his grip on the wheel.

He accelerated around a corner and the tiny Smart car the Candlestick Maker had taken off in came into view, passing by a row of houses with twinkling Christmas lights in the windows.

"Go!" I shouted and the engine roared as we tore up the road behind him.

The Smart car swerved down a side street and Church took chase as I dropped the window and lifted the gun, taking aim at the back tyres as the winter air swept over me.

"You've got five seconds," Church called. "Take the shot, Miss America, but the moment we hit the end of this street we'll be on camera every which way for miles."

I nodded, narrowing my eyes and focusing as I leaned half way out the window, lining up the shot.

I fired, the kickback from the gun resounding through my fingertips, but the asshole swerved the car a second before I did and the bullet hit the tarmac instead of blowing out his tyre.

Gus made it to the end of the street and Church fisted his hand in the back of my cami, yanking me back into the car and I lowered the gun out of sight as we bumped onto the road, turning the wheel hard so hard that I was pressed against my door.

The nodding bulldog on Church's dashboard came sliding violently towards the open window beside me, looking like it was in a rock concert as its head bounced up and down. I sat back, about to let the thing fly to its doom out the window when Church released a pained cry, swiping for it with a desperation that made him look like a kid who'd just let go of his helium balloon. "Barkley!"

I caught the stupid thing before it took a tumble to its death and Church threw me a look that said I'd just won myself the best orgasm of my life.

Church slammed the car into the fourth gear as we chased the Candlestick Maker down and we raced along a side street where clubbers were standing outside smoking and drinking, one of them singing a Christmas carol at the top of her lungs. They all screamed as the Smart car ploughed through them and one guy got clipped on the ass by its wing mirror, falling flat on his face before we raced past him in the Mini.

"Fuck a duck," Church exclaimed, laughing loudly and the sound was so infectious I laughed too.

A siren started up somewhere in the distance and our laughter fell away as we shared a look. We were on a time limit here and if the police showed up on our tail, we were fucked.

"Sorry, beautiful," Church muttered and it took me a second to realise he was addressing the car and not me as he pressed his foot to the gas, closing in on the Smart car and ramming it hard, nearly sending it spinning off the road. But the Candlestick Maker managed to keep control of it, pulling away from us again and taking a sudden turn.

Church followed, spinning the wheel hard and I braced myself against the door as the air whipped around us, my hair flying everywhere and my heart leaping into my throat. I swear the left wheels nearly came off the ground as Church made that turn and sped after the Candlestick Maker once more.

My breaths came heavily and excitement rushed through to my core. I realised I was turned on as hell and one look at the bulge in Church's dark jeans said he was riding the same high I was.

It was a combination of him and the adrenaline rolling through me like a tsunami hitting shore. And as the sirens cried out in the distance, I jammed my thumb against the radio, turning it on and Get Back by The Beatles poured out of the speakers like it had been waiting for me to come find it.

If this was my last night on earth, then at least let it be the best one I'd ever fucking had.

CHAPTER FIFTY TWO

Danny was leading us on a merry little dance as we hounded after him, racing through the more crowded streets into central London, forcing us to chase him rather than fire on him thanks to all the witnesses and potential casualties.

No matter how hard we pushed he managed to stay ahead, losing us in the crowd more than once before we spotted him tearing away down another street.

I'd muttered more than a few of my intentions towards the motherfucker who had killed my brother while we ran, and Benny hadn't said a word against them, but I still wasn't certain he had accepted how this had to end.

I got it. Danny was his brother just like Olly had been mine. Difference was, his brother was a fucking animal and he needed putting down. I just hoped he got that and wouldn't make it harder than it had to be, because I was owed my pound of flesh and I wasn't gonna go without.

"Where is he?" I shouted as we lost him again and I stopped at a crossroads, whirling around as I tried to see him through the crush of bodies that made it fucking impossible to keep him in our sights.

"There," Benny said suddenly, pointing towards the stairs which led down into a tube station and I cursed as I spotted him too, sprinting into the underground and heading out of sight.

We took off again, muscles burning and breaths labouring as we shoved between drunk arseholes, and I managed to knock a kebab clean out of one fella's hands.

He took a swing for me, but I caught his arm and whirled him around, sending him crashing into a row of bin bags and making his friends all yell out in alarm as he landed amongst them with a cry of horror.

I was gone before any of them could decide to try and play the big man, chasing after Benny as he ran down the steps and into the brightly lit tunnel which led to the tube.

"Danny!" Benny roared, his voice echoing offa the white tiled tunnel while Danny's laughter bounced back to us in reply.

We vaulted the ticket barriers, making a group of drunk girls in tiny dresses wolf whistle and shriek as we sped past them and headed onto the enormous escalators which delved beneath the ground.

We ran down the escalators, knocking into anyone who wasn't standing fully on the right side of the steps as they descended and we kept Danny in our sight while he closed in on the bottom of the thing.

We leapt from the escalator when we reached the lowest steps, looking left and right for our prey as the bustling crowd made it damn near impossible to spot him.

"Northern Line!" Benny yelled as the tunnel split in two directions and we ran towards the signs for that tube, marked with a black line beneath the red and blue station logos which decorated the space.

We shoved our way past more people, skidding out onto the southbound platform and spotting Danny as he leapt onto the train just as the doors began to close.

Benny sprinted forward and jumped through the doors, grabbing hold of them as they began to close and forcing them to stay open just long enough for me to get onboard too.

He dropped the doors and they closed as we turned and looked along the carriage, spotting Danny though the glass in the door which led to the next train car.

I pushed past Benny, running the length of the carriage as Danny took off again and I ripped the door open to let myself onto the next car.

"You shouldn't do that," some jumped up little Karen shouted and Benny slapped her cheeseburger out of her hand in reply before darting after me while she wailed in horror.

The air of the open tunnel rushed past us in the little space between the carriages and I yanked open the door that led into the next car, not letting myself think about what might happen if either of us took a tumble onto the tracks, immediately taking chase after Danny who had made it through into another one already.

A drunk arsehole stumbled into my way as we ran after him and I threw him aside so forcefully that he was knocked out by his head hitting the pole he should have been using to hold himself upright.

Several people screamed, but I didn't pay them any attention, running down the middle of the train car as the light beyond the windows brightened and we arrived at another platform.

The train slowed to a halt and I swore as the doors opened, a huge crowd of arseholes clamouring to get on while I tried to force my way out through them and the recorded announcement reminded everyone to mind the gap.

Benny took his gun from his pocket and fired a shot in the air, making them all scream and leap aside. But by the time we forced our way out, I'd lost sight of Danny on the platform again.

Benny grabbed my arm and started running towards the exit, heading for the stairs which Danny must have taken to get out of here.

The train pulled away behind us, the air in the tunnel ruffling my jacket and I turned my head, a furious roar escaping me as I caught sight of Danny's wide grin in one of the carriages as he waved to us in farewell half a second before the train disappeared into the tunnel. And he was lost.

CHAPTER FIFTY THREE

The Smart car was fast, but we were faster, and Church rode its bumper the whole time, blasting the horn and trying to drive the Candlestick Maker off the road. But somehow, he kept making turns, swerving through traffic and staying ahead just enough to keep us from stopping him.

Christmas lights glittered above us and people were out in droves on the street all dressed up in their winter hats and coats. They all seemed to be heading in one direction and as the Smart car raced around another corner and we followed, a cry left my lips. "Stop!"

A Christmas parade filled the entire road, a huge float ahead of us where Santa sat atop a wide wooden sleigh.

The Smart car veered left through the crowd and people dove aside with screams, snatching their children out of the way as it disappeared into a tiny alley.

Church drove the Mini forward to mount the pavement and I gasped, clutching the dashboard for support as he tried to follow but he slammed on the brakes before he even attempted to do it. The Mini was small, but it wasn't as small as that Smart car which was whizzing away down the narrow alley with its wing mirrors grinding against the walls either side, and there was no chance we could follow.

"Fuck!" Church bashed his fist against the wheel before pressing his other hand to the side of my seat and looking over his shoulder as he reversed wildly, the back of his car colliding with a wooden reindeer and crushing it beneath the wheels, getting us stuck on a lump of it.

"Oh that's just great, aint it? Rudolph the red nosed fucking cunt is fucking up my car!" Church barked as children started screaming and bawling their eyes out at the sight of the reindeer being mercilessly chopped up beneath Church's back wheels. In fairness, it was fucking late and they should have been at home in bed. What kind of parade went on at this time of night?

"Daddy!" a little girl wailed.

"Look away, darling," he said, scooping her into his arms and shaking his head at us.

For the carnage Church was creating, there was an awful lot of tutting and backs turning instead of the outcry there would have been in Vegas for this. Church probably would have been at gunpoint by now if he'd fucked with Rudolph in America.

The car jerked forward and we took off, leaving Rudolph shredded in our wake and I braced myself again as Church sped around a corner in the direction the Candlestick Maker had taken.

He flew down the road, but as we rounded the next street the flash of red and blue lights caught my eye. Church slammed the car to a halt, threw it in reverse and nearly smashed into a car coming up behind us before making such a tight maneuverer in the narrow road that I couldn't breathe until we were sailing along again in the opposite direction of the cops.

"You're a maniac," I said roughly, a note of reverence in my voice and Church threw me an unhinged look which confirmed that statement.

The sirens wailed behind us and Church didn't slow down for a second, taking turns so fast, the world became a blur until we left the cops in our dust, but in doing so, we lost all chance of catching the Candlestick Maker too.

He eventually reached a parking lot, speeding down the ramp and taking a ticket so that the barrier lifted before us. Then he proceeded to drive furiously up a corkscrew which led us all the way to the top of the lot, leaving my head spinning violently by the time he came to a halt. As my gaze settled on the view of the river over the low wall we were parked in front of and the sight of Tower Bridge ahead, a laugh fell from my throat.

"What are you so happy about?" Church growled, shoving his fingers into his blonde hair as he took out his phone and texted Benny. "We fucked it."

"When you've lived in a jar your whole life, it feels fucking amazing to spread your wings." I spread my arms, one hand hitting his chest while the other stretched out of the open window to my left.

"We're gonna have to lay low here for a bit until the coppers call off the hunt," Church said moodily and I dropped my arms, arching a brow at his grumpy little face.

"You're a sore loser," I pointed out.

"So?" he grumbled.

"The joy's in the game, not the winning," I said.

"It's definitely in the winning," he insisted.

"Why don't you win another game instead then?" I unclipped my belt, climbing onto his lap and pressing my knees either side of him on the seat, resting my hands to his shoulders. "Let's see how fast you can make me come."

His eyes fell down my body and a slow smile spread across his mouth, the anger lifting from his eyes. "Game on, Miss America."

I leaned down to kiss him, but he pressed me back so I sat on his knees, crushed between him and the steering wheel in the tiny space.

"Hang on," he said. "I need to put myself in sport mode." He unclipped his belt then pressed a lever on the side of the seat so that the back of it reclined so fast I squeaked and fell on top of him.

He lay beneath me as we both started laughing, our lips coming together in a frantic kiss which spoke of how much he'd really enjoyed that drive.

But the fun wasn't over yet, and I planned on giving him the ride of his life while we hid here in the dark and made use of the adrenaline which was surging through our veins.

CHAPTER FIFTY FOUR

I strolled down the dirty little alleyway which led to the safehouse old Gussy had found for us to hide out in while we got our acts together and made our plans to deal with my dear brother and his band of fucking clingers.

It was nippy out as the sun began to rise over the streets of London town, jack frost biting at my hands and makin' me rub them together as I blew on them, the little cloud of breath doing little to help.

I rubbed my finger over my gums, the habit annoying me as much as it helped me deal with the cravings, and I tugged my hand away again almost as fast as I'd lifted it.

I had expected Benny to figure out who I was holing up with quick enough, but my mind was buzzing now as I thought on the way that shit had gone down last night. He'd seemed surprised to see me there. And not just that, he hadn't been wholly focused on getting hold of me either. No. Churchy and the little whore had turned tail and taken chase after my dear old friend the Candlestick Maker instead of coming for me, and that had me seriously curious.

I took my shiny new phone from my pocket and turned it over in my hand, wondering if I might just have found a way back into my brother's good graces as I dialled my old number by heart and lifted it to my ear.

"Yeah?" Benny grunted sleepily after way too many rings, and I huffed out a breath as I realised the arsehole hadn't even bothered to keep hunting throughout the night for me.

"Am I disturbing you?" I snapped, the sound of a feminine groan in the background of his call making my jaw tick angrily as I realised he was with the whore. Of course he was.

"Danny? Where are you?" he demanded, sounding more with it all of a sudden and I grinned, liking the fact that I had his full attention at last.

"Don't you worry about that, we'll be back together soon," I promised him. "But I do have a question."

"Go on then, don't fanny about, if you've got something to say then let's have it."

I tutted at the tone he was taking with me but went on anyway. Me and him were overdue a bit of a throw down to cut through this bullshit tension we were harbouring, but it could wait a little longer.

"I wanna know why you want the Candlestick Maker," I said simply. "What's he done that's got you all hot and bothered?"

"Really? That's your question?" he asked and I held my tongue while I waited on my answer. Benny sighed like I was testing his patience, but he went on all the same. "He overstepped is all. Pushed into our turf, took a cut of our money. You know I ain't gonna stand for that. Besides, killing him will make someone I care about happy."

"The whore?" I asked in a low growl.

"Watch your fuckin' mouth or I'll cut your damn tongue out the next time we see each other," he hissed. "And no, it has nothing to do with my wife. It's business is all. For The Firm. You remember that? The thing you were supposed to be taking care of while I was banged up?"

"Huh." I let that mull around my brain for a few minutes, not missing the way he'd said *our* turf and *our* money. I could read between those lines. He still called it *ours* because that was what it was. The Firm belonged to the Butcher boys and we were the only two of those. He wanted me back. But he needed to see that I was sorry first. "Alright. I guess I'll be seeing you soon then."

I hung up on him and turned the phone off while my brain went around and around in circles, trying to fix on the hidden messages he'd been relaying to me there. He often did that. Setting me cryptic little tasks which I would only ever be able to interpret because of our bond. It was beautiful that. Real poetry given life.

I made it to the dirty black door at the far end of the alleyway and rapped my knuckles against it sharply, grinning at the arsehole who slid the little shutter aside to peer out at me and check who'd come calling.

The shutter snapped closed again and the door unlocked a moment later, Gus's man pointing me deeper into the building while he remained on watch by the door.

I followed the sound of male grunts and shit music until I found a door standing open an inch and stepped into a grubby looking lounge area. We were in the middle of some shitty old warehouse which was still at least partly in use commercially, so it wasn't a proper renovation, just a few couches, a coffee table and a TV all clustered together with an electric fan heater working to banish the cold from the room and failing. It was a shit knock off of mine and Benny's warehouse, as if this wanker thought he could be anything like us. But he was just a cunt in a plastic crown. We were the real kings, the real power, and maybe it was time he remembered that.

Gus was reclining on the faded red sofa, an emaciated looking girl sucking on his cock while he grunted his approval and pushed her head down onto it.

His hooded gaze met mine as I glanced around at the other fellas in the room, three of them as shit faced as he appeared to be and two standing ready with weapons close to the door.

There was a brick of coke already sliced open on the table, some pills and bottles of booze mixed in with it and I stepped forward greedily as my gaze zeroed in on my drug of choice.

"Mornin'," I greeted, dropping to my knees and taking a hit without waiting for the offer to be made officially. I took two more bumps before my brain stopped aching and my thoughts snapped together all the clearer.

I exhaled loudly, tension falling from my body as I closed my eyes and bathed in the pure bliss of that feeling as my skin began to tingle and everything in the world finally seemed to shine a whole lot brighter.

I enjoyed my moment in the light until the initial high faded then opened my eyes once more, my gaze falling to the Candlestick Maker where he sat to my right.

"Just a second, Danny," Gus panted, his hips thrusting as the girl moaned loudly, slurping on his cock so loudly that I had to assume her hit depended on her managing to suck him dry.

With a loud groan he finally finished, and I dipped my fingers into the coke, rubbing some white powder over my gums as I got to my feet once more, looking around the room.

"I could do with a bit of privacy for this, Gus," I said to him, my heart pounding to that frantic beat I loved so fucking much as the drugs began to do their worst.

He looked to me while buckling his pants up and the girl practically dove towards the table, lining up her own hit and moaning far louder than she had been around his cock as she snorted a line down.

Gus licked his lips, glancing to his men before nodding and waving a hand to dismiss them, sending them outa the room and telling them to take a long walk before they came back.

The girl stayed where she was, biting her lip as she looked between us and the brick of cocaine, the need in her haunted eyes clear.

"You know the deal," Gus snipped as she made a move to get herself another hit. "You get one line. You want to earn another one then find someone else to service."

Her gaze instantly went to me and I shrugged, not really having much feeling about the offer one way or another which she took as a yes.

The girl moved to kneel before me, unhooking my belt and I slipped my hands into my coat pockets as I let her have at it.

"I gave Benny a call," I said casually, my eyes meeting Gus's as he licked his plump lips.

"Oh?" His bald spot was gleaming as the drugs he'd ingested gave him a healthy dose of the sweats and my nose wrinkled.

The girl had my dick in her mouth now, but it was in no way hard and the more I looked at the fucking Candlestick Maker, in all his sweaty, unwashed glory, the less likely it seemed to be heading that way either. Not that I bothered telling her to stop.

"Yeah. I wanted to see if we could come to some kind of understanding, get him offa our backs, you know?"

"And did he bite?" Gus asked keenly, his gaze slipping to the coffee table and the drugs laid out on it as a clear tell of what he wanted next.

"Don't hold back on my account," I said, gesturing to the table and fingering the wire in my pocket as the darkness in me stirred with interest. Gus chuckled and moved to his knees, lining up his hit while I went on. "But yeah, as it happens, I think he did bite. It's always a tricky one with me and Ben. He has a way of laying out these little tests for me and I have to try and figure them out before we can move past our differences."

"But you've figured out what he wants?" Gus asked, leaning down to snort his first line.

"It just so happens I have," I agreed, my pulse really pounding now, exhilaration pushing into my veins.

I gave the girl a bit of a shove to get her offa me, my dick not in the least bit interested in whatever she'd been attempting and she scrambled onto the couch with a look of utter disappointment on her face which made me chuckle.

"Well whatever it is, let's get it done. I don't want to be stuck in this place any longer than I absolutely have to." Gus leaned down to take his next hit and I moved right up behind him, pulling the wire from my pocket and winding it between my fists.

"My thoughts precisely, Gus. My thoughts precisely."

He snorted the coke down and lifted his head with a sigh of contentment right in time for me to snap the wire tight around his thick neck.

His cry of panic was cut off sharply and my thundering pulse hit a crescendo as I half lifted him offa the ground with the force of my weight leaning back against the wire.

Gus kicked and flailed, blood spraying as the wire sliced into his flesh and a whoop of excitement left me as the girl began to scream in fright somewhere at my back.

His spasming legs sent the coffee table crashing to the ground and drugs and drink flew everywhere while I fell back onto my arse on the sofa, still very much holding onto the wire.

My heart thundered with the best fucking feeling I knew as my entire body buzzed, the thrill of my high only heightened by my love of the kill.

Finally, the fight went clean outa him and I was left panting with his corpse in my lap and the key to my brother's forgiveness all wrapped up in a pretty little bow.

"Fuck," the girl gasped from somewhere beside me and I laughed as I finally released my hold on the wire and kicked the Candlestick Maker's corpse to the floor.

"Well don't just stand there staring, sweetheart. I'm rock fucking hard now. So do you wanna earn yourself another hit or what?"

A laugh tumbled from my lips as her horror turned to hunger and I leaned back in my seat as she scrambled to her knees before me to earn herself the only thing on this green earth that she really gave a fuck about.

And through the act I loved most in the whole goddamn world, with a little bit of bloodshed and carnage, just like that, I knew I'd bought my way back to my brother's side. He'd wanted that fucker dead and I'd delivered. And once we were reunited, all would be well at last.

FRANK

CHAPTER FIFTY FIVE

I sat in silence with my tea cooling in front of me on the coffee table while the others discussed everything that had gone wrong last night and John Boy gave his account of the brawl. A couple of our guys were in the hospital, but beyond that our side of the fight had come out on top.

There were plans which needed to be made about how far we were gonna push into their turf and shit like that, but I wasn't interested in it.

All I kept thinking about was the smug as fuck look on Danny's face as that train had pulled away while we'd been left watching him escape us like a pair of fucking plonkers.

John Boy headed out and Benny locked up behind him, turning to look at us with a heavy sigh.

"We need to discuss what comes after this," I ground out, raising my gaze to look at him in the clean tracksuit he wore. Dylan had dropped by to give us the once over last night, taking our bloody clothes to destroy and making sure we all got cleaned up properly before we got a few hours sleep, but after Danny had called we'd all ended up awake, watching the sky lighten beyond the windows and trying to figure out our next move. "What happens when I catch up to Danny."

Church shifted uncomfortably in his position on the other end of the couch to me, and Anya looked between us uneasily from where she sat in the large armchair.

"We need to get hold of him," Benny said. "He still knows things about the time I spent in jail which could be vital to maintaining our hold over this city."

"Bullshit," I spat, getting to my feet and challenging him with a look which I knew he understood well. "You want to protect him from my wrath because he's your blood. You want to save him from death because even after all he's done, the way he abused your wife, the people he's destroyed in the years you've been absent, the fact that he murdered Olly in cold fucking blood, you can't just forget that he's your kin."

Benny glowered at me, but he said nothing because everyone in this room knew that if there was a single man who had been responsible for any one of those sins aside from Danny, we wouldn't even be discussing this. His death would be as inevitable as breathing.

"Look," Anya said slowly, rising to her feet and moving to stand between the two of us like she could sense the violence brimming in the air. "None of us even know where Danny is. He's going to go to ground just like the Candlestick Maker and the biggest problem we're going to face will be in trying to find the two of them. I think we should just focus on finding them and then once we have Danny, we can have this discussion. Right now, all it's going to do is cause more bloodshed and I'm tired. Surely you're all tired too?"

She held a hand out towards me but I just leaned back in my seat and shook my head. Church and Benny gave in to her command though, each of them turning and heading upstairs to bed, Church muttering something about needing to get some sleep before taking his car into the chop shop to get her fixed up.

I didn't watch them leave, my gaze settling on my hands as I fought to reign in my temper, but I could feel Anya's eyes on me and I knew she hadn't moved a muscle.

"I'm not much company at the moment," I said in a low voice, the darkness of all I'd lost eating into me as I sat there and wallowed in the memory of that tape, watching my brother die over and over again on repeat in my head.

It was torture but I couldn't stop it. I was stuck on a loop and there was no way out of it for me. Not until I made Danny Butcher bleed for what he'd done.

The sound of Anya's soft footsteps carried to me and the lights flicked off a moment later, letting me know she'd left me to it and the ache in my chest only intensified.

I could hear Olly's last words, Danny's laughter, the slick sound of the knife piercing his skin. It was getting louder and louder and I was going to drown in it before I could find a way to make myself break free.

Music started up, cutting through my thoughts and making my fists clench as Wake Me Up When September Ends by Green Day filled the room and I found Anya standing before me, her fingers reaching out to tilt my chin up.

"Do you need to take it out on me?" she breathed, a hitch to her voice which said she wanted that, to feel my grief so that I could be relieved of it.

I said nothing as I looked up at her and she dropped her trousers, pulling her t-shirt off too and revealing her body to me, her eyes full of all the pain I knew too well as she waited on my answer.

My mind ticked over all the things I could do to her body to release some of this anguish in me, but as my gaze trailed over the healing cuts which Danny had carved into her skin, I found myself not wanting that for once.

I didn't want to make her hurt any more than she already did inside, even if that pain was its own kind of therapy. Right now, it wasn't what I needed.

"I just need you," I said in a low voice, reaching for her and trailing my fingers down her thigh, avoiding the cut there as I looked into her eyes through the darkness of the room and feeling the way her skin shivered at my touch.

"You have me, Frank," she breathed. "Every piece."

I wasn't sure if I drew her closer or if she was the one to close the distance, but she was taking her knickers off and climbing onto my lap one way or another, her mouth finding mine and her kiss devouring every bit of dark inside me like it was all she ever needed.

That kiss held no pity, it held no mistrust or hatred, it was pure and real and full of all the pain we shared mixed up with this desperate kind of hope for a better tomorrow.

She exhaled my name as I pushed inside her, and with her in my arms and our bodies merged as one, I somehow found my way out of that pit of despair which had been beckoning me in. I found a taste of salvation on her tongue and worship in her arms, and amongst all of that I just found *her*. Because somehow, she'd become that one thing I needed. The only thing I wanted. The light to pull me from my dark.

Her.

I woke to the sound of heavy banging against the front door, jerking upright and tightening my hold on Anya where she lay in my arms in Benny's bed.

Church shoved out of the covers on the far side of the bed, taking a gun from the bedside table and cursing as he moved towards the door in his boxers.

Benny sat up too, his body placed before Anya's as he raised another gun and I couldn't help but like the feeling of the three of us standing between her and danger. She felt safe in our pack of wild dogs, protected in the heart of a nest of monsters. No one would ever get past us to lay a hand on her.

The banging continued for another few seconds then stopped abruptly, leaving the three of us looking between each other and waiting for something to happen. But as the seconds dragged on and there was no further sound, we relaxed a little, getting out of bed and stalking towards the door.

I tugged a pair of jeans on and followed the others out onto the walkway, flicking on the lights and scouring all the darkened corners of the open space as we headed downstairs, but finding nothing out of place.

Benny checked the feed for the camera which was positioned outside the door, flashing me a look at the image which showed a gift wrapped box on the front step.

He unlocked the door, aiming his gun into the darkness before bending down to pluck a card from the top of the box.

"It's from Danny," he said, showing us the envelope which was addressed to him. "Grab the box, Church."

"Got it." Church handed his gun to Anya and bent down to retrieve the large box, lifting it into his arms and giving me a clear look at the blue and yellow wrapping paper which was covered in toy cars. It was pretty big, filling his arms easily and making me frown as I wondered what was inside it.

I locked the door behind him as he carried it inside and he set it down on the kitchen island so that we could all cluster around it.

"What does the card say?" Anya asked.

Benny slit the envelope open and pulled out a happy birthday card with a pair of happy puppies on it, reading the message aloud for all of us to hear.

I thought I'd start the celebrations early this year, brother. One week until we party together again.

Church tugged on the ribbon to open the box as the rest of us exchanged concerned looks and Anya snatched his hand with a gasp of alarm.

"What if that's a bomb or something?" she hissed.

Church barked a laugh, shaking her off. "A bomb? Hark at Miss America over here with her casual expectations of bombings. Where exactly do you think Danny woulda got a bomb? Down the local Bombs and Books?"

He was still laughing as he ripped the wrapping paper open and lifted the lid from the box, ignoring the way Anya winced as he tossed it aside and I snorted a laugh too.

"Danny wouldn't send Benny anything that would kill him," I reassured her. "If there's one certain thing about that prick then it's his obsession with his brother."

"Oooh, nice," Church said as he pointed into the box at the birthday cake which sat inside the top part of it.

"Do you think it's poisoned?" Anya asked warily as Church grabbed a handful out of the side of the cake and stuffed it into his mouth like a savage.

"Nah, it's just a Victoria sponge," he said through a mouthful of frosting and Anya's lips fell open in alarm. "No harm ever came from eating a Victoria sponge. Especially a nice moist one like this. Mmm."

Anya stared at Church in horror like she expected him to drop dead at any second.

"You can't seriously imagine Danny spending the night baking and frosting a fuckin' cake, just to lace it with poison can you, Cash?" I teased and she snapped her mouth shut, pouting at me.

"Well there's no way I'm eating it," she muttered. "What the hell is a Victoria sponge anyway?"

"This," Church said, holding his cake covered hand out towards her like she might be tempted into taking a bite and she recoiled into me.

"That looks like a pound cake to me," she replied. "And no, I don't want your psycho birthday cake. You shouldn't be eating it either."

"First it's bombs then it's poison, next she's gonna suspect he's crawling through the ventilation system with a knife in his mouth like he's John McClane or some shit," I mocked, making Church laugh, but Benny was still frowning at the card in his hand, saying nothing and scowling like he was trying to figure something out.

"This ain't good, boys," he muttered, eyeing the box and arching an eyebrow as he pointed to the bottom of the thing where a deep red stain was slowly seeping through the wrapping paper.

"Lift that cake outa the way, Church," I said, stepping closer as he reached in and took the cake out, revealing a second layer of wrapping paper beneath it.

"Still think I'm being a dramatic American now?" Anya asked dryly as Benny pushed between us to tug the ribbon open himself.

"Maybe not," I muttered, holding my breath as I waited to see what was in the bottom of it.

"Well fuck me," Benny cursed as he tugged the lid aside and we all looked down into the lifeless eyes of the Candlestick Maker's severed head.

"He's gone on a fuckin' bender, ain't he?" Church said darkly and we all knew how bad shit could get when Danny went on a bender.

"Is it a coke bender or a blood bender though?" I asked, my gaze roaming over the severed head while Anya wrinkled her nose in distaste and backed away from it.

Benny looked up at us, his eyes hooded in darkness as he spoke. "Buckle up, fellas," he said darkly. "I think this might be both."

Fuck.

CHAPTER FIFTY SIX

"Ah, my favourite new friends," The Czar stood from a plush armchair as his manservant led us into his conservatory. Rain pattered relentlessly down on the windows and the greenery of his garden was just a blur beyond it. Huge potted plants stood in every corner of the room by the gleaming windows and smaller ones sat on expensive looking tables too.

The Czar wore a pinstriped suit as if that was everyday house wear and he moved to embrace Benny tightly, clapping him on the back before lunging for me. The hug he gave me left my skin crawling, his hands tight against my lower back and his breath heavy against my ear. When he released me, he held onto my arms, giving my outfit a long look as he took in the tight red and black dress I wore which was paired with high leather boots.

Benny's hand came down on The Czar's shoulder, forcing him back as he grinned playfully, but beneath it was an animal waiting to attack.

"Do you want the good news or the bad news first, mate?" Benny asked as he released him, placing his arm tight around my waist instead and yanking me against his side.

The Czar frowned. "The good news."

Benny took out his phone, opening up the photo of the Candlestick Maker's head in the box Danny had gift wrapped for us and offering it to him. "There ya are. He's deader than a doornail just like you asked."

A breath of relief went out of The Czar as he gazed down his nose at the photo.

"We made him pay for betraying you," I promised, though hell if I knew if he'd suffered. Knowing Danny, he likely had.

The Czar's light blue eyes flicked up to meet mine, lust filling his gaze. "Were you there? Did you make him bleed?"

"Yes," I said huskily. "I painted myself red."

"Did you now?" he breathed, staring at me like my husband wasn't right there at my side.

It made me want to gouge his eyes out and crush them beneath my heel, but instead I smiled like I enjoyed his attention. We had to pull this con off today, and The Czar needed to stay as sweet as sugar throughout it until his money was deep in our pockets.

"So here's the bad news, mate," Benny said. "That duck's not being sold in The Marketplace by the Candlestick Maker, he musta sold it onto the Albanians. And not just any Albanians, the fucking Kafshëts."

Benny had told me all about the violent gang which had a brutal reputation in London. He had them under control within The Firm, paying their monthly tythe just like everybody else, but as The Czar had no idea about that, he wasn't going to question Benny's hesitation to go after them for that duck.

"Blyad'," The Czar cursed in Russian.

"Yeah. So we're in a pickle, mate, because I can't send my men after them, it'd be world war fucking three." Benny sighed and I rubbed his arm as I frowned up at him.

"I see," The Czar sighed, looking distressed.

"Now, I know I took a bit liberty here, but I went and twisted the arm of a friend of mine by the name of Den Dazzler – he works a bit of magic between the gangs, he does. Right handy buggar to have up your sleeve. So he's gone and gotten you registered for the auction today. I know it ain't much, mate, but if you truly want that duck back, I'm afraid you're gonna have to pay for it."

The Czar swore colourfully in Russian and I moved closer, lowering my voice as I spoke to him.

"Think of the man who wronged you. Of what that duck represents. It proves you're a powerful man who overcame his enemy. You showed him what you were made of when you destroyed him and seized back what he took from you. You can't let that diamond fall into someone else's unworthy hands."

The Czar's chest puffed up at my appraisal of him. "I suppose you're right. Money is a small price to pay for bringing home what is rightfully mine, Mrs Butcher." His eyes moved to me and my skin itched as I gave him a lust-fuelled look in return. The lust I was feeling was all centred around chopping pieces off of him while he screamed for mercy, but of course he didn't need to know that.

"We should hurry if you want to get your hands on it though, the auction is about to start," I said and The Czar scowled furiously.

"I resent having to pay to get it back, but alas, I must have it," he said. "Come, Mrs Butcher, I need the luck of a beautiful woman at my side while I make the bids." He offered me his arm and I took it, letting him guide me from the room while Benny walked after us. "Come, Henry," he clipped at his man who ran forward so eagerly that he stumbled a little. "I do miss Yuri," The Czar muttered under his breath. "Fucking Interpol."

We echoed the sentiment and I schooled my expression as we headed into an office with a dark wooden desk and old editions of books lining bookcases on the walls. The Czar led me to a love seat in one corner, pulling me down onto it beside him so I was almost in his lap and his hand rubbed my knee for a moment while Benny's back was turned.

Henry set up the laptop between us as Benny took the seat beside us, lighting up a cigarette with a match from his matchbook like always and inhaling deeply on the end of it. His eyes ignited as the cherry reflected within them and I could see the monster lurking in him as he watched The Czar.

The Czar slipped on some reading glasses and leaned forward to peer at the screen.

I looked over at Benny, feeling like we were two beasts circling our prey together as a little smile curled up his lips.

"The item is next on the list," Henry announced as a rhino horn was bid for in the auction.

The bids flashed up beneath a picture of the item and when it sold, the winning bid was announced on a banner across the screen. I wondered how easy it would be to track down the people trading in ivory from beautiful animals like that and turning them into the prey for a bit of my own sport, making a mental note to suggest it to Benny later. We never had gotten a honeymoon after all.

"Time to bring home my sweet love," The Czar growled, sitting forward in his seat as the photo of the crystal duck appeared alongside the fat diamond beside it. A starting bid was set at two hundred thousand pounds and my pulse raced as I wondered how much we were about to steal from The Czar for this. Church and Frank were currently at home ready to push the bids higher with bids of their own when they needed to apply some pressure, and I wondered how much The Czar really could be milked for here.

"Wish me luck, Mrs Butcher." The Czar urged and I leaned in, my mouth close to his skin without me having to actually touch him as I whispered good luck in his ear.

He shivered, looking to me with a grunting noise before adjusting the crotch of his pants and staring back at the screen.

Benny shifted in his seat, smoke coiling out of his lips as he watched me, his inked fingers digging hard into the arm of the chair.

The bidding started at a million pounds and every time The Czar placed his own bid, I cheered and bounced in my seat, clapping and praising him every time he took the lead. He was clearly distracted as fuck, looking from me to the screen in a daze as he kept placing higher and higher bids while I smiled encouragingly.

It grossed me the fuck out, but it was seriously working and The Czar was up to four million with no other bids coming in when a bidder called Barkely Buttplug joined out of nowhere and bid five hundred grand more than him in the last thirty seconds of the auction.

"No!" The Czar cried, frantic as he started tapping on the screen, offering an extra two hundred grand. But Barkely Buttplug immediately placed a bid for another hundred and The Czar shrieked like a wounded animal.

"You can take him out, I know you can," I encouraged, shifting closer to him as I worked to squeeze as much cash from him as possible. "You're The Czar," I said in his ear. "The most powerful man in the world." I bit my lip, encouraging his mind to head to a place I absolutely did not wanna go, but we were down to ten seconds and Barkley Buttplug – who was without a doubt Church and Frank – was about to win the duck.

The Czar looked to me, panting, his eyes ablaze then he turned and tapped out another two hundred grand on top of the massive bid he'd already dropped and hit enter with one second to go.

I didn't breathe as I waited for the bid to be confirmed, to make it through in time and win that fucking duck. He had to. We were relying on this working out, but I didn't know if Church and Frank had played too risky a game.

Five million.

Five. Fucking. Million.

Holy shit.

I glanced at Benny as the butt of his cigarette sat forgotten on his lips while he waited for confirmation, ash building up on the end of it.

"YES!" The Czar roared as the banner appeared on the screen, announcing him as the winning bidder.

He leapt to his feet and I leapt up with him, clapping excitedly and jumping up and down for our win while The Czar thought I celebrated his. The Czar drew me into a hug but Benny barrelled into us too, crushing us in his powerful arms and shielding me from any lecherous intentions.

"You fucking did it, mate!"

"I am the king of this world," The Czar laughed as we broke apart, but I knew who the real king in this room was, because I was goddamn married to him.

Henry appeared, lurking around my husband and bowing his head. "Excuse me sir, your car is blocking the driveway and we have a delivery. Can you move it, please?"

"Here." Benny took out his keys, pressing them against Henry's chest, clearly not wanting to leave me alone.

"Oh, I um, can't drive, sir," Henry murmured, glancing at The Czar.

"For fuck's sake," Benny huffed, shoving to his feet as he snatched his keys back. "Fine."

He looked to me, hesitating a second but I gave him a stare that said I could handle myself with The Czar.

"I'll be two minutes." Benny strode out of the room and I was left with The Czar's hands still firmly on me, making me instantly feel too close to him.

"Now he is gone, you don't need to pretend you don't want this," The Czar murmured.

"I don't want anything," I said lightly, wanting to diffuse this situation fast.

I backed up, but he followed, leaning forward as if he was going to try and kiss me and I gasped, turning my head away.

"What are you doing?" I growled, and his mouth suddenly dropped to my neck, his tongue raking over the skin.

I shoved his head back with the heel of my palm, a snarl leaving my lips and he looked at me with a burning intensity in his eyes like I was just playing the game he liked.

"You know exactly what you're doing to me, Mrs Butcher. We have unfinished business, don't we?" He shoved his weight against me, crushing me to the wall and I brought my knee up to strike his balls, but he shifted his hips so I couldn't.

"I'm going to have you," he told me, his breath hot on my face. "My cock is going to rut between those pretty thighs after you're done punishing me like the bad Czar I am. I'll pay any price for it."

"My husband won't ever sell me," I said, trying to keep my tone level as I held off on attacking him.

We needed him to pay up that money for the duck and I knew how much Benny was relying on him investing fully in his development too. I had to be careful not to fuck that up.

"I've had them sweet and pure with tears running down their cheeks while they take my cock, but you'll take it like the warrior you are," he said, starting to pant like he was getting himself into a frenzy over the idea and hatred seeped under my skin over what this man had done to other women. He leaned in close until he was all I could see and his breath was fluttering against my mouth. "I will have you. I always get what I want. And you're my latest obsession. There has never been anything in this world I've wanted that has not become mine."

The Czar's hand moved up under my skirt, forcing his fingers between my thighs and tracing the line of my panties as he shoved his knee between my legs to keep them open. Rage spewed through me and I cracked, shifting my weight forward with a snarl and forcing him back a step.

My knee came up between his thighs as I finally got an opening, crushing his balls and he wheezed, sinking down onto the seat behind him and clutching his manhood with a groan of agony. But he still had that glint in his gaze like that had only made him want me more and I suddenly got the awful feeling that he would go to any lengths to ensure he got me. Men like him didn't live within the law. When Benny refused to accept his offers, what would happen if he took other measures to get hold of me?

Benny suddenly returned and he glanced between us, sensing something was off as The Czar released his balls and stared up at my husband with flushed cheeks. "Name any price for her. Any price at all, Mr Butcher," he demanded, speaking about me like I was nothing more than a piece of meat to be sold between men, like my opinion on the matter meant nothing at all. I knew I'd been playing a dangerous game with The Czar, but maybe I'd bitten off more than I could chew. Shame flushed my cheeks. I didn't want Benny to think I couldn't handle this asshole.

"She ain't for sale," Benny said, an edge of warning in his voice. "Don't ask me for a price again, or you'll cross a line with me which you won't come back from." His powerful aura filled the room, seeming to suck all the light out of the space like we were in the presence of a demon.

The Czar shrank before my husband's might, nodding slowly in agreement.

"I didn't mean any offence," he said carefully and the silence stretched as Benny's dominance seeped through every corner of the room and made a shiver of desire track down my spine. That right there was the real king of London showing his true colours and no one in their right mind would try to stand against him.

"It's been a lovely afternoon, shame about the rain, eh? We'll let you know when The Marketplace arranges a spot for the exchange and we'll show up for the purchase to make sure it all goes smoothly for you too," Benny said conversationally as he moved towards me and pulled me against him, glaring unblinking at The Czar as his arm rested possessively over my shoulders and the knot in my gut instantly loosened. "Have a spiffing fucking evening."

He towed me out of the room then started marching at speed down the corridor, keeping me tight against him as his jaw ticked and fury blazed in his eyes.

"Benny," I breathed, but he didn't answer me, snatching our coats from a servant's hand by the door and leading me out into the rain.

It instantly soaked us through as he pulled me along towards the car, yanking the back door open and pushing me inside.

He climbed in after me, tossing the coats down in the footwell as he flattened me to the seat, crushing me down beneath him as his mouth came down on mine. I arched into him as he pushed his tongue between my lips and kissed me punishingly, writing a message inside my mouth that was as clear as day, even before he said it.

"Mine," he growled, leaning back to glare down at me. "What happened in there?"

A lump pushed at the base of my throat and I carefully picked my words. I wasn't going to lie to him, and if he demanded every detail of me then so be it, but I also knew that I was in the company of pure violence right now, and no matter what money he could get from The Czar, he'd fuck up everything and go and kill him this very moment if he knew what The Czar had done. I didn't want to be the reason this whole con went to shit. I'd sworn I could handle that creep, and I could. Maybe when this deal was all done and the development was set in stone, I'd get a chance to exact my own revenge on The Czar with a blade between his ribs.

"He told me he wants to buy me. That he'll do anything to have me," I admitted and a deep, guttural noise left Benny's chest, rumbling right down to my core.

"You shouldn't have started this game with him. I should never have allowed it," he hissed.

"It got the job done." I cupped his cheek. "I'll stay away from him now. We don't need anything else from him. He's all in with the investment for the Soho development. And once he pays up for the duck, we've got everything we need."

Benny nodded though he still looked half tempted to walk back in there and murder the asshole.

"Come on." I kissed him, nibbling on his lower lip. "Let's go home."

"Home?" he echoed, catching on that word and a smile drew up my lips as I realised I really did have a home here now. One that felt more real than any other place I'd known in my life.

"Home," I confirmed. "With you, and Church and Frank. You're all I want. All of you."

Benny traced his mouth gently over mine, a sigh leaving his lips as the monster within him receded, those words clearly offering him as much peace as they offered me. And as his kiss deepened, we forgot all about The Czar, because it didn't really matter.

I knew in the depths of my being, that no one could take me from this man or the dark souls who kept his company. But that wasn't because I was caged, no, I was choosing this life as it had chosen me. And it was the most beautiful thing to be free.

CHAPTER FIFTY SEVEN

We stood by the docks, just far enough along the riverbank that we could see the Millennium Dome in the distance, the white canvas exterior lit up in the darkness across the icily cold water.

The headlights of my Mini Cooper backlit us as we stood like statues in the dark, me Benny and Anya alongside The Czar and his men, waiting for the exchange to go ahead on the duck.

This part of the plan needed to go smoothly, and obviously Frank couldn't be here what with The Czar thinking he'd been an Interpol agent who we'd conveniently executed for him. But he was close by. Up in one of the buildings, his eyes on us through the scope of a rifle as he kept an eye out for anything that might come at us unexpectedly.

Not that we anticipated any trouble. This play had gone as smooth as a shot of whiskey after a good fuck. And I was planning on enjoying the warmth of it in my belly for a long damn time to come.

I stood a little behind my boss and his wife, my eyes glued to Anya's arse in that tight black dress she was wearing where the roundness of it showed beneath the hem of the faux fur coat she wore to stave off the cold.

The Czar kept cutting looks her way, but Benny had planted himself firmly between them. He'd told me about the offer the arsehole had made to buy her and there was a switchblade in my pocket ready to cut his pretty throat open if he made any kind of move towards her tonight.

I knew his type. And Benny mighta thought that he could warn him off with a stern refusal, but I doubted that would do it. Motherfuckers like him didn't understand the word no. They just saw it as the opener for a longer negotiation. So he mighta said that he understood the answer he'd been given, but I knew he hadn't. He was just priming himself to make a stronger offer at the next opportunity.

The two women from The Marketplace stood to our right, a small fold-out table ready and waiting in front of each of them so that they could inspect the duck and count the money once everyone arrived. They didn't so much as look at us. Just stood there in their perfectly presented packages and waited like a pair of fuckin' statues.

A car finally pulled down the little road which led to the waterfront, momentarily blinding us with its headlights before the driver shut them off alongside the engine.

A pregnant pause filled the air while John Boy took his sweet time in getting out of the car, playing up to his part as an Albanian mobster a little too enthusiastically as he made us wait.

I shifted my weight to my other foot, eyeing the two heavy bags which The Czar's men held ready to make the purchase.

"It's tempting to kill him right here and now," The Czar muttered. "That duck is rightfully mine."

"Not a good shout, mate," Benny replied casually. "You know the auctioneers will have a rifle or four pointed at us as we speak. We gotta play by their rules. Besides, the Albanians bought it fair and square – the Candlestick Maker was the one who did you up the duffer and we took care of him, for ya, didn't we? So I'm afraid you'll just have to suck up the price of this one."

The Czar scoffed irritably but made no further suggestion about trying to dick John Boy over and steal the duck back - which was a good shout because Benny hadn't been lying about the ruthlessness of the people who ran The Marketplace, and even though we'd used their system to run this con, they would still be expecting their cut. Even we wouldn't try and do them out of that. I liked my life far too much.

John Boy stepped out of the car, a few more of our men climbing out of the back, flashing us a good look at their weapons while he moved forward and took the duck from his pocket.

"Here it is," he said in a flawless Albanian accent. Like honest to shit, that man shoulda been in films. Though I guess it mighta been hard for him to play a role when no one could remember what he looked like. But damn, he'd have given it a good shot. "Is that the money?"

"It is," The Czar agreed, flexing his fingers like he was itching to get his hands on the thing.

"Let's not waste time," one of the auctioneers said loudly, drawing our attention to her as she snapped her fingers and pointed to the tables which stood before her and her associate. I wondered if she always stood so ramrod straight or if she had to work hard to maintain that stuck up look at all times. Not that it mattered much to me either way.

Benny stepped forward and took bag after bag of cash from The Czar's men, striding over to the closest auctioneer and setting them down on her table.

He gave her a wide smile, but she ignored him entirely, setting a cash counting machine down beside the bags and placing a large wedge of fifty pound notes into it.

John Boy sauntered up to the second auctioneer, putting the duck down and giving her a less than subtle once over as she took an eyeglass from her pocket and released the diamond from the hidden compartment. She raised the diamond to the light as she inspected it and seconds ticked by while we waited with nothing but the whir of the cash counter and the lap of the water in the Thames to fill the silence.

"It's all here," the woman with the cash announced finally, stacking the money back into the bags as the total flashed up on the machine for all of us to see, making me salivate at the sight of it. Well butter my bagel, five million quid. She took a healthy slice from the total for their cut and set it aside then pushed the bags towards John Boy across the table.

"The diamond is authentic," the other woman agreed, placing it back into the duck and setting it on her table too.

They gestured for everyone to claim our portions of it and John Boy grabbed the cash while The Czar snatched the duck with a Russian exclamation which made his evil little eyes light up.

"Congratulations!" Anya gushed, clapping excitedly while The Czar smirked triumphantly, sauntering over to us once more.

"We should celebrate," he announced loudly, ignoring John Boy as he turned and got back into his car with all of our glorious money.

The two auctioneers silently pocketed the chunk of cash that they'd taken as their cut, packed up their tables and left without another word too.

The Czar's attention was entirely fixed on our girl and my hackles prickled as I took in the look he was giving her, shifting my weight once more as I moved a little closer to him.

The Czar dropped the duck into his pocket and Benny congratulated him, fobbing him off with some excuse about having other business to deal with tonight.

"Then why not allow me the pleasure of your wife for the evening? We can't have her waiting at home for you while you work," The Czar pushed and I slipped a little closer, my gaze trailing past him to his men who were eyeing the surrounding streets for any sign of a threat and not paying me nearly enough attention.

"I plan on joining my husband for his work tonight," Anya objected. "There's a man who's been skimming from our cut and I've asked for the pleasure of dealing with him myself."

"Have you now?" The Czar asked, his voice dipping as he moved into her personal space and Benny laid a possessive arm around her shoulders. "Tell me more."

I drew even closer, my hand slipping into The Czar's pocket as Anya leaned in, smiling darkly as she replied. "I plan on whipping the skin from his bones," she breathed, her voice laced in sin and making my cock jerk to attention as I drew the duck into my palm.

The Czar shifted, his head beginning to turn my way, but Anya gripped his chin suddenly, tilting his head so that she could speak into his ear while I flicked open the secret compartment and dropped the diamond straight into my own pocket, replacing it with the cut glass replica we'd gotten made for the job.

"I love the way fresh blood feels dripping over my skin," Anya purred. "It makes me all kinds of…intoxicated."

The Czar groaned sexually and Benny laughed as he tugged her out of his reach, the movement covering for me dropping the duck with its fake diamond into the bastard's pocket and I fought a grin as I took a step back.

"Name your price, Mr Butcher," The Czar pleaded but Benny just shook his head, laughing louder as he turned Anya away and led her back towards my car.

"That's the problem mate – this one is priceless. So you're asking the impossible," he called over his shoulder. "By the way, if I were you, I'd lock that duck up somewhere no one will ever reach it. You don't want someone half inching it from you again."

"I will have it sent to a vault this very night," The Czar agreed and I grinned at that. Because so long as that little ducky stayed locked up in the dark, no one would find out that the diamond up its arse was as fake as a Kellogg's cornflake posing as a Coco Pop.

I hurried after him and dropped into the driver's seat as the two of them climbed into the back, all of us ignoring the hungry look The Czar was giving her as I started the Mini up and threw her into reverse, speeding towards the street with a whoop of victory building in my chest.

"Fuck yes!" Benny roared the moment we were out of sight, and I took the diamond from my pocket, holding it up so the passing streetlights made it sparkle like crazy.

Anya plucked it from my fingers and I glanced at her in the rear view mirror as she rolled it between her finger and thumb.

"It's so beautiful," she muttered, the light scattering over her face.

"It's got nothin' on you, darlin'," I replied.

"Fuckin' nothin'," Benny agreed. "Now get us home, Church. Our woman is looking in need of a real celebration and I plan on the three of us giving her one before this night is done."

"Yes, boss," I agreed with a smirk, slamming my foot to the floor and speeding down a bus lane, making Anya shriek in a mixture of excitement and fright.

With an offer like that on the table, I wasn't gonna dick around and I had a feeling that none of us would be getting much sleep tonight.

CHAPTER FIFTY EIGHT

We'd been celebrating so much in the days since we'd pulled off the con on The Czar, that I swear my clit was ready to take a vacation. The guys enjoyed fucking so much, it was a miracle we got any sleep at all, and though I was hardly complaining, I'd woken early to take a hot bath and rest my aching body while the others were piled into Benny's bed.

It was Benny's birthday today and as I was now officially earning my own cut from The Firm and even had my own bank account, I'd been able to contribute towards the present me, Church and Frank had bought him. We'd booked him a helicopter flight over London and a meal at his favourite exclusive restaurant in the centre of town next week. He was gonna lose his shit when we told him, and I couldn't wait to see the smile on his face.

After a while, the door opened and Frank walked in wearing a pair of navy boxers, his muscles firm as he watched me with his shoulder propped against the doorway.

"Morning, Cash."

"Morning, Frankie boy," I said with a teasing smirk and he stepped into the room, moving to the toilet and taking a piss.

While his back was turned, I eyed the huge scar on his back of my family's crest and discomfort crawled through my skin as always. He washed his hands then turned to me, frowning at the look on my face.

"I'm never gonna be able to pay for all that Nikolay did to you," I said as he picked up a large bath towel and gestured for me to get out. I did so, my hair still up in a bun so it was only my body that was wet as he stepped forward and wrapped the whole thing around me, gently working to dry me as my gaze stayed set on his face.

"Pain and torture are my trade, and they're your brother's too. I ain't saying I forgive him, but I do understand him. Besides…" He turned me away from him, working to dry my back as tingles travelled along my skin from his attention. "I have claimed penance in the purest form. I've fallen in love with his flesh and blood." He kissed the back of my neck as I gasped at those words. "I love her to my bones and there ain't no pain in this world I wouldn't suffer through to be standing here at her back. This was my road in life, and I'm glad I took no other turns because it led me here to you, Anya. I've claimed you from your brothers in a way. You're mine. Ours. You may be a Volkov, but you're a Butcher now too, and better than that…you're a Forget-Me-Not." He dropped the towel and traced his fingers over my right hip. "Now we just need to find a place to mark it on you, would you like that Cash?"

"Yes," I admitted huskily, loving the idea of branding the same tattoo on my body which bonded the three men I'd fallen for. I didn't even entirely hate the brand on my ass anymore either, because I *was* a Butcher now. The wife of the Butcher king, a member of the Butcher gang, and when a knife was in my hand, I could be a butcher too. "And I want you to know, I started to love you the first time you played a chord on your guitar. That first note you sang, and every moment since with you because it's felt like music playing in my soul. You're the one who made me realise I don't need my headphones anymore, you tuned me into life and showed me how much it's worth staying present for every beat of it. Even when it hurts."

He ran his fingers up my spine then tugged my hair, forcing my head around at a painful angle to steal a wicked kiss from my lips. He'd always be punishing me, but now his punishments felt like worship too. And I would happily pay my debt to him for as long as I still drew breath.

"Happy birthday to you, happy birthday to you, happy birthday to Benny," Church sang loudly down the hall. "Happy birthday to *you*."

"Argh!" Benny cried. "You fuckin' muppet. Get offa me."

I grinned, running out on the walkway butt naked before racing down the hall and throwing open the door to our room, finding Benny being wrestled into the sheets by Church as he smeared cake all over his face and punched him in the kidney.

The two of them fell about laughing, but Benny's laughter stuttered out as he spotted me and Church whipped around to look too.

"Well fuck me," Benny breathed, taking in my naked body as Church slid off of him and sucked the frosting off his fingers. "That's the best damn birthday gift I ever saw."

Frank's chest suddenly pressed to my back and though my vagina screamed for more of a vacation, damn these boys were tempting.

"Here, darlin'." Church grabbed a fistful of cake from a plate on the nightstand and shoved it into Benny's boxers, making him grunt in surprise.

"Cake's up."

I swallowed greedily, climbing onto the bed and leaning over Benny, licking a line of frosting from his stomach. But before I could get too carried away, the doorbell rang downstairs and I paused.

"Who the fuck is that?" Benny grumbled.

"Leave it," Church insisted, eyeing me like he was as eager for me to start mouth fucking Benny as my husband was himself.

"I'll get it," Frank said, clapping his hand to my ass and squeezing. "You show the birthday boy a good time, Cash. If he hasn't come before I get back here, you'll be in trouble." He stalked from the room, my pussy throbbing with that lasting comment and I wasn't sure whether it might be worth denying Benny just to see what Frank would do to me for disobeying him.

Church bounced eagerly on the bed, leaning forward to paint a line of frosting along the edge of Benny's waistband. I followed his finger, kissing and sucking my way across his skin as Benny groaned and bucked his hips, his huge length begging for attention as I continued to deny him it.

"Get down here!" Frank boomed urgently from downstairs and I lurched backwards in alarm as Benny cursed loudly and Church grabbed a gun.

We all shot to our feet and Benny tossed me a shirt which I pulled on as we ran downstairs together. Frank stood there with a large box by his feet and a childish birthday card in his hand with a picture of two bunnies on it. A cold pit of dread opened up in my gut as I hurried towards him.

"It's from Danny," he growled, passing the card to Benny which had bloody fingerprints stained on it.

"*Hoppy* birthday, brother – Jesus, that's a shit pun - meet me at pa's grave like old times. Let's make it a day to remember," Benny read it aloud.

"Oh fuckin' hell, whose head is gonna be in this box then?" Church asked and Benny stepped closer to me as Church flicked it open. Movement stirred within it and in moments Frank had produced a gun from somewhere, Benny rolled his shoulders and Church snatched a knife from the nearest table. But instead of an attack, a blue balloon floated up out of the box with a bloody hairpiece sitting on top of it. There was a smiley face drawn onto the balloon which look seriously sinister.

"Oh no," Benny sighed. "Not Mickey Hairpiece."

"It's more than his hairpiece," Frank said darkly as he stepped forward, peering into the box and I moved nearer too, finding a bunch of fingers and toes all bundled up and tied to the end of the string like a balloon weight.

"This can't go on," Benny growled. "I have to go meet him before he kills any more of my men."

"I'll go with you," I offered but he shook his head, stepping forward and cupping my cheek. "You're stayin' right here where these two can protect you. I ain't takin' no for an answer, that's an order, bombshell."

The fear in his eyes stopped me from pushing the subject and I nodded, giving in to his desires. It was his birthday after all, and it looked like Danny was right. It really was going to be one to remember.

CHAPTER FIFTY NINE

I didn't like it. Didn't like it one fuckin' bit, but there it was and here we were.

All week we'd been trying to track down Danny in and amongst the rest of our business and having more than our fill of my sweet, Miss America, who was too damn tempting for her own good. But we hadn't found a single trace of him.

Deep down, I'd known we wouldn't find him. Not after the little gift he'd sent last week.

Danny had wanted it to go down like this and of course he'd chosen their birthday to do it.

I wasn't at all happy to have watched Benny stride outa the door no matter how confident he was that Danny wouldn't kill him. It ate at me. But he was right. Even Frank could see that. This was a fortress and Danny wouldn't be able to breach it.

We all knew from past experience what lengths Danny would go to to get rid of anyone he saw as a threat to his bond with Benny, and right now that meant his aim was gonna be fixed on Anya and the two of us.

It wasn't fear that had stopped us from going on out there with our boss though. It was just common sense. Benny was confident that he would be able to talk Danny down and get control of him again, and we'd been forced to agree that it was the safest way to deescalate the situation. Danny wouldn't hurt his brother, that much we knew for sure. So I wasn't worried about my friend, but I was worried about what that psycho had planned.

Frank was in a mood over it of course and I wasn't exactly feeling the party spirit anymore either, but we had to have faith.

Benny would be fine, Danny would be caught again and then…

My gaze shifted across the room to Frank who was sitting on the sofa with Anya, strumming a song on his guitar while she bit her lip and watched him with an expression that was just one shade shy of pornographic.

She was a clever little minx, distracting him with that. She'd quickly figured out what he needed to help calm him and provided it. No doubt she was getting a lot out of it herself too.

I, on the other hand was a ball of tension and I couldn't help but keep wondering what the hell was going on in that graveyard and whether or not Benny had even made it there yet.

Fuck, this tension was going to do my ticker in.

I watched Frank and Anya for another few minutes, smiling at her as she turned to look for me, liking the fact that even with him working his hardest to soak her knickers, she still had attention to spare for me too. But I shook my head when she beckoned me over, jerking my chin towards the stairs and pointing at the frosting which was still smeared on my chest after my little tussle with Benny earlier.

The others had gotten themselves dressed along with Benny as he'd been preparing to head out but I'd been too distracted to get myself cleaned up, lingering down here and checkin' in on as many members of The Firm and The Butchers as I could just in case Danny had gotten to any more of them. But so far as I could tell, nothing else had gone down besides Mickey Hairpiece disappearing.

My genius plan to watch our girl use Benny as a breakfast platter filled with cake and sausage had gone to shit fast, and I was now an hour into the drying stage of buttercream against my skin and in need of a shower.

Anya gave me a sexy little pout as I denied her and my smile widened before I turned and headed up the stairs.

I really needed to make another trip home for some more of my shit. This week I hadn't spent a single night back there and I had no intention of doing so again any time soon either. Benny's super king was the only place I planned on laying my head at night, easily within reach of my girl and surrounded by my boys. It was fuckin' bliss on a microfiber pillow and I was good with taking my fill of it.

I strode into the bathroom, reaching out to set the water running in the shower and moving to the sink where I grabbed my toothbrush and began to scrub at my teeth, having missed the chance to do it with the excitement of the morning.

Steam billowed out from the shower, obscuring the mirror and I gripped the edge of the sink as I leaned forward to spit the toothpaste from my mouth before tossing my toothbrush back into the little china pot alongside the others.

A shadow shifted in the mirror as I looked up at it once more but as I made a move to turn my head, a hand slapped down over my mouth and a hard body crashed against my back.

I threw an elbow back as shock rattled through me, but it wasn't fast enough to stop the knife which slammed into my gut in the next heartbeat.

Pain and horror radiated through my body as I looked down at the knife which was sticking out of my tattooed flesh just in time to see my attacker rip it free, spilling my blood across the white tiles before stabbing me again. And again.

I kicked off of the sink, throwing my weight back into the fucker and sending us crashing against the wall behind me, but his hand never once shifted from my mouth and his blade just punctured my skin over and over as he stifled my cries. A throaty laugh escaped him as my blood sprayed all over the room and the strength was stolen from my limbs.

Agony ripped through my body at the countless puncture wounds and my bare feet slipped in the blood which coated the tiles, causing me to lose my balance and fall.

My attacker let me drop to the floor, kicking me over and forcing a pained groan from my lips as I rolled onto my back in a puddle of my own blood and looked up at him, finding Danny grinning down at me, the bloody knife in his fist.

"It's been a long time coming, Church," he hissed. "Say hi to Olly for me though, yeah?"

I opened my mouth to try and yell out and warn the others, my lungs screaming with the pain of my stab wounds as I sucked in a breath.

I could feel death's cold fingers locking around my heart and tugging me into his embrace, but the organ continued to thrash and pound in my chest, beating on uselessly for the girl who had laid claim to it and begging me to save her from this monster. But Danny's booted foot swung into my face before I could get a single word to spill from my bloody lips and everything surrounding me fell to darkness as that cold hand on my heart ripped me away.

I was left with nothing but my own failure coating my tongue and terror for the people I loved to keep me company on my journey away from this place of sin and vitality.

CHAPTER SIXTY

I was captivated by the strum of Frank's fingers against the guitar, no pick in sight as he drew music from the beautiful instrument with nothing but the pluck of his hands. He was singing Blackbird by The Beatles in a low voice and I watched his lips wrap around the words, staring at him as desire burned a path through my body.

When his fingers played out the final notes of the song, I leapt on him, shoving the guitar aside and taking its place, jealous of the damn thing as it stole all of his attention.

Frank groaned as my mouth met his, his fingers rolling down my spine and playing my body as beautifully as they had played those strings, causing a noise of utter desire to escape me.

He curved his hands around my ass, tugging me harder against him as my heart raced and my need for him sharpened. He was my dark, vengeful god, casting his judgement across the land and I'd invoked his wrath, but it was so fucking sweet sometimes that I was starting to think he didn't want to punish me at all anymore. He'd fallen for a mere mortal and now I was his, tethered to him as we devoured each other's pain and left nothing but peace in each other's hearts.

A whoosh of air brushed my cheek a second before a heavy crack sounded and Frank jerked forward so hard that I was thrown backwards, my ass hitting the floor and my feet still on Frank's lap as I stared up at him in confusion.

A looming shadow stood behind him and fear slashed across my chest as I found Danny Butcher stood at his back, a baseball bat in his grip and a manic grin on his face.

Frank's expression mixed with shock and pain from the whack around the head he'd clearly just taken and he slumped forward as if in slow motion.

I screamed as I scrambled to catch him, but his weight knocked me sideways, his hands grabbing for the coffee table and sending it skidding forward as he failed to stop his momentum.

Frank was dazed, blood staining his hair as he pushed to his knees and tried to rise.

I sprang to my feet in fear, snatching a flick knife from the coffee table and snapping it out as Danny regarded me with a dark grin.

"Stay back!" I cried, but Danny climbed over the back of the couch, swinging the bat at me and I had to jump aside, narrowly missing the swing of it.

"Run," Frank rasped, trying to get to his feet from his hands and knees, the blow to his head clearly affecting his movements and my heart twisted in terror for him as I was forced to retreat further.

"No one's running anywhere," Danny growled, diving towards Frank as he raised the bat once more and I cried out in panic, lunging for him as he swung it towards the man I loved.

I rammed the blade into Danny's back, aiming for something vital to stop him as his arm swung powerfully. Blood spilled as the knife sank deep, but my attack did nothing to slow him and Frank hit the floor with a sickening crack as the bat connected with the back of his head.

The scream that left me was all terror and I yanked the blade out of Danny as he snarled in rage, driving it towards him again, determined to kill him.

He whipped around, the bat slamming into my shoulder and knocking me onto the couch before I could sink the blade into him for a second time and pain radiated through my limbs.

Danny was on me in the next moment, pinning me in place and wrestling the knife out of my grip as I kicked and thrashed. I managed to punch him in the face while he fought to get the knife from my other hand, but he ripped it from my grasp and pressed it to my throat, forcing me to still.

Danny glared down at me with his teeth bared, the knife pushing into my skin just hard enough to hurt without piercing it as his chest rose and fell heavily. His eyes were alight with the thrill of the fight, blood staining his shirt and making me fear for Church as he failed to appear at the sound of our struggle. Where was he? How long had Danny been inside the house?

Danny had dropped the bat behind him, the thing slowly rolling across the hard floor and into my line of sight. Horror coursed through me as I spotted the blood staining the end of it. Frank's blood.

I tried to fight back, to get him off of me, but he pressed his weight firmer to hold me in place.

"None of that," he hissed. "It's my birthday, and I get what I want on my birthday, yeah?" His eyes were the exact same shade as Benny's, though nothing but hell and drugs lived within them. He was coked up, his pupils full blown and his manic expression told me his demons were out to play in full force.

"Alright," I breathed, knowing I needed to do anything I could to keep him away from Frank. Church must have heard the fight, he'd be on his way down any second and Danny would die at the end of his gun. I refused to believe any other version of the truth. "How did you get in here?" I asked, trying to buy some time while he watched me with a look which said he hadn't quite decided on his next move yet.

"It's funny that, actually," he said. "If it wasn't for Frank over there, I never woulda done it. But about a year ago we got into a bit of bloodshed on the far side of town and he forgot to bring the spare keys out with us. I almost killed him when I couldn't get inside and he started yelling at me, telling me I shouldn't blame him for me losing my keys and shit like that. Then he went and told me that I should start leaving a key under the doormat if I needed a safety net for my fuck ups."

"There was a key under the mat?" I asked with a frown, because there wasn't even a mat outside the front door and I was certain he couldn't have snuck in through it without us noticing even if there had been.

"Don't be a daft bitch, of course there wasn't. But I did loosen the window frame in my bedroom so that I could get into it from the roof if I ever had to." He smirked triumphantly as I stared up at him in horror. "Before now, I couldn't get close to the place to climb up onto the roof easily, but I had a plan which all came together today. Birthday luck, that."

Danny caressed my cheek with the knife and Frank let out a groan that made relief stagger through my chest at knowing he was alive.

"Stay down, Frankie boy, you absolute machine," Danny said with a wild laugh. "He's like the fuckin' Terminator, that one. Church was easier. All those British tattoos of his always made my skin itch, but now they're punched full of holes, I feel a lot better."

Dread washed over me, cold and thick. "What have you done to him?" I snarled, shoving his huge chest, not caring about the knife he held against me because my men were in trouble and I had to get to them.

"See, this is your problem. You don't listen." He tapped my ear with the knife, locking his other hand around my throat as I punched and shoved him, desperate to get away. He winced as I jolted the wound on his back and I was pretty sure if he wasn't so coked up he'd have been more bothered by it, but he was barely human right now. "One more fucking punch and I'll cut your eyes out."

He held the knife under my left eye and I fell still, knowing I was no use to Frank and Church cut to bits.

"What do you want?" I spat.

"You and me are gonna take a little drive," Danny said, lowering his hand and taking a coil of rope which was tied at his hip. He slid the knife between his teeth and snatched my wrists, binding them tightly together in front of me before taking the knife back into his grip and pointing it at me.

"That's it. Good girl," he said, smirking at me before rising to his feet. "Now sit tight while I get a nice toasty fire going for your boys. We wouldn't want them to catch a cold on this wintery morning now, would we?"

He walked off into the kitchen and I got to my feet, running to Frank's side and dropping to my knees to help him, my heart splintering as he tried to push himself up.

"What did I fuckin' say?!" Danny roared as he returned to us. "Sit fuckin' tight!"

Danny no longer had the knife in hand, he had a bottle of lighter fluid and a box of matches. So I shoved to my feet and ran at him with a shriek of defiance, colliding with him, reaching around and throwing my bound hands into the wound on his back.

He cried out as he stumbled into a cabinet, the two of us falling to the floor and I grabbed a glass candle holder as it came tumbling down beside me, smashing it over Danny's head. He bellowed as it shattered against his skull, glass scattering in his hair and blood spilling.

Danny threw a punch at my chest which knocked me backwards and I was thrown to the floor again. I spotted Frank moving, crawling towards me as he fought to stay conscious, desperately trying to get up. My heart cleaved apart as I scrambled towards him too but Danny got to his feet, dragging me up beside him by the throat and pinning me to the wall.

"Who taught you to fight like that, you little Russian cunt?" he barked in my face, spittle flying over my cheeks.

I kicked at him, trying to get my knee between his legs, but he slammed me against the wall once more, making my thoughts scatter as my skull impacted with the brickwork.

"Stop it! Stop fuckin' wriggling!" he roared. "You're just a whore to him, you know that?! He loves me, not you! You almost ruined everything for us, but I'm done lettin' him be blinded by your pussy. It's me and him, it always was. You had no right to show up here and take him from me!"

He tossed me to the floor, the wind knocked out of my lungs as I landed in the broken glass from the candle holder and my arms were slit open.

I tried to get hold of a piece big enough to cut my binds or use as a weapon, but Danny swept his foot across the floor, kicking it all away from me.

"Sneaky, that's you." He snatched up the lighter fluid and matches where he'd dropped them, squirting the liquid all over the sofa, the rug and the nearest curtains, doing a sloppy job as he sprayed it everywhere in the lounge and then the kitchen until it was empty.

I crawled towards Frank, my dark hearted solider still trying to get to me and I reached out my bound and bloody hands towards his. His fingers locked around my binds, tugging with the last of his strength just as a loud whoosh was followed by the scent of fire and smoke tangling in the air as

Danny set the place on fire.

I didn't look away from Frank's eyes though, the terror and need in them so keen I could feel it down to the centre of my being.

He desperately tried to get me free, but the knot was too tight and I could see the panic rising in him.

"It's alright," I promised him in a choked voice as tears built in my eyes and he looked to me with a shake of his head, refusing this fate.

Danny strode up behind him while our gazes were still locked and I screamed in horror just before his boot slammed down on the back of Frank's head and he went still beneath him.

"Stay down, you fuckin' lout," Danny barked as he lowered into a crouch and took Frank's phone from his unmoving body, plucking it out of his pocket and dropping it into his own where I spotted Church's phone too. "Jesus fuckin' Christ, he just keeps kickin'."

Danny came at me while I sobbed for Frank, my fingers biting into his though he wasn't holding onto me anymore as I willed him to wake up again.

Danny gripped my blonde hair in his fist and yanked me upright while I sobbed and tried to lurch back towards Frank, a gun now in Danny's grip as he pressed it into my stomach.

"Stop fighting," he growled and I spotted the open cabinet across the room where he must have found the gun, the fire curling up around it as it took root quickly in the lounge. "We've got somewhere to be, and we're already late."

He locked me tight to his side, keeping the gun aimed firmly at me as he dragged me to the front door, snatching all of the keys from the hook beside it and stepping outside. Then he shut it and locked it tight while I began to shake and tried to figure out what to do.

There was no sign of the usual group of gangsters who hung around outside the warehouse and my heart pounded in fear as I hunted the shadows for them, my last hope for help falling away like sand into the ocean of despair I was feeling.

Because two of my men were in there and that fire was going to steal them from me if Danny hadn't already. They were hurt and I needed to be with them, but I was out here, bound and in the arms of a monster, about to be used in some sick game which I'd never agreed to play a part in.

"Happy birthday to us, happy birthday to us," Danny sang under his breath as he shoved me towards Frank's car, opening it with the keys he'd stolen. "Happy birthday to the Butcher boys, happy birthday to us."

CHAPTER SIXTY ONE

Pure agony tore through my skull, dragging me back to consciousness and making me blink the blood from my eyes as the scent of smoke choked me and made me cough violently.

I rolled onto my side, squinting into the space surrounding me and taking in the flames licking against the far wall, the sofa and coffee table already consumed by them and the thick black smoke blanketing the entire room.

A pained groan escaped me as I pushed myself up onto my knees, my hand going to the throbbing, bleeding wounds on the back of my head and my heart jackhammering as I remembered what had happened. Who had been here.

"Shit," I breathed, looking around for any sign of Anya before remembering her screams as he'd dragged her out of here and the way they'd called to me in the darkness of my mind, urging me to wake up, do something.

Fuck, how had we let this happen? How the hell had he gotten in here? And what the fuck had he done to Church?

I managed to get to my feet, coughing again as the room spun around me, my head wound making me dizzy and my thoughts slow.

I stumbled towards the front door, gripping the handle and shaking it against the heavy locks, trying to remember where I'd left the keys before realising there wasn't a single set on the hook beside the door. Every one was gone and as I checked my pockets, I found my phone missing too.

I slammed my fist against the door, yelling to whichever Butchers had been posted out there but getting no reply.

I didn't know if they were dead or had turned on us, but it didn't matter now. I was locked in a burning building and the woman who owned me was gone, taken by that fucking psychopath and out of my reach.

My sluggish thoughts wrapped around each other and I coughed harder as the smoke made it almost impossible to breathe, my eyes moving to the stairs as the heat of the fire made sweat run down my spine.

Someone would see those flames. They'd call for help.

They had to.

But as I looked across the room to the blazing furniture and kitchen units, I realised Danny had thought of that. This fire hadn't been lit from the outside which meant no one would see it until it consumed this place alongside me and Church as well.

"Church?!" I called, coughing once more and cursing as I got no reply.

I needed to get out of here, to warn Benny, go after Anya, a hundred different things with a thousand different outcomes, but right now, escaping this fire was the most pressing issue.

I cursed as I stumbled towards the stairs, flinching away from the kitchen as the flames there ate through everything they could and the acrid smoke they belched out made my lungs burn too.

I tripped as I reached the stairs, blood dripping down my forehead and into my eyes as I bowed my head and the room spun violently once more.

There was something seriously wrong with me. Something I refused to focus on but which was making every movement I made harder, take longer.

I gripped the railing and heaved myself up the stairs, my feet bumping against the steps and the smoke thickening until I was blinded by it, coughing and hacking every breath I choked down.

I almost fell over as I made it to the top of the steps, unable to see in the smoke-filled space and my balance way off.

I reached for the closest door, stumbling into the bathroom and instantly slipping over in a puddle of blood which stained the floor.

I smacked my head against the tiles, pain threatening to split my skull in two as a choked cry escaped me and I found a body lying on the tiles at my side.

"Church," I wheezed out, gripping his cold arm and shaking it while fighting a battle against my own body as I demanded it to stay conscious.

Church didn't reply, his arm just flopping back and forth as I tried to get a reaction from him and grief formed a vice around my heart as I shook my head in denial, trying to make out his face in the thick smoke of the dark room.

"Come on, Church, our girl needs us," I hissed, moving my hand to his chest and finding blood there. So much fucking blood which stuck to my fingers and made the foundation of my being crumble into dirt.

My head was throbbing and the smoke was utterly suffocating now, my coughs turning to wheezes as my lungs burned with the need for oxygen.

"Church," I panted again as I fell forward, my forehead pressing to his and his blood soaking through my jeans where I knelt at his side.

The smoke was growing thicker with every passing second and I coughed again, the sound feeble now, my lungs on fire and the dark pressing in on me, calling me away.

“I’m sorry,” I breathed. To him. To Benny. And to her. Because wherever she was now, I wasn’t going to be there. Death had finally come to claim me, and as the smoke and the dark tugged me into its embrace, I was helpless to do anything at all to stop it, no matter how much I wished I could.

CHAPTER SIXTY TWO

I sat with my arse perched on the edge of our pa's grave, the huge angel statue which stood over the extravagant stone tomb shadowing me from what little light made it through the fog.

It was a dim day, drizzle pouring from the clouds and soaking into my clothes, dampening my cheeks and sparking a chill in my bones. But I just waited where I was, the graveyard quiet, though I had noticed a fair few Christmas bouquets and little trees left alongside headstones on my way in. This was the time of year when people tended to think about their lost loved ones a little more after all.

Our ma had said we were her little Christmas miracles when we were born and she'd told us that over and over again as the years passed, despite our birthday being the week before the big event.

Thirty-five years sure seemed like a long time while I sat here waiting on the man I'd shared a womb with. I'd certainly done a whole lot of living with the days I'd been gifted on this earth.

But now I was going to have to decide if I planned on living on without my brother in this world. Because that was what this was coming to. Danny had always been a wild dog, hard to control and unreliable at the best of times, but now he'd gone rabid. There was no reeling him in at this point. I could try to catch him again, keep him locked up like the animal he was. But then the threat of him would always be there. The worry that he'd escape and come after the people I loved.

I didn't know what to do.

No. That was a lie. I knew he needed to die. I just didn't know if I could pull the trigger on him. Because no matter what he'd done, no matter how much I might have hated him and wanted him to suffer, he was still my twin brother. And despite the many things I'd done in this life to paint my soul in sin, I had to wonder if I could survive the tarnish his death would leave on me. The pain it would cause our poor, oblivious ma.

I'd bet our pa was turning over in the grave beneath me right now. He'd have done it. I was almost certain of that. I'd seen him put down his own men on more than one occasion for putting The Firm at risk or for betraying him. The organisation had been his beloved firstborn. Danny and I were just additional. And I knew he'd have put a bullet in his feral son if he'd seen what Danny had fallen into, no matter how fond he'd once been of the bloodlust in him.

Footsteps drew my attention to the space between gravestones ahead of me and I perked up as two figures approached through the fog.

I frowned as I looked at them, seeing the way the smaller figure seemed to be walking awkwardly, their feet stumbling as the bigger one pushed them ahead.

I was on my feet before their features had even become clear to me, my gun in my hand and pointed right at my brother's face as he shoved Anya into the space ahead of him, a fist in her hair and a gun jammed to the back of her skull.

"Happy birthday, brother," he said, grinning at me while Anya's fear filled eyes met with mine.

"He killed them," she gasped, tears staining her cheeks as she looked at me like her heart was breaking and mine plummeted right through my body and bottomed out hard.

"I didn't want this," Danny said, shaking her roughly and glaring at me. "You know I didn't. But you had to push and push, didn't you? So here we are."

"What did you do?" I hissed, my gun still aimed squarely at him but there was no way I could take the shot while he held Anya like that. Fear for my friends blinded me, but there was one thing I could see as clear as day suddenly and it was that I wasn't going to let him do a single thing more to the people I loved.

"I got rid of the problems standing between us, that's all," he replied. "Just like you knew I'd have to. Just like you know this is on you."

I eyed the way he was holding my wife, the blood from her split lip which showed me clearly that he'd laid his fucking hands on her again and the furious agony in her eyes over whatever he'd done to Church and Frank. My heart was galloping like a racehorse destined for the glue factory if I didn't get this win, but I held my tongue. I held it and tried to figure out how to survive this game because I knew my brother. I knew him and I knew what this was about.

He didn't give a fuck about Anya, not really. He only cared that she was standing between us. In his eyes, with her gone, the two of us would be free to do things the way we had once upon a time in his rose-tinted memories of our rise to power.

But one thing became clear to me as he stood there with the woman I loved at his mercy and the men I'd chosen as my own brothers fallen in his wake. I didn't have any questions about whether or not I could kill him anymore.

Now it was only a matter of getting the job done.

CHAPTER SIXTY THREE

"Toss your weapons, Benny, toss 'em now or I'll end her without any more bother on the subject," Danny snapped.

Benny bit his tongue on a reply, clearly hearing the truth to that threat and pulling a knife from his pocket, hurling it away into the fog along with his gun.

Danny shoved me in front of Benny, cutting the binds on my hands with his knife and pressing his gun to the back of my skull as my bare feet sank into the frost bitten grass at the foot of the grave.

"Choose!" he barked at his brother. "It's me or her. I'm done fuckin' about waiting for you to realise it's always been about us, Ben. Look this whore right in the eyes and tell her straight how it is. How it's always been us. How we don't need no one else and never will."

I stole a glance at Danny, a tremble running through my body as the tears in my eyes dried up. Frank…Church, I didn't know if they were alive or dead. And now I was left standing before my husband wondering if either of us would survive to see night fall.

Danny's face was taut with emotion and for a moment I saw what he really was, just a boy who'd never grown up, who'd been born different and was broken inside in a way I could never really understand. He was violent because he was hateful and hurting, and his need for his brother was all he really had. He seriously believed that killing the people Benny loved would bring his brother back to him, would fuse them together more tightly and keep everyone else away. He was fucked up, delusional, and there was only one way to handle that.

"Tell him," I begged of Benny. "Tell him the truth." I laid it on thick, letting him see the imploring look in my eyes and Benny's attention moved from me to his brother, his shoulders slumping.

"Of course it's you, Dan," he said quietly. "It's always been you and me, ain't it?"

Danny nodded eagerly, buying into those words like they were everything he'd been aching to hear for who knew how long.

"That's right. You see now, don't you?" he growled at me. "You're just a distraction. He don't love ya like he loves me. He can't. We're made of the same flesh, born outa one womb, we have matching DNA. You can't beat that, love. There's no one in this world who can." His eyes blazed and he licked his teeth like he was hankering for a sniff of his favourite addiction, his finger twitching against the trigger of his gun and making tension coil tighter within me.

"Let's go, Dan," Benny said, stepping closer. "Just you and me. We can go have a pint together, how's that sound?"

Danny inched forward, the gun still butting against my skull as he looked to Benny hopefully. But then he stopped himself, shaking his head. "Nah, look at you. You're all jittery. It's her, ain't it? You're still thinking about *her*."

He shoved me so hard I fell to my knees, the frozen stalks of grass crunching beneath me as the fog swirled tightly around us like it was desperate to watch this play out. I knelt at Benny's feet and Danny shifted to his brother's side, aiming the gun down at my forehead.

I stared up at my husband, my throat rising and falling as fear made my heart thrash. I was unsure if I'd ever rise to my feet again and I let myself be consumed by the sight of Benny before me, a man I'd fallen for so completely I'd never recover from it. And I never wanted to.

"It ain't worth the trouble with the Russians if we kill her," Benny tried, nudging Danny as he tried to get the gun away from me, but Danny held it firm. "Fuck her. We can just leave her here. Let's go. Just you and me, mate."

"Yeah…alright, yeah. Let's go." Danny let Benny turn him away from me drawing him along and I stared after them with my fingers pressing into the mud, unable to breathe as I watched them go, the fog shifting between us and attempting to swallow them within no more than a few steps.

But then Benny threw a glance back at me, the truth unveiled in his eyes as he begged me to run with that single look and Danny caught it.

"No! You fuckin' liar!" Danny roared, throwing his hands into Benny's chest, knocking him into a large gravestone and falling on him ravenously, knocking him down beneath him.

The moss covered gravestone caved beneath their weight with a crash as Benny fought to get the gun from his brother. They threw feral punches, cursing and snarling at one another as the beasts within them were brought to the surface of their skin and they were shown for the savages they were.

They fought like animals, kicking and punching and biting, there was no rules or honour between them just this barbaric, desperate need for victory.

I got to my feet, running forward with my breaths falling furiously from my lungs as I pinned my gaze on my husband and vowed to help him, hunting the ground for any sign of the weapons he'd cast aside or even a rock to beat his psychotic brother's skull in with, but there was nothing to be found in the foggy landscape and I had no time to waste hunting.

Danny pinned Benny down and pistol whipped him around the head, making him curse as blood poured from a wound in his temple and my heart lurched in panic at the thought of Danny getting the upper hand.

"She has to die, Ben. It's the only fuckin' way to get you back. To make you see things straight. Fuck the alliance and all of that shit – no one can come at us and win when we're united."

"She's my wife!" Benny shouted, rearing up and throwing Danny off of him like those words had summoned a god's strength within him. The gun went off and my heart juddered just as I collided with the two of them, grabbing Danny's wrist as I tried to wrestle the gun out of it while Benny fought to pin him to the ground.

"She's always going to be my number one," Benny spat, shoving Danny's head into the dirt as I bit into Danny's wrist to try and make him let go of the gun.

"She can't have you," Danny wailed, a noise of grief leaving him. "You're mine. My Benny. It's me and you. In this world or the next if it has to be."

"Danny – no," Benny gasped and I screamed as blood splashed my cheek, turning in shock.

Benny had a knife stabbed deep into the joint between his neck and his shoulder and Danny yanked it free again with a noise of pain leaving him. I was frozen in place as Danny abruptly slashed the sharp blade across his own throat, blood spurting and rising in his mouth, his eyes widening with victory. Like he'd finally found an answer to his maddening obsession with his brother.

But as Benny clapped a hand over his own wound, lurching away from his twin in horror as he began to bleed out beneath him, Danny clearly realised the wound on Benny wasn't fatal.

Danny yanked his hand free of my grip, whipping the gun up to point directly between Benny's eyes, the intention to drag him into the afterlife with him clear on his deranged face.

But for the briefest of seconds, Danny's finger hesitated on the trigger and I came to my senses fast, shoving my entire weight at my husband with a scream as I defied every law in this universe and forced him to move aside before that gun went off.

But it still did, and the bang resounded so loudly all around us that my skull rattled. Though that was nothing to the pain which ripped through my chest, the bullet tearing through muscle and bone as I fell awkwardly on top of Benny, the heat of my blood spilling between us.

Benny bellowed in rage, snatching the gun from Danny and tossing it as far away as he could.

"What have you done?!" Benny cried as he dragged me into his arms, but Danny was choking out, barely present as his cut throat pissed blood onto the grass and he slumped back onto the dirt of a grave.

Everything around me was darkening as Benny rolled me onto my back, pressing his hands to the wound on my chest as I found I couldn't move my limbs, the weight of my body so heavy like it wasn't mine at all anymore.

"Hang in there, Anya," Benny commanded, telling me to defy death while the fog rolled around him and the sun fought to burn through it fruitlessly. And I tried. I really fucking tried.

He pressed down desperately, fighting to keep the blood from spilling out of my body, and I couldn't feel anything but pain as panic clutched Benny's features.

"Stay with me, bombshell. Don't leave me behind." He stared into my eyes and I forced them to stay open, the dark calling to me as the sound of my last heartbeats drummed in my ears like the final song I'd ever hear.

"I'll wait for you," I whispered but I wasn't sure he heard me.

I realised something as I stared up at this man I'd vowed to kill once upon a time. Fate had driven me into his arms and placed a wedding band on my finger even while I'd fought it every second of the way. And not only that, but it had offered me two other perfect villains as well, like an offering for all the years I'd spent alone. And though our time had been brief, I had to be grateful for every single moment I'd been granted with them, every laugh and thrill and pleasure-filled gift.

They were my awakening, my path back to life, and if they had to be my death too then so be it. My story would end here in a country I'd been born to love. And I'd own those boys even as I died on the soil of a kingdom that had claimed countless lives before mine, my blood sinking deep into the earth to join that of royals, poets, conquerors and soldiers. It was just like Church had said, London would leave its mark on me, and I hoped my death would leave my mark on it in return.

My eyes failed me and I lost sight of my husband, the king of London, ruler of my heart. And all fell still.

EPILOGUE

AN' YA

THOUGHT IT WAS ALL OVER

CHAPTER SIXTY FOUR

Dying wasn't how I'd imagined it to be. I'd thought it would be frightening. That I'd feel the nothingness, be aware of all that I'd lost. But death was a quiet, gentle creature which came to take the pain away.

The loss was left in the living. And here, in this dark, ever present void, all was numb. All was silent. It was what I'd tried to find for most of my life, a place where the world wasn't loud, where the hurt wasn't sharp. But I found I missed the beauty in all of that, because even when life was at its worst, even when it crushed your heart between two iron walls and it seemed you'd never escape from it, it was still better than nothing. Life was a gift I'd wasted on trying to be dead.

I'd spent too long taking no risks, too many years disappearing, believing that if I could find a place where no feelings existed and hold onto it permanently, I'd be in nirvana. But I'd missed so much because of that. I'd missed out on friends, I'd placed barriers between me and my brothers, I'd even lost the chance to truly grieve my mother because in place of tears, I'd chosen music.

I'd worked so hard to keep myself from hurting that I'd lost countless opportunities to smile. Because it turned out, there was no good without bad. Neither could exist without the other, and every life held both. Every person in the world could experience purest joy, and the most desperate of griefs, but if our hearts and eyes were closed then we'd live beneath the surface of it all, never truly experiencing either. And though it may have seemed like we were saving ourselves from unimaginable pain, we were really keeping ourselves from unimaginable happiness too.

So in the brief window I'd allowed myself to feel it all, offering myself to three men whose hearts had been as black as mine, I'd discovered what could have been. The potential of a lifetime drenched in jet fuel and set alight. A fire that burned so goddamn sweetly.

A beat started up in my skull, an unfamiliar music which was missing lyrics. It took an age to realise it was more than just the beat of a drum, it was my own heart, thumping away in my head while the noise was echoed by a far off beep.

The weight that had seemed to hold my eyes closed lifted and confusion washed through my mind.

If I was dead, then how was I waking?

Light filtered through my eyelashes and holy fuck, did it burn. It was like a knife to my skull and a laugh rose in my throat, falling from my lungs and filling the room I was in. I was alive, a breathing, living thing with endless possibilities before me once more.

Three sentinels stood around my bed, as black as night compared to the blinding whiteness of the ceiling and the glaring lights within it. I knew them before their faces became clear, I'd know them anywhere now, but for a second each of them could have been the other, indistinguishable, like a creature split into three parts, yet sharing one soul. And I was pretty sure I was a part of that creature too.

"Bombshell," Benny's voice came first, his hand winding around mine, his thumb caressing the ring on my finger. "You've been out of it for days, Anya. But you're here now, you're back with us where you belong."

His face came into focus and a dreamy smile pulled at my lips. My husband. Royalty at its finest, his beauty hiding the darkness within him so well.

"Why does she keep smiling like that, is she alright?" Frank asked anxiously.

"You're okay, aren't you Miss America?" Church asked. "Say you're alright, darlin'."

"Maybe we should get a doctor," Benny said in concern as I drew my fingers from his, lifting my hand to admire the ring adorning it. There were half healed cuts along my fingers, but I didn't care. Somehow, we were all here, all alive and okay, and that was all that mattered.

"Why won't she say somethin'?" Church moved forward, cupping my cheek in his rough palm and I stared up at him, finding his body bound in bandages instead of a shirt. My heart tugged at that, but there was a brightness to his eyes which said he was going to be just fine. And I was unbelievably grateful for that. He was my sweet sinner, as kind as he could be cruel, a walking juxtaposition and I loved every shade of red, white and blue within him.

"Who are you?" I breathed and Church's eyes rounded in alarm.

"She don't know me," he said and Benny muscled him aside, his hand taking the place of Church's on my face.

"Anya, say my name," he growled frantically.

"B…Brian?" I said, watching as panic danced in his eyes.

"Benny," he said urgently. "It's Benny, love. Look at me. Tell me you know me."

Frank knocked him back and leaned forward to take up my view. God he was everything, his eyes like liquid sin come to drown me. I lifted a hand, my fingers running around to the back of his head, finding a row of stitches there beneath my fingertips. How the fuck he had survived so many whacks to the head, I'd never know. Maybe his bones were made of steel, I wouldn't even have been surprised.

"Are you the doctor?" I asked and Frank shook his head, lurching back and looking to the others in anger.

"I'm gonna break that surgeon's fuckin' legs. He's made her forget us," he barked.

"Calm down, Rambo, give her a second, she'll come back to her senses. She can't forget us, we're the fuckin' Forget-Me-Nots," Church insisted and I started laughing, the sound growing louder and louder as they all turned to me in astonished confusion.

"I know you, assholes. How could I forget?" I said when I'd caught my breath, but my joke was apparently not so funny to them.

"You little buggar," Benny said and Church cracked, roaring a laugh and lunging at me, crushing me to the bed as he stole a kiss from my lips, though he hissed in pain at the movement, giving away the fact that he still had a whole lot of healing to do.

Pain burned in my chest too, but whatever drugs I was on were keeping that bitch of a wound from causing me too much discomfort right now so I just enjoyed his attention.

Church was shoved aside and Benny's mouth came down on mine, his fingers pushing into my hair as a relieved noise left him.

"Don't you play games like that with me ever again, love," he growled then he was yanked back by Frank and he kissed me next, his fingers gripping my throat in a gentle hold but it still set my skin sparking with energy.

"How the hell did you survive?" I asked as Church slumped down into a chair beside my bed, a pained noise escaping him which betrayed how bad his injuries really were.

"Fuckin' John Boy saved us, didn't he?" Church said.

"Really?" I asked, my chest swelling at the thought. "When Danny pulled me outside, the gang wasn't there. I thought maybe he'd killed them or-"

"He tricked them. Waited for me to leave then went back and pretended to be me – told them all there was a fight kicking off in Lewisham and had 'em all race off to join it so he'd have a clear shot at the warehouse without them around. Only John Boy ain't no kipper and he got the feeling something was off while he was on his way to Lewisham. So when the others all left to take part in this fictional fight, he followed his gut and headed back to the house. Found it burning from the inside out with not a soul in sight."

"And he got you out?" I guessed, feeling endless gratitude towards the forgettable man as I realised I had him to thank for my world being returned to me.

"He had to drive a car into the front door to take it down," Frank explained. "Fuckin' hero he is. I came to as he was dragging the two of us down the stairs, wrapped in wet towels like a couple of little wet pigs in blankets."

"He managed to carry you both out?" I gasped.

"Yeah. He's a strong bugger that one. Then he threw us in the back of the car and got us to the hospital in time for the doctors to do their magic. I thought Church was a fuckin' goner, couldn't believe it when they told me they'd found a pulse," Frank said, shooting a look at Church which spoke of how much fear he'd felt over that.

"What car did he use?" Church asked with a frown. "No one ever said, but John Boy don't have his own car. So what was he driving when he smashed the front door down and-"

"Anyway, point is, they didn't die," Benny said loudly, cutting him off.

"Oh Jesus," Church breathed. "Don't tell me it was Britannia…"

"The Mini is called Britannia?" I asked, unsure why that even surprised me.

"It was," Benny said, wincing as Church let out a howl of grief.

"Why?" he cried like finding out the car had been wrecked would have been a worse fate than him bleeding out or burning to death in that house.

"So, er," Frank carried on as Church buried his face in his hands. "The doctors managed to stitch Church back together and give him a shit load of blood, and as you can see he'll be fine and dandy once he's all healed up again."

I looked over the countless bandages which covered Church's chest and abs, frowning as I counted at least nine of them, hating the fact that he'd suffered through that while Frank and I had been unaware and unhelpful right downstairs.

"They gave me Scottish blood," Church said conversationally as he recovered from the shock of Britannia's fate. "I've come over all highlanderish since they did the transfusion."

"They…I don't think that's a thing, Church," I said, breathing a laugh. "How did you even find out it was Scottish anyway?"

"I can just tell," he replied defiantly, raising his chin and Benny shook his head like he'd already heard this a hundred times. "I have a northerly feeling in my veins and it's making me feel all Scot-like."

I exchanged a look with the others who seemed to have absolutely nothing to say to that nonsense and decided that I didn't either. If Church wanted to go all Scottish in his recovery then that was fine by me – the main thing was that he did recover.

"And how the fuck did you survive that baseball bat to your head?" I asked, moving my attention to Frank who just shrugged.

"I've got a metal plate in my skull after the last time some fucker cracked it, don't I? Doctors said he'd never before told a person they were lucky to have had a head injury before."

Benny chuckled and I frowned. "This happened to you before?" I questioned.

"No. Course not. It was a bottle of whiskey the last time. But don't you worry – the other fella came off worse in that one. I heard he still walks with a limp." Frank smiled at me and I groaned, letting my head fall back against the pillows as I tried to process all of that from John Boy busting in like a super hero to the fact that everyone in this room was still breathing.

"Jeffrey?" a woman's voice came from the corridor outside my room and Church cursed as he tried to push himself out of his chair just as a nurse pushed through the door. "There you are! What have I told you about overexerting yourself?"

"Jeffrey?" I questioned, laughing as I realised she meant Church and his scowl deepened as he let Benny help him to his feet and was corralled from the room by the nurse.

"Not a fuckin' word," he grumbled, shooting me a death glare, but there was no chance of that. I was absolutely going to be pulling the Jeffrey card on him as often as humanly possible from now on.

"Give him a few more days to heal before you tease him over that one, bombshell," Benny said softly, reaching out to brush his fingers along my face. "He was putting on a brave face for you, but he really was in one hell of a way. We came as close to losing him as we did you."

I swallowed thickly, looking from him to Frank and knowing that was the truth, having felt death calling for me while I hovered between this place and that. But I had so much to live for now, it was no surprise to me that I'd fought my way back to my pack of heathens.

"Still," I said slowly, my lips lifting at the corners. "Jeffrey."

"You wanna know something even worse?" Benny asked, leaning down conspiratorially and I nodded, captivated by the mischief in his dark eyes. "He ain't related to Winston Churchill either."

"What?" I gasped and Frank smirked.

"Nah. His ma dropped her knickers for half the fuckers in town and we figured she never wanted him to know that she couldn't tell his pa from the postman, so she made up that bullshit heritage when he was a kid and just never gave him the truth. We only know because we ran a genealogy thing on him about ten years back for his birthday – we did it in secret, wanting to surprise him with an official record of it, but then the truth came out. Turns out his pa hails outa Germany of all places. So if anything, his ancestors probably fought on the other side of the war."

My mouth fell open in shock and then a hysterical kind of laugh escaped me as I leaned back against my pillows and tears pricked my eyes.

"You can't tell him," Frank added. "Me, Benny and Olly all swore to keep it secret after we destroyed the test results – we figured it would be a bit of a bastard thing to steal his heritage from him seeing as it's such a big deal to him and all that."

"I'll never breathe a word," I swore, my amusement fading as I turned my mind to the final piece of this puzzle as I tried to figure out the rest of what had happened after I was shot.

"What happened to Danny?" I asked.

"He bloody survived somehow. He's as goddamn unkillable as the rest of us fuckers apparently." Benny nodded to Frank with a smirk. "He's gonna be committed once he's made his recovery," he added and I looked to Frank with a frown, shocked to find out that he was still breathing too. How the fuck was that possible?

"Are you okay with that?" I asked him, knowing how badly he'd hungered for that revenge.

Frank thought on it before slowly nodding. "He ain't well. And there ain't no better way to suffer in this life or the next than in the company of your own demons. Death woulda been too easy for him, I reckon. He'll be stripped of his addiction and placed in a padded cell where he can't have a single one of his vices ever again. I think that's a punishment fitting for a monster like him."

I squeezed his fingers, a sigh of relief leaving me as I looked between these mafia men who'd staked their claim on me. And even though I knew I was in for a bitch of a recovery, I didn't care. Because we'd get through it together. And now that I'd had my life handed back to me, I didn't plan on wasting a single second of it ever again.

CHAPTER SIXTY FIVE

NINE MONTHS LATER…

"Cor, it's as hot as a pig's arsehole here," I muttered, wiping sweat from my brow before realigning my view down the sights of my rifle, observing the enormous elephant as it moved between the greenery just south of the watering hole.

"Shh. You'll scare it off," Anya hissed, glancing over at me with a frown and I eyed a few of the platinum strands of hair hanging down from the knot she'd tied in her hair before looking into her dark eyes.

It was okay for her though, in her tiny shorts and crop top, with her skin kissed golden from the sun, her childhood in Nevada clearly paying off as she drank in the heat of the African sun like she was a fuckin' pelican or some shit.

"Well we ain't all made for this climate," I grumbled, adjusting my hold on the powerful weapon and blowing out a harsh breath of air which was way too fuckin' hot for my liking.

"We're sick of hearing it, Church. Why don't you just reapply your sun cream and head back to the hotel if you can't hack it out here?" Benny suggested and I shot a scowl at him too.

Benny was also kissed golden by the unrelenting sun which shone out here, baking us normal, English folks to a crisp. It wasn't natural. Not for me. I needed a strong rainstorm and some gale force wind in my life.

Frank chuckled because of course his skin was doing just fine with this bullshit too. I hated them. Every last one of them. Almost as much as I loved them.

Here I was, baking my arse off in the South African desert, with lobster red skin no matter how much factor fucking fifty I slapped on and to top it all off, the mosquitos thought I tasted like top shelf bourbon too. Not the others though, oh no. They didn't have bites on their ankles the size of fuckin' walnuts, did they? Apparently my blood was fucking mosquito heroin and every one of those tiny cunts who drank it told a hundred more of their mates about it too.

"I thought this was meant to be a honeymoon we could all enjoy," I grumbled and I was pretty certain they really were all sick of my shit by this point, but I couldn't help it, I just wasn't made for this heat. "'How about a safari?' you said. 'It'll be fun' you said. Well this ain't my idea of fun and I want it to be known. I am not a man inclined towards extremely high temperatures and when I die of skin cancer in twenty years time, I want you all to remember that it was your fault."

"How about this?" Anya suggested, shifting in her position so that she was leaning on her elbows and tipping her weight to the side so that the rounded bump of her belly wasn't squashed to the ground where we were all lying in wait of our prey. From the new angle, I could see the forget-me-not tattoo which she'd gotten over the scar where she'd been shot by that gobshite Danny and my heart beat a little harder. I fuckin' loved that mark on her. "If you get a kill shot with your first round, you can have the entire night alone with me. Any way you want me, everything you'd like. Frank and Benny can go get drunk in the bar and I'll be exclusively yours."

"Why am I sensing a but here?" I asked suspiciously when neither Benny nor Frank objected to that, letting me know they must have already been in on this plan.

"But," Anya said, confirming my suspicions, her lips hooking up in a wicked little grin which I wanted to kiss clean offa her face. "You can't complain about the sun, the heat, your sunburn, the mosquitos or the way 'the cuisine doesn't agree with your British constitution'-"

The others joined in on quoting that little saying back at me and I scowled at them because it fuckin' didn't and they knew it. I was getting stomach cramps just thinking about whatever the fuck might be on the menu for tonight – we were staying in a five star exclusive suite with giraffes who stuck their heads in the windows at breakfast time for fuck's sake, why couldn't I just eat a nice chip butty for dinner?

"Well it doesn't," I muttered petulantly.

"We're sick of hearing it," Benny said firmly. "So that's the deal, Church. Shut up, get the kill shot and spend your night drowning your sorrows by burying your cock between our woman's thighs without the intimidating reality of having to compete with me and Frank for the night. Or keep bitching like a little twat and you can spend your night in the bitch hammock."

"What the fuck is the bitch hammock?" I asked.

"It's a hammock out on the veranda where you won't even be able to see what we're doing to Anya to make her moan so loud, and you'll have to keep one eye open in case any predators come calling in the night," Frank explained helpfully. "Plus we'll take your mosquito net away and let 'em have at ya."

"Sounds like hell," I said.

"All the more reason to get the kill shot and shut up with the bitching then, yeah?" Anya suggested, her attention shifting away from me as she looked down the sights of her rifle once more.

"Challenge accepted," I replied, propping my rifle up again too and releasing a long breath as I looked at the elephant through the scope again.

Several minutes passed while we all kept our silence and we waited for the perfect shot, eyeing the long, white tusks on the stunning animal and knowing we would be well rewarded once we got our kill.

"I've got the shot," Benny hissed.

"Like fuck you have," I growled in reply, my sights locking on the group of big game hunting wankers as they crept closer through the long grass at the top of the hill on the other side of the valley to the elephants.

"I've got the cunt in the hat," I announced, lining my shot up right between the eyes of the rich motherfucker as he raised his gun.

"I have the one on the left," Anya replied.

"I've got the right," Frank said.

"I guess I'm taking the prick with the binoculars who just spotted us then," Benny replied.

The man I was aiming at suddenly raised his eyes to look at us as the binoculars fucker clearly told him we were there, but before he could even figure out what the fuck we were doing, I pulled the trigger.

The shots rang out in near synchronicity, cracking through the air and dropping the piece of shit big game hunters like a rack of dominos and leaving them to bleed out while the elephants they'd been stalking ran from the noise.

A whoop of celebration escaped me as I shoved to my feet, yanking Anya up with me and stamping a kiss to those fuckable lips of hers.

"I think I just won myself a night of worship," I teased, though in all fairness, we knew that I would spend the night worshipping her far longer than she would spend it worshipping me.

"Only if you can keep the complaints to yourself between now and then," Benny reminded me, slapping me on my sunburned arm and making me curse like a sailor from the sting of his handprint.

"Well I say we head back to the air conditioning inside the suite and start our night right now," I suggested, scowling up at the relentless sun overhead and letting it know without words that I preferred to see it through a healthy layer of English cloud cover. Though I had to admit, it felt damn good to have finally killed those motherfuckers after spending months tracking them down through their connections to The Marketplace. It had been Anya's idea and it had seemed like the perfect excuse to combine our favourite hobby of killing arseholes with a honeymoon in the sun – at least until I'd remembered that the sun hated me and I would be the colour of a tomato for the duration of my stay anyway.

"Come on then," Benny agreed, turning and heading back towards the track where the park rangers were waiting for us to return from our little hunting trip. They were really nice fellas – they'd even passed on a healthy bribe to the local law enforcement to help make certain that a certain set of dead hunters' bodies were never found and ended up left out here for the hyenas to eat.

"How are you feeling, Cash?" Frank asked, slipping closer to Anya and placing a hand over her bump. She was only five months gone but the three of us had become right sappy fuckers over the little rascal which was currently growing inside of her, and we were making it our mission to keep her fully cared for at all times, no matter how often she told us to back off and leave her to it. We couldn't help it.

"I'm good. Baby likes the heat," she replied with a warm smile, letting Frank take her rifle from her and leaning into him a little as they walked.

"You need to get off your feet," Benny said, glancing over his shoulder at us. "Don't demand too much from her if she's tired tonight, Church."

I scowled at him for suggesting that, but Anya replied before I could.

"I'm not an invalid, Benny. And I'm insulted that you think Church could wear me out. I fully intend to be the one wearing him out and you know it."

Benny chuckled, biting his lip as he looked back at us.

"Maybe you should make me a home video then. In fact, you can even come inside her tonight, Church. It's not like you can get her pregnant, is it? Now that she's got a Butcher in her belly, I don't see why you should have to hold back."

I cleared my throat, glancing at Frank who quickly cut his gaze away, pointing at a herd of antelope in the distance to distract Benny from the guilty as fuck look on my face.

Anya hurried forward to watch the herd race by, not seeming to notice the tension or maybe just not giving a fuck about it as she took Benny's hand and cooed over the stunning view.

"On a scale of one to ten, how likely is it that that baby ain't Benny's?" I hissed, leaning in to hear Frank's answer.

"I mean, it could be his," he replied in a low voice. "I reckon I only finished in her like…eight times the month she fell."

"Eight?" I almost yelled, slapping my own hand over my mouth and looking to Benny, thankfully finding him still fully occupied with the view and his wife. "I thought three was bad."

"Huh." Frank scratched at the stubble lining his jaw. "Well how many times do you reckon Benny did? 'Cause if it's more than eleven then the odds are still in his favour. It's probably fine."

I cleared my throat, glancing at Anya's bump once more and shrugging. "Yeah. Probably. On a separate note, I'm thinking we hide all the weapons in the house when it gets close to her due date."

Frank eyed Benny cautiously then nodded. "Yeah. For the baby's sake. Can't risk it getting hold of a gun. Or anything sharp. Wouldn't want it to hurt itself."

"No," I agreed. "We wouldn't want that."

The antelope herd disappeared in a cloud of dust and the four of us continued back to the honeymoon suite without any further discussions of paternity or people getting murdered, or babies who might look suspiciously like anyone other than Benny. It wasn't that big of a deal anyway. We still had a good few months before we needed to hide the guns.

CHAPTER SIXTY SIX

THREE MONTHS AFTER THAT…

The low buzz of my cell door opening made my eyes snap open even though I hadn't been sleeping.

It was quiet in here. And so fucking loud at the same time.

I was all alone and yet surrounded by more monsters just like me. But not like me at all.

The cravings had never left me even when the sweats had finally subsided and the shakes had stopped too. They'd weaned me off my drug of choice, but they'd never removed my need of it. Never would.

I ached for a taste of it almost as much as I ached for my brother to end this punishment.

But maybe today was the day.

I grinned at the six big motherfuckers who they'd sent to escort me from my cell today.

They only sent the largest assholes to deal with me these days and I guessed they weren't taking chances with me anymore after I'd come close to killing that fella with the chair a couple of months back.

I didn't protest as they led me away down the corridor though. Not today. Not a cocky taunt or a bid for freedom from me, because my heart was racing and my palms were slick with the knowledge of who I was on my way to see.

I'd been locked up inside Broadmoor for a year now. A long, lonely year where I swear I'd almost lost my mind the way they claimed I had before I got thrown in here.

I could barely contain myself now though. I was damn near twitching at the thought of where I was headed and who would be waiting for me beyond that door.

The corridors were long and endless, and the men escorting me never so much as upped their damn pace no matter how much I tried to encourage them along. By the time we finally reached the visitation room, I was all on edge and desperate to get on with this.

The door finally swung wide, revealing the lone chair for me on this side of the table and the man I'd been aching to see who sat firmly on the other side beyond the glass which divided us.

"Benny," I breathed, drinking him in, my shoulders slumping and my heart pattering wildly at the sight of the only man I'd ever loved while he remained impassive and immobile before me.

I hurried into the room, dropping onto my seat and dragging it as close to the glass as I could get, not paying any mind to the man behind me as he warned me of the rules of this visit.

"You came," I breathed because there had been a few times when he hadn't shown up and those times had damn near broken me.

I'd even ended up in isolation, strapped to a bed for my own safety after throwing myself face first into the wall of my cell repeatedly when he'd refused to come.

I needed him. I fucking needed him and he knew it.

When he'd refused to let me visit him in prison I'd had blow, blood and whores to distract me from the pain of our separation, but in here I had nothing. No one. Only the time between his visits and the bliss of his company when he arrived.

"You look like shit, Dan," Benny said roughly, his hand going to his pocket like he'd been hoping to pluck a smoke from it before dropping into his lap as he remembered they'd cleared his pockets out on the way in here.

"Have I paid yet?" I hissed, leaning so close to the glass that my forehead pressed to it while he remained reclined and stoic in his plastic chair. "Are you going to pull some strings and bring me home?"

I asked him that every time he came here, and his answer never changed. But it would. One day it would. He needed me just like I needed him. That was why he came. Why he visited despite it all.

"You ain't ever getting outa here, Dan," he replied coldly. "You belong in this place and you'll rot in it too."

A whimper built in my throat, the sound causing me pain as the scarred tissue from where I'd tried to end my life was aggravated by the noise. My voice was different now. A lot of things were different now. But I was still kicking and so was he. That had to mean something.

"You don't have to keep punishing me," I said, unable to keep the plea from my voice. "I promise I won't touch the whore again. You know I can play nice. I'll play real nice with her, I swear it."

My tongue darted out to wet my lips as I thought of all the ways I could play with the Russian bitch. It would be nice for one of us anyway, that wasn't a lie. And when she was gone and her poison went with her, he'd remember who he was. He'd remember it was me and him.

"You know the rules," he growled, his eyes flashing with the violence we both loved so much. "You don't speak of her or any of them. Not a fuckin' word, Dan, or I'm gone and you can climb the walls in here for the next six months without a single fuckin' word from me."

"No," I gasped, reaching for him and hitting glass instead as my fingers scrambled for a way through to him despite it.

Benny shifted in his chair, his eyes as unforgiving as they always were when he visited me, but he still came. That was what proved his love for me, even when he wanted to deny it.

"You know what I'll do if you stop visiting," I warned, touching the scar on my neck as proof of my capability to perform that threat.

"Sometimes I think I should just let you do it," he replied darkly. "Cut your throat, hang yourself, whatever the fuck you fancy. Only then I remember that death is too good for you, brother. So if my attendance to this place ensures your suffering then I'll gladly pay the price of it."

I breathed a laugh, shaking my head. "You don't want me to suffer. You come because the idea of a world without me is as painful to you as the idea of a world without you is to me."

"Nah." Benny pushed to his feet and my heart began to race in panic as I realised that he was going to leave already. He'd leave me here and I'd be alone again, with nothing but my empty cell and emptier life to keep me company until the next time he came. "That's not it, Dan. Because I already have a world without you and let me tell you, the flowers never smelled so sweet. When I walk out that door, I'll forget you're even here while I live my life with the people I love and my mind never so much as wanders your way. But you – you'll think of me, won't you?"

"You know I will," I hissed, the venom of his words burning into me and making my head spin with frantic, terrifying thoughts.

"Yeah. You'll sit in your cell and pine and rot while I forget all about you. My words will haunt you and cause you pain and while they do, I want you to remember that the reason they hurt so much is because of what you hurt of mine. An eye for an eye, Butcher boy. Remember when Pa used to say that?"

"Pa thought we'd rule the underworld together," I cried as he moved to the door. "You're breaking his heart by not fulfilling that legacy."

Benny barked a laugh as he pulled the door wide. "You're forgetting, Danny, Pa never had a heart. Have fun pining over me while I'm gone – because I've forgotten I was ever here already."

He snapped the door shut behind him and I roared a demand for him to come back, screaming his name even though it ripped into the scar tissue in my throat and made agony pour through the old wound.

I threw my fists against the glass and yelled a demand for him to return even as the door behind me opened and the guards poured in to drag me out.

I kept screaming his name while I kicked and fought them all the way back to my cell, and I didn't stop even when they locked me inside with nothing but the dark, my fears and my need for my twin consuming me until I felt like I would break apart from the inside out and shatter all over the floor.

"Benny!" I roared into the silence.

But there was no reply. It was just me and my demons in here and they were utterly fucking ravenous.

CHAPTER SIXTY SEVEN

SEVEN YEARS LATER THAN THAT…

Today was the day I finally sold my wife.

I sat on the closed lid of the shitter in the expensive as fuck hotel suite, my phone in my hand as I waited out our mark.

"Bobby hit my ear," Cora complained, pouting at me as she held Frank's phone and took over the video call I'd been having with him. She was six and had all the fire of her mother along with the stubbornness of the motherfucker who had fathered her – which had not turned out to be me.

Of course, one look at her gorgeous little face had made it damn hard to be angry over the fact because she'd been fuckin' perfect, even when she was all covered in blood right after Anya gave birth. But I had beaten ten bells out of Frank a few days after we got her home in punishment for him breaking our deal.

"Bobby is a baby, love," I reminded her. "He can't even crawl yet, so I doubt he meant it."

"I dunno, Ben," Church piped up from somewhere out of sight. "He took a good swing at her. I think he'll be a knockout when we get him started in the ring."

I couldn't help but grin and Cora's eyes flashed with murder. "It's not funny, Daddy!" she shouted before snarling like a tiger in a trap and storming off, dropping the phone on the floor again as she went.

“I didn’t say it was,” I called back, but she was gone. No doubt off to put her little boxing gloves on and get some of that rage out by taking a few swings at the punch bag Santa got her for Christmas.

Edith picked up the phone before Frank could get to it again, holding it upside down as she gave me the kind of huge grin only a two-year-old could manage while Maggie waved from behind her, a sharpie in her hand which gave me palpitations.

“What’s your big sister doing with that pen?” I asked, wondering if I’d just managed to catch our resident artist before the act or if we were going to find yet another freshly decorated wall somewhere.

Maggie burst into laughter, racing away as Church took chase after the four-year-old and I wondered for the millionth time where the fuck she kept finding those sharpies.

“Hello, Daddy,” Edith said, ignoring the carnage as Church raced around the furniture in the background and tried to rugby tackle a toddler before she could draw on anything.

“Hello, beautiful, what are you up to?”

“Poopy,” she replied seriously and I nodded.

“Wanna try the potty?”

“No!” Edith launched the phone away from her and ran off too, leaving me with a view of the carpet for several seconds before Frank picked it up again.

“The girls have my backbone,” he taunted as he looked at me and I scowled.

Three fucking girls, all of them with Frank’s DNA instead of mine because he was a fucking animal who couldn’t keep his dick out of my wife for long enough to let me knock her up myself. He likes to joke about it now because the twins had finally arrived to complete my end of the treaty with the rest of the mafia families, and I was no longer beating his arse at every chance I could get for knocking my wife up three times in a fucking row before I could.

“You’re lucky I’m not there to give you a smack,” I muttered, though there wasn’t any real bite to my threat. I mean, yeah, it had been irritating as fuck that he kept managing to knock her up, but just like with Cora, I’d gone and fallen for Maggie and Edith, loving them too much to be able to stay mad for long over it.

“Did Teddy eat his broccoli?” I asked, noticing the kids’ plates on the kitchen counter behind him which looked to have a suspiciously large pile of green stuff on one of them.

“Like hell he did,” Frank replied, heading across the room and turning the camera to face the twins where they both sat in their highchairs, happily eating yogurt and flicking it at each other.

They were a pair of little ruffians, just like me and at least with them I didn’t have to question who the father was. They had Anya’s blonde hair which was starting to curl as it grew out and a cheeky look in their eyes which promised trouble the way only an east end boy could deliver it.

It was a damn relief too, because the other mafia families had been making comments as the years passed without me and Anya finishing our part of the deal by mixing our blood, but now, finally, we'd made good on our promise and it was done. No thanks to Frank for the hold up.

"I just got confirmation that the last of the money from The Czar has cleared," Frank said, turning the camera back to face him and bringing a dark smile to my lips.

"Good. Did you tell Anya?"

"I shot her a text just before I called you."

"It's been a long time coming," I said, taking the knife from my pocket and turning it over in my palm as I thought about all the things we were gonna do to the motherfucker who had laid his hands on my woman all those years ago.

When Anya had come to me with this plan and the admission about what he'd done, I'd been pissed. Really fuckin' pissed. I'd been damn close to driving straight over to that bastard's house and doing him in right then and there. But like always, my wife had been the voice of reason and she'd had a plan which I hadn't been able to deny in the long run.

So she'd kept him on her hook, making sure every penny of the two hundred million that he had been investing into the Soho development had gone through and that the construction was complete. He'd never even blinked at the fine print in the contract which stated his shares would revert back to my construction company in the event of his death.

And now, under the guise of us celebrating the completion of the project, I had finally given in to his unending pleas to buy a night with my wife. Ten million pounds. I had to give it to the bastard, he was singular in his tastes and his dedication to claiming her from me had never wavered.

I would be damn glad to end this fuckin' dance now though. We'd milked him for all he was worth, fucked him over, stolen his diamond, ruined his sex trade bullshit empire and now we were done dicking about. His time was up and the Butchers were coming for him.

"You alright with the kids for the night?" I confirmed as Church cursed in the background and I spotted him lying on the floor with Edith and Cora both holding him down while Maggie used the sharpie on his face.

"Yeah. We got this," Frank said with a chuckle. "You and Anya have fun."

He cut the call and I breathed a laugh, my heart beginning to pump faster as I turned the blade over in my hand and waited to hear from John Boy who was currently sitting in the bar with his eyes on Anya, waiting to let me know when it was time to party.

My phone pinged a few moments later and I grinned like a wolf as I read it.

John Boy:
He just walked in.

I pushed to my feet as my pulse pounded in anticipation of the kill and waited in silence for Anya to lead our prey right into our trap.

Let the games commence.

CHAPTER SIXTY EIGHT

The Czar roamed towards me through the hotel bar, victory settling over his features as a dark smile spread across his lips. He wore a pale shirt beneath his plum jacket, his hair a little whiter than it used to be, his age beginning to show. He didn't age gracefully either, he had spent too much time in the sun and his skin was beginning to wrinkle and crack. His teeth had clearly been whitened recently and they flashed at me as he arrived before me, stinking of cologne and too much fucking money.

He took my hand, leaning down to stamp his mouth to the back of it and I cringed internally, the only thing stopping me from striking him the knowledge of what was to come.

"It's a delight as always, Mrs Butcher. Shall we have a drink?" he purred, moving to take a seat beside me at the bar, but I got to my feet. I was wearing a pure white silk dress which hugged my figure. It had been a bitch to get my body back in shape after birthing the twins, but I'd managed it by sheer determination, though it had been a helluva long time since I'd had to wear something as clingy as this.

"Let's have it in your room…alone," I said eagerly, linking my arm through his and his eyes shone with that idea as he nodded.

I could spot every single one of his men in this room, all armed to the teeth no doubt, but they wouldn't follow us upstairs. This hotel was owned by The Czar, and he felt as relaxed here as he did at home. The Soho development was done and dusted, his money spent and gone while we profited daily on the Butchers' expanded empire. Now, The Czar wasn't of much use to us anymore, and I'd finally decided to tell Benny my idea for how to pay him back for all his help.

He dropped his hand to my lower back, guiding me along at a hurried pace out of the bar and towards the glitzy gold doors of the elevator. The moment we were alone inside it, his hand moved to squeeze my ass and his mouth fell to my ear. "I've waited so long for this. Ten million pounds was worth every penny for a night in your company. And I shall spend every hour of it enjoying you." He was sweaty and panting and I shoved him back hard enough to make his spine hit the mirror, giving him a firm look.

"You're going to be a good boy or you'll be in trouble," I growled and he dabbed at his glistening brow, moving back towards me and pawing at my waist.

"Yes, I will be good for you, Mrs Butcher. But then I will be so bad that you'll never forget the feel of me within you."

I smiled in place of the grimace I wanted to give him and the elevator doors slid open, giving me some air to breathe which wasn't laced with stale cologne.

The Czar gripped my hand, tugging me along again as he fumbled a key card out of his pocket and as my gaze fell to his pants, I realised he was already hard. He tapped the card against the door to his room and I was half dragged into a huge suite with a view right across the river to the impressive tower of The Shard. The final blood red rays of sunset gilded the mirror-like windows and made it look like a giant blade jutting out of the heart of London. There was a twisted irony in that and I smiled at the beauty of it as The Czar released my hand.

He moved to where a bottle of whiskey and two glasses were waiting in a seating area before the view, the super king bed beyond it making me think of all the women he'd likely brought here and fucked with or without their permission.

We'd destroyed his sex trade enterprise at least. Back in the wake of the Candlestick Maker's death, we'd managed to catch several of his men who were willing to sing for their lives and had gotten all the information we needed to tear that sick industry apart and rip it out of our city. That had been a fun, bloody few months of carnage.

He shed his jacket, dropping it on the back of a chair before loosening some of the buttons at his throat and opening the whiskey bottle.

"Come here, Mrs Butcher," he purred and I moved to join him, pressing my shoulders back as I stood before the window and took in the view.

He dropped onto the seat, taking a sip of his whiskey like he was taking a taste of me.

"Undress for me," he asked, his eyes hooding as he watched me and I caught a glimpse of the evil in him dripping from his gaze.

I reached around the back of my dress, slowly unzipping it and shrugging it off of my body, letting it pool at my feet as I let him look at me in the strapless white bodice and lacy thong I wore beneath it. It reminded me of the items I'd worn beneath my wedding dress all those years ago. He placed his whiskey down as his gaze dragged over my flesh to the tops of my suspenders, then he spread his legs and ran his hands over his thighs.

"I've paid for countless women to dominate me since that brief time I spent with you striking my flesh, Mrs Butcher," he growled. "But I have not found a high like I did with you. You are forbidden fruit, belonging to a brutal man who could sever my head from my shoulders if he wished it. And on top of your sheer class and murderous habits, you are simply one of a kind. When I've had you, I know I will want more. And Butch has assured me I may claim you in all the ways I desire. Do you understand what that means, Mrs Butcher?"

"Explain it to me," I said lightly, my eyes sharpening on him as I stepped closer, feeling the burn of the dying sun against my back.

"It means you may strike at me and make me yours for a while, but once I am bored of that, I will return the favour. I don't mind if you fight me, in fact, I think I might prefer it. You see, Mrs Butcher, I do not just want to own you, I want to destroy you. I want you returned to your husband with my mark forever left in your flesh. I am the power in this town, you see? Not him. Money always speaks louder than violence. So yes, it may hurt at times, but I have paid my price and you are now my possession until the night is done. Does that make you afraid?"

"No," I said truthfully, moving so close to him that I stood between his spread thighs.

"It should," he said, leaning forward to reach between my legs but I smacked his hand away hard and he snatched it back against his chest with a whimper. His eyes lit and he licked his lips. "I may have to bring a man or two in here to hold you down. Does that not even strike fear in the Butcher queen's heart?"

I dropped to my knees between his thighs, reaching up to release my hair from the bun it was wound in and letting it spill all over my shoulders.

"You are a truly unique creature," he said breathily as I ran my fingers up the inside of his thighs, the sharp little knife that had been twisted into my hair concealed against my palm.

"Let me see it," I demanded and he swallowed visibly.

He unbuckled his pants frantically, shuffling them down his legs along with his boxers and exposing his horrible little cock and balls.

I smiled up at him, rubbing his inner thighs as I ran my fingers up them, running my tongue across my lips like I was desperate for that shrivelled thing to be in my mouth. I'd literally rather jump out the window than give him that though. But I'd give him something alright. Something that he'd never fucking forget.

I moved my hand beneath his cock as if to cup his balls, but instead of that, I stabbed the deadly little knife into them and a pillow slammed down on his face as a scream ripped from his throat, my husband's inked hands holding it in place.

Blood poured as I twisted the knife and The Czar thrashed, trying to punch me while I yanked the knife free and stood up, smiling at the monster who'd come to play demon with me.

"Hello, wife," Benny said through a grin, yanking the pillow away and pushing a gun with a silencer on it deep into The Czar's mouth to shut him up as he walked around the chair to my side.

The Czar fell very still, his hands cupping his bleeding balls as full on tears rolled down his cheeks.

I tiptoed up to kiss Benny, watching The Czar's eyes widen in horror as he took us both in, the whole room cast in a deep red glow as the sun said its final goodbye for the night. It would be the last glimpse of it this asshole ever saw.

"I've got a little gift for you in my pocket, bombshell," Benny said gesturing for me to get it and I reached into his back pocket, finding two silver knuckle dusters with forget-me-nots engraved along the inner side of them.

"Benny," I breathed in awe. "They're beautiful."

"How about you try 'em out, love? Show The Czar here how well your boxing has come along with Zoya's training."

I slid them onto my fingers, flexing them as I admired the perfect fit of the weapons and curling my hands into fists around them.

Benny slowly pulled the gun out of The Czar's mouth, pointing it at his forehead, but stepping back enough to give me room to get closer. "Not a peep, Czar, or your brains are gonna make good friends with that rug behind ya."

The Czar trembled in complete terror, staring at Benny like he was one of the four horsemen of the apocalypse come to collect him. But it wasn't him he should have been afraid of right now.

I threw my first punch into The Czar's face, knocking out a couple of teeth which went skittering across the floor. The Czar failed at keeping quiet, crying out instead and Benny waved the gun in his face.

"Now moan, you fucker, pretend like you enjoyed that," he commanded and The Czar sobbed, shaking his head. "Fuckin' moan or I'll end you right now."

The Czar managed it, moaning loudly and I threw another punch that slammed right into his gut, the next to his chest then throat. He coughed and spluttered, forcing moans out between my strikes and when I was satisfied at how bloody he was, I stepped back to stand beside Benny.

"W-why?" The Czar whimpered. "We're f-friends."

"Friends?" Benny scoffed, the darkness in him crawling out and spreading through the room. "No, mate. We were never your friends. You were a job. All these years, just a big juicy teet of money we liked to squeeze all the time. And that was how I liked it until my wife told me somethin' very interesting, Czar. Very interesting indeed." He stepped forward, his shoulders tightening. "She says you haven't always kept your hands to yourself, and that just got my blood really pumpin', Czar, because no one touches my fucking woman. Especially not against her wishes. And you touched her, you fuckin' piece of shit."

"You sold her to me," he rasped, still clutching his bloody balls like he could save them.

"Nah, mate, that's the thing. I wouldn't sell that woman if there even was a price in this universe that could be put on her. But I let you think I did. I let you think you really could have a slice of her perfect flesh when I was never, ever gonna allow that to happen."

He reached into his pocket, taking out the diamond we'd had all these years. With all the money we'd acquired from The Czar and the rest of the Butcher empire, we hadn't needed to sell it yet. And it had clearly been worth holding onto it for this very moment as I watched confusion and horror flash across The Czar's face.

"That's right," I said with a smirk, taking the diamond from Benny and holding it up to the light, letting the red rays of the sun refract and dance across our prey's face. "We've had it all this time. We were the ones who stole it from the Candlestick Maker and the ones who sold it back to you too. Then we just stole it all over again after you'd paid up. It was all a set up."

"No," he gasped.

"Yes, you old cunt," Benny said, smiling cruelly as he moved forward and the tension in the air made my breath hitch with anticipation. "Do you hear the bells of death tolling in the streets of London once more, mate? Do you see the moon rising to watch your bloody end?"

"No, no, listen to me," The Czar tried. "I have more money. I'll pay anything for you to spare me."

"See, I don't want more of your money, mate. I've got my pockets full of your cash already and once we sell that diamond, I'll have even more of it. You ain't got any more bargaining chips. And now I'm gonna show ya what happens to people who touch my wife without her say so. For I am England's king, a monarch forged in tribulations and the tides of death."

He placed the gun against The Czar's throat, pulling the trigger and I gasped as blood sprayed and The Czar flailed, desperately trying to staunch the gaping wound.

Benny kicked his chair over and he went sprawling across the floor, making my heart thump and my breaths quicken as I watched the carnage play out just for me.

Benny started kicking him in the chest, stomping and stomping as his hair fell forward in his eyes and his muscles bulged against his shirt. "My power runs deeper than any other king who has ruled before me," he spat. "For I am the culmination of their savagery. A monarch's blood runs thick in my veins because I have claimed this land as mine, and all who defy me shall succumb to my pyre, built with the bones of traitors. I am the X marking your door, I am the hooded executioner at your back, and when I swing my axe, your head will roll and the earth will quake with my merciless fury, so all standing in this here city shall tremor with the force of me. This is the age of the Butcher King. I will protect my own and destroy all those who oppose them. Fear my ire, for if you dare try and take my throne, your screams will join those who have died before you in the vengeful soil of Britain, and you will know what it is like to die in torment at the hands of a cutthroat *king*." With that final word he stamped down on The Czar's head, ending him for good and I stood panting and aching for my husband as he pushed his dark hair out of his eyes and heaved deep breaths into his lungs.

I ran at him in a flash, leaping into his arms and he caught me as I wrapped my legs around his waist, my mouth clashing with his. He moaned, carrying me to the window and driving me up against it as our tongues collided with a desperate need.

Benny dropped me to the floor, flipping me around by my hips and kicking my legs apart as he grabbed hold of my thong, ripping it off of me. Fuck it, we had time to kill before Dylan made it here anyway.

I was flattened to the cold glass as he freed his cock and shoved it inside me, his forearm pressing to the back of my neck as he forced me to look down at the streets of London, and telling me with every pump of his hips that this was our dominion.

He fucked me with the ruthlessness of the barbarians who had once invaded this land and seized it as theirs, and I knew Benny was like the heathens who had once come to this city with swords in hand and declarations of war. He had crowned himself, clawing his way to the throne and terrorising those who tried to thwart him.

"See that, love, that's our kingdom," he growled in my ear, his savage thrusts becoming deeper. "And every kill I make, I make for you. Because I may own this city, but you own me, Anya. You're formidable." My clit ground against the glass and my pussy tightened on him as I started to come, his cock demanding it as he fucked me relentlessly. "You're exquisite."

I moaned loudly and he came with a growl, gripping my hips tightly as his mouth fell to my neck and he kissed me in worship.

"And you're mine."

CHAPTER SIXTY NINE

TWO YEARS AFTER THAT…

I dropped back into my seat as we sat around the pool in the basement of our house, watching the older three girls as they raced to swim lengths while the twins splashed in a little puddle beside us, encouraging little Betty to splash along with them.

Benny had a smirk on his face as he watched them too, the two trouble makers laughing wildly every time Betty was tempted into their game and she slapped her chubby little hand down in the water next to their feet. Mr Buttons was firmly clamped in her other hand, the dog-eared looking rabbit having been passed down between all of the kids ever since Anya had sewn his button eyes back into place for Benny and made him cry. Of course, he said that something had gotten in his eye when she gave the stuffed toy he'd loved as a kid back to him all fixed up and as good as new, but I was calling bullshit and reminded him regularly about the way he'd blubbered like a baby over it.

She was only ten months old, and I was already getting the impression that she would have every one of her siblings wrapped around her little finger and at her beck and call by the time she turned one.

"Betty is looking more and more like Frank every day, isn't she? Maybe we should let you have a free shot at the next one, Churchy," Benny said with a smirk as he reclined in his chair, rubbing Anya's feet for her where she'd placed them in his lap. "Me and Frank could give you one month with no competition to see if you can get our girl knocked up."

"Don't you think six is enough?" Anya asked, before Church could reply. "It seems like it's enough to me."

I chuckled because she'd said that after the first baby and then second, and every one of them following that. But then when one of us suggested vasectomies or anything else that might stop her from getting pregnant again, she would burst into tears and change her mind, saying she wanted just one more and then she'd be done. It was a vicious cycle and sometimes I wondered how many kids we would end up with if she didn't actually put her foot down about having more.

The three of us definitely weren't going to be saying no. So far as I was concerned, the more chaos in the house the better, and we had more than enough love to go around for a whole football team if that was what she wanted.

"Tough luck, Churchy," Benny said, placing his hands behind his head as Anya shifted upright and smirking like an arsehole. "Looks like your swimmers just weren't fast enough to pass on their DNA."

"Seriously?" Church asked, arching a disbelieving brow as he looked over at the twins with their golden curls and silvery eyes before looking to Benny again like he was waiting for the penny to drop. But the boys were almost three now and Benny hadn't figured it out yet, so I doubted he would in the next five minutes either.

"Ignore him, Church," Anya said soothingly, her hand brushing over his thigh and Church hummed irritably, looking out to the pool again as Edith cut through the water like she'd been born half fish.

"Maybe you should get yourself checked out," Benny teased and I winced because I knew that'd do it.

"I'm gonna say it," Church snapped, pushing to his feet.

"Church," Anya warned but he shook his head in refusal, pointing at Benny.

"No. I've had enough. I'm saying it and then it'll be said and then it'll be out there and that will be that," he said.

"What the fuck are you talking about?" Benny asked, arching his eyebrow while Church lost his shit and the kids all gathered a little closer for the show.

"Twenty quid on Pa," Cora hissed to Maggie who giggled as the bet was placed on Church before shaking her head.

"Na, Daddy will kick his butt like last time."

"I think Mummy will throw one of them in the pool," Edith added in a whisper shout, her eyes glimmering hopefully while the twins started chanting, "In the pool, in the pool, in the pool!"

"It's only us!" Dylan's voice came from the stairs and Anya heaved out a breath as she jumped up to greet him and John Boy.

"Thank god," she said, hurrying over to embrace them one after another before tugging John Boy's hat from his head.

"What have I told you about that? You know it confuses the kids when you wear a new hat," she teased and he laughed.

"Yeah but Dylan loves it, don't you, babe? It's like fuckin' a stranger every time I get a new hat with the perks of commitment whenever I take it off again."

I'd been more than a little surprised when the two of them had made their on-again-off-again situation official a couple of years back. But John Boy had gotten all up on his hill about it one day, announcing to every fucker in The Duck and Dog that he was off to 'lock down his man', and after a week during which none of us knew if either of them were even alive, they'd emerged from Dylan's house looking thoroughly fucked and grinning way too much while telling the world they were all in.

Dylan had of course thrown an elaborate party in a sex club to celebrate, and I had a lot of seriously vivid memories about what me and my family of heathens had gotten up to in that place of sin while Benny's ma had the kids for the night. There had been a lot of pink feathers and a few things we didn't bring up in polite conversation, but I still gave that night credit for Betty's conception no matter how often I woke with my heart thrashing wildly from the memories of the stuff we'd tried out in that club. In fact, I was more than tempted to suggest we spend another evening in one of their back rooms again the next time we had a night to ourselves.

"Oh stop," Dylan gasped, slapping John Boy's chest and blushing as he fanned his face and leaned in to speak to Anya like they were sharing a secret. "He's not lying though. His anonymity is really something when we play pretend. Not to mention the way he gets me going when he does his Albanian accent."

Benny slapped his hands over Edith's ears as she laughed loudly and he heaved her up out of the pool.

"Come on, you pack of scallywags, your uncles need you dry and dressed if you're going to the zoo."

The girls all squealed in alarm at the thought of being left behind, and the six of us each claimed a kid to get dressed so that they could leave. I lucked out with Betty who hadn't figured out the art of kicking like a horse yet and I had her dressed in record time while the others all fought the rest of them into their clothes with varying levels of success.

It took about fifteen minutes to coral them all back up into the main part of the house we'd had built for our family to live in after the warehouse was destroyed.

It took us a while to find shoes, hand over strollers, changing bags and what was arguably a bucket full of snacks, but eventually Dylan and John Boy had the kids all rounded up and the four of us were left waving goodbye as they set off in the minivan.

I shut the door behind them and turned to look at Anya with a dark grin on my lips and all kinds of sinful ideas in my head, but of course Benny couldn't just let sleeping dogs lie.

"Spit it out then, Church," he barked the moment the door was locked.

Anya sighed in a resigned kind of way, heading towards the stairs and shrugging out of her dress as she went.

"Alright then," Church said, so riled up that he didn't even seem to have noticed our woman was stripping for us as she headed up the wide staircase to the floor above. The house was all open space and Victorian high ceilings, right in the heart of the city we loved and big enough for us plus the six rascals. It had cost a pretty penny, but it was worth every one.

"But once I've said it, it can't be unsaid. So don't forget you wanted this," Church warned.

"Just spit it out," Benny snapped.

"Fine. I first got suspicious about the twins when they were born and they had a look of Winston Churchill about them."

"What?" Benny asked and I groaned, knowing there was no way back from this now.

"It just seemed strange to me how like an ancestor of mine they appeared when you were claiming they had Butcher blood running in their veins."

"All babies look like Winston Churchill, you fuckin' dipshit. What is your point?" Benny demanded and my gaze caught on Anya's as she kicked her shoes off, beckoning me after her in her underwear.

I slipped away from the argument as subtly as I could manage, wondering if they'd keep it up long enough for me to have her to myself. Fuck knew it was hard to find a minute alone with her these days and I wasn't gonna pass up the opportunity if it presented itself.

"Whatever," Church went on. "Even if you want to ignore that obvious clue then explain to me why they're blonde?"

"Because Anya is blonde," Benny growled.

"Well there's not a granny along this street or the next who doesn't comment on how much they look like me either," Church pushed.

"The twins aren't yours if that's what you're trying to say," Benny snarled, looking to me and stopping me in my tracks as I reached the bottom of the stairs. "Tell him, Frank. They're twin boys – of course they're mine."

"Err…I can see why you would assume that," I hedged.

"Yeah. So can I," Church agreed. "But what about their eyes? Or their dimples? Or the way they used to look like Churchill?"

"You're off your rocker," Benny scoffed.

"I knew you'd say that," Church snapped. "So I went and got a DNA test done."

"You what?!" Benny roared and I gave up on trying to be subtle as Church stalked away to find the results which me and Anya had talked him out of sharing when he got them a few weeks ago. We knew exactly what would happen when Benny realised the truth, and though I could admit that I'd laughed myself silly over it, Anya had wanted to see if he would figure it out for himself or not.

"Come here," I growled as I tossed my shirt aside and stalked after my woman, catching her around the waist as she pretended to run from me and capturing her mouth with mine. I knew my chance at having her to myself was running low so I didn't waste another second, pushing my hand into her knickers and stroking her soaking core with a lustful groan.

"They're mine, Ben - not yours. It's here in black and white. And I know we all love them the same no matter the paternity, but I won't have you tarnish the good name of my little English swimmers anymore!" Church yelled, his words punctuated by Anya's moan as I sank my fingers inside her and she hastily unbuckled my belt.

Several silent seconds passed while Benny read the paternity report on the twins before a bellow of rage escaped him and the sound of him punching Church reached us.

"You fucking cunt!" he yelled, losing his shit like we'd all known he would. "Why can't either of you just pull out before you come?"

"Watch it, Ben, you're coming mighty close to saying you wish the kids didn't exist," Church warned because we'd all long since figured out that that was the off switch to his infuriation over this situation, so we used it regularly.

"Fuck you," Benny barked. "You know I love the bones of those kids and I wouldn't wish a single thing different. But you also know that all of our lives depend on me upholding this fucking treaty and merging my bloodline with the Volkovs too."

"They looked like Churchill, Ben, all the signs were there."

"You're not even related to Winston fucking Churchill!" Benny shouted and I froze with my fingers deep inside Anya's sweet pussy, the two of us forgetting what we were in the middle of for a moment as the air seemed to be sucked from the room with that accusation and we looked down the stairs to Church's horror stricken face.

"You take that back," he demanded but from the fury in Benny's eyes, it was pretty clear to me that he was about to dump that bucket of shitty truth all over Church's head and damn the consequences.

"Benny," I growled before he could do something he would regret, and I had to question my own sanity for what I was about to do because my dick was fucking throbbing and I really didn't want to give up this moment in Anya's arms. "Seventh time's the charm, eh?"

Benny looked from me to Anya who was still panting against the wall in her little black underwear and I began to move my fingers again, making her moan and tempting him away from the brink of insanity.

"Yeah," Benny said slowly, glancing back at Church and sighing as he shook off his anger in favour of something far more interesting. "Seventh time's the charm."

"Fuck it," Anya panted as I kept fucking her with my hand. "I always wanted seven kids anyway."

"Really?" I asked her in surprise but she only nodded, biting down on her bottom lip as she came for me, her pussy clasping tight around my fingers and making my dick jerk with need.

Benny reached us at the top of the stairs, his shoulder butting against mine as he shoved me aside and unbuckled his belt.

"You sure about this, bombshell? I don't want to force you to have another one if-"

Anya punched him in the jaw, giving him a dark look which made it clear that that was for almost bursting Church's little bubble.

"Apologise for being a dick and tell him to come here," she said firmly.

Benny glanced down the stairs to where Church stood, his brow pinched from the words Benny had hurled at him, and he huffed out a breath before doing as he was told.

"Sorry for being a cunt about your heritage," he said obediently. "I didn't mean it. I'd just had a shock."

"That's alright," Church replied with a shrug, his attention moving to Anya as she panted against the wall and the expectation grew between the four of us as our breaking point approached. "I know you're all jealous about me and Churchill," he said. "I can't help being born from greatness. Besides, it's kind of a relief to find out they're mine, ain't it? I mean we were all worried that one of the twins mighta been a Danny if they'd been yours, but now we don't have to worry."

Benny narrowed his eyes, his lips parting on a reply but Anya got there first, reaching out and grabbing his cock in her hand.

"Stop wasting time and come put a baby in me, husband," she demanded. "Before one of your men beats you to it again."

"Bitch," Benny growled, shoving her knickers down and throwing his own clothes off while me and Church drew closer like moths drawn to a flame.

"Asshole," Anya tossed back.

Benny caught her by the waist and hooked her legs around him, sinking his cock into her drenched core and making her cry out as he began to fuck her roughly.

"Bloody hell," she gasped and I smirked as the little Englishism slipped out, then Benny claimed her mouth to devour her cries.

Church and I moved closer without needing an invitation, working together to remove her bra before our mouths fell to her neck, her breasts, our hands meeting on her clit and giving her everything while Benny's powerful thrusts rocked her body between us.

Anya's hand pushed into my boxers and the groan of desire that left Church told me she'd taken command of his dick too, owning all three of us the way she always did and demanding we be a part of this as well.

Her hand shifted up and down my shaft and I groaned as I alternated between watching her take Benny's cock and sucking and kissing any piece of flesh I could reach.

Church's fingers tangled with mine as we worked her clit and I pushed my other hand beneath her thigh, driving my fingers into her alongside Benny's dick until she was screaming so beautifully that I couldn't help but come for her.

Benny thrust into her a few more times before finishing with a roar and filling her with his seed. Church swore as he came too, the four of us sagging back against the wall in a tangle of utter bliss.

"Well if you ain't pregnant after that then you're never gonna be knocked up by me," Benny growled while we fought to catch our breath and I laughed with the others as we just enjoyed this little piece of heaven we'd stolen for ourselves inside the depths of our world of sin.

CHAPTER SEVENTY

TEN MORE YEARS LATER…

The helicopter soared over London while Frank's fingers wound between mine. Church and Benny sat opposite us and I swear my guys' attention was more fixed on me than the view. We did this every year on Benny's birthday, the flight having become something of a tradition while Dylan and John Boy babysat for us.

Benny had finally fulfilled his end of the treaty in the form of a little girl called Tilly, though the bloodline thing had never made a difference to how he treated our other kids. He loved them all equally, and the three of them made such good fathers despite the sins that stained their souls. Our children were the centre of our world, and there was nothing that had brought us closer than them. Our patch of forget-me-nots had flourished and multiplied, and now we lived in a meadow of our own creation.

Seven kids. Fondly known as the seven sins by everyone in the gang, and boy was that the truth. The oldest girls were teenagers now and we were fully into the swing of hormonal temper tantrums and them throwing fits of rage over all the boys they knew being too terrified of their dads to date them. Which had only really served to make my men more protective of them than ever.

The river Thames stretched out beneath us towards an endless horizon and I smiled serenely, every part of this country so deep in my blood now it was like I'd never lived anywhere else.

"I'll never get enough of this sight," I breathed and my men all assented, but when I turned to them they were still looking at me.

I smiled, heat burning two lines along my cheeks as I gazed from one to the other of my corrupted knights.

"Where's the music, mate?" Benny asked over his headset and the pilot started playing In My Life by The Beatles just for us.

But there was an even better song than that playing in my flesh. It was a tune more beautiful than any other, because it was made of grit and power, love and redemption. It took hold of me and pulled me in, marking me forever. It was *our* song, and I wanted to listen to it always, wide awake and facing every lull and every high it had to offer. It belonged to us down to its core and I wanted it to be played so loudly it was like a bomb going off into the end of time, heard right across the universe.

The four of us were a harem forged in blood on the streets of an ancient city. We were a terrible symphony, a cutthroat composition and a blood soaked harmony. Between us, we had written the song of the Forget-Me-Nots and it roared like a beast rising from hell, branding itself into the scorched heart of this earth. Even when we one day passed into the afterlife, it would still echo on into the end of time. And the world would forget us not.

AUTHOR'S NOTE

Kapow! We did it – one standalone book without any cliffhangers delivered right to your brain for your reading pleasure. I mean, yeah, there were a couple of little cliffs in there between the different parts. And yeah, we worked hard to try and hurt you the way we know you love and expect us to. But in the end, everything turned out just fine, didn't it?

This book was a real beastie. We were aiming for somewhere around 200k words but it came in at 275k in the end because these characters just wouldn't let us finish with them and we fell in love with them a little too deeply.

This was the first time we have set one of our books in a real life place too, and we hope you enjoyed the little slice of London we gave you as much as we enjoyed striding the streets of our home city in the name of research (and in hunt of our own pack of Butcher boys – who we sadly did not find).

So that's it, goodbye to this band of cutthroat gangsters and on to more of the dark and deadly men and women who reside inside our brains (hey, pipe down, I hear some of you crying out for a Danny Butcher spin-off with a redemption arc, you little psychos. That is an UNACCEPTABLE and very tempting idea). Anyway, don't you worry – if you are missing the agony of a cliff at the end of this book then we promise to leave you hanging again really soon.

Thank you so much for your love and support of our books, each and every one of our readers means so much to us and we love you eternally. If you want to keep up to date with everything we write then don't forget to join our newsletter and come hang out with us in our Facebook reader group which is now full of almost 40 thousand amazing readers just like you who are desperate to talk all things books at all hours of the day and night. Or you can always come stalk our weird asses on TikTok here and here.

Love you guys,
Susanne & Caroline xxx

ALSO BY

CAROLINE PECKHAM

&

SUSANNE VALENTI

Brutal Boys of Everlake Prep
(Complete Reverse Harem Bully Romance Contemporary Series)
Kings of Quarantine
Kings of Lockdown
Kings of Anarchy
Queen of Quarantine
**

Dead Men Walking
(Reverse Harem Dark Romance Contemporary Series)
The Death Club
Society of Psychos
**

The Harlequin Crew
(R*everse Harem Mafia Romance Contemporary Series)*
Sinners Playground
Dead Man's Isle
Carnival Hill
Paradise Lagoon

Harlequinn Crew Novellas
Devil's Pass
**

Dark Empire
(Dark Mafia Contemporary Standalones)
Beautiful Carnage
Beautiful Savage
**

The Ruthless Boys of the Zodiac
(Reverse Harem Paranormal Romance Series - Set in the world of Solaria)
Dark Fae
Savage Fae
Vicious Fae
Broken Fae
Warrior Fae

Zodiac Academy

(M/F Bully Romance Series- Set in the world of Solaria, five years after Dark Fae)

The Awakening
Ruthless Fae
The Reckoning
Shadow Princess
Cursed Fates
Fated Thrones
Heartless Sky
The Awakening - As told by the Boys

Zodiac Academy Novellas

Origins of an Academy Bully
The Big A.S.S. Party

Darkmore Penitentiary

(Reverse Harem Paranormal Romance Series - Set in the world of Solaria, ten years after Dark Fae)

Caged Wolf
Alpha Wolf
Feral Wolf

**

The Age of Vampires

(Complete M/F Paranormal Romance/Dystopian Series)

Eternal Reign
Eternal Shade
Eternal Curse
Eternal Vow
Eternal Night
Eternal Love

**

Cage of Lies

(M/F Dystopian Series)

Rebel Rising

**

Tainted Earth

(M/F Dystopian Series)

Afflicted
Altered
Adapted
Advanced

**

The Vampire Games
(Complete M/F Paranormal Romance Trilogy)
V Games
V Games: Fresh From The Grave
V Games: Dead Before Dawn
*

The Vampire Games: Season Two
(Complete M/F Paranormal Romance Trilogy)
Wolf Games
Wolf Games: Island of Shade
Wolf Games: Severed Fates
*

The Vampire Games: Season Three
Hunter Trials
*

The Vampire Games Novellas
A Game of Vampires
**

The Rise of Issac
(Complete YA Fantasy Series)
Creeping Shadow
Bleeding Snow
Turning Tide
Weeping Sky
Failing Light

www.ingramcontent.com/pod-product-compliance
Lightning Source LLC
Chambersburg PA
CBHW030346310726
48979CB00001B/208

* 9 7 8 1 9 1 4 4 2 5 2 1 9 *